The
FALLEN
WORLD

THE COMPLETE SERIES

Published in the United States by Lavabrook Publishing, LLC.

LAURA THALASSA

The
QUEEN
of All that
DIES

CHAPTER 1

SERENITY

I CAN BARELY remember a time before the war. The green, orderly lawns, the rows of houses, the neatly assigned shelves of food. That quest for perfection was the first thing to go when the king turned his attention to our land.

The first, but not the last.

War felled more than just order. We once knew casual compassion—politeness even. People smiled for the sake of smiling. Laughed because they couldn't contain their joy. One positive emotion begat another, and it spread like the most decadent disease.

And the colors. Every once in a while I still dream in such vivid colors. What I would give to live in such a bright place again.

The world we knew is nothing like the one I live in.

But none of this, none of it was so costly a price as the one we eventually paid. Somewhere along the way, my people lost the most precious thing of all.

Hope.

Well, most of us lost it. Most, but not all.

AN ALARM GOES off in the barracks, and I groan. My roommates—all seven of them—slide out of their beds before I do. But they hadn't stayed up late learning about international diplomacy.

I pull back my threadbare blanket and swing my legs out. As soon as my bare feet hit the cold concrete, I begin moving, grabbing my fatigues and changing into them. Most of the women next to me have already shoved theirs on and left. They're the smart ones. There might not be any breakfast by the time I get to the mess hall.

I sit on my bed and pull on my boots, wishing for the hundredth time that there was natural light in this place. For the last five years I've lived in this bunker nestled belowground. No matter how much I get used to this way of life, I can't adjust to this one thing.

Once my shoes are laced up, I jog out of my room and down to the cafeteria. Just as I suspected, I'm too late. The line winds out the door.

My stomach contracts painfully; it's a familiar ache. We're all underfed here. Most of the land above us has been razed, which makes food scarce. No one will admit it, but the war is coming to an end. It has to; our people are slowly starving to death.

Despite the long wait, I stand at the back of the line anyway, hoping there might be something left over by the time I reach the front. I can't bear the thought of waiting until dinner to eat.

I've been standing in line for almost fifteen minutes when a hand wraps around my arm and tugs me out of line.

"Wha—?" I glance up at Will, the general's son. He's handsome, has the dirtiest sense of humor, and he's responsible for getting me into trouble over the last five years. If circumstances were different, we might have dated, married, then had kids. But this isn't the world my grandparents grew up in.

"Did you have to pull me out of line?"

His face is serious, but his eyes shine excitedly. "The representatives want to see you—your father himself sent me here to get you."

Instantly my mood changes from annoyed to suspicious. "Why? What's going on?" The people near me glance in our direction.

Will's eyes flick to them before returning to me. "Not here, Serenity," he says quietly.

I look longingly at the cooks serving up oatmeal and accept the fact that I'm going to go hungry for the rest of the day.

I nod. "'Kay, I'll bite." I'm curious what put the twinkle in Will's eyes.

I follow him down the dimly lit halls until we arrive at the bunker's conference room. This is where the American representatives of the Western United Nations gather. The WUN is a collection of countries that make up North and South America. It's a coalition that's been fighting the eastern hemisphere for almost fifteen years.

Not the eastern hemisphere, I think darkly. *King Montes Lazuli.*

When we stop outside the room, I can't help but swallow. The last time I was called in here on official business, the representatives had decided that I would begin training as the next emissary. My father currently holds the role. Poor Will has been training to become the next general for even longer than I have. I don't envy him, but I'm also guessing that no one envies me. If we lose the war, we'll likely be killed or imprisoned.

Not that the thought scares me. I'm already dying.

WILL KNOCKS ON the door, and a moment later my father opens it. He smiles, but there's a tension that pinches the corners of his eyes. "Serenity, glad you could join us," he says. He nods to Will and opens the door for us both to enter.

Unlike me, Will's now required to attend these meetings with the representatives. I consider it a blessing that I haven't yet been asked to sit in on them, but judging by the assessing looks I'm receiving as I step inside, I have a horrible feeling that is all about to change.

The two dozen men and women seated around the table are all that remains of our political leaders. King Lazuli has killed off most of the presidential line of succession. We who live in this bunker are all that's left.

"Serenity Freeman," General Chris Kline says. Will's father. "Good morning."

I incline my head, my hands clasped tightly together. "Morning."

Will places a hand on my back and leads me to a free seat next to my father. I can tell my dad's nervous by the tense set of his jaw.

I sit down, Will following suit. A quick glance at the faces around me tells me that no one here has gone to bed yet. My clasped hands squeeze even tighter together. Whatever is going on, it's big, and I'm somehow involved.

"The WUN is in danger of collapsing." The general just comes out and says it. I've always appreciated his bluntness, but now it makes my stomach clench. He's as good as told me that we're all dead men here. "The eastern hemisphere is much larger than we are; nuclear warfare has crippled our numbers and our economy. We're not going to last much longer."

All this information I'd pieced together on my own. I just don't understand why General Kline is telling me this.

I nod and glance at my father. He won't look at me.

"It's time to think about peace and what's best for our people."

My eyes widen. Now I think I do know what he's talking about. The representatives want to forge the terms of surrender.

A sick feeling twists my gut. I already know the general's next words before he says them.

"As the emissary of the WUN, your father is expected to go to Geneva, where the peace talks are to be held." The general pauses. "And as your father's apprentice, we think it's best that you go along with him."

I swallow; my eyes sting. Our leaders always come back in body bags after visiting the king. And we can't do anything about it. The WUN has tried to assassinate him dozens of times, but somehow he always survives. The Undying King, as some call him.

My death sentence just got bumped a little sooner. As did my father's.

I look at my dad again, and I can see his eyes are red, his face anguished. I place a hand on his forearm and squeeze it. At least we'd be going in together. I prefer that to him going alone.

I turn back to General Kline. "I accept whatever duties are required of me."

A muscle in my father's forearm jerks beneath my hand. It's the only indication that this situation is tearing him up. I'm all he has left; he's all I have left. The thought of losing the last person in the world that loves you is terrifying. But no one in this room has the luxury of being selfish.

General Kline smiles grimly. "Good." He glances down at the paper in front of him. "You and your father will be representing the entire WUN."

What he means is that Canada and Central America are too splintered to send someone over. And the political infighting in South America makes them too fragmented to attempt this.

"We've already contacted our correspondences overseas as well as the king's retinue," General Kline continues.

I curl my lip at the term *retinue*. The king has people who wait on him hand and foot while we starve.

"They are expecting our arrival in Geneva on Wednesday."

"So soon?" I manage to get out. That's three days from now.

The general's eyes move to mine, and they flash like my fear disappoints him. I can't help it. The king is the boogey man; no weapon scares me as much as that deceptively charming face of his.

"You will be filmed," he says, ignoring my question. "The world will be watching. This means you must tread lightly. If you do well, you'll boost the morale of our citizens. If you or your father are killed, it will prove to the world just how vulnerable we are."

His words make me lightheaded. I'd assumed that death was the worst outcome, but no. The worst outcome is that we never get the chance to work on a peace agreement between the two hemispheres. We've heard stories of the conquered lands. There's a reason we've waited this long to surrender.

3

"Ignore your normal routine starting today. Lisa will swing by your room in an hour to get you fitted for some appropriate garments. Tomorrow you'll be boarding the jet for Geneva. Try to get some rest before then."

This is what I've been preparing to do ever since I became my father's apprentice. Forge alliances. I've learned a lot of useful skills, but I've never had the opportunity to implement them as I do now. And now the fate of the entire western hemisphere depends on my father's and my ability to negotiate with the enemy.

CHAPTER 2

SERENITY

NINE YEARS AGO I watched my mother die. That was also the day I received the scar that runs from the corner of my eye down my cheek, a permanent tear for all the souls the war has claimed.

At the time the eastern hemisphere had just fallen and the new king had set his sights on the west. In the wake of oncoming war, my father started working nonstop, leaving my mother and me to keep each other company.

That Saturday morning was just like any other. I laid under our coffee table flipping through a magazine, while my mom sat on the couch reading.

The only indication that something was about to happen was the trembling ground beneath me. I heard Mom's mug rattle on the glass side table next to her.

My mother's gaze met mine. Even then we knew enough about the war to immediately think the worst. But never had the enemy attacked civilians on our own soil.

A whine started up, distant at first. The sound got louder.

"Serenity, get down!" My mother lunged for me.

She wasn't fast enough.

The whine cut out, and for the briefest of moments, all was quiet. Then our front yard lit up, the windows shattered. A howling, fiery blast tore through the house, throwing my mother forward.

That was all I saw before the force of the explosion blasted the coffee table away from me and I tumbled, my body a ragdoll. Debris sliced against my skin, none so deep as the gash across my face.

Other than those cuts and what I later found out was a fractured wrist and several bruised ribs, I survived the explosion unscathed. Sheer providence kept me from further harm.

In the distance more bombs went off, the sound a whiplash to my ears. Each time they did, the ground shook violently. I whimpered at the pain in my arms and chest. But not even that could distract me from the sight ahead of me.

My mom's eyes had always gleamed like she had some secret to share.

Now they were vacant.

THERE'S A KNOCK on my door, and a moment later Lisa walks in.

"Hi sweetie," she says. The endearment always amuses me. As though I'm some innocent flower. I'm not.

"Hey Lisa." I can't muster much enthusiasm. Before the war, Lisa owned a wedding dress shop, so she's been the residential seamstress since her husband and the rest of her family moved in.

Her husband, like most of the men and women here, was an important figure when we still had a functioning government. My best guess is that he was a badass dude—the kind that can't actually tell you their profession because of national

5

security. I see a lot of those types around here. The bunker only has a finite amount of space, so only the most essential men and women are allowed to live here with their families.

Lisa drops the pile of material she carried in onto my bed, and my eyes are immediately drawn to the vibrant colors I see. Bright red, gold, rose petal pink. Iridescent beads catch the light.

I finger a bit of lace that pokes out amongst the pile. "Please tell me these aren't my outfits." They're all beautiful, but the thought of wearing such flashy garments is horrifying.

She gives me a rueful smile. "Sorry babe, but orders are orders."

"And what orders are those?" Surely I'd have heard about this. I thought I'd be wearing drab suits just like the rest of the men and women that meet for diplomacy talks.

"To have all eyes on you."

My jaw slides open, and I look at her in disbelief. "Why would the WUN want that?" My father was the one they should have their eyes on. Not me.

Her eyes are sad. "Because you are young and attractive. It's easier to sympathize with someone who looks like you than someone like your father."

It makes sense. Of course it does. The representatives have to leverage whatever they can. Still I grind my teeth together. Those who watch the peace talks might sympathize more if I dress like this, but they will also see us as weak. No one is afraid of a pretty bauble, and that's just what I'll be.

"Time to remove your clothes, sweetie."

I shuck off my fatigues and stand in my bra and panties. Lisa doesn't say anything about the sick way my collarbones stick out or my flat, empty stomach, but her brows pull together while she takes down my measurements, as though it pains her to see me this way.

There was a time when obesity was the losing battle our people faced. Not so anymore. As soon as food became scarce, curves became coveted.

Lisa puts away the tape measurer and rifles through the clothing, removing garments that she knows she can't tailor to fit me.

"Where did you even get all of these?" I ask.

"They're not mine. These are property of the WUN—and no, I have no idea where and when they came by these."

I try some of the remaining garments on, and Lisa tugs and adjusts the material, writing down notes in her notepad on adjustments. After the better part of an hour, she packs up her stuff. "I'll finish these tonight and have them packed for you tomorrow," she says. "And I'm supposed to tell you that Jessica's pulled out of kitchen duty to cut your hair and show you a thing or two about makeup."

I almost groan at the thought. Getting a haircut is one thing, but makeup? I've never worn it. I'm going to look like a clown. All for a televised meeting that will be viewed mostly by the enemy.

Few people in the WUN will even be able to watch. The king destroyed a large portion of our electronics years ago, and he has since halted the sale and distribution of all devices manufactured in the Eastern Empire. We have only a limited number of functioning electronics left.

Lisa cups my face, bringing me back to the present. She stares at me for a long time, and I can tell she wants to say something profound. Her eyes are getting watery, and I'm getting distinctly uncomfortable.

All she ends up saying, however, is, "You've got this, sweetie."

I nod my head once, not trusting my own voice. Because the truth is, I don't. *We* don't. This is really, truly the beginning of the end.

MY ROOMMATES HAVE long since gone to bed when I sneak out of the barracks, my hair several inches shorter from Jessica's ministrations. At night the florescent lights that line the subterranean hallways are turned off to save energy, so I make my way through the compound based on touch and memory.

When I get to the storage cellar, most of the group is already there, waiting for the meeting to begin.

Someone whistles. "Is that makeup, Serenity? And here we thought you were a dude this entire time."

I flip off David, the guy responsible for the comments. All he does is laugh.

Will nods to me and pats an empty crate next to him. I make my way through the cramped room to sit down. We wait five more minutes, and when no one else shows up, Will clears his throat. "This is the North American WUN command center. Let's commence the hundred and forty-third meeting of the Resistance." His voice is being recorded and streamed to other meetings occurring throughout the globe.

As the general's son, Will became the de facto correspondent with the Resistance. The group of us sitting here—all former soldiers and children of the various representatives—gather and relay information back to our leaders.

We make these meetings as clandestine as possible. While the WUN needs the information the Resistance feeds us, we don't want to be openly associated with them. While we share a common enemy, they're a terrorist organization.

"What are the casualty numbers this week?" Will asks first.

A crackly voice comes on over the Internet. "Ten thousand, three hundred and eleven globally—that's the official number. As usual, we have reason to believe there are several thousand more unreported casualties that have died from radiation sickness and biological warfare."

Next to Will, David jots these numbers down.

I rub my forehead. As much as I'm dreading the visit to Geneva, the WUN is at its breaking point. Our hemisphere's population is only a fraction of what it was before the war. It's not just fighting that's felling our numbers. People are sick.

Will's mouth is a thin line. "Any news on the enemy?"

"They're still holding the Panama Canal, and reports in the area say that they've taken over the hospitals and research clinics in the neighboring cities—just as they have in all other conquered territories."

"Have our spies figured out what the king's men are doing in these locations?"

"Same as all the others—a little of this and that. Stem cell research, the regeneration of cells, you know, the usual work up."

And we still had no idea what real medical developments the king was actually researching. He's managed to keep that under wraps for as long as we've been fighting this war.

"There was, however, one thing unusual about this takeover," the Resistance member says. "Many of the technicians the king let go were dazed."

"What do you mean by 'dazed'?" Will asks.

"They were confused. Couldn't answer our questions."

"Any ideas what might've happened to them?" I cut in.

The voice on the other end pauses. "None except the most general."

"And what would that be?" I press.

"They lost their memory."

THE NEXT DAY a knock on my door signals that it's time to go. I sit alone in the barracks, fingering my mother's necklace around my neck. I'm already wearing one of the dresses that Lisa tailored for me.

I despise the thing.

The door opens and Will pokes his head in. The sight of him brings me back to last night's conversation with the Resistance. The king's overtaken the Panama Canal; no wonder the WUN's folding. The war's ending soon if they've wrangled control of it.

And the hospitals … everywhere the king goes, he infiltrates the labs first. Initially we'd thought it was to decimate any chance of medical relief—and yes, he does do that. But when stories of his unusual research trickled in, we began to take note.

"Mind if I come in?" Will asks. His eyes widen as they move over me.

I motion him inside, banishing thoughts of the king. "What are you doing here?" I ask once Will closes the door behind him.

"I wanted to say goodbye to you," he says. He shifts his weight, sliding his hands into his pockets. His eyes flick over me again. "You look really nice."

I snort. "Yeah, if by nice you mean I look like a giant peacock," I say, picking up a piece of the dress and letting it flutter back to my side.

Will sits down next to me. "You make it look good," he says, his eyes full of that same intensity I'd seen him wear earlier.

Suddenly I get the impression that this isn't just a friendly goodbye. Will's not looking at me like I'm the soldier who fought alongside him. Nor is he looking at me like the friend who would stay up late talking about anything and everything that crossed our minds.

He's looking at me the way a lover should.

"Serenity, you're going to save our country," he says, clasping my hand.

I shake my head. "Don't put that on me, Will. We both know how this ends."

"No," he says, squeezing my hand tightly. "We don't. And the representatives wouldn't send you if they didn't think you'd sway the king."

The king. I'd have to speak with him, smile at him, pretend that he didn't destroy everything that I held dear.

"But more than that, you have to come back because I'll be waiting for you."

My throat constricts. I can't tell if it's from this strange ardor of his or that, in this moment, I realize I will never experience love. Not given my circumstances.

Will's expression softens. It's such a foreign emotion on him that I almost laugh.

And then he leans down and presses his lips to mine.

For a moment, I'm so shocked I do nothing but sit there. And then I recover and kiss him back. I would've thought my lips would be clumsy, but they're not, and the kiss … the kiss is nice.

When it ends, I blink at him. Will has a whimsical look on his face. It relaxes his hard features, and it speeds up my heart to think that I'm responsible for it.

I take in his dark eyes. "I didn't know."

"Now you do." He's looking at me like he's waiting for something else. Something more.

I touch my fingers to my lips. "I wish things were different," I say, because it's the only thing I can.

The sharp lines return to his face. "So do I." He eyes the door across from us and clears his throat. "We should probably get going. I'm supposed to be escorting you out."

I nod and grab my bag. As I sling it over my shoulder, both Will and I hear the clank of metal inside it.

Will raises his eyebrows. "They're not going to let you take your gun."

"Then they're going to have to pry it away from my cold, dead hands." And I mean it. If I'm going to die on enemy soil—and I have no doubt that I am—I want the few beloved possessions close by. One of those is the gun my father gave me. Morbid, I know, but during the last ten years it's become a dear and trusted companion.

A smile spreads along Will's face. "I'm not sure even death could take that gun away from you." His smile slips as soon as he says the words, and I get the impression that he's vividly imagining it. My death.

"C'mon, let's go." Will takes my hand, threading his fingers through mine. This is the first time he's held my hand that I can remember. I can't help but think that it's too little too late.

I take one last look at the barracks as we slip out the door. The room is the closest thing I've had to a home for a long time now. But as I take in the narrow beds, the cement walls and floor, the basin all eight of us use to wash out hands and faces, I can't say I'm all that sorry to leave.

My heels clack as we walk through the bunker, drawing attention my way. The people we pass stop and stare. News has spread that I'm going to Geneva for the peace talks. I'm now the girl walking to her execution in a dress. But some look hopeful, and their hope gives me courage.

Will's palm slickens the closer we get to the stairwell, which will take us to the surface. As soon as we round the corner and see it, his hand tightens on mine.

"This is where I leave you," he says.

I nod. Swallow. No one goes outside unless ordered to. The radiation from the blasts is still too dangerously high. And if the radiation doesn't kill you, your fellow citizens might.

Will tugs on our clasped hands, pulling me to him. "Make it back here alive," he says. His lips brush my forehead. It's not a goodbye kiss, and I really appreciate that.

After a moment, he lets me go. I back up to the stairwell door, watching him. I feel hyper alive. It's the same feeling I have every time I fight on the battlefield. I can't figure out if it's the sudden, startling possibility of Will and me or the prospect of meeting the king that has me feeling this way, but it's not an unpleasant sensation.

"I'll try my best to come back alive," I say.

Will gives me a small smile. "I'm holding you to that, Serenity."

I CLIMB THE stairs for what seems like ages. When I finally reach the top, the floor closest to the surface, several people wait for me. Among them are the general and my father.

My father's eyebrows nudge up when he sees me. This is the first time I've ever looked remotely feminine.

"You look … just like your mother," he manages to say. I blush at this—that's the best compliment my father could've given me.

General Kline grunts his approval. "Now that you're here, Serenity, it's time to get moving." As he speaks, the general begins leading the group to the garage, where all our vehicles are kept. "We're sending a dozen guards to go with you two," the general says to my father and me. "They are there to protect you should negotiations dissolve."

The general, my father, and I get into one of the military vehicles. The rest of our entourage piles into two other cars.

"I want you both to report to me every night," General Kline continues. "Be sure to watch your words. Let's assume the king can hear everything you say to me. You both know the code words."

In front of us the cement floor tilts up until it kisses the ceiling of the bunker. As I watch, the ceiling slides back, and the leaves that helped camouflage the hidden door fall into the bunker like confetti.

Natural light streams in, the first I've seen in months, and the sight of it takes my breath away. The washed out sky beyond is not the same blue that haunts my memories, but it's still one of the most beautiful sights I've seen in a long time.

Once the ceiling slides back far enough, our caravan pulls out. My eyes drink in the war-scorched earth. Out here in the middle of nowhere, the damage isn't as apparent as it is in the heart of our once big cities, but if you stare long enough, you'll see it.

It's a five-minute drive to the hangar that houses our jet. Short enough that if the representatives ever needed to make a quick escape they could, but long enough that if the hangar were ever to be attacked, the bunker would remain unharmed.

We pull into it, and inside several aircraft wait. One sits in front of the rest, and several men and women already swarm around it, loading the jet, and checking up on its general maintenance.

"Ambassador Freeman," the general turns to my father, "this will work."

I see a muscle in my father's cheek flex, and something unspoken passes between the two of them. Whatever it is, it has my father angry.

Beyond us, the rest of our group is beginning to load themselves onboard the aircraft. I grab my bag, clenching my jaw at the airy way my dress swishes around my legs—as if I am some delicate thing that requires only the lightest of caresses and the softest material.

I stare at the jet that will take me away from this miserable land to one that's already fallen to the king. The same king that's taken everything from me. I'll come face to face with him. I take a deep breath.

Time to dance with the devil.

CHAPTER 3

SERENITY

EIGHT YEARS AGO my father put a gun in my hand for the first time.

That morning when I walked into the kitchen, he sat at our table sipping a cup of coffee, a wrapped box in front of him.

I halted at the sight of it.

"Thought I'd forgotten your birthday?" he asked, glancing up from his laptop.

I had. He hadn't mentioned it, and I hadn't bothered reminding him. He'd been so busy. So weary. It made me feel guilty any time I thought of mentioning it to him.

I continued to stare at the gift.

"Well?" He closed the computer screen and pushed it aside. "Are you going to open it?"

Tentatively I approached the kitchen table. "You didn't have to get me a present," I said, even as I reached for the box.

He gave me a gentle smile, but something in his eyes warned me to curb my enthusiasm.

Carefully I peeled away the wrapping, savoring the fact that my father had remembered. Beneath it was a worn-out shoebox advertising men's loafers. I raised my eyebrows, earning me a chuckle.

"Open the lid, Serenity," my father said, leaning forward.

I lifted it like he asked, and balked at what rested inside.

"Go ahead and grab it—gently."

Reaching in, I touched the cold metal and wrapped my hands around the handle.

"Do you know what that is?" he asked me.

How could I not know? "It's a gun." I tried to curb my disappointment. I wouldn't be getting any new toys this year. Not on my father's watch.

"No," my father said. "That is a death sentence."

I stared at the weapon in my hand like it was a snake.

"I know you've seen the street gangs shooting up property for the hell of it," he continued, leaving his seat to kneel at my side. "That is not a toy. You point that gun, then you aim to kill."

My eyes widened at that. Of course I knew guns could kill, but my father was gifting me the weapon. As though he expected me to kill.

"Do you understand?" he asked.

I nodded.

"Good," he said. "Then get dressed. We're leaving in an hour."

"Where are we going?" I asked him.

He flashed me a small, sly smile. "The shooting range."

NINE HOURS AFTER we left D.C., the flight begins its descent into what was once Switzerland.

11

My father takes my hand and squeezes it. He's not a man of many words, but throughout the flight he's been even quieter than usual.

"I never wanted this life for you," he says, looking at me.

I squeeze his hand back. "I know, Dad."

But he's not done. "You've had to grow up so damn fast. And now this. I've delivered you into the belly of the beast."

I look at him, really look at him. "You are all that I have left," I say. "I'd rather die here with you than live alone underground until the war ends." *And I'm captured.*

My father shakes his head. "You don't know what you're saying," he says. "You have your whole life ahead of you."

What he doesn't say is that my lifespan isn't all that much longer in the bunker than it is here. The real question is what would kill me first—starvation, capture, or my failing health.

"And what kind of life is that?" I ask.

He's quiet for a moment. "Will likes you. Has for a while. And I've seen the way you look at him when you think no one's watching."

My brow creases at this, and my cheeks flush. Out of all the horrible things I've seen and done, why does this one embarrass me so much?

"Dad, that couldn't ever happen." Even as I say it, I wonder if it could. Will seemed interested in starting something.

My father sighs. "I just wish."

And that's all we do these days. Wish.

THE JET TOUCHES ground and I hold onto my seat as we bounce. Outside the sun is brighter than I've ever seen it, and the sky bluer. I don't know how it's possible that the world can look this lovely.

Outside the runway, a large crowd has gathered. My head pounds at the thought that they are waiting for my father and me.

I unbuckle my seatbelt as the aircraft coasts to a stop near the crowd. By the time my father and I stand, our guards are already waiting in the aisles, their faces grim. I know each and every one of them, which makes this whole situation worse. Now I have over a dozen people to worry over, to grieve for should anything go wrong.

One of them takes my bag from me, and now all I can do is twist my hands together.

Half our guards leave before we do. Then my father exits the jet. I linger back a moment, take a deep breath, then step out to face the enemy.

The air is cool, crisp, and the sun blinds my eyes. I blink against the glare as they adjust. Once they do, my breath catches. The crowd gathered cheers when they see us.

At first I can't figure out why they're cheering. And then I do. My father and I are going to discuss the terms of our surrender. The end of the war. In their eyes, they have won, we have lost, and the world might now return to the way it once was.

I descend down the stairs, keeping my attention focused on not falling in these heels.

On either side of me a camera crew films my entrance. The footage is likely being streamed across the Internet. Anyone who wants to view it can. Will is watching, I know he is, and that thought makes me raise my chin a little higher. I am a soldier, a survivor, and I represent the WUN.

A group of men wearing suits and earpieces waits for us in front of a car—our car. They look too clean, too slick, their hair combed and gelled into place, their suits tailored precisely to their body types. These must be the king's men. The king, I notice, isn't here. He's probably too busy figuring out how to best kill my people.

When we reach them, one steps away from the rest. "Ambassador Freeman, Serenity," he says, reaching a hand out to my father, then to me. I start at the sound of my name spoken from his lips. Of course they know who I am. "My name is Marco, and I am the liaison between you and the king."

I have to bite my tongue to keep from responding as I take his hand. Anything that comes out of my mouth right now will only make the situation worse. Instead I nod. Belatedly I realize that this makes me appear demure.

"Nice to meet you, Marco," my father says, smooth as silk. My father's good at this, masking his true feelings behind a pleasant façade. Me, not so much.

THE DRIVE TO the king's estate, where we'll be staying, is long and quiet. This is the first time I've gotten a good look at the city I'll be staying in.

When we descended into Geneva, I couldn't see the extent of the damage done to the city. Now that I'm in the car, I can. Bullet holes in the walls, piles of rubble where buildings and walkways have crumbled, graffiti, boarded up windows.

Amidst the damage I can see the city's efforts to rebuild. Construction trucks, fresh dirt, piles of building materials. Geneva is already recovering.

I read in history books that this place used to be neutral territory, but it didn't change Switzerland's fate. Once the king sets his sights on a country, he'll do whatever he needs to secure it. This was what he did to peaceful countries; I'd seen firsthand what he did to rebellious ones.

The king's estate rises like a phoenix from the ashes. The walls gleam an unearthly white, the roofs the blue-green color of oxidized copper. The asshole has the audacity to flaunt his wealth in a broken city.

The hatred that smolders in my chest expands at the sight. It's a good thing the gun I smuggled in is currently packed away, else I might be tempted to reach for it and end the peace talks before they've begun.

I feel a hand cover mine. My father's looking at me with a warning in his eyes. I'm being too obvious about my emotions. I fix my expression into something bland and pleasant. At least the cameras aren't here to capture whatever it was my father saw flicker across my features.

"When we arrive," Marco says, breaking the silence, "I'll show you and your entourage to your rooms. King Lazuli is hosting a welcome party tonight. That's when you'll officially meet him. Tomorrow morning the peace talks will commence."

Our car passes through the gates and the security checkpoints. A row of Italian Cypress trees lines the drive. Beyond them is an expanse of green lawn. The symmetry and colors assault my eyes, and something sharp and painful lodges in my throat. A dim memory of how things used to be. The king's estate reminds me of life before war. But the beauty here is duplicitous; the king lives a fantasy. The city outside these gates—that's the unpleasant truth. The world is a mess, and no amount of paint and landscaping can cover that up.

Eventually the car comes to a halt in front of the estate. The doors open and someone reaches for my hand—like I need help exiting a car. Brushing aside the offer, I step out of the vehicle.

I gaze up at those white, white walls, and the only thing I can think of is that, somewhere inside, dwells the devil.

And tonight, I'll meet him.

CHAPTER 4

SERENITY

SEVEN YEARS AGO I killed a man. Four men, in fact. I was only twelve. My father was off at work, and I'd just gotten home from school when I was ambushed. Four men had followed me back to my house. I'd watched them hang back behind me, far away enough to appear as though they were casually strolling. But I'd seen them before, heard rumors about them. No one tells you that in war, sometimes the enemy is your neighbor.

So as soon as I entered my house, I moved into my room and opened the lockbox that held my gun. Just in time too.

The front door smashed open and the men were shouting, no doubt to work me up into a frenzy. And it worked. I screamed at the sound. My heart hammered in my chest.

The weapon was preloaded for an occasion just like this. I clicked off the safety and knelt at the foot of my bed, breathing slowly to calm my racing heart. Gripping the gun with both hands, I aimed at the doorway to my room.

It only took them several more seconds to find me. As soon as the first man came within my line of sight, I pulled the trigger. The bullet hit him right in the middle of the chest. I'd mortally wounded him, but he wouldn't die instantly.

Two of his friends pressed into the doorway, their eyes wide. They were now more interested in what was going on than grabbing me. I shot both of them before they could react.

The fourth man must've seen his friends go down because I heard the pound of his footfalls moving away from my room.

If I didn't kill him now, he'd return for revenge. That was how this new world worked. I knew that even at age twelve.

By the time I'd left my room, the three other men lay on the ground moaning, the fourth man was already out my front door. I sprinted down the hall, past the living room, and followed him outside. As soon as I made it to the front yard I saw him running down my street. I knelt, took a calming breath, aimed, and fired.

His body jolted, then collapsed unnaturally.

By the time the ambulance arrived, all four were dead.

I got away with it too. The courts were too flooded with other cases to hear about the twelve-year-old girl who killed her would-be assaulters. The justice system proclaimed it self-defense, and the case was closed.

AS EVENING DESCENDS in Geneva, I sit in front of the vanity in my new room. The yellow glow of the light makes my features soft. With my hair loosely curled and a touch of makeup on my face, I realize for the first time in maybe ever that I'm pretty. It's a shock, and not a pleasant one either.

In war, beauty is a curse—it catches your enemies' attention, and you don't want that. Better to blend in. But sitting here in my borrowed scarlet dress, blending in is the last thing I'll be doing.

My eyes move to the room behind my reflection. A four-poster bed large enough to swim in rests directly behind me, and next to it are shelves and shelves of books. The ceiling is a mosaic of painted tiles.

In this lavish place, I might not blend in, but it appears I might just fit in.

There's a knock on my door, and one of my guards pokes his head in. "Your father and Marco are waiting for you out here, Serenity," he says. Out there in the sitting room.

Back at home I slept in a room with seven other women; here I have an entire room to myself, my father has another, and the guards another; we all share a sitting room.

I stand up and take in my appearance one final time. My scar catches the light. I might look sweet as syrup, but here in the lion's den I won't hesitate to kill my enemies, diplomacy or not. We're still at war, after all.

Out in the sitting room my father chats amicably with Marco. I'm not fooled by it at all. My father's lethal ability is presentation. He can lie like he's telling the truth. And not just about the little things, either. He can pretend entire relationships into and out of existence. It's not a very honorable talent, but it's the least violent means to an end in war.

In order to convince your enemies you must convince yourself—believe your own lies for a moment. One of his primary rules of diplomacy.

Time to put it into practice. "Hello Marco," I say, cutting into their discussion.

Marco's eyes move from my father to me—or rather, my plunging neckline. "Miss Freeman." He nods. "How do you like your rooms?"

They are a constant reminder of your king's corruption, I think. Instead I say, "They leave little to be desired. Your king is very generous to host us here," I finish off the sentence with a brittle smile. I don't think I can make a long-term career of diplomacy; those words felt like poison coming out.

In contrast to my own disquiet, I can practically feel my father's approval across from me.

"Yes, he is," Marco agrees. "And speaking of the king, he's waiting to meet you in the grand ballroom."

My heart slams in my chest. The king who can't be killed. The king who's caused the death of millions. He's more legend than man. And he's one of the few things that scare me. Because I can't understand how someone can be that evil.

"Well then, what are we waiting for?" I ask, smiling amicably, as though I'm not screaming inside.

Marco assesses me. "What indeed?" he says. I don't like the way he looks at me, as though he's trying to understand my motives.

Marco leads us out of the room. Luckily no cameras wait for us here. Tomorrow I won't be so lucky; the estate will be crawling with them.

As soon as we're in the hallway, I thread my arm through my father's, and our guards fan out around us.

"You clean up well," I say to my father. He's wearing a suit, and it brings out his fine features—high brows, sharp cheekbones, tan skin, wavy hair the color of dusty wheat, bright blue eyes. The fatigues I'm so used to seeing him in wash out his features and make him look his age.

He glances at me. "Thanks—that'll be the only compliment I'll get all evening standing next to you." His eyes light with humor, and I flash him a genuine smile.

"Tell me that again when you're fighting off all the cougars later tonight."

My father chuckles, and for a moment I can pretend that we are not in our enemy's house.

The faint sound of music, conversation, and tinkling glass drifts from down the hall behind two large, closed doors. In front of them stand two of the king's guards. As soon as we approach the doors, the guards open them, and we enter the ballroom.

I blink, just to make sure I'm not seeing things. The room spread out below me is full of warm light, crystal chandeliers, and walls of mirrors. Everything else is covered in gold. People twirl on the dance floor while others talk off to the sides. Here it's as though the war never happened. Here violence, dirt, and death don't exist.

We must be as exotic to the people in this room as they are to me, because it takes mere seconds for the room to quiet. The momentousness of this situation slams into me then. The two of us represent an entire hemisphere of the world. We are the figureheads of the final territories still free of the king. Free, that is, until we leave—*if* we leave.

The cameras that I thought would be absent tonight are waiting for us. A film crew off to our left captures our entrance. At the bottom of the stairs before us another crew waits.

Next to me, Marco announces to the room, "The emissary of the Western United Nations, Ambassador Carl Freeman, and his daughter, Serenity Freeman."

My hand tightens around my father's arm as I stare out at the crowd spread out before me.

And then someone steps up to the base of the staircase. Someone who's haunted my nightmares since I was little. The face I saw when I killed.

King Montes Lazuli.

THE KING

JUST WHEN I thought the evening was going to be another dull meet and greet, the WUN emissary walks in, and on his arm I see her.

The emissary's daughter. Serenity Freeman.

The world doesn't stop moving, the room doesn't go quiet, but I swear something inside me just broke and reformed the moment she turned her devlish eyes on me—and that's the only way to describe those eyes of hers. Devilish. She's a wicked soul, through and through.

Just like me.

She's unlike the women I'm used to. Her arms are sculpted, and her body is lean beneath her dress. It's an almost laughable contrast to the soft women that fill the rest of the room. I'm dying to lift her skirt, run my hands up those legs, and get to know just how toned the rest of her is.

As pretty as her body might be, it's not what's captivated me. I can't look away from her face. In another life it might've been sweet. But not in this one. A wicked scar slices down the side of it. It's the most obvious warning that she's a dangerous creature.

I wish I got off on fear and hate, because both are burning in her eyes the closer she gets to me. I've killed others for less than the expression I see in them, but this woman, she is someone who knows violence intimately. I'm almost positive that death doesn't scare her. But apparently I do.

And the strangest thought yet pops into my mind: I don't want this intriguing woman to fear me.

I know she's a trap. I know the WUN sent her here with her father because they're desperate, and they're hoping to bait me with a woman. Those clever fools probably never thought that what would attract me to her was everything that lay beneath that pretty skin of hers—the viscous, hardened soul that looks so similar to my own. She's the best challenge I've seen yet.

I need to get to know her. She might've just changed everything.

CHAPTER 5

SERENITY

SIX YEARS AGO Washington D.C. was leveled. It was sheer dumb luck that on that particular day, at that particular time, my father and I had driven to a shooting range on the outskirts of the city.

We stood outside, taking turns firing from one of the stalls. I steadied my stance and focused my aim when my peripherals caught sight of something they shouldn't have.

The blast rose into the sky, unfurling like some fiery flower. The sight was incomprehensible—too bright, too big, too breathtaking.

Too dreadful.

I tore my eyes away, and looked to my father. He was already yelling commands at me, but we both wore earmuffs, so they fell onto deaf ears. When he jerked his head towards the building that housed the indoor shooting range, however, I understood.

Flicking on my gun's safety, I shoved my weapon back into its holster just as my father grabbed my arm. Together we sprinted for the building; the few other people outside followed our lead.

I chanced a glance back. The explosion had expanded, and a thin white cloud haloed it. I knew in the pit of my stomach that we had until that cloud reached us to find safety.

My father and I ducked inside. He whipped off his headpiece and began shouting orders to the people loitering on the first floor. I didn't hear his words, but judging from the way men and women made for the stairs down to the basement, he'd said enough for them to seek shelter belowground.

He hadn't let go of me since we'd entered, and now he steered us to the same destination.

In the muffled silence I noticed all the little things that made the moment real: The way one man's jowls shook as he pushed his way past us. The coolness of the earth as we descended further into it. The controlled panic in my father's eyes, like fear sharpened his logical reasoning skills. It had. It's one of the many traits we share.

When we reached the basement, the stairway opened into a hallway. Tugging my arm, my father led me away from the crowd to the end of the corridor. We hooked a right, and my father pulled us into an empty office that had been left open.

He locked the door and overturned a nearby filing cabinet, further blockading it. Next, he flipped the desk. I began to tremble as my father directed me to a corner of the room, dragging the now sideways desk towards us until we were barricaded in.

Atomic bomb.

That was the first time I'd really put a name to what I saw. And it was all because of that damn desk, which looked so similar to the overturned coffee table I'd once read under all those years ago.

My father fit his earmuffs back on his head then wrapped his arms around me, and it was exactly the physical comfort I needed.

It didn't take much longer for the blast to hit us, though *hit* is the wrong word. It passed over us, tore through us. I threw my hands over my head as the blast slammed us into the desk. The explosion roared so loud that I heard it over my earmuffs. It was a monstrous symphony to the end of the world.

And then it was over—if you could say such a thing. The land we returned to hours later was not the same one we'd fled from. Gone was D.C., gone was the White House and every great monument I'd gazed upon with wondrous eyes. Gone was our home. Gone was my former life.

Later we discovered that all big cities across the western hemisphere had been hit. That day the nations that once were lay decimated.

No, the blast wasn't over. Far from it. If anything, it was just the beginning.

MY EYES LOCK with the king's, and I suppress a shudder. He's even more handsome than the pictures I've seen of him. Black, wavy hair, olive skin, dark eyes, sensual lips. But it's more than just his features; it's how he wears them. Like he is something regal, something you want to draw closer to. It's not fair that evil can wear such an alluring mask.

His eyes move over me like a predator sizing up prey.

I make a noise at the back of my throat, and my father places a hand over mine. We can't talk here, not when the cameras are rolling.

I breathe in, then out. I can do this. For my country, I can. I step forward, and we descend down the staircase. I know my father can feel my trembling hands. It's a miracle that my legs are holding me up at all. The entire time the king stares at me. Not my father. Me.

It takes all my energy to keep moving and look calm. In reality, I can't hear anything over the pounding of my pulse and the ringing inside my head. Not until we reach the bottom, until I stare into the king's deep brown eyes. Then the moment comes into hyper focus.

The king peels his eyes away from me to greet my father. "Ambassador Freeman," he says, "it is my pleasure to host you here for the peace talks." It's frightening to see that the king shares my father's talent for camouflaging himself to fit his audience. The king doesn't need peace talks to get what he wants, but he plays along, lying effortlessly through his teeth.

I drop my hold on my father's arm, and he takes the king's outstretched hand as cameras go off. "King Lazuli, it's an honor to finally meet you," my father says. "I hope that our two great hemispheres can come together to foster future peace." My father lies just as effortlessly as he stares the monster in the eyes and shakes his hand.

Now it's my turn.

The king turns his attention away from my father, and my stomach contracts painfully. This is the man who killed my mom. The man who leveled my city and all my friends living in it. He's the man who I've seen shot on national television, yet still he lives.

Unlike his response to my father, I can see the king's genuine interest in me. His eyes look lit from behind. "Ambassador Freeman, I presume that this is your daughter, Serenity Freeman?" the king asks.

Next to me my father's body goes rigid, and I know he senses the king's interest in me. "She is," my father says.

The king gives me a slow, sly grin and grabs my hand. I fight the overwhelming impulse to yank it free, cock my fist, and smash it into his face. Instead I bare my teeth as the cameras go off. I know it looks more like a snarl than a smile, but it's the best I can do at the moment.

King Lazuli brings my hand up to his lips, and I close my eyes to block out the sight of his mouth against my skin. I only open them once he pulls my hand away from his lips. "It's a pleasure to meet you Serenity."

He means it. Heaven help me, I've caught the attention of the king.

"King Lazuli," I choke out. I can feel tears burning my eyes, blurring my vision. I can't cry, not on television.

"Montes," he corrects me quietly. His eyes flick to my father's. "I believe the negotiations in the upcoming days will go quite well. I have a feeling for these things." The king is still holding my hand, and I feel him squeeze it.

None of this gets past my father, who nods once, his mouth a grim line.

The king's eyes move to mine and drink me in before returning to my father. "Mind if I whisk your daughter away for a dance?" the king asks.

My eyes widen. *No.* No, no, no. I don't know how to dance, but that's not even the issue here. The thought of spending any more time in the king's presence has me nauseous. I'm either going to get sick, or, more likely, I'm going to try to kill him.

"Not at all," my father says, his words clipped.

"Fantastic." The king flashes him a smile, and his attention returns to me. He raises an eyebrow. "Shall we?" he asks, as though I've already agreed to it.

"Only if you ask nicely." The words are out before I can attempt to censor myself. I shut my mouth before I can say more.

Those around us fall quiet. Out of the corner of my eye I can see the camera crew, my guards, and the king's retinue shifting nervously, their eyes darting between us. I don't know what reaction they're waiting for, but it's not this.

The king cocks his head, a small smile growing across his face. He raises an eyebrow. "Would you like to dance with me, Serenity?"

"I'd love to." I bite the words out because I have to say them.

Once I accept, the budding tension releases.

"So would I," he says, and again I can see he's being genuine. He gives the hand he's still holding a tug, and I'm gently whisked away.

I can tell everyone there is already aware of us—or him, more precisely, though I can feel curious eyes on me. As soon as we walk onto the dance floor, the king tugs me close. Too close. I can see the rough skin of his jaw, the gentle wave of his hair, the flecks of gold in his brown eyes.

His hand presses into the small of my back, and we begin to move. After glancing at other couples, I move my free hand to his shoulder like the other women do. The footwork, however, completely confuses me.

"I don't know how to dance," I say.

"Then it's a good thing I'm leading," the king responds, his expression amused. He glances down at my chest. "Beautiful necklace," he says, though I know it's just an excuse to stare at my chest.

"It was my mother's."

"Mmm," he says, and that's the end of that.

"She's dead."

"I'm sorry to hear that."

"No you're not." I can't get my mouth to shut up. Not right now when I'm caught in the arms of my mother's killer. "She died when your army dropped a bomb near our home."

Now I've caught his attention. His eyes narrow, but he doesn't look angry. More like I intrigue him.

"It was the same day that I received the scar on my face," I continue.

The king's gaze moves to my scar. "It seems I've caused you a lot of pain. I'm sorry for that."

I smile sardonically. "Save your lies for someone who will believe them."

The king's grip on my hand tightens. I'm in dangerous waters. "What makes you think I'm lying?"

"A man who was truly sorry would never have dropped the bomb to begin with." My breath catches as soon as the words leave my mouth. Have I gone too far?

The king scrutinizes me, and then ever so slowly, a smile appears. "I could have you killed for what you've said to me."

Fear grips my heart, but I call his bluff. "You won't."

He spins me. "Oh, and why is that?" he asks, raising an eyebrow.

"Because I amuse you." It's hard to admit that all I'm good for here is his entertainment.

His gaze drinks me in, and he presses me closer to him. "You do. Keep it up and the WUN might not face total annihilation."

I raise my eyebrows. "The truth suits you well." Even if it is psychotic. But I'd prefer hearing the ugly truth than a pretty lie.

My dress swishes around me as we twirl. It's not lost on me that that's what I am right now—a pretty lie, a soldier disguised as a lady.

"*You* suit me well," he says, his gaze sweeping over me. It sickens me that he seems to approve of what he sees.

My fingers dig into the muscles of his shoulder. "Sorry, but I don't mix business and pleasure."

"There's always time for firsts," he responds.

I'd gut him before that ever happened. I thin my eyes as I study him. "And why would I do that? I've considered you my enemy all my life."

The king smiles at me, thoroughly enjoying himself. "I don't really care about your personal problems." He's clearly warmed up to telling the truth.

"I can't imagine why you've been single this whole time," I say sarcastically. The song we're dancing to ends and a new one starts up.

His lips quirk. "Why get married when there are so many beautiful women who already want to be with me?"

I close my eyes and breathe through my nose. "Maybe you should go back to lying."

"Hmm," he muses, eyeing me, "the lady doesn't mind talking about destruction and death, but throw in a little sex and she gets demure."

My face flushes before I can help it, and the king chuckles. "My, my, have you never … ?" He gazes at me curiously. "How old *are* you?"

Even through my burning cheeks I give him a nasty look. "Nineteen."

"Nineteen? And you've never been romantic? Did you just get out of an ugly phase?"

Despite his offensive words, I flash him my first real smile of the evening. "I was too busy killing your men to bother with love."

Now he looks mad. It's nice to know that the king might actually care about the death of his soldiers. "Watch your words," he snaps.

I decide to back off. If I anger King Lazuli too much, my father and I could easily find ourselves on the wrong end of a gun.

He watches me, and I can practically see the anger flow away from his face, replaced with that predatory look I saw when I first locked eyes with him. "You were a soldier?" he asks.

"Yes."

"But not anymore?"

"I will always be a soldier," I say, "but right now I fight with my tongue rather than my fists."

He gives me a slow smile. "Perhaps we can put that tongue to other uses."

"Then perhaps I will resort to fighting with my fists."

"I welcome the challenge." In his eyes is a promise that he'll make good on.

Tonight I'm sleeping with my gun.

I RIP MY dress off and run my tongue over my teeth as soon as I enter my bedroom. The representatives knew. They *knew* there would be a chance that dolled up I might catch the king's attention. Of course. All other tactics hadn't worked with him. Everyone else came back in a body bag. Why not give it a shot and tempt the king with flesh? It was the oldest trick in the fucking book. And it worked.

I tear the rest of the clothes off of my body and change into a pair of pajamas.

"Serenity?" my father calls from the sitting room.

"What?" I ask as I untuck my hair from my shirt. My voice is angry.

He fills up the doorway to my room and takes me in. Neither of us needs to say anything—and we wouldn't dare anyway, the room had to be bugged. But he doesn't need to. His anguished expression tells me how he feels about our current situation.

"I'm sorry." He shakes his head.

"Why did no one tell me?" Even as I say this, I wonder if that's what had my father tense around the general when we left. He might've known then what I'd only just figured out.

I can't bring myself to be mad at him. We were all just pawns at this point.

My father pinches the bridge of his nose. "It was never official. You're a soldier and a future emissary. We wanted you to do what you do best—represent the WUN."

I read into what he can't say under the king's roof: acting was never my strength. I can barely hold my tongue; pretending to like the vilest man I know is beyond my abilities.

"We should check in with General Kline right now," he says.

I nod, my hands balling into fists. "I'd love to talk with him."

"Serenity." My father's voice carries a warning.

I sigh. "Let's just get this over with." I had a bad case of jetlag, and I wanted to get some sleep before tomorrow's peace talks.

I follow my father into his room, where his laptop rests on a side desk. I grab a nearby chair and pull it alongside my father's.

Once we're situated in front of the computer, my father calls up the representatives. They answer almost immediately.

"Ambassador Freeman and Serenity Freeman checking in," my father says.

On the other side of the screen I can see the bunker's conference room and the representatives sitting around the table. Now that I'm here inside the king's house, in this place filled with glittery objects and natural light, the conference room looks especially bleak.

"Good to hear from you Carl," the general says. "How's it going?"

My father's eyes slide to mine. "Fine so far. Have you been watching the footage?"

"Yes. Is Serenity there?"

My father turns the laptop so that my face takes up the screen. "General Kline." I nod to him.

"Serenity, aside from that comment you made during your introductions, you seem to be doing well making the king's acquaintance."

There are so many things that I want to shout at the general, none of which I can voice, one because he's still the leader of my country, and two, because I have to assume we're being recorded.

So instead I say, "Surprised? I was too." I lower my voice. "You've thrown me to the wolves, General." That's the closest thing I can come to the truth, that I'm here to persuade the king through more carnal means.

"Serenity, nations rely on your actions. Now is not the time for weakness." General Kline's practically chastising me.

My throat works. "He killed her." My father reaches over and squeezes my shoulder, his subtle way of telling me to shut up, that I've said too much. But the king already knows what I've just spoken out loud—that I blame him for my mother's death.

"And you've killed mothers, fathers, sons and daughters. War has taken something from everyone, Serenity. We can end that. You can end that."

His words sober me up. He's right, of course. The only difference between the king and I is that the king's body count is much higher, and for most of his kills he never had to dirty his hands.

My gaze moves from the general to his son who sits further down the table. "I'm sorry, Will," I say. His face is too grainy to make out, but I'm sure the expression he wears is not a pleasant one.

"There's nothing to apologize for," he says. "Negotiate an agreement and make it back here safely. That's all I want."

My throat constricts and I nod. Now that the cat's out of the bag, I know what I must do.

I'm going to have to charm the king into giving the WUN what it needs.

CHAPTER 6

SERENITY

FIVE YEARS AGO my father and I moved into the bunker. By that time we were in a full-scale war with the eastern hemisphere, and the king had started picking off those political leaders not already dead. Located several miles outside of D.C., the bunker was an asylum for what was left of our government officials and their families.

It also offered some measureable protection against the high radiation levels caused by the nuclear blasts. Not that it mattered. The radiation was in the water, in the earth and the food supply. We'd lived with it long enough; the damage was already done.

The day my father and I moved in, when I first saw the beds that lined a single room, my chest tightened. I realized that the world I thought I knew had been gone for a while now and somewhere along the way *people* had become synonymous with *threat*.

My wariness eventually wore off, and my next reaction was excitement. I might make *friends*. I had to dust that word off; I'd shelved it from my vocabulary for so long.

The bunker, however, came with its own sacrifices. No natural light filtered into our new home, and I had once been a self-proclaimed child of the sun. An unpleasant schedule came to rule my days. And social interactions were difficult to maneuver; I found I was way more skilled at making enemies than I was friends.

Still, I was safe, surrounded by people that didn't antagonize me, and I had reliable food and shelter. For the first time in a long time, I felt hopeful.

"I HATE DRESSES," I mumble as one of my guards zips me up.

He snickers.

"Shut up. It's not funny." I can't breathe in this thing.

"Freeman in a dress? Hell yeah it is," my guard says.

I throw him a look just as Marco knocks on the door to our suite.

The guard squeezes my shoulder. "Own those negotiations," he whispers.

I leave my room as my father opens the door. "Morning Marco," he says, grabbing his briefcase.

Marco nods to him. "Ready to go?"

My father looks over to where I stand.

"I'm ready," I say, now that my wispy dress is on. I glance back at my room. My gun lies underneath the pillows on my bed. It's hard to walk into the peace talks in my flimsy outfit without my usual protection.

"'Kay, then let's do this," my father says.

We follow Marco out into the hall, our guards shadowing us. At least they are allowed to carry holstered weapons. I've seen most of them in action, so I trust their skills.

We move to the other end of the king's mansion, where the negotiations are to take place. I fist my hands in the black folds of my dress. I've learned a lot about diplomacy from my father, but I've never been able to apply any of my lessons. I know how negotiations with an enemy state work in theory, but not in practice, and I fear that something I say or do might cause irreversible damage.

I can identify the conference room from all the way down the hall. Cameramen and film crews cluster around the door. Flashes of light are already going off, which makes me think that the king must have arrived before us.

My heart pounds a little faster at the thought. Last night felt like we danced on the edge of a knife. One wrong move and I'd cut myself.

Despite the obvious danger that comes from dealing with the king, yesterday he hadn't struck me as particularly … evil. Nor, for that matter, did he seem immortal, though he did appear to be younger than his true age. If I had to guess, I'd say the king is in his mid thirties. King Lazuli, however, has been conquering countries for nearly thirty years.

My thoughts are interrupted by a flash of light, and then the camera crews are on us, snapping shots and filming our entrance.

Unlike the conference room back in the bunker, this one is full of light and gilded surfaces. It is a room that a king does business in, and the sight of it reminds me all over again just why I despise the man who rules over half the world.

King Lazuli waits for us inside the room. His eyes find mine almost immediately. Once they do, they don't bother looking away.

In that moment I can feel in my bones that my father and I are merely toys here for the king's entertainment. Nothing more. We have no real power, so the king is allowed the luxury of gazing at the emissary's daughter and ignoring everyone else in the room.

I can still see flashes of light from my peripherals, but my attention focuses on the table. Someone's set placards in front of each seat. I look for my name, not surprised to find it placed next to the king's chair.

"How … convenient," I murmur quietly as I pass him.

King Lazuli pulls out my chair and leans in. "Convenient—yes, I do believe that word sums up our relationship."

I didn't notice it last night, but there's a subtle lilt to his words. English is not his first language. I wonder what is.

"We have no relationship," I whisper back to him. Luckily, there's too much going on around us for our conversation to gather unwanted attention.

His eyes linger on my face, moving to my scar, then my lips. "You won't be saying that by the time you leave."

I hold his gaze and suppress a shiver. As much as I want to fight his words, I fear they're true.

MY FATHER TAKES a seat across from me. His eyes move between the two of us, but other than that, there's no indication that the seating arrangement bothers him. I'm not deceived. He hates the king more than even I do.

Someone places a document in front of me. It takes me a minute to realize this is a peace treaty, a tentative contract drawn up listing the conditions that need to be met in order for the war to end.

King Lazuli's arm brushes mine from where he sits to my right. My eyes flick to him, but he's not paying attention to me. "Ambassador Freeman, Serenity," the king says, nodding to each of us, "in front of you is a draft of the terms of your surrender."

I see flashes of light go off as each media outlet allowed in here captures the beginning of the negotiations. Each one distracts me from the matter at hand.

My father pulls out the document the WUN crafted up that catalogues our terms of surrender. After reading it on the flight over, I can rattle off the essentials: Our people must be provided with medical relief, first and foremost. Then steps must be taken to clean the environment—too much radiation has seeped into the earth and the running water. It's in our food, and until we can expel it, people are going to keep getting cancer.

Once those two requirements are met, then our secondary measures are to boost the economy and reestablish the social order that existed before the war.

The king takes the document from my father and flips through it. Suddenly he laughs. "You think I'm going to let your country revert back to the materialistic, wasteful state it was in before the war?" he says, his eyes moving over the page before lifting to meet my father's gaze. The irony of his statement isn't lost on me, here in this opulent palace of his.

Across the table, my father relaxes into his seat, looking at ease when I'm sure that's the last thing he feels. "The WUN is not suggesting that. We merely wish to get our economy back on its feet."

The king's eyes flash. "Your hemisphere will never be where it once was."

THE NEGOTIATIONS DRAW on for a long time even after the king makes it known that he wants to cripple our economy. I shiver at the thought. Though pretty much anything would be an improvement from the current state of the western hemisphere, I know from history that there'd be long-term problems if the king decided to purposefully weaken our economy.

I page through the king's document in front of me. Most passages are long-winded discussions of the terms of the agreement. I keep looking for the medical relief the king would provide for our people, but I can't find any mention of it.

"Where can I find the terms of medical relief you'll provide the WUN?" I finally ask, turning to the king.

He swivels his body to face me. "There are none," he says.

I blink at him a few times. "None?"

"None."

I stand suddenly. "You'd leave our people to suffer? To die?" I don't know what I'm doing. It feels as though someone's squeezing my lungs because I can't seem to get enough air.

The king leans back in his seat. "Only some of them." He gives me a challenging look.

My anger obscures my vision. I ball my hands into fists. "This isn't a game!"

Silence.

No one moves.

And then a whole lot of things happen at once. The king stands, and judging by the vein throbbing at his temple, he's pissed. Behind me several people push forward, and my guards press in close.

King Lazuli leans in, his eyes flashing dangerously. "Yes, Serenity, this is a game. One you've already lost."

I'M ESCORTED FROM the negotiations for the rest of the day. The king's guards take me back to my room. They linger outside it, standing guard in case I try to leave.

Now that the anger has dulled somewhat, embarrassment and guilt quickly follow. I can't act like that, even if I think I'm defending the WUN. No one's going to thank me if the negotiations dissolve because of my emotional outbursts.

I hear the door to our suite open and, a few seconds later, a knock on my door. My heart hammers away in my chest. I stand, and my muscles tense. Knowing my father, he's not going to yell, and his quiet disappointment is so much worse to bear.

The door opens, but instead of my father, King Lazuli stands in the doorway.

My eyes widen. "What are you doing here?" My earlier anger hasn't simmered back to the surface yet. I'm too surprised.

He closes the door behind him and strolls into my room, taking a look around. "How are you liking the palace so far?" he asks.

I raise my eyebrows. "It's fine."

"*Fine?*" It's his turn to raise his eyebrows. "Surely it's more than just fine."

Now my anger's returning, like a dear old friend. "Okay, it's more than fine. It's absolutely repulsive that you can live around such opulence when the rest of this city is so broken. I'm sickened to hear you deny my people basic medical relief while you host dinner parties inside your palace."

The king approaches me. "There it is. The truth: you hate everything about me."

I suck in a sharp breath of air. "*Yes*," I breathe.

King Lazuli holds the crook of his arm out. "Walk with me."

I take a step back, eyeing his arm like it's poisonous. I just admitted to the king of the eastern hemisphere that I hated him.

When he sees my hesitation, he says, "I don't bite."

"No," I say, "you kill."

"So do you, soldier."

We stare at each other a moment. Not one fiber of my being wants to touch him, but I remember General Kline's words yesterday. I need to play my part.

Reluctantly I slide my fingers through the crook of King Lazuli's arm, and he leads me out of my room.

"Where's my father?" I ask as soon as we pass his empty room.

"He's still in discussions with my aides."

"And you're skipping out to what—give me a tour of your mansion?"

The king glances down at me, a small smile playing on his lips. "Something like that."

I frown at his expression and a sick sensation coils through my stomach. I can practically smell the desire wafting off of him.

The thought makes me want to puke. I've been rude to him since we met. I stood up to him; I admitted that I hated him. He must truly be psychotic if that excites rather than angers him.

He leads me outside to the gardens. "How lovely," I say, "you pay someone to cut your hedges into cute little animals. I'm so impressed."

His lips twitch. "I'm pleased to hear you like them so much. I'll have the gardeners shape another just for you. Perhaps a gun? Or are you more of a hand grenade lady?"

"How about you simply uproot the hedge you plan on shaping and watch it slowly die? That would be a more accurate representation of me and my people."

The king sighs. "You do not know the first thing about power."

"And you don't know the first thing about compassion," I bite out.

To our right, a large alcove has been cut into the hedge that borders the gardens. Inside it sits a marble sculpture. The king pushes me into the alcove.

My back bumps into the nearly solid surface of the hedge as the king presses his body against mine. "You think you know something about compassion? A soldier trained to kill?"

"Yes," I say.

"Then prove it."

I raise my eyebrow, still pinned between him and the hedge. Despite his closeness and his heated emotions, I'm not scared. I know how to take him down if I need to, and I trust him more when he's not so composed.

"How exactly would you suggest I prove it?"

His gaze flicks to my mouth. "Kiss me."

My breath hitches. "I think you've confused passion with *com*passion."

"No, I haven't." His eyes glitter, and I have to remind myself that he's a sick human being, because right now all I'm noticing are his expressive eyes and sensual mouth. "Compassion is showing kindness towards the man who killed your mother."

"You want to see compassion? Fine." I take the hand pressed against my shoulders and kiss his knuckles. "I've now kissed the hand of my mother's killer."

Before he has time to react to my chaste kiss, I bring my other hand up and slap him.

His head whips to the side. "I'm also a vindictive bitch," I say.

Slowly he moves his face back to where it was. There's a dull pink handprint across his cheek. His eyes flash, and I'm already learning that this is when he's at his most dangerous. "And I don't play fair," he admits.

The words are hardly out of his mouth when he closes the distance between us and his mouth captures mine.

There's nothing sweet or diplomatic about this kiss. His lips move roughly against my own, and his hand runs down the length of my side, as if even a kiss isn't enough to satiate him.

I will my mind to go blank before I kiss him back. I press my eyes tightly closed as I force myself to wind my arms around his neck and lean into him.

As soon as he feels me respond, the kiss deepens. His lips part my own and his tongue presses against mine.

Oh God, I don't think I can do this. It's too much. I turn my head to the side to break off the kiss.

I swallow down my bile. "Enough," I say, my voice hoarse.

He steps away from me, and I pull in a deep breath of air. The king's staring at my lips, as though looking at them long enough might cause them to resume their former activity.

29

I gaze at him, feeling like a cornered creature. This is when *I'm* my most dangerous. He must sense it as well because he steps aside. I brush past him, and he catches my wrist. "I want to see you tonight." His meaning is clear.

"No," I say.

"Yes."

"Not until you offer full medical relief to the WUN with no strings attached." It's a ballsy move, manipulating him like this. But this is why the WUN sent me.

"I could simply have you killed if you don't agree."

"Then kill me," I say, tugging on my wrist. I am more than ready to leave the king and his empty threats. Chances are, he will eventually kill me, but not like this.

He doesn't let go of me. "I'll think about it," he finally says, and I know he's referring to the medical relief and not having me killed.

"And all I'll do is *think* about visiting you until you make your decision," I say.

The king tugs my wrist hard enough for me to stumble into him. "Stop toying with me," he growls against my ear, his voice low and lethal.

I pull away from him. "Unlike you, I don't play games, *Montes*."

His eyes trail down my face to my lips. "And I get what I want. Always."

I yank my wrist out of his grip and back away from him. I can see the cold calculation in his eyes.

"There's always time for firsts," I say, and then I walk away.

"*WHAT WERE YOU thinking?*" Unlike my father, General Kline yells when he's angry.

Next to me, my father broods. When he returned an hour ago, he looked at me and shook his head. That's all it took for me to break down and apologize. I wanted him to be proud of me, not disappointed.

General Kline, on the other hand, could kiss my ass.

I flash him a vicious smile and hold up my index finger, signaling him to give me a moment. Seizing a nearby pen and sheet of paper, I scrawl a note on it.

The king came to my room after that incident, we went for a walk, and he kissed me. I've promised to do more if he negotiates medical relief into the peace agreement.

My cheeks burn as I hold the paper up to the camera, and my father looks away.

I've already told my dad about my little walk in the gardens. I can't imagine what he's feeling. Of the two of us, his is the worse task. He has to pretend to negotiate with a dictator while allowing that same man to take advantage of his daughter. At least I have some agency in the matter. He has none.

I pull the sheet away from the screen and hand it to my father, who will have to burn it later. This is the securest way to communicate.

The conference room in the bunker is quiet. I'm sure the situation doesn't sit well with anyone in there. I feel like a harlot, trading sex for promises.

The general bends over the table and scribbles something onto a sheet of paper before approaching the screen.

Good job, Serenity. Hold him to that and leave the rest to your father for now. If you try to leverage anything else, he's going to figure out what's going on.

AS IF THE king hasn't already. It didn't take a rocket scientist to deduce what my role here was. I'm just surprised that it's actually been working so far.

The general removes the note from the screen and returns to his seat a short distance away. "From now on, control yourself during negotiations," he says gruffly.

I work my jaw, but nod.

Behind me, I hear a distant knock on the door. My dad and I glance at each other.

"I'll get it," I say.

I push out of my chair and leave my father's room, making sure to close the door behind me. I pass through the apartment's common area and open the front door.

Marco stands on the other side. "The king requests your presence at dinner," he says, giving me a sullen look. The feeling's mutual.

"Request denied," I say, closing the door.

Marco's foot shoots out and catches the door before it can latch shut. "You can't deny the king's request."

"Well, I am." I give Marco's foot a good kick. He yelps and pulls it back, and I slam the door shut.

"What was that about?" my dad asks when I return to the room.

"The king requested my presence at dinner."

"And?" my father asks.

There's loud knocking on the other side of the suite door.

"I politely declined."

My father raises an eyebrow while the representatives watch from the other side of the screen. "Are you going to answer the door?" he asks.

"No."

My father lets a small smile slip out, just enough to tell me that I'm humoring him.

The general clears his throat. "You should go to dinner with him."

"Well, I don't want to."

"That's not a good enough reason, Serenity," the general says.

I lean in close to the screen. "You want me to use my womanly wiles to secure a favorable peace agreement? That's exactly what I'm doing," I say. "Let me do my job." The truth is that I'm not trying to play hard to get—I don't know the first thing about attraction. I simply can't stand the thought of being close to the king right now.

THE FOLLOWING MORNING I'm back in the conference room, sitting across from my father while we wait for the king.

The king pushes open the conference room doors. He holds onto two documents; one he drops in front of my father, the other he drops in front of me.

He leans in next to my ear. "I expect to see you in my room, tonight," he whispers.

I stiffen, watching him as he takes a seat next to me. His leg brushes against mine, and I flinch from the contact. Across from me my father's eyes move between the two of us.

"Here is a revised peace treaty that has been adjusted based on yesterday's discussions," the king says.

My father and I flip through the document, and I can't help the way my hands shake, crinkling the paper. I already know what I'm going to find before I read it.

"Medical relief?" My father says, looking up from the document in front of him. His voice carries both confusion and hope.

"Serenity happens to be very persuasive," the king says, glancing at me. My stomach clenches at his heated look. I try to tell myself that I'm merely nauseous at the thought of what's coming tonight. But it's more than just that. It's that in some dark corner of my mind, the thought of being alone with the king excites me.

I close my eyes and breathe in and out. When I open them, my father's gaze rests on mine for a moment. Just long enough for me to read the sheer panic in his own.

"YOU DON'T HAVE to do it, Serenity," my father says. He's sitting on a side chair in my room, his hands clasped so tightly together that his knuckles are a bluish white color. I'm flipping through the dresses I temporarily own.

"Dad," I throw him a glance, "you and I both know that's not an option." There's no telling what the king would do if I backed out after he'd held up his end.

My father scrubs his face and pushes himself out of the chair. "Come here," he says, opening his arms.

I stop rifling through my clothes to look at him. His face is weary—old. And as he stands there with open arms, I realize that he might need my comfort more than I need his.

I walk into his embrace and he envelops me in a hug. He speaks into my hair. "I'm not okay with this." His hold on me tightens. "I've been ordered—" My father's voice catches. "I've been ordered to let this happen."

"I know." I'd assumed as much. The general is the mastermind behind this idiotic plan. It doesn't matter how much my father disagrees with it, if General Kline ordered it, he's duty bound to follow through. As am I.

He holds me for a long time, and I'm hesitant to pull away before he does. I'm afraid of what I'll see on his face.

"You'll never know how proud I am of you."

I give a humorless laugh. "There's nothing honorable about what I'm doing."

My dad draws back to look at me. If he cried while he held me, all traces of his tears are gone. "Your life has never been easy, Serenity. The world has always demanded something from you—war is a series of hard choices—but you haven't let it break you. Not even now, when this is being asked of you. No father could be prouder of his daughter."

I blink back tears and swallow. "Thank you," I say quietly.

THIS EVENING, WHEN Marco knocks on our suite's door, I'm armed for battle. I have a plan that will keep the monster at bay.

I open the door. "The king requests—"

"Yeah, yeah, I know," I say. "Let's go." I push past Marco. The guards won't come with me tonight, not for this sort of thing.

Marco jogs up to me. "You're going the wrong way Miss Freeman," he says, catching my arm and spinning me around.

"Oh." I let him lead me in the opposite direction, and I smooth down the fabric of the lacey plum colored dress I wear. For the millionth time I wish I was wearing my fatigues. The tight bodice and high heels limit my movement.

We tread down the halls, and I memorize every twist and turn Marco makes. I'll need to since I doubt the king will escort me back to my room before he gets what he wants.

Every so often someone passes by me in the hallways. Their eyes dart to mine, then away. I sometimes receive this reaction from people who notice my scar. Tonight, however, I wonder if this has more to do with the filmed negotiations. I never considered the fact that people might recognize me once the footage hit the Internet, but they must.

Marco and I climb a set of stairs and turn down a hall. I can tell we're nearing the king's private rooms. There's a stillness about my surroundings that the rest of the mansion lacks.

I follow Marco up to a door and wait while he knocks. A servant opens the door and ushers us in. A quick glance around the room tells me that this is a private dining room. The lights have been dimmed, and a small round table has been set for two.

Romantic. I believe that's how one would describe the setting. Unease gathers in the pit of my stomach.

The king steps into the room from some side chamber, fiddling with a cufflink of his suit. When he catches my eye, I see him pause. His eyes move over me, his gaze searing. I can tell he doesn't want to simply have his way with me, and that realization surprises me.

"Thank you, Marco," the king says, "you may go now."

Marco inclines his head and backs away. I watch him leave us. Only once the door clicks shut, do I turn to face the king.

He's studying me. "Are you happy?"

"About what?" I ask.

"Your precious medical relief."

"I'll be happy once I see the finished peace agreement with the medical relief included. Until then, I remain skeptical." The king could always withdraw that clause of the treaty once he gets what he wants from me. That's why I'm going to have to make sure he doesn't.

"You don't trust me?"

I guffaw. "I don't have the luxury. In my world trust will land you a knife in your back and an early grave."

"So cynical," the king says, *tsk*-ing. He approaches me. "Why didn't you come to dinner last night?" he asks. His eyes gleam. He's not a man to take rejection well.

"I thought we just went over my opinion on trust."

King Lazuli cups my face and tilts my head up. His thumb strokes my jawline as his eyes dance over my lips. It takes most of my self-control to let him do this. Even this small touch feels extraordinarily intimate. "You don't trust yourself with me?" he asks.

"*Especially* not with you," I say, holding his gaze. My pulse is in my ears.

He drops his hand and moves away from me, a smile playing along his lips. "Hungry?" he asks, indicating the table.

I'm not, but pretending to eat is better than the alternative. I nod. "Starving."

I make my way over to the table, where King Lazuli pulls out a chair for me. I give him a strange look as I take it.

"Are you not used to a man pulling out your chair for you?" he asks.

"Where I live, a man would sooner mug me than pull out a chair for me." It's not completely true. I wouldn't get mugged in the bunker. But out on the streets where resources are scarce? Absolutely.

The king frowns at this. "Once this war is over, I will teach your country's men how to treat women."

I can't help it, I laugh. There are so many things wrong with his statement. "One, King Lazuli—"

"Montes," he corrects me, walking around the table and taking a seat across from me.

"—the men of my country aren't savages by nature. *Your* war has made savages of us all, me included." Of course the megalomaniac across from me would twist a problem he created into some form of cultural sexism. "And two, you are the last person on earth who should speak of how to treat women."

I went too far. I can see it in the way the vein at the king's temple throbs. We stare at each other for a few long seconds, and I can practically see the king's internal debate. In the past he's killed off everyone who speaks out against him, but clearly he's hesitant to do that to me, now that he's gotten me in his private rooms. But how to handle the situation?

The moment is interrupted by what appears to be the king's personal chef. She sets a covered plate in front of each of us, and then removes the metal lids. "Filet mignon served with a red wine sauce, fried gnocchi, and caramelized shallots. Paired with a cabernet sauvignon."

I stare at the plate in front of me. I don't recognize any of the food items the chef just rattled off, and I can only identify the reddish-brown lump on my plate as meat. But from the smell wafting off the food, it will taste delicious.

The chef pours a small serving of wine into the king's glass, and I watch, fascinated, as the king swirls the liquid, smells it, and tips a portion back into his mouth. After a moment, he nods, and the chef pours more wine into the king's glass, and then mine.

"You make food look like an art form," I say.

"That's because it can be," the king responds.

I shake my head and glance down at my meal. He will never understand how insulting this is to a girl who is always underfed.

"Go ahead," he says, "try it."

I lift my knife and fork and try a bite of the meat. I have to close my eyes as I eat it. I'm not sure I've ever tasted anything so delicious.

I hear the king chuckle across from me and my eyes snap open. "Now try the wine." His voice lilts, reminding me that he's just as exotic to me as his lifestyle is.

I reach for my glass. I've only had sips of alcohol up until now. Not too many people in the bunker bother with the stuff, but I've tasted it enough to expect the strange flavor that hits my taste buds. What I don't expect is the warm richness of the liquid. It heats up my throat, and then my stomach. I didn't know any substance could do such a thing.

"It's good," I say reluctantly, and then I take another drink. And another.

"Just good?" There's a twinkle in the king's eyes. "That's the best you can do?"

"Yes."

The room gets quiet, and I know that we're both remembering my earlier words. I wonder why he hasn't brought them up again.

"Tell me about yourself," I finally say, because I can't think of a more open-ended question to distract us.

The king raises his eyebrows. "What is it you want to know?" he asks.

I shrug. "Whatever it is you want to tell me."

"I'm an only child," he starts.

"Me too," I say, taking another swig of my wine.

He nods. "My mother passed away when I was eight, and my father passed away when I was twenty-two."

"I'm sorry," I say, and I mean it. Regardless of who the king is, I can empathize with the pain of losing a parent.

"Thank you," he says, holding my gaze. In that second, my pulse speeds up. I'm a fly caught in a spider's web, a moth drawn to flame. He's pain and death, yet I'm falling into those dark eyes of his. Perhaps he truly is something supernatural if he can coax this response from me.

King Lazuli glances away. "I enjoy playing football—soccer—I sing in the shower—"

I raise my eyebrows. "You sing in the shower?"

The grin that spreads along his face is pure sin. "I can always give you a demonstration, but you'd be required to join me."

"I think I'll pass." I reach for my full glass of wine and take another drink. I glance at it once I pull it away from my mouth. I could've sworn I'd almost finished the wine. Those servants of his should double as spies; they're shadows, slipping in and out of the room, refilling drinks, removing silverware—essentially seeing to our every need.

"How about you?" the king asks, tipping his own glass back.

I chew the inside of my cheek and stare at my wine. "I live in a room with seven other women. This trip is the first time I've seen natural light in months, but what I miss the most about the sky are the stars—oh, and I love to swim, even though I haven't been able to for several years."

The king holds my gaze. "Would you like to?"

"Like to what?" I ask, drinking more wine.

"Go for a swim. I have a pool."

My eyes widen, though I shouldn't be surprised to learn about this. "I don't have a swimsuit," I say. What I don't mention is that it seems wrong to enjoy myself when so many others can't.

He waves away my concern. "That's not an issue. Marco can get you one." The king stands up. "Give me a moment." He walks out of the room, presumably to talk to one of his servants.

As soon as he's gone, I eye the door. I could slip out now and return to my room. Where would that leave me, though? No, I need to stick around a little longer.

At least my plan is unfolding as I wanted it to. So long as I keep the king talking I don't have to do anything physical with him. But more importantly, if the king sees me as more than just a pretty face with an attitude, I'll have more leverage.

The king comes back in the room. "Grab your glass of wine," he says, seizing his own glass and the wine bottle that sits next to it.

I glance at our half-eaten plates. "What about the food?"

"It'll be here when we come back."

I know he says that for my benefit. I doubt the king would eat a reheated meal. But he's probably learned enough about me to know that I'd balk at wasting it.

He takes my hand and leads me to the door. I stare at our joined hands. The backside of his is tan, and I don't know why that particular detail makes me wistful, but it does.

Ashamedly, I savor the warm press of his palm. I can tell that he's used to being touched by the way his focus is on other things. And now, horror of horrors, it sinks in that I actually like skin contact with the king.

"What are you thinking about?" he asks.

"Nothing." I respond too fast, and the king's lips twitch. "Why do you ask?"

"You had a small smile on your face for a minute there. It was nice."

I look away, mortified that the king caught me smiling while I was thinking about him. Scratch that, I was embarrassed that the king caused me to smile in the first place.

"And the lady shuts down yet again. I should add smiles and compliments to the growing list of things that make you uneasy," King Lazuli says.

"You are what makes me uneasy," I say.

His grip on my hand tightens. "I know." He looks down at me, and I see the desire in his eyes.

I swallow. Tonight is going to be long.

I HOLD MY towel tightly to myself when I leave the bathroom. It's a good thing the alcohol is really starting to hit my system and lower my inhibitions. Otherwise there's no way I'd have the courage to do what I'm doing now.

King Lazuli waits for me in the room that houses his pool, wearing a swimsuit that leaves little to the imagination. I suck in my cheeks. I'd expected the king to have thin, doughy arms and a shapeless stomach under all those suits of his. I hadn't expected him to be toned like a soldier.

Our eyes meet across the room. "Are you going to take off your towel?" he asks.

"As soon as I get more wine." I probably shouldn't drink more. I'm already starting to feel a little queasy from the alcohol and overly rich food.

The king grabs my glass from where it rests on the edge of the pool next to the wine bottle, and he brings it over to me. "How about a trade: your glass of wine for the towel."

Instead of answering him, I take the wine in his hand, down it in two long gulps, and then let go of my towel.

It drops to the ground, and I'm left standing in only a black bikini. The king takes a step back, his expressive eyes brighter than usual. I know what he sees—a lean body toned by war. He might even see some of my fainter scars.

I never thought there was anything particularly beautiful about my body. It is useful, and in my war-torn country, that's the best I can ask for.

Only now, as Montes's gaze drinks me in, I realize he's savoring me like he does his wine. Like I am something rare and refined and he wants to take his time enjoying me. The thought makes me aware of every inch of exposed skin.

He takes my empty glass and sets it on a nearby ledge, his eyes serious. I sway a little on my feet as I watch him; the alcohol is already affecting me.

When the king turns back to me, he bends and scoops my feet out from beneath me.

"What are you doing?" I gasp out.

"What do think I'm doing?" he asks, carrying me to the shallow edge of the pool, where steps trail down into the water.

Alcohol swirls in my stomach, and I'm not sure whether I like the heady way it makes me feel. It's causing me to notice the way the king's dark hair curls at the base of his neck, and the golden skin that covers his strong muscles.

My body dips, and I hear the first splash of water as the king steps into the pool. He gazes down at me, and I catch my breath.

I'd never much cared for those epic love stories I'd heard growing up—Romeo and Juliet, Tristan and Isolde, Helen and Paris. All couples who'd placed love above all else; I thought the whole lot of them were idiots. But the way the king is looking at me ... now I can see why so many loved those stories. There is something to forbidden passion. One heated look has me feeling like I'm on the edge of a precipice, waiting to jump.

My body dips again as we descend down the last two steps. The water kisses the bare skin of my back, but I'm still staring at the king, and he me.

I blink rapidly. I'm here to seduce the king, not to actually feel something for him. I need to remember that at all times.

To distract myself, I focus on my surroundings. The white walls dance with the strange patterns the water makes. "This place is beautiful." I forget for a minute that this beauty represents everything I despise about the king. Right now I'm able to let go of some of my hate.

"If you think this is beautiful, you should see the pool at my official headquarters."

"Is that an offer?" I joke, still staring at the beautiful light that dances above us.

"It is."

My gaze snaps back to the king. "You should seriously leave the lying for the cameras," I say.

We move into deeper water. "I'm not lying," he says, his eyes trained on me.

I blink at him. He's serious. "Why would you invite me?" I ask.

"Because I enjoy your company." His statement is proof that he's out of his mind. I've been nothing but mean and malicious to him.

"I hate you, remember?" With all the alcohol thrumming through my system, I can't put emotion behind the words.

"I'm starting to think you don't, though." His eyes laugh at me.

I push myself out of his arms, enjoying the way the water ripples over my skin. I do hate the king, just not right now. In the morning I will.

I hope.

I swim over to where the wine bottle sits. "I think I need more alcohol for this conversation." I'm actually feeling plenty buzzed as it is, but I do need to change the subject before the king corners me into agreeing to the visit.

Just as I reach for the bottle, I see movement out of the corner of my eye. I jolt at the sight of King Lazuli. I hadn't heard him swim up next to me.

He grabs the wine bottle and moves it out of my reach. "I think you've had enough for now, Serenity." I shiver at the way he says my name. "Me on the other hand ..." He flashes me a wicked smile before he tips the bottle back and takes a drink from it.

My abs clench at the sight of him. If I didn't know better, I'd say I was feeling lustful. He sets the bottle down, and when his eyes meet mine, heat pools low in my stomach.

"Let's play a game," I say quickly. He raises an eyebrow. "I'll ask you a question, and you can choose to answer it, but if you decide not to, you're going to have to take a sip of wine." That'll loosen his lips.

The grin he gives me is full of mischief. "I'll play your little game, but only if I'm allowed to ask questions as well."

I nod. "Okay." I can live with that. "I'll start you off with an easy one: what's your favorite color?"

"Blue. What's yours?" he asks.

"I'll answer that only if it's your official question."

"It is."

I watch the way the light from the water dances over his skin. I want to hold onto this moment, where we are no longer enemies. Merely a man and a woman discovering each other.

"Yellow." The color of the sun and the stars, the color of happiness.

"*Yellow?*" The king's eyebrows nudge up.

"What, you thought I'd like the color of spilled blood or something?"

He tips his head back as he weighs my words. "Yeah, I kind of did."

"Next question: where are you from?" I ask, thinking about the roll of his words.

He pauses, watching me with an amused smile on his face. "I was born in the country formerly known as France."

The water laps against us as I file away this new bit of information.

"Are you enjoying yourself at the moment?" the king asks.

I search Montes's eyes. I could lie, make up an answer, or I could also pass. I do neither.

"I don't know," I answer honestly. "Maybe."

"Maybe," King Lazuli repeats. "I'll take it."

I glance out the window, where I can make out the moon. "How old are you, really?" I ask.

The king grabs the bottle of wine and drinks rather than answering.

"How old were you the first time you killed someone?" he asks.

"Twelve. And I killed four someones that first time."

"Four." He's looking at me like he's having trouble believing me. "What—?"

I hold up a hand. "My turn, remember?"

His eyes drop to my lips and he nods.

"Have you ever personally killed anyone?" I ask.

"No."

His answer doesn't surprise me. The king strikes me as the kind of man who doesn't care about other's suffering so long as he doesn't have to see it. He survives his cruelty only because he removes himself from it. I think in some ways I might be the more brutal of the two of us.

"Why did you kill those four men?" he asks me. I knew he was going to ask me this.

"They were going to rape me," I say. I look away from him as I remember.

So much is left out of my statement. How brain and bone flecked the floor like confetti. How one of them took an agonizing ten minutes to die. The entire time he begged me with the ruin of his mouth to put him out of his misery.

When I look at Montes again, his face is studiously blank, like he's trying to hide his reaction. I realize then that my life might shock the king as much as his life has

38

shocked me. I still can't comprehend the sheer quantity of lives he's taken through his wars, but maybe he is also having a hard time believing that I can kill so easily.

"Tell me how a decent man can be okay with leading a war," I say.

"That's not a question, and I'm not a decent man," he says.

"You're right, I forgot for a moment."

The king presses in close to me so that my back is up against the wall of the pool. His hands rest against the tiled edge, trapping me between them. "Told you," he says, his voice gravelly.

"Told me what?"

"I don't think you really hate me."

"That's just wishful thinking on your part," I say, but silently I worry that he's right, that a few hours with him have weakened my long-held beliefs.

"Okay," I say, changing the topic, "if you don't answer the question I just asked you—"

"Statement," King Lazuli corrects.

"—then you can at least answer this one: why do you like me?"

A sinful smile spreads along the king's lips, and he shifts his body so that his slick skin rubs against mine. "You're clearly new at this," he says. I bristle at his words. "Attraction and chemistry don't follow any logical rules. You're not the prettiest girl I've ever met, nor the smartest, nor the funniest."

I narrow my eyes at him.

"But you are the girl I've altered a peace treaty for, and you are the girl I'm spending the evening with."

"You're evil and deceptive," I say.

"And you're a kindred spirit."

That stops me. It stops me completely. I've never thought of it that way. That the two of us might be the same. The more I think about it, the more frightening similarities there are between us.

The king shifts against me, drawing my attention to the sculpted muscles of his chest and the arms that pin me to the wall. My eyes trail up and rest on his mouth.

The slow burn of the alcohol allows me to focus on only one thing at a time, and right now I'm focusing on those lips.

I blink slowly, the wine churning unpleasantly in my stomach.

"Are you going to let me kiss you?" the king asks.

"Does my answer even matter?" I flick my gaze up to his.

"No, not when you're looking at me like that. But I still want to hear you to say it."

"I won't. Not for you." Admitting I want him to kiss me feels too much like I'm betraying my nation.

He moves his left hand from where it rests to lift one of my legs. He wraps it around his waist. I swallow and fight the urge to close my eyes against the feel of his fingertips on the sensitive skin there.

He's challenging me to stop him with his eyes. I don't.

The king sets his hand back against the edge of the pool and removes his right hand to wrap my other leg around him.

My gaze moves between his eyes, his dark, fathomless eyes. "You can't make someone love you," I say.

"I don't need you to love me."

I'm sure that buried beneath all the king's narcissism and conceit, there's a man that wants companionship, affection—acceptance. That's what all humans want. But perhaps I give the king too much credit.

He leans in slowly, watching me, daring me. At the last minute I turn my head away from him.

"You don't get to have me," I say. "Not after you've taken everything from me." I don't know when the evening became so serious, and now the wine has loosened my lips. I'm saying things I shouldn't be saying. Not if I'm supposed to be seducing my way into an advantageous peace treaty.

"Is that a challenge?" King Lazuli's gaze dips to my breasts, and his knee rubs the fabric of my bikini bottoms against me. He knows what he's doing—I'll give him that.

"No, I'm just stating a fact." I have to coax my voice to sound normal.

"Just like you hating me is also you stating a fact."

"Exactly."

"Good," he says. "Now I know that you have absolutely no idea what a fact is."

My mouth drops open, and he uses that opportunity to lean all the way in and kiss me.

He was right earlier when he said he didn't play fair. His lips press hotly against mine, and his tongue caresses the inside of my mouth. I use my own tongue to shove his out, but this is where I make a critical mistake. Kisses are just as much a battle as they are a joining of desires, and in my ignorance I've unknowingly deepened the kiss.

The king reciprocates with force, his tongue scorching my mouth. I've never been kissed this way before, like I'm some desperate desire of the king's. He rubs himself against me, and I can feel him harden.

No. This can't go any further.

I push him away from me, and I scramble to get out of the pool. My exit is not very graceful, but that's the last thing on my mind.

I'm breathing heavily when I turn to face the king. He's treading water, studying me with a predatory look in his eyes. Or maybe it's lust I'm seeing. It doesn't matter.

"Scared?" he asks, taunting me.

"Yes." I sway on my feet, feeling lightheaded.

His tone changes. "Are you okay?"

I shake my head. The wine's no longer a pleasant buzz, but something more insidious. I feel my stomach cramp and nausea rise. "I think I drank too much."

I stumble over to one of the nearby chairs and lean my head between my legs. This position doesn't feel so bad.

When I feel a hand on my arm, I look up and see the king crouched in front of me. I must be losing my senses; I didn't hear him exit the pool and approach.

His gaze looks concerned. "We should probably get you to bed."

I nod and get up, grabbing a towel and wrapping it around myself.

The king escorts me back to my room, which surprises me. I'd assumed he'd send Marco or one of his other men to accompany me. Or that he'd lead me to his quarters. I can't make sense of the king when he does something even slightly honorable.

Once we stop outside my room, the king brushes a kiss across my lips. "Feel better," he says. And then he's gone.

CHAPTER 7

SERENITY

FOUR YEARS AGO the western hemisphere went dark.

I was doing rounds when it happened. I sat in the back of a military issued vehicle, a gun slung across my body.

An older bunker member—a retired colonel—sat up front, driving the car around the perimeter. It had been a quiet night. Usually at least one incident cropped up during my shifts, but tonight I seemed to be getting a break. My gaze drifted up to the night sky. I searched for my favorite constellations, but light pollution from the nearby city of Annapolis obscured them.

My eyes had only just begun to travel back to my surroundings when the sky lit up. It flashed, blindingly bright, turning night into day. Then the light shrank away.

Another bomb.

"Shit."

Less than a minute later I heard the blast. It sounded like the devil was shouting, like he was going to consume me and the earth. The wave of energy hit me, throwing me back into the bed of the vehicle. Beneath me the earth shivered, and the car engine faltered, the front lights flickering before it decided it wasn't going to die after all.

And then there was silence. Ominous silence.

"What in the fucking hell ... ? Serenity, you okay?" the colonel shouted back to me.

"I'm fine," I said, pushing myself upright.

By chance my gaze fell on Annapolis. The city, which only a moment ago had been ablaze in light, was dark.

I beat the colonel to the radio. "A bomb's been dropped. Repeat: a bomb's been dropped."

I was so shaken that it took me a moment to realize the message hadn't gone through; the radio was off. I went to click it on, only to find that it had already been on. I glanced back up at where Annapolis should be. Now it was shrouded in shadow.

Later I learned that King Lazuli had detonated several nuclear bombs high above the WUN's territories. The explosions had released EMP pulses that took out all electronics that weren't heavily shielded from them.

Most electricity. Many cars. Virtually all mobile devices. Nearly every computer. All snuffed out. Only the bunker and a few other heavily fortified locations—most belowground—survived the EMP pulse unscathed.

The rest of the WUN got set back decades that day.

BRIGHT RAYS OF sunlight wake me. I wince at the sight of them and rub my eyes. My head pounds once, then a few seconds later it pounds again, and again. A horrible headache blossoms, worsening with each passing second. All I want is to

41

fall back asleep, but the churning pain in my stomach has me throwing off my covers and running for the bathroom.

I lift the lid of the toilet and vomit. My stomach spasms while I bend over, letting me know it's only just warming up. I spend the next thirty minutes huddled around the porcelain bowl, retching until there is nothing left in my stomach. I flush it all down, pretending that last night's wine is responsible for the crimson tint of the water.

I feel weak, and my head is screaming at me. I might as well have drunk poison last night; it would have the same effect on me. I push myself to my feet and lean over the sink to catch my breath. I wonder briefly if the king also feels this way.

My skin heats at the thought of him. Last night I got to know him too well. We shared secrets, drank wine, kissed.

Oh God, I'm going to see him soon.

And that's when I notice it. The strange silence of my suite. Surely my father would've poked his head in by now. I haven't seen him since I left last night.

I pad back into my room and take another look out my window. It's late morning, but that can't be right, not unless …

A sick feeling that has nothing to do with my hangover washes over me. Did I sleep through the negotiations?

I cross the room and fling open my door. In the common area a lone WUN soldier waits.

He sees my face. "The king requested that the remainder of the negotiations be done without your attendance," he explains.

"What? Why would he do that?" I ask, furrowing my brows. My worry is quickly morphing into a more familiar emotion. Anger.

The guard shrugs. "You're probably doing your job a little too well."

I give the soldier a sharp look, and he holds up his hands.

"All I'm saying is that the king probably wants to make sure he's still in control of the situation. Having you there might affect his decisions."

Because one really shouldn't mix business and pleasure. And last night I established that I was here for the king's pleasure.

The guard is still talking, but I can't hear him over the noise in my head. I leave him, slamming the door to my room a little harder than I had intended.

I clench my hands. I want to scream—no I want to hurt something. I want to slam my fist against skin until it bruises.

The king wasn't drunk like I was last night. No, he's been busy orchestrating a plan of his own. One where he makes no consolations to the WUN, or to me, or to my father.

Just like I had hoped last night, my hatred is back; however, what stokes it is not my country's wrath, but my own.

I'VE ONLY BEEN awake an hour when I hear a knock on the door. The WUN soldier answers it before I do.

"The king wishes to deliver a present to Miss Freeman," I hear someone say on the other side of the door.

That's all I need to hear. "Don't bother taking the gift," I yell at the soldier. "I won't accept it."

My guard shrugs to the person standing in the hallway. "Sorry sir, orders are orders," he says before closing the door.

Once it clicks shut, the guard shakes his head and glances at me, a twinkle of respect in his eye. "The king's about to learn just what a ballbuster you are."

"The king's a fucking prick."

The guard snorts. "Tell me something I don't know."

I'M STARING OUT my window, bathed under the dwindling sunlight, when I hear my father enter the suite. As soon as I do, I rush out of my room, ignoring the faint pound of my fading headache.

My father rubs his eyes, his face weary.

"That bastard," I say.

"Serenity, watch your language," he says.

The irony is that I've been ruder to the king's face than this.

"What happened?" I ask.

My father takes a seat on one of the couches in the common area and drops a package he came into the room carrying. "Other than the medical relief you managed to wrangle from him, King Lazuli's not budging on most of his conditions—and they're the important ones."

"He kicked me out of the peace talks," I say quietly.

My father meets my eyes. "I know," he says, his voice resigned. Of course my father knows.

As we stare at each other, I feel another strange pang of sympathy for the man in front of me. The situation is unfolding how he feared it would.

"I'm sorry," I say.

"You shouldn't be the one apologizing," my dad says.

But that's exactly why I'm apologizing—because he blames himself. My father has a whole lot of insight, yet none of it could prevent what's happened. What a burden it must be to perceive the future yet be unable to change it.

His eyes shift to the package at his feet. "You have a present from the king."

"He can take his present and shove it up—"

"*Serenity.*"

"Yeah, yeah," I grumble. I grab the package and walk it into my room. Once I'm alone, I rip open the cardboard box. Inside is a pale yellow dress, and resting on top of it is a necklace made of yellow diamonds. Yellow, because it's my favorite color.

I work my jaw at the sight. How many stomachs could these items feed? How much medical relief could they afford? Everything that comes from the king is blood money.

My hands shake when I pick up the card resting on top of the pale fabric. The note is simple.

Forgive me, and feel better.

I crumple up his note. Forgive me my ass. The king is not sorry. But he will be.

MARCO RAPS ON our suite five separate times before I decide to meet the king. He has my father to thank for that.

The entire time my father sits in the corner of the room, peace treaty on his lap, his hands threaded through his hair. He hasn't turned the page since the knocking began.

Marco bangs on the door once more, and my father stands suddenly. Throwing the document on a nearby table, he strides towards the door.

"Dad, what are you doing?" I say, standing up from my own seat.

"I'm going to tell Marco that you will not see the king."

Crap. I hadn't meant for this.

"Wait, no." I cut him off, and stop him with a hand. "Dad, it's fine."

"It's not fine, and I can't watch this."

If my father intercedes now, it could be game over. Scenarios dance through my mind, none of them good. The ripple effects could be disastrous. I can't let that happen.

"Please, Dad. Sit down. I'll answer the door."

"I can't ask this of you," he says. "None of us can."

My throat works at his admission. "It's alright. This arrangement isn't forever. Just please, go sit back down."

My father stares at me for a long time, his nostrils flaring. For a man who's good at masking his emotions, he's not doing so well at the moment.

Finally he nods and walks back to his seat, his movements mechanical.

Hurrying to the door, I grab the handle and fling it open before I can reconsider my actions.

"Evening Marco," I say when I step out into the hallway.

"The king requests—"

"I know," I say, pushing past him.

"He wants you to wear your gift," Marco says to my back.

"And I want to live in a world where I don't have to worry about radiation poisoning, but neither is going to happen anytime soon."

I can hear Marco's huff, but he's smart enough to realize a lost cause when he sees one.

This evening Marco leads me to a different area of the mansion. We stop in front of a solid wood door and Marco knocks twice.

"Come in Marco." I can hear the king's muffled voice on the other side of the door.

Marco twists the handle and ushers me inside. The king's back is to me and he's staring at the walls of the room.

I suck in a breath of air. The walls are covered with maps of every nation on earth. Strings crisscross the images, connecting one section of land to another. Pins hold the strings down, and beneath a few of these pins are images. Most are of people whose faces have been crossed out; only a precious few remain unscathed. My earlier nausea rises.

"Feeling better, Serenity?"

"Fuck off."

The king turns to face me, his expression unreadable. "You're not wearing my gift."

"You can't bribe me into liking you."

The king's eyes flick to Marco. "You can go."

Behind me Marco's footfalls fade, and a moment later the door clicks shut. There's no one else in this room but the two of us. No guards, no servants. Like the pool last night, it's just the two of us.

"I can't have you clouding my judgment during negotiations," he explains without me asking.

My hands fist. "Right. Because how awful would it be to compromise for once in your life?"

"I haven't spent the last decade waging war with your country to finally compromise."

"No," I agree, "you haven't."

The king glances away from me at the maps that line the walls. "I'm not an idiot," he says, not looking at me. "I know the WUN sent you here to seduce me."

My body goes rigid. I have no idea why his confession shocks me; it doesn't take a scientist to put two and two together.

He laughs, the sound hollow. "The problem is, it worked." His eyes move over me, and something in them softens for a moment before he shutters the expression.

"Uh huh."

His lips curl into a smirk. "You find that hard to believe?" he asks. I'd say that he was mocking me, except his eyes are too serious.

I fold my arms over my chest. Of course I do. "Why are you telling me this?" I ask.

"To warn you."

"Warn me about what?"

"I get what I want. Always."

"You keep telling me that, yet I haven't seen any proof."

"You want proof?" he says. His eyes are calculating, and the smile dancing on his lips is sly. He's no longer the man I talked to yesterday; he's the man who's been taking over the world for the last three decades.

I take a step back. I shouldn't have spoken just now; my words were careless, and around the king, careless words could mean the difference between life and death.

I shake my head and close my eyes. "No, I don't want proof. I just want this to end." I open my eyes. "I don't want to see any more crossed out faces on those maps of yours." I jut my chin to the wall behind him. "I don't want to be hungry all the time. I don't want to see the hollow-eyed looks of the people I live alongside."

"I can give you that," he says, slowly walking towards me, not stopping until the two of us are dangerously close.

"Of course you can—but you won't."

"That's because no one's offered me the correct price yet." He says it like this is a simple matter of haggling.

I throw my arms up. "You can't expect the WUN to willingly cripple our future economy for you."

The king eliminates the last bit of space between us and fingers a lock of my hair. "That's not the price I was referring to." Almost lackadaisically, his eyes move from my hair and land on my face.

And now I get it. I take a step back, then another. I furrow my eyebrows; I think I'm going to be sick. "No."

"Why not?"

"Even if I believed that was a legitimate trade—which we both know it isn't—no."

"You could end this all now, and you refuse to agree to it?"

"You're asking me to make a deal with the devil."

"You and I both know you already signed your soul away a long time ago, Serenity."

"Because of you and your stupid war. I already told you last night, you don't get to have me."

The king prowls towards me, closing the distance between us once more. "I'm not just talking about sex," he says.

But sex would be included in the arrangement. "I'd rather die than do anything with you."

"If it's death you wish, we can arrange that."

The king reaches out to touch my arm, and I slap his hand away. "Don't. Touch. Me." I'm shaking; this was never supposed to happen. I'm getting played by the king, and I don't know how to get myself out of this situation.

King Lazuli sticks his hands in his pockets and leans in conspiratorially. "You know the thing about strategy? It takes knowing when to act and when to be patient."

I take a good look at him. King Lazuli's been waging this war for almost thirty years, yet he looks to be little older than thirty himself. I've seen footage of him shot, blown-up, and stabbed, yet he hasn't died. He's unnatural in more ways than one.

"If you try to force me into this plan of yours, I will find out your secrets," I say, "and once I do, I will kill you." I stare at him long enough for him to see the vehemence behind my words. And then I turn and walk away from the king and the sick tapestry that hangs along the walls of the room.

I'm almost to the door when he speaks. "I plan on making you love me before that happens."

CHAPTER 8

SERENITY

THREE YEARS AGO I saw combat for the first time.

I was allowed to fight despite being underage. Many of us were. The war had raged on long enough that the military would take almost all willing and able-bodied soldiers—even underage ones, so long as they were over the age of fourteen and their guardian agreed to it. My father had consented—albeit, reluctantly—and so had Will's.

Will and I, members of the same platoon, had been stationed in New York, near where New York City once stood. The two of us hunkered down outside the skeletons of former buildings, our breaths clouding in the chilly night air. Our battalion had reappropriated the ruins and turned them into makeshift barracks.

"We're missing all the action," Will complained, picking up a pebble and chucking it at an abandoned car across the street.

Because we were younger. Our military might recruit minors, but they tended to shelter them from action if they could.

Several minutes later one of the other members of our company whistled from a block away. "The king's men are dropping out of the sky!"

I glanced above me and sure enough, the dim outline of parachutes obscured the patches of the sky. There looked to be dozens of them.

"Oh shit," Will said.

My heart slammed inside my ribcage. We were being ambushed. I grabbed my mother's necklace and kissed it for good luck. I'd killed before, but never under such treacherous circumstances.

Shots pinged in the distance—likely other soldiers from our company trying to shoot the king's men out of the air. From what I could tell, it had no effect.

Will raised his weapon.

"Don't shoot," I said, staring up at the sky.

"Why not?" He lined up his gun's sights.

"We don't have enough bullets to waste." Not when our targets were too far away to aim with accuracy.

"So you think we should wait?" He sounded incredulous.

"Mmhm." My hands trembled.

Will shook his head but lowered his gun. "This better be a good idea, 'cause I feel like we're missing a perfect opportunity."

"Just wait for them to get within range."

He huffed, his way of agreeing without conceding his point.

It took an agonizing five minutes for the enemy to get close enough to shoot. When a man managed to land on our block, Will and I jogged over to him as the soldier extricated himself from his harness.

"I got this one," Will said, aiming his weapon.

I nodded next to him, my gun also trained on the enemy soldier.

Will hesitated, readjusted his grip, then hesitated some more.

"What are you waiting for?" I whispered.

"Nothing."

I cast a look over at Will. His hands fidgeted, his eyes were wild.

He'd never killed a man. I'd assumed he had. We lived in the kind of world where violence was inevitable.

The soldier was now glancing up at us as he frantically fiddled with the straps of his parachute. In several more seconds we'd lose the advantage we now had.

Next to me Will shifted his weight, his hands adjusting and readjusting their grip on his weapon. He wasn't going to finish the enemy in time.

Steadying my breath, I aimed my weapon and fired.

The bullet took the soldier right between the eyes—a quick, painless death. That was as compassionate as I was going to get out here, given the circumstances.

For ten long seconds neither of us moved.

Will finally lowered his gun. "I froze up." I could hear the embarrassment in his voice.

"Nothing to be ashamed of."

I pushed down my nausea. By now I'd learned that it wasn't physical. It was more of a soul-sickness. Another piece of my humanity chipped away.

"*You* were able to kill him," Will said.

You, a girl. That's what he meant. Like owning a vagina made me inferior in some fundamental way.

I gave Will a long look, then shook my head and began walking towards the body. I expected most of the teen boys in my platoon to be sexist, but not Will.

"I'm sorry," he said to my back.

I waved him off. "You'll get another chance to kill tonight. I'm sure it'll help your wounded ego recover."

Will did in fact kill for the first time that evening. And when he saw the woman's lifeless eyes, he vomited all over my shoes. The machismo act fell away after that. It didn't stop either of us from continuing to slaughter enemy soldiers, but by the end of the night, Will was no longer so eager to take lives.

Once upon a time, we were innocent. And then we were not.

THE NEXT FEW days at the king's estate are strangely quiet. Our time here is almost up. Not much progress has been made between my father and the king as far as negotiations go. My father enters our suite each day weary and beaten down. The WUN is not in a position to make an advantageous agreement, and the king is making that clearer now more than ever.

If we can't reach an agreement in the next two days, when our flight is scheduled to leave, the king will continue to wage war on us until we're forced to surrender, and then the WUN will have to agree with whatever demands he asks.

The twisted king hasn't tried to see me since our brief interaction in his map room, yet our last visit managed to spook me. I can't tell how much of what he said was true and how much of it was a lie. The king is a tactical mastermind, that much I know. So I can trust that whatever he decides will be solely in his best interest. I'll get used, and so will the WUN.

And now I have to see him in less than an hour. King Lazuli's hosting some bigwig dinner, and we're the guests of honor. It'll be the first time I'm in front of the cameras again since I was banned from the peace talks.

I carefully apply the makeup I was packed with. I've probably spent more time on this trip poking myself in the eye with the eyeliner pen than I have learning the ins and outs of the king's proposed peace treaty. And I've spent hours poring over that thing.

I turn away from the mirror and glance at the far corner of my room where I shoved the king's gifts. I don't want to put the gown or the jewelry on; to me it symbolizes all the broken families and defeated nations he's claimed.

But so close to when we have to leave, my mind is haunted by the possibility that I could do something for the WUN. Tonight.

I retrieve the king's gifts from the corner. I give the pale yellow dress a dirty look. Somehow the king managed to spoil my favorite color. I remove the towel wrapped around my torso and pull the gown on.

Once I do, I frown. My entire back is exposed. The rest of the dress falls suggestively over my curves. It fits me perfectly.

I grab the diamond necklace that goes along with the dress, and before I can think too much about it, I clasp it around my neck. It feels like a manacle.

I finish applying makeup and arrange my hair so that it lies in loose curls over my shoulders, and then I leave my room. I look nothing like the elegant women I've seen here, with their perfectly coiffed hair and painted faces, and for that I'm glad. I can still recognize myself in the mirror.

Outside my room, my father speaks animatedly with one of our guards. Gone is the devastated man who considered defying orders for me.

A wry smile passes over his face when he catches sight of me. "You almost pull off the sweet and innocent look," he says. "Almost."

"What ruins it? My scar?" I ask. I grin back at him.

"Nope—it's all in the eyes and the jaw. And that smile doesn't help. You look like you want to gut someone." Now my dad's grinning.

"You can dress up a pig, but it's still a pig."

My dad comes over to me and grasps my hand. "Not a pig," he says, staring me in the eye, "a soldier."

MY FATHER AND I follow Marcus to the banquet hall, our guards shadowing our procession. Inside, people haven't yet sat down to eat. Instead they mill about the room, sipping on champagne and chatting with one another.

The room stirs as we enter. You'd think that the king's stuck-up friends would get used to the sight of us, but they haven't. Nor have the camera crews. I notice that most of their lenses zoom in on me. I guess their audiences are more interested in my (lack of) involvement in the peace talks than they are of my father's or the king's.

My father leans into me. "You need to interact with these people tonight. Talk, be friendly, and try not to scare anyone too much. I'm leaving you to mingle."

He must see the fear in my eyes as he pulls away because he pats my shoulder. "Make me proud."

I give him a look that tells him what I think about that statement. He grins at me and winks before moving away from me to talk with an elderly man—the former prime minister of what used to be England.

My skin prickles; I can sense the king watching me. I turn and lock eyes with him. He swirls the wine in his glass as he assesses me. His eyes meander down my body and back up, and as he does so, an approving smile spreads across his face.

I suppress a shiver at his gaze. I imagine this is how he looks at unconquered territories.

The camera crews crowd me, despite the WUN soldiers standing guard. I keep my expression bland so the world doesn't see the terror coursing through me. The king has always been my boogeyman, but boogeymen aren't supposed to be real. They're the things of nightmares, the things your parents kiss away.

But he's real. And he wants me. And the entire western hemisphere might benefit if I simply face my fears.

The plan I've toyed with for the last several days comes to fruition. I will do this, even if it's as scary as running headlong into battle.

I roll my neck like I do before I work out and push my shoulders back. I'm going to give the cameramen one hell of a show.

I stride towards the king, who stands on the other side of the room. I let my body sway a little more than usual, just to pull eyes to me.

Up until now, all anyone knows about the king and me are rumors—if that. I'm about to blow those rumors open.

I can hear the uncertain shuffle of my guards keeping formation around me and the eager clamor of camera crews. They're like carrion circling a wounded creature—they can practically sense a story about to happen.

I'm gathering stares; I can feel the way they crawl along my skin. The king looks amused—no, transfixed—as I make a beeline for him. He too knows something is about to happen.

The crowd parts for me, and the buzzing chatter in the room dies down. I close the remaining distance between the two of us until I'm standing in front of him.

"Miss me?" I ask.

King Lazuli's face is serious, but his eyes smile. He's definitely enjoying the show.

"I haven't missed anything more," he responds smoothly, like the slick politician he is.

"Then why haven't you kissed me yet?" Now the room goes quiet.

This, this is a gamble. On the one hand, the king might reject me in front of a crowded room—scratch that, in front of the entire world. That I can handle; I haven't believed he's been sincere about his feelings for me since the day we met. And if he does reject me, the WUN will have definitive proof that the king's just toying with all of us.

On the other hand, if he goes along with this, the world will anticipate favorable negotiations with the WUN—if he's openly friendly with the emissary's daughter, he's surely friendly with the nations she represents. My hope is that it will increase the odds of an advantageous peace treaty for us.

This possibility scares the crap out of me. It means more contact with the king. Intimate contact.

Montes raises his eyebrows, his eyes twinkling like mad. This whole exchange delights him. He takes the final step that removes all the distance between the two of us, and I feel the press of his tux against my chest.

A roguish grin lights up his face. He slides a hand along my jaw and cups the back of my head. My heart speeds up, and I can't tell whether fear or a thread of desire is responsible for it.

His cool breath fans across my face. "Just remember tomorrow that you started this," he says quietly.

I don't know what to make of his words, but then I don't need to. His lips are on mine, and they move softly, sweetly against my mouth. I kiss him back, parting my lips and running my tongue over his.

The murmurs around us quiet, and in the silence that follows I can hear the frantic shuffling of camera crews that want to capture what could be a pivotal moment in the negotiations.

But even that is background noise compared to being completely and totally enveloped by the king. His fingertips touch my cheeks with the lightest of pressure. There's a kindness to the touch, and I have the oddest urge to weep that someone can be this gentle to another human being. That it's the king who caresses me like this … I can't rectify my conflicted emotions.

One of King Lazuli's hands moves to the small of my back, holding me close, his thumb stroking the bare skin there. I move my own hand so that it cups his jaw, and I'm shocked by its roughness. Shocked perhaps because he feels more like a man than a nightmare.

Our poolside evening together bubbles to the surface of my thoughts. He was a different person then, and right now, while his lips move against mine, he's that same person. The thought makes me forget that I'm in the arms of the enemy, and that my country might consider me a traitor for my current actions—actions I make on its behalf.

The kiss ends, and the king draws away slowly, his eyes lingering on my lips. Desire and a trace of something else flare up in his eyes.

Around us the room is silent. I can feel half a dozen cameras focused on me and the king. I'm sure several are capturing my father's expression as well, but I'm too busy staring down Montes to care much about that.

Whatever this is, it's no deception on the king's part. It's something far, far worse.

Someone whistles on the other side of the room, and then I hear the tinkling of silverware on glass. More join in; some people even tap the side of their glasses with a knife.

I look from them to the king, my brow furrowed.

"They want us to kiss again."

I feel my cheeks heat. My courage is all used up. King Lazuli dips down and brushes his lips against mine. My mouth responds, moving languidly over his, even though the entire situation freaks me out. At least we've definitely given the world a show.

This time when the king pulls away, his lips skim over my cheek to my ear. "You're cute when you blush."

My nostrils flare in annoyance, but I compose my face before anyone takes notice. The king's hands linger, one in particular gets comfortable around my waist.

His eyes drop to my gown. "You look gorgeous—the dress fits you perfectly."

The mention of this hateful gown reminds me that the king is more than just silky words and soft caresses. He's the enemy.

I give him a tight smile since I can't be openly rude to him while so much attention is on us.

King Lazuli seems to understand this, and a sly grin spreads across his face. "Like the color?"

"Uh huh." I clench my jaw so much it hurts.

The people who cluster around the king have focused their attention on me, and I know my pleasant exterior is cracking. I entwine my fingers around the king's, and pry his hand from my waist.

"Mind if I steal the king for a moment?" I ask the crowd.

The group shakes their heads and shrugs. "Thanks—I promise I'll only be a moment." I drag the king away from the crowd, not that he seems to mind it in the least. The camera crews start to follow us, so I turn and give them all a death glare. It's enough for them to keep their distance. For now. I know I've caused too much of a scene for them to stay away long.

Once I get the king a safe distance away from the crowd, I drop the act. "I'll do it."

"Oh? And what exactly is it that you'll do?" the king asks.

I narrow my eyes. "Whatever it is you want with me."

I can see the king's breath catch. He's getting exactly what he wants, just like he promised me he would.

"But—" I say, "I have a condition."

The king raises his eyebrows and waits for me to continue.

"You need to compromise with the WUN—don't cripple their economy, don't withhold needed funds. Give my homeland enough benefits to get them back on their feet."

"You do realize that's incredibly vague," the king says. What he doesn't say is that in his world, ambiguity is an exploitable weakness.

I touch his arm; I'm going to have to get used to his touch if I go through with this. He glances down at where my hand rests, then back to my face. His eyes are vulnerable.

"I'm asking you to be honorable," I say. I give him a long look, and I see some of his humanity seep into those bright eyes. "Please, you don't need to blackmail me or the western hemisphere to get what you want. I'm coming to you freely."

The king cups my chin, and I see real tenderness there. "I'll come up with a final agreement, but your father will have to approve of it for us to have a deal."

A deal. That's what this is. I nod.

He bows his head and steals a kiss from me. "Good. Then I look forward to a long and prosperous future for all parties involved."

I did it. I just sacrificed myself for my nation.

CHAPTER 9

SERENITY

TWO YEARS AGO I became my father's apprentice.

He hadn't always been our land's only emissary. I hear we used to have many. Men and women appointed by the government to engage in diplomacy with foreign nations.

When the Western United Nations was formed, this branch of the government was refashioned. A single position—that of WUN emissary—was created. It proved to be a fatal one. Half a dozen men and women died before my father, who'd once served as the Secretary of State, had been elected into the role.

He managed to hold onto the position and his life, mostly because he hadn't set foot onto the Eastern Hemisphere.

There should've been another round of elections since my father took the title of emissary. He should've abdicated the role to another official, along with all the other representatives that lived in the bunker. But once the western hemisphere went dark, our electoral system disintegrated almost overnight. In it's absence we had to revert to an archaic system of power: bequeathing titles from parent to child. And now my father was passing the position onto me.

I knew all of this the evening he called me into his office. I'd seen and lived so much that this shouldn't have scared me. But it did.

Once I shut the door behind me, my father glanced up from his papers. "Do you know why you're here?"

I gave him a sharp nod. "You want to teach me how to be an emissary."

My father scrubbed his face. "I don't want to do this—that you've got wrong. But neither of us have much of a choice."

"Dad, I'm no good at diplomacy."

He cracked a smile. "You're my daughter. You're good at everything."

I rolled my eyes. "You're a little biased."

"And you're a little humble."

His words were proof I'd never have his sharp tongue. He always knew the right thing to say to diffuse a situation. I was more likely to punch someone in the face than I was reasoning with them.

That first lesson was brief, unlike the hundreds to come. By the end of it, my father left me with one final bit of information. "Serenity?"

My hand was already on the door. I turned back to face him.

The wrinkles around his eyes and mouth deepened. "As an emissary, if an accord is ever to be reached between us and the Eastern Empire, you will likely be a key player in it."

I swallowed and nodded. I now carried a heavy responsibility.

"Do you know what that means?"

I waited for him to finish.

His gaze lingered on me a long time before he finally answered his own question. "One day you'll meet the king."

That day had come.

THE ROOM IS quiet as my father contacts the representatives. I barely made eye contact with him after my kiss with the king. I couldn't. The whole situation still gives me the heebie jeebies.

My dad, for his part, seems to be at a loss for words. So we wait in silence, until the representatives flash onto the screen. We do the usual greeting, and then there's a pause.

"Serenity," General Kline says, "you gave the world quite the show. The Internet's blowing up with it."

What he doesn't say is that everyone's calling me a traitor, a whore—whatever unoriginal names they can come up with. There will be no honor to my sacrifice. Women who have filled the role of temptress have always been looked down upon.

"I got King Lazuli to make another agreement," I snap, my voice bitter.

My father turns to me, surprised.

"Tomorrow," I say to the general, "if there's a semi-decent bone in the king's body, the WUN should have a fair and equitable peace treaty."

All's quiet for a moment, and then my father speaks. "What did you agree to, Serenity?" he asks, worry tingeing his voice. The rest of the representatives wait for my answer.

I glance down at my hands. "I don't exactly know."

I'M NOT SURPRISED when I hear knocking on the suite door. I glance at my father's closed off room. He's locked himself away in there since our talk with the representatives. His excuse is that he's relaying updates to those nations who couldn't send their own emissaries. I know better. I heard his muffled weeps. He can't stand the situation, so he's hiding from it.

Now the room's ominously quiet. My father knows what waits for me in the hallway, just as I do, and he's decided to ignore it.

If only I had that luxury.

Be brave, Serenity, I tell myself, because no one else is here to comfort me in this moment.

I rise from my seat, setting aside the WUN's proposal, and answer the door.

Marco stands outside. "The king requests—"

"Yeah, yeah." I could go the rest of my life without hearing these official missives. Particularly when they involve illicit business. I step out of my room and follow Marco through the palace. We pass the king's private dining room and continue on, eventually stopping in front of an ornately carved door.

Marco opens it. "This is where I leave you."

If I speak, he'll surely hear my fright, so I nod instead and step inside the room. I glance behind me in time to see the door close and Marco's form vanish from sight. It might as well have been the iron bars of a cell slamming shut.

I am trapped.

I turn my attention to my surroundings. I'm inside the king's richly decorated sitting room. It's beautiful and lacks for nothing, save the king.

I step up to a window. Below me, lamps cast the king's estate in shades of amber and orange. The city beyond lies in darkness. My hands slide along the windowsill. The greatest irony here is that the king lives in the light, the innocents in the dark. The king belongs to those shadows that lurk outside the light. As do I.

"You're still in my dress."

I swivel around, startled to find the man himself leaning against an open doorway, hands tucked in his pockets. He still wears his dinner attire, only now his suit jacket is gone, and the cuffs of his sleeves have been rolled up past his elbows. Aside from his swimsuit, this is the most casual I've ever seen him.

"I knew you'd come for me," I respond, touching my sternum in a poorly masked attempt to hide my cleavage. It only serves to draw the king's attention to my chest.

There they linger. Seconds tick by, and neither of us moves. I don't know what's passing through his mind, but terror and excitement consume mine. I'm incapable of moving, even if I tried.

The king's gaze flicks back up to mine, his dark eyes intense in the low lighting. Pushing away from the wall, he prowls forward. The trance is broken. Something's changed, and things I know nothing of are about to happen. With each step the king takes, I can see a little more of that fire burning in his eyes.

What have I agreed to?

Taking my hand, Montes leads me to a fainting couch. I allow him to guide my body onto it. The entire time I watch him like he might tear my throat out if I look away or move too quickly.

The king kneels next to me, a hand dropping to one of my ankles. It slips under the silky seam of my skirt and glides up my calf. Over my knee.

My heart's in my throat; I can feel it pounding there, cutting off my breath.

Up his hand delves, over my thigh. Then stops.

"You're shaking."

I close my eyes. His words carry no inflection, so I can't tell whether he considers this a good or bad thing. I have no idea what the hell I'm supposed to be doing either, but chances are, if I take an active role in whatever's going on, I will end up attacking him, the Undying King. That can't happen.

That won't happen.

I lick my dry lips. "I've never … done this."

"This?" the king repeats like he's confused. His fingers brush between my legs.

The small burst of pleasure tightens my stomach, and I glare at him. "Yes, *that*."

His hands slide out from under my skirt. "What *have* you done?" Curiosity smolders in his eyes.

"I've been kissed."

"That's it?" Again, his words are inflectionless. He lays a hand on my hipbone

"That's it."

He swears under his breath, his grip tightening. I can tell conflicting desires war within him because he's looking through me more than at me. I also know the moment they resolve themselves.

He hesitates, then rises to his feet. "Leave."

I don't move. This is not how it's supposed to play out.

"Move, Serenity, before I change my mind."

Slowly I stand. The fear is fading, replaced by confusion. I consider the man in front of me. Logic is telling me that he's letting me go because of some moral

55

compass he carries. My emotions are telling me any moral compass he possesses is so warped and eroded he wouldn't know a good deed from a bad one.

"I'm giving you tonight," he says, not looking at me. "Enjoy the company of your father. Tomorrow, you'll be at my side, not his."

CHAPTER 10

SERENITY

A YEAR AGO I discovered I was dying.

First my appetite diminished. I'd skip breakfast because in the morning I couldn't keep even the tasteless oatmeal down. Better to leave the food for people whose bodies wouldn't reject it.

Life continued that way for a couple months—long enough for people to notice. Long enough for them to assume I was pregnant despite the fact that I'd never even been kissed. Will took a lot of heat for that. But when months passed and no baby came, people forgot.

All save for me.

The nausea fled as quickly as it came. For a while I could pretend my health issues away, until one morning when my nausea returned. I made it to the bathroom in time, only what I retched up wasn't simply food and bile. Blood tinted my vomit red.

I breathed heavily as I stared down at the irrefutable evidence that I was sick. I never told my father. I never told Will.

The sickness never fully went away.

THE NEXT MORNING, I watch my father leave the room, worry creasing my brows. I hardly slept last night, I was so worried about what today's outcome would be. I half waited for the knock of the king; I'd assumed that he'd change his mind and collect on my side of the deal before he approached my father today.

But the knock never comes. Strange enough, my worries morph from what the king will do with me once the treaty's signed to what will happen if the king decides that whatever I have to offer isn't good enough.

The WUN soldiers watch me as I pace. When their stares become too disconcerting, I move to my bedroom and begin to organize my dresses by color, then make my bed. It takes twenty minutes in all, and it does nothing to calm my nerves, so I stretch and do several sets of pushups and sit-ups.

Once I have a nice sheen of sweat along my body, I hop into the shower, letting the water calm me. But even that can't relax me, not when I start to feel guilty about wasting clean water while my friends in the bunker share a dismal basin's worth each day.

I dry off and change, pulling on one of the more bearable dresses I've been packed. Today I was supposed to board a flight with my father. Now, in between fretting over what waits me after the sun sets, I wonder how I will possibly let the man who raised me go.

I've just finished applying mascara when the door to our suite is thrown open and my father storms in. "Grab your things, Serenity."

"What?"

"We need to go, *now*."

I switch to soldier mode. "What do I need?"

"Shoes you can run in and anything you can't live without. You have three minutes."

I don't waste another second. I grab the gun my father gave me long ago and load it before turning the safety on and shoving it down the bodice of my dress. It's not the safest place to carry a loaded gun, but my guess is that being unarmed in the king's palace at the moment is even less safe.

I pull on my combat boots, wondering just what words were exchanged between my father and the king. Clearly, the king hadn't made good on his promise to be honorable. Otherwise, my father wouldn't be acting this way.

I don't have time to change out of the ridiculous dress I'm wearing, but I rip off most of the skirt so that I can run better. The sound of tearing fabric is unbelievably satisfying.

As I finish getting ready, I can hear the WUN soldiers gearing up around me. There's a buzzing excitement in the air, the thrill that comes before battle.

"We're going out the rear windows," my father says, "and then we're going to cross the gardens and exit through the back of the estate, where a car will be waiting to take us to our jet."

My eyes widen. I hope I'm one day half as good as my father at these things. He's had our escape plan prepared way ahead of time.

My father glances at his watch. "Okay soldiers, your three minutes are up. Let's move to the back of the room."

The words are barely out of his mouth when there's a pounding on the door. I glance at my father.

"Don't answer that," he says, his voice deadly serious.

"Wasn't planning on it."

The pounding gets louder, and then I hear a key inserted into the lock. My eyes go wide as I look at my father. The soldiers fan out around us, covering us just as the door opens and Marco comes in with a dozen palace guards.

What could've possibly gone on during negotiations?

"Ambassador Freeman," Marco says, "the king has ordered me to retrieve your daughter."

My heart pounds at the mention of my name.

"I did not agree to the terms of the revised peace treaty, so he does not have that kind of authority over her," my father says.

I glance between Marco and my father. He didn't agree to the king's proposal. Why?

"You can agree to the peace treaty or not," Marco says. "Either way, the king is not going to let Serenity leave here."

I hone my attention on Marco. The king thinks he can keep me around despite the negotiations. Of course, this is his back up strategy to make sure he gets what he wants.

"Dad, what were the terms of the peace agreement?" This is the question I've been dying to know.

My father doesn't answer, but Marco does. "Money, medical relief, a series of programs to revitalize your hemisphere's shithole economy." I hear the acid in Marco's voice. I always had the feeling that below Marco's smooth exterior there was a dick of epic proportions. Now I'm finally meeting him. "The king would freely give all of this so long as you stayed here with him."

My gaze moves from Marco to my father. "Is that true?" I ask.

My father's focus is on Marco, but he nods in answer.

"Dad, if it's true, then why didn't you agree to the king's terms?"

Now my father looks at me. "I won't sign away your life, Serenity. I've already made too many personal sacrifices; I will not make this one."

What my father says brings tears to my eyes. He's choosing me over a nation—over an entire hemisphere. It's the most foolish decision he's ever made, but it's also the moment I feel the sheer force of my father's love for me. He won't let the boogeyman touch me.

"That's your official decision?" Marco asks.

"It is."

"We have to take Serenity," Marco says. "And we will use force." At his words, the WUN soldiers cluster around my father and me, but it doesn't make me feel safe. The king's soldiers outnumber ours, and they're better equipped. Not to mention that I no longer have a clean shot with them blocking me.

My father grabs my hand and pulls me behind him. Unlike me, my father's tall stature doesn't shield him from our enemies. Not completely.

"Dad—" I whisper.

"You're going to have to go through me," my father says to Marco, ignoring me.

My hand twitches and I barely breathe. Something's about to happen, and now I can't see anything beyond the cocoon of bodies surrounding me. Around us WUN soldiers are casting my father sideways glances. Right now he's the commanding officer, and they're waiting for him to make the call. I already know he won't be the first one to spill blood.

"So be it," Marco says.

Before I can so much as grab for my gun, someone fires a shot, and then another. Blood and bone spray down on me, and then my father is falling, my father who's now missing the back of his head.

I can't hear anything, the shots are still ringing in my ears. But I know I'm screaming, and now I've crumpled to the ground, holding my father's broken body to me.

My father, who taught me how to ride a bike, how to shoot a gun, how to be a diplomat and a decent human being. My father, my last remaining family.

My father.

My father. Murdered in front of my eyes.

Around me, I can sense movement, and I hear more gunshots go off. I stand, letting my father's slick body slide off my arms.

I've heard stories before about how grief can turn into bloodlust, but I've never experienced it before. Not until this moment. It builds like poison in my veins, converting my expanding grief into something violent.

Now I am a force of nature; I am the embodiment of rage. Enemy soldiers are coming at me, and I force my elbow into the neck of one and the solar plexus of another. I grab the gun from my bodice, and I begin shooting the enemy alongside my guards. Headshots. All of them.

I'm still screaming, and I can feel blood and tears dripping down my face. I know I look ferocious, and this gives me pleasure. Their fear and their pain give me pleasure.

I keep firing, even as more guards rush in. Amidst the chaos I see Marco run for the door.

I lift my gun, aim, and fire at him. The bullet grazes his arm, and then he's gone. I've missed my opportunity.

The king's soldiers, who are streaming into the suite, aren't shooting at me. They should be. They're not going to take me alive. I'm leaving this place one way or another. If it's in a casket, so be it.

"Soldiers!" I yell to what's left of my men. Five are still standing. That's all that's left. "Get to the window. We're getting out of here!" I can barely hear my own voice from all the gunfire. I signal to the back of the room just in case their hearing is as bad as mine.

The WUN soldiers move to the window, and I'm taking out the king's men one at a time. I back up to the rear of the room, shoving my now-empty gun back into my bodice and snagging another two from the bodies at my feet.

I throw a leg over the open window. I'm the last one out. We're on the second story, so I have to jump. I glance down and see one of the WUN soldiers waiting to catch me, the other four guarding the soldier's back. Beyond them I can see to the end of the king's property and the road beyond. That's where the car my father spoke of should be waiting.

A hand wraps around my arm. I don't think; I bring my arm up and shoot to kill. The king's soldier falls away, but more come after me. They'll shoot my guards if I don't do something first.

I aim and fire. One, two, three, four go down before the gun clicks. I drop it and grab another from the carnage. I shoot three more men and drop the weapon. I pick up two more guns before I'm able to focus on jumping down. This is all the ammunition I'll have between here and scheduled pick up, so I'll have to restrain myself from shooting anything that moves.

I make eye contact with the soldier waiting for me below, and then I jump, my arms pointing to the sky since I'm carrying two loaded weapons. He catches me, easing my impact.

"Let's go!" I shout.

The soldiers surround me, and we sprint through the king's stupid gardens. I pass the alcove he pushed me into, and I have to suppress the desire to shoot the balls off the marble statue that rests within it.

The quiet is eerie, and I know not to be deceived by it. The king's guards are regrouping, setting something up. I pray to any god willing to listen that our ride will still be waiting for us, that we'll get past the king's people, and that we can get the hell off this godforsaken land.

The gardens taper off, and beyond them is open grass. The trees and hedges have hidden us from view until now, but that's about to change.

I don't need to tell the soldiers this; they've noticed. Our collective speed picks up. We exit the gardens, and I spot the wrought iron fence running along the back of the king's estate.

A shot rings out and blood sprays as a soldier ahead of me takes a bullet to the head. What remains of his body collapses, and I have to jump over him to keep from tripping. There's nothing we can do for him at this point.

"Sniper!" I shout. The remaining soldiers and I scatter, running wildly left and right. I've trained with these people; we work soundlessly as a unit. Only now I'm their commander. Because my father ...

My eyes move over the fence, until I spot a car waiting about a hundred yards down to my left. I whistle and point to my men. Their movements are still wild, but they're moving towards it. I hear the sound of another gunshot, and the soldier running ahead of me falls.

I snarl and glance over at the mansion. It's impossible to see a sniper from here, so I can't do anything about it. But someone does catch my eye.

The king, standing on his back balcony. He's too far away to shoot as well, otherwise I would. He's also too far away for me to make out his expression. I hope he's hurting, I hope he knows I slaughtered his men, and I hope today causes him unending grief, like it will for me.

I know it won't.

I turn away from him and focus on the fence and the car, some heavy SUV with tinted windows. Another shot rings out, and I hear it ping against the car's armor. At this point, I can only hope it didn't destroy anything vital, or else we're out of an escape.

Ahead of me, someone—probably our ride—has cut away two of the wrought iron fence posts, leaving an opening wide enough for a person to slip through. The soldiers exit through it and jump into the car.

I'm the last out, and I follow my soldiers into the back of the SUV.

Our driver, a burly, bearded man, guns the engine and peels down the road, constantly checking his rearview and side view mirrors.

We skid around the corner, the car fishtailing, then we're accelerating until my surroundings blur. Three official-looking cars pull onto the road behind us. I glance at our driver. He doesn't look nervous. No, he smiles when he notices the vehicles. If I didn't know better, I'd say he's just as bloodthirsty as I am.

I hear a distant, high-pitched whine, and then the first car behind us explodes in a burst of flame. The sound of crumbling metal follows a second later, presumably as the two cars following the first crash into it. Someone laid in wait for those cars. And someone shot them with a grenade launcher.

Our driver whoops and slams his palm triumphantly on the driving wheel. "That's how it's fucking done!"

Rather than join in, I feel myself weaken as I release the last of my adrenaline. I lean back in my seat. "Who are you?" I ask.

The man pauses a beat. "I am a part of the Resistance."

He eyes me in the rearview mirror. "And judging by the fact that you have more blood on you than a butcher, I'm guessing that you aren't as traitorous as everyone's making you out to be."

I look out the window. My hands are shaking. Soon the rest of my body will follow suit, and then I'll have to truly feel again. Once that happens I'm going to wish I were dead. As it is, my head pounds as it tries to disassociate itself from all that just happened.

My father's dead.

His body lies in enemy territory.

I bury the emotion that's rising. Just because I'm not running and shooting at the moment doesn't mean I'm safe. I can't allow myself to fall apart now, not when I have three WUN soldiers whose lives I can still save.

I digest this. "Thank you," I finally say, "for risking your life to get us out of there."

The man grunts in response. "Did you kill him?"

I don't need any clarification to know whom he's asking about. "No," I say darkly.

Silence falls over the car, and for several minutes there's a strange kind of calm. It's not real, not when the blood of a dozen different men drips down my body and I tightly clench two guns in my hands, safeties off. Not when the car we're in is careening through the city of Geneva, zipping around other vehicles and pedestrians.

The sound of blades slicing the air catches our attention, and our driver swears. "That was faster than I expected," he says, looking up at the sky. I follow his gaze, and I see a helicopter heading our way.

Our driver makes another quick turn. "I'm going to pull into a garage in about thirty seconds. Once I do, get ready to jump out. You'll be entering a nondescript blue car, which I'll pull up next to. Got it?"

"Yes," I say. The men next to me grunt. They're even quieter than me.

The SUV fishtails as our driver takes a turn at breakneck speeds. The chopper makes a beeline for our car.

"You must've been some kisser," our driver mutters under his breath.

The wheels of our car squeal as our driver makes the tight turn into the parking garage to our left. As soon as we enter, the car accelerates to the other end of the structure, where a beat-up blue car idles.

Our driver slams on the brakes once we're almost upon it, and the WUN soldiers and I pile out of the vehicle.

"Thank you," I say over my shoulder, my voice hoarse. I push down the emotions. I need to hold out just a little longer.

Our driver nods. "Stay safe."

THE HELICOPTER DOESN'T notice the dingy blue car that leaves the garage. Instead its attention is focused on the black SUV we were in a minute ago.

I swallow down my worry for our previous driver as I watch his car careen down in the opposite direction, drawing attention away from us. As soon as the king's men realize I'm not in the car, his life will be in danger.

The rest of our drive is quiet, and the trip stretches on and on. I have no idea where we're going or what we'll find when we finally stop. To be honest, I don't really care at this point.

We move out of the city and pass through several more. As I stare out at the foreign landscape, a hand lands on my shoulder and then one of the soldiers pulls me into his arms and squeezes me tight. Only then do I realize I'm crying. I press my face into his chest, and heave great sobs.

So many people died today—some at the hands of the king's men, some at the hands of me and mine. So much death. The emotions are welling up; I can hear the keening sound work its way up my throat.

The soldier rubs my back. He's older—closer to my father's age than my own—which only makes the ache inside me hurt more acutely. His actions are so much worse than the usual tough guy act soldiers love to play, because at least aloofness separates us from the pain. This is the exact opposite. I can't avoid, can't suppress, can't hide from it anymore.

I sob harder into the soldier's chest as the events replay over and over through my mind. I feel anger, pain, regret, and pity. Gruesome images play alongside sweet memories. I'm being torn apart and restitched into something awful.

"Shhh, it's going to be alright," he says.

But it won't be. Not ever.

CHAPTER 11

SERENITY

I STAND IN front of the jet's staircase. The engines are still slowing down, and the pilot won't let me exit the aircraft until they come to a complete stop. It's a comical precaution in light of all I've been through in the last twenty-four hours.

Outside I can hear the crowd of WUN citizens waiting. Whereas my send off had been rushed and private, my arrival looks to be a bit more public and celebratory. The crowd sounds excited, but it's unclear what they know. Do they think a peace agreement has been reached? Do they know one was never signed? Do they know my father is dead?

I glance down at my blood-soaked body. The men I was with wouldn't let me and the other soldiers change or wash off. The world would need proof of what occurred in Geneva for the story to be as believable as possible.

And what then? Even if the image of me covered in blood sparked one last great push to fight against the king, we are doomed to lose the war.

The pilot's attendant shoos me away from the door so she can lower the staircase. My heart pounds in my chest. I know I'm about to cause a riot, and I'll be expected to talk. After all, I am now the WUN's emissary. The thought has me choking back a sob.

The attendant clears her throat to get my attention. I can tell she doesn't want to touch me—not that I blame her. "Whenever you're ready, you can go."

I look behind me at the three WUN soldiers, all that's left of our original entourage. Just like me, they are still covered with gore.

The soldier who comforted me hours ago now nods to me. I take a breath and walk out of the jet.

I screamed and cried my last tears several hours ago. I've got a good hour or two of respite before the grief swallows me up all over again.

Now is not the time for weakness. Now is the time to show my strength. So I square my shoulders; I need to send the message that I am not scared. If the king is my country's worst nightmare, I'll be his.

I step into the doorway and stare out at the crowd that waits. Once people catch a glimpse of me, they go quiet. The posters some hold wilt in their hands. Whatever their expectations were, it's clear that this is not it.

I descend down the stairs and touch my country's soil for the first time since I left. It's the first time I've ever set foot in my homeland without my father.

People holding cameras rush at me. I already knew this would happen. The woman locking lips with the king two nights ago is now covered in dried blood; this is as sensational as it gets.

My eyes find the representatives. They're all here, along with Will. They've decided to temporarily lift their safety precautions and leave the bunker all to welcome my father and me back.

I breathe heavily through my nose and walk to them, ignoring the WUN soldiers holding the crowd at bay and the ancient-looking cameras that follow my every movement.

I'm not a part of this moment; I'm seeing this all through a long, dark tunnel. The representatives' stoic expressions, the horrified screams of the crowd, which are now mixing with the increasing cheers by those who thirst for enemy blood.

Will looks shell-shocked. I can't get over how strange the sight is when he's usually so unruffled.

The general pushes his way to me. "What happened?" His brows are furrowed, and his nostrils flare. He can smell the death on me.

I lean in to him. "I'm only going to retell the story once," I say. "If you want this to go down in WUN history, you're going to have to give me a microphone and make a show of it."

He looks me over, his face grim, and he nods to the side. "We already have a makeshift stage ready." I glance to where he indicates. Sure enough, there's a small podium set up, probably meant for my father. But now it's there for me.

"Are you sure you want to record this?" the general asks. "It could be used against you once the war is over."

"I will be killed for my crimes, regardless," I say. This is the sick truth I've known since I could think properly on the flight over. There's no other alternative for what I've done.

The general stares at me for a long moment; I can see the morbid curiosity behind his eyes. "This footage is not going to appear to the public until we've okay-ed it—*if* we okay it," the general says.

"I understand." I approach the stage with the general at my side. Will appears on my other side, hovering but not touching me. I can see his concern etched into his crinkled brow. Underneath it I see fear, but I can't tell if it's fear for me or fear of me.

When the crowd sees what I'm doing, they creep closer to the stage.

I stop when I reach the podium. The microphone—probably one of the few still in existence on this side of the world—is angled for someone much taller than me— my father. That's why the king's men shot him in the head—because he was that much taller than everyone else.

I try to blink away the memory of my father cradled in my arms, but when I look down, I see his blood—now dried—still discoloring the skin of my forearms.

The crowd is staring; everyone's waiting for me. Time to get this over with.

I take the microphone from where it rests. "Over a dozen men and women of the WUN left for Geneva—only four of us have returned." I pause to collect myself. "This blood," I hold out my arm, "is the blood of my father, who was shot before my eyes because he would not agree to the king's peace treaty. We know this is how the king deals with dissension.

"This is also the blood of our fallen soldiers, who died trying to help me escape." I pace the stage. "And it is the blood of my enemies, whom I killed when they tried to capture me."

The crowd roars. Without meaning to, I've worked them up into some kind of frenzy.

Fatigue sets in. I haven't eaten or slept since we fled. "I want peace, and I was willing to pay the highest price—my own freedom." The crowd quiets. "If you watched the negotiations, then you saw me with the king. You saw me kiss the king.

You saw a traitorous woman doing what traitorous women always do, right?" There are uncomfortable murmurs in the crowd.

"Wrong," I say. "The king has killed every one of my family members. He's taken my friends and family from me. I hate him with every fiber of my being.

"The king wanted me—so much so that he changed his peace treaty on my behalf. He thought he'd keep me in Geneva with him. And when my father refused to let that happen ..." I close my eyes and breathe slowly, "the king had him killed."

There's angry murmuring. People are confused, and I don't have it in me to clarify the situation more. In fact, I don't have much of anything left in me, period.

I place the mike back where I found it and walk off the stage. There. I've done it. Said what I needed to say. And now I can quietly fall apart.

THE REST OF the day blurs. Will is beside me for most of it, except while I bathe. I'm actually afforded a real bath, not just a basin of water and a washcloth like usual. It has nothing on the king's showers, and it's still not enough to wash off all the blood, but it is familiar. And familiar is what I need at the moment.

Since I returned to the bunker, the representatives—minus me and Will—have been locked inside that room of theirs, no doubt trying to figure out what to make of this mess.

Once I finish bathing, I return to my room. Will's already there, waiting for me. I walk right into his arms and allow myself this closeness. I rub my face into the rough material that covers his chest, enjoying the feel of a body.

The sensation reminds me of the king's skin pressed against mine. The dark promise in his gaze.

I pinch my eyes shut. The last thing I want is to remember him fondly.

Will's arms encircle mine, and we stay like that for a long time, saying nothing. I can feel Will shaking; the situation bothers him too.

I finally pull away from him. "I need to sleep."

"I'll stay with you," he says.

I shake my head. "No. I want to be alone."

Will frowns. "You'll be okay?"

No. "I promise." I give him a small smile to further convince him.

He looks torn.

"Seriously Will," I say, "the representatives need you more than I do."

He flinches at my words; I hadn't meant them to sting.

"Please," I say, "find out what's going on with them so you can tell me when I wake up." Which might be never.

Reluctantly he nods. "If you need me, you know where to find me," he says. He hesitates, and I can see he's trying to figure out whether he should kiss me.

"Go," I say, giving him a push; I don't want anyone's lips on mine in a long, long time.

I DON'T KNOW how many hours I lie there, locked somewhere between sleep and wakefulness. Long enough to hear my roommates come in and whisper to one another as they get ready for bed. Long enough to hear them leave sometime later, and long enough for several people to crack open the door and poke their heads in only to quickly retract them and leave.

At some point I realize I'm no longer sleepy, merely weary. I haven't eaten in a while, though someone has left a plate of food and a glass of water next to my bed. A sick part of me wants to never again eat. I want to waste away until I join my parents in death.

Eventually someone comes in, and they don't leave. I feel a hand shake my shoulder. "Serenity, wake up," Will says from behind me.

I'm too tired to even tell him to go away, so I merely lay there.

"Serenity, the representatives need you. They've made contact with the king."

I BURST INTO the conference room, feeling more alive than I have for the last day or two. The king's face is plastered on the enormous screen. He looks tired, his eyes sad.

"You haven't eaten," he says. I don't know how he can tell over the screen.

The representatives glance between Montes and me. They know that something happened between us, but they don't know what.

Behind me Will puts his hand on my shoulder. The king's eyes flicker at the movement.

I shrug Will's hand off and approach the camera set up in our conference room, just so that the king can see my anguish more clearly.

"Why?" I whisper.

He watches me with solemn eyes but stays silent.

"I was willing to do what you asked, so why did you have to take the one person that mattered to me?"

His face is stoic.

"Why?" I ask again, this time louder.

When he doesn't answer, I scream like a wild animal. "Answer me!" I shriek. Hot tears snake down my cheek.

Instead of doing just that, the king's attention returns to the general. "Do we have an agreement?"

I follow the king's gaze to the general. "An agreement?" I ask. How could the WUN and the king agree to anything at a time like this?

I glance at Will. Only now do I notice that his eyes are red rimmed. My gaze darts back to the general, who's rubbing his eyes. He drops his hand and looks at me for a moment before returning his attention to the screen.

"We do."

My heart patters away in my chest.

The king's eyes find mine, and he stares at me for several seconds before moving his gaze over the room. "Congratulations ladies and gentlemen. The war is officially over."

MY MOUTH IS gaping long after the king's image disappears. The room's quiet, abnormally so.

I'm the first to speak. "What just happened?"

My eyes land first on Will, who looks like he's only barely holding it together. Then they move over each of the representatives. None of them will meet my gaze.

My breathing speeds up, and at the back of my mind I worry that I might pass out from anxiety. I'm weak enough that it's a distinct possibility.

"Why won't any of you look me in the eye?" My voice rises.

No one responds.

"What. Just. Happened?" My voice cracks.

Still no response. I put a hand to my head; I'm feeling faint.

"Sit down, Serenity."

"No," I snap. "Not until someone tells me what's going on."

A muscle in the general's jaw twitches. "The king approached us with a peace agreement."

"And you accepted it. In the wake of what happened, you still accepted it." I am a hair's breadth away from losing it.

"The king gave us everything we wanted and then some," he says.

"Uh huh." I can feel more hot tears cascading down my face. People are shifting nervously in their seats. The last time they saw me, I was covered in blood. I'm a wolf amongst a flock of sheep.

"Serenity," the general says, "this peace agreement will save the lives of millions. It's better than anything your father saw up until the day of his death."

I let out a strangled cry at the mention of my father. "Why didn't you include me in the decision making?"

"You weren't in a sound state of mind."

I nod, because he's right. I choke down my pride and vindictiveness. The representatives did what they had to do to ensure the well being of the western hemisphere.

"Tell her," Will says.

I look away from the general to his son. Will's hands are balled into fists, and he's crying as well. Only now do I realize that there might be a reason Will hasn't tried to comfort me like he would've a day ago. There might be a reason why the representatives can't look me in the eye and why there's an agreement at all in light of recent events.

"What is it?" I ask, returning my gaze to the general. Dread coils at the pit of my stomach.

The muscle in General Kline's cheek jumps again. "The king had one condition in the agreement."

"No," I whisper. The king wouldn't—the representatives wouldn't. There must be one decent person amongst the remaining leaders of the world.

The general's face is grim. "In return for peace, we're to deliver you to the king."

CHAPTER 12

SERENITY

I STARE AT the general for a moment, not allowing myself to comprehend his words. And then they sink in. Bile rises up my throat, and I barely have time to grab a nearby trashcan before I retch.

Someone places a hand on my shoulder, but I shrug it off. I wipe my mouth with the back of my hand and straighten.

The general's still speaking, but I'm no longer listening. I feel my legs buckle, and then Will is there, scooping me up and carrying me back to my room.

My entire body shakes.

I can't go back.

"Serenity, he's not going to kill you," Will says as he lays me on my bed. He crouches next to it so that we're at eye level. His gaze moves to my lips; he looks pained. "The king's not going to kill you—or imprison you." He takes a deep breath. "They've been talking about the possibility of a wedding."

I go still. "A wedding?"

Will nods, and I can see his throat work. He closes his eyes and I see his body shudder.

"I have to marry the king?"

Will opens his eyes. "That's what it sounds like."

"I have to marry my father's killer?"

His face crumbles and he looks away. "It's better than death or imprisonment," he says, his voice rough.

"Get out."

"What?"

"*Get out!*" I scream.

Slowly Will gets up and backs away from me. "I'll make this right, Serenity. I swear it."

I pretend I don't hear his words. I'm tired of promises. Of vendettas. Of posturing. Of politics and death.

Once he leaves the room, I curl into a ball and pretend nothing exists at all.

I STAY IN bed for another two days, shaking, sometimes rocking myself. Eventually I eat the food that someone's left for me, one small bite at a time. My stomach contracts painfully as each piece of food enters, and I have to fight off my rising sickness. I drink some water, if only to get rid of my splitting headache.

By the end of two days, the most painful emotions have dissolved away. I still feel like one giant, open wound, but I can think through it. I can be rational. Somewhat.

So I get up, wash myself, get dressed, and head to the conference room. Not surprisingly, when I get there, the representatives are in session. I've rarely seen them outside this room.

The group quiets when they see me. "I'm here to cooperate," I say, striding into the room. "I'll do what you want for the good of the country. What do you need of me?"

For a moment no one speaks. For all their smooth words, I've managed to silence these politicians several times over the last few days. Then the general approaches me, and in a rare show of emotion, he envelops me in a hug.

"You are the daughter I never had," he whispers into my ear. His voice is gruff. "I'd hoped you'd make my son happy one day."

I wince at his words. He doesn't know that he's making this so much worse for me.

He pulls away. "Has Will told you anything about what's going on?"

I glance about the room. I don't see the general's son; I wonder if he's been playing hooky just like I have.

"Only that I might be ..." my throat works, "*marrying* the king." The words burn coming out. "Whose idea was that?" I ask.

The general's lip curls with disdain, and he shakes his head. "His," he says.

After I killed the king's men, I'd assumed that if he ever got his hands on me, he'd execute me, regardless of his feelings. In the end, that's what war is, a string of revenge killings.

But his men hadn't tried to kill me, and they'd had many opportunities during my escape. He always wanted me alive.

I wonder if the peace agreement the representatives agreed to was the same one the king presented my father. If it was, then the man that raised me would've died in vain. I suppress my shudder.

The general clears his throat. "The king has a jet here waiting for you."

I raised my eyebrows. "Why didn't anyone wake me?"

"He gave us orders to leave you be until you were ready."

I'm struck by two things the general has said. One, the general is taking orders from the king. For as long as I've known the general, he's been the de facto leader of the WUN. It's strange to see him abdicate his leadership role.

And two, I'm stunned that the king gave those particular orders. Had circumstances been different, I'd say it was kind of him. But I've come to learn that this is the king's style—to cut you up then kiss the wounds he inflicted.

"Now that you're here," the general continues, "we will contact the king's retinue and let them know you're awake. They'll probably have you board the flight as soon as possible once this happens; they are going to assume you're unwilling and dangerous."

I nod.

"Once you arrive at the king's palace, he's planning on announcing the end of the war and your engagement."

I scowl at this; the thought of being engaged to him causes me physical discomfort.

"It sounds like there are already wedding preparations in the works," the general says. "It'll be filmed and aired over the Internet—the thought is that the wedding will symbolize the marriage of two hemispheres. It's quite brilliant, actually—it should go a long way to encourage peace."

"*Don't*," I say. My breaths are coming out quick and ragged. I can't bear to hear more on the subject.

The general puts a hand on my shoulder. "You'll be okay, Serenity. The asshole actually seems to care about you."

My eyes flick to the king. "Don't lie to yourself, General. I'm marrying a monster."

WILL AND THE general lead me up to the surface. They're the only ones I allow to accompany me. We reach the top of the final set of stairs, and I stare at the door to the garage. On the other side of it, the king's men wait for me. These are my last moments with the people I know.

I reach for the door and pause. "What will happen once I'm gone?" I ask the general. I've wanted to know the answer to this question since I left my bed. I knew my fate, but I knew nothing about what would happen to the WUN and its former political leaders.

The general gives me a sidelong glance. "The western hemisphere, under the governance of the king, will begin to receive medical relief in those areas that need it the most. There will also be additional efforts to cleanse the land of the radiation that's gotten into the soil. After that, the king's focus will then be rebuilding our economy."

I fidget. "What will happen to you and Will and the rest of the representatives?" I ask.

"The king has granted us amnesty and allowed us to continue to govern these territories under the supervision of his men."

I raise my eyebrows. "That's ... really good news." We'd always planned on being executed if we lost the war. I'm still not convinced that won't happen. After all, there are no checks on the king's power.

The general nods. "It is. The peace agreement is better than we'd ever anticipated—or hoped for."

I shift my weight. We've come back to the elephant in the room—that I'm leaving because of the agreement.

The general must realize how callous his words sound—spoken to the one person who will lose everything—since he takes a step back. He looks between Will and me. "I should let you two have your own goodbye." The general salutes me. An unbidden tear drips from my eye as I give him a small smile and salute him back.

Will and I watch him leave, neither of us willing to speak until his footsteps completely fade.

Will steps in close to me and cups my cheek. "It was never supposed to be like this," he says.

I wrap my hand around his wrist and lean into his hand. "A lot of things were never supposed to happen like they did." I close my eyes. I might never see Will again. That thought constricts my heart, and I have to force the thought from my mind. My body can't take much more emotional pain.

He leans his head against mine; I can tell by his ragged breathing that he's trying to keep it together for my sake.

"If this is the last moment we get, I want to make the most of it," I say. One final memory of the man and the life that will never be mine.

Will nods against me, his hand sliding to the back of my head. He presses his lips to mine, and our mouths move urgently. I'm memorizing the taste of him even as I'm saying goodbye.

When his lips finally leave mine, they move to my ear. "You have to kill him, Serenity."

My body goes rigid against him. "You work for the king; you can't say things like that anymore," I whisper.

"The Resistance—those people who saved you—they will spread to the western hemisphere. Once they do, I'm planning on joining," he says.

"And what do you hope to accomplish?" I ask. The war is over; we lost. The best any of us can do now is make the situation as bearable as possible. I'm not sure that killing the king would actually make the world better, or if it would just open the position to all the other power-hungry people out there.

"No one man should have that much power," Will says.

Silently, I agree with him, but it doesn't change the fact that the king might be the world's best chance at getting back on its feet. More fighting will only prolong our suffering.

"And what happens once he's dead, huh?" I ask. "They'll kill me too."

Will shakes his head. "No, they won't. We have the footage of your arrival still, remember?"

My skin prickles. I don't know whether this discussion fills me with fear or excitement, but I do feel my mortality in that moment. I'm certain I'll die before my time—not that I'd ever believed otherwise.

I back away from him and grab the handle of the door. "I'll think about what you've said."

"Do."

"Bye Will."

He tips his head. "Goodbye my future queen."

AS SOON AS the aircraft leaves the ground, the king's men relax. Not completely, but they're not encircling me the same way they had been when they picked me up in the bunker's garage.

One of them has my gun; he took it off of me when they patted me down for weapons. I keep my eye on him. I will kill for that gun. It's the last piece of my father I have.

I glance out my window and watch my homeland get smaller and smaller. This high in the sky, the land looks beautiful. You wouldn't know that the earth is poisoned with radiation, and its people are desperate, scavenging things.

I don't know when I'll be back here, if ever. It feels like a final goodbye. There's nothing much that I'm leaving—a few final friends, my past, my old way of life.

I can feel the wary stares of the king's men. Their animosity practically rolls off of them; I meet their gazes and give them each a slow, predatory smile. It pleases me to see the lines on their faces deepen. They've either seen me kill their comrades, or they've been warned.

It takes me a few minutes to realize that I'm causing them pain to feel better about my own. Once I do, I close my eyes and lean my head against the window and let myself nod off to sleep.

THE SENSATION OF falling wakes me up. I look out my window and see the rosy light of dawn as the jet makes its descent. When I look down at the scenery, I suppress a gasp. Small islands dot the blue expanse of ocean.

"Where are we?"

No one answers me. Big surprise.

As the aircraft descends and we draw closer to the small islands, the scenery comes into focus. It's not quite arid, but not quite tropical either.

A larger landmass looms in the horizon. I know in my gut this is my destination. The jet passes over it and circles back. I can see a small airstrip ahead of us. And then we're landing.

Once the aircraft coasts to a stop, I stand, ignoring the way the guards tense as they fall into form around me. The sick part of me enjoys how skittish they are.

The engine dies, and the jet's stairway is lowered. The guards ahead of me begin to move, and I follow them out. This is the second time I've arrived on enemy soil. And it is still that. To everyone else, the war might've ended, but it never will for me. Not so long as I live with the king.

This moment reminds me of a story my dad told me a long time ago. There was once an ancient battle, fought for ten years. The Trojan War. At the close of it, the Greeks, on the edge of defeat, surrendered and left in their place a huge wooden horse—a gift to their victorious enemies, the Trojans. Little did the Trojans know that waiting inside the wooden beast were Greek soldiers.

The Trojans brought the horse into their walls and celebrated their victory long into the night. Once the Trojan citizens had all drunk themselves into a stupor and gone to bed, the Greek soldiers left the horse and slaughtered the enemy. They won the war this way.

The king has only demonstrated his excellent talent for destroying things, but scant few at rebuilding the world. And now that the war is over, he's let the enemy into his house.

Perhaps Will is right and the king needs to be destroyed once and for all. I smile grimly. Perhaps I will be his Trojan horse.

CHAPTER 13

SERENITY

A SMALL GROUP of people wait for my arrival off to the left of the jet. Judging by how small the crowd is, I'm guessing the king has kept quiet about my bloody escape. I wouldn't be surprised if the world thought I'd never left the king's side.

The guards lead me towards a limo. As they do, my eyes drift back to the small gathering that watches me. The crowd shifts, and my steps falter. The king stands in the middle of them, dressed impeccably in a suit. Our eyes lock, and a small sound escapes from me. The sight of him splits open the wound I've been carrying inside myself.

I veer towards him. My guards are on me in an instant. Their hands wrap around my arms and pull me back. I push against them, my legs buckling.

The king approaches me slowly, his face unreadable.

"*Why can't you just leave me alone?*" I scream.

The king stares unwaveringly at me, but I could've sworn for a moment something like shame passed through those dark eyes of his.

"You killed him!" His face blurs as tears form. Emotionally, I've regressed back to the day I escaped. "You can't have me Montes! Not ever!"

"My king," a voice near me says, "should we administer the sedative?"

"I will never forgive you!" I shriek. "You hear me? Never!"

"I think that would be best." The king's voice glides over me like the smoothest silk. He's not even listening.

Someone extends my arm, and I buck against them. They drop their hands, and I elbow the guard behind me. He makes an *oomph* noise, and his grip loosens. I use the opportunity to wrench my arm free, and I slug the guard closest to me.

That's as far as I get. The rest of the king's guards close in and grab me, lowering my body to the ground. I thrash against them, but it's useless. They pin me down.

I'm sobbing horrible, heart-wrenching cries.

"Serenity, it's going to be okay," the king says from above me. I can feel his hands brushing my hair from my face.

I want to slap them away. I want to tell him to stop being nice when he's so evil. Instead I continue to sob.

I feel cool wetness rub against the crook of my arm, and then a slight sting. It doesn't take long for the numbness to overwhelm the pain.

I open my eyes. "Why?" I ask the king weakly.

But I never get my answer. The king's form blurs and fades with the last of the pain.

WHEN I WAKE up, I'm on a bed. I blink as I sit up, noticing the satiny comforter beneath me.

Where am I?

I glance around and jolt when my eyes land on the king. He sits in the chair next to my bed, pinching his lower lip in contemplation.

Looking at him hurts—he reminds me too much of all that's broken within me—but I can't tear my gaze from him.

"Hello Serenity," he finally says.

"Montes."

"Feeling better?"

I guffaw. "Like you care."

"You're right," he says, "I don't." He says the words so cavalierly, but his face betrays him. He's lying, and I really wish I couldn't tell. It's harder to despise him when he acts human.

"I want my gun," I say.

"And why would I give you that gun? You're difficult enough as it is."

His condescension is barely tolerable. "It's one of my only possessions. I want it."

The king tilts his head. "That's the gun that killed several of my men, isn't it?"

I say nothing.

"I've gotten a good look at it," he continues. "It's old but well cared for. Obviously it's important to you. Perhaps it was a gift from someone who once loved you?" He's openly taunting me and coming dangerously close to the truth.

Without realizing it, I've fisted my hands. I want to hit him. It's taking most of my self-control not to. I can see what he's doing

"You're a sociopath," I whisper.

"And you're a kindred spirit."

He's said that before. "I am nothing like you," I snap.

"You're right," he says. "I've never killed over a dozen people and then worn their blood like a trophy for an entire day."

I'm on my feet in an instant, and so is he. "I watched my father die that day, shot dead on your orders," I hiss. "I held his body in my arms as he bled out on me. So yes, I took pleasure in killing those men that harmed him."

The king steps closer to me. "I never ordered your father to be killed."

His words are a slap in the face. Still, "It's too little too late, Montes."

"No, it's not. The war is over."

"Ours isn't."

He works his jaw. "The wedding is at the end of the week," he says. "It's happening whether you want it to or not."

I slam my hand down on the bedside table next to me. "Goddamnit, Montes, you can't control everything—that's not how the world works."

"It's how my world works."

"And that's why you're going to end up alone." Preferably under six feet of soil.

"You need to learn about forgiveness."

I flash him a vicious smile. "Or else what? You'll kill me? Your threats hold no power over me. I've already lost everything I care about."

"Or else you'll never be happy," he says.

"I wouldn't recognize happiness if it stood right in front of me," I say.

"Clearly," the king says.

I narrow my eyes at him as he walks to the door. He pauses when he grabs the handle. "We're announcing the end of the war and the wedding this evening," he says. "A lot rests on how convincing you are. So if you don't know what happy is, I'd suggest you learn to fake it fast."

I DON'T KNOW what day it is, or what time it is, and I can't decide if I am jet lagged, or if my tiredness stems from my emotional and physical exhaustion. I stay in the room the king left me in. For all I know, I'm on some sort of house arrest.

Not that I mind. A servant comes in several hours after the king left, bearing food. I try to eat some and vomit it back up. I've gone too long without eating.

It's as I flush the toilet and clean myself up that I realize I want to live. In spite of the wedding, in spite of my father's death, in spite of every other fucked-up part of my life, I'm not ready to fold my hand. So I walk back to my food and eat it agonizingly slow, taking long breaks between bites to let my stomach settle.

I take a shower, and for once I let myself enjoy the way the water pelts my skin and force myself not to feel guilty that so many others don't have this luxury. I am in the unique position to change that—to change the entire world if I so desire. I am going to be the king's wife. The queen. Now that I've stopped running from the idea, I realize the doors it opens.

CHAPTER 14

SERENITY

MISERABLE. I AM absolutely miserable.

"Emerald green or orchid pink?" my wardrobe manager—*wardrobe manager*—asks me, holding up each dress.

"Neither."

She nods absently, as if that is the conclusion she's come to as well. "Yes, these colors are too casual—we want something that's hopeful yet regal." She stares at me for a beat, and then her eyes widen and she snaps her fingers.

I'm in the ninth circle of hell.

"I just had a thought. I'll be right back!"

"Can't wait," I mutter.

The hairstylist standing behind me yanks my hair, and my head snaps back. "Ow!"

"S-sorry, My Lady," the woman stammers. She sounds frightened, and she has good reason to be. I'm already rethinking this whole will-to-live bit if it includes being manhandled.

"Don't call me that," I growl out.

She nods her head and bites the inside of her cheek.

I'm being too abrasive, as usual. This is why friendship never came easily to me.

I reach up and place a hand on her arm. "I'm sorry," I say, gentler this time, "I'm just not used to people touching me." Or caring about my appearance at all.

In fact, over the last few hours I've repeatedly fantasized about grabbing my father's gun and ending all our lives. And then I'd remember that my gun was confiscated. Probably for the best.

My wardrobe manager comes waddling back into the bathroom with a shimmery golden dress draped over her arms. "Is it not perfect?" she says, holding the thing up so I can get a good look at it.

The thing is absolutely hideous; all that gold is giving me a headache. If I had a choice, I wouldn't be caught dead in the garment, but the same could be said for any dress I've crossed paths with. At this point, the sooner I agree to wear a dress, the sooner this will be over.

"There are no words," I say.

The wardrobe manager flashes me an eager smile. "I was hoping you'd say that. The king's going to have a hard time keeping his hands off you once he sees you in this."

I manage a weak smile. "Lucky me."

SHORTLY AFTER I'VE finished getting ready and my stylists have slipped out the door, I hear a knock. I grab the handle and open the door. On the other side King Lazuli waits.

His eyes widen when he sees me, and I watch as they slowly drink me in. When his gaze makes its way to my face, his eyes change from something hungry to something regretful. I recoil at the sight, and he pretends he didn't notice my reaction. We just managed to have an entire conversation solely based on body language.

"What, no guards?" I ask, noticing that he came to my room alone. It isn't the first time either. Earlier this morning he came alone as well, which means despite all he's done to me, there's a level of trust there. That, or he really can't be killed.

He takes my hand and kisses it. When he returns it to my side he says, "I hope you've been practicing how to pretend to be happy."

"Your beloved empire will be fine. I can be convincing when I want to be."

The king's eyes search mine. "I know."

He places his hand on my lower back, and I suppress a shiver. I'm not supposed to feel like this. I'm not supposed to react to his touch after everything.

"Ready?"

I take a breath and nod. "Let's do this."

The king leads me through his palace. This place is different from his mansion in Geneva. Both are grand and feel like stuffy royalty, but the king's palace here is larger and it seems more lived in than his other house. But like the mansion in Geneva, the floor plan here is hopelessly confusing.

"Where are we?" I ask.

"In the hallway," the king says.

I roll my eyes, and he laughs when he sees my expression. I realize too late that to him, exasperation is a better emotion that hate, fear, or sadness. And it is. It means that I can feel something towards him that's softer than what I have felt since I arrived.

"You know what I mean," I say.

The king's lips curve upwards at my interest. He should know that his reaction is only annoying me further. "We're in the Mediterranean—but you'll have to figure out what island we're on."

I file this information away and try not to think about how far away we are from my homeland. I'm dying to ask about the WUN, but I keep my mouth shut. I'm going to have to ease my way into a position of trust. For now I'll be the agreeable fiancée.

"How many houses do you own?"

"We," he says.

I flash him a questioning look.

"*We* have many houses. By the end of the week they'll be yours as well as mine."

My eyes widen, and then I glance away. I can't wrap my mind around all the implications of being married to this man.

Married.

To my parents' killer.

Suddenly the food I ate earlier doesn't seem like it's content to stay in my stomach. I stop walking and breathe slowly.

The king leans in so that he can peer into my eyes. "Are you alright?"

I hold up a finger, and he patiently waits. The nausea passes, and I begin walking again.

"What was that?" he asks.

"It's my body's reaction to you."

"I'm glad I leave you short of breath."

"Don't flatter yourself; I was trying not to barf."

The king's concern fades into an amused smile. We walk in silence after that, but with each passing second I feel the heat of King Lazuli's hand spread through me.

It angers me that my body reacts this way. Hell, it angers me even more that the king considers every emotion of mine that's not hate or pain a small victory..

He leads me outside to a limo. Photographers and cameramen swarm around us almost immediately, and again my stomach roils, this time from claustrophobia. A chauffeur holds the door open for the king and me, and I all but dive into it. I thought the publicity we'd received before was bad, but it seems I'd only received a taste of it in Geneva.

The king follows me into the car, I'm sure taking in my wide eyes. "I hope this is not you being convincing, because you're horrible at it," he says.

"Shut up."

Again, the king smirks, and I want to throttle him. Even if there wasn't this terrible baggage between us, there'd still be something about him that gets under my skin.

As soon as we pull away from the palace, I roll down the window. I can feel the king's eyes on me, but I ignore him. Once the window's all the way down, I stick my head out, then the rest of my torso.

For a single blissful second the air sings in my ears and streams through my hair. Then I feel a firm pair of hands wrap around my waist and yank me inside. I yelp and tumble into the king's arms.

"Are you trying to kill yourself?" the king asks, raising his voice. I can see that vein in his temple begin to throb.

"You caught me," I say sarcastically, "I was trying for death by moving vehicle."

"Be serious," he commands.

I raise my eyebrows. "Is that the tone you use on all your subjects? Because frankly, it—" My voice cuts off when the king leans forward and runs a hand through my hair.

He's fixing my hair. I don't know why this action of his catches me so completely off guard, but it does. Maybe because the gesture is affectionate, especially when I notice the slight quiver of his hands.

"Did you really think I was trying to kill myself?" I ask.

His hands pause, and they loosely cup my hair and my chin. "What do you think?" He stares at me, and I see concern in them.

"I'm thinking that there are far more effective ways of killing myself than jumping out of a moving car through the window." Seriously. I'd just use the door.

"Your father died a week ago."

I flinch at his words. Why would he bring that up?

"You had to be sedated when you arrived," King Lazuli continues. "I'm going to assume the worst until you prove otherwise."

I frown at him and push his hands away. "Well, I'm not planning on killing myself, so your concern is not needed."

The king doesn't leave my side. Instead he reaches around me and rolls up the window, and I feel my skin sear in every place his body presses against mine. The window seals shut, yet he doesn't move away. My eyes crawl over his arm to his shoulder, to his square jaw, to his mouth. There they pause, and then I meet his gaze.

My breath catches as we stare at each other.

He's the enemy.

It's too bad my body doesn't think so. It's ready to say *que sera sera* and forget the past.

The king leans in slowly, giving me plenty of time to pull away. There's no reason to fight him now that I'm forced to marry him, but that's not why I hold my ground. No, if I'm honest, it's because I want to feel something other than pain and hate.

He stops short of my mouth, though. Reaching up a hand, he traces the scar that drags down my face. "I'm sorry."

"No, you're not," I say.

"This time I really am."

A lump forms in my throat. "Don't say that." *Or else there will be no one left for me to hate but myself.*

He drops his hand, and something tugs at my heart. Regret? Yearning? I can't tell, but it's an emotion I don't want to feel.

"Where's my father's body?" I ask. It's been on my mind lately. I'm not sentimental over death; I've seen it, seen the way a soul leaves a person's eyes. The body is just a vessel—once whatever animates it is gone, it's just flesh. Still, I can't help but want to put my father's body to rest.

"It's being kept in a morgue in Geneva." The king's expression is cautious. He's watching me like I might snap. This conversation brings up all that's passed between us.

"Geneva?" I say, my throat hoarse. That is a punch to the gut. "I want his body returned to our homeland."

"I can arrange that," he says.

I stare at him for a beat, then nod once.

We sit in uneasy silence for the remainder of the drive. When the car finally stops and I look out the window, my heart drops through my chest. There are hundreds of people streaming into what looks like an amphitheater. This is really happening.

"Are you sure you're ready for this?" the king asks.

"Like I have a choice."

His leg brushes mine as he moves towards the doors. "Good point." His eyes slink over me. "I forgot to tell you—you look lovely."

Lovely. I want to laugh at his words. "You shouldn't have bothered with the compliment," I say "I'm many things, and the least impressive of them is lovely." I push past him just as someone opens the car door.

Lovely. What a load of bullshit.

CHAPTER 15

SERENITY

THE KING'S BEEN onstage for only a couple minutes when he calls me out. His voice booms out on the loudspeakers. "I have some important news I want to share with the world, and I want Serenity Freeman to help me announce it."

I know what's coming next, and I think the audience does as well. There's a buzz throughout the crowd. As I walk out onto the stage, I plaster on a smile and act as though my legs aren't wobbling beneath the dress I wear. Around so many people, my brain's having trouble processing what Montes is saying.

I come up next to him and stare out into the crowd. My smile wavers as I take in the hundreds—no, thousands—of occupied seats. A strong hand takes my own. I look down at the hand then back up at the man who holds it. He is the king of the entire world. He's a man who can't die. A man who doesn't age. He's a man who's made my life a living hell since the war began, and he's the man I'm forced to marry.

"The Western United Nations and the Eastern Empire have come to a peace agreement. The war is over."

I've never heard this many people cheer in such a confined space, but it seems to resonate through my bones. I smile at the sound, and it's genuine. Peace, at last.

The cheering goes on for a minute, maybe more, before the crowd is quieted and the king resumes his speech. "Now that there is peace between the two hemispheres, we can begin to look forward to the future."

The king turns his focus on me, and my heart drums faster. "There is no one I'd rather spend it with than the woman standing next to me." The look in his eyes is genuine; he's good. He's almost convinced me.

And then he does something I really wasn't expecting. He gets down on one knee. My heart is hammering away in my chest, and I'm sure if a camera got close enough, they'd capture the whites of my eyes on film. I'm about to take a step back when I pause.

You need to convince them.

He pulls out a small box and opens it, revealing a ring inside. "Serenity Freeman, will you marry me?" he asks, smiling. His eyes are vulnerable.

In a room full of thousands of people, it's absolutely silent.

I put a hand to my heart. Beneath my skin I can feel it pound. "Yes," I whisper. Only my whisper blasts across the sound systems thanks to the mike hooked up to me.

The crowd roars their applause, and the king's face breaks into a blinding smile, one that brightens his entire face and reaches his eyes. There's genuine happiness there, and I wonder if I might be the only person in the world that's not pleased by the situation. I think of Will.

No, I'm not the only one.

Taking my hand, the king removes the ring from its case and slides it onto my finger. It's a band made up of yellow diamonds. I can't decide whether it's the ugliest or prettiest thing I've ever seen.

The king stands, and without giving me a warning, he cups my face and his lips touch mine. I freeze for a split second, my mind and body conflicted, before I move my lips against his and return the kiss. I can feel a low burn starting at the bottom of my stomach and work its way through my limbs.

I touch a hand to his cheek and stroke the rough skin there. My abs clench. Aching want. Guilt. Divided loyalties.

The crowd continues to cheer, although now some whistles join the noise. It unsettles me that we have an audience—that we're doing this *for* an audience.

The kiss ends and the king takes my hand, lifting it into the air. The motion swivels my body so that I'm now facing the audience. I focus on my breathing as I stare out at the crowd.

"May our marriage symbolize the peaceful joining of two hemispheres and the future prosperity of the world," the king says. His words grate on my nerves. Of course, he's marrying me because it's the easiest, most secure way of controlling the entire world and snuffing out potential rebellions. A political alliance based on matrimony. What bothers me more than this realization is that the king's motives make a difference to me.

The crowd's cheers seem even louder now than they did before, and I force out what I hope sounds like a giddy laugh as I gaze at the king. His eyes stare back at me with that intensity I've come to recognize. And in this moment, I realize my mind is a small thing. Much smaller than the tide we're being swept along, smaller than the king's empire, smaller than the number of people who have fought and died to lead us to this moment.

But most of all, it's smaller than the heart, and that's the cruelest irony of all.

IT'S LATE BY the time we finally return to the king's palace, and by then I'd shaken hands with hundreds of people, smiled until it felt like my face must've broken, and withstood the flash of dozens and dozens of cameras. Tonight I got my first taste of what it will be like as the king's marionette. It made me want to shoot someone— preferably the king.

King Lazuli met my seething looks and barely contained anger with uncharacteristic patience, which only pissed me off further.

Our shoes click on the marble floor as Montes escorts me back to my room.

"Why are you still making an effort with me?" I ask, breaking the silence between us. "We have always been enemies, and we will always be enemies. Why try to force together puzzle pieces that will never fit?" I ask.

The king's hands slide into the pockets of his suit, and he bows his head, like he's actually thinking deeply on my question.

Finally, he speaks. "That first moment I saw you," Montes says, "I felt a jolt right here," Montes places a hand over his heart, "and I knew with certainty that you were mine."

"I'm not a possession, something you repeatedly seem to forget."

"Your heart is, and I wish to own it—I will own it."

I give him a curious look. "So confident."

We walk a few more paces in silence. "What is it that interests you?" Montes asks, glancing at me. "Apart from slaying, that is."

I ignore the barb and don't hesitate when I respond. "World affairs."

I glance at Montes to gauge his reaction, but he seems unsurprised. I was an emissary before I was his fiancée, after all. "Any areas in particular?" he asks.

Perhaps he means regions of the globe, but I interpret the question differently. An image of burned skin and patchy hair comes to mind. Another of the palsy a former soldier developed. All were the result of radiation poisoning and biological warfare. Not to mention that strange things are occurring in the king's labs, things he's kept quiet on. I want to know what those secrets are.

"Health," I say. "Innovations that will help people's quality of life."

He watches me for a long time. "You will make a great queen."

I press my lips together to keep my upper lip from curling at the title.

"The people need a leader who listens to their needs," the king continues as we come to a stop in front of my door. "Cares about them."

At his words, I close my eyes. I'm not sure I want to hear what he has to say. It means committing to my role as the king's wife, as the queen. I'm not ready for that.

His hand cups my chin. "Open your eyes, Serenity."

I do.

"If you are genuinely interested in health and technology as it relates to world affairs, I will give you access to that information."

I raise my eyebrows. "Really?" Excitement creeps into my voice.

His smile is sly. He knows I've taken his bait. "As soon as we're married and you've proven that you're not planning on killing me or yourself, then absolutely."

And there's the catch.

I scowl at him. "I already told you, I'm not going to do anything."

He touches a finger to my lips, and I pretend his touch does nothing to me. "I need more than just your word," he says. "I need proof."

I DON'T SEE the king again until the next evening. He's been busy all day with ruling the world, and I imagine that he will be especially busy for many months— hell, many years—to come.

When he knocks on my door, I just about bound out to meet him. Sure he's a slimy bastard, but men and women have been in and out of my room all day taking my measurements, asking questions about my personal preferences, and abusing my skin, nails, and hair in the name of beauty. There are forms of torture less painful than that.

"Someone seems happy to see me," he says.

"You are a sadistic bastard." I brush past him and out the door, glancing both ways just to make sure no one else is about to ambush me into picking out a color scheme for God-knows-what.

Somehow the king knows exactly what I'm referring to. I can see the laughter in his eyes. "I thought all women liked getting pampered?"

I narrow my eyes at him. "Do I look like the kind of woman who enjoys that?"

The king places a hand on my back and leans down to whisper in my ear. "You look like the kind of woman who shoots and asks questions later, and it's a turn-on."

My head whips back to look at King Lazuli. He's gazing at me hungrily. "You are a twisted son of a gun."

"Look who's talking."

I open my mouth to retort when the king cuts me off. "I want to show you something." He takes my hand and pulls me down the hall.

"Where's your little henchman, Marco?"

The king's hand tightens on mine. "He's around, but I've asked him to keep his distance."

"So, he's still working for you?"

"Yes." King Montes doesn't look at me when he says it.

I pull my hand out of his. "That's it? He kills my father and he goes unpunished?"

"Watch your words." Now the king turns to face me, and his eyes flash. "You and your men killed and injured some of my best men, and you got a peace treaty and a promotion out of it."

I stop in my tracks. "A *promotion*?" My voice only gets quiet like this before I do terrible things. "You consider this a promotion?"

My hands clench and unclench. The king eyes them before he speaks. "From emissary of a dying nation to queen of the entire world? Of course it is."

I pull my fist back and slam it into his face. My knuckles split as they connect with the king's cheek. It's the most pleasant sting I've ever endured.

His head whips to the side, and I hear the click of his teeth as his jaw snaps together. Montes staggers, but only for a moment. I hear the pounding of several footsteps as some of the nearby palace guards run to help the king. He waves them off and rubs his jaw while he watches me, his eyes sparkling dangerously. Blood trickles out the side of his mouth. He must've cut himself with his teeth.

"So the king bleeds—I wasn't sure," I say.

He smiles. That's all the warning I get. Then he's on me. He swipes my feet out from under me, and I slam to the ground. The king follows, straddling me. He grabs my hands and holds them over my head. "Are you finished with your tantrum?"

"Not even close," I growl.

I try to buck him off my body, but it only serves to tighten his grip on me. The king's legs press into my sides, and he squeezes my hands. It takes me a few seconds and a couple deep breaths to realize that we're in a compromising position.

As if reading my mind, the king's eyes flick to my lips, a wicked grin forming along his own. I want to scream, but instead I force my strained muscles to relax. It's even harder to swallow my pride.

"Are you going to get off of me and show me this surprise of yours?" I ask, trying to sound exasperated. It's not very convincing, considering the series of events that led up to now.

"Hmm, I'm not sure," King Lazuli says, pretending to ponder my words. "It's not very often that I get my bloodthirsty wife-to-be on her back."

My face heats both with anger and embarrassment. He removes one of his hands from where they grip mine to brush his thumb over my lower lip. Heat ripples through my stomach. I don't want to react this way, not in the middle of some hall in the king's palace in front of palace guards. Not with him, and not after he's just tackled me to the ground.

I lie there, watching, waiting for what he'll do next. He gazes at my lips, and then he leans in.

He's a hair's breadth away from my mouth when I speak. "Don't," I say.

"Why not?" The king's breath fans against my lips. He's smiling down at me rapaciously.

I don't speak. There are a hundred reasons why this shouldn't happen right now, but my mouth can't form a single one.

"I'll tell you what," he says, his voice low. "I won't kiss you if you can offer me something better."

"I'm not your fucking employee, and this is not a business transaction," I snap.

His grin deepens. "You're right, it isn't." His mouth presses against mine, and my stomach clenches. His tongue strokes my lips, encouraging them to part. Caught up in the moment, I let them. I'd forgotten how much I enjoyed kissing and how good the king's, in particular, are.

His tongue brushes against mine, and I relish the heady taste of him. With Will, my mind had loved him while my body had remained unmoved. In this situation, it's the exact opposite. I hate the king, yet I crave him. I want him to suffer, but I also want this.

Love and hate really aren't so very different.

He bites my lower lip, sucks on it, and I all but moan at the sensation. The king pulls away from me, and I lazily open my eyes, not realizing I'd closed them to begin with.

I just got owned, and the king knows it. I can tell by the way he bites his lip. He releases me and stands up.

I push myself up on my forearms and watch him. He reaches out a hand to help me up.

When I don't take it, he says, "Do you want to see my surprise, or would you rather I get back on top of you?" he asks.

I run my tongue along my teeth and take his hand, giving it a hard yank as I get up. He doesn't flinch.

I follow the king out of the palace. The cool night air raises goose bumps along my skin, but it's the sound of crashing waves that captures my attention. This is the first time I've been outside the palace since I arrived, and it's ecstasy.

I take a deep breath, relishing the smell of the salty sea breeze and let myself forget my past. The sea and the sky can do that—make me feel like an ageless thing.

This is the surprise, I realize. I'd like to be snarky about it, since it's so simple, but instead I feel a little unnerved. This is the best thing he could've surprised me with: escape.

I lift the skirt of the dress I'm wearing and run towards the waves, kicking my shoes off in the process. Behind me I can hear the king jogging, and I wonder if he's worried that I'm going to throw myself into the water like some tragic Greek maiden. 'Cause he should be. That's exactly what I'm going to do.

I yip as my feet hit the water and then I dive in, ruining my outfit and my hair and my makeup. Good riddance.

When I come up for air, I'm laughing. A moment later I feel hands wrap around me and haul me to my feet. It takes the king a moment to realize I'm fine.

He swipes the wet strands of my hair away from my face. "Jesus," he says, "you scared the shit out of me!"

I can't see him in the dark, but if I could, I bet I'd see that vein in his temple throbbing. "If I didn't know better, I'd say you were concerned."

"Why would you think otherwise?"

Water laps around us, swirling with the tide. My dress tangles itself around the king as he holds me to him. I taste saltwater on my lips and try to ignore the way Montes's dress shirt clings to his chest.

"Oh, I don't know," I say, "maybe because you killed my parents, destroyed my homeland, and are now forcing me into marrying you." My voice comes out flinty.

Rather than responding, the king releases me. He walks out of the water and back onto the beach, leaving me staring after him.

"Oh, *now* you walk away!" I yell at his back, mostly just to rile him up.

It works.

He comes stalking back into the water. "What do I have to do to prove myself? I've already moved mountains—an entire half of the world will prosper because you wanted it to be so. What more do you want me to do?"

"I want you to leave me the hell alone."

He grasps my jaw and holds it firmly, and in the dim moonlight I can just barely make out the shine of his eyes. "That is the one thing I cannot do."

He lets me go and leaves, this time for good.

CHAPTER 16

SERENITY

THE DAY OF the wedding I sleep in. Normally I'm loathe to waste away the first hours of the morning, but not today. Today I want to forget that I have to get married. To the king. I make a face in my pillow.

People have been knocking on my door for the last two hours, and up until now I've done a pretty good job of ignoring them. But the pounding on my door right now is louder and more insistent than the others.

When I don't answer, the pounding stops. I smile into my pillow until I hear the click of my lock being thrown back. The door opens and footsteps cross the room.

My bed dips as someone sits down on it, and then I feel the feathery touch of fingertips on the bare skin of my shoulder. "You need to get up now."

My eyes snap open at that voice. "I thought you were ignoring me?" I say to King Montes. He's leaning over me, and his nearness is doing strange things to my body. I haven't seen him since that night in the ocean.

"When it comes to you, that's impossible."

I bury my face in my pillow. "I want to sleep in."

"We're getting married in two hours."

"Don't care," I say, my voice muffled.

"Fine. We'll skip the wedding part and go straight to the honeymoon." He pulls back the covers and begins to slide in next to me. I yelp and jump out of bed.

The king steps away and sticks his hands into his pockets. He's wearing a uniform with a sash, and it takes me a minute to realize that's what he'll be wearing today when we get married.

I rub the sleep from my eyes and give him my best glare.

"Just so you know, you're not frightening at all in the morning," he says, smirking. "You look like a pissed-off kitten."

"Say that again, and I'll castrate you with a butter knife."

His lips quirk. "Ah, lucky me to have such a blushing bride."

"Isn't it bad luck to see me before the wedding?" I ask, folding my arms over my chest.

"What, you think our luck can get any worse?" the king says, raising an eyebrow. He has a point.

Before I can formulate a response, he walks to the door and ushers in a group of women who carry bags of makeup and hair supplies. I grimace at the sight.

"I'll see you in a couple of hours, Serenity," the king says, and then he's gone.

BY THE TIME I'm sitting in a small room waiting to be ushered down the aisle, a cold emptiness has settled in me. I'm wearing a dress I didn't pick out, holding flowers I don't care for, wearing makeup and hair someone else has styled, and I'm waiting to be married to a man I don't love because of orders someone else gave.

87

There's a rap on the door, and it opens after a moment. A young guard sticks his head in. "We're ready for you."

I shake out my arms and crack my neck. I'm supposed to be gathering my courage, not falling apart. I nod and follow him out, bringing the bouquet up to my chest.

Flashes go off, and cameras pan in on me. The photographers press against the velvet rope they're prohibited from crossing.

All I need to do is march down this hallway, then the aisle.

Easy, I tell myself.

I'm a horrible liar. I might as well be walking the plank. I'm just as frightened as I would be if my life were on the line. I have no one to hold my arm, and even though I don't believe in giving someone away (my current situation case in point), it'd be nice to not face this alone. That thought makes me think of my father and how unhappy he'd be if he could see me now.

Time's up, regardless. I turn the corner and stare at two large oak doors guarded by two of the king's men. Inside is the royal chapel, where hundreds of guests and dozens of camera crews eagerly wait. I can hear music softly playing from inside.

When the tune abruptly changes, the guard at my side nods to the two men in front of me, and they grasp the door handles. "Congratulations," he says, stepping aside as the doors swing open.

I stand there blinking as I take in the foreign faces that watch me from the pews. I'm too terrified to smile, so I simply stare straight ahead. My eyes meet the king's, and strangely, in this moment, the sight of him grounds me.

He stands with his hands clasped, smiling at me. I can't help it, between my nerves and his smile, my mouth curves up. I don't look away as I walk towards him; ironically, he's the only thing that's keeping me from running out of here screaming. And I don't want that—not if this is somehow supposed to symbolize future peace and unity.

It seems like an eternity before I get to him. Once I do, relief washes over me that I'm no longer doing this alone. I pass my flowers to someone standing nearby, and the king takes my hands. I know he can feel them shaking by the way he squeezes them reassuringly.

The priest officiating drones on in Latin, and my pulse calms down a bit. At some point he reverts to English and asks King Lazuli to present me with the token of his commitment.

Montes reaches into his breast pocket and procures a ring. Giving me a soft smile, he slides it onto the finger where the engagement band already rests.

The stone of this new ring is dark blue, and flecks of gold are caught in its matrix. It looks for all the world like I'm wearing the night sky on my finger. Because what I love most about the sky are the stars.

He remembered.

It's also not lost on me that the stone is lapis lazuli; I'm wearing the king's namesake on my finger.

Someone passes me a ring, and with trembling hands I slip it onto the king's finger.

I gaze into his eyes as the priest speaks. They shine, and right then I feel beloved—by the man in front of me and the world that's looking to me.

Then I remember my father, and why it is that I'm up here. The lives the king has taken because of his selfishness. The façade is gone just as the priest says, "You may now kiss the bride."

My movements are jerky and automated. I kiss the king, but I'm not really present. My skin crawls as his lips caress mine. When he pulls away he smiles, but I can see something like uncertainty there. I want to laugh that I can make someone like the king feel vulnerable, but I'm too consumed by my own personal pain.

The priest announces us to the chapel, and I feel a tear drip down my cheek. I just married the monster under the bed.

THE KING AND I stand outside the palace, on the grassy lawn that overlooks the water. From the ice sculptures to the overabundance of flowers, it's clear the king's spared no expense on our reception. It had to cost a fortune of money better spent elsewhere.

A constant stream of people approaches us and congratulates the king and me on our union. I give most of them flinty looks. I know it's not fair of me to be hostile to people I don't know, but I'm insulted that anyone could assume I'm happy about what's happening to me.

"Congratulations my friend. You deserve all the happiness in the world," says the politician in front of us. He looks frighteningly similar to a walrus, and he eyes me like the object I'm supposed to be.

Montes nods and shakes his hand, "Thank you," he murmurs.

When the man reaches for my hand, I level a glare at him. He gets it.

Bowing, he says, "Congratulations again," and backs away.

The king watches him as he leaves. "I don't like the way he looked at you," he says quietly.

"That makes two of us."

The king nods to himself. "Then I'll take care of the situation."

I blink a few times. "Are you psychotic?" I hiss at him under my breath. "You can't just punish everyone who slights you."

"Of course I can," he says.

Before I can respond, the next guest approaches, this one a crusty old man who spews praise at the king. Once he moves along, I lean into the king. "Brownnoser, that one."

The king snickers, and I cringe that, at the moment, we are coconspirators. For the king, this seems to elicit the opposite reaction. He wraps a hand around my waist and rubs my side affectionately. I think I'm going to be sick.

A couple approaches us, and thankfully King Lazuli has to drop his hand from my side in order to greet them.

"We are so happy for you," the woman says, "and we hope that this union brings prosperity to your home—and lots of children," she throws in, flashing me a sly smile. Like what every woman wants is a snotty baby.

I sway on my feet at the thought. "That won't ever happen," I say before I can help it. The idea of carrying the king's child is just too much for me to process at the moment.

The woman glances at me sharply, and the king stiffens at my side. "Er ... I can't have children." It's not even necessarily a lie, considering all the radiation I've been exposed to.

"You poor thing," the woman says.

"The queen doesn't know what she's saying," King Lazuli says. "She *can* have children."

I try to hide my swallow at the way the king looks at me, like my reproductive system is now at the forefront of his mind.

"Oh." Now the woman glances back and forth between us in confusion.

"Great to see you Claudette—Roger." The king nods to both of them and they take the cue to move on.

I watch their retreating forms. "Do you even have any real friends?" I say. "These people make me want to blow my brains out."

"What the hell was that about, Serenity?" King Lazuli says.

"Nothing," I say quickly.

The king studies me. "This discussion isn't over."

An older, regal woman greets us next.

"I'm so glad to see you settle down," she says to King Lazuli.

The king smiles back at her. "Thank you, Margot."

She squeezes his hand with her wrinkled one. I eye her withered beauty. She wears strings of pearls and gaudy gold jewelry. My upper lip curls. It changes into a grimace of a smile when she focuses on me.

Her eyes widen when she sees the scar that trails down the side of my face. I've gotten this reaction all day. And just like the others, I get the feeling that the woman in front of me has never seen violence firsthand. She's never killed a man, never watched his blood slowly seep out of him and the light fade from his eyes. I'd wager that she came from a nation that either allied with the king, or surrendered before war broke out.

She recovers from her shock and pats the side of my face. "My, my, what a pretty thing you are." My smile slips at her words, and she must see the killer in me because she recoils.

The woman clears her throat. "Congratulations again you two," she says, nodding at the king and trying hard not to look at me. I watch her as she walks away, and just as I suspected, she throws a final, spooked glance over her shoulder, like she can't help herself.

I narrow my eyes and give her a slow, predatory smile. Her eyes widen and she hurries away from us.

"Stop scaring our guests," King Lazuli says next to me.

"You mean your guests," I retort.

The king's eyes drift to my bare arm and move down. The sight is possessive, hungry, and it makes my stomach churn.

I won't think about later tonight. I won't.

"They are our guests now, my queen," King Lazuli says.

"Don't call me that." I rub my shoulder against my neck, as if to wipe off the stain of his words from my skin.

"You better get used to it. That's what you'll be known as from now on." The king seems satisfied by the thought.

I snag a champagne flute from a passing waiter. The waiter looks between me and the king, mortified. The caterers are controlling the amount of alcohol I'm consuming, probably on behalf of the king's orders. It's a clever move too, since if I had it my way, I'd already be twelve drinks deep and unwilling to stop until the liquor killed me.

Before the king can take the glass from me, I throw it back. It's only my third drink of the night, but I can already feel the warm, tingly sensation of the alcohol sliding through my veins. King Lazuli scowls at me as I remove the now empty glass from my lips and flash him a triumphant smile.

The waiter snatches the champagne flute from my hands the first chance he gets, as though his attentiveness now can make up for the fact that he blew it.

The boy stutters apologies at the king, who waves him off. I watch longingly as the tray carrying champagne is whisked away.

I can feel the king's eyes on me, and I'm strangely interested in what he's thinking—not because I care about him, but because I want to know what his motives are for marrying me, a woman who loathes him.

The only answer that comes to mind is the obvious one: that this is some archaic form of a political alliance—marrying into power. Not that I have any power in my own right. But ideology is the most powerful currency in the world—it can start wars, and it can end them—and to the citizens of the nation, the king of the eastern empire and the emissary of the WUN symbolize two hemispheres tonight made whole.

However, feeling the king's eyes on me, I can't help but wonder if the marriage might be more than just a power play. I know the king finds me attractive and that he enjoys verbally sparring with me, but could something more be there?

The king waves Marco over. Marco, who's just as responsible for my father's death as the king is. Perhaps more so, if the king really didn't order my father killed.

This is the first time I've seen him, and I give him my most lethal look. The fact that Marco is not rotting in a jail cell or a coffin, but instead attending my wedding, has me seeing red.

He flinches, but that doesn't stop him from approaching King Lazuli.

"The queen is tired," the king says to Marco.

"No, I'm not."

Marco flicks me an annoyed look. I get perverse satisfaction knowing that it bothers him that I undermine the king.

The king ignores me. "We're going to head to our suite now. Think you can handle the rest of the wedding without us?"

"Absolutely. Go enjoy your wedding night," Marco says, smiling at me as he does so. It's his underhanded form of payback.

I work my jaw, then let my gaze flick back to the king. "I'm not tired. Please." I've resorted to begging. Anything to put off the inevitable for a little longer.

The king's eyes move over my face. "You want to stay now? I could've sworn that you said you wanted to blow your brains out at the thought of being around *our* guests."

I slit my eyes at him and he smiles. He places his hand at the small of my back and leads me towards the palace. I can feel the mounting stares of smiling guests. Why are they so happy? Why is anyone happy? They still have a tyrant ruler who's now married to a strange girl from the last conquered land.

The looming palace looks like my prison, and in some ways it is. Here I will always be watched, assessed, guarded. But I will stick to my decision. I'll leverage my new status for my people, I'll figure out the king's secrets, and when the time is right, I will kill the Undying King.

We pass into the palace. In here it's quiet, too quiet. The king and I ascend the stairs, and I follow him down the hall to a room I've never been in before. Our room.

He cracks the door open and turns back to me. "I think this calls for tradition." He bends and wraps one arm behind my knees and another across my back, then lifts me.

I yelp, and before I can think about what I'm doing, I wrap my arms around his neck. "Put me down, Montes."

Instead of putting me down, he pushes the door further open with his foot and carries me inside. The large canopy bed is the first thing that catches my eye. And we're moving towards it. Next I notice a wall of windows that open up to a balcony. Beyond them I can see the starry sky and the dark ocean.

The king places me gently on the bed, and gazes at me like I'm his next meal. I scramble off the mattress.

"I-I need to use the restroom." I bolt for the gleaming bathroom before he has a chance to respond.

I close the door behind me and lock it. Then I lean against the wall and let myself slide down. I rest my head between my knees.

This is no worse than death I try to tell myself. But in some ways it is. I'm protecting a nation by following through with this wedding, but I'm dishonoring my parents. What I despise most is that, beneath all that anger and hate, I actually feel something else for the king. Sometimes desire—he is beautiful, after all—sometimes camaraderie, sometimes amusement, and sometimes ... compassion.

I get to my feet, my legs shaky, and lean over the counter. When I glance at my reflection I see a strong woman, one who's had to skirt right and wrong her entire life. I can do this.

I leave the bathroom without pretending to flush the toilet or wash my hands—the king's not a fool. He knows I'm scared as hell of what lies ahead.

When I enter the bedroom, Montes lounges on a side chair. His tie is loosened and his jacket has already been removed. He doesn't move for a moment, just takes me in.

Then, ever so slowly he gets up and makes his way to me. "I'm not a nice man," he says.

"I couldn't agree more," I say.

"This is happening tonight."

My throat works. "I know."

"Good." Then he closes the remaining distance between us and kisses me. At first, all I do is stand there, unresponsive. But eventually, I give in and move my lips. I wonder if this is how royalty felt when they were forced to marry one another. The repulsion, the nervousness, the sense of duty—all of it. I wonder if any of them felt perversely excited, as I do. Perhaps in this I am well and truly alone.

The king backs us up until I fall against the bed. He kneels between my legs to remove my shoes. First one comes off, then the other. But he doesn't remove his hands. Instead he slides them up my leg until they brush the lace of my panties.

I gasp, and struggle against the urge to rip his hands away. A second later his hands are gone, but only so that he can remove his tie. Once he's discarded the garment, he begins unbuttoning his shirt.

I squeeze my eyes shut. When I open them, he's shirtless. His body is all sculpted muscle. I appreciate the sight on a physical level, but it bothers me that he can care so much about his body and so little for entire nations.

Then again, perhaps he has to keep himself in shape in case he ever needs to use his physical strength. It's not like he doesn't have enemies. With that thought, I scour his body for bullet wounds. He's been shot before.

I reach out to his chest and run a hand over the smooth skin that covers his heart. "Where is it?" There should be scar tissue where he'd been shot. It was filmed on live T.V. I've seen him bleed in front of my eyes.

He closes his eyes slowly, as though he's relishing the feel of my skin on his. "Don't you know, my queen?" he says, opening his eyes. "I can't be killed."

I frown. "Stop calling me that."

"No."

I drop my hand and the king resumes undressing himself. I scoot further back on the bed as I watch him remove his shoes, then his socks, and then his pants. I fist the comforter beneath me to give my hands something to do.

When he stands in just his boxer briefs, his stomach muscles rippling, he returns his attention to me. "Come here."

I don't move.

He sighs. "You need to take your dress off, Serenity, and you need my help to do so." He says it like he's the most reasonable person in the world. As though I'm being ridiculous by wanting to keep on the dress I despised so much earlier. What he doesn't realize—or maybe he does—is that it's my last defense before we get intimate.

Reluctantly I scoot myself off the bed and pad over to him. I feel like the world's most wretched person that my eyes linger on all the sculpted lines of his body. He turns me around and begins unfastening the buttons that trail down my back. I can feel the brush of his fingers along my skin. They draw out goose bumps.

Slowly my dress peels away from me. Montes removes the last of the buttons, and the gown glides over my hips and pools at my feet. Instinctively I cover myself. I'm still wearing lingerie, but it hardly leaves anything to the imagination.

Montes pulls my arms down from where they hide my chest. He gives me a surprisingly gentle look, and I close my eyes.

"Open your eyes, Serenity."

"Then stop looking at me like that."

"I can't."

I press my eyelids shut harder. "You're heartless."

"Most of the time. But sometimes … sometimes I'm not when I'm around you."

I open my eyes at that. He's being genuine. And this is the worst. A bad guy with a change of heart. I'm not his redemption; I'm going to be his executioner.

He kisses me, and this time I don't fight it. My lips move against his, and I tangle my fingers in his hair, relishing the fact that I'm ruining it. He makes an approving sound in my mouth and lifts me so that my legs are forced to wrap around his hips.

The king moves us to the bed and then places me on top of it. He reaches under my back and unsnaps my bra. I wince as he tosses the flimsy garment aside.

And then he's touching me, kneading my breasts, moving his thumbs over my nipples, and I can't figure out whether this situation disturbs me or turns me on. Both, I think.

Montes's mouth replaces his fingers, and his teeth skim the tender flesh. I shiver at the sensation, and he flashes me a smile.

"Still a virgin?" he asks.

"That's none of your business."

"I'll take that as a yes," he says, "which means it's my job to make sure you enjoy yourself tonight."

"That's not going to happen."

"We'll see what you say after all is said and done."

His fingers hook under the thin fabric of my panties and he pulls them off me before removing his boxer briefs. When he returns to the bed, he lays his body over mine. I've never experienced so much skin-on-skin contact, and I'm surprised to find that it feels good.

Really good.

He rolls to my side and moves his hand until it's touching the most intimate part of me.

"*Montes.*" I jerk away from him before I remember myself.

He pushes me back down against the mattress and kisses my collarbone. His fingers slip inside me, and I jerk again.

"You're already wet," his whispers in my ear.

I get the logistics of female anatomy, but not how it works when expert fingers strum it. Judging by the king's smug tone, I can piece together what I'm missing. The way he touches me has me throwing my head back and closing my eyes.

My breath catches and picks up as his fingers rhythmically stroke me. Sensation is building up inside of me, and my eyes flutter closed to better experience this.

The king lets out a satisfied chuckle under his breath, then removes his fingers. I'm left bereft only for a moment before he rolls back onto me and positions himself. My eyes snap open and gaze into his. Oh God, it's happening.

"This might hurt," he says.

And it does, briefly. Then I feel him fully inside me.

Montes's hands brush back the hair of my face, and he presses a kiss along my cheek as he withdraws.

The optimist in me wonders if this is it. Show's over. Then Montes glides back into me, and I suck in a breath at the pleasant throb. The man who ruined my world, killed my parents and most of my people, is now my husband, and he's making love to me. And I'm enjoying it. It's so wrong it makes my skin crawl.

A stray tear streaks down my cheek. "I hate you," I say to him.

"You won't always feel that way," he says, thrusting into me.

"I will. I swear it."

"Give it up," he growls, pushing into me harder. "The war is over."

"Not for me. It won't ever be over for me."

CHAPTER 17

SERENITY

I LIE AWAKE for a long time afterwards, staring at the ceiling. Next to me the king's breathing is steady and even. He fell asleep a while ago. When I can't take it anymore, I push his arm off of my waist. The king makes a noise in his sleep and rearranges himself.

I slip out of bed and grab the silk robe that someone had set out for me earlier. The smooth material makes me want to shrug the garment off. After wearing rough fatigues for most of my life, such soft fabric feels unnatural against my skin. Instead I cinch the robe around my waist and walk outside.

I grip the stone railing. Here, wherever here is, the night is pleasant. I can smell the seawater carried along the breeze.

Now that no one is watching, I bow my head and allow myself to weep. Weep for my life, for all those who've killed or died because of the war, and for the uncertain future of the world.

When I've cried myself out, I lie down on the cool floor of the balcony and stare at the stars. I make out the Pleiades, a constellation my mother taught me years ago. *Make a wish upon the seven sisters*, she'd whisper to me when we'd catch sight of them.

And I do so now. *I wish I could be up there with you.* I gaze at them until my eyes drift closed.

Sometime later I feel my body lifted off the ground and the warm press of skin against mine as I'm tucked back into my bed.

I'm pulled from sleep once more when I feel a light kiss on my lips, and the sensation of hands caressing my skin. I make an approving sound at the back of my throat and stretch like a contented cat.

Then my situation comes rushing back to me. My eyes snap open, and I stare into Montes's deep brown ones. His hair hangs down around his face, and I can't help but notice that the ruffled look suits him well.

The sky outside has a predawn glow. It's not morning yet, which means …

"Again?" I widen my eyes. Of course we weren't going to do this only once. I'd just hoped that it wouldn't happen again so soon. I enjoyed it far too much the first time.

"I plan on acquainting myself with you many times."

I feel his erection press against me, and my breath catches. Just like last night, his fingers touch the soft skin between my legs. His thumb dances circles around my sensitive flesh until I moan. I bite back the sound, but it's too late.

Montes wears a knowing grin, and his finger moves faster. "Like that?" he whispers against my ear.

"This changes nothing," I gasp out.

"I think it does." I can feel myself getting slick against him, and the bastard's fully aware of this as well. He removes his hand, and I feel the hard press of him against my opening.

I'm still sore from last night, so when he pushes himself inside me, air whistles through my teeth as I inhale. And just like last night, the soreness is soon replaced by the first stirrings of pleasure. The whole thing is wrong, wrong, wrong. Then again, I'm not the most morally righteous person; war hasn't afforded me that luxury. So instead of retreating into my mind, I tentatively begin to touch the king.

First my hands glide over his shoulders and arms, stroking the bunched muscles beneath the skin. Above me the king stills, and I meet his gaze.

"What are you doing?" he asks.

"Discovering my . . . husband." It's hard for me to call him that—to think of him like that, but some wars are won by surrendering certain, doomed battles, and this is one of them.

He watches me, unmoving, and I squirm against him. "Why have you stopped?"

Something a whole lot like affection—or maybe victory—brightens his eyes. He leans in and kisses me, and the feeling of being joined in two places nearly throws me over the edge. Who knew that beneath my tough exterior was a sex-starved woman?

When the kiss ends, he begins moving again. "Does that feel better?" he whispers.

I close my eyes and hum in response. We continue like that, enjoying extremely sinful and morally questionable sex for a while, before I open my eyes again and run my fingers down his cheek. His large, dark eyes shutter at my touch and his tempo increases.

Heat builds at my core, and finally I cry out and clutch him as my orgasm lashes through me. His strokes become harder and deeper, and I feel him throb inside me as he finds his own release.

He collapses against me, and we're both slick with sweat. In some ways sex is a lot like the lifestyle I'm used to, and that surprises me. I'd always imagined that it was something purely soft and sweet, but what we've done tonight proves otherwise. That there's something primal in the act—some strange combo of pain and pleasure, an adrenaline rush, exertion—just like there is in war.

I'D NEVER REALLY thought through marrying the king. The horror of it eclipsed any curiosity I might've had at being someone's partner. I'm greatly surprised to find that in private the king can be gentle and—dare I think it—caring.

I watch him as morning sunlight streams through our balcony windows and find I want to touch him again. His tan skin dips and rises over corded muscles. I see a solitary freckle just below his shoulder blade.

He's human.

It's the stupid freckle that reminds me. He may be broken and wicked and narcissistic, but he's human. He bleeds, he feels.

Thinking like this is risky, particularly when I still plan on killing him. I don't want to grow close to this man, but I can't seem to help myself, even after all he's done. Maybe he doesn't need to die. Maybe he can be changed.

I scoff at my own ridiculous thought. If nothing has swayed the king into growing a conscience before now, I doubt I'll be what does.

His thick hair dusts his cheekbones, hiding his features. Before I can think twice, I reach out and push the dark locks away from his face. In sleep, he's lovely. At my touch, he stirs but doesn't wake.

I didn't quite realize humans could savor each other the way we did last night. In the bunker, people didn't talk about these things, and if they did them, they kept their business private.

The bed shifts next to me, and when I refocus my attention on the king, his eyes open. "What is my queen doing up?" Sleep roughens his voice, and again, I'm reminded that at the end of the day—or the beginning of it, rather—the king is just a man.

He scoops me to him when I don't respond, and we spend a minute staring at each other. "Sore?" he finally asks.

I feel my cheeks flush. I hate that this subject still makes me uncomfortable. "I'm fine."

His fingers brush across my face. "Hmm. I thought we were past the lies."

Lying and discussing this with the king seem like two very different things. My eyes move between his. "Are you happy now that you finally have me?"

The king shakes his head. "I don't have you—yet. But I will."

SOMEONE BRINGS IN strawberries and champagne shortly after we wake up, and now it's clear that not only can one enjoy good food and good sex, but also enjoy the two together. It seems outrageously gluttonous, but it doesn't stop me from reaching over to the platter and picking up a strawberry while the king pours champagne.

Just as I open my mouth, the king catches my hand and makes a *tsk*-ing sound. "This, I believe, is my job."

He takes the strawberry from me and presses a champagne flute into my hand.

"So now I'm permitted to drink?"

"As long as I'm the one pouring, you are."

"You're a control freak."

The king scoops cream onto the strawberry from a nearby bowl. "This surprises you?" he asks.

"No, but you could try loosening up for once in your life."

He raises an eyebrow. "What, exactly, do you think I've been doing for the last twelve hours?"

"Punishing me," I say without missing a beat.

He sighs. "You keep lying. Hasn't anyone told you the key to a healthy marriage is trust and honesty?"

I scoff at him. "There are so many things I could say to that statement."

The king smirks and lifts the strawberry like he wants to feed me.

"Do that, and I'll bite your fingers off."

"You like my fingers too much to do them harm. Now, open your mouth."

I eye him like a wary creature even as I part my lips and he feeds the berry to me. My annoyance with him is less compelling than my desire to eat the fruit.

My eyes close as I bite down on it and enjoy the taste. I can't remember the last time I had a strawberry.

When my eyelids lift, Montes is watching me with fascination, like he craves these reactions.

That sense of wrongness comes back. I shouldn't be doing this with the king while the world toils on. I feel like the traitor everyone made me out to be.

I flash him a cautious look, and never taking my eyes off of him, down the champagne.

Bad idea. Whether it's my empty stomach, all the alcohol I've imbibed, or the rich palace food, something's not sitting well.

"Serenity?"

I scramble out of bed. I don't bother grabbing the silk robe on my way to the bathroom. I barely make it in time. The water's tinged red, and I can't tell if it's from the berry or the blood.

Behind me, the king swears. What's he doing in here?

"Get out," I say weakly.

"Last I checked, I'm the king, not you."

I flush the toilet and rise to my feet. I'm more fatigued than I should be. I fear that just when I decided I had the will to live, my body decided it didn't.

Montes presses a button built into the wall of the bathroom. "Marco, get me a doctor—"

"No." My voice is sharper than I intend it. "Please," I add, leaning against the counter, "the alcohol didn't sit well. That's all."

"Your Majesty?" Marco's static-y voice blares into the room. Just the sound of it makes my trigger finger itch.

The king scrutinizes me for a long time before he turns back to the intercom. "Scratch that, Marco. Just bring some broth, crackers, and something with electrolytes in it. Oh, and I believe it's time to put the queen on my pills."

My ears perk up at this.

"Consider it done," Marco says, and the line clicks off.

"Pills?" I inquire. "Trying to poison me?" I fish.

Montes's gaze lands meaningfully on the toilet. "Seems like you're doing a perfectly good job of that on your own."

"Then what are they for?"

"Your long-term health," he says cryptically, and that's the last he'll say on the subject.

EVEN ON THE king's honeymoon he has to work; it's one of the drawbacks of being the leader of the entire globe.

"I'm coming with you," I say, as he buttons his cufflinks.

The king assesses me. "You're fatigued. You should spend the day resting. One of the servants can give you a massage if you'd like."

I yank a dress from a hanger in our closet. "I wasn't asking."

"Nor was I."

Today I'll discover what happens when two stubborn people reach an impasse.

"You're going to have to physically stop me from leaving, then." I've been cooped up for too long. I need to get back to the world of the living.

"Don't tempt me. I can get creative." The look Montes is giving me makes me flush. I wouldn't mind his methods one bit, and I've made peace with this disturbing realization.

His words, however, don't stop me from getting dressed. When he's about to leave, I block his exit. "I'm coming with you."

"No, you're not."

I reach up and trickle my fingers over his jaw. I've learned that the king enjoys any casual affection I give him—likely because I have so little to offer. "Find something for me to do, Montes. Surely you have more than enough work to keep the both of us occupied."

I'm more than ready to begin healing the damaged lands of the world. I need to prove to myself and to my people that I haven't turned my back on my past.

He scrutinizes me, then sighs. He must have figured out what I already know: if he leaves me alone, I'm going to get myself in more trouble than if he simply drags me along.

"Aw," I give him a fake pout, "is someone having buyer's remorse?" The king's finally realizing just what a handful I can be.

He catches my jaw. "You believe you can push me without repercussions. You can't, and you will be repaying me for this later."

The king should know by now that threats don't scare me. I hope he can see in my eyes that I don't give a flying fuck about his words.

When I don't back down, Montes drops his hold so that he can reach around me and open the door.

I turn to go, but he catches my wrist, reeling me back in. "Serenity?" he says, his lips brushing against my ear. "I'm glad you're not frightened by my words, but you should be."

FIVE HOURS LATER, I'm sitting in a conference room, trying to keep my lunch down. The king flashes me a concerned glance, like he has been all day. Perhaps part of the reason he's come to rule the world is because he misses nothing.

I finger the document in front of me and focus on evening my breaths. It helps with the nausea. If I concentrate long enough, I can ride this out. I shouldn't have let myself go following my father's death. My body's paying for it now and making it painfully obvious that I'm not okay.

"Reports suggest the Resistance is growing in unprecedented numbers," one of the king's political advisors says. "They've raided the Toulouse research facility and bombed the Department of Defense in Berlin. There have also been threats to air footage of the queen."

I suck in air too quickly and choke on my own saliva. I begin to cough, and once I start, I can't seem to stop.

Next to me Montes stands. "Bringing you along was a bad idea." He's been waiting for an excuse to say this. "You should go back to the room and rest."

I wave him off but continue to cough. My lungs seem to rattle with the effort, and my whole body shakes. Finally I manage to clear my throat. As I draw my fist away from my mouth, I notice the bright red speckles.

Blood.

I drop my hand before the king can see what I have. "I think I will."

The king's brow crinkles. If anything, my easy agreement only worries him more.

I stand to leave, hiding my hand in the folds of my dress. The king's eyes dart to the action, then up to me. He doesn't say anything, instead waving his royal guards over. "Escort the queen back to our rooms," he commands.

"I'll be back in a few hours," he says to me. "If you need anything, you only need to ask the staff."

Without waiting for further direction, I nod and leave the room. Behind me the guards scurry to catch up. My heels click as I cross the halls. I should be wondering what the king thinks about my behavior, or what will happen if the footage of me leaks.

Instead I think of my dwindling health. I've never coughed up blood before, but I've known people who have. This is the moment of truth, the one I've ignored for so long.

It's starting. The beginning of the end.

CHAPTER 18

SERENITY

A HAND GLIDES through my hair, and I blink my eyes open. Montes sits on the edge of the bed. He's fully dressed, while I'm only clad in skimpy lingerie. I pull the sheets a little tighter around me before I realize that he's already seen it all, touched it all.

His lips quirk when he sees what I'm doing. "You have an appointment," he says.

"What are you talking about?" I ask, edging away from him. Outside the sky is dark. I can't imagine any appointment occurring this late in the day.

Instead of answering, Montes crosses the room, opens a drawer in a nearby dresser, and pulls out a pair of stretchy-looking pants and a cotton shirt. I almost cry out with joy when I see that the outfit is, one, not a dress, and two, made out of something that's neither too soft nor too itchy.

"I need a shower," I say. I already took one, but between Montes's news, and the determined set of his jaw, I'm pretty sure I want to avoid whatever it is he's arranged.

"It's going to have to wait," he says. "We need to go right now."

This can't be good.

I SHAKE MY head. "No. No, no—"

"Yes," Montes says to the doctor that's trying to hand me a hospital gown.

I fold my arms. "You're going to have to force that thing on me."

A doctor's appointment, that's what Montes had in mind this evening. The king was right not to say anything earlier. I'm practically shaking from nervousness. Most people don't fear the doctor; they have no reason to. I do. War has given me plenty of reasons to.

"If I must." Montes casts a lazy glance at the two guards who stand on either side of the doorway. "Guards, why don't you help your queen remove her clothing?"

I flash them a heated look. "You touch me, you die."

Five minutes later, I'm screaming as Montes and his guards hold me down. The doctor has a pair of scissors poised over the thin cotton of my shirt.

"Fine, *fine*! I'll put on the goddamn robe, just get your hands off of me!"

I will say this for Montes, his methods may be inhumane, but they are effective.

Montes nods to his soldiers, and they back off immediately. He flashes me a victorious smile as he pushes himself off the ground and holds out a hand to help me up.

I ignore his hand and snatch the robe from the doctor. "Where's the bathroom?"

"Uh-uh, Serenity," the king says. "It doesn't work like that. Not after that little demonstration. You're going to have to change right here."

101

My nostrils flare as I stare him down. I'm the first to break eye contact. I shake my head and strip off my shirt. Instead of looking at the king, I smile at one of his guards while I take off my pants.

The king glances between the stoic guard and me. Just as I reach back to unclasp my bra, the king steps in front of my line of sight, his eyes narrowed. I smirk at him and finish sliding off my bra.

Montes's eyes draw down to my breasts. For a moment his look is hungry. Then he shutters the expression. He takes the thin cotton hospital gown from me, shakes it out, and holds it open for me to step into.

I thread my arms into the gown while the king ties the strings in the back. Once Montes is done, I move to the sole hospital bed in the room and lie down. A strange device arches over it.

"This is for yesterday's comment, isn't it?" I ask, remembering the way Montes looked at me after I stated that I couldn't have children.

"I want an heir ... eventually," he says, coming to stand next to me.

I snort at this. "As if you'd ever give up the throne," I say.

"All good things must end at some point." His fingers press against the bare skin of my leg.

"That they do," I agree.

"More importantly," he says, "I want to make sure you're in good health."

He knows. Somehow, after only spending a full day in my presence, he's figured out what no one else has: that something other than grief has weakened me.

I'm struck that he cares. Something uncomfortable catches in my throat at the thought. Right when I assumed I was the loneliest creature in the world, I find out I might matter to someone.

The doctor comes over and starts up the machine that's centered over my lower abdomen. I'm beginning to guess it is some type of scanner.

Montes sits in a chair next to me and takes my hand. The whole situation should be ridiculous. It's not.

The scanner thrums to life and begins to travel over my abdomen and up my body.

Behind the doctor a wall of computer screens come to life. The main one catches my eye. On it I can see my skeleton, and fainter but no less clear, I spot my reproductive organs, then my intestines, then my heart and lungs, and lastly my head.

The doctor scrutinizes the computer screens for a long time, looking over the images and the readouts. "There are no cysts, no apparent scarring or obvious swelling. I don't see anything that might indicate you're infertile, Queen Lazuli."

The king's hold on my hand loosens with his relief.

"Great," I say, lifting my torso off of the bed. "That means I can go, right?" I ask, trying to rush this along.

The doctor hasn't looked away from the main screen. "Hmm," he says.

Montes's grip tightens again, and he pushes my chest back down. "What is it?" the king asks.

The doctor sucks in a breath, and the king's hand begins to crush mine.

"Ow." I pull my hand out of his.

"Sorry," Montes says, distracted. He recaptures my hand and watches the doctor.

My heart thumps. Montes actually apologized. For squeezing my hand too tightly. The man who apologizes to no one.

"What is it?" King Lazuli asks the doctor.
The doctor pauses. "The queen has cancer."

CHAPTER 19

SERENITY

THERE IT IS, the burden I've been hiding for a year now. Radiation-borne cancer. It was common in the WUN, especially in and around big cities where the king deployed the nukes.

Montes stands up and drops my hand. "Cancer?" I've never heard that tone in his voice. Like devastation and disbelief wrapped into one. Surely I'm not the source of that anguish.

"We'll have to do a biopsy to be safe, but judging from the imaging here," the doctor says, returning his attention to the screen, "it's overwhelmingly likely that what I'm seeing is cancer. It looks like it's metastasized."

And that's the other discovery I made earlier today when I coughed up blood. I've had stomach problems for the last year, not lung problems. However, I'd seen several bunker residents suffer through the various stages of cancer. I know this is the tail end of the process.

The Pleiades granted me my wish. I'm going to join them soon.

Montes glances down at me, and I see true fear in his eyes. "What can we do?" he asks the doctor.

"It depends on the particulars. The queen will need to be placed in the Sleeper to remove the cancerous tissue where possible."

The Sleeper?

"She'll also need to be put on the same medication as you, Your Majesty." The doctor gives Montes a meaningful look.

"It's already done," Montes says, and there's something fierce in his voice now.

I glance at him, my heart constricting. I've fantasized about killing the king—there have been times in my life where I wanted nothing more than to see him suffer and die for all the pain he caused me. And yet now that the tables are turned and my life is in danger, the king seems to want to do everything in his power to keep me alive.

I can't stand that my ethics might be more corrupt than the king's.

The doctor comes over to us. "Have you experienced any unusual symptoms up until now?"

I give him a long look. "I've lived most of my life in wartime conditions. I have no idea what 'unusual symptoms' might be."

The doctor's eyebrows dart up. "Were you exposed to radiation during that time?"

"Of course." It was everywhere—in the soil, the drinking water, the crops. No one living in the western hemisphere could totally avoid it, but especially not me, who lived so close to D.C.

The king's hand squeezes mine, and I glance at him. His expression is carefully blank, but that vein is pulsing in his temple.

War tears down everything. Morals, loyalties, lives. Its aftershocks can ripple long after it ends. This is merely one more way that it's ripped my life apart. And now, maybe for the first time, it's affecting the king's life on a personal level.

"We will fix this," the king says in that commanding voice of his, like this is just another minor obstacle.

Suddenly, I pity him, because some things simply cannot be conquered, and this might be one of them.

THE NEXT EVENING we sit on a jet flying to what was once Austria. Next to me, Montes drums his fingers on his armrest, his leg jiggling. His eyes keep returning to my stomach.

"Cancer," he murmurs. He's said that word several times today. Stomach cancer, to be precise. It's one of several types of cancer caused by radiation.

I can't help my next words. "Ironic that you caused the cancer you're now trying to stop from killing me." There's poetic justice in that, though only the king gets the luxury of justice. The rest of us just pointlessly suffer.

He rubs his eyes. "We—*we* are trying to stop it from killing you." I notice that he doesn't address the other part of my statement. I guess he has to pretend it all away, otherwise he might actually realize what a despicable human being he's been.

"Have you taken your medication?" he asks.

I shake my head. It's the same mystery drug the king takes. Neither he nor the doctor told me what it does, but it leaves me wondering what exactly an undying king would need a prescription for.

Montes digs through a bag at his feet and pulls out water and a bottle of pills.

I take them with me into the small restroom and shake one of the small white pills into my hand. Staring down at it, I try to divine its use. Perhaps I'll turn into the same douchey prick the king is. The thought makes me smirk, despite my circumstances. I unscrew the bottle of water and toss the medication into my mouth before taking a long drink.

Almost immediately my stomach clenches. I'm sure even a healthy stomach might rebel against this medication if it were as empty as mine.

I lean against the counter and take slow, steady breaths. The jet chooses that moment to hit a patch of turbulence. I barely have time to turn my body to the toilet before I start to retch. Hot tears roll down my cheeks as my stomach tries to force its contents out of me.

I'm still bent over the toilet when the bathroom door bangs open, and the king strides in. He pulls back my hair while I dry heave, and once I'm done, he gathers me to him and strokes my face as I shake.

"How did you manage to hide this from everyone?" he asks, his voice soft.

I'm still too nauseous to answer. I curl up into him and bury my face in his shirt. "Don't leave me," I whisper. I don't know why I say it; I don't know why I'm giving or receiving compassion from this man. But I do know this: only compassion can redeem someone. Even the king. Even me.

THE KING CARRIES me out of the bathroom and lays me out on one of the jet's couches. I won't let him go, and the feeling seems to be mutual by the way he cradles my torso in his arms.

He pulls one of his arms out from under me and brushes my hair away from my face. "You're okay," he whispers over and over again. His eyes look frightened, like I might die right here and now.

Gradually my stomach settles, and I feel a bit better. The king kisses the skin along my hairline, and I continue to cling to him. "I'm supposed to hate you," I whisper.

He laughs humorlessly. "Are you finally admitting that you don't?" he asks, his throat catching.

"Never," I whisper.

"Liar."

I curl up against him, forgetting for a while that he's the culprit behind every bad memory I possess, and eventually I fall asleep in his arms.

OVER THE NEXT two days, a biopsy is taken, and it's confirmed that I have cancer. Then come the X-rays. By the end of my second day, I'm scheduled for surgery.

The hospital allows me to stay with the king for the evening. As soon as I see the fluffy bed in our room, I collapse onto it. The mattress dips as the king joins me.

We're in yet another one of his estates. I'm no longer surprised at the excess of it all.

I feel Montes tug off one of my shoes, then the other. Next he rolls me over and begins removing my pants. I raise my eyebrows but say nothing; I'm not completely opposed to sex.

But the king doesn't try to seduce me. Once I'm undressed, he strips down and joins me on the bed, gathering me to him. Our exposed skin presses together and it feels exquisite. Never in a million years did I think I'd enjoy casual intimacy with the king.

Since finding out that I have cancer, Montes has revealed this other side of him, one that's inexplicably compassionate. It's made me realize something else: the king is lonelier than even me, and he desperately doesn't want to be.

"Don't make me go in for surgery tomorrow," I whisper. I'd kept quiet about the cancer because everything about illness frightens me. Declining health, doctors, medications, surgery.

The king doesn't answer for a long time. So long, in fact, that I assume he won't.

"My father killed himself," the king finally says. "Died at the hand of his own gun. And like you, he was the last family I had."

I stiffen in the king's arms.

"Why are you telling me this?"

The king touches my temple. "You have that same look in your eyes he had. It's been there from the first moment I saw you. And I fear both he and you know a secret I don't."

I watch the king for a long time, my throat working.

"We do." Never had I imagined my life leading me here, to this moment. Yet now that I'm here, I wonder if there is a beautiful design to things.

"Then tell me what it is," the king says. Those intense eyes are fully focused on me.

He doesn't know; he really has no clue when it's quite obvious. It's the secret he continually hides from.

"Everything that lives must eventually die."

THE SURGERY HAPPENS the next day, and just like the last time I was in the presence of a doctor, soldiers have to hold me down while the doctor administers the sedative.

The ordeal is one that should be solely reserved for the worst inhabitants of hell.

"Why are you fighting this?" the king asks me as he holds down my shoulders.

It's a good question, especially since I want the cancer out. "That needle better not come any closer to me," I say. Like I wield any power in this situation.

"Serenity, you need to be put under. You know this," the king replies.

"No—please, no."

"Christ," the king says looking away, "Stop begging. I can't take it."

"Montes, please."

"I'll have to leave if you don't stop."

I lock eyes with him. *"Don't leave."*

He nods and I hold still. I squeeze my eyes shut when I feel the needle enter my skin. The doctor kneeling next to me begins to talk. "I'm going to count back from one hundred. Follow along with me. One hundred, ninety-nine, ninety-eight, …"

I repeat the numbers in my head, focusing on his voice until my eyes drop and my mind drifts off.

CHAPTER 20

SERENITY

WHEN I WAKE up, the king is at the side of my bed. He's smiling and holding my hand. Almost reflexively I smile back at him. It's strange to feel this way about anyone. The fact that the king is the one who's opened my heart is just proof that fate is a cruel bitch.

"How long have I been out?" I ask.

"Not long, although now the entire hospital knows you snore."

I narrow my eyes. "I don't snore."

The king smiles slyly. "You're not the one who has to fall asleep next to you each evening."

"Most people bring their loved ones gifts; instead you bring your effortless charm."

He squeezes my hand tighter, and he leans in until his lips are barely an inch from mine. "How do you think I came to rule the world?"

"You're an asshole," I say, staring into his eyes, "and as an asshole, you've done a lot of asshole-ish things—including marrying me. *That's* how you came to rule the world."

The king touches my cheek. "Hmm. I think I like your dirty mouth better in the bedroom," he says, and then he closes the remaining distance between our lips.

My mouth moves against his, my tongue enjoying the taste of him. It's frightening how right he feels pressed this close to me. He has the same dark soul I do; he knows and embraces my sins, and I'm learning to accept his. I know he is dangerous to be around—dangerous to love—but my heart doesn't seem to care.

I lift a hand and run it through his hair, my fingers rubbing a strand of it together. This thing of my nightmares is just as human as I am.

Finally, he pulls away. "I have a meeting I've been putting off until you awakened." He glances at the clock hanging in the room. "I can't put it off too much longer, but ..."

My hand slides from his hair to his cheek. "Go. I'll be waiting here for you to return."

He stands, looking reluctant to leave.

"The sooner you leave, the sooner I'll be out of this godforsaken place," I say. The shudder that ripples through me is very real. My skin crawls even now at the smell of disinfectants and sickness that lingers in the room. An epidemic tore through this land years ago. I'm sure many people filed through these doors only to perish.

The king bends down and kisses my forehead. "Promise me you won't shoot anyone until I get back," he says.

My lips waver before they tug up at the corners. "I won't make a promise I can't keep."

THE KING

IT'S NOT UNTIL the door to Serenity's room clicks shut that I let the façade slip. I run a hand over my mouth and jaw, feeling my age even if I don't look it. If my guards notice, they don't say anything. Not if they want to continue getting their cushy paychecks.

She's dying. The phrase repeats over and over in my head. That's what the doctors here seem to think. They aren't the only ones to think this, either. The royal physician had also pulled me aside, shook his head, and murmured his fears. Nothing official—it was a concern, not a diagnosis.

But several of the world's best doctors sharing the same fears? I'd be a damn fool not to take their words seriously.

I grapple with emotions I've never fully experienced before. I hadn't realized the depth of them—hadn't realized I even could feel this way about someone.

I'd wanted Serenity's affection, her fire, even her love—I just hadn't realized I'd give anything back in the process.

I rub the skin over my heart. The thought of losing her after I've only just gotten her makes it twinge.

Marco meets me at the end of the hall. "Your Majesty," he says in Basque, as he often does when he wants privacy, "how's the queen doing?"

"Fine."

Marco peers at me. We've known each other—trusted each other—since we were kids. The man can read me like a book.

"You talked to the doctor then?" Marco guesses.

Of course Marco would piece it together. I nod.

"And?"

I rub my eyes. "Doctor said the cancer had spread. The Sleeper reversed the damage, but ..." I take a deep breath. My hands tremble slightly, "we don't have the knowledge to stop the mutated cells from continuing to replicate." Which means the cancer is still, at this moment, producing more malignant tissue inside Serenity.

The Sleeper can fend it off so long as it doesn't move to her brain. But it inevitably will, and as soon as it does, it was game over. Not even the Sleeper has the ability to replicate the intricacies of the mind.

"So she's ... ?"

"Yes, I believe so," I say, before Marco can finish his thought. We'd bought Serenity time, but not much.

"Have you considered keeping our queen in the Sleeper until a cure's been discovered?"

I hiss in a breath. That's months—maybe even years—away.

My gaze snaps to him. "Of course I have. That's a last resort."

I've spent all this time pouring money into destroying healthy bodies and perfecting a body that isn't broken. Scant few of my efforts have focused on fixing sick ones.

"Hasn't it gotten to that point?" Marco asks. "She's dying. This could halt the damage."

Something thick lodges itself in my throat. It comes down to the Sleeper or death, and either option still takes her away from me. It's been hard enough waiting out her recovery during the last few weeks.

"Since when do you care?" I give Marco a sharp look.

"Since you started to."

Just like that, his words deflate my rising anger. I rub a hand over my mouth. "She might spend years asleep in it before we have the technology to remove the cancer forever." My voice comes out strong and smooth; I can't let even Marco, my oldest, closest friend, see how vulnerable I feel.

"Your Majesty," Marco pauses, picking his words carefully, "if you want her to live for as long as you will, this might be the only way."

SERENITY

I WATCH THE door for several minutes after the king leaves, making sure that he's not going to double back to my room. When nothing happens, I fling the hospital sheets off of me, more than a little surprised that my body doesn't scream at the movement. In fact, I feel fine—not at all like I've just woken from an operation.

I'm right in the middle of an Eastern Empire hospital, one of the most coveted and secretive places under the king's control. It's where cutting edge medical research takes place.

Now is my chance to find out what exactly that research is.

Before I leave my bed to go explore, I gather up my gown to take a look at the extent of my surgery. I don't want to accidently reopen the wound and find myself a patient here for longer than absolutely necessary.

I lift the thin cotton fabric and reveal inch after inch of skin. I unveil my stomach, and a strange sort of disbelief twists inside my core. Just to be sure I'm seeing correctly, I run a hand over the smooth skin.

There are no surgical marks, no scars. Nothing. The only indication that something's happened to me is that a dark freckle that should've lingered near my bellybutton has now vanished as though it never existed in the first place.

So what did they do?

I PEER OUT the door of my room.

"What are you doing, my queen?"

I yelp at the sound of the voice. A guard stands off to the side of the door. Of course the king left a guard outside my room. Now I'm going to have to figure out how to shake him.

"I need to talk to a nurse," I say, slipping out the door and walking past him. Now that I'm up and about, I can feel my exhaustion after all. I'm not quite as fine as I assumed I was.

"Wait—my queen!" the guard calls from behind me. "You should not be out of bed."

I ignore him and continue towards the main desk on this floor concocting a quick plan to ditch my extra shadow.

The nurse manning the desk glances up when she hears my guard and me coming. Her face lights with surprise—I'm now that recognizable—before falling back into a careful mask.

"Do you need anything, my queen?" She doesn't demand to know why I'm out of bed, nor does she rush to get me back in my room.

Whatever operation was performed on me, she seems to feel I'm in good enough health to walk around.

"Can I speak with you in private?"

The nurse nods, her brow wrinkling. My guard still stands behind me, and I shoot him a look.

"I've been commanded to not let you out of my sight if you leave your room," he explains.

I turn back to the nurse and lean in close. "I need to use the bathroom and I'd like to not be shadowed like a prisoner."

The nurse's gaze moves from me to the guard.

"Is there anyway you can make sure he stays out here?" I whisper.

The nurse mulls this over, then finally nods. "I think that'll be just fine," she says, her voice low. "Need anything else?"

"Just directions to the bathroom."

"Down the hall and to your left." The nurse nods in the appropriate direction.

Perfect. I'll be out of the guard and the nurse's line of sight.

"Thanks," I say, flashing her a genuine smile.

I push away from the counter. My guard is now looking at me suspiciously. I brush past him. When he begins to follow me, the nurse clears her throat. "Sir, sir— yes *you*," I hear from behind me.

I don't wait to listen to the rest. I move down the corridor and turn left, just so that it looks like I'm going to the bathroom. At the end of this hall is a stairwell, and right before it, a storage closet hangs slightly open. I stop by it and peek in. Medical supplies and a spare pair of scrubs rest on the shelves. I grab the scrubs and change into them quickly, just in case whoever left the door open is about to come back.

As I unfold the soft material, a keycard slips out. I pick it up and glance at the face of the male nurse whom these scrubs belong to. On it is a barcode, probably to allow him access into restricted areas.

The whole thing could not have gone better had I planned it.

I finish changing and palm the keycard. Slipping out of the closet, I enter the stairwell and take it down. It takes me ten minutes to locate where the research labs are, and I'm sure I only have minutes before the guard sounds the alarm that I'm missing.

I enter the lowest basement of the hospital. My first glimpses of this subterranean floor aren't promising. Paint peels from the walls and the exposed metal pipes I see. It smells like mildew and rot down here—not exactly the ideal atmosphere for cutting edge medical research.

Despite my misgivings, I begin to scrutinize the hall. The floor is abandoned.

A shiver races down my back. An epidemic preceded the king's war, culling the Eastern Hemisphere's population to little over a third of what it once was. I'd never noticed what exactly that looked like until this moment, when I stood in one of their understaffed hospitals.

I go for the first door I see. Locked. Damn. I place my head next to it; I can hear lugging noises on the other side. It must be a boiler room. The next door I come to is the morgue. I wrinkle my nose at the thought. As curious as I am to see if any of the research occurring in these hospitals has landed test subjects in here, I decide against it. Who knows if victims of biological warfare are in there? It would be a damn shame to survive cancer only to die of a virus.

The next door is unmarked. I try the handle. Just like the boiler room, this one is locked. Next to the handle, however, is a scanner. I lift the plastic card in my hand and hold it in front of the device. It beeps and a light flashes green next to it. I try the handle again and the door opens.

I slip into the room and flip on the lights. Whoever normally works here is gone for the time being. I glance around, almost afraid to touch anything. The counters are covered with racks of vials, strange machines, and data readouts.

I don't know where to start or what I'm looking for. I never thought my problem would be making sense of the research I came across. Hell, I don't even know if I'm in the right place.

I begin moving, my eyes scanning the papers strewn across the counters. I see numbers and percentages, but nothing that I recognize. Moving further into the room, I scan the counters, the machines, the spines of books that are sitting out.

I want to scream. Nothing here corroborates the Resistance's sparse findings.

I'm about to leave when the title of a document catches my eye: "Recent Medical Advances in Memory Recall and Suppression." It looks like an article from a medical journal, and the publication date printed below it is from a month ago. Recent. I read the abstract at the top of the page, which summarizes the content of the article.

There are more scientific terms than normal jargon, but from what I read, the topic seems to have to do with repressing long term and short term memories as well as reversing memory loss.

Those dazed technicians the Resistance had reported on when I'd been back in the WUN... they'd been in the king's research labs. Could their predicament be related to this?

The very non-scientific wheels of my mind whir. Why *would* anyone want to repress a person's memories? The answer is so simple that I'm embarrassed I asked the question in the first place.

Control.

THE LAST THINGS I read are the news articles someone's taped to the wall. They all have to do with biological warfare. Some discuss the pathogens involved, and some go over the cures the king doled out once a region fell.

Death and health were the stick and carrot the king regularly used to gain control of a new land on the eastern hemisphere. He still doesn't seem to understand that repairing that which he broke doesn't make it new again. It makes it scarred.

I try the other doors in the basement. All are locked, and none will open with the key card in my hand. It makes me think that I never entered the room where the real research is occurring. A simple nurse might not have that kind of clearance.

I'd like to explore the rest of the hospital, but I've already been gone too long. So I walk back to the closet, change into my hospital gown, and place the scrubs where I found them.

"Last time I checked, the bathroom was across the hall."

I spin, only to come face-to-face with my guard. Despite his soft-spoken words, he's angry.

My first instinct is to become defensive. So I do the opposite. "What does it matter to you? I'm the queen."

He grabs my upper arm. "You need to get back to your room, now." He begins leading me down the hall.

"I'm going to tell the king that you're manhandling me," I say, as I yank futilely against his grip. "He's not going to like that."

My guard chooses to ignore me. He opens the door to my room and pushes me inside.

"Hey—!" The door slams shut behind me.

What an ass.

I lean against the wall, not ready to get back in bed, and let my eyes drift around the room. They land on a calendar that hangs across from me.

I still. It says it is May, but it should still be April. I'm about to shrug it off when my hand goes to the smooth skin of my stomach.

What if some new technology was used on me—the same one that removed all traces of the king's bullet wounds from his body?

Perhaps I'm being paranoid, reading into things that aren't there, but that thought doesn't stop me from reaching for the door handle next to me and slipping back out into the hall.

"Your Majesty," the guard growls, blocking my exit. I feint to the right and duck under his arm, hurrying to the main desk.

"Can you tell me what day it is?" I ask, breathlessly to the nurse behind the desk, the same nurse who helped me earlier.

A moment later my guard comes to stand beside me, but he doesn't drag me off like I worried he might. I guess threatening to narc on him was effective after all.

The nurse across from me looks baffled by my request—or maybe just the fact that I'm out here again. "Of course, my queen," she says. She turns to the screen in front of her. "It's May tenth."

I do the math in my head. That would mean that it's been almost three weeks since I married the king and over two weeks since I came here for the operation.

"Is something the matter, Your Majesty?" the nurse asks.

I shake my head, my mind still far away. The surgery should've taken hours, not days, and definitely not weeks. I'm not being paranoid after all. Something did happen to me.

"You're sure that's today's date?" I ask.

The nurse glances from me to her screen again, looking uncomfortable. "Yep. May tenth." She smiles warmly at me, but it falters a bit when she takes in my expression. "Would you like me to escort you back to your room?" The nurse eyes me and the guard at my side, missing nothing.

"I'm fine." I back away from the main desk.

"I'll have someone check in on you in five minutes," the nurse says. She says it to comfort me, but I know her true motives are to make sure I'm okay before the king returns.

I walk back in a daze. Why would Montes not mention that I'd been out for weeks? And, more importantly, why *was* I out for that long?

THIRTY MINUTES LATER, I hear the click of expensive shoes on the hospital linoleum. The king is coming back to my room, and I'm ready for him.

As soon as the king takes up the doorway, his eyebrows raise. I'm sitting on top of my bed in my hospital gown, my forearms slung over my knees. In one of my hands I'm playing with a scalpel that I lifted from the nurse that checked on me.

"Where'd you get that?"

I narrow my eyes at the king. "You don't seriously expect me to answer that question, do you?"

He smirks, totally at ease with the fact that I'm playing with a scalpel in his presence.

Behind him I see Marco and some of the king's bodyguards flank the doorway. "He," I jut my chin at Marco, "better make himself scarce, or else this scalpel is going to find itself lodged into his chest."

King Lazuli saunters into the room. "There is no need for threats, my queen."

My eyes shoot daggers at Marco.

"Marco and his guards are going to wait outside while I spend time with my recovering wife." The king's mouth curves up at the last word.

Marco opens his mouth to speak. As soon as he does so, my hand tightens around the knife, and I rearrange my grip for throwing it. Marco's eyes flick to my hand, and his mouth closes. Without a further word, he slips out of the room.

"You need to stop threatening my men," the king says.

"Or else what?" I ask insolently. "You'll divorce me?"

He sighs. "Is that what you're trying to do? Make me regret my decision to marry you?"

"Absolutely." Gone for the moment are my blossoming feelings for the king. Instead I can't help but feel deeply disturbed once more by the king and his science.

The king leans in close—close enough for me to stab him if I desire it. He knows this too. I can see him daring me with his eyes.

"If I wanted to punish you for threatening my men, I'd find something infinitely more creative than divorce."

I flip the scalpel around in my hand several times, a small smile forming on my lips. "You're right. Divorce would hardly be punishment."

Montes's fingers touch my jaw, angling it to better face him. "Why are you so angry?"

"What have you done to me?"

The king's brows lift. "This is about your surgery?"

"See, there's where you've got it wrong," I say. "Surgeries require this—" I raise the scalpel, "—and they leave scars. Most importantly of all, they don't take *two weeks*."

"My doctors have access to the latest technology. You were placed in a device called the Sleeper. It removed the cancer and regenerated healthy tissue."

The king has equipment that can do that?

Before I can respond, the king wraps his hand around the base of the knife and tries to pull it from me.

"Hey—" I can tell I'm about to lose the scalpel, so I give it a good yank and slide it against the king's skin.

The king curses as the knife cuts into the flesh between his thumb and forefinger and blood pools.

I let go of the scalpel just as the door to my room is thrown open. Marco comes in, gun drawn, a group of guards spreading out behind him.

I roll my eyes at Marco and very slowly relax my coiled muscles. Despite appearing indifferent, I'm not. I'm staring down the same gun barrel that my father had. The one that might've killed him.

"Your Majesty," Marco says, taking in the scene, "is everything alright?" His eyes flick to the king's bloody hand. "You're bleeding."

The king holds out the scalpel for Marco to take while studying me. "I'm fine," he says as Marco takes the knife from him. "I just cut myself while I took the scalpel from the queen." The king's giving me a strange look. I get the impression he's trying to figure me out.

"Your Majesty?" Marco says, not buying the story.

"That's all Marco," the king says.

"But sir, your hand ..."

"Later Marco," the king says, his eyes never straying from mine. "Leave us."

Marco hesitates, piercing me with a look that says just what he'll do to me if more harm befalls the king. I flash him my most nefarious grin as he backs out of the room.

"Must you terrify everyone you meet?" The king asks, grabbing some paper towels out of a dispenser to cauterize the flow of blood.

"Yes."

The king comes back to me, and that strange look is back in his eyes. "Why did you cut me?"

My skin prickles, not because of his question, but because he's not angry at all. He's *curious*. It's the wrong reaction, and it makes me worry that there indeed is something very, very wrong with the man I married.

"I wanted to see if you could bleed," I say. My words sound cruel and calculating even to my own ears. There is also something very wrong with me.

"No, you didn't," the king says. "You've already seen me bleed." He comes closer to my bed. "You want to know how I heal, don't you?" he says, his eyes ever so inquisitive.

My heart thumps. "Yes," I admit.

The king nods slowly. "You thought because I refused to tell you how I died before, I'd always refuse to tell you."

"How you *died* before?" I go completely still. Already he's admitted so much more than I expected.

"Perhaps 'died' is the wrong word." He sits on my bed and cups the side of my face. In his eyes I see something I hoped not to. I don't know what love is, and I doubt the king does either, but the expression he wears seems awfully near the mark.

"You really want to know?" he asks.

I nod.

He lets out a breath, then making a decision, he says, "All right. I'll tell you the whole sordid story—it's a long one."

This moment strikes me as terribly anticlimactic. King Lazuli, the feared ruler of the entire globe, is about to tell me his biggest and most well kept secret. A secret men have killed and died for. A secret that used to bring goose bumps to my skin.

He presses his mouth to my ear, exhales, and breathes the first line. "But not here—"

The sound of shots ring out.

The king pulls back, and we stare at each other for a moment. Then we're moving.

Ambushed. Someone knows we're at this hospital, and we're being ambushed.

On the other side of the door, I hear Marco's voice. "Montes, Serenity," he shouts, dropping our titles, "stay inside." Then his footfalls move away from us.

He expects us to hide in this room like sitting ducks, but I've had too much military training to ever act like a civilian again. Oddly enough, Montes seems to have the same idea. He tries to push me behind him as he approaches the door. Instead I brush past him.

The king catches my hand. "Serenity—"

I turn and look at him. "I know what I'm doing."

He opens his mouth, then closes it. Montes tugs me to him and kisses me.

"I'll follow your lead," he says when he breaks away. "Just don't get hurt—that's an order."

I pull away from him. "I won't." I just hope I'm right.

CHAPTER 21

SERENITY

I CRACK THE door open and peek out. Just as I do so, my guard, who has been stationed at the door, turns toward us.

"Get back inside," he commands.

"You and I both know we're outnumbered," I say. That's the only way a group would be ballsy enough to infiltrate the hospital. "We need to leave this place."

The guard hesitates, and in that span of time, a series of shots punctuates the silence.

Now is the perfect time to kill the king or, at the very least, severely injure him. It's an unpleasant realization that I don't want him to meet his end here.

"Can you help me get the king out?" I ask.

I can feel Montes press in behind me.

The guard's eyes flick from me to the king. "There's a back way out of the hospital where a car should be waiting," the guard says. "I can get him to it so long as the enemy isn't waiting there to ambush us."

Having been in communication with the Resistance for so long, I know how these groups work. They probably jumped on the unusual opportunity to attack the king while he was in a vulnerable position. It's a toss up whether they know the layout of the place or not.

"I'll go first," I say to the guard. "You'll have to navigate."

"No." Montes's hand falls heavily on my shoulder, like he's considering physically restraining me.

"My queen," the guard says, "it's my job to protect you too."

The sound of gunfire is getting closer.

"If the king dies, the world will be leaderless when we need one the most." I shouldn't be worrying about the king's death. He can't be killed. But I've seen him bleed just as easily as I do and watched him take medications like any other person might. I am beginning to think the Undying King isn't quite so resilient as he might have me believe.

"Serenity—" Montes begins.

I swivel to face him. "I'll be fi—"

The king shoves a gun into my hand, and for a beat I stare dumbly at it. I hadn't even realized the king was carrying.

"Don't hesitate to use it," he says.

My fingers curl around the weapon, and I nod. I open the door wider and pull Montes out with me.

To the king and the guard I'm sure I look resolute. That's not how I feel. Inside I'm battling years of conditioning. Two months ago, I would've used this opportunity to assist those who are attacking us. Now I am protecting the very person I once hated.

"Where do we go?" I ask.

The guard points down the hall, and we begin to trot. We pass the nurses' station, which is now abandoned.

The sound of gunfire is moving, but I can't tell where it's coming from.

At some point the guard yells, "Stop!"

I halt and turn to him and the king. The guard pulls out a key and inserts it into a door that blends into the wall.

My eyes move to Montes. He looks surprisingly calm, and I have to wonder how often he's been in this situation. As for me, I'm breathing heavily, but I feel exhilarated.

The guard opens the door and beckons us through. I enter first and glance around. It's a stairwell.

"The car is down two floors," the guard says.

I begin moving, ignoring the chill that seeps into my bare feet. The gunfire has died down, which means that someone's soldiers have been dealt with. I hope it's theirs rather than ours, then cringe when I realize just how quickly I changed sides.

The silence that follows has my heart pounding. This isn't a good situation, us being here in this stairwell with only a single guard to protect the king.

I descend the second flight of stairs. A narrow hallway branches off of it, leading to a door that exits to the back of the hospital. Through the narrow window a nondescript van stands out against the inky black night.

"Is that the getaway car?" I ask.

"It is," Montes responds from behind me.

I turn to gaze at him. "I'm going out there first."

"No, you're not," Montes responds.

I glance at the guard.

"I take my orders from the king," he says.

I work my jaw but nod. I have to assume that everyone here can take care of themselves.

"Jose," the king says to the guard, "you'll go first, I'll go second, the queen will go last."

I open my mouth to protest, but Jose is already moving. I jog to keep up. Once Jose reaches the exit, my stomach clenches. If someone's waiting for us, we're either going to meet our maker or be in a whole lot of pain in the next few seconds.

Jose pushes open the door and sprints to the van. The king's right behind him, and then I'm out the door moving, gun in hand, my skin prickling at the cold night air.

The shot takes us all by surprise. I see Jose and the king flinch in front of me at the same time my body jerks. I already know whose been hit before the pain sets in.

I stumble and fall forward, clutching my side. Dark liquid seeps under my hand, and then the fiery sting of the wound explodes across my skin. I grind my teeth together at the lacerating pain.

The king shouts, and Jose muscles him into the car. Above that I can hear the pound of footsteps coming closer.

"Go!" I scream at them. I want to say so much more, but I can't seem to formulate my feelings into words. Not now when the pain is pushing every other thought to the wayside.

More shots blast my eardrums, and I jump at each one. Bullet holes dent the van frighteningly close to the wheels. Luckily the night makes the shooters' aim less accurate.

I lift the gun in my hand and fire in the vague direction of our attackers, but it's no use when I can't see them.

I hear the van's engine turn over. The king will make it. My sight blurs, but I can still see Montes struggling to leave the vehicle, and Jose's hand pushing him down so that he's not in the shooter's line of sight.

The pounding footsteps get closer and I glance behind me. A man and a woman wearing black fatigues jog towards us, their guns raised.

I aim my weapon and fire off three more shots—all misses due to my trembling hand—then the gun clicks empty.

Tires screech and the van peels out. Several more shots ring out, and bullet holes puncture the side of the van. The last thing I see before rough hands grab me is Montes's face.

It's a mask of despair, and that, more than anything frightens me. If the king is already in mourning, then I am as good as dead.

"WE GOT THE queen," the man radios to his accomplices. I guess I know which side survived the gunfire. "We're going to load her and take her back to the warehouse."

That can't be good.

Rough hands lift me from where I'm crumpled against the ground. I scream at the sensation. The woman grabs my arms and the man grabs my legs.

I shriek as they lift me, and salty tears sting my eyes. My wound feels like it's ripping me in two; warm liquid exits it and slides across my skin.

They carry me to a nearby ambulance and load me on a stretcher. I'm already starting to shiver.

"She's losing a lot of blood. Think she'll survive the ride?" the man asks the woman.

"Nadia will make sure she does."

I groan from the pain and squeeze my eyes shut, trying to forget just how my life led me here. Given the situation, I hope the wound takes me. Chances are good that if I live through it, I'm going to die a much more painful death.

The door to the ambulance opens, and I see the nurse I talked to earlier. "So you're the traitor?" I wheeze.

"I'd say the same thing to you." She glances at the man hovering over me. "Get the car started. The rest of the team is leaving."

She turns her attention back to me. "Let's get you fixed up." This must be Nadia.

They shot me only to stitch me back together. "This is why I hate doctors," I whisper.

"I'm a nurse," Nadia says, snapping on gloves. And then she touches the wound.

I scream. What she is, is a sadist.

I BLINK OPEN my eyes, confused about where I am. I twist my body to look around, and pain lacerates me everywhere. I yelp and still. My side throbs long after I stop moving, and I quickly fill in the gaps of my memory.

The king and I were ambushed. He escaped. I didn't. I'd been operated on and passed out at some point, either from the pain or the blood loss. And now I'm here.

I no longer side with the Resistance. That realization leaves a bitter taste in my mouth. They'd been my allies for so long. But I'd made the choice to defend the king—my husband—when I could've let him die. I find I don't regret it, either. *And now the Resistance and I are enemies.*

I'm still wearing the hospital gown, and crusted blood and bits of tissue cake it. I run my hands over my ribcage and waist and feel layers of gauze encircling the bullet wound. They've done a good job dressing my injury.

I sit up slowly, careful not to jostle anything. The glimpse of my room isn't promising. Cement walls and floor, a cot—which I'm resting on—a table and two chairs, a T.V. mounted near the ceiling. But my absolute favorite two details are the one-way mirror and the stainless steel toilet. If I need to go to the bathroom, I'll have an audience.

Someone must be watching me because the knob to my room twists and the door opens. I watch it, my face carefully arranged to look disinterested.

But the mask slips when I see exactly who steps through the door.

CHAPTER 22

SERENITY

"WILL?" I'M NOT sure whether to be horrified or elated that he's the one entering my cell. I do know that I'm shocked.

He's wearing the same black fatigues as everyone else, and I notice that he's carrying his weapons on him. Either he's planning to use force, or he hopes to intimidate me.

He crosses the room in three long strides and then I'm gathered in his arms. I wince from the pain.

"What are you doing here?" I ask, standing. "What's going on?"

"I'm now the head of the western chapter of the Resistance. And I'm here to help you kill the king." He lets me go long enough to cup my face. I swear for a moment he considers leaning in and kissing me, and I can't help but rear back. His hands drop, looking confused at my reaction.

"Will, you're still a part of the Resistance? What were you thinking? If the king finds out, he'll kill you." My heart pounds at the thought. Then the implications of Will's new position sink in. My eyes widen. "*You* ordered your men to shoot me?"

He cocks his head, like he doesn't understand me. "It needed to be believable."

"Believable for what?"

He leans in, his voice hushed. "Everyone thinks you're with the king except for me."

I give him a disbelieving look. "Will, I *am* with the king." That was why the representatives made me marry Montes—to glue together two warring hemispheres.

Will stares at me long and hard, like I might really be the traitor everyone else claims I am.

Surprise morphs to anger. I sacrificed so much for the good of my friends and my nation, and Will still wants to play soldier, to gamble with lives like this is a game.

"Does your father know of your actions?" I ask.

"Leave him out of this."

"He doesn't," I state.

Will shakes his head. "That's not the point, and that's not why we dragged you here." He grips my upper arms. "The king can be killed," he says, shaking me slightly.

His words catch my attention, temporarily distracting me from my current situation.

"How?" I ask.

Will releases me. "He hasn't told you?" He actually sounds surprised.

I hesitate. "The king was going to tell me once I recovered," I finally say.

Will's head tilted. "Is it true then? Do you have cancer?"

"If I answer your question, will you tell me how you know the king can be killed?"

He gives me a sharp nod, and I exhale, glancing down at my soiled gown. "It's true," I say quietly. "All that radiation ... I have stomach cancer."

As I speak, Will's brows draw together, and in the silence that follows, he glances away. One might think that he was overcome with emotion, but I know what he's really thinking—it's the same thing that plagued my thoughts for a while. He's wondering why the hell the king is trying to save my life.

"Did they get the cancer?" Will asks.

I fold my arms over my chest. "I wouldn't know. I was shot and kidnapped before I heard the prognosis." Voicing this only throws the absurdity of the whole situation in sharp relief: Will allowed Resistance members to shoot me even though he knew I might be sick. Right now his heartlessness is giving the king a run for his money.

Will grunts, and that's the closest he'll come to saying, *point taken.*

"I shared my news," I say. "Your turn."

"One of our members found out that the king takes a certain prescription," Will begins.

My mouth dries, and my fingers grip the skin of my arms tightly.

"We were able to get ahold of a sample of it and study what it does," Will continues.

I wait with bated breath.

"The thing's the fucking fountain of youth in a pill. Test subjects reported that their sunspots vanished, their wrinkles disappeared, and their hair regenerated—and that's only what they noticed. The truth is that daily doses of this drug lead to denser bones, stronger muscles, better eyesight—you name it."

I swallow. A pill that could effectively make you immortal. And I was now taking it. "Are there any side effects?" I ask.

"Don't know. However, this is the kicker: we found medical journals on this drug from almost thirty years ago."

I purse my lips. That was more than a little odd.

"Want to know who funded the bulk of the research?" Will asks.

I raise my eyebrows and nod for him to continue.

Will smiles grimly. "Your husband, Montes Lazuli."

I'M REELING FROM this revelation, though I shouldn't be too surprised, given the king's nature. Sometime in the shadowy bowels of history, Montes had come across this wonder pill. He could've been taking it that entire time—no, not could've, he *must've.*

I marvel at the thought that his real age might be close to sixty. Montes always struck me as ageless—not twenty, not sixty, not a hundred. There simply wasn't a number I could ascribe to him. I find that even now, even knowing he's as old as he is, my opinion of him doesn't change.

I'm still pondering this discovery when Will turns my chin to face him. "The king is not immortal." He enunciates each word.

"If he's mortal," I say, playing devil's advocate, "then how do you explain him surviving getting shot? Or the explosion?"

Will shakes his head. "Another one of his medical discoveries—that must be at least part of the reason why he took over the hospitals first."

I admit, it makes sense, especially after being healed by the Sleeper. I've seen firsthand what the king's medical devices can accomplish. And it makes more sense than the king actually being immortal.

Strange, I preferred him an unnatural thing. It made who he was and what we had more okay in my mind.

"You can find out the rest." Will still holds my chin in his hand, and his eyes move to my lips. "Find out what makes the king supposedly indestructible and kill him."

"No."

"What?" Wills looks genuinely surprised.

"What makes you think I'm willing to work with you and the Resistance?"

He drops his grip on my jaw. "Why wouldn't you? Serenity, I'm trying to make things right."

I laugh at that. "This is you making things right? *Wow.*"

He crowds me. "I'm not giving you a choice. We can torture you until you agree to this, if you want to be difficult. We also have enough damning material to blackmail you into following through should you get cold feet."

His words are a slap in the face, and at first I think he's joking, being hotheaded and speaking before he's thought through his words. But one glance at his eyes tells me that he's serious.

"You'd do that?" I ask, incredulous. "Blackmail me? Torture me? All just to get what you want?"

Will's jaw clenches.

God, he *would.* I suppose I shouldn't be surprised; this is the role he's trained for. To be a general, one has to make hard choices, to set one's feelings aside for the good of the people. Still, I can't wrap my mind around this side of him. This is not the Will I remember.

"What happened to you?" I ask, peering at him.

"What happened to me? What happened to *you?*" he retorts. "If I didn't know better, I'd say you were in love with the king."

I fist my hands. "Fuck you, Will," I whisper. "You don't have to lie with your parents' killer every night. You don't have to live with the guilt and disgust that comes with trying to make that situation work, because as queen you have the opportunity to benefit the world."

There's a flicker of remorse in his eyes, but I'm not done.

"I've given *every* ounce of myself," I say. "How dare you question my motives."

Will reaches up and touches a lock of hair. "I love you Serenity, you know that," he says. "But this is larger than us—we're talking about millions of lives here. Millions of lives that we can save."

"What do you think I'm trying to do right now?" I ask.

He shakes his head. "Whatever it is, it's not good enough."

I lift my chin. "What happens if the king dies? Who leads the world then?"

"You would, Serenity, along with whoever you appointed."

My breath catches. The Resistance's plans are all so painfully simple. If I came into power, I'd push the agenda I'd been raised with, and I'd likely employ those trusted few people I'd worked and fought alongside. Will would be one of them. Hell, he and the Resistance might've taken this a step further and assumed Will would replace the king.

A little piece of me dies; it's been dying since the moment I realized my friend allowed me to get shot.

I'm surrounded by bad men.

"You are blinded by power, Will." When had this happened, and how had I never noticed this metamorphosis?

Will raises his eyebrows and barks out a disbelieving laugh. "You think *I* am blinded by power?" He leans in, his lip curling. From his expression, I can see that my lack of cooperation has fermented into some more poisonous emotion. "The king has you under his thumb, just where he wants you. Who knew all it took was a little romance and a little dick?"

In one smooth motion I cock my fist back and slam it into his face. I can feel the agonizing movement across my entire body, and I bite the inside of my cheek to smother my cry. Still, hitting him is incredibly satisfying.

Will reels back, holding his nose, but I know it's not broken. I'm too weak at the moment to put much force behind the punch.

A moment later the door to my cell opens up, and a Resistance soldier steps a foot into the room. Will waves him away. "I'm fine," he says.

The man's eyes dart between us, but he steps back and closes the door, leaving us alone once more.

I step in close to him. "You and the rest of the WUN traded me for peace," I say, my voice rising. "If the king brainwashed me, that is your fault. If I'm falling for the king, it's only because you forced me to marry him." I'm shaking I'm so angry. "You don't have the right to use me anymore. *You already gave me away.*"

Will reels back, and I see genuine emotion in his eyes. Remorse. Regret.

I square my jaw. "I won't do what you ask," I say, my body still burning with fury. "You will have to torture me."

"Serenity." Will's voice drops low. "Please."

"Screw you, asshole. No."

Will exhales. "Fine." He looks over his shoulder at the one-way mirror beyond. "Omar, can we run that clip of the queen?"

A few seconds later the screen in the interrogation room winks on. It glows white for a moment, and then footage appears. I suck in a breath at the sight.

I watch myself step into the doorway of a jet. The short dress I wear is in tatters, and it flaps in the breeze. But it's not what flares my nostrils as I watch myself descend the stairs to the ground. Maroon blood is caked all over my body, and strange dark flecks of what must have once been flesh are splattered across me. I want to puke at the sight of myself.

"That's what will hit the Internet," Will says. "The king won't be able to sweep that under the rug—and if he does, we'll start posting the recordings and emails from the Resistance meetings that incriminate you until he is forced to do something about it. He will kill you. And he'll enjoy it. Still want to refuse my offer?"

I close my eyes and swallow. "I never thought you'd be the one to betray me, Will," I say.

"That's not an answer."

I open my eyes. "If you want to sentence me to death, so be it. You already received my answer."

Will's nostrils flare. He strides to the table, grasps a chair, and flings it at the one-way mirror. "Goddamnit Serenity, stop being an idiot!"

I watch him. "Is that supposed to scare me?"

His chest heaves. "You will be imprisoned, tortured, killed if you don't agree to do this. Do you care so little for your life?"

"I live with the devil. I've already died and gone to hell. So no, I don't care." The truth is, I don't want to die, and torture scares the shit out of me. But I've already bent to the will of too many men. I'm done compromising.

Will stands motionless. I can tell he doesn't know what to do. He probably assumed that I'd willingly agree to his plan, and that if I didn't, pain would sway me. He hadn't counted on me folding out altogether.

An alarm in the corner of the room sounds, and then someone radios Will. "The king's men have found us. The warehouse has been infiltrated."

For a split second, Will's distracted. This is my chance to escape. I don't want to be the Resistance's pawn anymore than I'd wanted to be the WUN's or the king's. I lunge at him, my hand reaching for his weapon.

In one smooth move I flick open his holster and pull the gun out. I see a flash of betrayal in Will's eyes when I point the weapon at him, but I feel no remorse.

"So what, you're going to shoot me?" he asks.

"I'm seriously considering it, you fucker." My words burn like acid.

Will tilts his head. "You really are a traitor queen."

I pull my arm back and slam the gun into his temple. He crumples to the ground in front of me, unmoving.

I crouch next to him and avoid looking at his face. It's hard to reconcile this discontent man with the strong, kind friend I grew up alongside. Of all the ways I thought war would affect me, this is one I hadn't predicted. I never imagined that I could lose one of my closest companions.

Beneath my fingers I can feel Will's pulse. It's a little sluggish, but he'll be fine. For now.

Shots ring out somewhere around me, and I can't help feeling like a sitting duck in this room, even though the king's men have come for me. *They've come for me.*

I search Will's pockets for a key or a card—something that will get me out of this room. But he has nothing on him, and judging by the look of the door handle, there isn't a keyhole nor is there a keypad. It seems the interrogation room has been designed to only unlock from the outside. Just my luck.

Five minutes later the door bursts open. I already have Will's gun trained on the door, ready to blow away anyone who considers using me as their ticket out of the warehouse. But instead of a Resistance soldier, one of the king's men surges into the room.

We make eye contact and I can see the relief soften the expression on his face and loosen his taut muscles. I drop the gun in my hand and kick it away.

The guard grabs a radio from his belt and calls in. "The queen is alive and secure. Repeat, the queen is alive and secure."

Will moans on the floor at my feet, and the guard's eyes snap to him. The guard glances down at my bloodied hospital gown and sucks in a breath. He cocks his gun and points it at Will.

"It wasn't him," I say. "This wound was from when I was shot outside the hospital."

The guard radios in a second time. "The queen is injured. Repeat, the queen is injured. Requesting a stretcher."

"I am *not* leaving this building on a stretcher," I growl out.

Over my dead body would that happen.

I GLARE UP at the hallway's florescent bulbs as I'm wheeled out. Around me several guards push the gurney, and I swear they're suppressing smiles. Pricks.

Somewhere ahead of me, one of the king's soldiers leads a handcuffed Will. But most of them surround me.

From the brief glimpses I get as I'm rolled out, I see bodies littering the floor, most lying in pools of their own blood. One of them is Nadia, the nurse that stitched up my gunshot wound, her eyes glazed and empty. The Resistance members here have been massacred.

My throat works. I shouldn't feel anything for them—not after they were so willing to hurt me. But these were once people I worked with. People whose courage I admired. Sorrow wells within me. Wrong is right, and right is wrong.

Somewhere ahead of me doors open, and early morning light pours in. I squint at the sunlight shining down on me.

Above me several helicopters circle the warehouse. I can't see my surroundings well, but by the looks of it, the king has brought most of his army here.

I hear a cheer rise through the air, but I can't tell who's watching.

Suddenly a head eclipses the light, and I make out the dark eyes of the king. My stretcher stops as the guards halt. The king cups my face and bends over me.

I feel a drop of water against my cheek. A tear—the king is crying. Over me.

He presses his lips to mine, and I feel the brush of his wet eyelashes against me. I've never seen the king cry—no footage has ever captured this side of him.

"I thought I'd lost you," he says, his voice choked.

My heart thumps painfully in my chest. It should never have been this way. My comrades turning on me, my enemies saving me. But worst of all, I should never have felt anything other than hatred for this man, the king. Definitely not this, this warmth that thaws my soul.

I stare into the king's eyes. I am Isolde, I am Juliet, I am Guinevere.

I am every one of those idiots because I've fallen for the king.

CHAPTER 23

THE KING

I WILL MURDER every last one of them. I will rip every last survivor from limb to limb, I will torture them for days for what they did to Serenity. For what they tried to do to me.

I can feel small pricks of pain behind my eyes, but I hold back my tears. She's safe now.

I thread my hands behind my head and pace outside Serenity's hospital room, where she's been resting since she returned.

Henry, the lead investigator of my secret service unit, approaches me. "Your Majesty, the prisoner who was found with Serenity in the interrogation room—we have reason to believe that he's the leader of the western division of the Resistance."

This is news. What is the leader of the western division doing here? And why was he the one in Serenity's room?

Cold dread settles in my stomach, but I keep my resolve steely.

"We're trying to figure that out at the moment." Henry's lips thin. "That's not all, Your Majesty."

I wait for him to go on.

"The prisoner is William Kline, the son of the former general of the WUN, Chris Kline."

HE KNEW HER. He knew her. He knew her.

And he betrayed her. He betrayed me. Hell, he probably betrayed his father.

There's nothing I hate worse than a traitor.

I watch him through the one-way mirrors as he's being tortured for information. Funny how quickly he's gone from being interrogator to interrogated.

Usually I stay far away from these sessions. They're a little too gruesome for my taste. But while Serenity is still sleeping off her latest surgery to undo the mediocre medical attention her bullet wound received, I'm savoring justice in its most savage form.

"Why did you kidnap Queen Serenity Lazuli?" the interrogator asks.

The general's son is silent.

"Still not going to talk?" the interrogator asks.

When William, the general's son, doesn't reply, the interrogator grabs the metal pliers and moves it over to an untouched finger. The table he sits in front of is already slick with blood.

"Stop!" William shrieks as another fingernail goes. This isn't even the worst part yet.

"Do you want to talk?" the interrogator asks calmly. Civilly.

William is sobbing, and sweat drips down his pale face.

"Perhaps I should move to chopping off fingers ... or other things," the interrogator says.

The Resistance leader's jaw clenches.

"No? Then perhaps we'll just have to drag your father into it."

William's face pales further. "I—I'll talk." I can hear the defeat in his voice.

What the boy doesn't know is that my men are already on their way to execute his father. It's long overdue.

SERENITY

WHEN I WAKE up, my golden hair fanned out around me, I'm alone in the hospital room. The monitors beep and whirr.

I throw my legs over the side of the bed, the pads of my feet touching the cool linoleum. Not surprisingly, I feel like I've been rolled over by a tank. It doesn't matter. I can't take it in here. Not one second more. I've been either injured or recovering for the last few weeks in the hospital; I'm done being sick.

I rip out the IV drip taped to my wrist, only wincing slightly when I feel the momentary pain. A monitor next to me goes off.

Out of curiosity I lift up my hospital gown to look at my wound. Unlike the last time I was here, my body shows evidence of surgery. Clean bandages wrap around my torso. Relief floods me at the sight of it; it means that I haven't lost days or weeks.

I pull the cloth gown back down and exit my room.

In the hallway a swarm of guards keep watch outside my door. I guess the king didn't want to chance an attack again. As soon as they see me leaving, they try to coerce me back into the room.

"My queen, you need to—"

"The first person who tells me to rest will find themselves castrated," I say, piercing each guard with a glare.

The guards go silent, and I smile. "I want to see the king," I say.

"But—"

I narrow my eyes on the guard who spoke and whatever he was going to say dies in his throat. "Take me to him—that's an order."

I FINGER MY spare clothes as I follow the guards through the secret service building. My arms shake; they've been doing that since I was told the king was extracting information from Will.

The guards glance nervously at one another. "You have my word you will not get in trouble for this," I promise.

I can tell which interrogation room Montes is in by the cluster of officials standing around it.

A couple of them see me and try to cut me off. "My queen, you can't—"

"I am fucking tired of hearing I can't do things today," I say. "Let me through or I will force my way through."

One tries to grab me. My fist snaps out, but he blocks it with his forearm. Another closes in, pressing a finger to his ear and speaking in low tones. I know what this is—containment.

"*Montes!*" I shriek.

Hands are on me, and the guards that led me here are nowhere to be seen. Pansies.

"Let me *go*," I snap, yanking at my arms. They won't release me. My anger spikes; there is nothing so infuriating as being physically helpless against another human being.

The door opens and Montes walks out. "What is going on?" The moment he processes that I'm being detained against my will, his face hardens. "Let the queen go." His voice is steel.

Hands release me, and I glare at the guards.

"Serenity, what are you doing out of bed?"

"I want to see Will."

The king's jaw works. "You can't."

There's that command again. That I can't. And now I've heard it one time too many.

I push past the king and dart for the door he's come out of. I've barely managed to open the door when arms wrap around my midsection and pry me away. But not before I catch a glimpse of the viewing room, and beyond it, the interrogation.

All I see is crimson blood and all I hear are Will's screams. The outer walls must be thick to silence such agonized cries. The king's wrath is just as frightening as I'd always feared.

My mouth parts as I'm dragged away. "Oh God." My words croak out. "Stop," I whisper.

"Serenity—" The king's voice comes from behind me. He's the one restraining me.

"*Stop!*" I scream.

The king's hand rubs my skin, as if I am a child needing soothing from a nightmare. "We need information from him," he says.

"I don't care." I'm shaking all over. I've seen and done many horrifying things, but it's this one that undoes me. "This needs to stop." I'm no longer just talking about Will's interrogation. I'm talking about war—about being a woman raised on a diet of pain and punishment. Where evil is avenged with more evil. It will never be enough to remedy the world.

The king feels me trembling beneath his hands. "You need to rest."

"I'll do whatever you want, Montes, just please, stop torturing him." A tear leaks out. It's Will, after all. I might hate what he's become, but torture … I don't wish that on my worst enemy.

The king sighs. "If we don't get information out of him, then your life might still be in danger. I can't allow that."

"Montes," I say, my hands clutching his arms. "*Please.*"

That vein near his temple throbs, and I'm sure he's going to say no.

His hold on me drops. "Get the queen out of here." The king eyes each one of his soldiers. "And I don't care what threats the queen made to get here, the next time you defy my direct orders—it will be your head."

He raises an eyebrow at me—the warning is for me as well—then he turns on his heel and re-enters the interrogation room.

"*Montes!*" I yell after him. The door clicks shut; the bastard ignored me.

I stare at the room as I'm dragged away. My world is completely falling apart.

The walls of this place might be thick, but they don't muffle everything. I'm halfway down the hall when I hear a bang. My body jumps at the sound, and a tear leaks out.

Gone. Will is gone.

THE KING

I'M GETTING TOO soft. That sentiment is running on repeat as my men drag the Resistance leader's body out of the interrogation room.

I've been the master of strategy and power plays since the beginning of my career. I don't compromise, ever. Yet here I am, watching the cleanup crew wipe up the boy's spilled blood. I did as Serenity asked—I put the traitor out of his misery. Thanks to listening to my bloody fucking heart instead of my brain, I threw away the opportunity to learn the locations of dozens of Resistance cells.

Deep in my gut, unease pools. Killing him was a mistake, one I can't correct. And it's one I might repeat if I become too compassionate. I rub my mouth.

"Your Majesty," Henry, the lead investigator, enters the room.

"Hmm?" I glance up at him.

"There's something you need to see, and it concerns the queen."

"THE RESISTANCE RECORDED the queen's interrogation," Henry explains as he leads me to one of the station's conference rooms.

That horrible rage that I've kept in check since we retrieved Serenity now rears its ugly head once more. That anyone would dare harm my wife. No one crosses me and gets away with it.

"Show me the footage." I know Henry doesn't miss the flinty edge to my voice.

Henry grabs a remote control sitting on the conference table and points it at the large screen that dominates one of the walls.

A grainy black and white image of a cinderblock cell flickers on. I lean my knuckles heavily on the desk, and I lean forward. My blood pressure rises as several Resistance members drag an unconscious Serenity into the room and dump her onto a cot.

Henry's time lapsed the footage so that it fast forwards several hours. During all that time, my wife's form barely moves. The sight of her looking so fragile does something to me.

The tape slows; several seconds later, Serenity's eyes open. After taking in the room, she sits up. I only have to wait a minute more before the door to her cell opens and William Kline joins her.

The sound is even grainer than the video, but I can still make out the words. I grit my teeth as William cups my wife's face. He touches her like he has a right to. Now I doubly regret my decision to end his life.

As I watch and listen to the entire interrogation—which really isn't an interrogation at all—my breathing slows. The Resistance knows so much more about me than I believed. I thought this might be the most worrisome aspect of it, until William threatens my queen.

"She's associated with the Resistance," Henry says.

"I can damn well see that," I snap.

I glare at the man on the screen. I should've gotten more information out of this piece of shit. They've set their sights on the throne, and they plan on using my wife to usurp me. This needs to be suppressed stat.

I'm a cold-blooded bastard. I know this, the world knows this, and most of all, the queen knows this. Yet as I watch her, my heart pounds madly. She's vicious and frank, and she's not giving into their demands.

If I didn't understand her, I might've worried that she was some sort of double agent. But Serenity doesn't hide her violence and anger. No, she puts the worst parts of herself out on display and hides the best aspects of herself. Even that she's not so good at because she's risking torture and death by defending me.

She's the most fearless person I know.

My opinion of her only increases when she slugs Will, and again when she pulls his own gun on him.

It doesn't take a genius to know I married up.

CHAPTER 24

SERENITY

I'M RETURNED TO my hospital room where I languish until I'm questioned on my time spent in the warehouse. It's a sad day when giving a statement is preferable to the alternative—leaving me alone to my thoughts.

After the stunt I pulled with Will and the king, I have extra guards watching me throughout the day, none of whom want to make small talk. I burned that bridge either when I killed their comrades, or when the king threatened them with death for listening to me.

Hours tick by before I see Montes again. By then the officers are long gone, as are the painkillers I've been fed. Several sets of shoes click against the linoleum floor outside my room.

The king doesn't knock. He stalks inside, his men filing in behind him. My eyes flick to them.

Montes crosses the room, cups my face, and kisses me long and hard. It's over before I can react.

"Let's get the queen out of here," the king orders his men. There's shuffling.

"Does this mean I'm all better?"

He returns his attention to me, and he's looking at me funny. "I'm not making the same mistake twice," the king says, evading my question. "We'll be finishing your treatment in a more secure location."

That's when I know, I just know, I'm not all right. Not at all.

Things happen quickly after that. A nurse comes in with another round of pain pills, and I take them to distract myself from the king's unnerving expression. He's either deeply worried or deeply moved by me. Neither emotion is particularly welcome.

It's only as I'm moved to a stretcher and wheeled out that I realize something's amiss. My eyelids droop.

"What did you give me?" My voice slurs.

Montes is there, his brows pinched. "A mild sedative."

"Am I going to die?"

"No, Serenity, you're going to be fine."

THE KING

THE RESISTANCE MAKES good on their threat of blackmailing the queen. The first leaked file hits the Internet shortly before we land in Geneva.

Serenity's still unconscious, her body encased in the Sleeper, and she'll remain in there for the rest of the week. The machine is busy regenerating the muscle and skin destroyed by the gunshot wound and removing the cancerous tissue that's regrown since her last treatment. I could keep her in there like Marco suggested, but I'm a selfish prick and I want her out and by my side as soon as possible, cancer or no.

Marco himself is down in the hull of the aircraft with her, stashed away in another Sleeper. He also barely made it out of the hospital alive. The thought that I almost lost both Marco and Serenity to the Resistance has my fist curling in on itself. They're going to regret pissing me off.

So far the Resistance has released just a single audio file from one of their meetings, one where Serenity's taken an active role in the discussion. But even this small piece of evidence is damning. Serenity's promised the Japanese Resistance members weapons in return for information.

The leader in me admits she's good—shrewd, assertive, compelling, and empathetic when the conversation calls for it. Too bad she's on the wrong side of the conflict.

Already the Internet is blowing up with this. The audio has been compared to that from the peace talks here. It matches.

"I want those sites shut down," I say to the advisors onboard with me. "Have all the major search engines do a sweep for this audio file and have them block all the links they find. I want my top guys to trace the leak back to its source."

"Your Majesty," one replies, "it's likely encrypted."

"I don't fucking care. Have them find the source, or you're all out of jobs. I'm going to hunt these assholes down."

When I get my hands on them, I won't kill them.

They will wish I had.

SERENITY

I BLINK MY eyes open. An unfamiliar room stares back at me. My hands finger a velvety comforter, and around me a fresco covers the walls.

I push myself upright in bed, belatedly realizing there's no more pain. My eyes flutter shut as my hand brushes over my torso. Someone's removed the gauze, and where a bullet hole should be, there's only smooth skin.

The king's technology has cured me once more. The thought pisses me off, mostly because I got duped. Montes does what he wants when he wants to whomever he wants.

Flinging the sheets off, I begin to storm out of the room. Halfway to the door I realize I'm still in a hospital gown. I practically growl as I rip the thing off of me and search the dresser and closet for real clothes.

Five minutes later, wearing tight pants, a loose shirt, and ass-kicking boots, I stalk out of the room. My hair whips wildly around me. I couldn't care less how I look. In fact, the scarier the better.

Outside the room a guard intercepts me. "Your Majesty," he says, scurrying after me.

"Where's the king?" I demand.

"If you'll follow me, Your Majesty."

His acquiescence surprises me. I guess the king's learned that he can't keep me stationary unless he locks me up.

I trail after the guard. My body receives a shock when I realize we're back in Geneva, inside the king's estate, and not the palace where I married him.

Why stop here and not there?

My thoughts are interrupted when the soldier halts in front of a door. Before he can politely knock on it, I push past him and throw the door open. Storming inside, I catch sight of over a dozen important people, including my husband. A tape recording immediately blares throughout the room.

I freeze as I hear a familiar voice—my own.

CHAPTER 25

SERENITY

"SERENITY," THE KING says, pushing his chair back and rising to his feet, "I wasn't informed you were awake."

I can hear the surprise—and happiness—in his voice. That's where the two of us are now. Caught between hate and love, between our grim reality and what might be.

Montes comes to my side while someone else clicks the recording off. He runs a hand through my hair, tilting my head to get a better look at me. "Are you feeling all right?"

"Don't baby me, Montes." I hear several of the king's men suck in air at that. I want to laugh. I've said so much worse to this man.

Montes's mouth curves at my words. He likes me best with my claws out.

I lift my chin a little as my gaze flicks beyond him to the other people in the room. Amongst them is Marco; guess he survived the hospital melee. Shame.

"What's going on?" I ask.

"The Resistance is blackmailing you," the king says.

My throat catches. "How bad is the situation?"

Montes lets out a breath. "People's opinion of you was already shaky since we were still at war with you only months ago. But you also participated in this terrorist group."

I don't deny it. I don't even try to.

"The Resistance is capitalizing on that. Over the last week they've begun a smear campaign, and they're targeting you."

I'm preoccupied with another portion of his statement. "A week?" I say. "Is that how long I've been unconscious?" I can't keep the accusation out of my voice.

"Yes." He's remorseless. Seems neither of us feel the need to defend our actions. I can respect that.

I turn my attention back to the situation at hand. The Resistance followed through with their threat; they'd already begun to disclose the incriminating files they had on me.

"How are people reacting?" I ask.

"Exactly how you'd think they might—they're getting worked up. Our statistics suggest that there's been a surge of new recruits in the Resistance."

All because of some audio files from when the king and I stood on opposite ends of the war. It's the ugly elephant in the room, this volatile history of ours. When we were more likely to kill than kiss. There will always be that looming shadow, and now it might mean more battles and more violence on the horizon.

I saunter towards the conference table. The rest of the room's been quietly watching the king and me up until now. I can tell by the glares of some of the king's men—and they're all men—that my presence isn't welcome. They could go screw themselves for all I care.

"I'm going to need to make a statement," I say, swiveling back to face the king.

He shakes his head, following me to the table. "They're waiting for that. As soon as you do so, they'll release the footage of your bloody arrival into the WUN. It'll undermine your credibility."

"We could release the footage first," I say. It would still be a shitshow, but at least we'd control the chaos somewhat.

Again the king shakes his head. "Better to let my team attempt to delete it from the Internet before it catches on."

I press my fingertips onto the conference table and nod. "Well, now you all know I've worked with the Resistance." When I look up, I give each one of the men in the room a piercing look, then turn back to the king. He's scrutinizing me, a small smile tugging at the corners of his mouth. I'm giving him a show, one that he seems to greatly enjoy.

"That means you might want to actually utilize me. I'm good for more than just staring at."

Next to me, the king's mouth tilts further up. "Yes, why don't we?" He places a hand on the small of my back and leads me to his seat while someone fetches him another chair. Finally, for the first time since we've met, I can tell the king doesn't just see me as a distraction.

He sees me as an equal.

"THE RESISTANCE HAS moles everywhere," I say to the men in the room. "And I do mean everywhere. When I was with them, they'd infiltrated many of your research labs. Now, however, they seem to have focused their attention on King Lazuli and me, which means they'll focus on the king's homes as well as those places we visit."

A muscle in Montes's jaw jumps. "You mean you believe there are Resistance members here right now?"

"Absolutely."

The king slams his fist into the table. "That should be impossible. We do intensive screening."

"Montes, tens of millions of people have died fighting this war. There are plenty of identities one can take on, and the Resistance excels at scrubbing them down. You'd never know."

This causes the king to pace, his hands clasped behind his back. He pauses and scrutinizes the men in the room. Suspicion flares in his eyes.

"Usually Resistance fighters take on positions that allow them to disappear," I say. "Maids, drivers, cooks, and so on. It's unlikely that any of the men in this room are in the Resistance's pocket ... though not impossible."

One of the king's advisors, who's been staring at me with intense vitriol, now speaks. "Your Majesty, how do we know the queen's not still working with them?"

The king stops pacing.

I tense, and not from the accusation itself. I couldn't care less what the king or his men think of my loyalties. I owe no one an explanation.

No, my muscles coil up the moment the king's shoes stop clicking against the floor because something bad is about to happen.

My eyes move over the men at the table. Like me, everyone's frozen in their seats.

I hear the squeak of the king's shoe soles as he swivels to face the man who spoke. "Are you questioning your queen's loyalty?" I can hear the dangerous edge in his voice.

Don't speak, I want to tell him.

I can see the man's body shaking. "N-no, merely—"

"You said 'how do we know the queen's not still working with them?' didn't you?"

"Yes, but—"

"How do we, indeed?" the king says. "Perhaps, you know something I don't about the queen's loyalties? I'm sure she's had plenty of time to deceive us between getting shot and fighting cancer."

The man's gone pale. The officers sitting at his sides are scooting away from him, like being too close might make them guilty by association.

When I glance at Montes, a smile is playing on his lips. He's a cat that's caught a mouse and is now toying with its food. "Or maybe it was when the Resistance kidnapped your queen and threatened her with torture?" Montes snaps his fingers. "Oh wait, she never gave into their demands."

My breath catches when I realize that my interrogation must've been recorded. Somehow the king got his hands on it.

Montes's voice goes cold. "How do we know you're not working with the Resistance, Ronaldo?"

The man, Ronaldo, shakes his head furiously, a sheen of sweat coating his forehead. "I'd never do such a thing. Please, Your Majesty, forgive me."

I and every other person in this room—including Ronaldo—know there's nothing he can say that will save him. This is a witch-hunt, and guilty or innocent, Montes has found his first suspect.

The king nods to Marco, who's seated to my right. I'd managed to ignore the asshole so far, but now my eyes move to him. Marco pushes out of his chair and approaches the man who spoke, the king's guards leaving their stations to flank him.

Now I understand why these men have kept so quiet. Speaking means catching the king's attention. Defeated nations everywhere can testify that garnering his attention is never a good thing. Hell, I can testify to that.

Montes has murder in his eyes. I stand abruptly, my chair scraping back. When his gaze meets mine, I shake my head. "I will not sit by and watch this."

The room's fallen silent, save for Ronaldo's quiet sobs as Marco and the guards drag him out. The king's just proved how he responds to challenges of any kind.

I, however, don't give two shits.

The king's arms are folded and he pinches his lower lip as he studies me. "You don't get a choice."

"I do if you want my help."

The king takes two ominous steps towards me, until he towers over me. "You might be my queen, but I am the leader, Serenity, and I make the decisions. And fuck it if I'll let you make demands of me."

So much for being equals.

I push past him, and he grabs my wrist. "I haven't dismissed you," he growls.

I laugh. "I don't answer to you, Montes. You better fucking remember who you married." There are millions of demure ladies who would've done his bidding in a heartbeat, who would've carved out their own identities to become whoever they thought he wanted. And yet he chose me, the one woman who won't do that, the one woman who's as likely to explode as he is.

Yanking my wrist out of his grip, I stalk out of the room, and no one stops me.

I don't know where I'm going, but it's a good thing I'm unarmed or else someone might get hurt. As it is, I'm eyeing the coat of arms that's on display ahead of me, and I'm seriously considering maiming the thing.

Behind me the door opens.

"*Serenity.*"

I rotate and see Montes headed towards me, his eyes angry. When he gets to me he wraps a hand around my throat and pushes me up against the wall. A knee slides between mine.

"You really shouldn't have left the room."

I should be pissing my pants at the look in his eye and the way he presses himself against me, but I'm not. I'm no longer frightened of this man. I don't know when that happened. The king has always been my nightmare. But he's not anymore. It's just further proof that I'm maladaptive.

I lift my chin. "Are you going to cart me away like you did Ronaldo?"

"I'm considering it."

I don't get the chance to reply.

Montes captures my mouth with his. Fear, anger, lust—they must all function on the same wavelength because one moment I'm pissed at the king, and the next I'm twining my tongue with his, my breaths coming in short, heavy pants.

His free hand grabs my hip and pulls me even closer to him. Close enough that I can tell he wants me. I find it curious that insubordination—and the resulting anger—could turn him on. Do people get intimate when they really just want to throttle each other? If so, I believe I'd excel at it.

"I think I will cart you away after all," Montes murmurs. He bends to pick me up. I'm slammed back into reality.

I rip my mouth from his. "We can't do this right now."

The king's eyebrows rise, and he smirks like I'm funny. "We're the rulers of the entire world; we can do whatever it is we want."

"But I still want to punch you in the face."

The king clucks his tongue. "My queen has never heard of angry sex. I think a woman like you would enjoy it."

The door we exited from opens. "Your Majesty, the Resistance just raided one of the warehouses of our weapons supplier. They took most of the armaments stored inside, including technology that hasn't officially hit the market."

Montes curses. His hold tightens on me before he releases me—though not completely. His hand slides down my arm and clasps my hand. He begins walking, tugging me along behind him.

I halt in my tracks, causing Montes to glance back at me. "I don't want you to hurt Ronaldo."

If I'm conceding something by returning to the king's conference room, then he's going to have to concede something, his earlier words be damned.

Montes narrows his eyes. "That man was the one who coordinated the atomic blasts that destroyed your nation all those years ago."

The news is a slap in the face.

"Still want to save him?" the king presses.

My throat constricts, but I force my words out. "Killing him will not resurrect my people."

The king tilts his head, like he has all the time in the world to ponder my request. "I know what you're doing, Serenity," he says, finally. "He'll return unharmed if you come with me and assist us with intel on the Resistance. If you don't, I can promise you that you'll never see Ronaldo again." I can see it in his eyes too; he'll end that man's life.

Bastard. Now look who's blackmailing whom.

"Deal?" He smiles like the devil he is.

I run my tongue over my teeth and nod. "Deal."

I SPEND THE rest of the day and well into the evening discussing what I know of the inner workings of the Resistance. My words will jeopardize hundreds of Resistance members, people I once worked with. The thought leaves a bad taste at the back of my mouth, but it doesn't stop me from telling Montes and his men everything they need to know.

The war's over. We should be focusing on healing communities, not more violence. Yet we can't. Not when stolen military weapons are in the hands of a terrorist organization. Because that's what the Resistance is and what it's always been, a terrorist organization. Vigilantes that use intimidation and coercion to fight for a cause they believe in.

When I stood with the WUN, I never minded their activities. It was enough that we were fighting a common enemy. Now that the war is over, the violence is no longer excusable. No matter where my allegiance once lay, I can't risk more innocent lives lost by staying quiet.

By the time Montes and I head back to our room, the mansion has a stillness to it that only comes with the deep night.

The king's hands are shoved into his pockets, and there's a vertical crease between his brows.

Once again my opinion of the king subtly shifts. Worries plague him. Another weakness. Another sign that he has a conscience.

He catches me looking, and the edge of his mouth tips up. He reaches for my hand.

We are the epitome of dysfunction. Our marriage won't work—it shouldn't. We are miserable human beings. And yet, when he laces his fingers through mine and I feel the thrill of contact, that tiny flame of hope I carry around flares up.

Anything's possible. From darkness to light, war to peace—hate to love.

The king brings the back of my hand to his lips and presses a kiss to it. The entire time he stares at me like we're sharing a secret. We are. We're two monsters that might not be quite so monstrous after all.

Anything's possible.

CHAPTER 26

SERENITY

BEFORE WE LEAVE Geneva, there's something of great importance to me here. A visit I've been anticipating and dreading. I come to find out it's the reason the king stopped here instead of his Mediterranean palace.

I enter the morgue alone—well, as alone as I'm allowed outside the king's estate. Today that means two guards flank me. Montes has wisely made himself scarce.

My eyes fall on the body in the middle of the room. He's already laid out, and suddenly, he's the only thing I have eyes for.

In four quick strides I cross the room. The medical examiner stands off to the side, and my guards fall away. It's just me and him.

My father.

Before I can think twice about it, I take his hand. It's cold and the texture is somehow all wrong. He's been gone long enough that, even embalmed, there is no pretending that he's a living thing. Still, I can't seem to let him go.

My gaze travels to his face. The blood has been washed from him, and the bullet hole in his forehead's been sealed up.

A tear drips onto the metal table beside my father's head. "I was supposed to die with you," I whisper to him.

The loneliness of my situation slams into me. How am I supposed to live if the one person who mattered most to me is now dead?

Killed by my husband's people. How could I forgive Montes for this? What kind of weak woman would that make me?

"I'm so sorry, Dad." For a moment I wait for him to respond. I know what he would say: *Don't be. I'm so proud of you.*

A memory from two years ago floats in. I'd been so angry at the king, angry at all the senseless death.

My father placed a hand on my shoulder.

"Do you know why your mother and I named you 'Serenity'?" he'd asked me.

I shook my head; I had no idea where he was going with this.

"Serenity means to be at peace," he explained. "When your mother was pregnant, she said the thought of you gave her that—peace."

Ironic that my life had known so very little of it.

"You'll never live up to your namesake if you don't forgive, Serenity."

"Dad—" He managed to use my one weakness, my mother, against me.

"No," he shook his head, "this is not an argument. What you choose to do with all that anger is your business. But you can't control the world; someone will always be there to wrong you. It's your choice to let it go. Only you can decide the woman you want to be."

It's finally time to let it go. I'm not excusing Montes's atrocities, nor all the monstrous acts that his war brought with it. No, I'm releasing my bitterness so that I can find peace within myself. I want to be that woman my father spoke of, the woman my mother might've imagined I'd become.

Perhaps my father was against my current circumstance. It doesn't change the fact that he always wanted the best for me. He'd want this, serenity.

BY THE TIME we arrive back at the king's palace by the sea, my father's remains are on their way to becoming ash. I didn't think he'd want to be buried in the ground after spending so many years down in the bunker.

Once he's cremated, I intend to scatter his ashes over our homeland, just like we did my mother's.

I walk into Montes's room—our room—and see the bed I lost my virginity in. I have mixed feelings about this place, but it's definitely better than Geneva, where memories of my father haunt the halls.

Montes comes in behind me. His arms weave around my torso and across my stomach. It's clear what feelings this room stirs in him.

He places a kiss along my neck. This hasn't happened in awhile—angry hallway encounter not withstanding. Surgeries, kidnapping, and healing wounds have kept us apart. But as the king's hands glide down my torso, I can tell that's all about to change.

I turn my head to face him. The look he gives me commands attention—demands I quiet my thoughts so that I can be filled with his. I see his charisma, his charm. It's what everyone notices, but below all those hardened layers is a shred of the man he must have been long ago. Someone who wasn't nearly so cruel. Perhaps it isn't just me who's capable of becoming a better person.

His fingers hook under my shirt, and he peels it off me.

"I hate you," I say quietly, without any of my usual venom.

Montes tosses my shirt aside. "I know—you've told me many times." He doesn't stop undressing me.

"But."

The king's hands still on the button of my pants. "But?" he repeats calmly. I know his cool demeanor is a ruse, especially when his eyes slowly travel up to mine.

I press the palm of my hand to the side of his face. "But it is not the only thing I feel for you."

The king's eyes smolder at my words. He understands what I'm saying even if I can't really put words to it.

He threads a hand behind my neck and pulls me to him, and I catch sight of it: a flicker of something vulnerable and compassionate on the king's face. His lips press hard against mine, kissing me like I'm his oxygen. This is magic, this is heaven, this is everything my life has denied me.

We begin tugging off our clothes. My hands grasp the collar of Montes's shirt, and I yank it open, popping buttons as I go. He growls low in this throat. The sound makes me pause until I realize that this is an approving sound.

The king pushes me up against the wall, and my back hits hard.

"Fuck," the king swears quietly, "did that hurt?"

There's that shred of humanity again in his eyes. Too bad it's misplaced. I am most comfortable with pain.

I tunnel my fingers into his hair and drag his head back harshly. "Don't stop."

The king's eyes hood, and he recaptures my mouth, his tongue forcing its way in.

For all his rough ministrations, his hands and his gaze are gentle. While his chest pins me to the wall and his mouth pillages mine, his fingers trail down the skin of my arms and my torso. They come to a halt low on my belly, and there they linger.

It's the area where a woman carries a child and just below the epicenter of my cancer.

The king falls to his knees and kisses it. I lean my head back and close my eyes at the tender gesture. We both know the king's plans for an heir will be put on hold indefinitely—at least if he wants one that shares my blood. It's one of the many things that go unsaid between the two of us because we can't seem to acknowledge things that waken our cold, charred hearts. Like the fact that I'm still dying.

He unzips my pants, tugs them off, leaving me in only my lingerie. That's what I wear now—scraps of lace. I only tolerate them because I'm obviously not wasting material.

Montes stares at them, and I can see his thoughts turning wicked. "I wouldn't have guessed my wife would go for these." His eyes move to mine. "I always assumed you were more of a cotton panties lady."

"Better be careful what you say when my knee is that close to your face."

A wolfish smile breaks out on his face. His lips skim over the material, and then he drags them off of my legs.

Suddenly I feel far too exposed. I've only done this with Montes a handful of times, and before that, never. I'm not used to baring myself, and the king is at face-level with the most intimate parts of me. I reach down to cover myself, and the king catches my hands.

"I don't think so." He pins them to my side.

When he moves his mouth to my core, I yelp. "Montes!"

I'm scandalized; I wasn't aware that anything could still shock me.

The king lets out a husky laugh, then his lips return to the sensitive flesh. I don't last long. My legs buckle, and Montes is there to catch me. He stands and picks me up.

He quiets me with another kiss, and carries me to our bed. When he lays me out on it and removes the last of his clothes, I swear his eyes shine in the dim glow of the room's light.

Where I'm modest with nudity, the king isn't. Once he's fully unclothed, he approaches me, completely unselfconscious. My eyes stray to all the pleasing lines of his body. He is mesmerizing to look at.

He prowls over to me, his hands stroking my legs as he watches me, a slight smile playing along his lips. I can't stand just laying here, so I push myself to my knees.

Reaching out, I stroke the king's chest for no other reason than I want to. After all, he's clearly put his fingers—and lips—everywhere that pleases him.

The king's eyes close, and he covers my hands with his own. They're warm and they dwarf mine.

"Don't stop," he murmurs.

I blink. I hadn't realized that his touch had stilled my own. I move our hands down, over the ridges of his abs, across his obliques, to the hard, lean muscle of his thighs. Here the king's hands tighten over mine.

He releases his hold and softly pushes me back against the bed and follows me on, his body blanketing me.

There's something to be said about physical touch. I've gone so long without it that the sensation is better than the sweetest of the king's liquors. I don't believe I'm the only one that feels this way. Montes is stroking my skin.

It hits me: he's been with far more people than I have—he told me so himself—yet he's acting as though I'm something coveted.

One of the king's knees slink between my legs, spreading them apart. His hips settle heavily over me, and I can feel him right at my entrance. He shifts his pelvis, and then he's pushing into me.

The king enters slowly, watching me the entire time. This isn't the rough sex I expected. Somewhere along the way our frenzied movements have turned into this.

My lifelong enemy is now the person who's physically closest to me. And I don't mind. The remorse I felt on our wedding night is gone.

Montes thrusts into me, and the sensation is overwhelming. He's overwhelming—over me, inside me.

Something about the languid way he moves and the way his eyes track mine makes me think this is more than just physical for him. That I might now consume the thoughts of the man who consumes mine.

A small smile tugs at the corners of my lips.

Montes stills. "That's a first," he breathes.

I'm finally giving into whatever it is I feel for this man and forgiving myself for circumstances beyond my control. I'm drawing a new beginning. One where not everything is a battle.

LONG AFTER WE'VE finished, Montes clasps me to him. A light and fizzy emotion surges through me. Hope.

If not war, then love.

I don't know the first thing about it—love. I don't know if I'm even capable of it. But I also know that I have a limited time to learn. I'm still dying. If I hope to help the world before my time's up, then I'll have to work with the king to achieve it.

That's asking a lot of the two of us—working together. We're the last people for any of this. But it will happen. I'll make sure of it.

"Weeks ago you promised I could get involved with medical relief," I murmur.

Montes's fingers trail my back. "I did."

"I want to start tomorrow."

His fingers halt. They tap against my skin once, twice. "Then I'll put you in touch with the advisor on global health and wellness first thing," he says. Whether the king is actually doting on me or just interested in keeping me busy doesn't matter. I'll get to work immediately.

Neither of us speaks again for several minutes.

Eventually, Montes breaks the silence. "What do you fear above all else, Serenity?" he asks quietly.

It's a strange question, given our circumstances.

"You," I say automatically.

I glance up at him, but he's not looking at me. He's staring at the ceiling, a faraway expression on his face.

His thumb strokes my shoulder. "Is this another one of your 'facts'?" Now his eyes do travel to mine.

I give him a shove, even as my lips curve up. He has me there. One doesn't make love with one's fears. Not willingly. Then again … perhaps I am the poster child for immersion therapy.

"Aside from me, is there anything you fear?"

My brows furrow.

When I don't respond, Montes says, "You can't answer my question."

I can't. Death doesn't scare me. Nor does pain. I might've said I feared losing the things that I love … but I've already lost them all.

"What do *you* fear?" I ask.

He's silent. "I don't know," he finally says.

"You do," I accuse.

He sits up, the action causing the blanket to draw down and expose my breasts. I push myself up as well, dragging the sheet back over my chest.

"They kept blood and oxygen flowing to my brain," Montes says, rubbing his jaw. "That's how they did it—how they kept me alive even after I'd been shot. You can replace everything but the brain. If that goes, a person is well and truly dead."

My hands tighten on the cloth. I don't know why he's decided to confide in me now, but I don't stop him. People have killed and died to learn what he's telling me. And he's telling *me*, the woman who's threatened to kill him to his face.

He knows things have changed between us.

"The origins of this war began decades ago, when I was just a successful businessman trying my hand at politics. I'd caught wind of a company developing an Alzheimer's drug with unusual side effects. It could turn back the clock—it could return a patient to their brain's peak performance, reverse baldness and bone loss, increase skin's elasticity, repair torn tissue.

"I took a chance and bought the majority shareholding of the company, and gave it the capital needed to continue testing. The drug was further tweaked, and we found a way to prevent aging completely."

Will had been right; Montes had stumbled upon the fountain of youth.

"The company's shares skyrocketed, and for a while, there was real concern in the medical field that the drug had just made tens of thousands of health related jobs obsolete." The king gives a dry laugh. "It probably would've too."

That sounded ominous.

"A super-virus swept through the Eastern Hemisphere. It spread rapidly, killing seventy to eighty percent of its victims. People panicked. The world hadn't seen something like this in centuries."

Apprehension skitters through my veins.

"Then one of my researchers discovered that my drug could cure the illness—if taken in the right dosage for the right amount of time. "

The king stares down at his palms. "People demanded I mass produce it and hand it out for free."

It dawns on me, how these long ago events affected the present. "You didn't?"

"No," he says quietly. "I didn't. I sold it for profit instead. And as the world got sicker, I became richer."

Montes shoves a hand through his hair. "In the beginning, I didn't want power, I just didn't want to lose everything I'd built. But somewhere along the way the line between money and power blurred, until I became king of it all."

All those people that died when they could've been saved.

I cover my mouth with my hand and scramble out of bed, no longer caring that I'm exposing myself. My entire body is shaking.

"I should never have saved you," I whisper.

A muscle in Montes's cheek ticks. It's the only sign that my words affect him.

He pushes himself out of bed and stalks towards me. "You wanted to know what I fear most? Here it is: I fear I will always be alone. That no one who truly knows me will love me. Not even my wife."

I balk at this. "You've made piss poor life choices, and you want me to love you in spite of it? You're insane."

I swivel to grab my robe and get the fuck out of here when Montes catches me around the waist.

He tugs me to him, pulling me in close. "I'm not insane, Serenity," he whispers into my ear. "And you and I both know why you saved my life. It doesn't matter that you think I'm an evil bastard. You love me."

CHAPTER 27

SERENITY

"HERE THEY ARE," Nigel Hall, the king's head advisor on Global Health and Wellness, sets a crate of papers down on the desk between us, "the regional reports you requested. All two hundred and fifty-seven of them."

Montes made good on his promise to put me in touch with Nigel. That was three days ago, and it takes the king's advisor that long to collect and deliver all the information on the state of affairs in every corner of the world.

Tossing aside the cardboard top that covers the box, I pull out a handful of folders and begin flipping through them. There are hundreds of locations in need of medical relief. Places where the crime rate is exorbitantly high and the death rate is even higher.

This isn't just a medical issue; it was simple of me to assume so. I'll have to take a holistic approach: education, shelter, basic amenities, regional justice systems, health—they all need to be addressed if I want to do this right.

I thumb over the pages. "Who wrote up these reports?"

"The committees on health and wellness, environmental sustainability, regional economic …"

I tune him out after that. I've heard enough. These reports were all written in-house, which means they're skewed to please the king.

Just to test my theory, I interrupt him. "Where are the WUN's?"

He flips through the files still in the box and pulls several out. I open them up. The regions are strangely divided here. I realize why when I delve into the reports.

The Midwest is sectioned off from the surrounding land. The committees involved decided that it was the region in the most dire need of relief, and here measures will be taken to rid the earth and water of radiation, repair the economy, and get people back to health.

It's laughable. The Midwest was one of the most unscathed areas of the WUN's land. Our former representatives figured that the king had plans to make use of the miles and miles of farmable land. This analysis only seems to support our theory.

"Interesting," I say, snapping the folder shut.

"What is?"

"The data gathered. It's inaccurate."

Nigel balks at my words. "Your Majesty, I assure you, these are the most comprehensive reports out there."

"Oh, I have no doubt of that. They're the *only* ones out there. But they're still inaccurate. I will not be following your committees' recommendations."

Nigel looks scandalized.

"Has anyone gone into these communities and asked the people themselves what they need?" I ask.

"Your Majesty," he says my title disparagingly, like how an adult might talk to a small child, "most of these areas are far too dangerous to enter."

"All the more reason to find out how to change the situation. I want you to pull together a team and begin plans for us to visit these places."

"'*Us*'? No, no, no. I'm afraid that's not possible. The king will have my head."

"You'll do this or *I'll* have yours."

"But the king—"

"I don't give a shit about the king's opinion on this." I talk over him. "I vow on my life I will offer you protection from him, Nigel, but this *will* be done." Montes owes the world that much.

Someone raps on the door. "Your Majesty." It's Marco. Abominable, douchelord Marco.

"I'm busy," I say, staring down a panicked Nigel.

"Not for this," he says. "The video has leaked."

WHEN I ENTER the king's conference room, I find him pacing. Behind him, footage of my entrance into the WUN plays in loops across the screen. When Will had showed the tape for me, I couldn't see all the meaningful details. Now I can. My face is alarmingly calm.

Marco shifts uncomfortably next to me as he catches sight of the footage. In fact, most of the king's advisors sitting in on this meeting stare at me with a mixture of anger and horror.

"We've been deleting various uploads of the video all morning, but it keeps surfacing," Montes says.

"Why now?" I ask, my eyes traveling over him.

Three days ago, this man admitted to me how he stayed ageless and how the war came to be. I still can't wrap my mind around how he can look at himself in the mirror every day, or why my heart hasn't stopped aching for him.

Montes turns to look back at the screen. "We've destroyed numerous cells over the last several days."

The cells I'd told the king about. So this was a direct result of my efforts.

"How bad is it?"

That vein in Montes's temple pulses.

"You haven't been able to completely stop the leak, have you?" I say. He'd been so sure.

That's how kings fall. Hubris.

Montes glances away from the screen, piercing me with his gaze. It's an explosive look, one full of vicious protectiveness. For all his wicked deeds, he doesn't just care about himself. No, he cares fiercely about me too.

"It'll be taken care of," the king says. The edge in his voice makes me think more people will die.

I back out of the room and leave the king to his collusions. This isn't my battle. It once was, but no longer. I've already surrendered.

OVER THE NEXT week, Bedlam breaks out across the globe. The king isn't able to suppress the footage of me, and it's done exactly what the Resistance intended: sparked rebellion.

Uprisings pop up across continents, some more organized than others. The Resistance spearheads many of them, and they're the most destructive. Provincial governments are demolished, the king's research labs burned, armories ambushed.

Reports suggest the group's numbers have nearly doubled since the video leaked, and membership was already in the hundreds of thousands.

I rub my forehead, trying to focus on the files Nigel gave me a week ago. I sit out in front of the palace soaking up the morning sun as I flip through them.

I've never been more unsure of myself than I am now. A year ago, I knew exactly who I was and what I stood for. The king was the enemy. He was evil and he wreaked death and destruction.

Now I'm married to that very man, and he's no longer so easily compartmentalized. The Resistance, whom I'd sided with for so long, is now the one perpetuating violence when the world's finally found peace. Right and wrong are lovers; I can't have one without the other.

I lean back against my chair and try to discern fact from fiction in these reports. I could be sifting through this inside, in the fancy new office I've been given, but I haven't had the luxury of lingering out in the sun for some time, and feeling the warm rays on my skin is better than even the king's most luxurious rooms.

I glance up from the report when I hear the distant sound of a car coming up the drive.

I squint my eyes. Not one car. A battalion of them. And not just cars. Armored vehicles.

I stand, dropping the file on the stone bench beside me.

I hear a familiar whine; my mind sharpens at the sound. That ransacked warehouse, those missing weapons. I'm now facing them down.

The whine turns into a hiss as a rocket arcs across the sky from the bed of one of the cars. It's headed straight for the palace.

So today's the day I die.

CHAPTER 28

THE KING

MY MEN GET the call while I'm setting up provincial governments in South America. I see their fingers go to their earpieces one moment, and in the next, they're surrounding me.

"Your Majesty," one says, "we need to get you out of the palace. Now."

"What's going on?"

The explosion knocks me over the desk, the sound a roar in my ears. The walls shake as dust and plaster rain down on me.

Someone bombed my palace. *Someone bombed my palace.* Anger and incredulity war for dominance.

"Security breach! Front gate!" a guard yells, and then my soldiers are pulling me to my feet and dragging me out of the room.

The front gate? Serenity's out there. A bolt of panic flares through my veins.

I yank the hands off of me. "I'm not leaving without the queen." I need to see her now.

"Our men are already on it."

I hesitate, forcing my guards to drag me out of my room and propel me towards the map room, where escape waits.

Oh God, what if something already happened to her?

SERENITY

THE MISSILE SLAMS into the west wing of the palace, and the building erupts in a plume of fire and stone. I barely have time to cover my face before the wave of heat slams into me.

After all their years of planning, the Resistance is finally making their big move, and now I'm on the wrong side of the fight.

Go figure.

"Your Majesty!" The guards who've shadowed me all morning now sprint towards me as I rise to my feet.

When they reach me, I don't think. I grab the gun from one of the guard's holsters.

For a split second he looks at me like I've betrayed them. No, I have something much stupider in mind. "We need to cut them off."

The words are barely out of my mouth when one of my guards lays a hand on my shoulder. "We need to get you out of here. Now."

Perhaps if I'd grown up in a world without violence, I would've readily agreed to this. Instead I duck under the guard's arms and begin running for the front gate. I pump my arms; I can hear the king's men behind me.

I fall to one knee and line up the gun's sights, and then I fire, aiming at the leading car's front window.

A miss.

I correct my aim and try again.

Another miss.

I can see the line of vehicles a little better. Someone's reloading the rocket launcher in the bed of that truck. I bite my lip and pull the trigger. I miss my target—I am too far away for much accuracy—but my bullet punctures the driver's side window.

That's all it takes for the car to swerve, sending some of the men in the back over the tailgate.

A pair of arms wrap around my midsection, and I'm lifted off my feet. One of the king's vehicles cuts across the expansive lawn and lurches to a stop behind us. More of Montes's soldiers grab me and throw me into the car.

Fighting my guards' orders any longer will only get more people killed. This isn't a battle I'm equipped to fight in.

I right myself and glance out the window. Behind us I can see the Resistance's vehicles still barreling full speed ahead towards the gate. Other palace guards stationed near the palace entrance are already firing their weapons, but it's making no difference.

The gate lets out a sickening groan as the first car rams into it, and it's torn from its hinges. The palace has now been breached.

"Where are we going?" I ask.

"There's an escape route inside the palace that leads to a launch pad. The king's already on his way there."

Our car slams to a stop at the fancy courtyard in front of the palace's front doors.

"Move, move, move!" one of the soldiers shouts as we exit the vehicle. And now I understand; wherever this exit is, we're not nearly close enough to it.

A black cloud of smoke rises to my left, where a third of the palace lies in smoldering ruins.

I sprint towards the entrance of the palace, shielded by a cluster of guards. Behind us I can hear gunfire. The soldier next to me grunts and grabs his arm. A man to my left goes down.

This all has an eerie sense of déjà vu to it. There's even a good possibility that those shooting at us will avoid hitting me. Political figures tend to have higher currency alive rather than dead.

Though I doubt it'll do me any good surviving this if the enemy captures me. Torture, humiliation, and a slow death likely wait at their hands.

We burst through the front door. Inside, plumes of smoke and dust hover in the air.

At our backs a car screeches to a halt and car doors slam. They're practically nipping at our heels.

I still have the guard's gun, and I can't help swinging around and firing off a shot. My bullet hits a Resistance fighter square in the chest.

Finally made one goddamn mark.

"Come on, my queen." Hands are on me, dragging me back.

I rotate around and begin running again. "Where to?" I shout.

"Montes's map room."

"Is the king still alive?" I ask. I hate the way my pulse jumps when I ask the question. I've been trying to shove him out of my mind. Worrying can sabotage a soldier so quickly. In my experience, the harder you think about your fears, the likelier they are to manifest themselves.

"Aye," one of them says.

Relief courses through me. I've gone from wanting the man to die in the worst possible way to fearing for his safety. I'm sure there's some unhealthy explanation for this, but I am also far beyond caring. I'm a recovering monster that cares about another soulless creature.

Behind us I hear shouts, gunshots, and the sound of shattering objects. Anything that the king once held sacred is likely getting desecrated.

"There she is! I see the queen!" someone yells on the other end of the hall.

The soldiers tighten their guard around me. "Keep moving!" one of them shouts even as bullets begin to spray. "We're almost there!" I sense rather than see the soldier at my back go down. The tight circle around me shifts to close the space.

We take a sharp turn and the firing stops. The silence is a welcome relief until I hear the sickeningly familiar sound of an object clattering against the floor behind us.

"Grenade!" I shout.

My men shove me to the ground. I split my lip at the impact, but I don't register the pain before the grenade goes off. I feel the heat on my back, hear the yells and groans of the men who've taken the hit, breathe in the smoldering air.

My leg burns, but that's it.

The Resistance soldiers are already moving—I can hear their footfalls—and most of the soldiers that surround me are still.

I can tell the men above me are dead. I roll their bloodied bodies off me. Something sharp lodges itself in my throat at their instantaneous decision to cover me; they surely knew they were sacrificing themselves.

"Anyone alive?" I shout.

"Aye," comes a pained voice beside me. Someone else grunts.

The survivors—two currently—are working their way out of the dog pile. None of us have any hope of escape unless we can get to that launch pad.

Pulling a gun out of one of the unquestionably dead men, I rise to a knee.

The Resistance fighters are already closing in on me, but all I see are targets— heads, hearts. I aim, fire, and move on to the next target. Rinse and repeat.

I'm in my element. Anger and aggression flood through my veins. I hit four soldiers before they get wise to my ways, and one shoots my arm. I scream as the bullet rips through skin and muscle.

Fuck that hurts.

I fire back before the shooter can clip me again. My aim's off, and the slug buries itself into the wall instead of his heart. Behind me I hear another gun go off and a Resistance soldier falls.

I can't turn, but I know it's one of my surviving guards. I rise to my feet and back up towards him. Before I reach him, his head whips back. I see blood and bone spray onto the walls and floor around him. He's gone.

I empty my gun and two of the three remaining men go down. The final man left standing reaches for his radio as I grope around for another weapon.

I feel like a grave robber as I lift a gun off a dead body. People who've never seen action think there's something honorable in this—giving your life for a higher cause. This moment is proof that the human spirit is capable of nothing baser than war. The indignity of death. The desperation and apathy. I've been raised on it, but even I grasp the horror of it all.

I swivel and point the gun, but the Resistance member is gone, likely getting backup before he comes at me again. I push myself to my feet, hissing in a breath as I put weight on my scorched leg.

"Anyone alive?" I call out.

No one answers back. The second soldier who'd called out to me earlier must've died during the shootout.

I waste several seconds grabbing another gun and shoving it down the small of my back.

Move, I command my broken body. I have no idea where the king's map room is in this palace of his. I only saw the one in Geneva. And without a clear destination, I'm essentially a fly caught in the spider's web.

I limp down the hall, towards the first door I see. I doubt it leads to some promising destination, but I open it anyway and peek inside. Guest room. Not promising. I continue on.

I can hear shouting in the distance and those damn footfalls that herald another wave of Resistance fighters.

Hitting the end of the hall, I glance to my left and to my right. The walls have caved in one direction. I've hit the edge of the destruction. In the other direction dust is still settling from the blast.

One of the soldiers had said we were close, and this hall looks vaguely familiar. I might be able to find the exit on my own.

A moment later as I move down the remaining corridor, I spot the door to the king's conference room. The king's map room must be close by. Hope flares up in me. I hurry down the hall until I come across a door that looks like it leads to an important room. I try the door. Locked.

The footsteps are getting closer. No time to waste at this point. This is my only option. As soon as I step back to gun down the door, I hear voices on the other side.

I think I've found the map room. And here I thought I had the world's worst luck.

"Help!" I scream and begin to pound on the door. "It's the queen!"

I've got seconds left to get inside; otherwise, I'm as good as dead.

The door opens just as Resistance fighters turn down onto the hall. I level my gun and begin firing at them.

"Your Majesty!"

"Serenity!" The king's voice rises above the fray. What is he still doing in the palace? He should be gone by now.

Someone grabs me around the waist and drags me inside the room, and I suck in air through my teeth as my injured arm is jostled. The door slams shut, and I'm surrounded by the king's soldiers.

"Can you walk?" one asks.

I groan. "Yeah, but not quickly."

The king pushes through his men and comes to my side. His hands don't know where to touch me, so he settles on my face.

No words are exchanged. They're not needed. I can see relief mingling with panic. And then he kisses me.

It's cut short by banging on the door. The door shudders. Several of the king's soldiers hang back to watch the room's entrance. It won't hold for long now that the Resistance saw me enter.

I'm assisted to a blast door propped open at the back of the room. I've seen these before, I know that once this door closes, there will be no getting it back open. Beyond it I can see a sleek passageway; I'm sure this is the escape route the soldier mentioned earlier.

Outside the room, the muffled pounding of footsteps lessens. Not a good sign.

The king's men lead him through the escape passage first. Marco stands to the side, waiting to follow us in. I notice something in his hand, but I never get a good look at it. Behind me I hear a muffled clink of a heavy object out in the hallway.

"Grena—!" My words are cut off by the explosion.

My body's thrown forward, right into Marco. The two of us fall in a tangle of limbs just outside the passage entrance. A plume of ash and dust obscures the room, but I can hear the tread of feet.

"Close the door!" Marco shouts.

The king roars something in response, but it's cut off by the slam of the blast door. The sound is a death knell; there will be no escaping now. Once again, the king's been shuffled away while I remain in the fray, this time with Marco, one of the men I revile most in the world.

I scramble to get up when Marco's hand presses me back down into the floor.

My gaze flicks to his. "Get the fuck off of—"

The side of Marco's fist slams down against my chest, and I choke on my words. A sharp, burning pain punctures my heart. I can't make sense of it until Marco withdraws his fist, and with it, an empty syringe.

"What've you done?" I ask, drawing in a ragged breath and touching my chest.

Shots are fired on the other end of the room, and I have no idea who's killing whom.

"It's a serum to make you forget."

My eyes widen in surprise. Those dazed technicians, that article on memory suppression—I'm staring down the terrible invention behind it all.

"The king's told you his secrets," Marco explains. "They'll torture them out of you unless they're not there."

"You bastard," I whisper. My memory is all I have left. I'll forget who I am, where I came from. I'll forget my father, my mother, my entire life.

I want to scratch the liquid out of me.

"The king possesses an antidote. It's reversible."

I huff at that. "Like that's going to do me a lot of good if I can't remember the king."

The sounds of gunfire are getting closer.

"He'll find you. Trust me, he will."

Marco rolls off me and pulls out a gun.

My breath catches. "What are you doing?" I ask, scrambling to sit up.

He clicks off the safety. "I only had one vial."

Marco doesn't hesitate. He places the gun barrel against his temple and fires. Blood and viscous things hit me.

And that is the end of Marco. For only a moment I find it strangely poetic that my father and my father's killer both died from the same wound. Then the thought is whisked away from me.

I try to snatch it again, but it's somewhere beyond my reach.

The serum is already working.

I press the back of my bloodied hand to my mouth. Whatever he gave me, it's puncturing holes in my memory almost at random. I remember entering this room, but not how I got here.

In the next breath I can't remember the name of the dead man in front of me, only that I hated him. The memory should scare me, but it just serves to piss me off.

I grab the dead man's gun and the one shoved down the small of my back and begin to shoot the encroaching militants. I'm not even positive who they are, or what they want, but they're approaching me like an enemy would.

My guns click empty, and I throw them as hard as I can at some of my attackers. I clip one and miss another.

Now I'm weaponless and I can't remember how I got here.

A handful of guns are trained on me, but they're not shooting. *Death is better than whatever they have in store.* I know this on some deep, instinctual level.

As soon as they come within range, I kick out at one and slam my fist into another. A man tackles me to the ground and yanks my wrists behind me. The movement tugs at my injuries and I scream out.

"Shut up," he growls.

"Fuck you."

He takes a fistful of my hair and smashes my head into the ground.

Once my wrists are bound, a black bag is dragged over my head, and the world goes dark.

I'm pulled up to my feet and led out of the room, and the men who've captured me start barking out questions I don't have answers for. Questions they expect answers to.

"Where is the king?"

"Why did you betray your country?"

"How do you kill the king?"

When I don't respond, they begin hitting my injuries until my body simply gives out and they have to drag me away.

I'm bound and blinded, but those are not nearly so constricting as the confusion running rampant in my head.

There are only a handful of things I understand with complete clarity at the moment: I'm a woman without a past, and these people need to access it. And if I can't remember it soon, I'm going to die a very painful death.

I know I'm someone powerful, someone dangerous. A grim smile tugs at my lips despite my current circumstances. I know I'm not afraid of pain or death. And these men and women? They should be afraid of me. Because whoever I am, I am violent, and I will be having my revenge.

The
QUEEN
TRAITORS of

I LOVE YOU as certain dark things are to be loved, in secret, between the shadow and the soul …
—Pablo   Neruda

CHAPTER 1

SERENITY

CONFUSION.

Am I conscious? Everything's dark.

A moment later, pain flares my body to life. I'm awake, I have to be to acutely feel every inch of throbbing skin.

I grind my teeth together against the agony, but I can't stop the tears that leak from my eyes. I'm lying on my side, my weight pressed against my bad arm, my wrists bound behind my back. If not for the pain, I wouldn't even know I had a bad arm.

I can hear people talking, and I smell oil and steel. But I can't see any of it. Something covers my face. I try to shrug it off with my shoulder, but I don't make any progress.

What's going on?

I search my mind, but there's nothing to grasp onto. I cannot remember a moment before this. What actions led my life here, cuffed and wounded. My past and my identity have been cleaved away, along with my freedom, and I have no idea what any of it means.

The floor dips and rises, and my bodyweight is thrown against my injury. The agony is instant and all-compassing. I can't hold back my gasp, but it cuts off as the pain overwhelms me and my mind shuts down.

I wake off and on to voices, pain, and jostling. I should know what's happening to me, but the explanation is a wil-o'-the-wisp; the more I chase it, the farther away it gets.

My entire existence is a series of shallow breaths drawn from damp, recycled air, my world contained within the bag that covers my head. I do not know my name, the color of my eyes, the shape of my face. Most importantly, I have no idea what's going on.

And now I'm being jerked to my feet, and now we're walking. I hiss in a breath at the pain. My legs can't hold me up. They keep wanting to fold under me, but my captors grip my elbows and force me to remain upright.

I can hear cheering as I'm carted away. A migraine pulses behind my eyes and along my temple, and the noise stirs it.

A crowd must be watching this procession. People begin to boo.

At me, I realize. The entire mass of them are booing at *me*.

Who *am* I?

Something smashes into the side of my head. I stagger, and my headache unfurls the full force of its power. I have to swallow back the bile that rises up in my throat.

"Move!" an angry voice shouts. A booted foot kicks the back of my knee, and I stumble forward.

Beneath the pain and the confusion, anger simmers. My cuffed hands curl into fists. If I wasn't restrained, I'd gladly endure more suffering to land a few good blows on my captors. I'm no helpless thing.

The air cools as I'm directed indoors. That doesn't stop the booing crowd or the objects flung at me. Whatever's happening, I'm supposed to be humiliated. They're wasting their efforts. I'm in far too much pain to care about what they think of me.

This goes on for a while, and I resign myself to enduring this for the time being. It's not until I hear the heavy turn of locks and I'm pushed forward once more, that my situation changes.

Now the noise from the crowd dulls and the thump of dozens of footsteps break away. I can't say how much farther we walk, or how many turns we take. I'm weaving on my feet.

The men holding my arms halt. Ahead of me, locks tumble and then another heavy door creaks open. A tug on my injured arm has me moving forward. We only walk a few steps forward before I'm stopped again. Behind me, the thick thud of a door cuts the last of the sound off completely.

Someone rips the bag from my head, taking some strands of my hair along with it.

The overhead light blinds me, and I squint against it, gnashing my teeth against the new wave of pain behind my temple. I sense more than see the men on either side of me.

I finally breathe in fresh air, and it shakes off a bit of my weariness. The last time air was this crisp ...

I stand in a moat of bloody bodies. Men in dark fatigues creep closer. I don't know who they are, but I know I need to fight them.

The memory's blurry, and I can't be sure it's real.

I blink, my earlier confusion roaring back to life. Why can't I place where I am? Who I am? I know I should remember these things, so why can't I?

And then there are the things that I inexplicably know. The fact, for instance, that I'm in a holding cell. The kind with a one-way mirror. I have no memory of this place or any like it, yet somehow I recognize exactly what it is. A room for prisoners.

That's what I am. I can't say what my crimes are, though I'm obviously someone important. Someone infamous.

As my eyes adjust, I notice three men in uniform standing around me. Soldiers of some sort. They appear wary of me, like I might get violent at any moment.

I think they're wise to be wary.

One of them shoves me to my knees. Roughly, he grabs my bound hands behind my back and unlocks the cuffs. Pain slices through my arms as they're released and sensation flows back into them.

I pivot on my knees, primed for attack. I may not know what's going on, but I have muscle memory, and it's leading me now.

I lunge for the nearest of my captors. Clumsily my arms wrap around his calves as I slam into him, and God, does my injured arm burn. The pain almost stops me. Almost.

He loses his balance and falls. Not good for him.

My instincts are directing me. Before he can recover, I move up his body and slam the fist of my good arm into his temple. Again and again.

I was right. It is absolutely worth every bit of agony to pummel one of these men.

Just as quickly as I find myself on my captor, I'm dragged off of him by the other two. The entire time they curse at me.

Like I actually give a shit.

I struggle against them, and even injured as I am, I still manage to slip their hold. One tackles me to the ground. "Your gun, man, your gun!" he shouts to his comrade.

I don't understand the order until I see the hilt of some military grade weapon raised above me. The butt of it slams into my temple, and I'm out cold once more.

WHEN I COME to, I'm cuffed to a chair in my cell. Across the table I sit at, an enemy soldier watches me with obvious disgust. That one-way mirror looms behind him. Someone's watching us. I can practically feel their eyes on me.

I catch sight of myself in the mirror. It's brief, just a flash of blood-matted hair and skin that looks more like overripe fruit.

I can taste blood in my mouth, and a tooth is loose. I don't think I have a concussion, but that's sheer luck. They hit me hard and repeatedly.

A chill slithers up my spine. Perhaps I already have a concussion, and that's why I can't remember anything about myself.

Standing guard next to the door of my cell is another soldier, a military-grade rifle in his hand. His finger loosely cradles the trigger. I can read nothing from his face. That, more than anything, convinces me that if I so much as flinch the wrong way, he'll shoot me.

Looks like my situation just went from bad to worse.

"I'm Lieutenant Begbie. Do you know why you're here?" The man across from me wears dark fatigues, and he has a gristly look about him, like he's held together mostly by sinew and anger.

"You want answers from me," I say.

"Yes, ma'am." He settles a bit more into his chair. "And you're going to give them to us."

"And if I don't?" But it's not *if*, it's *when.*

Begbie studies me, sucking on his teeth while he does so. "We're going to try this the civilized way first. If you answer our questions, we won't use force to get them out of you."

I raise an eyebrow, even though my heart pounds like mad. Torture.

"We'll start off easy. Tell me your full name."

I can feel the burn of the cuffs on my wrist, rubbing my skin raw. My body is a mass of wounds, and my head feels as though it's ready to split open. These are all injuries this man and his people gave me. Perhaps this little tasting of their wares is supposed to scare me.

I don't feel scared. And I don't feel very talkative.

But I am angry. I'm very angry.

"What's your name?" he repeats.

I lean to the side and spit out blood. Answer enough.

My interrogator's scowl only deepens.

The door to my cell opens, and angry voices from the hall trickle in.

"—I don't give a damn. I need to see her for myself."

My eyes flick to the man that enters.

Old, strong, his hair cropped close to his head. His features are hard, even his eyes. A man used to making tough decisions. I can already tell he'll show me no more kindness than the rest of them.

"Serenity," he says to me, "what happened to him?"

Serenity—is this my name? It doesn't sound like a name.

I stare at him curiously. Does this man know me?

"Kline." Begbie says the word—another name perhaps—like a warning.

The older man stalks across the room and leans over me. An intense pair of blue eyes fix on mine, and I see a mixture of anger and grief in them. "What did you and the king do to him?"

He rests his hands on the metal backing of my chair and shakes it to emphasize his point.

Air hisses out of me as the movement jostles my already screaming gunshot wound. The headache that's been pounding behind my temple pulsates with pain.

"For the love of Christ, Serenity, what did you do to my son? I want to hear you say it."

This man might know me, but he's no friend of mine.

"General," Begbie rounds the table and grabs the man's upper arm, "that's enough. We're in the middle of an interrogation."

The general—I assume this is a title—shrugs off Begbie's grip and gives a jerky nod, his gaze trained on my face.

"Get her to talk," he says. And then he turns on his heel and stalks out of the room, the door slamming shut behind him.

I stare at the space he took up. Whoever that man was, I did something to his son—me and this king they keep asking about—something that broke a hardened man.

I search the empty halls of my mind for a memory—even just a fragment of one. Nothing comes to mind. And now I have the general's cryptic words to add to my already addled state. The whole thing makes me weary.

I'm injured, locked up like the world's deadliest criminal, and being questioned about a past I can't remember. They're going to torture me, then kill me, and at the end of it all I'll have no idea why. It seems so pointless.

My interviewer runs a hand over his cropped hair. "Why don't we start where we left off?"

"What do you really want to know?" I ask, leaning back into my seat.

There's no use in me stalling. Torture's coming, either way.

"Where is the king?" the man across from me asks.

This mysterious king whom I can't recall. I must work for him. It makes sense.

"I don't know," I say, still distracted by my own thoughts.

My interviewer leans forward. "Surely you know where he would go."

"Maybe," I hedge, shifting my weight as the injury on my calf begins to burn. The movement causes the pain in my arm to flare up.

Would it be wise to reveal how little I know?

Begbie must read my expression because he says, "If you're not going to cooperate, Serenity, then we'll force the answers out of you."

Serenity must be my name.

"That I'm well aware of," I say.

My reflection catches my attention once more, and I shift my eyes away from Begbie. Aside from the bruises that cover my face, and I have a deep scar that runs from the corner of my eye down my cheek.

I look ... sinister. And hardened. Oddly enough, that gives me courage.

Begbie tries again. "What do you believe you're worth to the king?"

"I don't know."

The Lieutenant leans back in his seat and studies me. "Alright," he finally drawls, coming to some sort of decision, "what locations in the WUN do you believe the king will select for his armories?"

"I don't know."

Begbie touches his lips with two fingers; he taps one of them against his mouth as he watches me. I know he's trying to figure out the best way to crack me.

"I don't want to hurt you, Serenity," he says, "I really don't, but you have to give me information for this to work."

Contrary to his words, this man wants to hurt me very, very badly.

We stare each other down. I'm going to be killed either way, and that knowledge settles on my shoulders like a cloak. Whatever else happens, my words won't get me out of here.

He leans forward in his chair, his hand coming to rest on the table. "What *do* you know?"

This is one question I can answer.

"That my name is Serenity, and my memory is gone."

CHAPTER 2

LIEUTENANT BEGBIE ENDS the interview shortly after my admission, promising me "advanced interrogation techniques" if I can't come up with answers soon.

Suffice it to say, the man doesn't believe me.

After he finishes questioning me, he unlocks my cuffs, and this time I'm wise enough not to attack. The guard with the assault rifle looks ready and willing to use it. If I want to rebel, today won't be the day.

I make note of the fact that the lieutenant has a gun holstered to his hip, and he likely has another weapon somewhere on his person.

If what I know won't save me, then my actions must. I'm going to have to hurt people to leave this place.

That should bother me more than it does. I add heartlessness to my growing list of character traits.

Until then, I'll bide my time and figure out what, exactly, is wrong with my mind. Specifically, why I don't know who I am.

Once Begbie and the guard leave, I lean against the cement wall of my cell, my legs bent in front of me. I rub my wrists.

I haven't changed clothes since my capture. I wear black leather boots, fitted pants, and a crimson shirt.

At least, these were the original colors I wore. Blood and dust now cake them. My outfit's ripped in several locations, and the back of one boot's burned away. I can't remember how I got this way, which makes my past all the more intriguing.

I finger the material of my shirt. I have nothing to compare it to, but its softness, weave, and saturated color all scream *wealth*.

While I'd been unconscious, someone cut away the fabric covering my injured arm and leg. Gauze covers both wounds; these enemy soldiers went to the trouble of patching me up. I'd assume it was a small kindness, but after seeing the way they've treated me, they probably just wanted to make sure I live long enough to be of use to them.

Eventually I'll need to check the wounds and let them breathe. Even if they were tended by combat medics, staunching the blood flow and wrapping a wound up is no permanent remedy.

How do I know any of this?

I'm still absently rubbing the material of my shirt when light glints off my hand. My body stills as I hold it up.

I don't know which surprises me more: that I'm wearing jewelry, or that my captors haven't yet confiscated it.

If I'm someone important, they will eventually. Another truth I inexplicably know.

I study the two rings that adorn my hand. One is a band of yellow diamonds. Expensive. The other is a polished piece of lapis lazuli. Tiny flakes of gold shimmer amongst the dark blue of the stone, reminding me of the night sky. This one doesn't seem so expensive, but meaningful perhaps.

My heart thumps loudly in my chest.

I'm married.

I let that sink in. I don't think I like that. Even without the aid of memories, there's something constricting about the prospect.

Still, that means someone's missing me right now.

Around my rings, the skin is scarred—particularly my knuckles. Apparently the guard wasn't the first face these fists have dug into. My hands, however, are free of even the hint of wrinkles.

I add up what I know: I'm young, female—I gleaned that much from the mirror—married, dangerous, and valuable to these people's cause.

It's an unlikely combination.

Who am I to be so young and so experienced in the darker deeds of men?

I hold my hand up again, letting the rings catch the light.

And what kind of man would marry a woman like me?

TIME TICKS BY slowly in this place. No one's come for me again, but they will.

I lean my head back against the cool cement wall and close my eyes.

I'm at the back of the room. Cornered. Enemy soldiers creep closer to me. Between us, bloody men and women lay unmoving.

This is the first memory I have, and it's a struggle to hold onto it. I try to focus on the wounds of the fallen, but my mind won't give up those details.

The hiss of scraping metal snaps my eyes open. A tray slides through the slot at the bottom of my cell's door. Those crafty soldiers use the end of a broom to push it through; by now they've figured out that I'll take out a finger or two if given the chance.

I'm not a very nice person. I wonder if that's the result of nature or nurture.

My stomach cramps painfully as I stare at the food, and only then do I realize just how hungry I am. Adrenaline and pain had distracted me up until now.

I get up and grab the tray. The sight of the food tempers my appetite somewhat. If I were less hungry, perhaps I'd simply skip the meal. Instead I pick up the plastic utensil and try what can only be described as gruel.

It's over salted, and the more I eat, the queasier I get.

I set the food aside and steady my breathing. I'm all right, just a little too battle worn. It doesn't help that my arm wound pounds like it has its own pulse.

The memory of those dead bodies flash through my mind again, only now, when I don't bid it, do I see their injuries in all their gruesome detail.

I barely reach the toilet in time.

My entire body shakes as I vomit, and all the awful food I just forced down leaves my system. I feel weak, so weak, as I hunch over the toilet bowl. My stomach didn't just purge itself of food. There's blood in the mix as well.

From my injuries?

Behind me, the door creaks open. I don't bother glancing back. I'm too tired to defend myself, and I've already accepted the fact that torture will come. If it's right now, then there's not much I can do about it.

Instead, a chair scrapes back. Someone's taken to watching me.

"You're sick."

I recognize the voice. It belongs to the general, the man who knows me.

I'm not surprised he's come back, but I am surprised at the shift in his temperament. His voice even has a modicum of control to it.

Experience that I can't remember tells me not to trust his calmness. There's always a calm before a storm.

I reach a hand up to flush the toilet, then drag myself to the wall, leaning my back against it. I'm sweating, either from sickness, like the general mentioned, or my injuries.

"I hadn't realized ..." the general starts, taking me in. "When you were sick before, we assumed you and my son ..." He lets the sentence trail off. His Adam's apple bobs.

I try to process all that he is and isn't saying. Apparently this nausea is more than just fatigue, and the general's known me long enough to have some insight into this. More surprising, this man who opposes the king is father to a man I was once close to.

"Will?" I ask, remembering the name he threw out at me yesterday. There's something downright spooky about learning of a relationship and having no recollection of it.

The general bows his head and nods.

I'm afraid to ask what happened to Will. Afraid of what else this man knows about us.

"You really don't remember who you are?" he asks.

I stare at the rings on my left hand. "No."

I am a woman unmade. Something of skin and meat and bone and consciousness, but not a person, not in the truest sense. I have no opinions, no past, no identity. It's been stripped from me. And even here I can feel the wrongness of it.

"That bastard," the general whispers.

I glance up at him. All the earlier heat in his expression is gone. Now he just looks old and defeated.

He studies me, something like pity softening those hard features. "Our sources believed he'd been working on a memory suppressant. Never thought he'd turn it on you."

A memory suppressant. So that's why I lack an identity. Someone deliberately erased my memory—the king, if the general is to be believed.

He could be lying. About everything. For all I know this entire situation was concocted for some purpose I'm unaware of.

"Who are you?" I ask.

"I'm the former general of the Western United Nations—the WUN." He says this as though it should ring a bell. It doesn't.

"Who am I?" I ask.

"You were our former emissary."

Past tense.

"But I am no longer?" The cell is proof of that. Still, I want to know what changed between then and now.

The general rubs his face.

"No, Serenity," he sighs out. "No."

White whiskers grow along his cheeks and jaw. He doesn't strike me as a man who forgets to shave. Everything about him screams defeat, despite the fact that once he's done here, he'll be the one walking out that door a free man.

"What happened?" I ask.

I don't think he's going to answer me. I'm stepping out of line, the prisoner asking questions of her captor. But then he does speak. "The WUN surrendered to the Eastern Empire and you were part of the collateral."

I furrow my brows. What he says makes no sense.

"It's my fault," he admits, leaning forward in his seat. He threads his hands together and rests them between his legs. "I made the call to give you to King Lazuli."

Lazuli, like the stone on my finger. My stomach drops.

"'Give'?" He makes it sound as though I was nothing more than a commodity. Little more than what I am now—a means to an end for these people.

"It was the only way," the general says. He's pleading with me, and I can tell this long ago decision cost him. "The king was prepared to rip apart the WUN. You were the only bargaining chip we had, and God, he wanted you so badly. He was willing to give us everything we wanted."

Bile rises up in my throat again, and I swallow it back down.

"Why did he want me?"

He bows his head, staring at his clasped hands. "You left ... quite the impression when you and your father negotiated the terms of our nation's surrender."

"So you gave me to him ... in return for peace?" I say, making sense of his words.

He rubs his eyes. "Yes, I did."

Outrage flares up in me. I may not recall this decision, but I had to live through it at some point. This general offered me to our enemy. Never mind that it saved countless other lives. This was the same man I must've worked with—whose son I had some sort of relationship with—and yet he threw me to the wolves.

I stare at my ring as an even more terrifying idea takes form. "I don't work for the king, do I?"

The general sighs and meets my eyes. "No, Serenity, you don't work for the king. You're married to him."

CHAPTER 3

SERENITY

GIVEN TO THE king like a war prize.

"Do I love him?"

The general squints at me. "He killed your parents, razed your hometown, and if that sickness is what I suspect it is," he nods to the toilet, "then you have him to thank for it as well. No, I don't think you love him, but I do believe he's poisoned your mind."

I frown. This story is getting more and more twisted and harder for me to believe. This king sounds like the devil. Yet here I am, prisoner to the very people whose side I once fought on. I have to be missing something. No matter how heartless I might be, one doesn't go from hate to love or swap loyalties without a good cause.

"Why would I marry him?"

"You were forced to."

To be married to my parents' killer … a shudder works its way through me. I may be heartless, but even I don't deserve that kind of fate.

"Who are these people?" I glance at the one-way mirror.

"They're the last soldiers willing to fight the king. The world is now controlled entirely by him. The Resistance and other grassroots organizations are the only ones that stand in his way. Us and you."

Someone knocks on the door, and the general stands.

He hesitates, then says, "Perhaps it would do to take you outside and show what your husband has done to our world."

I raise my eyebrows. "I've never heard of a prisoner getting that type of privilege." Not that I've heard much of anything since my memory was wiped. It's a mystery how I know what a typical prisoner's experience should be, and the source of the knowledge left no maker's mark.

"You're not a typical prisoner," the general says. "For better or worse, you're the queen of this entire rock."

He pauses at the door. "No one here is going to torture you. Not if I can help it. But the reality of your situation is that your life is no longer in your control."

"Was it ever?" I ask, searching his eyes.

I genuinely want to know. Did I choose to do wrong by these people, or was I forced into it? The distinction matters.

The general hesitates. "No," he finally says, "it wasn't."

I FIND I miss the general once he leaves. I don't want to miss him. I have no illusions that he likes me, and by the end of our discussion, I'm not so sure I like him all that much either.

However, he knows me, and he's been civil enough, which is more than I can say about the rest of my captors.

I begin moving around the room.

Blanket, bed, wall, ceiling, floor. Rings, shirt, pants, shoes. The names of each item come without hesitation, but I have no memories to attach to each of them.

I move onto current events. Here I brush up against a barrier. Part of me wants to say that the world is suffering. Food's scarce, land's contaminated, war's prevalent. I don't know how much of this is me guessing from the snippets I've heard and how much is actual knowledge.

What year is it? I begin to pin dates to historic events. The 1700s, 1800s, and 1900s are all distinct enough from the present that I can write them off as the past. But the 2000s ... my knowledge of this century is muddled, and when I think of 2100s and later, I can't conjure anything. I actually huff out at a laugh. I've narrowed the year down—give or take a century or so.

I know what people look like, but I can't picture up anyone I know besides Lieutenant Begbie and the general. My head begins to pound from the effort.

I don't have a concussion after all, at least not one responsible for my staggering memory loss. The king did this.

The king, my husband. A man willing to tear apart the world to satisfy his own need for power, a man who forced me into marriage. This is not a man fit to rule over others. This is not a man fit for anything, really, except a swift, bloody death.

It's not until much, much later that anyone returns. By then I'm dozing on the thin mattress. The door to my cell opens, and Lieutenant Begbie enters, followed by a soldier.

I shiver as I'm roused awake. This type of chill comes from the inside out. I know without looking that my arm wound is worsening.

"'Morning," he opens.

I swing my feet out of bed and bite back a groan. Movement's agonizing. I roll my shoulders, crack my neck, and push the pain back. I can lick my wounds later.

Begbie rounds the interview table in my cell and takes a seat. The table's bolted to the floor, but the chairs aren't.

I've already considered everything in this room as a potential weapon. The sheets can choke, the chairs can bludgeon, my pillow can smother. Those types of deaths require intimacy and strength, neither of which I have at the moment. Hence, I've taken to assessing the soldiers that come into the room.

This time they pulled in a greenie to guard the door. I can see it in his jaw; he's forcing himself to look stoic. The more experienced soldiers don't have to force anything. They've seen and done it all, and if it hasn't broken their mind or their will, they become a whole new type of lethal, and sometimes they'll let you see the emptiness in their eyes.

This soldier's eyes are not empty, despite all his valiant efforts. I tear my gaze away from him before either he or Begbie notice my interest.

"We're in negotiations with the king at the moment," Begbie says.

The king. I don't want any part of his madness.

I take a seat across from Begbie. "He knows I'm here?"

"The way I see it, I'm the only one who should be asking questions."

Begbie leans back in his seat and folds his arms, getting real comfortable. "There's a rumor out there that the king is immortal, that he can't die. We have a clip of the king getting shot in the heart. Another of a grenade clipping him. Both were killing blows, but that fucker is still alive."

The general never mentioned this. Despite myself, the hairs on my arms rise. Memory wipe or no, I'm pretty sure immortality is impossible.

"He's responsible for the deaths of your friends and family, he's taken over your country, and he wants you back. If the rumors are true, you do realize there's no killing him, don't you? You'll have to live with him, the man responsible for the death of your countrymen, and he'll want things from you—sex among them.

"You'll continue to be dubbed a traitor, all while sleeping with your parents' killer. And, frankly, I don't see any end in sight for you."

I'm glaring at Begbie, though my vitriol is not aimed at him. Not really.

I don't believe him, however. Not entirely. The king may have killed my family, defeated nations, taken my memory and forced my hand in marriage, but I don't believe he's figured out the riddle to immortality.

I lean forward. "You're wrong, Lieutenant. Everything can die."

Love, hate. Even kings.

BEFORE HE HAS time to respond, a soldier cracks open the door and leans in. "Get the prisoner ready."

Lieutenant Begbie stands. "Put your hands behind your back," he orders me.

I could escape now. By the time the lieutenant figured out my motives, it would be too late. I'd steal that gun holstered to his side. I'd gamble the greenie wouldn't shoot me before I got a chance to fire at him.

I could do it, there's a confidence to my assessment and I already know I have the muscle memory. Yet every fiber of my being recoils from the thought. Whatever else, I'm not a monster by design.

Just necessity.

"Put your hands behind your back," Begbie says more forcefully.

I've missed my opportunity.

I do so, and he cuffs me rougher than needed. I run my tongue over my teeth, clenching my jaw as my raw wrists and my bullet wound sting. It doesn't help that the lieutenant jerks me up.

Pain is a warm companion. I must've known it quite well before today, whether at the hands of the WUN or the king. Probably both. It seems like they're two sides of the same coin.

Begbie and the soldier escort me out of the cell, and I get my first good look at the outside of my prison. More cement walls and fluorescent lights. No windows.

"Where are we going?"

No one answers me.

I might be walking to my death. Or to an interrogation chamber, the kind that leaves behind teeth and bloodstains. Now I know why I was so ready to kill, despite my disgust. Being soft doesn't save you in this place. Power does, fear does, and pain does.

If I have the chance to act again, I won't hesitate.

THEY MARCH ME down the narrow corridor. We make several turns, and I memorize each one. The drabness of this prison doesn't exactly change, but the atmosphere does. An increasing number of people wander the halls. When their eyes land on me, I see them react. Sometimes it's just recognition, other times it's fear or anger or pity.

They know of me.

What had I been expecting? I am the king's wife. Likely a public figure.

We stop in front of a door, and on the other side I can hear murmurs.

An execution, then. Torture doesn't require so many people, I think.

Only, when they open the door, my presumptions melt away. In front of me rests a camera and a chair, the latter currently occupied by a soldier.

But that is not what captures my attention.

At the back of the room is a large screen. My breath catches when my eyes land on it, and suddenly my pulse is in my ears.

The soldier sitting in front of the camera turns, then stands when he sees us. My guards march me forward and force me into the relinquished seat.

The entire time I stare at the man whose face takes up the screen.

I expected an abomination.

Not *this*.

Evil is supposed to be ugly, but he isn't ugly. In fact, this man—my *husband*, if my assumption's correct—is more than just a little pleasing to stare at.

Unlined, olive skin, dark hair brushed back from his face, a strong, straight nose, eyes that draw you in, and a mouth that promises secrets and slow seduction. Was that why I married him? God, I hope not. I don't want to know who I was if that were the reason.

My heart thumps faster. He is gorgeous, but it's not his looks that have moved me.

I recognize myself in his eyes. Even as fogged as my mind is, even as unaware of my past as I am, something about him resonates deep within me. I don't know what it is I feel or what it means, but already I can no longer think of him objectively.

"Serenity." He doesn't say my name the same way my captors do, like I'm the scourge of the earth. He says it like we're lovers.

We *are* lovers.

He wants me back. I can read it plainly on his face, in the way his pupils dilate. This is the man they all fear and hate. A man, if they're to be believed, that *I* fear and hate.

"King Lazuli," I return.

Why would he want me back, this man who's so willing to ruin my life?

"Montes," he corrects. I get the impression he's done that before—corrected me.

His gaze scours my face, and I realize his cool exterior is hiding a well of emotions. A vein in his temple pulses. "What've they done to you?"

This abomination of a human being *cares* about me. It doesn't add up with what I've learned of him.

And now, one wrong word and this house of cards will tumble. That's the kind of power I sense I wield, being the king's wife. He'll kill them all, and unlike me, he'll enjoy it thoroughly.

"I'm okay."

His jaw clenches ever so slightly. That and the throbbing vein are the only signs he feels. The king's tells are subtle, but I'm still shocked at how genuine his emotions towards me are. Whoever Montes Lazuli is, at the moment he's more man than nightmare.

Odd that right now, of the two of us, I am the colder one. My heart is made of steel and ice and I cannot muster emotion to match his.

"I'm going to get you out of there," he says. "You need to stay alive for me."

I can't go back to him. I can't. He has power over me, power that has nothing to do with pain and punishment. I'm enthralled by him, and considering the way he tracks my every movement through the screen, the feeling seems mutual.

"Time's up," someone calls. "We've proven she's alive."

"Alive and injured," the king says. A dozen threats lace his voice. I fear that if I live long enough, I'll see each one of them carried out.

At my back, several soldiers approach. I take in the handsome man on the other side of the screen a final time. "Whoever you are, I hope you were worth it." After all, torture and death are still on the table for me. I hope the Serenity who had a past was satisfied with it.

They drag me away after that.

"Serenity! Wait—" I can hear him at my back, his voice rising as he shouts at whoever will listen that he isn't finished talking with me.

Yes, my husband wants me back, and he'll guard me like a dragon does its treasure. I doubt very much that I'll enjoy that kind of protection.

An ache starts up in my chest as I stride back to my cell. I'm trapped between the king's wishes and this organization's, and there's no room for my own. As the ache grows, I realize it isn't fear or sadness.

It's rage.

Other people got me into this mess; they're not going to get me out of it. I will.

And I *will* get myself out of it, or I'll die trying.

CHAPTER 4

SERENITY

INFECTION'S BEGINNING TO set in.

My hands shake as I unravel the gauze over my arm. A shiver racks my body. I need to see just how bad it is, but I don't want to. My skin's already swollen above and below the bandages. It won't be pretty.

I hear nothing from outside the walls of my prison. If soldiers are watching, they've decided not to interfere.

My eyes burn, and as I remove layer after layer, I can tell I'm worse off than I thought I was. A foul smell emanates from my bandages, and it gets stronger the more I unwind.

The last layer of gauze is the worst. The material's fused to the wound. I clench my jaw as I peel it away. The pain blazes so brightly my vision clouds. I can't stop the agonized cry that slips out. My breath comes out in pants. Sweat beads along my forehead. With a final tug, I remove the last of the bandages.

I'd prepared myself for the savage sight of my injury, but it's still hard to look at. Blood and puss cover the wound. The dirty skin around it is so swollen it looks ready to burst.

Reaching over to the untouched tray of food I received a short while ago, I grab the cup of water. Taking a fortifying breath, I pour it over the wound.

As soon as the first drop hits my skin, the pain explodes. My teeth are tightly clenched, so my cry escapes as a hiss of air. My vision clouds again, and I'm blind for a couple seconds as I fight to stay conscious.

The empty cup slips from my hand, and I spend the next several minutes shivering and clutching my arm to my chest.

In the hallway outside my cell, I hear raised voices. They sound panicked, and they're getting closer.

Don't let the enemy see your weaknesses.

I need to rewrap my arm. The thought tightens my stomach.

Reluctantly I crawl over to the discarded bandages. Using my teeth, I rip off the soiled section of cloth. The agony's even worse this time around, so bad that I have to pause twice to vomit. The wound doesn't want to be bound, and my cheeks are wet by the time I'm tying the knot.

BOOM!

The earth quakes, and I nearly fall on my injured arm. I brace myself against the wall. I glance above me.

The voices in the hall turn to shouts.

BOOM!

The door to my cell opens. A soldier runs in and grabs me, cursing the entire time. I scream as he squeezes my injured arm. Before I consciously decide to hit him, my good arm shoots out and slams into his nose. I hear it crunch, and he cries out, releasing me to clutch at it.

The time for compliance has long since run out. If I don't want to die in this prison, now's my chance.

While he's distracted, I grab his gun from its holster. Flicking off the safety, I cock it and shoot him in the thigh. There's no hesitation to my actions. No uncertainty.

He howls, falling to his knees. I watch him dispassionately, and my lack of reaction terrifies me.

As he writhes on the ground, another soldier begins to enter my cell. I clench my jaw against the pain in my arm as I lift the gun and fire. The bullet clips him in the shoulder.

Not only can I injure without remorse, I know how and where to shoot a man without killing him.

I shake my head, more than a little curious just what kind of ball-busting broad I was before I lost my memories.

Before the door can click shut, I force my way out, ignoring the burn of my injuries as I step over the man and push my feverish body into action.

BOOM!

My back crashes against the wall. The fluorescent lights flicker.

Out here I hear shouting and the echo of dozens of pounding footsteps. Somewhere in the distance, rounds of gunfire go off.

A uniformed man runs past. Only after he passes me does he pause to glance back. I point my gun at him.

"Keep moving," I say.

This one is either smarter or less courageous than his comrades because he does.

I need to get out of here before someone decides I'm worth the trouble. I begin to jog, clenching my teeth against the pain in my calf. I hook a right, then a left, following the sounds to their source.

In the chaos, no one I pass stops me, though several of them pause when they recognize my face. The gun in my hand seems to deter them from doing anything more.

BOOM! The screams increase in number and volume.

The lights flicker again. We're going to lose electricity soon. I welcome the possibility. At the moment, I'm too recognizable.

Ahead of me, people herd into a stairwell and from my vantage point, they seem to be descending the stairs. Most, but not all, wear fatigues. I hesitate. Either escape or shelter is down there, but so are my enemies.

Making a spur-of-the-moment decision, I head into the mass of people, keeping my head ducked.

We shuffle into the stairwell, and the current of bodies tries to drag me down the stairs, but I don't want to go down. I want to go up.

It's as I try to extricate myself that I get noticed.

"Hey," a soldier next to me says, bending to peer at me, "are you … ? Shit, it's Queen Lazuli," he says, more to the people around him than to me.

People look over, and the murmurs begin.

"Queen Lazuli." "It's the queen!" "Someone grab her!"

I straighten; no use hiding now that my cover's been blown.

Just as the first hand reaches for me, I raise my good arm in the air, the one holding the gun. I aim it at the bare bulb lighting the stairwell, and then I pull the trigger.

The bulb shatters, and the stairwell goes dark. Around me, the crowd shouts and covers their heads.

"The next one goes in someone's brain!" I yell over the noise.

People fall away from me like I have the plague.

Pushing myself the rest of the way through the crowd, I head upstairs. No one else tries to stop me, too intent on saving their own lives.

The higher I climb, the more distinct the noises of battle become. I can hear shouted orders and the thump of machine gun fire—the kind that's mounted to a vehicle rather than a person. It's louder, you can hear the force of the kickback.

Again, I wonder how I knew that.

I lean heavily on the metal bannister as a series of shivers course through me. My eyes burn. It probably doesn't matter whether I manage to escape or not. I'm pretty bad off. I give myself another day before my fever takes me completely, and then it'll be up to Mother Nature to decide my fate.

The next floor is where the noise is loudest. Ground floor. I brace myself for the onslaught of soldiers, readying my gun, but the only people who enter the stairwell carry injured men, and they have no time for me.

I follow the stairs up two more flights to the top. All's quiet here.

Running on instinct, I slip out.

I understand immediately why no one's here. Building materials, broken furniture, and a couple bloody limbs litter the ground. The floor outside the stairwell slumps, and less than twenty feet away from me, it's crumbled away completely. In several places fires sizzle. I welcome the heat against my feverish skin.

The place got firebombed. No wonder nobody's here.

Beyond the gaping remains of this building, another building smolders across the street, lighting up the dark night. Between the two, I hear more than see the fighting. The air is filled with hazy smoke, and it smells like gunpowder and charred bodies.

Hell has come to earth.

The whine of a jet shakes the building as it swoops by, and I grab a wall for support.

My stomach clenches at the noise, like it knows something I don't.

It does.

When the explosion hits, the sound consumes me. It shrieks across my skin and as my body's thrown back, the last thought I have is that out of all the ways I thought I might die, this one's the most preferable.

I FIGHT AGAINST consciousness. Everything already hurts. I don't want to face it.

My body doesn't give me a choice. I moan as I stir.

I'm on fire. I must be.

The fever's fully set in, and I'm being cooked from the inside out.

I peel my eyes open and lick my chapped lips, tasting soot and plaster on them. Where am I?

Trash and debris litter the ground I lay on. I remember the mad dash I'd made up here and the sounds of fighting.

All's silent now.

The rays of early morning light stream in from the gaping hole, and my throat tightens. It's the most beautiful thing I've seen since I can remember.

I crawl to the edge of what remains of the room, where the floor drops away. I lay directly beneath a beam of that early morning light. It touches my skin and all the depravity of this place can't ruin this moment. I close my eyes as a tear trickles out.

I'm not going to die here. Not amongst my enemies.

I crawl back to the stairwell, grabbing my fallen gun from the debris. I must've dropped it during the explosion. Shakily, I push myself to my feet and tuck the weapon into the small of my back, flicking the safety on.

Everything hurts. God, does it hurt. I won't allow myself to focus on the pain or the unsettling silence.

When I make it to the ground level, nothing stirs. Only the dead live here now.

I make my way towards what must be the front of the building, ignoring several bodies that are slumped against the wall or splayed out along the floor. The bombs missed this section, and the front door ahead of me is still intact.

Only a fool would head towards the carnage, but I'm beyond playing it safe.

I step into the light on shaky legs. I blink away some of the fever-induced haze to take in my surroundings.

The pink rays of dawn touch scattered bodies. Dozens of them. Maybe hundreds. The morning light doesn't seem so peaceful anymore.

It's just like my first memory, only worse. A sea of soldiers surround the building I just exited. All dead. I don't even hear moans or their death throes.

My skin prickles, and I can't say it's from my fever this time.

Someone attacked them so thoroughly that none survived, and none of the living have come to collect them.

The king.

They've been picked off like fish in a barrel. It's not just from the explosions either. Their bodies are riddled with bullets, and some look bloated, their vacant eyes bulging from their sockets.

Snow hits me, tangling in my hair, and I'm distracted from the graveyard of bodies. It's snowing. Only, heated air blows on me like the devil's breath.

I catch a flake in my cupped hands, cradling it like I've captured a butterfly. I open my hands wide enough to peek at my find. It's gray and paper thin.

Not snow. *Ash.*

I glance above me. The sky looks bruised, as do the clouds. And it smells … it smells the way hell should smell. Of sulfur and spent kindling.

My gaze moves from my hands to my feet. Between bodies, piles of the ash swirl like fallen leaves. Up my eyes move. Up, up, until I see mounds of rubble and tilted phone poles. Crumbling streets, some with large sinkholes, stretch off towards the ruins of a city.

My carefully crafted memory never showed me this. It wouldn't know how to string together so many awful sights.

None of the skyscrapers are completely intact. Some looked chewed upon, like a giant creature came, got a taste, and found it lacking. Others look like they're decaying, slowly shedding their sleek chrome exteriors and tinted windows for steel cables and concrete skeletons. One skyscraper looks as though someone took a giant axe to it and felled it like a tree. Its upper half leans against another.

Then there are the gaping holes between some of them, like some of these behemoths have already collapsed.

Do people still live there? What sort of existence must they eek out?

I take a few more steps forward. The sight of this world—my world, the one I don't remember—robs me of breath.

The drone of an engine has me tearing my eyes away from the ruins and towards the sky. In the distance I can make out several aircrafts.

I was wrong to think there was any safety in the silence. The jets are not nearly done with this place. I begin to move, though all I really want is to collapse.

I catch sight of a military vehicle partially buried beneath the rubble. I stumble over to it. As I get closer, I can hear the low purr of an idling engine. The machine gun responsible for the earlier noise is welded to the bed of this vehicle. The body of a soldier slumps over the weapon.

The driver side window is shattered, and when I open the door, another body tumbles out.

I'm numb to the sight of death. I step over the dead soldier without giving him a second glance and hoist myself into the car.

The key's already in the ignition, so all I have to do is shift the car into reverse and press on the gas to get it going. I hear a sick thump as the body in the bed of the vehicle hits the metal wall that separates us. More sick thumps come as I drive over the bodies littering the ground. I white-knuckle the steering wheel as each one jostles my injuries and shakes my unsettled stomach.

My hands tremble, sweat drenches my clothes, and self-preservation alone sustains me. I maneuver the car out of the graveyard, and then I floor it.

The vehicle tears down the street that leads into the city. Wind gusts through the shattered windows, whipping my hair around my face.

I can no longer see the encroaching aircrafts, but there's no way I escaped undetected. The streets I drive are utterly abandoned. I've made myself a target simply by being on them.

Now that I'm free of my captors, I could simply pull over and flag down one of these jets. They're likely the king's. But I have no way of knowing whether they'd recognize me. They might mistake me for an enemy and gun me down.

And then there's a larger matter of returning to the king. If I want to live, he's my last chance. But what would a depraved king want with an injured, soon-to-be amputated woman who has no memory? I can't imagine I'd like whatever he has in store.

No, better to die on my own terms than to live on his.

A bottle of amber liquid rests on the seat next to me, and I grab it, unscrewing the lid and lifting it to my nose. The astringent smell of alcohol burns my nostrils.

I bring it to my lips and take several swallows. I grimace at the taste and my stomach roils. But in its wake, a pleasant warmth spreads down my throat, taking the barest edge off the pain.

Once I get the chance to stop, I'll pour the rest on my wound. At this point, I doubt it will do much good—the arm probably has to go—but I'm too desperate not to try.

Close up, the city is even worse off than I initially thought. I have to swerve around piles of rubble, and at one point, turn around and take an alternate route altogether. The structures that rise on either side of me have been tagged, and bullet holes riddle many of them.

There's so much evidence of civilization, and yet I see not a single soul.

A sound like thunder rises up behind me. When I glance out my side view mirrors, I see a helicopter heading straight for me. It quickly overtakes the vehicle, before banking left and circling around.

"Fuck."

I jerk the wheel and pull the car off into a subterranean parking garage.

Across the street a building rises high into the air. Most of its windows have long since fallen away, but it appears sturdy enough for me to occupy until the chopper passes.

Shoving the liquor bottle into my back pocket, I stumble out of the car and head for the skyscraper across the street. The stairwell inside cants a little to the side. The whole building is starting its slow slide back into the earth.

I make it up ten flights before I stagger out onto a random floor. This is the last push my body will endure. I can feel it in my marrow.

The plate-glass windows that once covered the outer walls are shattered. A howling wind slides through what remains, kicking up dust and stirring my hair.

The blades of the chopper beat outside, and I can hear a chorus of engines closing in on our location.

Somehow, the king has found me.

CHAPTER 5

I PULL THE gun from the small of my back.

Heavy boots jog up the stairs. Despair sets in.

Sick, injured, but not free. Never free.

I back up as the king's men pour out of the stairwell. There's at least a dozen of them and they're covered from head to toe in gear. Their guns are bared, but almost immediately their barrels swivel around the room, looking for threats other than the one in front of them.

One of men parts through the group and removes his helmet. I have to lock my knees to keep from falling.

The king.

My tormentor and my husband.

I don't remember him, and yet a part of me aches with such ferocity that I know he's imprinted in my bones. Or maybe it's just the look in his eyes. It's the first time I've seen compassion, and it railroads me.

There's also a good dose of horror in those eyes of his. They track each of my features. He can see my sickness and my wounds.

With a shaky hand, I point the gun at that face. I don't want to feel this way—like I belong to someone. I'd rather die than live a prisoner shuffled between two enemies.

Behind him, his men turn their weapons on me. The king holds up a hand and signals to his men to hold their fire.

"Put the gun down, Serenity."

I don't. I don't react at all. I'm incapable of reacting, frozen between my heart and my head.

He should die.

He must live.

He needs to pay.

He wants me safe.

"Put it down." I think he has an idea where my mind is because he's coaxing. "You're not going to shoot me."

I cock the gun.

His body tenses at the sound, but he's still edging forward. "You can't kill me. You know this. My men will take you out if you don't put the gun down and come with me."

"I can't." I don't know anything else besides this—fighting lost causes. I was always meant to go down with the ship, not to survive it.

"You can. My queen, you already have once before."

I waver, searching for a memory that isn't there.

My aim droops. A wave of dizziness passes over me and I stumble.

"Serenity?" Is it my imagination, or does the monster in front of me sound frightened?

I try to focus on the king, but my vision's clouding. I fight to stay in the moment, but my body is finally, finally giving out.

THE KING

SERENITY'S EYES ROLL back. Ignoring my men's warnings, I run the last distance between us and catch her as she falls, her gun clattering harmlessly to the floor.

This feral woman. I'd learned long ago that she was most ferocious once you peeled away her layers. Whatever happened to her over the last few days had done exactly that. She didn't know enemy from friend.

I pull off a glove and touch her cheek. She's burning up.

"Serenity." I shake her lightly. "Serenity!"

She moans but doesn't wake.

"Soldiers! I need a medic!"

Men rush to my side, and things happen quickly after that. A stretcher makes its way to our floor. They have to pry her out of my hands, and when they move her, she's limp, lifeless, this woman that burns so brightly.

Fear tastes like gunmetal and blood. How long it's been since I've feared for anything, save myself. I don't like it that the most important parts of me live inside a dying woman.

When we've boarded my jet, I follow the medics into the back cabin, where a hospital room and a Sleeper have been set up. I'd known that she would need medical attention, but I'd underestimated the extent of her injuries. Vastly so.

They cut away her clothes, and her head lolls to the side. One of the men working on her curses, drawing my attention. He removes the last of Serenity's bandages. I almost gag at the sight of the wound on her upper arm. It's swollen and festering. Another medic pushes me out, and I don't fight him.

I place a shaking fist to my mouth. No, fear doesn't sit well inside me. I'm the leader of the entire globe, and the Resistance dared to hurt *my* wife, their queen.

I head to the onboard phone and dial the head of my special weapons unit. "Move ahead with our original plans." By nightfall, that Resistance outpost will be obliterated. Everyone and everything that hasn't escaped by then will be captured, and I'll make sure they understand what happens to those that cross me.

SERENITY

I BLINK MY eyes open and stare at the white molding decorating the ceiling above me.

I don't know where I am.

A hand squeezes mine. "You're awake."

My entire body reacts to that voice. I've only met this man twice, and already his presence overwhelms me.

I turn my head to face the king. He sits next to the bed I'm in, my hand clasped in both of his. His eyes look sad, regretful.

I try to sit up and look around. Already my body's tensing. I may be a woman without a past, but I haven't lost the memory of the past few days. This world eats the innocent for breakfast, and it does far worse to those like me.

The king gets up to sit on the edge of my bed. He's too close. Gently he places a hand on my chest and pushes me back down.

"Not so fast," he says.

I'm a cornered creature. It makes me want to lash out.

"Let me up," I demand.

"Serenity, you're safe."

He can read me. That's good to know.

Rather than letting me up, he leans down. All sorts of unforgiving angles have sharpened his features. His expression's only tempered by his eyes, which are devouring me. When his mouth's a hairsbreadth away from mine, I realize what he's going to do. At the last second I turn my face away. His lips brush my cheek.

The king pulls away enough for me to think through the haze of his presence. Does he not know that I lost my memory? I assumed my previous captors told him, but in hindsight, they had plenty of reasons to keep this a secret.

"Is my wife suddenly shy?"

My cheeks flame.

One of his fingers trail my blush. "She *is*. How very titillating." He leans back in, his breath warm against my throat. "Let's see how long it'll take for me to make you forget your embarrassment."

He presses a kiss to my neck.

I can't hold it in any longer.

"I don't remember you." I stare at the velvet chair the king sat in not a minute ago, but I'm not really seeing it. I swivel my head to face him. "I don't remember you."

Above me, the king's fallen ominously silent. I feel the weight of it bearing down on me. Nothing this man does is subtle. Not even his silence.

"What do you mean?" he says carefully.

"My memory is gone."

THE KING

MARCO.

The Resistance made it appear that he'd died at their hands, but Serenity's words paint a new picture.

Marco carried the memory suppressant on him at all times in place of a cyanide capsule. When he and Serenity were cornered, he must've used it on her. He could've still died at the Resistance's hands, but if he'd had time to give her the serum, he probably had time to die, either by his own hand or knowingly by another's.

Faithful until the very end.

The crushing weight of his absence tightens my lungs. I force my grief down. I've had plenty of time to mourn him while the Sleeper pieced Serenity back together. I won't let it ruin this day.

I stare at my wife, flummoxed by this turn of events and more than just a little unnerved that she lost her memory and I hadn't noticed.

She remembers nothing.

All those reasons she hated me so viciously—gone. I could avoid her ire altogether. I could charm her as I had the many women who passed through my bed before her. It's tempting. But as I fall into her guarded, wary eyes, I find I want the old Serenity back.

I married my hardened, angry queen because her spirit was the twin of mine. Without her past, all her rough edges will be blunted; she'd only be a shadow of herself.

I touch her cheek. "Would you like your memory back?"

"You can do that?"

My thumb strokes her skin. I'm practically vibrating with the need to take action. The weeks spent waiting for her to recover have tested my patience. Knowing it'll be a while longer until my Serenity returns is almost too much.

"I can."

"Then yes," she says, "I want my memories back."

SERENITY

I DON'T LIKE doctors. Soon enough I'll find out precisely why.

The king still hasn't let me up from the bed. He has, however, stopped trying to kiss me. I'm horrified that mixed in with my relief is regret. His touch awakens all sorts of slumbering emotions.

I'm supposed to hate him, and yet he's the first person I've encountered who treats me like I'm something precious. It's heady, feeling cherished, and it's making me question everything I've been told about him.

I do, however, believe he's a bastard—otherwise, he wouldn't be holding me down while the doctor comes at me with a needle.

"Let me go," I growl, trying to push him and the other guard they called in off of me.

"I'm seriously questioning your memory loss," he mutters under his breath. Louder, he says, "It's just a needle."

I don't care if it's just a needle. I'm tired of people asserting their will on me.

The king nods to the doctor. The man in the white coat captures my arm and steadies it. Before I can pull it away from him, the needle slips under my skin, and he empties the antidote into my veins.

It's over before I can react. The king lets up as the doctor moves away. I glare at him as I rub the crook of my elbow.

Belatedly, I realize I'm rubbing my arm with my injured one. Only, it no longer hurts.

I've been too distracted by the king to notice what else about me is different. I roll back the sleeve of my shirt, expecting ... something.

What I don't expect is smooth skin.

It's gone—the wound, the infection, the scar that should mark it. My skin prickles. Not only has the king saved my arm from amputation, he's removed all evidence that there ever was an injury to begin with.

It reminds me eerily of my memory wipe, replacing the ugly and scarred with something new and unsullied.

"It's gone." I run a finger over it. When I look up at the king, I can tell he's drinking in my wonder. "How?"

"The East's medicine is better than the West's. You've been inside the Sleeper for a long time."

"'The Sleeper'?"

The doctor's lingering at the foot of my bed, and now he clears his throat. "Your memories won't return all at once," he says. "The bulk of them will come to you in three hours or so, but it'll take up to several days for the drug to fully reverse the effects of the memory suppressant."

"Is that all?" the king asks.

"Yes, Your Majesty." The doctor bows to the king, and then he and the guard take their leave.

It's just the two of us again.

My eyes meet the king's.

"Want to see the rest of our home?" he asks.

My heart skips. From prisoner to queen. I may be trapped in a whole different way here, but I much prefer the king's presence to that of Lieutenant Begbie's. We'll see if it'll remain that way once I get my memories back.

I nod to the king. Hopefully a tour of this place will break up the strange tension crackling between us.

He extends a hand to me. I don't bother taking it, not so soon after he held me down. I'm not above pettiness.

This, oddly enough, makes the king's eyes twinkle. "Some things, Serenity, not even memory can touch."

CHAPTER 6

SERENITY

NOTHING'S HAPPENING.

Granted, it's only been thirty minutes, but I've taken to stalking through what appears to be an honest-to-goodness palace. The king's sly smiles only serve to make my foul mood even fouler.

The man beside me, for his part, has been cordial and chivalrous and completely and utterly fake. It makes me want to rake my hands through his hair and shake him until the calculation in his eyes drips onto his tongue and out his mouth. He's acting like I'm a ticking time bomb and he's waiting for me to explode.

I hate it just as much as I hate each subsequent room I enter. I don't like the gold filigree that adorns just about everything, or the intricate designs carved into the very woodwork of this place. I don't like the white, white walls and the polished floors. The delicate art and the crystal chandeliers.

The sheer opulence of it is an insult to the land beyond the walls.

"They were right about you, weren't they?" I ask, rotating to the king. When I catch sight of him, déjà vu ripples through me, but I can't place it—yet.

He's already studying me, like I'm some fascinating creature he wishes to collect.

"Right about what?" He lays his hand on the small of my back, trying to steer me out of his drawing room—or is it his tea room? They all have absurd names and more absurd purposes.

"Your cruelty." I shrug off his touch, striding ahead of him.

The ploy doesn't work. He's much taller, his legs much longer, and in a few short paces he's cut me off.

The king looms over me, and he takes a step forward.

I stand my ground, though it means brushing against him.

"Have you not already figured that out for yourself? You've always been able to see right through me," he says, his voice low. The pitch is both secretive and threatening, and I can't stop the goosebumps that spread down my arms.

He's the boogeyman, and he's come to claim me all over again.

With that thought, I catch a memory. Just a snippet, really.

"Serenity?"

My hand was already on the door. I turned back to face an older man with hair the color of dusty wheat.

The wrinkles around his eyes and mouth deepened. "As an emissary, if an accord is ever to be reached between us and the Eastern Empire, you will likely be a key player in it."

I swallowed and nodded. I now carried a heavy responsibility.

"Do you know what that means?"

I waited for him to finish.

His gaze lingered on me a long time before he finally answered his own question. "One day you'll meet the king."

I blink, and the object of my memory is in front of me again.

The king tilts his head. "You just had your first memory, didn't you?"

I nod. The man from my past—the man I spoke with—he's at the edge of my mind and the tip of my tongue. I'm positive I know him, but his identity still eludes me.

"What did you remember?" He picks up a lock of my hair and rubs it as he asks.

He wants to touch me. He's been fairly obvious about this, but I sense his impatience increasing.

"Nothing that I can make sense of."

Those dark eyes probe mine. "That'll change soon enough." *And then you'll be mine.* I swear I hear the promise, though he never voices it.

The king backs off, but that stubborn hand of his presses into the small of my back again. There's no use fighting him on this; he's going to keep doing it, and I'm going to keep losing.

In the halls, men and women pass by, and they're just as ridiculous as the rest of this place. The people here wear fabrics with fine names I doubt, even if I could remember, I'd know.

Their outfits are intricate things that come in colors brighter than I knew existed, and each one is paired with decorative medals and sabers or ropes of jewels wrapped around necks and wrists. Their hair's too coiffed, their teeth too white, their skin too stretched, their bodies too soft.

It all looks so luxurious and impossibly fake.

I don't belong here.

The king must see my lingering attention on the people who side-eye me. He leans in, his lips brushing the shell of my ear. "None of them are as beautiful as you, *nire bihotza.*"

I scowl at him. "I don't care about your standards of beauty."

If anything, it annoys me. These men and women bask in the opulence of it. But how many lives has this lifestyle cost?

The king's gaze tracks my movements, and I wonder if I'm one of the lives it's claimed.

I suspect I am.

In the brief silence between us, a dizzying number of questions bloom. It's amazing how many a girl with only a few days of memory can have. I want to know more about who the king is, who I am, who my enemies are, why wrong seems right and right seems wrong. Most of all, I want to know how I've been bent and twisted into this person that seems to hate and be hated so fiercely by everyone, save the king.

"Why did you marry me?" I ask as we leave the king's grand ballroom. I won't even touch on the ridiculousness of a room dedicated to nothing but dancing.

"Ssssh. I'll answer your questions soon enough. Let me enjoy the last few minutes before you hate me again."

I know his words are meant to grate, but I doubt he realizes how ominous I find them. What would it take for a woman like me to hate him?

"When I was a prisoner, they told me you killed my family," I say.

"They told you that?"

"They told me many things. Is it true?"

His features are guarded. "You'll know soon enough."

And I do.

WE'RE IN THE palace gardens when it hits.

I stumble, reaching out for the king—Montes. After the bits and pieces I received inside the palace, I assumed the rest of my memories would subtly surface. I didn't imagine *this*.

This is a barrage of enemy fire. It rips through me suddenly and violently.

Montes's arms lock around my torso as I gasp, my messy golden hair dangling around me.

Every memory feels like an epiphany, and I can't possibly describe the euphoria that comes with each. Life is a series of experiences that stack, one on top of the other.

I see my mother and my father—the man from my first recalled memory now has an identity! I see bikes with training wheels. Suburbia. My parents hold my hands and, on the count of three, they swing me. There are candles and birthdays and mentions of war breaking out in Europe.

There are chalk drawings and games of tag with the kids on my street—some I've known for ages, some who are part of the recent influx of immigrants. Nail polish and days out with my mother while my father buries himself in work. My childhood crush that lives down the street.

The act of remembering is magic; I get to live a little of my life all over again.

And then …

And then, somewhere along the way, they turn.

For every ray of light each happy memory casts, there is a much darker shadow.

I moan as I hear phantom explosions. I see blood spray. This dark past is sucking me under.

I step out of the king's embrace and hold my head. "No, no, no."

One bad memory follows the last. My mom's broken neck, soldiers with glassy eyes. The first four men I killed—my friends watch me with wary eyes after that. A bomb that takes over the sky and hides the sun. My city, my home, my childhood crush and everyone else is obliterated in a single blast.

Then, radiation, everywhere. In the food, the water, our bodies. Civilizations swiftly fell into depravity when the last pillar of humanity gave out.

My father's body cradled in my arms.

I feel the loss all over again. Fresh. New. As though in this moment I lose my mother, my father, my land, my freedom all at once.

Through it all is a single face, the answer to all my anger and anguish.

Montes Lazuli.

The king did this. I blink back tears. He did this and now I'm his. Bound to the root of the evil I tried so hard to stop. It's almost unfathomable. There is no fairness in the world. There is no kindness.

A sick feeling twists my gut. I've laid with the king. I've let him into my body. Worse, I've let him into my heart.

I only have a moment to register that I'm going to be sick before I begin to heave. But there's nothing left in my empty stomach to purge. The queasiness doesn't abate.

"Serenity!" Montes's voice cuts through, and it's so concerned. I jerk myself away from the monster.

More memories force their way through and I press my palms into my eyes. I scream as bloody, broken bodies flood my mind. And behind it all, the kind's white,

white smile. I want to smash it in and not stop until those teeth rip up my knuckles and fall out of his mouth. I let out a sob because I *like* the very smile I also detest.

It's the face behind every nightmare I've ever had, and the face that awakened my heart. It's ripping, bleeding. This shouldn't be the way of things, hating and loving something at the same time.

But it's not enough for my mind to end there. I feel the squeeze of my heart as a memory of the king holding me sneaks its way in. Another of his fearful expression when he learned of my cancer. The unguarded face he wore when nothing separated us. And through it all I see his eyes, filled with a bottomless reservoir of emotions reserved for me.

The heartless king has found his heart after all. It rests beneath my ribcage. God save me, he swapped mine for his when I wasn't looking. And now we're stuck— me with the weight of his death count, him with the guilt of my suffering.

Flesh and bone aren't meant to contain all this. The mind shouldn't stay sane when the world's fallen to chaos, and love shouldn't be able to grow in the wastelands of our consciences.

But, God save us all, it does.

It does.

CHAPTER 7

SERENITY

IT'S OVER. FOR now.

But it isn't, because I have to live with a past I might've been better off forgetting. My memories are horrifying. I'm a woman remade—but into this *thing*.

I'd asked myself what kind of person married the king. Now I know. Now, I know.

I straighten, drawing in a ragged breath, my hand just above my stomach.

The world around me sharpens. The green hedges that rise up all around us, the cyan sky beyond, the marble statue of a woman holding her loose robes against her body.

"Serenity."

I focus on the voice. Montes stands in front of me, his brows pinched together. For once he doesn't appear overconfident. He reaches out for me, but lets his hand drop.

What feral expression must I be wearing to scare him off?

"What do you remember?" he asks.

"That I hate you." A hate so deep and vast that it's blackened my soul. Even now I fight the urge to lunge at him and make good my age-old vendetta.

"Ah, yes," he says, sliding his hands into his slacks, unaware of how close I am to snapping. "I'm well acquainted with your hate." He's not even fazed.

We've done this before. Traded words like we've traded wounds. That puts me at a disadvantage because I have more memories to unearth, and he knows how to handle me.

I don't like to be handled.

Montes doesn't remove his hands from his pockets, but he does extend the crook of his arm towards me, like I'm some kind of lady.

I dropped that ruse the moment my father died in my arms.

I'm about to reject him when I notice our audience. People have planted themselves everywhere—at windows, on benches, strolling by. They act as though they're not transfixed by us.

I have a duty to uphold. I married the king to save my land. My hate is a vulnerability, one the Resistance preyed upon when they took me. I can't let these people see it. The king and I have many, many battles ahead of us, and our relationship is the least of them.

The world's still in turmoil and the king—the ruler of it all—has used fear to win his subjects over. I know quite a bit about fear. It pulls people into line, but it also draws in the predators. The moment he shows weakness, they'll attack.

I can't let that happen, even now when I'd like to see him suffer. So I take his arm and let him lead me away like I'm a frail, dainty thing. All the while, I flash hard looks at those that catch my eye.

For I, too, am something to fear.

"Do I finally have my Serenity back?" the king asks, leaning his head towards mine.

"I am not yours."

"You are."

"No."

He stops us in front of a bubbling fountain, our audience still pretending not to watch.

His hand glides out of his pocket and captures my arm, reeling me in. "Yes, you are," he breathes. He brushes a lock of hair from my face. "Hello, Serenity."

"Let me go." I give his hold the barest of tugs, aware of the eyes on us.

"I'm glad to have you back." He smiles at me, and it's almost too much. "I missed you and your anger."

I narrow my eyes on him. "I never left."

"You did, and now you're back, and I want a kiss."

I look at him like he's mad—he *is* mad. I'm still trying to get over the fact that I have to kiss him at all, and now he wants me to freely give him affection amongst an audience?

Up until now, I've been careful dolling out my affection. That won't change today.

He must see that I'm not going to give in because before I have a chance to respond, his lips descend on mine and he takes matters into his own hands.

THIS IS SOMETHING else that the king does—he seizes what's not freely given. You could say it's a strength of his.

And now it's a kiss.

None of my memories could've prepared me for the sensation of being enveloped by the king. I taste him and breathe him in through my nose. How I'd forgotten his scent. It's unnamable, but I enjoy it nearly as much as the glide of his lips. Lips that took something that wasn't his.

I bite his lower lip. That only serves to ratchet up his hunger. His hands secure me closer to him, and he unleashes more passion, his tongue sliding over mine.

Montes's hands knead into my skin, coaxing me to give in further. If he had it his way, he'd probably strip me bare, ravish me here in the gardens, and then order everyone who saw us killed.

Like I said, he's good at instilling fear.

Someone whistles, and then I hear clapping. I break away from him at the sound, and he flashes me a triumphant grin.

The crowd continues to cheer, praising the king for what? His vigor? The ease with which he commands everyone, even his wife? That he's human enough to enjoy a kiss?

My money's on that last one.

Montes tucks me under his arm, and with a parting wave to the crowd, leads me back inside his palace.

We're still not alone here, but I've burned up the last of my patience. There's appearing weak to the outside world and then there's appearing weak to yourself.

I push his arm off of me and stride away. I've only taken a few steps when I realize this is yet another palace of his that I don't recognize. I know that I still have some memories left to remember, but I'm pretty sure I've never been here before, regardless.

"Where, exactly, are you planning on going?" Montes asks. I can hear the smirk in his voice.

"It doesn't matter so long as it's away from you." I can't do this with Montes right now. Not with all those memories so fresh. Even now they crowd my mind. The dead want vindication, and I can't deliver it.

"You have to kill him, Serenity." It's just an echo of a memory, but the voice and the vehemence of the words has me placing a shaky hand on a side table.

"You work for the king; you can't say things like that anymore," I whispered.

"No one man should have that much power," Will said.

"And what happens once he's dead, huh?" I asked. *"They'll kill me too."*

I finally remember Will, General Kline's son. We'd been friends, but something happened ... something I still haven't recalled. Now having had a taste of my memories, I dread that one.

The last remnant of memory echoes through me.

Perhaps I will be the WUN's Trojan horse. Perhaps I will kill the king.

I rotate to face Montes. I'd planned on killing him. Me, the dying girl, thought she could execute the immortal king.

"I wanted to see you die," I murmur. I don't know why I say it.

Montes flicks a glance at the people that linger in this area of the palace. "Leave us."

The servants and an aging couple vacate the room. The guards hesitate.

"Unless you'd like to be relieved of your duties," the king says, "I'd suggest you do as I say—and tell the men we are not to be disturbed under any circumstances."

Reluctantly, the guards leave. I see them eye me as they do so.

Once the room's emptied out, the king returns his attention to me. "You were saying?"

Not for the first time, I'm taken aback by this man. If his goal was to unsettle me, he's accomplished that.

"You've already forgotten? And here I thought I was the one with the memory loss."

"You wanted to watch me die," he says.

"Yes." Admitting this is high treason. Should he feel so inclined, the king could have me killed. It doesn't stop me from continuing on. "I wanted to be the one who killed you."

"And would you?"

My skin's crawling. I remember the horror of my situation as though it befell me yesterday. *"Yes."*

Montes strides forward much faster than I back up. I hate it that I can't help but flee this man. Maybe once all my memories return, I will wear them like armor so that he cannot get under my skin. But right now my emotions are raw, and I feel everything—my intense hatred for him, my budding feelings.

He corners me against the wall, and then there's no escaping him.

"You can't kill me," he says, and in this moment he looks every bit as unnatural as he claims to be.

"Can't I though?" I say, peering up at him. "You bleed the same as every other man."

He slides a leg between mine. "This isn't about my immortality. It never was. See," he tips my chin up, "I don't think you *would* kill me. I think you like me too much."

"Ask me that again when I'm armed, Montes."

"That won't change anything, lonely girl." He rubs my lower lip with his thumb. I swat his hand away, and he smiles.

"I'm all you have left," he says. "Your family is gone. The last of your people gave you up."

My hand strikes him before I even think twice about it. The slap snaps his head to the side. Already I can see the beginnings of my handprint forming.

It's not enough.

"*You* are the reason my family is gone," I say. "You are the reason I'm here. You forced everyone's hand and I will never, ever let you forget it."

He rubs his jaw and his cheek. "And you think that bothers me?"

His mouth lies, but his eyes don't. I'm starting to think that some of the things he's done do in fact weigh on his conscience.

The king leans in close. "If you wanted to scare me off, you went about it the wrong way." His breath brushes against my cheek and chin. "I love your anger and your hate, and I have many regrets, but marrying you is not one of them."

I'm glaring at him. I try to move, but his body pins mine to the wall. His lips skim my jaw, heading for my mouth. I turn my head away from him.

He places a kiss at the corner of my lips. "And if you think your reluctance will stop me, then you've read me wrong."

I have read him wrong, but not in the way he thinks. My mind needs him to be wholly evil, and he's not, and my spirit does not have the iron will that it should to keep him at bay. Even now, I react to his nearness. I want more of him, and that shames me. It is one thing to enjoy the mechanics of sex, another to enjoy this—our power plays, our magnetism.

He steps away. "I have something for you."

I straighten. "I don't want anything from you, Montes."

"Not true. You want many things from me; my body, my power—"

"Your head."

"Between your thighs," he finishes.

A flush crawls up my neck. It would help not to get embarrassed about this.

"On a stake," I amend.

He clucks his tongue. "I thought you said you didn't want anything from me."

I'm at a momentary loss for words, and that's precisely when he strikes. He takes my hand and drags me out of the room.

I would fight him, but a million different memories crowd my mind. I haven't had time to process the multitude of them, but now I do.

The hours leading up to my memory loss, the Resistance attacked the king's coastal palace. We'd been cornered, I'd been close to escape, but I never made it out. Marco, the king's right-hand man and my nemesis, and I had been left to face the enemies with the last of the king's soldiers.

With my free hand I rub the skin over my heart. That's when I lost my memory. The king hadn't administered the serum, Marco had—right before he blew his brains out.

I suddenly have context to attach to all the memories I acquired from that point on. The Resistance took me to one of their outposts, held me as they would any important prisoner of war, and tried to leverage me to their advantage.

General Kline … he'd been a part of it. Now knowing what I do, I can't decide how to feel about seeing him. He was my commander, and had my life not unfolded the way it had, he might've one day been my father-in-law. I respected him, and I was close to him. That makes the role he played during my capture that much worse. And yet, I'm not without blame either. I did something to his son, and he still managed to be civil with me.

Then there was that final day of my imprisonment. Had the king not firebombed the outpost, I would've died.

"How did you find me?" I ask Montes as he walks us down the hall. The guards posted along the corridor eye me warily as we pass. I have a reputation among their ranks. I remember slaughtering them after my father died.

Montes doesn't turn around when he replies, "The Resistance isn't the only one with spies."

"You bombed the place," I accuse.

All those bodies, all that carnage …

"And?"

"Were you trying to save me or kill me?" It's real rich of me to be critiquing his efforts right after I admitted I wanted to execute him.

But I never pretended to be a saint.

Montes stops and swivels to face me. "You were five floors belowground, and when my contact came to retrieve you, you put a bullet in his thigh. By the time my back up came to free you, you were gone.

"Death, Serenity, is the last thing I want from you."

Montes resumes walking, tugging me after him. He leads me to an office much grander than anything I ever saw in the bunker.

I enter the cavernous room. There's a wall of books to my left and a giant oak desk towards the back of it.

"Why did you take me here?" I ask, stepping away from him.

Now that I've got my memories back, the last thing I want to do is continue to tour the king's palace. Once you've seen one palace, you've seen them all.

Montes saunters in after me. "You'll figure it out for yourself soon enough."

I give him a dark look. The king and his games …

I meander towards the desk. When I reach it, my fingers trail over the wood surface. There are several photographs resting on it. I lift one of them up. It's a wedding photo of me and Montes. Not one of the official ones. Those I particularly relish—I'm glaring in most of them.

This is one of us outside at the reception. I'm smiling at something outside of the photo and Montes is beaming down at me. You would've almost thought we were happy in that moment.

I was terrified.

I set it down only to lift another. As soon as my eyes fall on the image, I drop it like it burns me. The heavy metal frame hits the carpet with a dull thud.

"Where did you get that?" I ask, my eyes locked on the photo. I don't want to look at it, it *hurts* to look at it, but for the life of me I can't tear my gaze away.

"Where do you think?"

Staring back up at me is a younger version of myself. In the picture I'm giving my father a side hug. He used to keep this photo in his office.

I can't breathe. I'm not sure I can keep that photo here. Seeing his face makes my soul ache in terrible ways.

I miss him, but that's not nearly a strong enough word to describe life without him. He was the sun; how do you go on living when something that huge gets extinguished?

And now to have him sit there day in and day out and watch this mockery of my life unfold. I don't know if I can stand that.

Montes picks the frame up from the floor and returns it to my desk. He doesn't say anything. He lost a father tragically too.

Resting next to the photographs is my mother's necklace. I pick it up, a slight tremor running through my hands.

The gold pendant catches the light. Montes left me the few items that have any value to me. I don't have many things to call my own, but what I do, I cherish.

"And my father's gun?" I ask.

"I'll give it back to you the moment I trust you not to shoot me with it," Montes says.

"So you *do* think I'll shoot you," I say, studying the necklace dangling from my hand.

"You're a woman that loves a good dare. I'm not gambling my life on your ability to prove me wrong."

He takes the necklace from me and clasps it around my neck. I run my fingers over the delicate chain. My eyes drift around the room.

It dawns on me. "This office is mine."

"It is—my queen needs a place to carry out world affairs."

He's given me an office before, not one that was outfitted with my personal affects. Not like this one. I don't know what I'm feeling, but it makes me uneasy.

"Why did you do all this for me?" I ask.

"This is such a small thing." He runs a hand over the veins of wood. His wily, conniving side disappears altogether. "You are my wife. I want to make you ... happy."

The man who always takes is now giving. And he wants me to be happy. Here. With him.

I don't have the heart to tell him that will never happen.

CHAPTER 8

SERENITY

MONTES SHRUGS OFF his suit jacket and throws it over my chair back before rolling up his sleeves. My eyes linger far too long on his tan, corded forearms. I'd forgotten that underneath all those layers of fine clothing was a fit man.

He then grabs a cardboard box sitting off to the side and heaves it onto the desk. Tossing aside the lid, he pulls out the first file and drops it in front of the chrome computer situated in the middle of my desk.

"Here are reprints of the files you were working on. Any notes you had with the originals are, unfortunately, lost," he says, sitting on the edge of the desk.

It's hard to focus on anything he's saying. He might be six feet and some change of a man, but his presence fills the entire room.

An unfamiliar part of me wants to step between those powerful legs of his and trail my fingers over the backs of his hands.

I could do it—I know he would welcome it—but I fight the impulse. He still feels alien to me.

I'll have to lay with him tonight.

An odd combination of anxiety and anticipation flares through me.

The king watches me with those penetrating eyes of his, and I swear they can see into my mind.

I try to stay as far away from him as I can when I open the folder in front of the computer.

"Ah, yes, these reports," I say, remembering them. I'd been reading through the files when the Resistance laid siege to the king's palace. The reports had been largely skewed for the king's purposes. I'm too ruffled to point that out. "Thank you," I say instead.

"'Thank you'?" He reaches out and catches my wrist before I can step away, then reels me in.

I end up between his thighs after all.

His other hand steadies my chin. "What's going on in my vicious little wife's mind?"

I try to jerk away, but he holds me in place.

"Montes, let me go."

"Not until you tell me what you were just thinking about."

I'm so close to kneeing him in the crotch.

However, neither of us gets the chance to see our actions through.

Not before another memory hits.

All I saw was crimson blood and all I heard were Will's screams. The outer walls must've been thick to silence such agonized cries. The king's wrath was just as frightening as I'd always feared.

I squeeze Montes's thighs as a memory rolls through me. I'm being swept up in its tide.

"I'll do whatever you want, Montes, just please, stop torturing him." It was Will, after all. I might hate what he'd become, but torture ... I didn't wish that on my worst enemy.

I was halfway down the hall when I heard a bang. My body jumped at the sound, and a tear leaked out.

Gone. Will was gone.

Back in the present, I choke on a gasp.

"You killed Will." After torturing him nonetheless. Death, at that point, had been a mercy.

I try to pull away again, and again Montes refuses to release me.

"Let me the fuck go."

He ignores my command and instead forces me to look at that pleasing face of his. "Yes, I did have my men kill him," he says, "and I'd make the same decision over and over again. In case you still don't remember, your friend Will had his men shoot you," the king says. That vein in his temple pulses. "He threatened you with torture.

"Anyone who thinks to torture you, Serenity, will be made an example of, and I don't give a damn how well you know them."

I stop struggling against him, though none of my ire is gone. "Well, I do."

He sighs. "Out of all the slights against you, that's the one you punish me with?"

He catches my fist before I can land the blow, and now he holds both my hands prisoner.

I try to knee him, but the angle is all wrong. The last of his mirth leaves his face. Using the grip he has on my hands, he yanks me onto the desk next to him and rolls over me. The file scatters and the computer monitor topples over as he pins my torso down.

That vein of his still throbs, and several loose strands of his dark hair brush my cheeks. He smiles down at me, but it's not kind. "You try that again," he breathes, "and you won't like the results."

But I have rage to match his. "It'd be worth it," I say.

"For you, I imagine it might." Slowly, the anger drains from his face. He doesn't let me go, however.

Instead, he moves both my hands into one of his, and he uses the other to reaches into his pocket. Pulling out a phone, he types something onto the screen.

A moment later, the guard enters the room. I'm still pinned to the desk, and Montes appears to be five seconds away from having his way with me, yet the guard doesn't bat an eyelash.

I renew my struggles against the king.

Montes readjusts his hold, his eyes trained on his man. "Please tell the staff to see to the earlier dinner arrangements we discussed."

The guard inclines his head and bows. As his footsteps retreat from the room, the king returns his attention to me. All at once he releases my hands and straightens.

I work my jaw as I push myself up to my forearms. The urge to hit him is still riding me hard.

"You will dine with me." *You will surrender to me.*

His mouth and his eyes say two very different things.

"No." I'm not interested in either.

I stand and brush myself off. I'm wearing a dress someone else clothed me in. This entire day has been one unpleasant experience after the last.

He steps in close and tips my chin up.

"Yes, you will, even if it means having my guards drag you to dinner. Fight all you want, it won't change my mind."

Even if I didn't already have a vendetta against this man, I would develop one quickly enough.

"I'll drop you off at our room and give you time to rest and get ready," he continues.

I step away from him. "Don't bother. I'll find it myself."

I DON'T HEAD back to our room because fuck him. Instead I spend the next several hours figuring out the basic layout of the palace. When I was with Montes I didn't want a tour of the place, and I still don't, but there is use in knowing how a machine like the palace works.

This one is U-shaped with east and west wings. Montes already showed me most of the central building and the west wing. Those appear largely to serve formal functions.

The east wing, on the other hand, contains the king's official business. I pass several doors fitted with placards of the king's highest-ranking advisors. Another conference room, and a room that bears a sickening resemblance to the map rooms of the king's other palaces. I leave before I can look at any of the crossed out faces too closely. The last thing I want to see is my father's face among them.

I head back outside. A maze of hedges rise up on either side of a central pathway. Beyond them are a series of structures.

I squint up at the sky. Pinks and golds have replaced the earlier blue. I won't have time to explore all of this place, not before the king drags me off to dinner. And I'm sure he will indeed drag me to it if I resist. Montes doesn't make idle threats. Like me, he stands by his words, no matter how perverse they are.

I take in the many buildings that sit off in the distance. Towards the far corner of the palace grounds, I notice a series of long, squat structures. The soldiers' barracks, if I had to guess. I have enough time to visit them, I think, before the king calls on me. So I head there next, ignoring the two guards that follow several feet behind me.

When I arrive, I can tell I guessed right. Several soldiers loiter between buildings, some laughing with each other. Of course, that all ends when they see me. Quickly, they stand at attention, bowing as I make my way through the barracks. I sense a good dose of that earlier wariness here. It's just a feeling—perhaps the soldiers' eyes are a tad too hard, their spines a bit too straight—but I know that I'm not entirely welcome. It doesn't stop me, however, from moving through the buildings.

Mess hall, sleeping quarters, and to my utter delight, several training rooms. This, I belatedly realize, is what drew me out here. Amongst all the soft, painted faces, I feel hopelessly different. But this place that lacks adornment and smells like sweat, this I understand.

I run my hand over a metal dumbbell stacked against the wall, the grips worn down with use. I decide then and there that I won't become what I detest. I'll come here to train, and I'll earn the guards' respect or I won't, but I will not lose the soldier in me.

From behind me, one of the guards now approaches. "Your Majesty, the king's called for dinner."

CHAPTER 9

SERENITY

WHEN I MEET Montes back inside the palace, he doesn't lead me to the dining room like I thought he might. Instead we head outside once more and cross the garden. The sun's already set and the sky is deep blue. I feel summer in the breeze, and it stirs such intense longing in me. The last time I felt like this, I still had my mother.

As we move beyond the hedges, it becomes clear the king is leading me to another one of the buildings sitting at the far end of the grounds. It's made of copper, marble, and most of all, glass. Hundreds of panes make up the dome alone. I've never seen a structure like this.

Montes holds my hand against the crook of his arm. I think he knows that if he lets go, I'll pull away immediately. But the gesture's strangely intimate

"Are you still angry?" he asks.

"When it comes to you, I'm always angry."

"Mmm, you must not have recalled all your memories yet. For instance, the last time I laid between those pretty thighs of yours, you were far from angry."

A blush spreads up my neck at the memory I do, in fact, recall. "Do you always get enjoyment being lewd?"

"My queen, *that* is not lewd. Lewd would be telling you how your tight little pu—"

"*Montes.*" My cheeks are flaming now, and I can't tell if I'm more embarrassed by his words or the fact that I still react like this. Both he and I are aware it's a weakness of mine.

He glances down at me, his eyes luminous as they catch the light of a nearby lamp. "That's not lewd, Serenity. That is just what it means to be your husband. And yes, I get enjoyment from making you blush. It's so very ... unlike you."

He squeezes my hand. And as I feel his fingers envelop mine, I'm reminded again that with him, intimacy isn't just a handful of memories. It's something that'll happen again, and sooner rather than later, if the intense look in his eyes is any indication.

"What are you thinking about?" he asks.

He must see all my nerves, all my anxieties, but I won't hand them to him on a platter by voicing the words.

I don't tear my eyes from his when I say, "I'm thinking that you'd give the devil a run for his money. In fact, he's probably worried that you'll set your sights on his territory next."

The corner of Monte's mouth lifts. "A good idea, Serenity. Perhaps I could consult you on hell's layout? I hear you're familiar with it."

God, I hate this man.

I turn my attention away from him, back to the structure he's leading me towards. We enter the building, and I realize exactly what it is.

A greenhouse.

My lingering irritation evaporates as my eyes sweep across the interior. I've never seen so many different plants so close together. Their leaves are waxy and their colors—I didn't realize so many different shades of green existed. But it's not just green. Pinks and yellows, reds and oranges, whites and purples and every color in between, each plant stranger and lovelier than the last.

Without thinking I begin moving through the clusters of them, inadvertently tugging the king along with me. I can feel his gaze on my face, drinking up my reaction. I pull away from him to pet a leaf.

It's a captive here, living in its own gilded cage.

Just like me.

Releasing it, I lift my gaze and take in the rest of the greenhouse. The glass panes are misted over, and the humidity is curling my hair. Hundreds of plants line the building. The size and beauty of this place is staggering.

After living in a gloomy, subterranean bunker for the last five years, the idea of a room filled with light and plants is almost incomprehensible.

So, naturally, the king has one of these places on his property.

"And my queen's frowning again."

"This is just another room with a ridiculous purpose."

He actually looks pleased, and I can't fathom why.

He takes my hand and leads me down an aisle. Then he begins pointing. "*Papaver somniferum*—the opium poppy. Extracts of the plant can be used as high grade pain relievers, amongst other things. *Camellia sinensis*—the dried leaves of that one make tea. *Coffea arabica*—the plant that's saved you from killing everyone before eight a.m."

"Not everyone. Just you," I correct.

He smirks and points to another plant. "*Cannabis sativa*—helps with appetite, sleep, anxiety, lowers nausea. A wonder drug, really.

"Many of these plants are already being used medicinally," he continues, "and outside of my greenhouses, they are hard to find. Many more of them are being researched and genetically modified, again for science."

And now I understand the king's smug expression. I assumed he didn't care about saving the world his war had broken. I hadn't imagined that maybe some of the laboratory testing he'd been working on was to benefit the people he'd so abused.

He steers me down the aisle we're on and we enter another room of the greenhouse. High above us I see the stars through the domed glass roof I'd caught a glimpse of outside.

The plants here cling to the edges of the room. In the middle of it all is a table set for two that's illuminated by candlelight.

I clutch the chain of my mother's necklace. I've never been romanced, outside of one other candlelit dinner also hosted by the king. And that last time, to my great embarrassment, it worked.

It probably will again.

Montes herds me forward, his dark eyes twinkling. It's even harder to not be drawn in by him when the room's dim glow draws attention to all the pleasing angles of his face.

He likes this, I realize. Indulging me in his lavish lifestyle. He hasn't yet figured out that it's a double-edged sword. I am a child of war and famine. I don't know how to indulge, and I don't want it.

He must see me backpedaling because he increases the pressure he places on my lower back. Reluctantly I let him steer me to the table. I approach it the way I would anything else that's too good to be true.

The plates and cutlery rest atop indigo and gold linens embroidered with the king's initials. I glance down at my rings. The colors match.

"Blue and gold—they're your colors," I say. I'm only now putting together the symbolism that's been woven into the king's rule.

"And yours as well, my queen that loves the stars and the deep night," he says, shrugging off his jacket and taking a seat across from me.

Just like earlier today, he undoes his cufflinks and rolls his shirt up past his elbows. And now I'm back to staring at his forearms.

This is carefully crafted seduction, and I'm defenseless against it.

"What do you want from me?" I ask, forcing my gaze up. His face isn't a better option.

I can't bear this. I was raised on duty and honor, and I can't find any in my situation. I'm trapped in a role where I'm everyone's traitor—even my own.

He gives me a penetrating look. "Everything."

"You know that's impossible."

"Is this another one your facts?" Montes asks, leaning forward.

Before I can answer, I hear the door to the greenhouse open. A long beat of silence stretches on while two servants enter, one bearing a bottle of wine, the other a tray with two plates on it.

"Here, I'll take that from you," the king says, grabbing the neck of the wine bottle from the server while the other one sets the plates in front of us.

Once the food has been laid out, both servers bow and exit the room.

Montes pours us each a glass of wine from the uncorked bottle he holds. "Let's play a little game," he says, handing my glass to me. "I'll ask you a question and you'll either tell me the answer, or you'll drink."

I narrow my eyes at him but take my drink from his outstretched hand. The last time I played this game, I slept through the next day's negotiations, and when I woke, I was sicker than a dog. A downside. I also kept the king from sleeping with me. An upside.

"I'll play, but only if you answer my questions as well."

His mouth curves up. "Of course. That's only fair."

As if he knows a thing about fairness.

He leans back in his seat, the flame of the candles dancing in his eyes. I might as well be seated with the devil; Montes is handsome enough and wicked enough for the job.

"You told me once that hate isn't the only thing you feel for me," he says. "What else is it that you feel?"

He starts with that? *That*?

I take a drink of my wine. Montes smiles, and I realize too late that my reaction was an answer in and of itself.

"Were you planning on killing my father and me before we arrived in Geneva?" I ask.

If he gets to ask hard questions, then so do I.

Montes's sighs. "This is supposed to be fun."

"It's not my fault you're a bastard," I say. "Now answer my question."

The vein in his temple begins to pound. "Tread lightly, my queen," he says softly.

We stare each other down, and I think we both realize we've met our match.

Finally, he says, "Death is always on the table when it comes to my negotiations. You know that."

He *had* planned to kill us.

"Did you order my father killed?"

"Ah-ah," he says, his voice jovial, but his eyes are hard. "Already forgetting the rules."

I glower at him.

"Why did you marry me?" he asks.

I go still. "It was me or my country."

"That was the only reason?"

"It's my turn." My voice is icy. I'm seconds away from overturning the table—or lunging across it and attacking the king.

"Did you order my father killed?" I repeat.

"No, Serenity, I didn't."

I swirl my wine glass, agitated. What had I hoped for him to say—that he had?

"Was saving your country the only reason you married me?" he asks.

Did he really expect any answer but yes?

"I vomited when I learned I'd have to marry you," I say. "Do you really want to rehash this all out?"

"No. What did the Resistance do to you while they held you prisoner?"

He tricked me out of a turn.

I grip the stem of my glass tightly and force myself to muse on his question. The man across from me is not a soldier. He has no true concept of torture and humiliation. But he is my husband, and he is the megalomaniac that has bent the world to his will.

I grab my glass and drink. With him, violence begets violence.

I tilt my head back and look at the stars that I can barely see through the domed ceiling above. I want to say I watch them because they are beautiful, but I can't lie to myself about this. I'm avoiding the king's reaction to what I'm about to ask.

I pull myself together. I'm not a wimp, and if I have the courage to ask the question, then I should also have the courage to face the king as I do so.

Leveling my gaze on him, I ask, "What do you feel for me?"

Surprise flickers through his features before he collects himself. Once he does, I wish I could draw the words back into my mouth.

Montes gives me a slow, smoldering smile, one that I feel low in my belly. He lifts his glass and takes a drink.

Neither of us has touched our food yet, and at that the moment, hunger is the furthest thing from my mind.

He sets his glass down, his gaze dropping to the base of my throat. "How old were you when you lost her?" He nods to my mother's necklace.

I wrap my hand around it, and already I'm shaking my head. No, he doesn't get to know about her. His war killed her, along with a million other mothers. She's beyond his reach now, and I won't give him what's left of her.

The wine I swallow down barely makes it past the lump in my throat.

It's my turn, and all the words I can think of have turned bitter on my tongue. "Tell me, what is the price of my life, Montes?"

Montes has been swirling his glass, but now he stops. "What are you really asking?"

"That," I say. "I'm asking that. What is the price of my life?"

I'm setting myself up for failure, and I want him to fail me. I want him to disappoint me with his answer because I don't hate him with all my heart, but I desperately wish I did.

He takes a sip of his drink.

That's what I thought.

Maybe my life is worth one country to him. Maybe it's worth less. Whatever the cost, he knows it would burn me worse than his silence.

I push back my chair and stand. "Some epic love you are," I mutter. My words carry no vitriol. Perhaps that is what makes him flinch.

"You love me?" He says.

And he latches onto that. I shake my head. "I don't blame you for it, you know. Thirty years is a long time to spend collecting countries like toys." Long enough to lose your conscience.

He stands. "Serenity."

I ignore him as I stride away, and there is something satisfying about unveiling the monster behind all the pretty prose.

"*Serenity!*"

I can hear his shoes click against the marble floor.

"You're wrong," he says when I don't stop. "You want to know why I didn't answer the question? Because I don't know the answer, and that terrifies me. But I do know this: what we have is epic. Why do you think our enemies want to separate us so badly?"

Now I halt.

"We were enemies before this all began," I say.

"I was never your enemy, Serenity. The world saw that when they watched the peace talks, and they saw it again when they watched our wedding. That is why the Resistance is trying to come between us."

I swivel to face him. Even this far away, he swallows up space. If anyone were to be a world leader, it would be him. He's mesmerizing, and not just for his looks. Maybe it's all those hidden years of his that take up space in this room because they can't be worn on his face. Whatever it is, it only makes him more of an enigma.

"You married me to secure your power," I say.

He laughs at that and takes a step forward. "Is that what you've convinced yourself of? That my primary reason for marrying you was to secure my power?"

The hairs on my arm lift at what he isn't saying.

"You and I both know I could've crushed the WUN under my boot if I so chose. They are more of a pain because I secured them peacefully."

The scariest things are those that you don't understand. That was what always frightened me about the king—I couldn't fathom his motives. I thought I was beginning to understand him for a while there, but I wasn't.

He saunters towards me slowly. "I'm afraid that when it comes to strategy, my queen, I've outmaneuvered you."

Adrenaline courses through me as my body gets battle ready. "Why would you marry me if not for power?" There's no more diving into a glass of wine for either of us.

I'm the ugly truth and he's a pretty lie, and we are always, always circling each other. I think that he's right. What passes between us is every bit as epic as I'd always feared.

He closes the last of the distance and reaches up to cup my jaw.

I tilt my head away from him. "Don't."

"Can't I touch my wife?"

It's so unlike him to ask.

There's nothing left for me to hang onto when he's like this. My hate's too ephemeral, my heart too hopeful.

I close my eyes and nod.

A second later the smooth skin of his fingers brush my cheeks, my mouth. They leave, and then his lips are caressing mine.

He tastes like a taboo. He's mine.

"It was better when I simply hated you," I murmur against him. My head and my heart are at war, and the fallout's ripping me in two.

"I know," he says, his lips still pressed to mine. "That won't stop me from trying to win you over, but I know."

I open my eyes. The king's dark, unfathomable ones stare back at me. My pulse quickens a little more. I'm not supposed to want to know what he's thinking or be pulled in by the same allure that's won over countries and officials.

But I do and I am. His life frightens me, but he's also a kindred spirit. His darkness complements my own.

"Sit back down," he murmurs against my lips.

I let him lead me back; I have nowhere else to go. He takes his own seat and reaches for his cutlery.

I lift my own fork and spear a pasta noodle. They used to serve us spaghetti in the bunker, but as soon as the flavor hits my taste buds, I realize this is a different beast entirely. If what I was used to was water then this would be wine.

Montes watches me the entire time.

I swallow. "Stop that."

"Then stop making that expression when you eat."

"What expression?" I ask.

"Like you're being sweetly fucked."

I shouldn't have asked. And I definitely need more alcohol for this conversation. Montes refills my glass right before I reach for it.

"I'm surprised by you," I say, eyeing my topped-off drink.

His eyes noticeably brighten. "Oh, really?"

This man and his ego.

"Feeding wine to the woman with stomach cancer." Last time I overdrank, I vomited blood up.

The luster in his gaze dies out a little. "The Sleeper's controlling the cancer."

That's good enough for me. I take a healthy drink.

"But I still have it." I place the glass back down.

"You do. But you won't for long."

I really want to kick my legs up on the table and settle into my chair. Instead, I take another bite of the pasta. It's heavenly.

Damnit, I think I *am* making a face while I eat it.

"We haven't discovered a cure yet," he continues, "but my researchers are close."

I take another drink of my wine. "I wouldn't hold my breath if I were you." Sure, there are experts galore, but Montes has only been funding those that furthered his war.

"What are you saying?" That vein begins pulsing again.

"I don't think you can save me."

Montes lets my words sink in, and for a split second he looks so reasonable. Then the bubble pops.

He stands swiftly, shaking the table as he does so. I stare up at him as he rounds it, his eyes sparking with emotion.

We're fire and gunpowder. Something's about to explode, and I lit the match.

He kicks my chair out and leans in, resting his hand along the back of it. "I can save you, and I *will*."

I meet his gaze. God save me, the man means it.

I swallow. "Montes, it's always going to be this way." I feel like a soothsayer as I speak. "Whether it's the cancer or the Resistance, something's going to get me."

My number's already been drawn. It's simply a matter of time. Montes is the only one besides me that's fighting it at all.

"Haven't you heard?" he says. "Death doesn't come to this house."

CHAPTER 10

SERENITY

IT'S LATE BY the time we return to the palace. Before I can think twice about it, I take off my shoes. I can't remember the last time I walked barefoot outside, and I shouldn't be taken by something as simple as my naked feet touching the ground, but I am. In times of peace, people probably don't have to think about wearing shoes, but I've always had to. You never know when you're going to have to run.

It's a little thing, this freedom, but I enjoy it. I steer us off the stone path to feel the sensation of grass between my toes. I have to bite the inside of my cheek to keep from smiling as I feel the spongy, moist earth beneath my feet and the itchy prick of the lawn. Right now I don't care that a dozen lights are still on in the palace windows, or that we're in view of several guards. Nothing can come between me and this small pleasure.

Montes must notice my fascination with the textures of the earth because he maneuvers us towards an area where the soil is free of grass and plant life. Neither of us acknowledges that I'm interested in walking through the mud and dirt.

He subtly steers me to another section of the palace grounds. Sharp pebbles bite into the pads of my feet. I curse, and suddenly, Montes's hand is trembling in mine.

When I glance over at him, he's laughing.

I push him. "You did that on purpose."

Now he's not bothering to curb his laughter. "I did."

"That's what I get for trusting you." The usual venom is gone from my words. I find I enjoy Montes's teasing at the moment.

"C'mon," he says. "I promise no more nasty surprises."

He leads me to a hose. Like many things here, this mundane piece of equipment is something of a novelty. I've seen and, on a couple occasions, used hoses before, and the WUN still had some running water when I left it, but no one waters their lawns anymore.

Montes turns it on and angles the spray at my toes.

"Lift your foot." I do so. He grabs my ankle and rinses the dirt off. I have to brace myself against his shoulder to keep my balance. It's oddly intimate. He lets go of my right foot and beckons for the other.

I study his features as he rinses me off. He's caring for me, I realize. This is what friends do, what family and lovers do. I must indeed be a strange, strange girl to covet these moments with the king more than the fancy dinners he arranges.

He releases my foot, and then we're moving again.

The king's palaces have always looked ominous to me, and tonight's no different. Beneath the stars, we have no ranking, no responsibilities, no civilization, but inside this building that all changes.

We cross the threshold, and I bid goodbye to the few threads of freedom I found outside. I let myself lose count of all the twists and turns that take us to Montes's room.

Our room, I correct as we step inside.

I hover near the door. A big four-poster bed looms in front of me. I have to get in it with the king. I sober up instantly.

Most of my memory has returned. I know what we do in beds like this one, but I still feel like a stranger in my own body. And after our dinner in the greenhouse and our walk through the gardens, I'm feeling strangely vulnerable.

The slick sounds of material sliding off jolts me. I glance over at Montes just as he removes his last article of clothing. His deeply tan body is fully on display, and I'm having trouble fighting my own impulses. It takes most of my energy just to pretend he's not every bit as lovely as he knows he is.

He pads over to me. His hands brush my hair off my shoulders. "Scared?"

How have I ended up here? With no family save for Montes, the very person that took them all away from me.

"Of you? No."

It's my conflicted emotions that scare me. They're sucking me under, and I'm afraid that once they do, I won't like the woman they fashion me into.

"Then come to bed."

It's not a request, it's a dare, and he punctuates it by pulling loose the tie around my dress. The fabric parts with a little encouragement from the king, and then my outfit slides off.

Montes circles me, his hand trailing across my flesh. With a flick of his wrist he undoes my bra. His fingers move to my panties, and he hooks them around the thin bands of material and yanks them down before returning once more to face me.

I blink, startled, as we stand naked across from one another.

Montes's eyes dip down and then he's backing up towards the bed. "Come, Serenity."

I hesitate, but even this is a lost cause. He's my husband. This is a part of the package.

Following him to bed, I slip beneath the sheets and keep my back to Montes. My muscles tense. I'm not going to fall asleep anytime soon.

An arm snakes around my waist and Montes pulls me against his chest. I can feel every naked inch of him pressed along my back.

He breathes in my hair, nuzzling the shell of my ear. "I will never let you go, and I will never let you die. You will be mine, always."

HANDS GLIDE OVER my legs. Am I in a dream or out of one? I can't tell.

I crack my eyes open. Early morning light filters into the room, and my lips crack into a smile. As long as I live, the sight of it will never grow old.

Montes's lips brush against mine, stealing my smile. The kiss is quick, gentle, and his mouth's gone before I can react at all.

He moves down my body, his hair tickling the skin of my chest as he drops lower.

I push myself up onto my elbows. "What are you doing?"

Montes skims a kiss along my ribcage, his rough cheek scraping my flesh. "Waking my wife up."

This isn't terribly out of character for him, but I'm still not used to it.

He presses my torso back to the mattress. His hand stays against my sternum until I stop resisting. His other slides lower. And lower.

I catch his wrist.

I'm so, so terribly conflicted, mostly because I enjoy doing this with the king.

"Let go, Serenity," he says, gazing down at me. His eyes are too dark, his skin too tan, his teeth too white. His features are unnatural, just like the rest of him.

"You first," I say.

Ever so slowly, he lifts his hand from my skin and holds it up in surrender. I don't trust him to play by any sort of rules when it comes to being physical.

A knock on the door interrupts us.

He sighs. "Grab a robe."

"Why?" I ask, but I'm already pushing myself out of bed and heading towards what looks to be a closet. The sheer quantity of clothing inside it has me reeling back. I'm not seeing a robe. This really would be easier if someone thinned out the clothes in here by a factor of ten.

I grab the first item I do see and don it. Too late I realize I've slipped on one of Montes's button-downs, and now the door's opening.

The king flashes me a heated look at my outfit. I want to knock the expression off his face. For his part, he's managed to slide on a pair of lounge pants.

A group of women enter the room, and—oh God. No, please, no.

They're carrying canvas bags in colors ranging from pink to black. I've seen those bags before. This doesn't bode well.

"What's going on?" I take a step back.

"Press conference in … " he strides over to a dresser and picks up a watch resting on it, "three hours."

"You're telling me this now?"

"Someone has to keep you on your toes." He flashes me a grin, like this is all good fun.

As soon as I reestablish myself here, I'm getting my own schedule.

The women bustle over to me, and my earlier fears are confirmed. They're here to primp me up.

"I can do this myself." I speak to the room in general, but it's Montes who answers.

"I didn't ask if you could."

They usher me over to a chair and get to work, touching my face, running their hands through my hair, brandishing sets of jewelry for me to try on.

The only things I tend to accessorize are my weapons.

Montes pulls up a chair next to me.

"Oh, staying this time are you?" I try to turn my head to him, but that earns me a firm tug on my scalp and a gentle admonishment from the hairstylist hovering over me.

I give myself fifteen minutes before the last of my patience runs out and I turn violent.

"I need to prep you on your speech." I can hear mirth in his voice. My trigger finger itches.

"What speech? Wait, *my* speech?" Just when I thought all of the morning's nasty surprises were over.

"The video of you returning to the WUN has been leaked. The world's seen the footage of you." The footage of me drenched with my enemy's blood.

And my father's.

"They also know that the Resistance captured you—albeit, briefly. The terrorist organization released video and a statement on the event, and I spoke about it shortly after you were taken."

For a girl who's lived underground for the last five years, there's an awful lot of media attention on me—and most of it bad.

"What do you want me to say?" I ask. I'm legitimately curious how the king handles affairs like this.

"What would you say if you were still an emissary for the WUN?"

"I'd tell them that you were the devil."

Above me I hear at least one woman suck in a breath.

"That's not what I meant," the king says.

"I know." And I do. "You want me to debrief them on my experience?"

"You don't actually have to worry. We have a speech already written for you. All you're going to do is read from the teleprompter."

"You're seriously trusting me with a microphone and your subjects?" I badly want to look over at Montes just to read his face.

"*Our* subjects. You've been practicing for this for the better part of your life, Serenity. This isn't just my world; it's your world and it's their world. Do right by it."

DO RIGHT.

Montes's words linger with me even as we slide into the car that will take us to the press conference.

What is right?

I don't know anymore.

I glance over at the king, who's flipping through a stack of papers one of his aides gave him.

He is so sure of everything, and I am sure of nothing. I can't tell which is the worse fate—to question everything, to be paralyzed by indecision, or to question nothing and move through the world blind to any other way of existing save for your own.

My thoughts are whisked from me as we leave the palace grounds. This is the first time since the king retrieved me that I see the world outside.

I place my hand against the window. Fields of weeds and wild grass float by. Wherever we are, it's far from any broken city. A morning mist clings to the ground, but with each passing minute it dissipates a little more.

"Where are we?"

I don't expect Montes to answer. He didn't last time. So I'm surprised when he does.

"We're in what used to be known as England."

I remember England from the history books. It was one of the first countries to fall. By the time my father and I flew to Geneva for the peace talks, the Northern Isles were one of King Montes Lazuli's most secure regions. The Resistance didn't have a great foothold there, which might be one of the reasons why the king and I are currently here.

It strikes me all over again how intent Montes is on keeping me safe. It's been this way since he learned of my cancer. The thought leaves my throat dry.

I grab a water bottle nestled in the center console of the car and take a drink of it before going back to staring out the window.

Nearly an hour goes by in that car. Sometimes we pass through villages that look completely unaffected by the king's war, and twice we pass through bigger towns that show only the barest hints of repair—scaffolding along the sides of some buildings and a temporary wall erected around a block. This might just be general maintenance. It's been so long since I've seen how normal cities function that I can't be sure.

When we reach the city, everything gleams. If there was once war here, the evidence has been painted and rebuilt away. People here stand by the side of the road, waving as we go by. They actually appear ... excited to see the king's procession of vehicles.

That's a first.

The car slows to a stop in front of what appears to be an enormous coliseum. We're shuffled past the waiting throngs of people, down a series of halls, and out to an outdoor stage.

"This is all you now," the king says. He peels away from me while the organizers direct me from the wings of the stage towards the podium.

I almost stagger back when I catch a glimpse of the crowd. There are thousands of them. The seats are all full. It's a far cry from the last speech I gave.

Covered in blood, my body shaking. My father was dead and I had to inform the WUN.

The crowd roars as they catch sight of me.

These aren't the same people who waited for me to disembark all that time ago. These people are foreigners with entirely separate histories. This new world of mine has been theirs for far longer. What could they possibly want from me? What would I want from me?

A leader. A real one. The world doesn't trust Montes.

They continue to cheer as I approach the dais. Their applause is a terrible, terrible sound because it's a lie. I've killed their comrades, their sons and daughters, their friends and neighbors.

I draw in a shuddering breath at the podium, and it echoes from the speakers. Montes stands only a handful of feet away, back in the shadows hidden off to the side of the stage, but we might as well be separated by oceans.

My eyes find the teleprompter. Just as quickly, they leave it. If I'm going to give a speech, the words will be my own.

I clear my throat. "I'm honored that you've cheered for me, given that most of you have seen the footage of me stepping onto former WUN soil."

Any remaining noise dies out at that, and I can see PR people gesturing wildly to cut off my mike.

I curl my hands over the edge of the podium and bow my head. The pain is right there. All I have to do is give it a little attention and I'll fall apart. Luckily for me, I have no interest in indulging it. I've spent the better part of a decade too busy surviving to afford the luxury of living inside my sadness. I won't start today.

"Several months ago, you were my enemy and my husband, the king, was the one man I most wanted to see dead."

More wild gesturing comes from the wings of the stage, but Montes must be refusing their requests because no one comes to drag me off.

"I was born in Washington D.C., the daughter of an American congressman. When I was ten, I watched my mother die. The aerial attack came from the sky. A few years later, a nuclear blast wiped out my city. Aside from my father, everyone I'd known and loved was gone in an instant."

My words are met with utter silence.

"I'm telling you this because many of you have similar stories. They might be older, but they're no less painful."

The ominous silence turns to murmuring. People are listening, some nodding.

"I may have married the king, but I am not him. I am one of you. I hurt like you, I love like you, and I can die like you."

The words flow out of me. I don't know if anything I'm saying finds its mark, but this is the best I have to offer.

"I've seen what war does to a place. It brings out the worst in us. But the war is over. It's time for us to not simply survive, but to thrive …"

The crowd's talking and shifting. People point to the erected screens and I follow their gazes.

I see myself, my face angled slightly away from the camera. Dripping from my nose is a line of blood. I reach up and touch it, staring at my fingers.

The noise of the crowd rises. People are shouting, and they're repeating one word over and over—

Plague.

CHAPTER 11

SERENITY

"IT'S GOING TO be okay."

Five words every soldier fears.

You can rephrase them, elaborate on them, parse them down, but the meaning is always the same: you're fucked.

It doesn't help that the royal physician—Dr. Goldstein, the man who administered the antidote to my memory loss—says this while wearing a hazmat suit. He's already swabbed my cheek and taken a sample of my blood for testing, and now he's cleansing my arm for a shot.

What no one's mentioning is that the king's pills should've prevented me from catching plague in the first place. Or that the plague has run its course in this region of the world.

"What are the odds that the shot will work?" Montes asks from where he holds me down alongside his guards. I've obviously been a little too transparent with my hate for doctors.

I don't fight them too hard, however. The king and his men have quarantined themselves with me inside this room in the palace, and judging from the bits and pieces I've gathered, they could be at risk.

Even the king.

It's unlikely, considering that prior exposure to the virus means their bodies should have the immunities needed to fight it, but it's not impossible.

The doctor's shaking his head. "Decent, though I'd need to see her bloodwork first."

He slips the needle under my skin, and now I do jerk my limbs.

"She can take a bullet, but not a shot," the king murmurs. I think he's trying to lighten the mood. He shouldn't bother. I know the odds. Despite what the king said last night, Death and I are old friends, and he's decided to pay me a visit.

TWO HOURS LATER it's clear the shot hasn't worked. I'm drenched in sweat, yet I have the chills. No wonder this plague killed so many. It has a swift onset and it escalates quickly.

My head pounds, my brain feeling far too swollen for the cavity it rests in. For once, there's no nausea, just an ache that's burrowed itself into my bones.

Montes sits at my side. "You're okay," he says, taking my hand.

My teeth chatter. "Stop saying that."

His lips tilt into a smile, and he brushes the hair back from my face. "This wasn't how I imagined getting you on your back."

"You're such an asshole," I say, but my lips twitch at his words. He understands that I don't want pity. I'll drink up his strength.

Unlike the others, he hasn't bothered donning even a mask. My eyes prick. Illness unwinds the last of my defenses. The immortal king risks his own health to be by my side. I'm too sick to wonder about this, but not too sick to be moved by it.

Montes wipes away a tear that leaks out the corner of my eye, staring at it wondrously. "She cries."

"Put on a mask, Montes." I can't think about the fact that I'm actually concerned about his wellbeing.

"I'll be fine."

I want to place my hands over his lips to stop him from speaking, but that might just increase his chances of catching whatever I have.

"Please."

A knock on the door interrupts us. A moment later the doctor, who had left to run my bloodwork, returns, clad once more in a hazmat suit.

One look at his face and I know whatever he has to say won't be good.

"Montes," he says, not meeting my eyes, "a moment please?"

THE KING

DR. GOLDSTEIN PULLS me to the edge of the room.

"I sent Serenity's bloodwork to the lab," he says when I approach him. He looks tired, which is not the expression I want to see on his face.

"The lab confirmed that the queen does in fact have the plague. However," the doctor looks more than a little concerned, "this strain ... it's new."

"It's *new*?"

How does a new strain of plague show up out of thin air and choose my wife as its first victim?

"Where did it originate from?"

"One of your laboratories—the one stationed in Paris."

It takes me a moment to register his words. I'm expecting him to say a general region like the Balkan Peninsula, not a specific location, and definitely not one of my labs.

"From what I was able to gather, it matches a strain of plague your researchers have been testing."

The news is a shock to my system.

"They're in the initial stages of creating an inoculation for this strain," Goldstein continues, "but an inoculation won't do Serenity any good now that she's already caught it. We've already given her the antidote for the old virus."

"What good is an old antidote if this is not the same illness?" My voice is rising. I pinch the bridge of my nose and pace. "And how the hell did this get leaked?"

Heads are going to fucking roll. Now I just need to figure out whose those will be.

"Your Majesty, we have no idea. No one at the research station in Paris has reported a contamination, but that could be a failure in oversi—"

"Don't feed me that bullshit."

This was a deliberate attack. Someone went into one of my laboratories and harvested a super virus to kill my queen with.

I run a hand down my face. I'll torture all those technicians one by one until I have my answers, and then I will hunt down whoever did this and I will kill them slowly. A point must be made: those who dare to turn my weapons against me and my own will die, along with many innocents.

"What's the kill rate?" I ask.

"Pardon?" Dr. Goldstein says.

"The kill rate. How lethal is this strain?"

"Your Majesty—"

"Just give me the goddamn number, Goldstein."

He shakes his head. "I don't know. Your researchers in Paris didn't know, but they thought it was somewhere around," he takes a breath, "eighty percent."

Eighty percent.

Eighty percent.

I've turned away from him before even realizing I've done so. I rub my mouth at the horror of it all. Four out of every five victims die.

I glance over at Serenity just as she lets out a wet, rattling cough.

"What happens at this point?" I ask, returning my attention to Dr. Goldstein. "Do we move her into the Sleeper?"

Goldstein shakes his head. "The Sleeper specializes in trauma, not illness. It won't work for this, just like it won't cure Serenity of cancer.

"Your Majesty," he continues, his voice already apologetic, "this is out of our hands. If the queen is to live, she'll have to beat this on her own."

SERENITY'S CONDITION WORSENS. By the evening, she's strapped to several different monitors, and I tense at every beep.

No one else in the room contracts the plague. It's not too surprising given that on this end of the hemisphere, people have either survived the plague once, or been inoculated against it. Goldstein speculates that this mutated strain is much less transmutable, meaning that while lethal, it won't readily spread. This only strengthens the argument that someone deliberately infected my wife.

And Serenity, who's never encountered the plague before, has no defenses against it. The pills that should've protected her from this pathogen, the pills that prevent me from aging, she hasn't taken since the bombing on the palace, which was a month ago. Any she took before then have long since been purged from her system.

I watch her toss and turn in the hospital bed.

I brought one of the victims of my war into my house, and she's brought the world's blights in with her.

I run my hand over hers. Scars mar her knuckles; it's the same hand that wears my rings. Love and war—they battle it out across her skin. I thread my fingers between hers and bring them to my mouth.

Serenity doesn't react to the touch, but I do. My hand trembles, and I can't be sure whether fear or fury are responsible for the palsy.

Even as I sit here, my researchers are being interrogated and punished.

It's not enough to slack my need for vengeance. Not nearly.

Serenity lets out a moan and tugs against my grip. Only then do I realize I've been squeezing her hand so tightly my knuckles have whitened.

That night in Geneva, when I first held her under the stars, I told her all the ways she was unexceptional—how she wasn't the prettiest, or the smartest, or the funniest person I'd encountered. I didn't bother to tell her that she was the most ferocious woman I'd ever met, or the most tragic. I didn't tell her that whatever combination of pain and hardship she'd endured, it enthralled me completely.

She's not dying. She can't. Serenity's final act is not succumbing to fever in a hospital bed.

Serenity will live—she must. I rely upon it, and humanity relies upon it. Otherwise, I won't rest until the world burns.

CHAPTER 12

SERENITY

THEY SAY IT took me five days to beat this thing.

They say that it was the most lethal strain of plague they'd yet seen. They tell me that four out of every five people die from it. That my compromised immune system saved me from death by a virus that primarily kills the healthy.

They say that someone planted the virus on or near me.

They say it was the Resistance.

I believe everything but the last.

"Trust me when I tell you that if the Resistance knew about your super virus, they would've taken advantage of it long ago," I say to the king's council.

I'm pacing inside one of the palace's conference rooms as Montes and his advisors go over the attack.

"It's been months since you were part of the Resistance," one of his men says—a former West African ruler. "How would you know that?"

The king's lounging back in his chair, his calculating eyes moving between me and the advisor. He's been quiet, and that's probably for the best. Usually when he talks someone ends up with a bullet between their eyes.

"You were the one that suggested that Resistance members are planted everywhere," the man continues. "Now we're missing a driver and an official car; one matching its description has been found near a suspected Resistance stronghold."

"Correlation is not the same as causation," I say.

The man guffaws, and I thin my eyes. The derision these men have for me is almost palpable. I know what they see: a young, pretty girl from a backwards nation who wishes to talk to them as equals. They can barely stand it. And while I enjoy their silent seething, I'm never going to make inroads with these men if they don't respect my opinion.

I place my hands on the table and stare him down, letting the civility bleed from my expression. I'm no delicate flower. I've seen more of war's atrocities first hand than most—if not all—of these men have.

"It's reasoning like that that's set the world back decades and dropped the global lifespan from the high sixties to the mid-thirties," I say.

He stares back at me with flinty eyes. "It's reasoning like yours, my queen, that's nearly gotten you killed multiple times."

"*Efe.*" Montes rises from his chair, his expression ominous. The threat is clear—an insult to me is an insult to him.

"They're both right." This comes from Alexander Gorev—or Alexei, as he prefers. I know him better as the Beast of the East. Everyone in the WUN's heard tales of the former general's penchant for torture and rape. He's the man who replaced Marco's seat. Now he's trying to be everyone's best friend to make up for the fact that he's new to this council. I'm having trouble not stealing one of the guards' guns and putting a bullet in his belly, right where I know death will come only after an agonizing ten minutes.

My gaze flicks to him, and whatever he was going to say dies on his lips. He must sense how close to death he is. Him I will kill eventually.

I don't understand why Montes has chosen this group of despots as his advisors, but I now understand why he uses fear to get them to cooperate. It's the only mechanism that they react to.

"I didn't come here to discuss my mortality," I say.

"Mmm, but I did." Montes's voice coils around us all. He'd barely let me out of bed this morning, despite being cleared for activity by Dr. Goldstein. Only my expert opinion on the Resistance and his own thirst for vengeance swayed him.

"We've been working on this for a week," he continues, "and we've made no progress. Who do I have to kill to make things happen?"

If only the psycho were joking.

His men pale. Already the whispers I've heard suggest that the king's killed off several people he suspected of facilitating my assassination.

"Perhaps we could start with you, Efe."

The man's eyes widen, but before he has a chance to plead with the king, Montes's eyes move to Alexei. "Or you."

I swear the Beast stops breathing. He hasn't become accustomed to the king's threats.

"Hmmm, no," Montes continues, "I believe the blame must lie with all of you. You have another day. Bring me something tomorrow, or I'll find myself new advisors."

People nod and murmur, some shuffle papers. Just another day in the life of a demagogue's advisor.

Someone clears his throat. "We should discuss the former WUN."

My hackles rise at the mention of my homeland. These men are predators ready to tear into their newest kill.

My eyes land on the speaker. Ronaldo. He was the one that orchestrated the nuclear blasts that wiped my country apart, the one whose life I saved in one of these last meetings.

"No." The word is out before I can censor myself.

Montes swivels in his chair, an eyebrow raised.

"*I* will be dealing with the WUN," I say. Not Ronaldo, who played a key role in destroying it. Not any of these other men that hold no love for the scarred land I once called home.

Montes's advisors look aghast. Their gazes move from me to the king and back.

"Your Majesty?" It's Walrus Man from our wedding who pipes up, the man with the bulging eyes and belly. I don't remember his name and I don't particularly care.

The king focuses all that disturbing intensity of his onto the advisor. "Yes?"

Walrus glances to either side of him, his face beginning to redden when no one else speaks up. Had he thought to dispute me? Was it his hope that breaking the silence would herald in more complaints from his colleagues? No one else seems interested in disputing the king's wife, despite the fact that many of them appear angry.

Such loyal comrades, these men.

"Nothing," Walrus says.

Weak, weak man.

"Good." Montes's eyes twinkle when they meet mine. He keeps me around because I'm still amusing to him. "Your queen's spoken," he says to the room. "All dealings with the western hemisphere will go through her from this day forward."

There's a collective exhale as twelve men hand over their balls to a woman. I can't help the satisfied smile that stretches across my face. I made a promise to myself that I'd help my homeland.

Today I've begun to in earnest.

"YOU DEFIED ME," the king says after the meeting.

The last of his men have left, and by the time we leave the conference room, there's no sign in the hallways that over a dozen of the world's wickedest men had convened here ten minutes ago.

"Taking control away from those men is not defiance."

The king's hand falls to the back of my neck, his fingers caressing the pulse points on either side of it. It's oddly sensual, but it's also an innate threat. Power flows from the king; for all my posturing I'm just his puppet.

He pulls the side of my head to his lips. "It is if I say it is," he said, his breath tickling my ear.

Even his words are some combination of sensuality and threat. My mouth usually gets me into trouble, I decide for once to muzzle it.

"How are you feeling?" Montes asks. He still holds my neck hostage, and he's using the grip to keep me even closer.

"Healthy."

Healthy is the last thing I'm feeling. The king doesn't know that half my bathroom breaks consist of me hugging the toilet rather than sitting on it, or that blood continues to speckle the evidence of my sickness. Up until today I've been on forced bedrest. I'm not about to blow my first taste of freedom.

"I was hoping you'd say so. Tonight we're hosting a very important dinner party; if you're feeling better, you'll be there by my side."

I've been cornered by a master manipulator. It's either attend the stuffy dinner party or languish in bed.

"This is revenge for speaking up today, isn't it?"

This twisted man.

"No, Serenity," the king says. He removes his thumb from my pulse point to stroke it down the back of my neck. "That, I will collect on later."

THE DINNER PARTY we walk into is identical to the ones I went to during the peace talks with the king. The only things missing are the camera crews and my father.

I swallow down the lump in my throat. Had I felt objectified then? It's nothing compared to now. The room's collective gaze fixes on me. I can feel their eyes studying my hair, my makeup, my jewelry, and my outfit. If only they knew that when I walked into my room several hours earlier, someone else had laid it all out for me. The woman they see is a stranger. Maybe one day I'll get just as used to wearing dresses as I do fatigues, but not today.

"Relax your features, my queen," Montes says, his voice pitched low for only me to hear, "you look ready to massacre the room."

"Don't tempt me."

Out of the corner of my eye, I catch a glimpse of Montes's smile.

Ahead of me, thirty odd people lounge in whatever this room is—a sitting room? A standing room? Does it even matter? Most of these rooms look identical to my untrained eyes.

The people here are just as interchangeable, and I have to study their features closely to distinguish them. What I find surprises me.

Some of the younger women wear their hair loosely curled. Just like mine.

Another sports a jewel just below the corner of her eye. It's on the same side as my scar. Several women wear pale yellow dresses. Another wears a gold dress eerily similar to the one I wore at my engagement announcement.

They're emulating me.

I work my jaw. I hate it. What's worse, I'm fueling this.

I don't think I can be civil tonight. Not here, not with these people.

I have to remind myself of all the lessons my father taught me. Not everything needs to be a confrontation.

Shortly after they catch sight of us, Montes's guests begin to approach. Many of the men are his advisors, but not all of them. The bejeweled, bright-eyed women join them, smiles fixed on their faces.

I'm glaring at all of them while Montes charms the group.

"Montes, can I steal your wife away?" This comes from the woman with the jewel at the corner of her eye.

"I'm right here," I say. "You can ask me."

She reels back slightly. "Of course, Your Majesty. Would you care to meet the wives of the king's advisors?"

I would care very much. But this is the world of politics and diplomacy, a world my father schooled me on. Study your enemies.

"It would be a pleasure." The words come out clipped. It's my one lie of the night. I'm tapping out after this.

The king flashes me a look. He knows exactly how deceptive I'm being at the moment.

I'm dragged away from the king towards the far left side of the room, where most of the women are grouped.

"I'm Helen," the woman says as she leads me. "I met you briefly at the wedding, but there were so many people."

She's apologizing for me, like I need or want an out for not remembering her name.

I stare at the rubies that drip from her ears. So this is how the rich bleed— elegantly.

"We're so excited to see the king finally settling down. We thought that he would never," she says as we join the group.

"Your Majesty," the women echo, dipping their heads.

"This is Beatrice, Anouk, Isabel, Katarina, …" Helen introduces. I forget each name the moment my eyes move on to the next. Some are old; most are young.

They can't all be the advisors' wives. The way some of them are looking at me … if I had to guess, I'd say that the king's mixed business and pleasure plenty of times in the past.

Jealousy lances through me before I can stop it. To think that any of them might've also experienced the king as I have …

The thought is followed by a good dose of self-loathing. For me to be jealous of the affections of the king—it's unconscionable.

I square my jaw, forcing my emotions down. I swear the group notices my anger. They shift a little restlessly. I'm a predator among prey.

Someone breaks the silence that follows the introductions.

"Beautiful dress, and—" she gasps, "are those heels from Vesuvio's summer collection?"

I glance down at my toes. Vesuvio?

"They are!" she exclaims. "I adore his entire summer collection. I would *kill* for a pair."

My jaw tightens. "Would you?" I say, looking back up.

The woman falls silent, and the rest of the group tensely watches the exchange, some clutching their jewel-encrusted necklaces. They must sense how offensive I find it to even jest about killing over *pretty* shoes.

Finally, someone breaks the silence and asks the woman next to me about some recent trip she took. As the group gets swept up in the newest conversation, I withdraw further inside myself.

These women are nothing like the ones I'm used to. They care about the length of their skirts and the color of their face paint and the weave of their clothes. They have no idea what goes on outside these walls.

The women I lived with sharpened knives and oiled guns. I saw one fight through a bullet wound to the stomach, even though it eventually killed her. Another performed CPR on an unresponsive boy lying in the streets we patrolled while we were being attacked by local gangs. They were some of the hardest women I ever met, but they would die for you.

And they'd never give a shit what you wore.

Remembering is all it takes.

I leave right in the middle of the conversation. At my back I hear a chorus of soft-spoken protests. I ignore them. Some people you can't change, and the effort of trying would be wasted.

My eyes sweep the room as I walk. The genders are divided. Men to one side of the room, ladies to the other. The women gossip and preen like all those exotic birds that died off first when war struck. They're just like them—pretty and soft and so unenduring. The men swirl amber liquid, their faces ruddy. They look so damn proud of themselves. I want to shout at them that anyone can destroy a city.

And, amongst them all, there's Montes. I never glance his way, but I feel his eyes on me the entire way out.

AS SOON AS I leave the room, the king's guards fall into step behind me. I come close to threatening them, but even if I promised them death, they still wouldn't leave me. Say what you will about Montes, he has some loyal guards.

I storm through the palace, heading for the gardens. I feel a great deal of disgust. This is what the new world order does while its citizens starve. I can't be a part of it.

Once I push open the palace doors and the cool evening air hits my skin, I give into the impulse riding me since I entered that dinner party. I kick my shoes off and wipe my lipstick away with the back of my hand. I pull out the few pins in my hair and shake my locks loose. I pass through the gardens and bypass the giant hedge maze.

I break the delicate clasp of first my bracelet and then my necklace, and let them fall to the ground. Only then do I feel like myself again. I'm still in my dress, and my hands itch to tear into the fabric, but I hold myself back.

I walk across the palace grounds until the back fence comes into view. I head straight for it, my mind replaying the last time I ran towards one of the king's fences. Odd how something as bland as a wall can conjure such memories.

My chest tightens. All my friends are ghosts, and all my memories are dust in the wind. Out here, beneath the stars, I can't help but remember that I am hopelessly, achingly alone.

I stare up at the wrought iron fence. It took losing all that I held dear for me to learn a valuable lesson: only when everything is gone are you truly free.

CHAPTER 13

THE KING

SERENITY CARVED A path of destruction in her wake. She's the untamable wilderness. Of course she can't palette civilized company.

The women are speaking frantically to one another, their eyes darting in my direction. They're worried about my anger, but I don't blame them for being sheep and my wife a wolf.

I'm done sharing my queen anyway. I don't want these politicians or their wives to have any part of her, and I don't want her to give herself away to anyone but me. So after some parting exchanges, I head after her, moving towards the back of the property where my soldiers indicate she went.

Serenity leaves me a trail of expensive breadcrumbs to follow. A satin shoe here, a diamond bracelet there. I follow them to the edge of the palace grounds. She's several feet away from the wrought iron fence that circles the grounds, and she's staring up at it like she's considering the best way to scale it.

"And here I was hoping that you might consider shedding your dress along with the jewelry."

She doesn't flinch at my voice, nor does she turn around.

"How do you live with yourself?" she asks, touching one of the wrought iron bars.

For one instant I fear that if I ever let her go, she'd disappear into the land, never to return. God, she'd want that. And I probably just caught her as she was tasting the possibility on her tongue.

I've been vacillating between anger and arousal since she stormed out of the palace. I settle on anger.

"You make a fool out of me and now you insult me?"

Finally she turns. Her wild eyes search mine, and it doesn't matter that she's broken in all the right places and whole in all the wrong ones. Or that out here with her bare feet and windblown hair, I catch a hint of the woman she should've been. That soul of hers, tempered by the hottest of forges, has been and will always be mine.

And it is probably the evilest thought I've ever had, but I'd ruin the world all over again just to be brought back to this very moment.

"You set yourself up for failure the second you decided to pursue me," she says. "I'm never going to be one of them." She gestures to the palace.

"No, you're not." And I'm glad for it.

"Then why bother making me try?"

"Serenity," I chastise. "I'd think you more than anyone would know the answer to that."

Her dress flaps in the breeze as she waits for me to explain myself.

"Ruling," I say, "isn't always about getting to be who you want to be. It's about sacrifices."

"And what sacrifices have you made? Bombing innocents? Taking a hostage wife?"

Usually I like the chase, but not like this, not when she's deriding me while eyeing my perimeter walls like she's considering escape.

"I am still your king, and you will *not* speak to me that way." My voice resonates in the evening air.

"Then kill me already, or let me go." She has the audacity to look exasperated.

Don't yell at her.

Don't threaten her.

Don't rip off her dress and fuck her.

I should just walk away. I have before when I wanted to shake her. She doesn't realize she's not the only one being tormented here. Instead I take her hand.

She tries to jerk away, but when I don't release her, she relaxes.

She steps in closer, and I only realize what she's about to do the moment before her fist slams into my face. Those scarred knuckles of hers that I admired only days ago now smash into my skin and teeth.

I stumble back at the impact, and she uses the distraction to throw me against the fence. Her hand goes to my neck.

"I am not something you can control, Montes," she says, and the way the shadows play on her face make her appear downright sinister. "I'll do many things for you—"

I raise an eyebrow, though I doubt she can see it out here.

"—but don't try to make me become one of you."

Had I thought I was angry or aroused before? It doesn't hold a candle to the way my blood now heats at her presumptions. She thinks she has me in more ways than one.

I swipe her feet out from under her. I may not have the combat experience she does, but I've had plenty of military training. A moment later, it's me that has her pinned. My legs straddle her torso, and I capture her hands in one of my own, pulling them high over her head.

She glares at me as I press my other hand gently to her throat, noticing the way her hair spills across the lawn. For a woman who has little time for appearances, she takes awfully good care of those golden locks.

"My queen," I say, "you're seriously misguided if you think you have any agency outside of what I give you. I will *allow* you some measure of control over our empire, and in return you will attend every dinner party I host. I'll chain you to my side if I have to."

She's moving beneath me, trying to pry my hold from her. It's only serving to display every pleasing angle of hers.

"Now," I say, "about those many things you'll do for me ..."

"Give me a knife and I'll show you."

I let out a husky laugh and move one of my legs to the inside of her thighs. "Still uncomfortable with sex, I see. I'm taking that as a challenge."

I remove my hand from her throat to grasp her freed leg. Her skirts pool around her waist. She looks indecent, and on Serenity, indecent is a good look.

She's no longer trying to free herself from my grip, and her chest's rising and falling faster and faster. From what I can make out of her expression, I'm thinking she has no idea what to make of intimacy in all its forms.

219

A spark of protectiveness flares in me. Despite everything this world's thrown at her, Serenity still maintains a shred of innocence when it comes to things between a man and a woman. That's going to disappear eventually—marriage will force her hand—but I'm not too keen on rushing her in this.

I'm a wicked man. I've never made bones about that. So I don't readily recognize myself when I get off of Serenity and extend a hand towards her. I'm not sure I like this side of me, either.

Slowly she sits up. I can feel her gaze on me. We've been here before. She doesn't take my hand, but she does stand.

She turns her head to the blazing lights of the palace. "We should probably go back."

I stick my hands in my pockets and study her. This is her peace offering. She'll go back inside what she sees as a bastion of depravity.

"Alright," I say.

And together we return to the castle.

SERENITY

SOMETHING'S HAPPENING BETWEEN me and the king. It's been happening for a while, but it's not slowing down.

I stretch my legs out in the tub. I can still feel the phantom fingers of the king as they moved up my calf last night. The sensation reminded me of another time he ran his hands up my legs, only then I'd been trying to seduce him. Both times, he'd backed off.

Both times, I'd felt conflicted by his reluctance.

I hear the rustle of sheets in the adjoining bedroom, pulling me back to the present.

The king's awake.

Heat courses through me, and I hate myself a little that he can make me feel this way at all. And that while I might be in the bath, my mind is with the king.

It takes him all of thirty seconds to make his way to the door.

I startle as it opens, water splashing against the walls of the tub. I cover myself with my arms.

"What are you doing in here?" I demand.

I hadn't locked the door because I had thought Montes would give me privacy here of all places.

I obviously thought wrong.

He's naked and sleep-ruffled, and in this moment, I can't possibly reconcile him with the evil dictator I've hated so passionately.

"There's my wife." Even his voice is rough and uncultivated in the morning. It's just one more small intimacy that I get with the king.

His molten eyes move from me to the water. "Now I know who's been using up the palace's water supply."

"Are you going to let me take my bath?"

"That's not a bath," he says, "that's a puddle." He bends down, uncaring that I'm clearly uncomfortable, and sticks his hand in the water. "And it's tepid." Montes turns on the hot water spigot.

"What are you doing?" I ask, alarmed.

"Taking a bath," he says, stepping in. "My wife thinks it's good to conserve water. I'm supporting the cause." By joining me. This man is slippery.

"You can uncover yourself," he adds. "Your nudity doesn't offend me."

My gaze slits.

He settles against the opposite side of the tub, stretching his legs out until they brush mine, and he drapes his arms along the rim. It's a good thing the basin is large enough to comfortably fit two people. Even so, he's still crowding me.

Is this what married couples do? Step on each other's toes until the notion of privacy is entirely done away with? I can't escape this man.

I uncover myself and lean back against the tub, all too aware of our nakedness.

Montes settles that heavy gaze of his on me, and he wears his acquisitive look. This isn't just a bath if he has it his way.

He picks up my foot and begins to rub it.

"Montes—" I try to jerk my foot from his grip.

"I'm helping you relax, *nire bihotza*."

"I will kick you."

He sets my foot back down and returns to staring at me.

"I have a question for you," I say.

He raises his eyebrows. "She has an interest in her husband? Who would've thought?"

"'She' is sitting across from you and 'she' would appreciate it if you stopped referring to her in the third person."

His mouth curves into a smirk. "No death threats for me this morning? I'm disappointed."

"If you don't stop referring to me in the third person, I'll drown you in this puddle—as you so eloquently put it."

"There's my girl."

"I'm not your girl."

He leans back in the tub. "Don't you have a question for me?"

I work my jaw, annoyed he's caught me in a web of my own making. "Why are there no women in your government?"

"There are."

"You know what I mean."

"You mean my inner circle of advisors and officers? There were once women. They ended up being too soft for the job."

"That's your reasoning? Fuck you, Montes, and all your sexist ideals."

"They're not ideals. The women couldn't stomach it."

And the one woman that—according to him—apparently can has stomach cancer. I'm not going to peer at that one too closely.

"Had you ever considered the fact that maybe what you saw as weakness was instead compassion?"

"What, are you a champion now for women's rights?" he says. "Odd since you seem to clash with most of them."

In fact, I got along quite well with the women I lived with. It's just the ones here that I can't stand.

"I clash with most people. That has nothing to do with it."

He pushes away from his end of the bathtub and moves towards mine. He's eating up the final space between us, and there's nowhere for me to go.

221

Montes looms over me, his glistening torso close enough to touch. That dark hair of his hangs near his eyes as he looks down at me. Just when I think he's going to make a move, he reaches up and shuts off the water.

It goes to show you how captivated by this man I am that I don't notice until now that the water level is past my shoulder.

Montes is hovering over me, his knees on either side of mine. The crook of his index finger dampens my chin as he tilts my face up. "We can hire more women. Is that all you wanted to talk about?"

"No—"

He cuts me off with a kiss, his hand moving from my chin to my cheek. His other one finds my hip and grips it tightly.

It hits me then. He wants me, badly; he's practically quaking with the need. I can taste it in his kiss, I can feel it in the pressure of his grip.

The entire time since my memories returned, Montes hasn't pushed sex on me. He takes many things, but not this. It's the barest glimmer of a conscience.

And here I was disappointed in him for it. I need to shed this shyness.

So I give in.

I let myself slide my fingers through his mussed hair and kiss away the droplets of water that drip onto our lips. Our mouths open and I taste this taboo that's forced his way into my world.

He's poison and radiation and he's seeping into my bloodstream, tainting me from the inside out. I'll never be free of him.

And God, he tastes just like me.

Montes moves between my legs and I help him angle my pelvis up to meet his. If he hadn't known before that I was willing, now he does.

The last of his restraint falls away.

I gasp into his mouth as he fills me. This is our world, this starved, desolate place. Both of us want things we don't know how to attain. So we seek solace in each other.

Our eyes lock as Montes draws away and pistons back into me. His hands are on my breasts and in my hair. I get the impression that he wants to be everywhere all at once. It's not enough to taste me and move inside me.

My hands glide down his backside, leaving watery trails in their wake, and I pull him closer. My hair floats about us, curling about Montes like it never had a problem with him in the first place.

Finally his restless hands find my face, and they cup it. We stare at each other while he moves in and out of me. My heart pounds as I fall into his eyes. We stay like that until the king's hot water turns tepid once more.

And for once the two of us make love instead of war.

CHAPTER 14

SERENITY

ALL PRODUCTIVE GOVERNMENTS have schedules and patterns. Reliable systems put in place to chart out the ruling of a country—or, in this case, the world. The king's is no different. So despite the early morning festivities, we both get ready for work.

We dress—me in black jeans and boots, the closest thing to combat gear I now own—and the king in a pressed suit.

Since the bath, we've both been keenly aware of each other. I don't think either of us is prone to softer emotions, but what happened less than an hour ago hasn't happened before.

We've had sex, yes, but we've never fallen into each other the way we just did. It wasn't supposed to be like this. Marriage—and sex—I'd agreed to. But not love.

I hadn't even thought I'd be vulnerable to falling for the king. I'd only ever meant to bide my time until I could thrust a dagger into his heart or a bullet into his brain.

But now I know that won't happen. Not now that I've seen the sharks he works alongside. Not now that I've grown to care for him.

"Ready?" he asks, extending his arm towards me.

I ignore his arm and reach for the door. Where I'm from, after all, chivalry is long dead.

"Happy to see that I put you in good spirits this morning," Montes says as he follows me out.

He doesn't know the half of it. My heart's still beating too fast, and every time I close my eyes I see the way he looked at me as he moved inside me. Like more than just sex passed between us. I hate that he's convinced me that there's another side to him. I hate that I want to drop back and take his hand, or hold his face in place while I memorize those irises that scared me for so long.

My own urges make me feel dirty. It's one thing to be taken by a monster, and quite another to be taken with him.

"You vastly overestimate your skills, Montes," I say. "I'm beginning to understand why you settled on world domination before marriage."

"My queen *did* enjoy herself," Montes says. He sounds so smug. "Perhaps a little too much?"

I run my tongue over my teeth. It would do me no good to respond to him. But it burns to not rise to his bait.

The palace is already bustling with people. Save for the guards, all the men are in suits, and the few women I see wear heels and skirts. I'm the only one wearing anything sensible. It's just another reminder that these people were once my enemy, and they were so untouchable that safety never dictated what they wore. They never had to worry about fleeing the palace at a moment's notice.

This den of iniquity is now my home, and at the moment I'd love nothing more than to burn it to the ground, just to let these people feel a shadow of what I have my entire life.

Ahead of us, the servant carrying tea is the only one, as far as I can tell, who's wearing shoes she can run in. Not even the others that mill the halls wear the same sensible black shoes she does.

Perhaps it's that small detail that has me giving her a second look. A linen cloth is thrown over her forearm, and the base of the silver teapot she carries rests on it.

She's only feet away from me, her eyes downcast. She's not looking where she's going, and even as I try to sidestep her, she manages to bump into me.

I feel the pressure of the knife sliding into me well before I feel the pain. That's all it takes for my training to kick in.

Working on reflex alone, I grab the woman's wrist and yank it behind her back. She cries out as I sweep her feet out from under her and follow her to the ground.

Jesus. Now I feel the pain. It only makes me more aggressive. I grind my knee into her back and pull her wrists more tightly together. My blood slips down the hilt of the dagger protruding from me and drips onto her.

"Nice try," I whisper in her ear.

"*Guards!*" Montes yells.

The people in the hallway stand frozen as guards run to our side, a few gasp as they catch sight of me. Here in their world, nothing bad happens.

The guards gently push me away as they take over restraining the woman.

I rise to my feet slowly, careful not to cut more of myself. Montes helps me up the rest of the way.

"We need a medic!" he shouts.

He's staring at the line of blood blooming across my abdomen, his face shell-shocked.

Two attempts on my life within a single week. Someone wants me dead. "You really should give me back my gun."

IT'S ONLY ONCE I'm standing that I realize the woman inflicted more than just a flesh wound. My hands move to my stomach as I sway.

"Serenity?" Montes's eyes are wider than usual. He turns to the guards not dispensing with the hit woman. "We need a doctor! Now!"

I place a hand on him to steady myself and stare down at the woman who's now being jerked to her feet by several of his men. That was bold of her, trying to kill me in the king's headquarters. She had to know she'd get caught. That she would be killed.

Montes holds my sides like he wants to draw me into him, but he's afraid of jostling me. His eyes follow mine to my attacker.

"Make her talk by whatever means necessary," he says. "Then make an example of her."

The woman hasn't said a word this entire time, and really what is there to say? She catches my eye as the guards drag her away. There's nothing there. No remorse, no anger, no fear. That's something else I've learned from war. Sometimes, violence isn't personal. Sometimes it's cold and passionless. And sometimes, you'll never know a person's motives.

As she's taken away, several sets of feet sprint down the hall. A handful of medics move towards us, pushing a stretcher between them.

Now I'm half considering removing this knife from my belly and attacking my attacker for making me face more doctors.

Once the medical crew reaches us, they make quick work of laying me onto the stretcher. I reach for Montes's hand and grip it in my own bloody one.

"Stay with me," I whisper.

His nostrils flare as he breathes through his nose. That perfect suit of his is now rumpled. "I'm not going anywhere."

I've heard that love was messy, but ours is downright bloody. It turns men into monsters, and monsters into men.

I don't care that soldiers, medics, staff, and politicians are watching. I bring his bloody hand to my lips and kiss his knuckles. And the entire time they wheel me away, I hold my monster tightly to me.

THE KING

THEY PUT HER in the Sleeper again.

She fought it. Again.

Her pain almost broke me.

Again.

I've never bloodied my own hands, but I'm honestly giving it thought at the moment. Someone's targeting my wife, someone wants her dead.

The Resistance had been the likeliest suspect. Serenity herself warned me that they had eyes everywhere. But Serenity's attacker never fully broke under interrogation, which in and of itself means that she wasn't just some crazed vigilante. What she did say was that someone paid her off. That's not how the Resistance does their dirty work.

But if not them, then who?

I sit outside Serenity's Sleeper, my elbows braced on my thighs and my hands shoved through my hair. I've taken to coming here between my meetings. This time, the doctor joins me.

"You had some information for me?" I say to Dr. Goldstein, staring at the Sleeper as it hums away.

"Yes."

My heart's thundering, though I don't let on that it is. I'm afraid, I'm desperately afraid of what this man is going to tell me about Serenity. Special news from Goldstein is almost always unwelcome.

"What is it?"

"Her injury's fully healed. The Sleeper is removing the malignant tissue it has detected. It should be done in another two hours, then she'll be out."

I already know this.

"If nothing is done for her ... the cancer will eventually overtake her system. It's only a matter of time. If you want her to live, not just for the next year, but for as long as you intend to, then I'd advise you to consider leaving Serenity in there for ... a longer stretch of time."

He wants me to leave her in there like some sort of vegetable until we find a cure for her cancer. Marco advised the same thing while he was still alive. And if we were talking about anyone other than Serenity, I might. But now that my oldest friend's gone, my wife is my closest companion, and she's swiftly becoming something more.

She could be in there for years, imprisoned in a box. A coffin, really. All that ferocity of hers forced to lay dormant. For Goldstein to even suggest that has my blood pressure rising.

I rub my knuckles. "No." I feel selfish, even as I say it. "We'll continue with treatment as we have been. Is that all?"

He lingers. "That … wasn't what I came here to talk to you about."

My cheeks suck in. "Then get it out already." If he gives me one more piece of bad news …

"Your Majesty, when I was looking at the imaging of the queen's cancer, the machine captured something else as well." He takes a breath. "Congratulations, my king, the queen is pregnant."

CHAPTER 15

THE KING

THE NEWS DOESN'T immediately take. I stare at the tiled floor as the doctor's words sink in.

Serenity is … pregnant?

With my child?

My gaze moves up slowly to the doctor. "She is?"

He nods.

She's carrying my child.

Serenity's carrying our child.

I draw in a lungful of air.

Now it takes.

Fierce joy surges through my system, followed on its heels by possessive, masculine pride. I can't stop my reaction. Now my heart's pounding for an entirely different reason.

A child.

We hadn't planned on this. I wasn't trying to get her pregnant, despite my eventual plans for an heir. I'd never considered kids, and now I don't know what to do with this strange elation I feel. If I'd have known I'd have this reaction, I'd have pushed the issue sooner.

I want to grab my wife and hold her. My eyes move to the Sleeper. Instead she's unconscious, hurt once again.

She and our child.

A burst of anger punches through my joy. Someone needs to die, and Serenity and I need to leave the palace. It's clear that if we remain, this will continue to happen. It grates me to flee my own home, but I'll do it for her and the baby.

I'm going to be a father.

Had I once worried that no one who knows me will love me? Already my wife's long-standing hatred is toppling. And my child—I rub my mouth. I'll make damn sure they love me.

"How far along is she?" I ask.

"Just shy of eight weeks—Your Majesty, I need to caution you, the child might not survive. Women like Serenity who have been exposed to high levels of radiation often have fertility issues. And if the child does survive, it might have problems of its own."

These words, too, don't immediately sink in. But when they do—and they eventually do—they slaughter me.

This is karma, giving me everything I want only to steal it away.

I'm shaking my head. I won't believe it.

Usually I'm a reasonable man. But reasonableness has nothing to do with this. Not now that I have a future to look forward to and something to hope for.

"The Sleeper can fix this." Serenity is a survivor. Maybe our child will be as well.

"The Sleeper, as we've previously discussed, has limits."

"Then fucking *enhance* it! Goddamnit, I will not sit here and listen to you tell me all the ways this won't work." I rise to my feet and get in Goldstein's face. "You're the royal physician. Consider your life now tied to my child's." I mean every word.

He blanches.

Good. Perhaps the threat will be enough to prompt him into usefulness.

Once he recovers, the doctor bows his head. "As you wish, Your Majesty."

"Leave—and tell no one of this." If my enemies knew of the pregnancy, they'd redouble their efforts to kill Serenity.

Goldstein exits the room, leaving me with my sick, pregnant wife.

I stare at the Sleeper, my excitement offset by Goldstein's warnings. I place a hand on the machine.

Deadly, savage woman.

Now that I'm alone with her, I realize Serenity won't react to the news like I have. I don't know quite how she'll take it, but I doubt joy will top her list. I remember her barely masked revulsion on our wedding day when the subject came up. It burns me raw to remember. She still hates me; I haven't won her over enough for her to forget the bad blood between us. And when she finds out she's pregnant with my child … it will set off all sorts of her triggers.

I'm a wise enough man to know telling her will earn me her famous wrath. I might not survive an angry, hormonal Serenity. Better she figure it out on her own.

I smile at the prospect of a pregnant Serenity stomping around.

I've only gotten the barest taste of this future, but already I know I want no other.

SERENITY

WHEN I WAKE up, it's in the king's bed.

I push myself up and rest my back against the headboard.

How did I get here?

I have to jog my memory to recall the knife wound.

The Sleeper. Of course.

Now I wear a dress someone else slid onto my body while I slept. I try not to think about that too hard. Same goes for the underwear I see when I lift the hem of the dress up. There really isn't anyone who I'd want to see me naked.

I continue to raise the material until I see the smooth expanse of my stomach. I touch the skin that had been split open last time I'd seen it. Nothing remains of that wound, not even a scar.

How many days did I lose this time?

I pull my dress back down and lean my head against the headboard. A glint of metal catches my eye, and I turn to the bedside table.

A row of bullets are lined up along the polished wood. Next to them are a giftwrapped box and a card with my name scrawled across the front. I reach for the card.

I thought you'd prefer this to flowers.

I run my thumb over the king's handwriting.

A reluctant smile spreads across my face. I do prefer bullets to flowers.

I pick one of them up and study it.

My smile falls away. This ammunition is familiar.

I turn my attention to the gift wrapped box. When I lift it onto my lap the weight, too, is familiar.

I tear away at the ribbons and paper that cover it. I'm breathing faster than I should be. And then, when I open the lid of the box, I stop breathing altogether.

Inside, resting on tissue paper, is a gift I have already been given once before. I pick up the piece of cold, hard metal. It fits in my hand like it was born there.

The gun had originally been a gift from my father, and ever since he'd given it to me, it had been the most constant of comrades.

Montes had held onto it this entire time. I can't stop the anger that rises at the thought. He'd taken away one of the few possessions I'd coveted.

But he had given it back. With bullets.

What a trusting, stupid man.

I'M LOADING BULLETS into the chamber of my father's gun when Montes storms in. His eyes capture mine, and he stalks towards me.

My anger is no match for the emotion pouring off him.

He doesn't bother removing the gun from my hand before he cups my face the same way he had the last time we'd been intimate. The same intensity burns through him now as it did then.

He takes my mouth savagely. When the kiss doesn't let up after a few seconds, I set aside the gun to better return it.

I can tell without asking that Montes's emotions simmer just beneath his skin. Usually I doubt his motives and intentions, but there is no confusion here: I'm no passing fancy of his.

He threads his fingers through my hair and his tongue invades my mouth.

It's not enough.

I can practically hear the thought running on repeat in his head. The man who owns the world has finally found something he can never have enough of, and he's trying to figure out a way to remedy that.

He breaks off the kiss and leans his forehead against mine. "How do you feel?"

"You gave me back my father's gun." Even as I speak, I reach for it.

"Thinking of using it on me?" His eyes are full of mirth, and any anger I was planning on directing his way now dissipates. He enjoys the vicious side of me; it's hard to threaten someone when they relish it.

I turn my attention from the king to the weapon. I flip it over and over in my hand. I miss my war-torn country and my father. I miss knowing right from wrong and friends from enemies. I miss knowing my place in the world.

I can feel the king watching me. The bed dips as he sits at my side. "Your gun had me thinking."

That train of thought can't end well.

His fingertips touch the scar on my face. "I have a serious question for you: Now that you're the unofficial representative of the western hemisphere, how would you feel about returning to the WUN?"

NOT TWO DAYS later Montes and I are on the plane heading to the last land to fall to the king.

Up here, the sky is bluer than I've ever seen it, and the clouds are whiter than even the king's smile. It hurts my chest that a day can be this beautiful.

We're not headed to the continent formerly known as North America. It's an odd mix of relief and disappointment to not be returning to the place I called home. It's all I've ever known, but there's nothing there left for me.

Instead, we're heading to the land on the other side of the equator. The king's having trouble pulling together the fractured nations of Southern WUN, and now, as the self-appointed representative of the western hemisphere, I'm to help him fashion some sort of cohesive government. I smile to myself as I stare out the window. What he wants to do is damn near impossible, and it may be petty of me, but I look forward to seeing the king struggle.

I steal a glance at Montes, who sits across from me, his legs pressed against my own. He's pinching his lower lip as he scrolls through a document on his tablet. Without warning, Montes looks up and our eyes meet. I squeeze my chair's armrests.

A wry smile spreads across his face. "Still plotting my death?"

I frown. I don't want this casual familiarity with him, no matter that it's inevitable.

Absently I touch my holstered gun. "You shouldn't remind me. The prospect is too tempting."

"So you *weren't* plotting my death while you were staring at me? Hmmm, I wonder what my queen was thinking." He leaves the thought hanging there.

More bait for me to rise to.

"This is where all your delusions of grandeur come from," I say.

"They're not delusions, Serenity, if they come true."

He has a point.

"Who are we meeting with first?" I ask, purposefully changing the subject.

We land in Morro de São Paulo, a city along the continent's eastern coast, in another several hours. The discussions don't begin until tomorrow, but I want to be ready. Not only is this a chance to establish my own abilities, I know many of these people either directly or indirectly from my time with the WUN.

"Luca Estes," Montes says.

I groan. "Don't tell me you're giving him a government seat."

"Not just a government seat, *the* government seat. He'll spearhead the South American region of my rule. You have an issue with this?"

"Yes." A huge one. "He's a sellout."

My eyes flick over the luxurious cabin we sit in. Greed, in the end, got to Estes. It's as corrosive to the soul as outright violence. After all, if not for greed, there would be no King Lazuli.

I click my tongue. "He's not a good person to have working for you. Before he was a politician, he was a thug. He only came to power once he killed enough people."

Something you two have in common.

"I dare you to find me a single person in office that hasn't gotten his or her hands dirty—including you."

I can't say anything to that. Our world is one of hard choices and bloodshed.

"After you detonated the nukes across the WUN," I say, "Estes began destabilizing many of the neighboring regions."

When I was just the daughter of an emissary, Estes had been one of the thorns in the WUN's side. He often pulled aggressive maneuvers on his allies rather than trying to come together and provide a united front against the Eastern Empire.

"That's because he was working for me the entire time."

Montes's words aren't surprising, but they are disheartening.

"So you would have a sellout—a traitor to his comrades—holding the seat of Southern WUN."

"South America," Montes corrects.

"What would you have me do?" he asks, leaning forward.

He really wants my advice, this man who's taken over the world.

"You have better experience with bad men than I do." He convenes with a whole room of them on a daily basis. "Perhaps you can handle Estes. But I'd listen to what the people here want."

"My reports indicate he's a favorite amongst the people."

I know all about Montes's reports. They'd serve more use as kindling than as information.

"Fear and love wear similar faces," I say.

"Not on you."

This is hedging too close to subjects I don't want to talk about. "You've never seen love on my face," I say, staring him down.

"I thought you and I were beyond the lies." He holds my gaze.

My fingers dig into my arm rests. I'm itching to unholster my gun, but not because I'm angry. Heaven help me, it's because Montes might be right and I can't bear that he of all people lured something as soft as love out of me.

Montes lifts a cup of coffee to his lips. After he sets it down, he says, "I will take what you say into account. For now, let's keep our friends close and our enemies closer."

"I already am, Montes." And that really is the problem.

CHAPTER 16

SERENITY

THE WORLD WE descend into is rapturous. There's no other word to describe it. From the sky, the world is a blanket of lush green. I know this place was hit hard by the king, but it's hard to appreciate the destruction from my vantage point.

The king's eyes are trained on mine as we step out of the plane. I've come across photos of jungles and the tropics, and long ago, before the war, my parents had taken me on vacations, but faded memories and two-dimensional images are nothing compared to this.

The air is a hot breath against my face; the humidity sticks to my skin. Beyond the tarmac, shrubs and trees press in, their stalks and leaves swaying in the light breeze. I can smell brine in the air. It's like war and corruption never touched this place. I know that's not true, but nature paints a pretty picture.

A small contingent waits for us. I scan the group for Estes or anyone else I might recognize, but these are just more of the king's aides and soldiers stationed here to guard us. They shuffle us into a sleek black car, and then as quickly as we arrive, we leave.

The damage to this place becomes apparent on our drive. It's not so much the broken buildings that tell the story of war. No, it's more subtle and insidious than that. It's the vines that grow between the skeletal remains of houses, the side streets that have been all but smothered by the plants.

Goosebumps prickle along my skin. Mother Nature is the apex predator here.

We crest a hill, and I see the deep blue ocean spread out before us. The king's managed to find one of the few places on the western hemisphere whose beauty is unsullied by war.

But it's like overripe fruit. To the eyes, everything's fine, but there's a sickness that's settled just beneath the surface.

It's no surprise when the car pulls up in front of a seaside mansion. What is surprising is the place's seclusion. We have no neighbors, and I already know we will be hosting no meetings here. It's not the kind of home that demands an audience, it's the kind made for secret rendezvous—or so I assume. I have no other point of reference save for my imagination.

"This seems a little underwhelming for your taste," I say, stepping out of the car.

He gets up behind me, and his lips press against my ear. "I'm not doing this for me."

I don't bother keeping the skepticism from my voice. "You thought I would appreciate the seaside getaway?"

"I thought you'd appreciate not having to worry about assassination attempts— and banal conversations with politicians and their wives."

I study Montes as he passes me. *Thoughtful* is not a word I would use to describe him—nor is *caring*—and yet both seem to motivate him when it comes to me.

"You and I both know we'll still have to participate in banal conversations, seaside getaway or no," I say, following him inside. Politics really only gets exciting when people are stirring up trouble. Otherwise the legislation can put you to sleep.

"Yes, but this way I won't have to constantly worry about you shooting those that piss you off."

"Do their lives really matter that much to you?" I ask.

He pauses in the living room. This may be no palace, but each lavish detail—from the painted tile to the carved mantle to the marbled archways—indicates just how expensive this place is.

"Not in the least. But I prefer to burn bridges on my terms, not yours."

I shake my head and wander through the kitchen. I head over to the stovetop and flick a burner on, watching the flames bloom in a ring. Instant fire. Does the king have any idea just how precious this one thing is? Turf wars have been started over less.

Stirring utensils hang along the wall. Jars of oils and seasonings sit on display in fancy glass containers. The line between food and art is blurry here.

For years now, meals are a morbid occasion for me. Everyone must eat to live, but when the food and water are in short supply and what's left is riddled with radiation, it feels a bit like Russian roulette. Will today's meal be the one that poisons your system? It's the reminder that while we stave off death for the day, we're always beckoning it closer.

But here in this place, food appears to be a joyous occasion. One that celebrates life and gluttony. I envy the lifestyle even as I reject it.

I head over to a faucet and turn it on. Clear water pours from it.

"The radiation … ?"

"Reverse osmosis filters it out. It's simple enough technology."

I run my fingers under the stream. "Not if you don't have running water to begin with."

I turn off the faucet. If this house is supposed to be inviting, it has the opposite effect on me. I don't belong amongst plush carpets and polished surfaces and crystal goblets made for delicate drinks that are to be sipped.

I belong around gunmetal and smoke, around the weak and the violent, the broken and battered.

But not here, not here.

I head up the stairs to the second story. An expansive bedroom takes up most of the space. A wall of glass doors line one wall, facing the water. They're already propped open, and a cool sea breeze blows through the room. I head out to the balcony beyond them.

Places like this make you yearn for things you can't put your finger on. I always imagined myself too hardened for something like whimsy, but even I feel a deep stirring in my heart.

I can't take it. Hope is a dangerous thing when you're in the business of loss. Better to expect the worst.

In this world, that's often what you receive.

THE NEXT MORNING, I wake to fingertips on my back.

They trail down my spine and I arch beneath them. I sigh, stretching out my body. I feel a kiss at my temple, then another where my jaw meets my neck.

This is Montes's wake up call, and each morning it happens, I enjoy it a little more. Unfortunately.

I flip onto my back and he continues to trail kisses down my throat, between my breasts, all the way to my stomach. There he stops. His hands move over the skin there, like he's cradling it. I've gained weight, not enough to lose my waist, but enough to fill me out.

He must notice.

I begin to move, about to slip out from under him, but he holds me in place.

"You're beautiful," he says, his gaze trailing up the length of me to meet my eyes. I can tell from his expression how much he means this. And he's looking at me like it should mean something to me as well.

"I already told you what I think of beauty," I say, fighting my own impulse to touch him. It's a losing battle, and I end up running my fingers over his jaw.

"Yes, you have very little regard for it." His hands are still on the swell of my stomach. "It doesn't change that you are."

His grip tightens on me. "You're also brave, fierce, reasonable, and despite all your violence, you have a good heart."

I trace his lips. "Compliments won't save you from my gun," I say. It's not a threat, not like my others which are said in anger. I don't know when that shift happened, when this easy camaraderie became a part of our relationship.

"Serenity, I'm serious."

I know he is, and he's forcing me to be as well. I don't want that.

I cover his mouth with my fingertips. "Don't," I say.

He removes my hand from his lips. "Don't what? Make you face this?"

"Caring for me doesn't change anything," I say.

Did my voice sound a tad distressed?

"It changes *everything*," he says.

I push my way out of bed and angrily begin dressing. He follows me.

"Serenity."

I try to ignore him. I can't. He's everywhere. On my skin, in my mind, inside my heart. I wear his ring, share his name and his empire.

He turns me. "Serenity."

"*Stop.*" I'm shaking.

"*No.*" His voice resonates.

We stare each other down.

"I don't care what you think of me," he says. "I don't care that you think I'm evil. We're both guilty of horrific things. Why do you think I wanted you in the first place? Death in a dress. That's what you were when you descended down those stairs in Geneva. I knew you'd either redeem me or you'd kill me."

"You and I both know there's only one way this ends," I say.

Six feet under.

He shakes his head. "No, Serenity. You want to believe that, but you and I both know this doesn't end in death."

He's apparently the keeper of wisdom, on top of everything else.

"Then how does it end?"

"In love. And life."

CHAPTER 17

SERENITY

I'M IN A foul mood when we arrive at some swanky hotel for the morning's first meetings. For one thing, the king cornered me into facing emotions I'd rather ignore.

For another, the people who packed my bags sent me away with a suitcase full of dresses. They look similar in style and cut to the gowns I wore during the peace talks. I hate them all. It's just my luck that I now have a style, one I didn't choose, and it's getting perpetuated.

To top it all off, we're going to a morning soiree before our first meeting so that the traitors of the southern WUN can rub elbows with the king and his newest acquisition—me.

Montes's hand falls to my back. His other waves to the audience gathered on either side of the roped-off aisle made for us. They scream when they see us, like we're celebrities.

The beads of my dress shiver as I walk down the pathway. I feel the brush of Velcro and metal as my leg rubs against my thigh holster. This was my compromise—I'd wear these ridiculous outfits and attend the king's stupid gatherings so long as I could carry my gun. It doesn't inspire much faith when political leaders walk into meetings armed, but considering that I'm now the queen of the not-so-free world, exceptions are made.

As soon as we enter the building, it's to more applause.

"Who did you pay off to make them all clap?" I ask.

"Mmm, no one, my queen. Here before you are the people who respect power and money above all else."

I stare out at the room. We might as well be back at the king's palace. The crowd's coloring may be slightly different, but they wear the same expensive clothing. These people, however, I take note of. They are the ones who ended up siding with the king before, during, or immediately after the WUN fell.

The room watches us while I watch them. I'd imagine they don't much care for me. Or worse, they think we're alike—westerners that turned their backs on their former allegiances.

I would sooner die than willingly become a traitor. The king and the general forced my hand on this matter.

The conference hall is more a resort than anything else. I can see the ocean out the back windows, and between us and it lounge chairs and umbrellas line the sand.

Waiters carrying delicate silver trays move throughout the room, offering hors d'oeuvres to guests. It's strange to not see them descending upon the food like their very lives depend on it. That's the kind of reaction I'm used to in the WUN.

A man steps into my line of sight, bowing low to the king before taking my hand and kissing it. "Your Majesties, it's an honor."

The hairs at the nape of my neck rise at that voice. I sat in on a lot of calls my father had with that smooth baritone. I snatch my hand away as he straightens.

Luca Estes wears middle age well. His salt and pepper hair is trimmed close to his head, as is his goatee, and he sports the same lean build that many active military members do.

His dark eyes glitter as he takes me in. "It's been too long since we last spoke."

My skin crawls, and I stop my hand from groping towards my holster.

"I saw the peace talks," he continues, "apologies for not joining. I hadn't realized until then just how much you've grown up, Serenity," he says, his accent barely there.

He rests a hand on my shoulder and turns to the king. "I've known your wife since she was a child."

That is stretching the truth quite a bit. He's known my father since I was a child; he's only known me since I began to train for my role as emissary.

I flash Luca a dark look. "Yes, we're practically family."

You sellout.

My father had all sorts of advice for dealing with political figures you didn't like. I was never very good at following any of it, and now, married to my archenemy and facing down another, I'm having a hard time controlling my emotions.

Montes studies Estes, his mask firmly in place. "I hadn't realized how close you and my wife were."

Tread carefully.

Montes's subtle threat sends a thrill through me. I find I don't mind them when they're lobbed at other bad men.

Estes turns to me, a smile plastered on his face. I can see just a touch of panic in the corners of his eyes. We're all having two conversations at the moment—one spoken, the other implied. He's only now realizing how treacherous knowing the traitor queen can be.

"Yes," he pats Montes's shoulder; the fatherly gesture is made all the more ridiculous by the fact that he has to reach up to do so, "well, congratulations on stealing Serenity's heart."

"He didn't steal my heart, Luca," I interject. "He just stole me."

That temporarily silences the corrupt politician.

"She's kidding," Montes says, giving me a look.

I raise an eyebrow. He knows I'm not going to muzzle my mouth.

Estes barks out a laugh. The whole thing is wooden and awkward, because the three of us know just how wicked both men are, and it's not something you're supposed to bring up.

So naturally, I'm going to bring it up.

"All those conversations, Serenity," Estes continues, "and I had no idea how quick tongued you were."

"She can do many things with that tongue of hers," Montes says.

That's it.

I'm reaching for my gun when the king grabs my wrist.

"Let me the fuck go," I hiss.

"She hasn't had her coffee yet," Montes explains calmly.

I'm seeing red.

"Apologies, you both must be hungry." Luca waves down a waiter.

"Whatever you give me is ending up on your shirt," I say while Estes is distracted.

Montes leans into my ear. "You keep this up and we won't make it through the first hour of meetings before I have you pressed up against one of these walls."

I think he's threatening me until I see the heat in his eyes. It's still a warning, but this one's of a wholly different nature.

His arousal only pisses me off more, as does my response to it. He told me once that I'd be good at angry sex. I think he's right.

"This is all just a game to you, isn't it?" I say.

"Of course." His face is only inches from mine. "But you already knew that."

I straighten and speak low enough so that only he hears. "One day you're going to underestimate the wrong person, and then your pretty empire is going to come crashing down."

"I'M STILL DEBATING shooting you," I say an hour later.

"I know," Montes says next to me. "My pants have been tight all morning because of it."

"You are a sick, sick man."

We're back to greeting people, just like we had at our wedding. The line of men and women eager to meet the king winds through the room and out one of the exits. This is not how I imagined changing the world—giving the privileged my time in a few empty lines of greetings.

"Perhaps I should just pull down your pants," I say after the next round of guests leave our side.

That gets Montes's attention.

"That way it'll be easier to bend you over and let everyone here kiss your ass."

King Lazuli stares at me for several seconds, then he lets loose a deep laugh, the sound carrying throughout the room.

He reels me in for a kiss. "Life is infinitely more interesting with you in it."

It takes another hour to meet with everyone, and then we're being shuffled down the hall to a conference room.

The entire time at least two cameras stay trained on us. They hover like flies, orbiting us, drawing in as close as they dare, then backing off before I get a chance to break their lenses. I've come close.

"They're fascinated with you," the king says as we walk. His silken voice raises my gooseflesh. "They've always been."

I give a cameraman a hard look, and he quickly retreats.

Montes is right, but he's also wrong. They're not fascinated with me so much as they are our relationship. I'm the blood-soaked soldier that defended the WUN, and he's the bloodthirsty king that captured my land. We're enemies that became lovers. Two terrible people that rule the world together.

Montes's hand skims down my back, and it's a far more intimate gesture than it has any right to be. He's undressing me with his fingers and his eyes, and even after all we've seen and done together, I still feel like a bug caught in a spider's web.

Estes is already in the conference room when we enter, along with a handful of other faces I recognize from my time spent as an emissary. Several of them my father communicated with directly or indirectly. Back then they'd worked for the

WUN—when they weren't challenging and usurping each other's territories. Now, only months after the war ended, they're here fawning over the king.

For once I would like to meet with leaders who weren't completely unfit for the job.

They eye me as I enter the room. Like Estes, they're trying to figure out whether knowing me benefits them or not.

I decide to help them out.

I stop at the table and take them in. "Corruption looks good on you all."

I render the room speechless—for a moment. Then, all at once, half a dozen people are speaking in Spanish, Portuguese and English.

Ah, southern WUN. They were always very vocal when they disagreed. It's nice to see they're consistent about at least something.

Montes cuts through the noise. "We're not here to talk about prior alliances. The war has ended. South America now needs some stability; let's focus our attentions on that."

Only the king has the balls to make me look like a bad guy and him the martyr.

I take a seat at the table, hyperaware of the tension I've stirred up.

Their anger revitalizes me. People are easier to read when they take their masks off.

The chair next to me scrapes back, and the king sits heavily down. He picks up the papers his aides have set in front of his seat and spends a good minute flipping through them while everyone else waits.

Finally he sets them back down. "Thank you all for being here. I figure we might as well just dive right in: what are the main issues standing in the way of a unified South America?"

And thus begins the first hour of meetings.

"YOU HAVE MANAGED, yet again, to get an entire room of people to hate you in record time," the king says as he closes our front door behind us. We're back from the conference after four nearly unbearable hours. The only people the South American representatives hate worse than me are each other. Everyone wants a piece of the pie that Montes is giving to Estes.

That was the main theme of the meetings—who was going to get what. The only time anyone brought up the region's general health and welfare was when they wanted to use it as a talking point for why they deserved something or why someone else didn't.

I almost pistol-whipped the lot of them.

If that wasn't bad enough, I have to see them again this evening at another one of those needless dinner parties.

I pass through the foyer, kicking off my shoes. This damn dress is a cage. It's too tight around my stomach and thighs, and if someone attacked, I couldn't run in it. I need it off.

"It's probably the first genuine emotion they've displayed since we arrived," I say, groping for my zipper.

Montes comes up behind me and drags the zipper down. Material peels away from my skin, and now those hands of his are coaxing the rest of the fabric off me.

"Perhaps if they weren't turncoats," I continue, "I'd be a little nicer—"

Montes pushes me up against the wall. He captures my hands in his own, "You know what I think upsets you?" he asks, his nose skimming my jaw as he breathes me in. "I think you see yourself in them, and you hate it." He pitches his voice low, and it drips with all sorts of dark intentions.

They and I are nothing alike. But Montes's words dig under my skin. Am I not for all outer appearances a traitor just like them? Perhaps, like me, they were cornered into this. And perhaps, like me, they too have lost themselves somewhere along the way.

The king captures my lips, his hand sliding up my thigh. I feel the remnants of my lipstick smear as our mouths move against each other.

He doesn't bother undressing. He simply unbuckles his belt, unzips his pants, and pushes aside my lingerie.

With one hard thrust, he's inside of me.

I gasp at the sensation. It's just on this side of pain, and that's when I love sex best. I could never indulge in something wholly sweet with the king. Not without at least a little grappling.

He lets my wrists go to grip my hips, kissing my neck as he does so. I feel his hot breath fan down the column of my throat. His pace increases, and each rock of his hips causes my back to pound against the wall.

I cradle him in my arms and arch my neck back. What I can't possibly understand is why anyone wastes time with war when they could be doing this instead.

Montes pulls us away from the wall. We don't break apart as he carries me to our room. We fall in a tangle of limbs on the mattress. The pins holding my hair in place are coming loose, and as I tug on the king's dark locks, his fancy gel disintegrates beneath my fingertips. Civilization is giving way to our primal savagery.

He thrusts into me, and dear God, I'm willing to admit that right about now, I love the king. It's fucked up, and if ever there was proof of my twisted nature, this would be it.

I don't give a damn.

I slide my feet along the back of the king's legs.

"Tell me you love me," the king says next to my ear.

His thoughts are clearly moving in the same direction as mine.

I grip his hair tighter and tilt his ear to my mouth. "*No.*"

He moves harder against me, the friction causing a moan to slip out. I'm far beyond caring that the king's torn down most of my walls and my modesty along with them.

"Say it," he breathes.

I don't.

As a result, he stops.

We're both panting like animals, and when he stares down at me, I see sweat beaded along his brow.

"Say it," he repeats.

Staring at him, our bodies joined and our limbs entangled, I almost do.

He moves against me, just a little. Enough to remind me that he controls the strings.

I shake my head. "I'm not giving that to you."

He flashes me his wickedest grin. "Has my queen forgotten who she's married?" he whispers, his nose dipping down to nuzzle my hair.

He cups a breast through the fabric of my dress. "I'll get you to say those words just as I have everything else."

I'm too far gone to give into his witty rapport. "Just shut up and fuck me."

And he does, but not before he says his final piece. "I will, Serenity. And when I do, you'll mean them, too."

CHAPTER 18

SERENITY

AN AFFECTIONATE KING. It should be impossible, but it isn't.

He hasn't stopped touching me in some way since we were intimate. And now that we're at Estes's estate for a dinner party, he's being affectionate in public.

To be honest, I'm not entirely opposed to it. The ballbuster in me wants to slap his hands away, but each touch regrettably also draws up memories of heavy breathing and slick skin, and when I meet his eyes, they're heated, as though he's ready to repeat the afternoon's activities at any given minute.

Like the one I wore earlier, this dress is far too constricting. That's the only reason why I can't catch my breath.

My eyes move around Este's extravagant home, and they latch on to each piece of wealth the man's accumulated. To think this was all acquired while his people starved—while *we* starved.

I see the guards posted at the four corners of the room. There are more outside, and even more stationed in the watchtowers that border the entrance to the estate. Everything here has been acquired through bloodshed and lies.

This will all come to an end. I vow it then and there.

A waiter passes by carrying a tray of various drinks. I snatch one of the champagne flutes. Just as my fingers wrap around the stem, Montes intercepts it.

I give him a disbelieving look.

"You really shouldn't be drinking this with your cancer," he says.

He can't be serious.

"Give the alcohol back to me," I demand.

"No."

"I thought it didn't matter to you whether I drank or not."

"I lied," he says. "It does. Now," Montes looks around, "Let's find you some sparkling cider."

I breathe through my nose. "Give me the fucking drink." The promise of alcohol was all that was keeping me from open mutiny.

He smiles at me and downs it.

People are watching, cameras are rolling. Our explosive interactions are on display. I can't just brawl it out like I might've back in the bunker. Here it's all about posturing.

I breathe in and out of my nose, and settle on glaring at him. "I hope you don't expect me to be nice tonight."

"You? Nice? I wouldn't dream of it."

Bastard.

I leave him as soon as the first group of politicians approaches. My violent tendencies are bubbling to the surface, and if I don't take them out on Montes, I'll surely take them out on the fuckers in this room.

I feel the king's eyes burning into my back as I walk away from him. He doesn't like parting from me. I'd written this particular detail off as an aspect of his controlling nature—and it is—but it's gotten worse as the attempts on my life have increased.

The most powerful man in the world has a single weakness, and that's me. And I'm not above using it against him.

"*LA REINA DEL mundo.* It's an impressive title." Luca Estes steps up to my side, a glass of amber liquid in his hand.

"Mmm," I manage, watching the room as the evening toils on. A warm breeze blows in from the open windows at my back.

At the moment, I'm mourning the fact that I left Montes to fend for myself among these people. Had I swallowed a bit of my pride, I might not have to bear Luca's company alone. Estes is one of those men that doesn't have a good side. He's corrupt, violent, greedy, lecherous. The only question is which side of him I'll see tonight.

"From what I hear, your father was against the match."

Apparently he's chosen asshole. At least he's no longer trying to be nice.

"My father's dead." I take a sip of my drink. I need something stronger than the glass of water in my hand.

"Yes, my condolences," he says, leaning in. I can smell the strong spirits on his breath.

"Fuck your condolences, Estes." I don't bother looking at him. "I know you didn't like him."

"I like him better than your new husband."

Now I glance over at South America's premier dictator. "That's because my father couldn't control you." Montes can.

He grunts in agreement and takes a swallow of his drink. When he glances over at me again he levels his gaze at my cleavage.

"Last time I saw you, you wore a shapeless uniform. This is a much better look on you."

Now he's being a *lecherous* asshole.

"You and I both know the last time you saw me, it was the leaked footage of my return to the WUN. I believe I was wearing a dress then."

"There was a dress under all that blood? Forgive me for not noticing."

I don't say anything.

The king throws a glance in our direction, which Estes notices. "He keeps you on a pretty short leash, doesn't he? If I didn't know better I'd say that he was obsessed." He swirls his drink, the ice cubes clinking against the glass. "Tell me, does the infatuation go both ways?" He looks over at me. "I suppose it wouldn't, considering what he did to your family—and your country."

Even before Estes approached me, I knew what kind of man he was. So his words shouldn't get a rise out of me, but they do. It's taking every last ounce of restraint not to smash my glass across his face.

"I've been wondering what sort of bed play comes out of that union ..." he muses.

Enough.

"In case you needed the reminder, I am '*la reina del mundo*', and I won't hesitate to use my position to remove you from power if I feel the desire. I am not half as decent as my father, so keep your sick perversions to yourself, Luca, and don't fucking cross me."

I stalk away from him. People give me wide berth, and I'm sure it has something to do with the harsh set of my face. The cameras begin panning in on me. I set my drink down on a sideboard and make a beeline for Montes. He's in the middle of a flock of admirers. They too give me wide berth the moment I cut into their circle.

Montes watches me, a dark gleam in his eyes. He always did like my flare for the dramatic.

I wrap my arm around the back of his head before I kiss him. I'm angry, and I'm sure he can feel it in the harsh movements of my lips. This is no passionate kiss. All my usual rage and violence is wrapped into it.

"I'm done," I say against his mouth. I've had enough fake smiles and false endearments for one evening. I should have had enough of the king as well, but instead, he feels like my one ally in a sea of enemies. It's an illusion, but I can't reason it away.

My father was right when he said appearances are everything. Let the world believe the king and I are some odd love match. Better that than the messy truth— that I hate him every bit as much as I care for him.

When I break away from the kiss, I take the king's hand. He's all too willing to follow me away from the quickly dissolving circle of admirers. But not five seconds later, he tugs my hand and reels me back into him until my chest is pressed against his.

He gazes down at me with amusement. "My vicious little queen," he says low enough so that only I can hear him, "you should know by now not to test me in public." His voice becomes husky. "And you should definitely know by now how to give your husband a real kiss."

I warn him with my eyes that I'm in no mood, but it does nothing to stop him from bending me backwards and taking my mouth with his own. In this position, nearly parallel to the ground, I'm at his mercy.

Wolf whistles and claps come from the crowd.

This is ridiculous.

I bite his tongue even as I grip his arms. He smiles against the pain. The psycho actually enjoys it when I get mean. He drags the kiss out longer than necessary, just to further push my breaking patience. Finally, with flourish, he pulls me back to my feet.

The crowd's still cheering.

Montes waves and steers me out. The last glimpse I catch is of Estes. He lifts his glass in salute. And then the front door closes behind us and all the pretty people are gone.

Our shoes click down the steps of Estes's estate.

"What did Estes say to you to put that expression on your face?" he asks as we descend the stairs.

"The truth." Isn't that what hurts us so much?

"My queen doesn't run from the truth. She leaves only after she's threatened someone. So what did he say?"

I push away from the king. "What does it matter to you? My business is my own."

The king makes a noise low in his throat. I can hear him at my back. "Your business is anything but your own. It's mine, and it's our empire's."

Our car pulls up to the curb.

"I don't know how many times I have to say it," I say, "but you don't get to have everything, Montes. That includes knowledge."

He grabs my arm and spins me so that I face him, and then he backs me up until he has me braced against the car. There are people out here. Not many—mostly just valets and guards, since the camera crews stayed behind—but we have onlookers all the same.

So much for appearances.

"You are very, very wrong." I think this is the same tone he takes right before he ends someone's life. His lips are a hairsbreadth from my own. "I do get to have all of you, whenever I want." He grips my thigh, and it's incredibly suggestive. "Even your conversations. Even your thoughts."

Estes was right. Montes is nothing short of obsessed.

The king kisses me, and even that feels possessive, like he's taking my lust along with everything else.

He hauls me away from the car and opens the door for me. "Everything you are is mine, and no threats of yours will ever change that."

CHAPTER 19

SERENITY

I WAKE UP in the middle of the night, clammy with sweat. If I close my eyes, I can still see the last moments of the dream—the blood, the shattered bones, the death throes of the mortally wounded.

I run a hand down my face. I'm used to nightmares; I have too many bad memories for my mind to prey upon. Tonight's just reminded me of the abyss I've traveled down since war broke out.

The king stirs, and his arm goes around my stomach. He drags me against his chest, his fingers stroking my damp skin.

"It's okay, my queen," he murmurs against my hair. I'm not even sure he's awake. "You're safe now."

Safety's not what I crave, and no one can rescue me from my life. I wait until I'm sure Montes is asleep before I slip out of bed.

My demons ride me hard. I change as quietly as I can, and I pad out of the room and onto the balcony.

I swing one foot over the ledge, then the other. Once I'm standing on the outside of the balcony, my arms wrap around the railing behind me. I gaze out at the dark sea. The surf crashes, calling to me.

All at once, I let go of the railing.

I feel weightless for an instant, and then my feet meet grass. I clench my teeth as the impact sends a stabbing pain through my knees and abdomen.

I head towards the ocean, and the lawn gives away to sand. I scoop up a handful of it and let it run through my fingers. The lamps out here are few and far between, and the nearly full moon casts the edge of the garden in shades of blue. The king's many guards patrol this place, but they've either made themselves scarce for the evening, or they blend in well. Either way, I can almost pretend that I'm alone.

Now that I have some small measure of privacy, I can finally settle my thoughts on things I'd rather keep from the king. I place a hand over my stomach. I'm dying, and not even Montes can stop it. I still vomit blood, my stomach still aches sharply. Whatever the Sleeper's abilities are, I'm not sure they're making things better for me.

I would've thought I'd be happy—it's finally an end to this sad life of mine. I'll return to the earth, just like everyone else I've loved.

But I'm not pleased about it.

"I'm sorry, Mom and Dad," I whisper to the stars above me, "but I'm not ready to come home yet."

I watch the sky. A cool evening breeze runs through my hair, beckoning me closer to the water. If I had it my way, I'd let the wind and the waves carry me far, far away.

I head over to the water and stick my toes in the sand.

"What are you doing out here this late?"

My spine stiffens at that voice, and I rotate.

Montes stands a few short feet away from me. He shouldn't look as handsome as he does. Moonlight pools against his features, illuminating half of them and casting the other half in shadow. He wears only loose lounge pants, and I have to force myself from fixating on his torso.

"Enjoying the view," I say, casting a brief look up at the stars.

"The one sleeping next to you wasn't good enough?"

All I want is to be left alone. Not even in the deepest recesses of night am I allowed this. "Not everything is about you, Montes," I say, weary.

"You can talk to me."

I almost laugh. I'm not sure this man could handle my past. But more than that, he gave me this past of mine. "I will never tell you my burdens."

He closes the distance between us. "You're lying again."

I search his face. "Why do you try so hard with me when you so obviously don't with anybody else?"

"Your heart has always been mine. I knew it from the moment I met you. I try because I cherish what is mine."

"I don't believe in love at first sight."

He laughs. "I'm not talking about *love*, Serenity."

"Then what are you talking about?"

He shakes his head. "Something else. Something poets know more about than I do."

I hate to concede anything to Montes, but I felt it, too. Maybe not the moment I met him—I had too much hate for that. But when I caught sight of him on the flat screen when I was the Resistance's prisoner, I still recognized him in a way that had nothing to do with memory.

"I will never forgive you," I say.

"I don't want forgiveness from you. I never did." His hand slides to mine.

My beautiful nightmare. That's what he is, what all of this is—the nightmare I can never wake from. And it doesn't frighten me any longer.

I take one look as the stars. "They're waiting for me. You know, they might be even more powerful than you."

"Who are you referring to?"

"The dead."

The king appears unnerved by my words. "I didn't know you were superstitious."

"I'm not." I sit down in the sand. The king joins me.

"Superstitions are nonsensical," I say, slinging my arms over my knees. "I've seen a person's soul leave their body. You can't *not* believe once you see proof like that."

"Is that what you've been dwelling on out here? All the people you've killed?"

"All the people *you've* killed."

The king leans back on his elbows and stretches his body out. My eyes linger first on his chest, and then those long legs of his.

"Throwing blame around doesn't change the fact that they're dead," he says.

"Dead, yes. But gone? No, they're not gone." If anything they are more present than ever. The dead haunt my memories and my dreams; I'll never be free of them. That's the penance you pay when you take a life.

Montes glances over at me, and lounging back on his forearms, he's the poster boy for irreverence. "Let the past go," he says. "Be happy."

246

I stare up at the lonely stars. "I don't know how."

WE SIT NEXT to each other in the sand for who knows how long, and somewhere along the way Montes sits back up and his arm finds itself around me. I pretend I don't notice. Better that than to admit I might actually enjoy him holding me close.

"Now that you no longer live in the bunker, have the stars lost any of their allure?" Montes asks.

I shake my head and smile. "None. If anything, they've gotten more beautiful."

When I look over at him, he's already watching me. The intensity of that stare makes me acutely aware of myself. Sometimes, like right now, I believe that if the king could, he would drink me up and swallow me whole just to absorb every single bit of me into him.

It's disconcerting, to say the least.

I glance back up at the sky to shake my strange awareness. Amongst a sea of unfamiliar constellations, I see a dear one.

"Want to know a secret?" I ask.

"Of course," Montes says. "If it has anything to do with you, I'm interested."

I will give the king this: he never does anything half-assed. Especially not when it comes to pursuing his cold wife.

"I have a favorite constellation," I admit.

In the moonlight, I see him raise an eyebrow. "Which one?"

I lean into him, for once uncaring at our closeness, and point far above me. "Do you see that cluster of dim stars?"

"The Pleiades?" the king says.

I nod and wrap my arms around my legs. "My mother taught me about that constellation. The Seven Sisters. She said those were the wishing stars. That if you wanted something badly enough, you need only to wish upon them and it would come true."

Montes is flashing me a rueful grin. "And have you ever?"

I give him the side eye. "Once or twice."

"What did you wish for?"

The end of the war. The end of my sorrowful life. "Things I won't admit to another soul."

"Not even to me?"

Now I laugh. "*Especially* not to you."

He pushes me back into the sand and rolls over me. "Why not?"

We're gazing into each other's eyes, and now I see the night sky in his irises, and I can only imagine what he sees in mine.

"Because you're my enemy, and you don't tell your enemy your secrets."

He captures my hands, like I knew he would, and presses them into the sand on either side of me. "But I'm also your husband, and you *do* tell your husband secrets," he says, threading his fingers through mine.

"You're going to have to force them out of me."

"Oh?" His interest is piqued. "Lucky me," he removes one of his hands from mine to slip it into my robe, "I know exactly the type of torture my wife likes best," he says, cupping a breast.

"Stop referring to me in the third person."

"Or what?" His lips are just an inch away from mine, and his voice is husky. "You'll *really* never tell me your secrets?" He thumbs my nipple as he taunts me.

Already my breath has quickened. "I sleep with my gun. You'd do well to remember that."

"And you know I'll take that gun away from you if I feel like you're abusing your power."

I guffaw. "Do you seriously want to get into a debate about the abuse of power?"

He laughs low in his throat. "I don't want a debate at all."

He takes my mouth then, his lips gliding against my own. I like to think myself a complicated, toughened person, but it never takes Montes long to pull me apart piece by piece.

I press my torso into his, and now he releases my hands so that he can skim his along my skin.

Beyond us the tide has risen, and it licks at our toes. I can feel it dampening the edges of my robe, which—thanks largely to Montes—is no longer serving any sort of proprietary function. I'm splayed open to the king, something it doesn't take him long to figure out.

First his hand, then his head dip down between my thighs, and my fingers are grasping uselessly at sand. My legs open further, and the king groans, pausing his ministrations to grip my thighs.

"I enjoy it when we fight," he says, "but I enjoy it even more when you finally give in."

"Ssssh ..." I don't bother clarifying that I was trying to tell him to shut up, but I couldn't get past that first syllable.

I've come completely untethered. I thread my fingers through Montes's hair, getting sea salt and sand all over the king's dark locks. I mess it up further, which I'm unashamed to say is a favorite pastime of mine.

I don't know how he does it, but the man manages to shed his pants while keeping me preoccupied. But then his mouth leaves my core and his bare chest slides up my torso. I laugh as the sand I put in his hair sprinkles down on me.

He kisses my mouth, and I taste myself on his lips.

"Maybe I'll make a wish upon those Sisters," he says between kisses.

"Mmm, you don't get to claim the Sisters on top of everything else," I say, nipping his lower lip.

"That's not very egalitarian of you." That wicked grin of his stretches against my lips.

"Wishes are for people who can't just buy what they want."

"Hasn't anyone told you, *nire bihotza*?" he says between kisses. "The best things can't be bought."

"What does that even mean?" I ask, fighting the impulse to move against him now that his weight has settled between my legs.

"'*Nire bihotza*'?"

I nod.

"Mmm, you'd like to know, wouldn't you?" He touches my scar. "Too bad it takes sharing your secrets to learn mine."

I huff. What he says is fair; it doesn't mean I like it.

"Now," he continues, "about that wish ..."

Back to this?

"Fine, make a wish, man-who-has-everything," I say.

He lifts my hips and slides into me, breaking away from my mouth to watch my reaction.

"I will: I wish that one day, you'll finally know happiness."

And, staring into his eyes, I fear that one day, I just might.

CHAPTER 20

SERENITY

MONTES SLIPS OUT of bed the next morning only to return sometime later, bearing a tray with breakfast on it. His hair is mussed from sleep and sex, and he smells like man as he sets the tray on the bedside table and runs a hand through my locks.

"Morning, my queen."

I stretch and force myself to sit up.

"Morning," I mumble, stifling a yawn. It's as pleasant as I can be. After the prior evening's late-night foray, I feel like I've gotten steamrolled by a tank. The king, on the other hand, looks positively refreshed.

"You know how to cook?" I ask, my eyes falling on the tray. I know maids have come in—that or the bed magically remade itself yesterday—but aside from that, I haven't seen any staff on the premises.

"I'm a regular Renaissance man," Montes says, winking at me.

I furrow my brows at his carefree expression, and then at the spread of food. I can't take him when he's like this—selfless. Sweet. Or that, for a girl used to waking up early and standing in line for breakfast, having a decadent one prepared and delivered to me is a significant gesture.

He reaches out and smooths the skin about my eyes. "You don't have to be conflicted about this. It's just breakfast."

I breathe in deeply, catching a whiff of bacon. A wave of nausea rolls through me at the smell. I wait for it to pass.

When it doesn't, I throw off the covers and run for the bathroom. I barely make it in time. My stomach spasms over and over as I clutch the toilet. It's even worse this time around—the nausea, the sharp pains that stab my abdomen.

Behind me, Montes lays a warm hand on my back. He rubs me affectionately while his other hand gathers my hair. First breakfast and now this. What does this man want from me today? I've already handed over my heart and sold him most of my soul.

Once the nausea passes, I flush the toilet and wipe the perspiration from my forehead. I stand, shakily, and Montes is there, wrapping an arm around my waist and letting me lean on him.

He has no questions for me, nor does he air his concerns about my worsening condition. He doesn't even glance over at the bottle of pills I'm supposed to take every day. Perhaps he's finally accepting the hopelessness of the situation.

He walks me back to the bed, and I sit down on the edge of it.

My body's trembling from exertion. It'll pass in another ten minutes, but until then I feel every inch of my mortality. How fragile the human body is when it's riddled with sickness.

He hands me a glass of water.

I look from it to him. "What's going on, Montes?"

He sighs. "Does kindness always have to have a price on it?"

"When it comes from you? Always."

I eye him over the rim of the glass as I take a drink. "You taught me that, you know—to never trust people's motives." Had I not lived through the king's war, I'd never have grown up so jaded.

"I know," he admits. "All your worst qualities lead back to me. And those are the ones I love most."

I shake my head, a reluctant, rueful smile tugging at the corners of my lips.

His eyes twinkle at the sight. We're sharing a moment, I realize. And it's not one based on hate, or humor, or lust. There's a chance we might actually be good together if we manage to not kill each other first.

"IF I HAD even half as much money as Diego's receiving, I'd actually be able to implement good ground control ..."

My boots squeak as I reposition them. I've taken to kicking my feet up on the conference table while the idiots around me fight over scraps.

"My holdings are twice as large as yours," Diego says. "Even with the money allocated to my territory, it won't be enough for ground control."

Day two of discussions has begun. We're only two hours in, but I'm just about done.

Next to me, the king sits back in his chair, running his thumb over his lower lip. That same hand held my hair back while I was sick.

The king never was like other people; I don't know why I keep allowing myself to be surprised by him.

A third person jumps into the debate. "My holdings are larger than either of yours, and our budget is one of the smallest here."

On the surface, every person here sounds reasonable. They have convenient explanations lined up for why they should be paid more. As though they're not going to use most of the money on personal expenses. Already the line item breakdown of many of these proposed budgets includes extravagances like extra planes, additions to homes, and hefty vacation plans.

"That's because no one lives in your territory," another says. "Mine is one of the smallest, but it's also the densest, and it's one of the most violent regions of South America. If we are going to implement ground troops, they should be concentrated in the city centers."

I've reached my limit.

"Alright," kicking my feet off the table, I stand, bracing my hands against the table, "if I hear one more goddamn reason why any of you deserve more than what you already have, I swear to God I will kill you myself."

The room falls silent. "No one is getting ground troops. Martial law is over. You will all set up your own police forces with the budgets we've already given you. Anything else will have to come out of pocket. And after reviewing your generous compensation plans, it damn well better.

"My husband may be king, but he has left me in charge of South America's affairs. *You* are one of those affairs, and frankly, I don't like any of you. You want to keep your jobs and your titles? I want to see some proposals tomorrow for government programs that will help your people. And they better use up every penny of your budgets."

Montes is now pinching his lower lip, his other hand drumming against his seat rest. His expression is pure satisfaction.

"Now get the fuck out of my sight if you don't want to lose your jobs right this instant," I say.

I've never seen a room clear so quickly. The silence that follows their exit fills my ears.

"Your father trained you well."

I turn to Montes. "My father would've been mortified by the way I handled that," I say, weary as I take my seat.

"This is not your father's world, and those men and women will take all that you have to offer and more unless you stop them."

"Then why do you deal with them? You clearly have no qualms about getting rid of people. Why keep the worst ones around?"

"Haven't you heard? All the good, honest leaders have been killed off. Only the weak and wicked remain."

We run in circles. It's no use telling him that before he rose to power the world had done a decent enough job keeping the sociopaths away from office. But in war, it appears they've popped up like weeds. Not just here, either. Montes's entire inner circle is made up of them, men too afraid or too evil themselves to stand up to the king.

"You handled that well, Serenity." There's genuine pride in his voice and I gain insight into something I hadn't noticed before.

"You really do want me to help you rule."

"Of course," he says.

But there's nothing obvious about this. "Why would you share that with me?"

He steeples his hands beneath his chin. "Despite everything, I trust you with my power."

I raise my eyebrows. "You really shouldn't. I've already admitted I plan on killing you."

He leans towards me. "And I've already told you, I don't believe you'll ever do it."

We stare each other down. Another battle of wills. I look away first.

"Do you really think they'll pull something together by tomorrow?" he asks.

I drum my fingers on my arm rest. "They better. Maybe for once they'll stop throwing parties and put their mind and their money towards something that actually matters."

"And what will you do if they don't?"

I give the king a piercing look. "Exactly what you would do—I'll make good on my threat."

He stands. "And you wonder why I give you a portion of my power. You know how to rule." He extends a hand out to me. "Enough plotting for a day. Come, my queen."

Together we leave the hotel. People who see us bow like I'm not just some dying soldier from a conquered nation and the king our tyrant ruler.

I am Montes's captive queen. I may have agreed to this fate for the sake of my people, but I'm a prisoner nonetheless.

It's my heart and the king's that have betrayed us both.

Our car pulls up, but I hesitate to get inside. I may be a prisoner, but I'm a powerful one.

"Serenity?" Montes says when I don't make a move towards the vehicle.

"I want to see the people here," I say, my gaze flicking to the king.

Montes glances around like that's a trick question. "You have."

I know enough about this region to know I'm seeing what powerful people want me to see. "Take me to the nearest settlement. I want to see how the impoverished live."

Montes studies me. "I don't need to warn you about the radiation."

He's actually entertaining this request. And here I thought I'd have to fight him.

"You don't," I say. I know better than most exactly what exposure can do to a person's body.

He squints and works his lower jaw as he considers it.

Finally, he says, "Ten minutes. Make them count because that's all you get."

IT'S EVEN WORSE than I thought.

Our caravan of vehicles pulls up to the edge of a shantytown. The houses are nothing more than bits and pieces of cinderblock, tin, tattered cloth, plastic, and palm fronds. The whole thing looks like it could be swept away by the first big storm of the season.

People stop what they're doing and watch us. It's not every day that shiny, fancy cars bearing the king's insignia stop at your doorstep. In my opinion, a day like that would be terrifying beyond belief.

As soon as our engine is idling, I step out of the car, uncaring that I've left Montes behind or that the king's men haven't cleared the area. The latter shout at me to stop, but I don't. What are these people going to do to me that hasn't already been done before?

My boots sink into the mud as I head towards the edge of the village, and I'm thankful that I decided today to wear boots and pants instead of another frilly dress. The place is muddy and it smells like open sewage.

In my peripherals, I can see the king's guards begin to flank me, but they keep their distance, and I can almost pretend that it's just me walking down the main road.

I don't get very far. Dirty, mostly naked kids run up to greet me.

"*La reina! La reina!*" Some of them call.

Even out here they know of me.

Their exuberance pulls a smile from my lips. "*Hola—hola,*" I say to each of them in turn.

Already I can see signs of malnourishment and ill health. Some have distended bellies, others discolored skin from radiation burns. I'm almost afraid to touch them for fear that I'll somehow hurt them.

"Someone take pictures of this," I call to the guards. I want to show those contentious politicians what really matters.

"*Tiene comida para nosotros?*" one asks.

"*Comida?*" Other kids echo.

"Do you speak the common tongue?" I ask. "*La lengua común?*"

"Yes!" I hear some kids shout enthusiastically.

Despite all they must've endured at the hands of their government, they're still happy to see me. The resilience of children.

"Do you have food for us?" asks a girl with stringy hair. Her eyes are far too aged.

Food. Water. I'm used to hearing these requests. They came up many times during my tour as a soldier. No one wants money. Currency means little in these areas when a single meal might be the difference between life and death.

"I will get you and your families some food," I promise. For once I feel like my position as queen allows me to do what I've always wanted to—to save lives instead of taking them.

She jumps up and down at my words and translates for the kids that don't understand English. Little squeals erupt from the small crowd.

Behind me, I hear the car door close. I don't look back, but many of the children do. I can tell by their widening eyes who they see.

"It's okay," I reassure them, "he's not here to hurt anyone."

I can tell they don't believe me, and why should they? We've all been spooked by tales of the undying king.

"Manuel!" "Esteban!" "Maria!"

I look up. The adults, who have been lingering outside their houses, now call their kids back.

It strikes me as odd—they're obviously frightened of the king but not of me. I'd assumed that people hated me worse than Montes, but out here it appears they trust a former WUN citizen a great deal more than King Lazuli.

Some of the kids peel away. Others hesitate.

"Go," I say. "Tell your parents I'll be personally arranging for food and medical supplies to be delivered to your families."

I watch them run off as the king steps up to my side. "This is why I fought so hard for medical relief in the negotiations," I say to him.

"I can see that." His gaze roves over the shantytown, and I can't get a read on his expression. Right now, I would give a lot to know where his mind is.

The people head into their houses. I can see them still watching us through their windows, but no one else approaches.

The king's hand falls to the back of my neck. He massages it as he says, "Your ten minutes are up."

It's a weak way to end the visit, but I doubt anyone would be willing to talk to us at this point, regardless. Not now that the king is among them.

If Montes is disgusted or unsettled by what he's seen, he never shows it. We get in the car, and our caravan leaves the desolate encampment these people call home.

This is what my sacrifices are for—making sure settlements like that one get what they need to survive and, eventually, thrive.

I glance over at Montes on our way back. "Why did you let me do it?"

The king in his ivory tower; I'd imagine a visit like that is far down on his list of things to do.

Montes lounges against his seatback. He lifts a shoulder and lets it drop. "You'd find a way regardless, and the radiation levels aren't too dangerous there. But most importantly, I want to get laid later."

I narrow my eyes at him.

"I expect I will too," he adds.

"You are a terrible person."

"I *am* terrible, and yet when I'm buried inside you tonight, you'll have your doubts. And tomorrow when I send the food and water to the village, your carefully crafted hate will die."

I glare at him.

"I wonder what will happen once we burn down all of it? What will be left of my queen when her fury no longer fuels her?"

I don't say anything. I can't. Already he's uncovered a very real concern of my own: how to hold onto hate when there's nothing left to feed it.

He leans forward. "I intend to find out."

CHAPTER 21

SERENITY

SEVERAL HOURS LATER, after reading a stack of reports on the South American territories, I head into the bathroom to change for dinner.

Another day, another dinner party. This one will be hosted back at the hotel where we're holding the discussions.

I give the black lace dress hanging on the bathroom door the evil eye.

I unbutton my shirt in front of the mirror. As I slip it off, I notice—really notice—what a difference a few months of living with the king have made. My hips and waist are fuller and my stomach slopes gently out. I run a hand over it. The skin feels taut. I'm still not as soft as I would've imagined.

I could still be getting worse. The king believes in the Sleeper the same way some people believe in religion. I, on the other hand, only have misgivings about the machine. To me the only thing it does is remove scars and kill time.

I slide the dress on, along with a pair of heels. I run my fingers through the loose waves of my hair and paint my lips a dark red. I still haven't gotten used to the type of grooming the upper echelons of society expect.

My hands move from the makeup set out on the counter to the neat case of pills I've been packed with. I hold one up to the light. This little thing is what keeps the king permanently young, and it's partly what started his war.

I swallow it, despite my compulsive desire to flush it down the toilet. After all the killing and dying, it seems too precious to waste.

The king knocks on the door. Giving my reflection one final look, I leave.

He waits for me on the other side clad in a tux. Montes leans back as I walk out, his gaze approving. He opens his mouth.

"Don't say it," I say.

"Can't I give my wife a compliment?"

"I don't want the compliment you're about to give me."

Montes comes to my side as we head downstairs. "Has anyone ever told you that you are a strange girl?"

"Because I don't like being called pretty? You all can take your stereotypes and shove them where the sun don't shine."

"Mmm, I'd prefer to shove something else there."

I glance sharply at him.

He looks unrepentant.

His hand falls to the small of my back. "You look lovely. I don't care that you don't want to hear it. I'm going to tell you over and over again."

"You don't get it," I say to Montes as I fold myself into the car waiting for us outside. "I don't want to be valued for my looks. That belongs to your world."

He follows me in. "You now belong to that world."

I think Montes enjoys having the attention on us. Not because he's a narcissist—though he is—but because it gives him an excuse to exercise his chivalry on me. He knows I won't fight him while we're being filmed.

But I don't. I belong to neither the old world nor the new one. I'm no longer one of the impoverished, but I'll never be one of the rich.

I'm a woman with nothing to her name but a few memories and a few more dreams.

"ARE YOU GOING to deprive me of alcohol again tonight?" I ask as we step out of the car. Immediately camera crews close in on us. I squint against the flashing lights. The king's guards step in and keep the media at bay.

"Yes," the king says, guiding me forward.

So the king's serious about preventing me from drinking. That's unfortunate. Talking to these people sober is its own kind of torture. I'll just have to snatch a drink or two when the king's head is turned.

He keeps his body slightly in front of mine, and he angles himself protectively towards me, as if the cameramen might suddenly pull out guns and start shooting us all.

"Tell me again why this dinner is important?" I take in the jewels dripping from one woman's neck as we enter the hotel's lobby.

These people and their beauty.

"Despite what you might think, not all my victories are won on the battlefield. If you charm the right people, you can get just as far without the bloodshed."

"Oh, so now you're a pacifist?" A waiter passes by, and I make a grab for one of the glasses of wine.

Montes catches my wrist. "Threatening works well too," he says, his eyes glittering. "No drinking, Serenity. I mean it."

I yank my hand away.

It wasn't the best strategy to go for it right in front of him, but I'm being slowly stifled to death by him and his rules.

"Or else what, Montes? All I hear from you are empty threats."

He raises an eyebrow, the corner of his mouth lifting. I think he's crafting some unusually painful punishment for me.

"So good seeing you both this evening," an older couple interrupts us. "How are you enjoying your stay?"

This inanity begins again. I think I'd prefer the king's punishment to it.

The couple eventually leaves, but not a minute later another couple takes their place, and then another. And so the evening goes.

My eyes drift away from one portly man's account of his last big game hunt. They move aimlessly over the crowd. I notice Estes is chatting with some of the other political figureheads that were in session with me and the king today.

Scheming, scheming, scheming. These men are always scheming. Sometimes I miss the battlefield for this very reason. The enemy is pretty obvious when they're shooting at you, and you have permission to shoot them back. Here the lines between friend and enemy blur.

I drag my gaze away from Estes. I'm about to check back into the conversation when I catch sight of a ghost.

I have to be mistaken. There is no logical reason why General Kline should be here in South America. And yet I swear it's him across the room bearing a tray of hors d'oeuvres.

He wears the same attire as the rest of the waiters—a white shirt and suit jacket and a bow tie at his neck. He looks thinner than he has in the past, but maybe I'm just getting used to the curves of the people here.

His head swivels, and I blanche as, for a moment, our gazes lock.

It *is* him.

The last time I saw the general, I was in a cell, my memory wiped. That feels like a lifetime ago.

My breathing picks up, something the king notices.

"Serenity, are you alright?" He follows my line of sight, but General Kline has already disappeared back into the crowd.

"Fine. I just need some air," I say, distracted.

I leave Montes's side before he can respond, though I feel his eyes on me the whole time.

I head towards where I last saw the general. It's slow going because, surprisingly, people want to talk to me. I nod to them, exchange a few words here and there, and push my way through the crowd. The entire time my eyes sweep the room.

I catch sight of the back of the general's head as he enters the kitchens.

I pick up my pace, no longer attempting niceties. If I don't want the general to slip through my grasp, I'll have to move a little faster.

My palms slap against the doors to the kitchen as I barge in. Inside, steam fills the air, and the staff shouts out orders. Once they see me, they bow their heads and their shouts turn to murmurs of "Your Majesty."

I stride past them, down the narrow kitchen aisle, following the retreating form of General Kline.

"General!" I shout.

Rather than slowing, he begins to jog deeper into the kitchens.

Damnit, this is why combat boots are far superior to heels. I pick up my skirts and run after him, accidentally elbowing some of the kitchen staff in the process. I don't care that I've probably committed half a dozen faux pas, or that a multitude of people have heard and seen me pass through. My former leader, now a high up Resistance officer, is posing as a waiter at a party I'm attending. I'm not going to wait for shit to hit the fan.

The general leaves through one of the kitchen's back doors. I can't see anything beyond it.

Adrenaline gathers in my veins, and I prepare myself for an ambush. Mistake number one was not telling the king that I saw the general. Mistake number two was pursuing him alone.

I don't much care, however, that I might be endangering my life. It's been up for forfeit a while now.

Reaching inside my skirts, I unholster my gun and click the safety off. I push through the back doors, my weapon ready, only to find myself in an empty staff parking lot.

"You always did have a fondness for that gun." The hard as nails voice wakes all sorts of memories of a time when I knew right from wrong and good from evil.

The general steps out of the shadows. "I see you got your memory back," he says.

How can he tell? Is it the gun? Or something I've said while cameras are rolling?

I lower the weapon. "Why are you here?"

He glances at the door I exited. We both hear muffled commotion coming from the kitchens.

The king will be coming for me soon.

General Kline returns his gaze to mine. "You need to leave South America—tonight if possible."

It's all I can do to bite back a "yes, sir." Old habits die hard.

"What've you heard?" I ask instead.

The general looks to my stomach. "Is it true?"

"Is what true?"

He opens his mouth, but he can't get the words out.

I furrow my brows. I've never known the general to be short of words. Not even when he delivered the news of my impending marriage to the king.

"What?"

The general grunts, squinting past me. He shakes his head. "The Resistance hears a lot of things—some true, some nothing more than rumors."

I already know this.

"Estes isn't planning on letting either of you leave here alive," he says.

I raise my brows.

"There are those in the Resistance that support him and his efforts, and I've heard whispers that they're just waiting for his call to take you out. That could be any day now."

Montes and I are scheduled to be here for another five days. If what the general says is true, then the attack will happen by the week's end.

If being the key word here.

"Where and how?" I ask.

"The men are getting the location when they get Estes's call. It's going to be messy, from what I hear. They won't just bomb you—they want proof of the kills."

They want our bodies, he means. It's easy to convince the world someone's dead when you show them evidence of it.

I rub the trigger of my lowered weapon. "Why are you telling me this?"

He slides his hands into his pockets. "You're the world's best chance at survival."

"If you really believe that, then why join the Resistance?" The king had let him keep his position as general.

"I'm not a betting man."

And I was a dying girl. Once I died, he'd need a backup plan.

The two of us have a strange relationship. I blame him for the ring on my finger and he blames me for his son in a casket. And yet here we are, working together.

"Now that really doesn't explain why you're telling me this—or why you're in South America for that matter."

"I'm a top operative for the Resistance, Serenity. I'm never far from you or the king."

Operative is a nice euphemism for an assassin. I'm sure the Resistance is also using the general for strategy as well, but in the Resistance's ranks, operatives are the ones that take out important figures.

"Why haven't you killed me?" I open my arms; I'm still holding the gun in one of them, but it's no longer pointed at the general. "You have your chance—but you better make it quick."

I can hear the king's men in the kitchen.

"You stupid girl," he says taking me by the shoulders and pulling me into a tight hug. "I *love* you. That's why I'm telling you this, that's why I'm not shooting you." He backs away as the soldiers' footsteps begin moving towards the door. "You were always the daughter I never had. Now do me and your father proud and right the king's wrongs."

My throat closes. How can just a few words undo me?

His hands slip away and he turns from me. I watch his form fade into the darkness.

He's almost disappeared entirely when I remember.

"Wait!"

I can barely make him out. He's already blended back into the shadows, but I think he pauses.

"Will's dead." I say quietly, but the night carries my words to him.

I'm not sure whether I'm relieved that I can't see the general's expression, or desperate for it.

"He captured me in the hospital where I was being treated for my cancer," I continue. "His men shot me, patched me up, then proceeded to interrogate me." It's hauntingly similar to my experience with the general. I suppose this is how the Resistance does things.

"The king ransacked the warehouse we were in and took Will." This last part's still hard. "The king had him tortured."

General Kline's quiet, but I hear a thousand things in that silence. We're talking about Kline's beloved son, the man set to take over the general's job.

War takes many things from people, but unfortunately, pain is not one of them. In some quiet, dark corner, when no one's around, General Kline will break down.

"I stopped the torture," I say. "That's why they killed Will."

The general steps back into the light, and his eyes meet mine one last time. He nods, and for that instant, we understand each other completely. The two of us have lived through a nightmare; we've both seen our worst fears realized, and we've been forced to make decisions no human should have to. We've lived more, done more, and stained our souls more.

The general disappears into the night, and the last of my past walks away with him. It's both liberating and crushing, being freed of your last ties. Once more I am the lonely girl that has everything and nothing.

CHAPTER 22

SERENITY

THE KING AND his men descend on me not a minute later.

"Serenity, what the hell are you doing out here?" the king says, jogging up to me.

Half of me wants to say, "Getting air." That was the excuse I parted with, after all. But I'm in no mood to taunt the king. Not when my body aches from wounds that leave no trace.

However, I can't tell him about the general, either. Not here at least. If the general's bending loyalties to save my life, then I can do the same.

"I thought I saw someone I knew ..."

It's the only explanation I can think of. I'm a fairly terrible liar, and the king has a built-in bullshit detector.

Montes cups my face, frowning. "If you think you see someone worth tracking, you tell me, you don't go chasing them yourself."

I run my tongue over my teeth. I've always been independent; I don't plan on stopping that now. And I certainly don't plan on trapping myself in the king's gilded cage so that he feels better.

He catches sight of my gun. Up until now he's been concerned, but not panicked over my departure from the party. I can see the moment he begins to take the situation seriously.

His hands slide down my cheeks to the base of my neck. "Who did you see?"

Shaking the king's grip off me, I slide the weapon back into its holster, uncaring that his soldiers are seeing a lot of leg in the process.

"A ghost from my past," I say as Montes steps in front of me, shielding even this exposure from his men.

It's too dark to be sure, but I believe that vein in Montes's temple is throbbing.

"Do I look like an idiot to you?" he says sharply. "Tell me who you saw, or my men will quarantine the area and start interrogating everyone. I promise you, you don't want that."

I've seen the king's interrogation techniques. They involve pliers.

"You are insane."

"No, but you are if you think to keep information from me."

There is no dealing with a man who's willing to hurt innocents for my compliance.

Several people from the party are drifting outside, drawn by us. Now's not the time to share secrets.

"I'll tell you, but not here."

SHE DOESN'T TELL me until we're back at our villa lying in bed. I think she only admits it then because I begin to stroke the soft skin of her stomach. She assumes it's an advance—not that I'm ever opposed to sex—but at the moment I only want to revel in the fact that she's carrying our child.

"General Kline was at the party," she says, staring at the ceiling. "That's who I saw, and who I ran after."

My hand stills. "You chased after the same man who held you hostage—who nearly let you die—only weeks ago?"

My earlier rage is returning with a vengeance. I don't know whether to be angrier at the general, who thinks he can come between me and my wife, or Serenity, who ran out to meet him with no regard to her life. She could've died, along with my child, for all her stupid heroism.

Worse, she covered for the man. That's why she's only telling me this now; she gave him time to get away.

I know my eyes are icy when they meet hers. "If you were anyone else—if I cared for you any less—I'd have you strung up by your thumbs and beaten."

She's right to think I'm full of empty threats. For all my violent promises, I wouldn't dare hurt her, and I'd turn my wrath on anyone who'd try.

"Am I supposed to be frightened?"

"Goddamnit, Serenity." I pull back and look at her. "I'm serious. I will put you on house arrest—I'll take away your gun, strip you of your duties, and keep you secluded to a single room if I have to."

She pushes me back into the mattress and leans over me. "Kline warned me that Estes is planning an ambush. The man you want to spearhead the leadership of this territory is going to try to kill us both at some point within the next week."

I stare up at her. My mind's primed for a fight; I expected her to lash out, not to divulge. If it were any other time, I'd turn Serenity's reaction over and over in my mind and find all the ways that she's changed since I first met her. All the ways she's begun to give into me.

Her words sink in. An attack. The former general sought my wife out to warn her of an attack.

My reaction is instant—*I will take out any who try.*

All that is evil in me rouses at the possibility.

However, plots to end my life are a dime a dozen. And considering where this warning came from, I have serious concerns over its validity.

There are a hundred and one reasons the Resistance would want us to leave this place early. The one that tops the list—sabotaging the discussions. Weeds like the Resistance thrive in the wild. There is no room for them in the civilized world. South America is still largely in chaos, but as soon as I place certain figureheads into—limited—power, the territory will come to heel.

"Is there any basis for this accusation?" I ask. I'm glad she confided in me, but a warning from the WUN's former-general-turned-Resistance-officer is not a reliable source.

"Does there need to be?" Her eyes are wild. She thinks *me* crazy for not taking this seriously.

Wrapping an arm around her waist, I roll us so that now she is the one laying prone on the bed, and I am the one hovering over her.

"Of course," I say. "Serenity, this is the same man who nearly let you die when the Resistance held you hostage. This is the same man whose son arranged for you to be shot. And this is the same man who willingly gave you to his enemy." I hold her in my arms, completely unashamed that *I* am that enemy. "How do you know he's not trying to force you into some plot of the Resistance's own making?"

"The same way you know I won't kill you," she says.

I don't bother to hide my surprise that she admitted this. I'm not the only one who doles out empty threats, but this one in particular she wraps around her like a safety blanket. To acknowledge that she'll never have her revenge ... this is another turn of events I have to mull over once the time is right.

However, the only reason she would admit this now is because she wants to be taken seriously.

I can give her that.

"Alright," I say, already groping along the nightstand for my phone. "I'll inform my men of the threat, and I'll arrange a morning flight for us."

And I do.

Perhaps that's why we never make it out as scheduled.

CHAPTER 23

SERENITY

SOMETHING WAKES ME up. I can only hear a phantom echo of the sound, but it's enough to have me sliding out of bed and pulling on my gear. Habit propels me into action.

Montes wakes just as I'm lacing my boots over my pants.

"Serenity, what are you doing?"

I must seem insane, getting hurriedly dressed as I am for no apparent reason. Just another difference between soldiers and civilians. I've been programmed to expect an attack.

Before I respond, I hear it. It's just a distant, dull thump, like someone sinking a dart into a dart board, but silencers also make that noise. It's so subtle that I almost discount it.

Almost.

"Get dressed," I say. "Quickly. Something you can run in. And keep the lights off."

Montes doesn't argue. As he's pulling on his clothes, I grab my gun from beneath my pillow and shove all my spare bullets into my pockets.

I recognize the sound of a jet in the distance. That's what woke me up, I realize. Before I even recognized the purr of its engine, I heard enough of its whine to set me on edge.

I cock my head as I listen to it. It's getting closer.

Shit.

Heading to the nearest window, I peer out. Shadows still cloak most of the yard, but I can make out one of the king's soldiers. He's splayed out on his stomach, near the edge of the property, and as I watch, two dark forms grab his legs and drag him into the thick foliage.

"Montes, your men are getting slaughtered. I think the enemy is approaching from all sides. Call whoever you need to." *But I fear we are alone.*

He swears. He's just finishing lacing up his own shoes when he swipes his phone and places a call.

War's taught me to be paranoid. I'm maladaptive in the king's decadent castle, but out here, out here I know how to survive.

That familiar, rising excitement begins to flow through my veins. I think I am addicted to this sensation. My mortality never means so much as it does now, when it could be seconds away from snuffing out.

Life and death are violent lovers, and today they do battle.

Moving to the sliding glass door, I return to watching our surroundings. I can see figures below, but I'm afraid to shoot when it's still so dark out. It won't stay that way for long; the sun's rising, and if we can survive the next few minutes, I'll be able to tell friend from foe enough to shoot.

"Montes, grab a gun if you have one," I say.

He nods, distracted. He's already on the phone, but judging by his tone, assistance won't be coming in time.

He covers the receiver. "I wasn't able to get ahold of my head of security." Montes's top guard, who's stationed here with us, wouldn't miss a call for anything short of death.

I'm sure death is exactly what befell him.

I hear another thump, and I turn my attention back to the sliding glass door. Two soldiers creep towards the house bearing guns; another man lays sprawled across the grass, a dark pool of blood widening around him.

They're closing in, and we're running out of time.

Opening the sliding glass door, I slip out onto the balcony and study the two approaching men. They wear helmets and Kevlar, which means I'll have to hit their necks if I want a kill shot. And as soon as I shoot, they're going to know my exact location.

The jet I heard earlier is almost overhead. This isn't some routine flight path. This is an orchestrated assassination.

We're dead if I do nothing.

Breathing steadily in and out, I clear my mind and line up my sights.

Aim. Fire. Aim. Fire.

The shots pierce the silence. Blood sprays as one of the bullets finds its mark; the other buries itself into the second man's vest.

Several things happen all at once. Montes shouts for me, enemy soldiers hiding in the dense shrubs bordering the property now run forward, and the king's men— what's left of them—scramble to meet an enemy that's snuck up on them.

I duck and run for the bedroom. Behind me I hear shots ping against the house's outer walls as that second soldier returns fire.

I've barely made it around our four-poster bed when a violent wind blows my hair, and the jet's purring engine shakes the house.

I spin just in time to face down the aircraft lowering itself to hover outside our balcony. I stare at it, and for a single second the melee quiets.

This is the moment I meet my maker.

"Serenity!"

Montes tackles me to the ground just as the glass sliding doors shatter, and the pilot opens fire on us. A barrage of bullets lights up the room. Furniture is shredded in seconds. Feathers and cloth dance in the air, and the wooden dresser splinters as the jet unloads its ammunition into the room. In seconds the walls are riddled with holes.

Montes shields me with his body the entire time. I breathe in the king's cologne as a familiar rush of adrenaline thrums through my veins.

We might live, but we'll probably die.

We stare at each other the entire time, and I think he might be trying to memorize my face.

He covered me; in that instant when he faced down death, he thought to protect me. I'd expected that from the men I fought alongside, but from the selfish, narcissistic king?

Not in a thousand years.

The firing cuts off all at once.

"Time to go," I say, even though I know he cannot hear me. I jerk my head towards the door, and Montes nods.

Staying flush with the ground, we crawl through debris towards the door. Dust, plaster, and the odd feather float down on us as we move.

"*Are you hit?*" I yell. The ringing in my ears is dying down, but it's still hard to hear.

He shakes his head. "*You?*"

I shake my head. A fucking jet. Estes called in a jet to take us out on top of his ground troops. This is sloppy. Dramatic, but sloppy. Estes must've learned of our plans to leave and rushed the attack.

Montes glances over at me. I see raw fear in them.

"What?" I say, reloading my gun and keeping an eye on the doorway out. I haven't heard anyone breach the building yet, but when they do, things will happen really fast.

His gaze moves to my stomach. He licks his lips, and his eyes return to mine. "There's something I need to tell you."

I wait for him to speak. Now is not a great time to have a heart-to-heart, but if he feels he needs to confess while our lives are on the line, I'm not going to stop him.

"You're pregnant, Serenity."

I stare at him, uncomprehending. I don't think I breathe for several seconds.

"What?" I finally say.

I'm aching to return my attention to the business at hand, but I can't look away from him.

"You're pregnant."

I recoil from him.

This conversation might be the one thing that can make me forget about the fight occurring right outside these walls.

I don't realize I'm shaking my head until the king says, "Yes, Serenity, you are."

Pregnant? With the king's child? Horror and disbelief war for dominance.

No. *No.*

Impossible.

He has to be wrong. How would he even know this?

"You're lying," I say.

Below us someone kicks at the front door. A second later, I hear a shot fired and the thump of a body hitting the outside wall.

"*Nire bihotza*, I'm not."

There is not enough air for me to catch my breath.

I still don't believe him. But each second that he stares back at me unflinchingly, I lose a little more confidence. We're about to die. He has no reason to lie.

I'm going to be sick. The king's child is inside of me. I've never thought of a baby as parasitic, but I do now.

I'm carrying a monster's child.

"How would you know whether I was … ?" I can't even say the word.

"It came up when you were in the Sleeper."

That was over a week ago.

I grip my gun tighter, but I'm not angry—not yet. At the moment I'm … *blindsided.*

I draw in a deep breath.

It doesn't matter. The situation, the deception, the horror of it all. None of this matters if we're dead.

I nod to the gun in Montes's hand. "Know how to use that?"

He looks affronted by the subject change. "Yes."

"Good. We're going to survive this so that I can kill you myself. Until then, I need your help." I nod to the window. "There are too many of them. I'll need you to shoot incoming soldiers."

His eyes follow mine. I can't read his expression, but I know where his mind lingers. I can't afford to think about what he's just confessed, and if he's to do his part, he can't think about it either.

Montes has never personally killed before. It's almost frightening that he's never gotten his hands dirty with death, mostly because that needs to change today if we're to live. Even the monster that is my husband has limits to his terror, and today I'm asking that he break one.

"Montes." I recapture his gaze. "This is target practice. Don't see people. See heads and chests. If they're wearing bulletproof vests and helmets, you'll need to aim for the neck, groin, or thighs. And be careful, once you fire the first shot, they're going to know your position."

That's all I can give him. It doesn't get past me how messed up the situation is— I'm giving the man responsible for the third world war tips on how to kill.

The man responsible for knocking me up.

I force down a wave of nausea and get up to leave.

"Serenity—"

I slip out of the room before he can finish whatever he'd been about to say. As far as I'm concerned, the time for talking is over.

I head down the stairs, both hands on my weapon. I can hear the pad of several sets of boots. The enemy is still trying to be silent and stealthy, which means they will be keeping their bodies crouched as they approach. I adjust my aim, knowing they will also likely be wearing Kevlar and helmets. It makes them harder targets, but not impossible to get past.

I peer around the corner.

A shot goes off, and the plaster just above my head chips away. I pull back and lean against the wall, closing my eyes and drawing in a deep breath. From the glimpse I caught, there are at least a half a dozen of them and one of me.

They've come outfitted for war while I have just a handful of bullets. This will take some creativity on my part if I want to survive the next several minutes.

I exhale and an open my eyes. I may not be used to the ways of queenship and polite society, but I'm intimately acquainted with death.

I push away from the stairs and sprint towards a nearby couch. As soon as I hear the first gunshot go off, I slide the last few feet behind the couch.

They're relentless. They must have a bottomless supply of ammunition to use it so carelessly.

Above me, Montes's gun goes off. He fires three separate shots.

I don't have time to wonder about what's happening outside these walls. The couch I hide behind is getting shot up with bullets; stuffing and scraps of material flutter into the air. I have to flatten myself along the floor to avoid getting nicked.

And then I hear a sound that makes my stomach bottom out.

A grenade clinks against the ground next to my head. My eyes lock onto it. I don't give myself time to think. I simply grab it and lob it back over the couch. The split second decision ranks as one of the stupidest, riskiest maneuvers I've made in battle.

And this time it pays off.

The grenade explodes seconds after I throw it. I hear shouts and the thud of large bodies as they hit the ground. The blast shoves the couch against me, and a wave of heat ripples through the room.

I peer over the back of the couch and level my gun at my opponents. Some are getting up off the ground, some aren't. I take advantage of their temporary disorientation and fire my gun. I aim for their necks.

Five out of the eight shots find their mark. And then my gun clicks empty.

Shit.

While my opponents are shouting and scrambling to regroup, I duck again behind the couch and tuck my father's gun into my waistband.

This is the moment where my chances of survival are the slimmest. I'm out of weapons and the enemy hasn't retreated.

In fact, more vehicles are approaching; I can hear their engines in the distance.

It hits me again: I'm pregnant. Whatever happens to me doesn't just affect my life anymore. It makes me hesitate when I shouldn't.

Behind me, several of the windows have been shot out. It's no honorable exit, but honor has nothing to do with this entire situation.

I begin to crawl towards them, keeping my body as low to the ground as I can.

Two successive shots pierce the air.

There's a moment, right after the shot is fired and before the pain sets in, where you actually don't know whether or not you're hit.

But then the moment passes and the pain doesn't come. I feel the ground vibrate as two bodies collapse.

I cast a glance over my shoulder.

Standing at the foot of the stairs, gun still raised, is the king.

King Montes Lazuli killed for me. The evilest man on earth killed for me and probably saved my life by doing so.

And, God, the look on his face. The vein in his temple throbs, and his eyes are cold and resolute. There's no shell-shocked expression, and he doesn't double over and vomit. He's remorseless.

I shouldn't be surprised. This is the king we're talking about. If anything, I should be worried that he'll get a taste for it.

I nod to him. "Thank you."

He takes his eyes off of his victims to nod back to me, finally dropping his aim.

I stand and head to the bodies. Most of the dead are missing appendages. Grenades are a messy way to go. Ignoring the gore, I begin to take what weapons I can. Montes joins me, and together we strap on guns, grenades, and ammunition.

When I begin to drape weaponry across my chest, he stops me.

"Kevlar first," he says. "To protect the baby."

My stomach drops at his words. It's real, this is real. We're in the middle of a shootout and I'm pregnant.

This is some sick parody of real life, and Montes is some twisted version of my knight in shining armor as he removes the bulletproof vest from one of the dead men and slips it on me. The thing's heavy, and the top left breast is soaked with blood.

I don't focus on that. Instead I string ammunition and guns across my chest while Montes dons a vest of his own. I check the men for keys, but come up empty-handed. They must've left them in the car.

Meanwhile the sound of engines is getting closer.

"We need to go, now," he says, and his order actually makes me smile. I hadn't imagined him to be an equal on the field, but it seems that's just what he is.

Together we sprint for the only car out in the driveway. In the early morning light, I make out several unmoving bodies sprawled across the yard. The jeep our attackers drove in is outfitted with a crate of explosives, semi-automatic assault rifles, and ammunition. The keys sit in the glove compartment.

"You drive; I'll shoot," I say.

Montes doesn't argue, which I appreciate.

While he cranks on the engine, I familiarize myself with my new weaponry. In addition to assault rifles, Montes and I lifted machine guns off of our attackers, the kind you can hold and fire continuously. They have a mean kickback, which means that if you're not stationary or bracing yourself well, your accuracy will take a hit. I'm neither of those things at the moment, but the sheer quantity of ammunition we've acquired makes up for it.

Montes floors the gas and the car screeches around the circular drive before cutting down the dirt road off the property. Mud and pebbles shoot out from under the wheels as I make my way to the back of the jeep.

Back here I can brace myself along the vehicle's exposed metal frame as the jeep jumps and dips over the uneven terrain. I peer at the crate filled with explosives. It's a dangerous thing to have in an automobile, especially when there's going to be a shootout in the near future, but I can't bear to dump them. Not when Montes and I are overwhelmed by the sheer volume of enemies.

I flip the lid off another crate, one I haven't yet looked into. Several grenades are nestled amongst wood shavings. I suck in a breath at the sight. This car is a moving bomb. One nicely placed gunshot and we're all going up in flames.

Ahead of us, two more military vehicles barrel down the dirt road towards the estate.

I don't wait for them to recognize us. Bracing myself against the top metal bar of the jeep, I begin to unload my round of ammunition, holding down the trigger as the bullets spray across the vehicles.

The shots tear through metal and glass, but none of the cars slow. If the soldiers were confused about why one of their own vehicles was leaving the estate, they are no longer.

The enemy begins to return fire, and bullets ping against the jeep's metal frame.

"Montes," I call out, crouching down to grab a grenade. His eyes meet mine in the rearview mirror. "Slow down when we pass them."

"What are you planning?" he says, his voice rising to be heard over the engine and the gunfire

"You'll see."

He doesn't show any signs that he'll do as I ask, but I have to trust that he will.

I return to gunning down the vehicles. One enemy bullet whizzes to the left of my head. Another pings against the metal bar I'm holding onto.

"Serenity!" Montes clearly sees who our enemies are trying to eliminate first.

"I'm fine!" I yell, keeping my eyes fixed on my targets. "Worry about yourself!"

I manage to take out the front tire of the first car, along with its driver. The second slams into it.

We're almost upon them. Out of habit, I kiss the grenade I clutch for good luck. It's a macabre custom of mine, but after you live through enough battles, you become superstitious.

Like I asked, the moment we begin to pass the row of cars, Montes slows. I pull the grenade's pin and throw the explosive into the second enemy jeep, which is now entangled with the first.

"*Gun it.*"

I have time to see the passengers widen their eyes, and then we leave the car in the dust.

The explosion rocks our vehicle forward, and I cover my head as the scorching heat rolls over me.

Once the initial wave of the explosion dissipates, I glance over my shoulder. Both cars are smoldering, and no one inside the vehicles is moving.

I move back to the front of the car and take a seat next to Montes.

He looks at me like he's never see me before. There's a healthy dose of shock on his face, and no little amount of awe.

I work my jaw. I don't want his respect. Not for killing.

At this point, we have two options: to attack our opponents head on, or flee. The problem with the latter is, even if we managed to get to the hangar undetected, Estes has likely paid off the staff that mans the aircrafts. We'd never make it out.

The problem with the former is that Estes has potentially thousands of men backing him. Montes and I, deadly though we can be, are no match to the sheer quantity of our opponents.

It's an impossible situation.

We're quiet for a minute.

My hand slides to my stomach, and I glance down at it. It's rounder than it usually is, but I attributed that to being well fed.

Montes's hand covers mine.

"You are so lucky I have other people to kill at the moment," I say.

"I know."

When I look up at him, I see he's serious.

"How far along—?" I begin.

"About two months."

I pinch my eyes shut. Fighting for your life has a way of throwing things into perspective. And really, what's bothering me is not that Montes kept this from me; it's that I never tried to prevent this from happening in the first place, and now that it has …

I have few fears left, the king gift-wrapped me a new one.

CHAPTER 24

THE KING

I'VE ORDERED EXECUTIONS, waged wars, withheld antidotes, neglected people into early graves, and now I've delivered death myself.

I didn't see the soldiers as targets like Serenity advised. I saw them as people. And I didn't distance myself from the violence like I know some killers do. I was there in that moment and I savored watching my enemies die.

Serenity is right to think I'm evil. The last salvaged bit of my soul burns for her. Other than that, I'm cruelty formed into the shape of a man, and I have no qualms about that.

"We need to leave the country immediately," I say.

Serenity looks out the window and rubs her belly absently. It's a knife to the gut, watching her come to terms with what is, and it's making me want to pull over, hold her to me, and force her to rejoice over the news the way I did.

"The hangar may be compromised," she says.

I nod. That very worry has plagued me since we left our villa.

Even if the airport isn't compromised, we could be shot out of the sky.

"And you think all of this is because …" Serenity glances back down at her stomach.

She can't bear to say it. As much as I would normally enjoy her being squeamish, right now it does nothing but worsen my mood. This is the last thing I want her uncomfortable with.

"You're carrying our child. Is it really so hard to accept?"

She opens the hand that cradles her stomach, staring down at it like it holds the answers. "Yes," she breathes. "I never wanted this."

I give a caustic laugh that does nothing to lessen my blooming fury. "Well you better get used to it because neither of you are going anywhere."

I am the king of the entire world; I picked her, a lowly former soldier and an emissary of one of the conquered lands to be my wife. Queen of the planet. Who is she to reject me and my child—*her* child?

She needs to fucking accept that this is the way things are.

SERENITY

THE KING THINKS he can keep me and this child of ours around. I still can't think about the situation without a fresh wave of nausea passing through me.

"If Estes hasn't already heard that we've survived, he will soon," I say.

I can tell the king hates that I keep changing the subject. I don't give a damn that he thinks I'm being subversive. He has no clue just how terrible the storm inside me is right now. I'm keeping it together only because we're in danger.

"I have a safe house an hour from here," he says.

"Do any South Americans know about it?" I ask.

"Some. You think it's compromised?"

"The WUN—the Americas—don't work the way the Eastern Empire does. Everyone here can be bought for a price, and if Estes is willing to fly in a fighter jet to gun us down, he sure as hell will be willing to pay off people for information."

"I can pay more," Montes argues.

He's thinking like a rich foreigner.

"Yes," I agree, "but Estes lives here. You don't. This is someone else's turf and the people here play by their rules, not ours. Trust me when I say that when we're this close to death, people here are going to remain loyal to Estes for fear of his future retribution."

"Then we're going to have to kill him," Montes says, grim.

"Yes." If we cut off the head of the snake, the orders stop trickling down to Estes's loyalists.

"Let's be clear about one thing," he says, "my first goal is to get you out of here alive. All our actions will stem from that."

I reappraise my husband. He didn't include himself in that statement. If we weren't in the middle of a dire situation, the magnitude of his words might've hit me a little harder.

Something worse than my nausea rises up my throat. Something worse than grief and violence.

I love this broken, broken creature, and damn him to the pits of hell for making me feel it when I should hate him all over again. If I could reason or suppress it away, I would. If I could crush it by sheer force of will, I would.

"Alright," I say, working to make my voice even, "we're clear about that."

"We need to strike before Estes has time to regroup."

Now *this* is the king I'm familiar with.

Already the humidity of this place has my hair sticking to the nape of my neck. I squint my eyes and look at the horizon. "Let's go pay the bastard a house call."

BY THE TIME we near Estes's estate, Montes and I have plotted out a rough strategy to kill the man. One that involves liberal use of explosives.

Neither of us know whether the man will be inside, but smug assholes like Estes are fairly predictable. Right now I'm both desperate enough and sure enough to bet all our lives on his being home.

I move back to the bed of the jeep and swap out the machine gun for a rifle. "If we live through this, I'm having a stiff drink," I mutter.

"Better ask those stars of yours to grant your wish, *nire bihotza*," Montes calls out behind me. "I'm not letting you anywhere near the alcohol cabinet when we get back."

I smirk. I don't know if the king's aware of it or not, but banter like this calms my nerves before fights.

The car curves down the road, and ahead of us I catch sight of watchtowers posted on either side of the entrance to Estes's estate. Two grim-faced guards manage them.

"Are you ready?" I say, lining up my sights. Once I shoot, things will happen very quickly.

"Do it."

I pull the trigger.

It takes seconds to shoot down the guards. I watch as one of their bodies tumbles from its post.

"Hold on," Montes warns.

I brace myself against the jeep's frame as we barrel towards the gates. Our car rams into the wrought iron fence. Metal groans and then, with an agonizing shriek, it rips away completely.

It's almost anti-climactic, driving guns a-blazing onto a quiet estate. But it doesn't stop me from taking position once more. I begin picking off guards stationed outside the house one by one as they struggle to grab their weapons and take position themselves. I don't give any of them time to aim. As soon as my sites lock on heads or chests, I shoot.

Our vehicle comes to a halt, and Montes joins me at the back of the Jeep. His normally coiffed hair is wild. Dirt and ash mar his skin and clothes. He has rolled up his shirt sleeves, and a bulletproof vest encases his chest. This Montes belongs on the battlefield; he looks like he was born to the profession. I definitely like this version of him better.

He bends and grabs a grenade. Flashing me a smile that looks even whiter than usual, he pulls the pin and launches it at one of the windows while I continue to take out anything that moves.

The glass shatters, and we hear a surprised shout. Then—

BOOM!

The explosion unfurls out the window, and I can only imagine what it's doing inside.

Montes already has another grenade in his hand, and he drives this one towards a downstairs room.

The screams start soon after that.

I train my gun on the house's main entrance. At some point, someone's going to run out of that front door that might not be evil like the rest of us. My heart and my soul weep for them. All soldiers that have seen considerable action can tell you that there are always these situations—the questionable ones. And often the innocents get caught in the crossfire.

I hope that doesn't happen today. I hope the people that have nothing to do with Estes's power plays are far away from here by the time Montes and I level this building. Because we *will* level the building, and we aren't taking any prisoners.

I draw in a steadying breath when the front door opens, and then I shoot.

Two guards and a woman I recognize from the meetings. No innocents so far.

I periodically flick my gaze to the windows and the sides of the house. That's where counterattacks will come from.

Montes throws a third grenade, then a fourth. The screams are beginning to harmonize, and the house is catching fire.

Now people are pouring out of the building, some on fire. I shoot those ones first; it's one thing to kill, another to watch a human being suffer, and even after all I've seen and done, I don't have the stomach for it.

"*I surrender! I surrender!*" Over the roar of the fire, it's hard to hear Estes's voice. It comes from just inside the front door. "*Don't shoot!*"

Like all good vermin, the rat managed to survive the explosions.

"Come out with your hands up!" I yell.

I cradle my trigger lovingly. I'd love nothing more than to pump this man full of bullets.

Through the smoke drifting out of the front door, I make out Estes's form. Hands in the air, he leaves the shelter of his house. Too late I see the small gun he clutches.

His gun arm drops and he fires off a shot a split second before I fire at him.

I hear Montes shout. Next to me, he stumbles, then pitches forward into the seatbacks, clutching his hip.

I can't breathe. This is my father all over again. The bullet, the blood, the emotion expanding, expanding, expanding inside of me. It's too large to contain.

Loss, agony, it's roaring, ripping through me, and I can no longer passively kill.

I lunge for Montes just as the South American dictator falls. I grab my husband, and there's blood everywhere.

Not again, please God, not again.

But Montes is breathing. It's shallow, and with every second that passes more blood slides out of him. I don't know where he's hit—whether it's his thigh or his torso; muscle, artery, or organ.

I'm scared.

I don't know when that happened—when this terrible man went from being someone I feared to someone I feared for.

Montes shakes his head as I try to help him. "Finish this," he grits out.

I don't want to. He could still die; every fiber inside me is warring with itself. My training demands that I stand and shoot, my heart is telling me to keep my husband alive.

Vengeance is a poison, and it slithers through my veins.

Estes tried to kill my husband. My monster. Father of my child.

Something cold and resolute settles on my shoulders. Montes *will* survive, and I *will* end this.

I lift my gun. The screams have turned into moans. I shoot at two more people who've caught flame. Everyone else is laying in pools of their own blood. Almost all are dead, and those that aren't will soon be.

I train my weapon on Estes and approach him cautiously.

He's been inching his way towards his gun, which rests several feet away from him. It must've slipped from his hand when he fell.

I reach his gun before he does, and I kick it away, keeping my aim trained on his heart.

The dictator watches me with angry eyes. "You won't get out of here alive," he says.

"We'll see."

I don't shoot. Even though he tried to kill me and Montes, I don't pull the trigger. Not yet.

For all his depravity, Estes is just one more WUN citizen who shares a past like my own.

"What?" he challenges when I don't shoot. "Do you want to know why I did it?"

"No."

I already know why. It's the same reason behind my mother's death, and my father's, and my land's. Power is the worst sort of drug. You can never have enough of it, and you'll give up every last good thing for more.

"Then what are you waiting for?"

It's a good question. I want him to redeem himself. I want proof that a soul as far gone as his—or mine, or the king's—*can* repent.

But he's not going to understand, and it's not going to happen.

"Who are you working with?" I ask.

He tries to laugh but ends up grimacing instead. "You and I both know I won't tell you." He's beginning to sweat. A gut wound is a painful way to go.

Estes has about seven minutes of life left in him. I won't get answers from him willingly or unwillingly. We both know it.

"Did you really think you could ever do what I do?" he says. "You have no idea. You're just a savage with a sad story. And the king wants you to rule the world? I won't be the last—"

I pull the trigger before he can finish the sentence. The bullet hits him in between the eyes. One instant the man was aggressively alive, and the next he's nothing more than bones and muscle and cartilage.

The smoke soaks into my clothes and the wind dries the blood on my skin as I stare down at him. The roar of flames is the only noise out here. The whole thing is a dark baptism.

I don't want to be this way. Killing and killing and killing. I'm a prisoner to violence, and I'll never be free.

I strap my gun back across my body and kneel before Estes. Threading my arms under his, I drag the dead dictator's body to the jeep.

There are a lot of horrific things that I've had to do throughout the king's war. This is just one more of them. The man's body is our ticket out of here. Just as Estes wanted proof of our deaths, I'll need proof of his to sway loyalists who would stop the king and me from leaving.

The stillness of the estate is eerie. All that's left of Estes's great scheming is me, a dying immortal king, and a whole lot of carnage.

I grunt as I pull the body along, pausing when I reach the back of the jeep to catch my breath.

Montes raises an eyebrow weakly.

I grunt again as I shove first Estes's upper body and then his lower half into the back of the vehicle. Montes's upper lip curls as he stares down at the dictator now lying next to him.

I round to the king's side and remove his hand from his hip. There's blood everywhere. My own hands are beginning to shake; they don't usually do that, especially not in the heat of battle. That's often when they're steadiest.

I take a deep breath.

I still can't tell what the bullet hit, and this is no place to doctor Montes back to health.

We need to get back to the hangar.

I hop onto the driver's seat and press on the gas. Behind me, I hear Montes groan.

A bloody hand grabs my seatback. A moment later, Montes hauls himself over the center console.

"What are you doing?" I say, aghast. "Sit back down."

"You are not leaving me to rot next to a dead man," he says. He grits his teeth as he forces his broken body into the seat next to mine. He didn't once cry out. The guy's made of tougher stuff than I would've guessed.

When I reach the end of Estes's property, I let the jeep idle.

"I don't know how to get to the airport," I say.

I can't meet Montes's eyes. I don't want more proof that my monster-turned-lover is now nothing more than an injured man. He's supposed to defy the laws of nature.

"I'll get you there," Montes whispers. "Just ... look at me."

I don't want to.

"Serenity, please."

I squeeze the steering wheel and force my gaze to meet his. He looks tired. Worn. Weak. All the things I feared I'd see in those eyes of his. And now these might be the last breaths of air he'll take.

"Do you love me?" he asks.

I'm shaking my head. "No."

"Liar."

He can see right through me.

"Now's your chance to kill me," he says.

I work my jaw. "What do you want me to say? That I can no longer do it? I already admitted that to you."

He gives me a wan smile. "Turn right."

I take my eyes off of him to do so.

"There's a Sleeper in my plane," he says. "You want to save me, then get me inside it."

I floor the gas pedal. Anger and guilt and confusion—they all vie for my attention. It's one thing to protect the king from death, another to try to save him from its clutches. I'm truly abandoning my own promise right now. I won't kill the king—not today, and not in the foreseeable future.

I grit my teeth against his groans as the vehicle hits rocks and potholes.

"Left," he says, when the road tees off.

There's a Sleeper at the end of this drive. I just need to get to the hangar, and then we can get Montes inside it. I even my breaths; I'm cool and collected, I can feel myself detaching from the situation.

Until I look over at the king. His head leans against the wall of the jeep, and his eyes are closed.

"*Montes*." I reach over and shake him. "Stay with me."

His head lolls as he tries to nod.

"I swear to God, I will fucking punch you in the dick if you don't."

That actually elicits a shadow of a smile. "Vicious ... woman ..."

Two minutes later, he slips away again. Luckily, I no longer need his instructions. I begin to recognize our surroundings—the skeletal remains of a home nature's reclaiming, streets that are nearly covered by foliage. I can get us the rest of the way there.

By the time I pull into the hangar, Montes is completely unconscious. The place is bustling with activity. I have to assume that all these men are in Estes's pocket. I hop out of the jeep, gun in hand.

"*Estes is dead*." I point to the back of our vehicle with my free hand, where the dictator's body lays. The men peer at the car, and some approach. "Whatever orders he gave you, they no longer apply. The king and I are getting on the king's plane. Anyone who stands against us will be shot on sight. Those that help us will each receive half a year's pay once we safely disembark."

That gets them moving. Men rush around the hangar, preparing our plane for takeoff. Each discreetly looks at Estes as they pass the car.

Once the aircraft is ready to board, two men help me carry Montes onto the plane. His skin is paler than I've ever seen it, and his body is dead weight.

"*El rey está muerto.*" The man speaking has two fingers pressed to the pulse point beneath the king's jaw.

"No." I push aside his hand and place my own where his was. I wait for his pulse. It never comes.

I stare down at the king's face. His head's rolled back, like he's fixated on the ceiling, but his eyes are closed and his mouth is slightly parted. Already the planes of his face are losing shape.

I cradle the side of his head. I don't realize I'm crying until the first tear trickles into my mouth.

People are wrong to say that the dead look peaceful. They just look dead.

"No," I repeat.

This man isn't beyond saving. Not now that I've fallen for him, not now that I carry his child.

The men look at me strangely, but they nonetheless help haul the king into the plane. Montes told me that the Sleeper would be onboard, but I've never seen it before.

"The Sleeper—we need to get him into the Sleeper."

Someone knows what I'm talking about because I begin to hear shouts of "*Compartimiento de carga! La carga! El durmiente! Más rápido.*"

We begin to move again, this time towards the plane's cargo bay. Inside, I can already hear the hum of the machine as it idles. It's bolted to the floor. My heart palpitates a little faster just locking eyes on it.

The king told me once that so long as the brain was intact, the Sleeper could bring the dead back to life. So it doesn't make sense, this irrational dread I feel when I see it. Perhaps it's that such technology seems just as unnatural as Montes. But right now I'm happy to set aside my superstitions if it means resurrecting a dead king.

We get him situated inside and I close the lid. I don't know what to do next, but the machine has a "Power" button. On a whim, I press it.

The humming sound turns into a whirr as the Sleeper wakes up.

I watch the small readout as it begins to assess the king's vitals—his now nonexistent ones. Then it begins scanning his body.

"Come," one of the men says.

"Not yet." I want to make sure that the machine is doing what I need it to. I know that means more time on the ground, more time for a potential counterattack should Estes's allies decide to rise up. I don't care.

It only takes a minute for the machine to get a respirator and something called a cardiopulmonary bypass device hooked up to the king. Five minutes after that, the machine begins cleaning the wound.

A gentle hand touches my upper arm. "Good?" one of the men asks.

I nod, backing away. Leaving is the last thing I want to do, but I need to arrange safe passage with the men here. If the machine can save Montes, it will.

If it can't, then the world will know the undying king can, in fact, die.

CHAPTER 25

SERENITY

I STARE OUT the plane's window, my hands resting on my gun and my chin resting atop my hands.

I have all the time in the world and nothing but my thoughts to occupy me. There's plenty to think about, and I don't want to dwell on any of it.

So instead I gaze out at the lonely sky and try to feel nothing. It doesn't work. Last I saw, Montes was dead, and even with the Sleeper's best efforts, he may stay that way. If he doesn't live, I'll be queen.

The world won't bow to me, the young woman who betrayed her land when she married the king. I might inherit Montes's empire, but I haven't earned the right to rule it. War could very well break out again. And I'd be the first to die.

That's no longer an option. Not now that I'm pregnant. I exhale a long breath. I will have to be more ruthless than I've ever been if I want to survive. And I'll have to be willing to get back inside that dreaded machine if I want to live long enough to have this child.

My thoughts turn to General Kline. I couldn't say what I feel in this moment. Gratitude? Grief? Melancholy for the life I once lived? He banished me to this fate the day he made a deal with the king, but I might have died today if not for him.

My thoughts circle back to the king. I'm used to greenies underwhelming me. Montes did the opposite. Before today I couldn't imagine him on the battlefield. I'm used to seeing him in pressed linens and suits, and while he has muscle to spare, I've never seen him exert true force.

Today he did, and he was relentless. He saved my life at least once, but in all likelihood, he spared me from death several times. Had he not so readily killed, we would never have left South America. Of that I'm certain.

The king who killed millions from his ivory tower now left it to kill several himself. That last bit of Montes's innocence was snuffed out today. If he wakes from the Sleeper, what man will rise? Will he be worse? Better? Wholly unchanged?

I find I really don't care. I just want him back.

It seems like a lifetime later that the overhead speaker clicks on. "We're beginning our descent into Geneva. We should touch down in another twenty minutes."

Geneva, the last place I want to be. Only a handful of months ago I'd fled that city, boarded a plane and crossed the Atlantic to flee the king. Back then I'd mourned the death of my father. Now here I am returning to the very place I'd once loathed, and I'm trying to bring the dead king who'd once tormented my people back to life.

The world has gone crazy, and me along with it.

It's dark outside as we descend, and few city lights illuminate the streets. The airfield, by contrast, is lit up.

When I exit the plane, it's to a crowd of the king's medics and his security team. They try to shuffle me off to look at my wounds. I elbow past them and head for the cargo bay. Behind me, I can hear their protests.

I make it to the back of the plane just as the flight crew opens the cargo hold. I'm the first one inside, despite the commotion behind me. I jog up to the Sleeper and scan the readout.

I blink back tears as I clench and unclench my jaw. Medics and security personnel move in behind me. Some grab my arms and gently guide me out. I let them.

The undying king beat death yet again.

THE KING

I WAKE WITH a start.

Reflexively, my body tenses. The gold leaf molding overhead is distinctly different from the exposed cross beams of the Spanish villa we've been staying in.

I feel skin beneath my hand. I trace the flesh with my fingers. It's soft, but the muscle beneath it is unyielding. My hand travels higher, rounding a delicate shoulder. Then the hollow above a collarbone. I feel soft hair slide under my touch.

I glance down at Serenity, who's nestled against my side.

My stomach tightens pleasantly at the sight. Savage woman. She hasn't left me, despite now knowing she's pregnant.

This pleases me immensely.

My last memories involved gunfire and explosions. Somehow I survived it, in no small part thanks to the woman in my arms. Not so long ago she told me she wanted to kill me. But she didn't take her chance when it was offered to her.

My hand delves into her hair and strokes its way down the golden locks. There is no name for what I feel right now. Not awe, not love, not gratitude. None of those are large enough to encompass this emotion that's not quite pleasure and not quite pain.

"Mmm." She moves against my side and opens her eyes. "You're awake."

I expect her to try to move out of my arms—not that I'll let her. When she doesn't, that feeling burrowed beneath my sternum expands.

Her fingers touch my side, where I'd been shot. "Did you know you died?" she says, her voice toneless.

My hand pauses its ministrations.

So my wife not only spared my life, she saved it.

"I don't want to outlive you, Montes," she says.

I squeeze her close and whisper against her temple, "Are you admitting you can't live without me?"

She's quiet for so long I assume she's not going to respond.

"Maybe," she finally whispers.

I'm not big enough to hold what I feel.

I touch the scar on her face and follow the line of it down her cheekbone. "Do you still hate me?"

"Sometimes," she says honestly.

I smile to myself. "Good. I like you feral."

She shakes her head against my chest. "You're twisted."

We fall silent for several minutes.

"I'm going to be a terrible mother," she finally whispers.

I pause. Serenity's *scared*. The woman who's killed legions of men is actually afraid. Of herself.

It's almost unfathomable.

I pull her in closer and kiss the crown of her head. I'm holding my family in my arms; I have literally everything I could ever want.

"You'll be the best mother," I whisper against her temple. She will be because she'll second guess everything and work to get it right. For all of my wife's ruthlessness, she has a wealth of compassion.

"You're not a great judge of character," she says.

I laugh. "When it comes to you, I am."

SERENITY

THE DOOR TO our room opens.

"Good morning, Your Majesty."

"Oh, I love the view from this room."

"Look at that flaxen hair of hers. I've tried to dye mine the same color, but I can't quite mimic it."

The female voices fill the bedroom, and I can hear them moving towards the bathroom.

I squeeze my pillow tighter. The cool metal of my father's gun brushes against my hands. I'm not going to look up; that'll make it all real, and I have at least another hour of sleep in me.

The bed dips and I feel a hand on the small of my back. A moment later, the king's lips press against my temple. "Serenity, you need to get ready."

I groan and bury my face deeper into the linen. If the king has it his way, then *I* am not going to get myself ready at all—a bunch of strangers are.

"Make them go away," I mumble.

One of Montes's hands delves under the pillows and finds me gripping my gun tightly.

"Don't you agree one massacre is enough per week?" he says conversationally.

I turn my head to face him so that I can glare. All that earns me is a kiss on the nose.

He gets up to leave, and I release my gun to snatch his wrist. I'm more awake now, more aware that the only time the king actually calls in a team to get me *prettied* up is when something important occurs. "What's going on?"

He stares down at me, and those conniving eyes of his hold such fondness in them. It both moves me and disturbs me that the king looks at me this way; I'll never get used to it. "Politics," he says evasively.

I squeeze his wrist tighter. "Give me more than that."

He raises an eyebrow. "And what will you give me in return?"

I'm not in the mood for his coy games. "This isn't a fucking exchange. I'm your wife."

Montes leans in. "With me, it will always be an exchange. Of wits, of wills, of affection, and of everything in between." He yanks his wrist out of my grip and walks away.

Two hours later I'm glaring at him as I exit the palace, my hair coiffed, my face painted, my body sheathed in another too-tight dress. He waits to the side of our ride, wearing his coat of arms.

Those deep eyes of his land heavily on me. "My, doesn't my wife look lovely."

"Fuck off." I stride past him and duck into the car waiting for us. I still have no idea where we're going.

He follows me in. "Dark blue is a good color on you."

I won't look at the asshole, who probably took a total of ten minutes to get ready himself.

"Are you going to finally tell me where we're headed, or do I have to guess?"

When I turn to face him, he's pinching his bottom lip and studying me with interest.

"We're going to church."

IT'S BEEN A while since I've been inside a church, and not just because I lived in the bunker for most of my teen years. After all, I spent a good amount of time topside when I was doing my tour with the military.

I lost my religion about the same time I lost my city. When it comes to war, people tend to go one of two ways: either they find God, or they do away with him. I fell into the latter category.

I never blamed him, not like some of the others that gave up religion. They seemed more like jaded lovers than atheists. God just never was a man in my mind. He was food, shelter, safety, and—ultimately—peace. And when all that fled, I realized that my world no longer had a place for him.

But now as I enter the cathedral, holding the king's arm like I was prepped to do, I can feel the weight of *something* fall on my shoulders. Maybe it's the dim light, or the silence in the cavernous space filled with hundreds of people, but it prickles the back of my neck.

I'm about to ask the king if we're getting married all over again when I catch sight of a crown at the end of the aisle. It rests on a pillow next to a priest—or a bishop, or a cardinal. I have no idea what title the holy man goes by.

My breath releases all at once.

The king's planning to coronate me.

I pause mid-stride. I want no part in this. It's one thing to be forced to marry a ruler, another to accept the position yourself. And this isn't just some parliamentary affair; this is a spiritual one as well.

No good god would sanctify this.

"Montes," I hiss. "No." That's all I'm willing to say in this place of silence.

"*Yes*," he insists.

I'm still fighting him, even as he drags me forward.

"Do it for our child," he whispers.

My heart pangs. I have a new weakness, and Montes just exploited it. If he thinks a crown will protect the baby, I'll go along with it. After all, I was willing to do much worse when I didn't know if Montes would survive the flight to Geneva. So I stop fighting him.

281

We're halfway up the aisle when he leans into me. "Once we get to the altar, kneel," he breathes, his voice barely a whisper. "When you rise again, you'll be a crowned queen."

Montes leaves me at the foot of the altar, where I do as he says and kneel.

The rites are read in Latin, and they go on and on and on. My eyelids are drooping by the time the holy man grabs the crown.

I blink several times as he approaches me with it. Lapis lazuli circles its base, and dozens of gold spikes branch off of it. I've never seen anything like it.

The holy man speaks more Latin as he places the crown on my head. He makes the sign of the cross before retrieving a robe made of velvet and ermine. The material settles over my shoulders, and he clasps it at the base of my throat. The weight of it all presses down on me; I'm sure the effect is intentional. This is very much a burden.

He gestures for me to stand. I do so, and the two of us lock eyes. I think for a moment we are wondering what kind of person the other one is. What kind of woman marries a tyrant ruler? What kind of religious man ordains a killer as queen? Staring at him, I realize we might both simply be decent people cornered into powerful roles. Everyone can be bought, but the price is not always power. I wonder what his was.

He speaks again in Latin, makes the sign of the cross again, and then indicates for me to face the crowd.

I swivel and find hundreds of faces staring back at me. But there's one face my eyes seek out. He's the only other person besides me and the man behind me who remains standing. His dark eyes gleam with approval.

For the first time since I entered the Cathedral, the man behind me speaks in English. "I present to you, Her Majesty Serenity Lazuli, High Consort of the King, Queen Regent of the East and the West.

"Long live the queen!"

CHAPTER 26

SERENITY

I'M STARING OUT the window of my room at Geneva's broken city. It presses up against the edge of the palace grounds and fans out to what I can see of the horizon.

I don't like this place; it holds too many bad memories. I keep wanting to hunt down the suite my father and I stayed in. It's macabre, but I feel like if I went there, I'd run into him—or at least see the stain his blood left on the carpet.

I touch my crown and prick myself on one of its points. They might as well be thorns. They look like thorns, they feel like thorns, the only difference is that these thorns are golden and shine in the light.

I pull the thing off and stare at it.

"It's not going to bite you."

I don't turn around when I hear Montes's voice. He'll demand attention soon enough—he always does—but I won't give him any immediate gratification. I've been whittled down to petty acts of rebellion.

"How long have you been planning that?" I ask.

"The coronation? Since we returned," he answers.

"I'm actually impressed," I say, running my thumb over the spires of my crown. "You coordinated an entire ceremony, a feat you managed to keep me in the dark about, and you executed it all without making me look like a fool."

I think he recognizes what I'm not saying.

You deceived me.

You made me vulnerable in a room full of wolves.

You forced my hand.

"Our enemies already recognize your position as my wife; it's time the people recognize it as well."

I rotate to face him. His eyes glint as he watches me. He wears a crown of his own, and the sight of it brings back all those months and years when he was just an evil so unnatural that he defied the very laws of nature. He seems just as inhuman now—just as dark, just as beautiful, just as untouchable.

I should renew that old vow and kill the king where he stands. My gun is holstered against my inner thigh. It would take seconds to pull it out, aim, and fire a lethal shot. Hit that terrible mind of his and destroy all chances of him ever being revived.

I won't act on the fantasy. This evil man has awoken my heart. I don't understand why or how, but he has, and even my ironclad will doesn't stand a chance against it.

Montes strides across the room and takes the crown out of my hand. He studies it.

"Whether you like it or not," he says, "you were always a queen. You were this morning before you woke up, you were the day I slid my ring onto your finger. You were the first time I laid eyes on you. You were queen the first time you drew blood, and the first moment you drew breath." Very deliberately, he places the

283

crown on my head. "The coronation makes no difference because here," he touches my temple, "and here," he touches my heart, "you've always been this way."

He has no idea that while he waxes on about queenship, I've been debating whether or not I could kill him.

"I'm calling bullshit," I say.

He laughs and extends his arm. "Come, Queen Regent, you have a coronation banquet to attend, and our child needs to eat."

And there it is, the final nail in the coffin: he has compassion, and now we share more than just bloody, deadly love between us. We share life.

WE HEAD DOWN the hall, towards the ballroom where I first met the king. The doors leading to it are closed, but muffled conversation and laughter still filter out. I'm hit with a powerful wave of déjà vu. Not so long ago I walked down this hall with my hand tucked into the crook of another man's arm and together we faced the same pair of closed doors. But then it was my father, and the dreaded meeting was with the king.

Now the very monster I feared is the one lending support at my side. I breathe in deeply.

"All you have to do is eat a little and nod to people you don't know," Montes says, misreading me. "Oh, and don't stab anyone in the eye with the utensils."

"Montes, I'm not going to stab anyone with anything." That's what my gun's for.

We stop at the doors and wait for the guards to open them. "It'll take an hour," he says, "and then we'll leave."

The doors swing open. The moment the room comes into view, the guests fall silent even as they rise to their feet. I wonder what they see when they look at me and the king. Their nightmares swathed in silk and crowned in gold? Or are we more benign in their eyes than that? I know what I see. This place is the bastion of extravagance and corruption.

"May I now present you with Your Majesties the King and Queen Montes Lazuli, Sovereigns of the East and the West."

Applause erupts and amidst the noise I hear shouts of "Long live the king! Long live the queen!"

Montes leads me down the stairs. As I pass by our guests, they bow.

The whole thing is more than a little unnerving.

The ballroom is now an expansive dining room. Everything that's not gilded at least gleams. The clothing, the jewels, the candlelight, even the guests' eyes and smiles.

There's a table at the far end of the room and at its center are two empty seats. I just need to make it there and then converse with people I despise.

It's times like these that I'm almost positive I somehow already died and this is my hell.

When we get to our designated table, the king pulls out my seat, just as he always insists on doing. I sit—and just about scream when I realize who is across from me.

I *have* died. This *is* hell.

"Congratulations, Your Majesty," the Beast of the East says.

I don't see him; I see a string of broken women.

This monster is going to die before the dinner is over.

I glare at the Beast—Alexei is far too innocent a name for this *thing*—until he looks away. Even that's not good enough. I begin tracing the serrated edge of my steak knife with my finger.

I don't care at this point that nearly a dozen cameras are capturing every second of this dinner. I'll kill this monster where he sits, and then I will stand on his corpse and laugh.

Not five minutes after we've taken our seats, the waiters begin bringing out dinner. The sight and smell of all that red meat ...

I think of the grenades tossed at Estes's estate. The smell of charred humans that drifted in the air. The sight of those bodies ripped open, their innards exposed.

My nausea is climbing up my throat. I press the back of my hand to my mouth. I thought morning sickness behaved its damn self and stuck to mornings.

"Are you alright?" the Beast asks.

I ignore him while Montes drapes his arm over the back of my chair and rubs my neck. He leans in. "Do you want me to send back the food?" he asks quietly, reading my reaction.

I look over at him. Is he seriously considering wasting every single plate of food all because of me? It's horrifying, this power I wield, this power the king seems happy to bestow upon me.

I rear back as I assess him.

The psycho is serious.

"Don't you dare."

"Very well." Montes still flags down a waiter and discusses something with him. The waiter's eyes focus on the Beast as he listens. Finally, he nods to Montes and leaves. A short while later a bowl of soup and a basket of bread are set in front of me.

I glance over at the king. He goes on talking to the men on his left, but the hand still resting on my neck gives a light squeeze.

He ordered me soup so I wouldn't have to eat the meat. It's just one more considerate thing the king's done on my behalf.

I break the bread and dip it into the soup. This I can palate.

I'm halfway through it when the king's lips brush against my ear. "Better?" he asks.

I turn into him, my lips brushing his. "Much."

This might be the first time I've been genuinely affectionate with the king in public.

"Good," he says, his voice roughening.

Someone begins clinking a knife against their glass.

When Montes smiles, I feel it low in my belly.

"Do you remember what that means?" he asks.

I do. They want us to kiss.

I lean in the remaining distance and press my lips against his. I can feel his surprise in the way he returns the kiss and the slow smile that gets incorporated into it. Our audience begins to clap, and though my skin prickles uncomfortably from the attention, I don't pull away until the kiss is done.

We break apart slowly. Montes is gazing at me, his brows slightly pinched, his mouth curved with amusement. He leans in and steals another brief kiss. Then he lounges back in his chair and reaches for his wine glass. Lifting it, he surveys the room, but it's me he looks at when he takes a lazy sip from it.

I grab my glass of water with a shaky hand. Either it's all the eyes on us, or my own actions, but I'm not nearly as composed as the king.

"How does it feel to be the queen regent?" the Beast asks, drawing my attention to him. He cuts into his steak as he speaks. Blood seeps out of the nearly raw interior.

My eyes drift from his plate to my own. I take a sip of my soup and pretend he doesn't exist.

Only he won't let me.

"I mean," he continues, "technically you were queen since you married our king, but today he handed over part of his empire to you." He shakes his head. "I never thought I'd see the day he shared his power with anyone. You must be something." His knife scrapes against the porcelain as he cuts into the meat again.

I can't take it anymore. The smell of the meat, the sight of this abomination, the stifling civility of these people. We're all barbarians here, and we know it.

I'm done pretending.

I lean forward. Somewhere along the way, I released the soup spoon and exchanged it for something a little sharper. I'm now gripping the steak knife in my hand and not wholly sure how it got there.

"I'm going to tell you this just once," I say. "If you so much as look at me wrong, I will castrate you with the nearest object." My voice is low and angry. "Then I will throw you into the worst prison I can think of. One of the ones where they'll have fun with you—and I'll make sure they do. And if I ever catch wind that you've *raped*"—I hear a gasp from one of our nearest guests, and feel Montes's eyes immediately on me—"anyone else, I will do all that and worse."

Other than looking a little pale, the Beast appears unruffled. Either he's schooling his features well, or he can't bother to be intimidated by me. It's probably some mixture of both.

He stares at me for a long second then inclines his head. "Understood."

"Good." I release the knife and return to my soup.

Conversation, which had quieted for a moment, picks back up.

My left hand rests on the table, and I feel the king cover it with his own. He leans in close. "I'd been almost positive I'd have to dig a knife out of Gorev's skull," he says quietly, eyeing the Beast, who is now in a conversation with the person to his left.

"This isn't funny."

The king's hand tightens around mine. "No, it isn't. Save the killing for when the cameras aren't around."

I give him an exasperated look, but I relent. The Beast is safe.

For now.

I WAKE UP in the middle of the night to terrible, throbbing pain. At first it simply stirred me from sleep. I'd roll, reposition myself, and go back to bed.

But now my eyes snap open as the pain rips through my abdomen like a knife wound to the gut. My skin is slick with sweat, and the sheets stick to it.

My hand drops my lower stomach, where it hurts the worst. Several seconds later another wave hits. I let out a groan and fist the comforter as it cramps up my muscles.

"Serenity?" Montes's voice is thick with sleep.

When he tries to pull me to him, I let out a gasp.

"*What's wrong?*" Now he sounds wide awake. He clicks on the bedside lamp and turns back to me.

I shake my head. "I don't know."

A healthy body shouldn't be doing this. Montes and his doctors have been swearing up and down that I'm alright, but right now I don't feel alright. I feel wrong.

Very, very wrong.

My pelvis cramps so sharply that I release a strangled sound. I'm being wounded from the inside out.

One of Montes's arms slides behind my back. The other touches my cheek and tilts my head to face him. "Do you need a doctor?"

I shake my head, then nod. I don't know. I grip Montes's upper arm as the cramps intensify.

Oh God, dear God, I think I know what's happening.

I squeeze his arm. "Montes," I say. "Our child ..." This is the first time I've openly acknowledged the baby as ours.

His expression doesn't exactly change, but I see it—fear.

I choke on a silent cry as the pain somehow gets worse. Warm, wet fluid seeps out between my thighs. I can't look away from him as it's happening.

Montes's eyes search mine, and there's such desolation in them.

He begins to pull away.

I latch onto his upper arm. "Don't leave me."

"Serenity, I need to call a doctor." He's pleading.

A tear slips out before I can help it. "I think it's already too late," I whisper.

CHAPTER 27

SERENITY

SOME DAYS I want to live, and other days, like today, I want to die.

I shouldn't feel this sadness, this overwhelming grief. I hadn't even thought I wanted a child. Especially not this one. Only once it was too late do I find out I did. Now I can actually admit that I might've even been excited.

But just like everything else in my life, all roads lead back to death.

I lean against the pillows propped up behind me like I'm some kind of invalid. The sheets have already been changed, the bloodstains removed like they never existed. I've now lost two family members within these walls.

This place is cursed.

"… These things just sometimes happen," the doctor is saying to Montes.

The king paces, one of his hands squeezing his lower jaw almost painfully. Other than that single tear I shed, neither of us has cried. We bottle up our emotions because to dwell on them might just destroy us, and the king and I, we won't let anything consume what's left of us.

I stare at the far wall, study the gilded edges of the molding. The impersonal art painted by an expert hand that hangs just below it.

"Serenity … *Serenity.*"

I blink and refocus my attention on the king.

He takes my hand. I don't realize that I've been fisting it until he smooths the fingers out. Each nail has left bloody, crescent-shaped wounds in the pads of my palm. "You're going to need to get into the Sleeper so that everything's been properly flushed out—"

"I'm not getting in your fucking machine ever again."

That's probably a lie. I'm speaking from my heart right now. The weight of this terrible existence is pressing down on me, and I can barely breathe through it.

I don't want more of this.

Montes's hand squeezes mine. "I'm not giving you a choice." He sounds as close to losing it as I've ever heard him. "Either you get into the Sleeper on your own free will, or it happens by force."

I narrow my eyes at him. He's not the only one close to the edge. But anger lifts the fog I've been under for the last couple hours.

What's happened to me today can't happen again. I won't let it.

Montes will force me into the Sleeper, that I don't doubt. But if I go willingly …

I run my tongue over my teeth. "I'll do it—on one condition."

Montes and the doctor wait for me to finish.

"I don't want to get pregnant again."

THE KING

THEY GIVE HER a birth control shot. It won't last forever like she wants it to, but it will keep her sterile for a while. Long enough for both of us to grieve and move on.

My hand covers my mouth as they sedate her and place her in the Sleeper.

Now I've lost two people in mere hours. Serenity will be fine in a few days, once her body has purged the last of the fetus and the Sleeper has expunged the most recent flare-ups of her cancer.

But I won't.

I leave the medical wing because I can't bear to look down on her sleeping face and envy her fate.

I head to the palace's training facilities, which I share here in Geneva with my soldiers and guards. When I enter the weight room, several of my men are already there lifting. They stand and salute as soon as they recognize me.

"Out," I say. It's all I can manage.

I wait until I can't even hear the echo of their boots.

I don't wrap my hands or change before I begin laying into the punching bag. It feels cathartic, releasing emotion this way.

I slam my fists into leather until my knuckles split and my body's covered in a sheen of sweat. Even then I don't stop. My grief is turning on me. I never did well with feeling helpless.

I embrace the rage that's willing to take its place. This is one of the fundamental ways I understand Serenity. Death makes us both vicious. It burns through us like fuel and we consume it before it can consume us.

Another hit. I pretend I'm hitting skin and bone and not unforgiving leather. The chains clang and the bag swings.

Such a little thing, this life we lost. Just a spark of a possibility, really. And that was snuffed out before it could grow into something more. I was warned. I didn't listen. And why the hell would I? I played God for the past thirty years. It's a rude awakening to realize I can really be powerless.

I slam my fist into the bag—left, right, jab, uppercut. The metal chain that it hangs from continues to shiver, the sound echoing in the empty space.

Eventually I stop and steady the swaying bag. I'm a bloody mess; it drips from my hands, and it's smeared into my clothes and on the leather.

I catch my breath, watching droplets of blood and sweat spill from me onto the floor. And then I begin to laugh. Two of the world's most terrible people lost a fetus—or is it an embryo? Whatever it is, it couldn't have survived on its own. It didn't have a gender—it might not have even had a heartbeat. It lived instead off of Serenity's scarred one. And we *mourn* for it—us, the two people who have staggering death counts to our names. This grief is madness.

And yet I can't shake it.

My laughter turns to ragged sobs. Not a single tear falls from my eyes, and yet my entire body weeps. I tried so hard and for so long to not feel this way. You can heal your body, but not your mind or your heart.

And how they bleed.

SOMETHING'S WRONG. I know it's wrong before I even fully wake. As I blink, I try to figure out why I feel so ill at ease.

The first thing I see is Montes. He grips my hand in his, and he's kissing my knuckles one by one. He looks troubled.

I sit up and look around. I'm back in our room, in our bed, and—

The last lucid hours of my life come back to me. I now have a name for that wrongness; it's called death.

The nausea comes on suddenly, and I run for the bathroom. Maybe it's the grief or maybe it's the physical aftereffects of a miscarriage, but everything hurts. My back hurts, my stomach hurts, most of all, my heart hurts. I heave and heave, but nothing comes. Even after the nausea passes, I don't bother moving from where I kneel in front of the toilet.

I hear Montes make his way in. He places a hand on my back. "*Nire bihotza*, I need you to get up."

I bow my head. Take a deep breath.

Keep moving. One of the many soldier creeds I learned in the military. So long as you focus on placing one foot in front of the other, your demons can't catch up to you.

Reluctantly I stand and turn to Montes. My hair's in my face. He brushes it away and cups my cheeks. Our eyes meet, and then he pulls me into a tight embrace.

The king hugs me like I might slip away if he doesn't hold on tightly enough. He doesn't say anything, and I appreciate it. When it comes to grief, words have no balm strong enough to soothe the soul.

His fingers run down my hair, and he buries his face in my neck. I breathe him in. How had I ever thought this man inhuman? He smells real enough, he feels real enough, he bleeds, he hurts.

I turn my head into him, my lips skimming his jawline. He pulls away and our eyes meet. I can feel his mortality beneath my fingertips, his anguish batters against mine. For perhaps the first time ever, I wish to consume him the way he consumes me.

His brows draw together as I lean in. And then I'm kissing him, marking him, making him mine. I grab the collar of his button-down and—*rip*. Seams split and buttons fly. The hard skin of his stomach is bared to me. I touch it, luxuriate in it.

My monster.

He nearly died. We all nearly died. I will hurt because of what we lost, but it could've been worse.

So much worse.

And now I want to savor what I didn't lose.

His hands grip my upper arms. He's staring at me like he doesn't know me—but he desperately wishes to. I like the look. A lot.

Montes backs us up, helping me out of my clothes and his. He doesn't dare speak. This side of me, the one that pursues him—he must think it's some sort of apparition. Smart man is not going to ruin the moment if he can help it.

We fall together onto the bed. Neither of us bothers kicking off the top sheets before I slide down onto him.

I close my eyes and exhale as I relish the feel of him inside me. One of my hands finds his corded shoulder. I run my palm over the muscle. Real. Alive. Mine.

He holds my hips tightly to his own. We both need to move, but neither of us wants the feeling of being connected to slip away.

"Open your eyes, my queen."

I do.

His dark, mesmerizing ones stare back at me.

No one ever warned me about feelings like this. That I could see something worth redeeming in the world's evilest man, or that he could see something worth saving in the scarred, dying girl he holds in his arms.

I touch his cheek. My hand looks pale and delicate against his olive skin.

Had I once despised the way his presence could overwhelm me? Now the way he envelops me, fills me, devours me is what I love most about this life I lead. He is what's real.

"Make me forget," I say.

And he does.

CHAPTER 28

SERENITY

LONG AFTER MONTES and I finish, I lay in bed awake.

Outside our windows, the night is dark. The city gives off no light, and for once it feels like the darkness is pressing in on me, rather than beckoning me away.

Next to me the king's breaths are deep and even.

My throat works as I gaze at the ceiling.

Event one—the king's palace comes under siege. I lose my memory in the process. Event two—I catch a strain of plague concocted in one of the king's laboratories, a laboratory nations away. A strain of plague no one else catches. Event three—the stabbing. Again meant solely for me. Event four—an ambush meant to end my life and the king's.

Four events spread over a couple months. All of them took place in areas the king deemed safe. All around people the king trusted.

There's a traitor amongst us.

My heart beats faster. The more I mull over it, the surer I am. No average Resistance member could know where the king's blast door was, the door Marco and I never made it inside. Nor could an average Resistance member know our movements enough to try to stab me or ambush me and the king. And to acquire and transfer a super virus like the plague—for that, one would need a scientist or, perhaps, a doctor ...

I bolt upright in bed.

Dr. Goldstein? Is it possible?

A terrible, terrible thought clutches me. On the evening of my coronation, I had a miscarriage.

Panic seizes up my lungs.

What if ... ?

The king reaches for me in his sleep, murmuring something. I move out from under his hand.

I need to know.

I slip out of bed, dress, and leave our room.

My boots click against the marble floors as I stride down the hall.

I touch the gun I holstered to my side. If what I fear is true, there is no place my enemies can hide where I won't find them.

It takes me almost ten minutes to reach the royal medical facilities, which are housed belowground. Even here guards are stationed along the hallways. They look on, impassive, as I pass them.

Ahead of me are two double doors. When I reach them, they're locked shut, but next to the door is a fingerprint scanner. I place my thumb against the surface. In theory, being queen essentially grants me access to anywhere I want to go, but this is the first time I'm actually testing that power.

A light next to the scanner blinks green and the door unlocks.

I don't question my luck.

I flip the lights on, and a moment later the fluorescent bulbs flicker to life.

The royal medical facilities are some strange hybrid of hospital and palace. The walls have gilded molding and the floors are made of marble, but the smell of the place is exactly what you'd find in any hospital.

The soles of my boots sound deafening against the floor, but there's no one here to startle.

I'm looking for the proverbial needle in a haystack. The chances of finding anything are slim, but I won't fall back asleep again until I know for sure whether the doctor has been compromised.

I move through the first set of sterile rooms towards the labs, using another thumbprint scanner to make my way into another room.

I hear the hum before I see the Sleeper. This machine holds none of the answers I seek. Still, I feel compelled to approach the hated device.

Over the last several months, I'd been in one of these things longer than I'd been out of it. At the end of this particular Sleeper is a window, similar to a porthole on a ship.

I hesitate. The machine's on; I have no idea what I'll see if I peer through that glass pane, and I'm not here to sightsee. But curiosity gets the better of me. Who else is important enough to incubate in one of these coffins?

My shoes click as I near it, I tilt my head and peer down.

I inhale sharply.

Dear God.

I recognize the dark, close-cropped hair and that hateful face that's so serene at the moment. I watched that very face kill my father, and then, later, himself.

Marco, the king's former right hand.

He's supposed to be dead.

But apparently he's not.

MY HANDS BEGAN to tremble. First the king's immortality, now this—resurrecting a dead man from his grave. Where I come from, things are simple: you live, you age, and then you die—in that order.

I back away.

This is unnatural. More than that, it's wrong.

"I see you found Marco."

I'm reaching for my gun before I fully recognize the king's voice.

When I turn, he's carefully watching me. His hair is swept back; he wears slacks and another button-down, the sleeves rolled to his elbows like he's ready to get his hands dirty.

Had he watched me as I dressed? Waited for me to leave before he dared to follow? I keep forgetting that no one can even sneeze in this place without the king learning of it. And when it comes to me, he always wants to learn.

"You sick bastard," I whisper. "What have you done?"

The king steps up to my side, but his eyes are focused on the Sleeper. "He was my oldest, most loyal friend." He touches the glass fondly, his eyes sad. "When you and Marco were sealed off—and then I found out that at least one of you was dead—" he shakes his head, "I wasn't willing to lose either of you."

"You can't change these things," I say.

293

Montes is shaking his head. "Do you remember what I told you?"

I furrow my brows.

"So long as the brain survives, the Sleeper can save him."

"Marco put a bullet in his brain. I saw him do it. By your own logic, Montes, the Sleeper can't revive him."

"You're right," the king says, leaning against the machine. "The man you're staring at is a vegetable. My friend is gone."

I shouldn't be affected by how desolate his voice is. Not after witnessing this.

I don't bother asking how Montes secured Marco's body. The king has his ways; if he wants something badly enough, he'll get it. I'm firsthand proof of that.

"Would you do this to me?" I nod to the Sleeper. "Leave me in one of these things rather than letting me die?"

This is an important question because I *am* dying.

The king doesn't say anything, just continues to gaze down at his fallen friend.

"Montes, would you do this to me?" I repeat.

His eyes flick to mine. And then very deliberately, he turns on his heel and walks away.

I STAND THERE for several seconds, processing that. I hear the far doors open and close. My husband left me with his silence. And in that silence, I have my answer.

Heaven help me, that was a yes.

He'd shove me into one of these coffins and prevent my body from dying.

Now I'm faced with the very real prospect that at some point in the near future, I'm going to need to take matters into my own hands. I rub my eyes. My heart's heavy.

After every sacrifice I've made, must I make this one too? Is it wrong to not want immortality? That the price I'd have to pay would be too steep?

My hand drops. I stare down at Marco as unease settles low in my belly. Had he known the king would do this? Had he rejected the idea as well? Was that why he took the bullet instead of the serum?

I force myself away from the device. I didn't come here to ponder Montes's plans. I wanted answers.

I begin rifling through everything. No one comes back for me—not Montes, not the guards. I'm sure someone's got eyes on me, but I don't much care.

I move out of the lab and deeper inside the facility. Back here the doors have bronze name plates fastened to them. I stop when I come to Goldstein's.

Using the thumb scanner, I enter his office.

Stacks of charts sit in piles around the doctor's desk. But it's the one sitting right in front of his computer that captures my attention.

It's mine. I read my name clearly along the tab.

Serenity F. Lazuli

On the front, a note's been paper clipped to it. I pick up the folder and begin to flip through it. The first page appears to be a form for a prescription. The only thing that's written in at the bottom of it are two drugs I can barely pronounce.

Behind this page are the latest readouts from the Sleeper, mostly x-rays of my brain and body. The doctor's gone through and circled certain sections. Malignant tumors, by the looks of them. Not that I know anything about this. I was trained to kill, not to heal.

As I flip through the x-rays, they appear time lapsed. Each gets smaller, but then, the dates get older. My eyebrows pinch together.

That can't be right. I spent weeks upon fucking weeks in the Sleeper in an attempt to reduce these. The machine might not be able to cure cancer, but it can remove a tumor.

I recheck the dates. My eyes aren't deceiving me; my cancer hasn't been treated. If anything, it's been expedited.

CHAPTER 29

SERENITY

A SHAKY HAND goes to my mouth. The warm breath of anger is pushing against my shock, and I welcome it. Dr. Goldstein tricked me and Montes.

An inside man.

I need to find the good doctor, but first I have to figure out the depth of the deception.

I fold the x-rays and scans in half and shove them into the back of my waistband. Carefully I put my file back on the desk where I found it.

My eyes move to the note paper-clipped to the front of the file.

I grab a pen and notepad from the doctor's desk and scribble down the series of numbers written on the note, followed by the medication I read on the first page of my file. Once I finish, I rip the sheet of paper from the notepad and, clutching it in my hand, I leave the palace's medical facility.

But I don't go back to my room. Instead I head to the office I've been using here in Geneva.

I sit down at my desk and boot up my computer. Time to find out what else the good doctor's been up to.

THE KING

SERENITY NEVER CAME back to find me. I'm pissed, both at her refusal to simply accept her situation and at my own burgeoning dependency on her.

Two hours after I left her, I leave my office. I thought that work—rather than lying in bed awake—would better take my mind off of her; I was wrong.

I'm going to find my wife, and then I'm going to make her understand that I am not a monster for wanting her to live.

I head for the medical facility, almost dreading the possibility that she's still there.

She has to know that I won't give her up to death. For Christ's sakes, she should be more desperate to live than I am. Why would she want it to all end when she knows I have the power to keep her alive, and that, one day soon, I'll have the power to cure her of her cancer?

Another thought chills my blood: what if she's already tried to kill herself?

She's the furthest thing from depressed, but if she got it in her head that she had to take her own life, she would. Without hesitation. It wouldn't be suicide to her; it'd be a mercy killing.

Now I'm running, my footfalls echoing against the marble. I can hear my pulse between my ears.

When I burst into the medical facilities, the lights are still on.

"Serenity?" I call.

Silence.

My heart rate continues to ratchet up, and the cloying sensation of dread floods my veins. I find myself holding my breath briefly each time I enter a new room, fearing that this will be the one that contains her lifeless body.

I should've hid Marco better. I should've simply known she'd react the way she did. I scour the facility for her, but she's not here.

Relief doesn't come.

Where would she go once she left this place?

Short of death, she might try to escape.

That thought sends me stalking towards the palace gardens. I consider asking the guards if she's passed this way, but I don't want to shed light on the fact that I can't control my queen. I'm not that desperate. Yet.

She's not outside. Not in the gardens. Not near the fence.

I head back inside, scrubbing my face. Where could she be?

Her office.

I go there at once. The lights are on, the computer's running, but Serenity isn't here. She's leading me on a goose chase.

I head over to her desk and pick up the thin pile of papers sitting on top of her keyboard.

At first they don't make sense. I'm looking at a rib cage, a pelvis. Another rib cage, another pelvis. Someone's gone in and circled orbs—tumors. As I flip through the scans, a horrifying pattern shows up. The tumors are becoming bigger, and more numerous. Some disappear, but those are the minority.

The last image I see is not an x-ray; it's a color-coded image of the brain. A small cluster of color is circled.

I nearly drop the papers. As it is, I stop breathing.

I'm almost positive that I'm looking at Serenity's cancer. The Sleeper should've minimized or altogether eliminated the growth of malignant cells. But these images suggest a different story.

The papers crunch in my hand. I bring my fist to my mouth.

While the Sleeper can't cure someone of cancer—yet—it is capable of controlling it. Yet I hold proof it hasn't done that.

This was a deliberate act of sedition. And it will cost Serenity her life.

Usually I'm a cold, calculating bastard. Not this time. My wrath is a living, breathing thing. Every ounce of fear I feel—and I feel a great deal—fuels it.

Goldstein is a traitor.

"Guards!" I bellow.

They come running into the room.

"Collect Dr. Goldstein and take him to interrogation," I order.

They leave just as swiftly as they came.

I promised the man that his life was tied to my child's. Not only did he ignore that warning, he also tried to take Serenity away from me. And he might have succeeded.

It's time to let him know just why no one crosses me.

NOW I *MUST* find where Serenity went. She's a smart woman, she knows I won't let her die, and it appears she's figured out before me that Goldstein played us both.

All this time I thought Serenity's symptoms had been the result of her pregnancy. *Fool.*

I'd been had.

The thought brings on a wave of rage so strong an animalistic cry forces its way out of my mouth. Without thinking, I grab the back of the bookcase next to Serenity's desk and topple it over.

I do the same to the filing cabinet. I hurtle a paperweight across the room, and it punches a hole through the drywall. I can hear my guards running back towards this room.

"Stay out!" I yell.

So help me God, I will kill the first man that comes through the door, and I'll enjoy it. Lucky for them, they listen to my order.

The quiet drone of the computer catches my attention. The screen is dark but all it takes is a jiggle of the mouse and it comes to life.

Two windows are up on the screen. The first is an informational page on two drugs. A single, chilling word pops up repeatedly throughout the article.

Abortion.

I taste bile at the back of my throat. For one sheer instant I believe my wife rid herself of our child.

Anger, betrayal, and soul-searing fear all move through me, and for one second I feel the devastation Serenity always alludes to. I feel as though I'm losing everything all at once.

And then I remember. The x-rays, the scans. She found her medical file. The site she left open gave her only a definition.

She didn't seek out the drug; she must've found evidence of it in her medical records.

The second wave of my rage rushes through me. Her miscarriage was no accident.

Goldstein killed my child.

I almost leave then. I already know that Goldstein will not die quickly, and I'm eager to see that man suffer as none have before him.

However, the second window catches my eye. On the screen is the palace's directory. It's listed in alphabetical order, and about five people and their corresponding contact information fill the space of the screen. Four of the names and faces mean nothing to me. But the fifth one, the fifth one I see almost daily.

It's my newest recruit. The Beast of the East. Alexander Gorev.

SERENITY

DR. GOLDSTEIN AND the Beast of the East. Two traitors who are in communication. Two traitors who are sharing my personal information. Two traitors who've tried to kill me—if my assumptions are correct—and succeeded in killing my child.

I smile viciously as I head to the office Gorev uses while in Geneva. This is one of the few times I'm actually pleased with my fractured conscience. I wanted an excuse to kill this sad sack of human flesh. Now I have it.

The random assortment of numbers scribbled on Goldstein's note referred to Gorev's fax machine, a number registered in the royal directory.

I don't bother going after Goldstein. Not yet. The doctor will face my wrath later, once the Beast is nothing more than ashes.

Do these men not realize what I did when my father died? Did they think it would be any different with my child? How cocky both must be to think I wouldn't find out.

I reach Gorev's office. Another thumb scan and I'm inside. I make myself at home. Immediately I begin to flip through his drawers. In the first one I find cigarettes, a fancy metal lighter, and a bottle of 186 proof whiskey.

A man's most important professional items are those closest at hand. Alexei's are his vices. He's not a man plagued by his demons; he's ruled by them. It actually makes me more curious about the Beast. What his motives are for getting involved in treason when he's just about as high up as one can be?

Then again, in the king's world, all roads lead back to greed.

I pocket the lighter and uncap the whiskey, taking a swig as I continue to peruse the traitor's office. I almost choke on the stuff. My eyes tear up as it burns its way down.

I glance at the label again. This stuff isn't alcohol; this is lighter fluid.

I find nothing else of interest in the office. Gorev is less careless than Goldstein when it comes to leaving damnable breadcrumbs.

I kick my legs up on the desk, and then I wait.

When the Beast walks in, I'm playing with fire.

I flick Alexei's lighter open and closed. Open. Closed. Open. Closed.

He stops.

My gaze is focused on the fire. "Do you know why I'm here?" I ask.

Alexei steps into the room and closes the door behind him. He leans back against it. No one in the WUN would be so stupid as to lock themselves in a room with the person they were betraying. When you live amongst casual violence, you never underestimate people. Not even a young, dying queen.

Especially not a young, dying queen.

But perhaps the infamous Beast of the East sees me as just another meek woman.

"You wanted to speak with me?" he says, one side of his mouth curving up. His eyes fall on the bottle of whiskey.

My mouth curves upward as well. "You're good, I'll give you that. Even when you know that I know."

He tenses, and it's the signal I need. Grabbing the 186 proof alcohol, I saunter around the desk. I stop in front of him.

He has no idea what I'm going to do next.

I tilt whiskey bottle to read the label better. "You know, what it really comes down to is this: you killed my child."

My eyes flick up to him, and before he has a chance to react, I backhand him with the bottle. Glass shatters against his cheekbone, and the force of the impact throws him to the ground. The alcohol soaks his face and his hair, and it drips down his neck and seeps onto his chest.

The Beast cradles his injured cheek as blood drips between his fingers. I must've cut him with the jagged edge I still hold. I drop it to the ground and smash it with my boot.

Then, ever so slowly, I stroll towards him.

He's drenched in whiskey and glass shards, and he's losing his calm facade as he crawls away from me.

"The attacks on my life—those I could've forgiven. The attacks on Montes's—well, you know my history. But you involve an innocent?" I kick him onto his back and flick open the lighter I still hold. "That'll bring out the sadist in me."

Now I'm seeing this hateful man's fear. Wrapped up in it is anger and incredulity. I'd like to think that last one has to do with my gender.

I hold the lighter over him. "Just how fast do you think you'll go up in flame?"

The cocky man who entered his office is gone. Alexei keeps swallowing, and I think he's desperately trying to hold back vomit.

"There's alcohol on you," he says. "If you drop that on me, I'll make sure you catch fire as well."

I flash him an indulgent smile. "You think I'm scared of death? Goldstein's been informing you on my health. You know how advanced my cancer is," I say. "The king can't stop it. I might be squandering ... oh, a few months if you do manage to kill me. But you know just as well as I do that with cancer, the final months are the worst.

"You, on the other hand," I continue conversationally, "probably have decades left." My gaze moves back to the flame. "I've heard death by fire is the worst way to go."

I let him see my eyes. My empty, empty eyes. I am the result of a life of loss. This is what happens when you live through every fear you've ever owned.

"Please," he says.

"Please what?"

"I don't want to die."

I stare down at him. My hand is practically shaking from the need to drop the lighter on his body and see him go up in flame. Vengeance is whispering in my ear, and it's such a seductive lover.

"Who else?" I ask.

He's looking at me with confusion.

"Who else is in on it?" I doubt his word is any good, but every once in a while someone squeals who's actually telling the truth the first time around.

He opens his mouth, but before he has a chance to talk, we both hear footfalls approaching the door.

"This could end very badly for you depending on who enters," I say.

Several seconds later the door bursts open. I shouldn't be surprised when I see Montes, but I am. Sometimes I forget just how resourceful my husband is. And this time, he's come alone.

His eyes take in the scene. He's seen me kill, but this is the first time he's ever seen me truly cruel.

"Do it," he says.

My eyes move back to Alexei. He knows he's a dead man.

"I'll tell you everything, just please don't kill me."

And then he begins to list off names.

CHAPTER 30

IT'S WORSE THAN we imagined.

The Beast and the royal physician aren't the only traitors amongst us. There's a whole ring of them, and most Montes meets with on a daily basis.

His advisors betrayed him.

He'd been right all along to begin that witch hunt amongst his councilors. At the time I'd been horrified at the thought of him killing one of them. I'd even saved one from death, an advisor whose guilt the Beast admitted to several hours ago.

I saved the man who helped plot my assassination. Who facilitated the death of my child.

I have to work to keep my features expressionless.

The advisors trickle in, all but Alexei. The king's newest advisor will never again take his seat, or walk, or eat, or conspire.

He's now nothing more than a lump of cooling flesh, and my only regret is that he didn't die slow enough. Those women he raped and tortured, they deserved better justice than I gave them.

I pick out a bit of glass from underneath a fingernail. My eyes flick to the king's remaining advisors. These fuckers, however, we haven't dealt with. They sit down in their expensive suits and chat idly as they wait for the king.

Next to me, Montes lounges in his chair, watching them all, a small smile on his face. He's utterly still—no bouncing legs, no drumming fingers. Whatever fuels my husband, he doesn't waste it on tells. Not even that vein in his temple throbs at the moment.

Suddenly, Montes's chair screeches as he slides it back. He stands, bracing his hands against the table.

The room falls silent.

"For the longest time I believed the Resistance was behind the attacks on Serenity's life," he begins. "But a king has many enemies." His gaze moves over his advisors, and the men eye one another uneasily.

The door to the conference room opens, and the king's soldiers storm inside. They head up either side of the conference table, boxing the advisors in.

It's a nice show of force; the soldiers even have their guns out.

"Half of you have committed high treason. Traitors do not get the benefit of a fair trial. I am your judge, jury, and executioner."

I glance over at Montes.

Executioner?

I'm about to stand when the officers aim their guns. It all happens so quickly. I only have a second to take in everyone's shock before half a dozen guns go off at the same time.

I jerk back at the deafening sound. Blood sprays across the room and mists in the air.

Foreheads and eyes are missing from a handful of the world's evilest men. The smell of meat and gun smoke fills the room as their bodies slump over. The rest of the councilors stare at their dead comrades with horror.

I draw in one shallow breath, then another.

Slowly I turn my head to Montes. He meets my gaze, and I see rather than hear him say, "I did what I had to do to keep you safe." And then he leads me out of the room.

He's holding my upper arm, and I realize it's because I'm weaving. I'm so goddamn tired.

I shrug his hand off me and walk ahead of him.

He grabs my arm again. "I did that for you—and for our ... child." He can barely even say it, now that it's gone. For once we actually created someone rather than destroyed them. In a sea of old experiences, this is a new, intimate one, and it binds us together in a way that nothing else can.

"I'm not mad," I say, weary. "I wanted them to die. Horribly." That's the problem. "I don't want to be that ruler, Montes. I don't want to be what you've become."

NOT TWENTY-FOUR HOURS later we get wind that the rest of Montes's advisors—as well as several of his staff, including Dr. Goldstein—have fled the king's palace. The next day, the king's intel alert us to their whereabouts.

South America.

The land of Luca Estes and now over a dozen more traitors.

The king's council has dissolved. I'll never have to attend another ridiculous dinner party with his men because they're either dead, or they've absconded to the wilds of the West.

Montes and I are all that's left of his inner circle: two enemies brought together by war and bound by peace. I was wrong when I believed that the king and the Resistance were two sides of the same coin; in reality, it's the king and I who are. The East and the West, the conqueror and the conquered. We complement each other nicely in all things, even ruling.

Montes and I sit next to each other in his cavernous map room. He hasn't taken down the assassinated men or his intricate war strategies plotted out across the map. I eye the web of thread and the crossed out faces with unconcealed disgust.

"It still bothers you?" Montes asks, not looking up from the paper he's reading.

"It will always bother me." But tearing down distasteful wallpaper is a battle for another day.

Our thighs brush as I return my attention to the latest reports, and concentrating on work becomes a task in itself.

"All seven of your advisors have been spotted in South America," I say, once we've gone through the documents.

They hadn't just been spotted in South America, they'd been spotted near the former city of Salvador. It's awfully close to a Resistance stronghold and the city of Morro de São Paulo, where the king and I nearly lost our lives.

Too close.

The vein in Montes's temple throbs, and one of his hands is curled into a fist so tightly his knuckles are white.

"Alexei gave us the wrong names." The Beast's final bit of treason.

The last laugh is on Montes—or us, rather, since I'm involved in this feud as well. Alexei tricked the king into killing his honest advisors.

"Do you think they were aligned with Estes? With the Resistance?" I ask.

"It doesn't matter." The king's quiet voice raises the hairs on my forearms. "They'll all die, along with every single person they have ever loved."

THE KING IS slipping into violence.

Whether it's the personal cost this war is finally having on him, or that he just can't bear to lose what he worked so ruthlessly hard for, he's falling deeper into that abyss.

"Leave the innocents out of this, Montes."

He turns his head to me slowly. "You are my equal in many ways," he says quietly, "but *I* am the man who conquered the world, and you will *not* tell me how to carry out my will."

What he is proposing is abominable. I know he's done this before, leveraged loved ones to force a person's cooperation—hell, he's done it to me—but even bad men have a code, and targeting innocents goes against that code.

I push up from my chair. "Yeah? Well you better make damn sure you kill those innocents. Because the survivors, they'll turn out just like me."

I walk away from him, my boots clicking against the floor. As far as I'm concerned, this meeting is over.

"In that case," he calls out to my back, "I have no need to worry at all."

His meaning is clear: I, and anyone like me, are fickle with our vendettas.

He is so wrong.

Swiveling back to him, I pull out my gun, cock it, and fire. The bullet buries itself into his right shoulder. It all happens so fast he doesn't have time to react until blood is blooming onto his expensive suit.

Shock and pain mingle in his eyes as he clutches the wound. Blood drips over and in between his fingers. "You shot me," he gasps out.

Normally I'm not this stupid. To draw blood from the king but refuse to kill him—that sort of thing doesn't go unpunished. With all that I've endured, I've just guaranteed myself more pain. But these days, pain is the only thing I really feel. Without it, I might as well not exist.

I holster my weapon. "Look into my eyes, Montes."

He's clenching his teeth, his breath coming in quick pants, but he makes eye contact.

"This monster, the one you created, the one you love so much, this is what I can do."

I can hurt those I love.

Montes doesn't need to know that my windpipes are tightening up at the sight of his agony. That even now I have to steel myself from running to his side and soothing the very hurt I caused.

But I don't do that. I need him to know the extent of my depravity.

Soldiers burst into the room right before I say my final piece.

"You don't want more of me around," I say, "and you should never, ever forget exactly what I am."

CHAPTER 31

SERENITY

I'M ON HOUSE arrest until the king's released from the Sleeper. That pretty much means I just have a shit ton of soldiers guarding me at all hours. And my gun's been confiscated. Again.

Because there are no more advisors to help govern the world, I find myself running the globe by myself.

I want to laugh that I did what so few could: I shot the king and received a promotion for it.

That all ends the day Montes is removed from the Sleeper. It's my turn to sit at the king's side and wait for him to wake. Of course, guards flank me. They no longer trust me alone with the king, but since he's given no orders to punish me for my crimes, they can't stand against the queen until the king wakes.

They won't let me touch him, but my fingers twitch with the need. I try to tell myself it's just curiosity, that I want to feel the smooth expanse of skin where his bullet wound was. But if I'm being honest with myself, what I really want is to stroke his dark hair back from his face. I want to run my fingers over the stubble that's grown on his cheeks and chin.

His eyelids twitch, then one of his fingers moves the barest bit. It takes another several minutes before his eyes flutter open. They immediately lock on mine.

Before he can help it, he smiles, and it's free of any duplicity. He's just happy to see me. His attention shifts from my face to the soldiers that flank me.

His eyebrows draw together.

I help him out. "I shot you. You've been recovering in the Sleeper."

His expression grows distant as he searches for the memories.

Montes sits up. "Wife doesn't bluff," he mutters. He looks to me again, and I can see him trying to make sense of me. His gaze flicks to the guards. "Leave us."

They hesitate.

"I gave you a direct order. *Leave.*"

Reluctantly, the guards do so.

"Am I no longer on house arrest?" I ask.

Montes's eyes burn. "Oh, your punishment is far from over."

THE KING

I STARE INTO my wife's mesmerizing blue eyes. I'm still wrapping my mind around the fact that she looked me square in the eye and shot me. But I always knew what I was marrying. I'd seen the bodies in my palace back when she was just the daughter of an emissary.

I will admit that I had underestimated her. I didn't believe she would hurt someone she loved.

"I know what you were trying to prove back in the map room," I say. "I could've passed on the demonstration, but I understand."

She leans back a little in her seat and I think I actually managed to make her uneasy. I doubt she expected her tyrannical husband to see her side.

"Have *you* been in the Sleeper?" I ask.

"Montes," she warns, "I'm never going in there again."

Her tumors are growing, the cancer has spread to her brain, and while I've been recovering, she grows closer and closer to the grave.

"You *are*," I insist.

"I will shoot you again before that happens."

She doesn't realize it, but she just sealed her own fate.

I reach out and cup her face. For a girl who has lost much, she seems awfully entitled. Queenship suits her all too well. "You won't shoot me again," I say, my thumb rubbing the corner of her mouth.

She glares at me, her lower jaw working. She might as well have just agreed. Whatever proclamations she's made about her lack of a conscience, hurting me cost her.

I frown to keep from smiling. I'm pleased beyond measure. I never meant to tame this creature, and to some extent she'll always be a wild thing, but she's given in to me—to us—far more deeply than I initially imagined she would.

A knocking on the door interrupts us.

"Come in," I say, not bothering to look away from my wife.

"Your Majesties," the soldier bows low to us, "I have word on your former advisors."

My mind is still a bit foggy from the effects of the Sleeper, but it sharpens at that statement.

"What about them?" I say.

"We think they're attempting to take over South America."

SERENITY AND I storm towards my conference room. It doesn't slip my notice that she's having trouble keeping up. She may be in denial, but I'm not. Her body is shutting down; her muscles and organs aren't working as they should.

Her illness has robbed me of the last of my fury. I cannot find it in myself to be angry with her when I fear for her life. I have no intention of punishing her, but what I do intend—she'll think it punishment.

I've been in denial, thinking that because Serenity acted strong she physically was. But no longer. As soon as I deal with this freshest calamity, I'll deal with her.

When we arrive at my conference room, several of my aids have already pulled down a large screen from the ceiling. A slideshow of photos and grainy video clips stream across the screen, many of them capturing my advisors in the middle of treasonable tasks.

Some of these men had been on my council for decades. We shared more than power and ambition.

Over the next twelve hours we hear from the band of traitors. The message is written in red. South America's militia and the Resistance turned on my soldiers. My government officials have almost all been summarily executed.

Serenity stumbles back when she hears the news that the Resistance has sided with my councilors. She should know by now that the Resistance holds no allegiance to her, that they crave power just as much as I do. Just as much as my former advisors do.

I rub my mouth with one hand and cradle my elbow with the other. I've nearly worn a hole in the rug where I've been stalking up and down. It's taken me most of the day to grow detached. Strategy doesn't come to those blinded by emotion. My young queen knows that on the battlefield, but she still struggles with it inside these walls.

I stop and stare up at the footage still being projected on repeat.

"Ready as many troops as you can—I want them coming from the air, the water, and the land," I say. "We'll need to disable their lines of communication first—satellites, radio towers, and whatever electronics we can. And then we'll descend on them."

This needs to be stopped immediately.

SERENITY

IT'S NEARLY FOUR in the morning by the time we finally make it back to our bedroom. I roll my shoulders. My muscles are tight from holding them rigid for so long.

Just when the king thought his pretty war was over, it reared its ugly head again. And for once, the king didn't orchestrate the bloodshed. In fact, most of the violence that occurred since the war ended has been reactionary, and all these events have been set off by a single catalyst—me. The moment the king found something other than his power to care about, the world began to plot.

One of the king's hands touches the back of my neck and he rubs the base of it. I lean into his touch.

My eyes fall to the bed. I've been running on nothing but caffeine and adrenaline for the better part of the day. My body still buzzes with the need to do something. It doesn't understand that in this situation, I can't fight or flee. Instead I have to watch from afar as more men fight and die senselessly.

The last thing I want to do right now is sleep.

Montes's hands slide down my back. He kisses the juncture where my neck meets my shoulders as he squeezes my waist.

My mind still remembers all the black deeds he's done, but my body is pliant beneath his hands, and my heart forgives, even though it shouldn't. Even though it knows a man like Montes never changes, not really.

I'm someone who will never really change, either. And what we have, it works. This twisted love that's endured so much more than it ever should've.

"Are you tired?" he asks.

It's a loaded question. I already know where his mind is.

"No," I say.

Montes's fingers grip the edge of my shirt and, pulling it over my head, he trails kisses along my now bare shoulders, and then my arms. He removes my bra and his hands smooth over my skin.

"Neither am I."

He releases me to remove his own shirt and toss it aside. The look he flashes me is all predatory. He makes quick work removing the rest of his clothes, and then he saunters towards me.

I back up until my skin brushes the ivory and gold wall trimmings. Montes follows, pressing his sculpted torso against mine. Already the sensation of skin meeting skin has me turned on.

His dark eyes are trained on mine, and as that alluring stare of his bores into me, he reaches a hand between us and flicks open the top button of my pants. The zipper goes next. His hand delves into them and—

"*Montes.*"

"Are you going to take your boots off, or am I?" That silken smooth voice of his is now coarse, husky with the first stirrings of passion. I like him the most when he's like this—untamed.

When I don't answer him, he crouches at my feet and begins unfastening my boots. He slides one off, then the other. My socks go next. Lastly, with one quick pull, he draws down the last of my garments.

Montes rises to his feet slowly, drinking in my nudity. My own eyes appraise the tight, flowing muscles that wrap themselves lovingly around his frame.

We're both naked from head to toe. My heart gallops as he grabs my hand and draws me to the bed.

Sometimes, when we're together, we're feverish. I don't have time to reflect on what exactly my heart's caught itself up in. But now, every move of ours is deliberate, and it gives me far too much time to savor each drawn out second.

With those depthless eyes trained on me, he drapes his body over mine.

"My vicious, hardened queen," he murmurs, cupping my cheeks, his thumbs stroking the skin beneath my eyes. "You are not so terrifying in my arms."

I know I'm not.

Devoid of my gun, my clothes, and my anger, I'm nothing more than a troubled, broken girl. And here in the king's arms, when all his intensity bears down on me, it's easy to pretend that nothing else besides his skin and mine matter. He's my Romeo, and I'm his Juliet, and even though we're star-crossed and our time's running out, we might fall into each other's eyes and live forever in this moment.

He enters me, and where there was two, now there's only one. Montes rocks his hips against my pelvis, moving languidly in and out.

The whole thing's gentle and slow, and he watches me the entire time.

The king has a growing habit of making love to me. It's more than a little disquieting, and it makes me feel like what he sees when he looks at me and what I see in the mirror are two very different people.

His chest slides along mine as I pull him closer.

His Serenity seems like a better person than the horrifying one I've known since war changed me.

Montes picks up the pace, and I begin to lose the last of my composure.

A wicked grin spreads across his face. "Say it."

I already know what he wants. "No."

He squeezes one of my hips. "Say it."

When I don't respond, he leans his forehead against mine. "Do I have to do it first?"

My eyes widen. I've never considered that the king could fall in love with me. Caring for me? Yes. Obsessing over me? Yes. Loving me? Not in the truest sense. Love takes too much selflessness for that.

But now he's essentially admitting as much.

He likes that he's shocked me.

He rubs one of his thumbs over my lips. His eyes move to mine.

"I love you," he says.

Instinctually, I cover his mouth with my hand, like I can push the words back inside him.

My eyes prick with moisture.

I don't want to know this. I don't want to feel hope like this. Happiness like this. He's going to ruin it, or I'm going to.

He moves against me, just enough to remind me of how intimately connected we already are at the moment.

His ruffled hair hangs down around his face. He removes my hand from his mouth and presses a soft kiss to my lips.

"I never meant to," he whispers against me, "but I do."

A tear drips down my cheek, and he kisses that away too.

"Tell me you love me," he breathes against my cheek.

I shake my head.

"Stubborn woman," he says, thrusting into me harder, "I *will* get you to say it."

He forces my orgasm out of me with several long strokes, perhaps just to prove how easily manipulated I can be. I don't care. I hold him close as my climax works its way through my body.

He comes on the heels of my orgasm, his body slick with sweat as he moves against me.

Once we break apart, Montes gathers me to his chest and holds me there. "Stay with me, just like this," he says, kissing my shoulder.

I press my hand to his heart as I lay against him and savor the thump of it beneath my palm. This is where happiness sneaks up on you, and you forgive evil people for unforgivable things because they give you a taste of a future you always thought was beyond your reach.

I wait for the king's breath to even before I whisper my secret in the dark. "I love you too."

CHAPTER 32

THE KING

SERENITY AND I have maybe been asleep for an hour when I'm awoken by one of her rattling coughs. The thing has got ahold of her body. Her entire frame shakes as she desperately tries to clear her throat.

"I'm sorry," she says in between the hacking coughs.

It's only after she says that, that I realize my hold on her tightened the moment I woke. She's clearly too sleepy to realize she's apologized to me—something she's made a point of avoiding at all costs—and my constricting grip is only making it harder for her to catch her breath.

I relax my hold and begin rubbing her back soothingly. I'm still not used to the tight ball of fear that's made a home for itself in my stomach, or the slow release of its poison.

I'm also not used to being caring, affectionate. The previous women I have been with can attest to that. But with Serenity, it comes naturally, perhaps because I know just how unused to it she is as well. It's easier to give another something that's never been demanded of you.

She's still coughing, and at some point several droplets of her sickness hit my chest. Concern trumps any disgust I might have. She hasn't stopped coughing; if anything, it sounds like it's getting worse. She rolls away from me.

I pull her back against my chest and press my lips to the back of her slender neck. "*Nire bihotza*, I'm not letting you go." I'm not sure whether I'm referring to this moment, or the larger trajectory of her life. She's mine. Her life is mine, her heart and her soul are mine.

"What does that even mean?" she rasps, choking down her cough to talk.

I swallow the golf ball sized wedge that's taken up residence in my throat.

A reluctant smile tips the corners of my mouth up. "'*Nire bihotza*' means 'my heart' in Euskara—Basque."

"That's your native tongue?" Her voice sounds painfully rough.

I run a hand down her arm. "Mhm."

"You've been saying that for a while."

My hand comes to the end of her arm, and I thread my fingers through hers. "It's been so since the moment I met you."

Even now I want to wrap myself up in her and make her the air I breathe and the earth I stand on. But she's not earth or air.

She has been and always will be fire. She's my light and my death, and I couldn't escape her unscathed even if I tried.

Serenity falls quiet after that. With relief I realize that her coughing fit is over, for now.

Finally she breaks the silence. "Montes?"

"Yes?"

"Bury my body in my homeland."

My hand tightens around hers. A single sentence shouldn't be so devastating. This one levels my heart.

No.

No, no, no.

I want to shout my answer at her. She's not leaving me. I won't let her.

"Go to sleep, Serenity."

She sighs.

I wait for her body to relax before I leave her side and go to the bathroom. Turning on the faucet, I splash water on my face then settle my palms heavily against the marble countertop.

War comes at steep costs. Everyone I've ever held in high esteem has told me this. I just never felt the breath of it until recently. Things I've never had trouble holding onto are slipping through my hands—friends, loyalties, countries, *lovers*.

When I glance back up at my reflection, I notice the blood speckled across my chest. I touch my fingers to it and look down at them. The crimson liquid is smeared across the pads of my fingertips. It hadn't been saliva that Serenity had coughed on me.

My last straw just broke.

I return to our bed and pull her back into my chest, attempting to get as much of her pressed to as much of me as I can.

"Fuck you and your bravery," I whisper. This hurts worse than the bullet she buried in my shoulder.

She murmurs against me.

For the first time in what feels like eons, tears spill from my eyes.

My eyes had burned when I found out Marco died, and they'd watered when we lost our unborn child, but it's Serenity who gets my tears. This is the first time since my father died that I let them freely fall.

I bite my lip to keep a sob from slipping out, and it takes most of my self-control to not squeeze her to me when it might trigger another coughing fit. I can't, however, stop my body from shaking as premature grief consumes me. It's almost unbearable, watching someone die. I've callously killed millions, but when my victim is my lover and she's dying in my arms, I can't bear it.

What I told her earlier was true. I never planned on loving her, but I do. I never planned on losing her either.

I still don't.

SERENITY

I GROAN AS I wake, stretching my limbs out and wincing when I feel a sharp lance of pain in my abdomen. I tilt my head to the side and stare tiredly out the window. The sun has an orange glow to it. For a moment I relish the fact that I can wake to the sun at all. Aside from my stint with the military, I've lived belowground for the last five years. I'm used to waking to total darkness or the bunker's sickly fluorescent lights.

Then I noticed that along with the deep orange light are the beginnings of shadows.

How late did I sleep?

I look over my shoulder. The other half of the bed is empty. And now that I think about it, I vaguely remember Montes bending over and kissing my lips.

That snake.

He slipped away before I woke to resume his post and help his troops fight the rebellions in South America. He left his weak, sick wife to sleep in.

For all his good intentions, he left me here, out of the action. I hate that. If there's trouble on the horizon, I don't want to be left in the dark about it.

I push back the covers. That's when I notice the blood. It speckles the sheets and my pillow.

Had the king seen this?

He couldn't have, otherwise he'd be riding my ass to get in the dreaded Sleeper. Even now I shiver at the thought of it. Months spent in stasis as my body heals and no memory to account for that lost time. Could you even call that living?

When I glance down at my hands, I see more droplets of blood.

Cancer's a frightening way to go. I always wanted a swift end for myself, for death to take me quickly. Not this.

I quickly change into a black shirt and pants. When given the choice, I will always reach for the outfit the leaves me the most mobile.

In the middle of dressing, I have to pause to run to the bathroom and vomit. After I rinse my mouth out several times and brush my teeth, I roughly comb out my hair.

Good enough.

I tuck my tight black pants into a pair of lace up boots and leave.

When I arrive at the king's conference room, it's empty. I try him in his map room next. Again, the room is completely vacant.

Where is everyone?

I run into a group of aides talking in the corridor. They glance up from their readouts and monitors.

"Where is the king?" I ask, glancing at each one.

"Your Majesty," the aide nearest me says, bowing as he does so. The rest of them murmur the greeting and dip their heads. I wave the title off.

One of the aides pulls me aside. He bends in close for a private word. "Last I heard, he was discussing the possibility of another aerial strike with some of the men upstairs. Third floor, east wing, fourth door on the left."

I leave then and follow the aide's instructions.

I climb up the stairs and head for the east wing. From the windows I get a panoramic view of the palace grounds and a glimpse of the world beyond. That world still represents freedom, and now that so many have seen my face, that freedom seems farther and farther out of my reach.

When I arrive at the room the aide referred to, I don't bother knocking. I simply storm inside.

The tea room—or whatever the fuck they call delicate little spaces like this one—that I walk into is devoid of life.

My first thought is that I've entered the wrong room, but I head back out into the hallway and recount the doors. I'm in the east wing, and the tea room is the fourth door on the left. I re-enter the room.

A few papers rest on one of the couches. I glance down at them. All appear to be printouts of the latest activities in South America. A cold cup of coffee rests on the side table next to the couch.

My second thought is that this is a trap, another intricately rigged situation designed to lead to my death. My heart palpitates at the thrill of it all. Bring the carnage, bring the destruction. I could use a good showdown at the moment.

I no longer have my gun, but half the objects in here could be weaponized.

I'm considering all the ways one can bludgeon someone to death with the bronze figurine resting on a nearby stand when I hear a familiar noise. The rhythmic stomping comes from beyond the windows.

Walking over to them, I peer outside. Two rows of soldiers cross the palace gardens, heading towards the east wing. I back away from the windows.

Something feels wrong about this situation. It shouldn't be unfolding the way it is.

I hear an echo of the footfalls in the hallway heading straight for this room. Understanding sets in. This is a trap, and it's one my enemy did set.

I just forgot for a while who my enemy really was.

I can taste bile at the back of my throat, and I realize I'm grimacing. My throat works and my eyes sting.

Oh God, I'm actually hurt by this.

Like this is anything compared to the atrocities the king's already committed. It was only a matter of time before he turned on me like he had everyone else close to him.

Still, when the door opens and Montes walks in, I have to physically swallow down the emotion rising up the back of my throat. Behind him I can see two armed guards, but I know there's more that I can't see.

I watch him warily.

"Serenity," he says, and the monster's eyes are actually sad, "don't look at me like that."

"Like what? Like you betrayed me? You never did." No, the blame lies with my own weak heart.

"I can't let you die," he says, and his voice breaks. The man is begging me to understand. "Not now when you're so close to death and my enemies are more aggressive than ever."

My muscles tense. Here I'd thought he was coming to dispose of me. That's usually what happens when someone betrays you. This betrayal, I realize, is much deeper and more intrinsic than I imagined.

He doesn't want to kill me, he wants to keep me alive in that Sleeper of his.

"How long?" I ask.

His shoulders relax. He thinks I am actually considering this. "Just until we find a cure." Looking into his eyes, I know it will be long enough to horrify me.

I nod, and I'm sure to him it appears as though I'm ruminating over this.

The idea of being in that machine for months or—heaven forbid—*years* has my breath picking up. I've lost my family, my friends, my land, my freedom, even my memory for a time. I can't lose this last sliver of my free will.

Montes's eyes are flat. He's already detached himself from what's about to happen to me.

My muscles are twitching, telling me I need to run, now. I take a step back, towards the windows. Then another. "What will happen to me between now and then?"

This is the man who married me. The man who held me when I was sick. This is the man I'd begun to fall in love with, the man who told me he loved me.

But he is also the man responsible for the death of countless people. He's the one who killed my parents, leveled my hometown, gave me cancer and the scar on my face.

He's the one that made me the monster I am.

I'm already studying the exits. We're on the third floor, which is probably intentional on the king's part. If I try to leave through the windows, I will surely break my legs. That leaves the door behind Montes.

I don't have a gun, and by now, there are probably over a dozen guards on the other side of the door, all waiting for me to try to escape.

If I want to leave through that door, I'm going to have to get past the king and many more armed guards who I can hear positioning themselves in the hallway. They're outside too, and they're getting closer.

Montes must see the realization in my eyes. He takes a step forward, then another. "Serenity, look at me."

That was why he called so many guards into such a futile situation, to smother any wild ideas I might get. He's the leader of the world; he knows a thing or two about strategy.

"You led me in here like a lamb to slaughter." I'm moving around the room. Resting on one of the side tables is a vase. On another is a lamp. Both are potential weapons.

He folds his arms, tracking me. "Are you seriously considering smashing that lamp over my head?"

"It doesn't have to be this way, Montes," I say. "Everything can go back to the way it was."

He takes a step towards me. "It will," he says. "Eventually."

Adrenaline buzzes just beneath the surface of my skin. "I will hurt you," I say. "I don't want to, but I will."

It's that, or hurt myself, and nothing in this room would kill me faster than the king could save me. Not even falling through those windows, I realize.

That's why the soldiers are outside. Not to prevent escape, to prevent a potential suicide.

The king turns away from me and glances at the door. "Guards!"

I begin to move before the words are fully out of his mouth.

I grab the lamp, but rather than throwing it at the king, who would surely duck, I lob it at the window.

Glass and porcelain shatter as the lamp obliterates it. Behind me, the door is thrown open.

I sprint away from the king, towards the broken window.

"Serenity, don't!" the king yells.

He thinks I'm trying to kill myself; he still doesn't really know who I am or else he'd know that this is my last desperate chance at survival. Then again, I can't blame him. Even after all we've been through, I don't really know who he is either.

I leap over furniture, ignoring the shouts coming from the guards.

I can hear them behind me, flooding into the room now that the charade of civility is up.

I reach the window and kick the last jagged bits of glass out before throwing one foot over the side. I swing the other leg over, and then I push off the sill.

"*Serenity*!" the king yells.

This is the second time I've exited the king's palace through one of his windows. And there's a moment after each leap of faith where I feel blissfully free. My hair whips around my face, my shirt flaps manically, and the ground rises up swiftly.

This time, like the last, there is someone here to catch me. Several someones. I land hard in their arms. I grip their starched uniforms as I try to right myself.

Brushing my hair from my eyes, I glance up. More soldiers peer from the room I exited. Distantly I can hear shouting, and people are running towards me.

A half dozen hands hold me in place; more join in as I struggle.

I bite my lip hard enough for it to bleed. The odds are now stacked far against me. I'm not getting out of whatever twisted plan the king has in store. There isn't a car waiting, nor are there Resistance fighters to protect me.

The normally stoic soldiers are yelling, trying to contain my struggles. Eventually they do, leaving me gasping out of anger and incredulity.

Servants are watching, the ladies of the court are watching, the men who might be politicians or just more elite individuals are watching. I have captured all their attention. And they look horrified. The queen who jumped three stories only to fall into the arms of her husband's waiting army.

I have a clear line of sight to the palace's rear doors. It only takes a minute for them to open and the king to come storming out.

This man who I have come to know intimately looks larger than life as he strides towards me, a doctor in a white lab coat at his heels.

He's really going to do it.

I renew my struggles. A handful of wild, animalistic cries slip from my lips as I vainly try to get away. The entire time my eyes stay locked on the king's.

His rove over my body. I can only imagine what he must see—the tangled locks of my hair, the whites of my eyes, the angry set of my jaw.

I grit my teeth as he steps up to me. This is it.

"What were you thinking, Serenity?" The vein at his temple pounds, and God does he sound angry. Angry and desperate.

"Montes, don't. Please." I have desperation in my voice to match the king's.

He tips my chin up. "I *love* you, Serenity. I'm not doing this to hurt you. I'm doing it to save you."

After all this time, he still doesn't understand. "This was never about me," I say as he steps back so the man in the lab coat can get closer. "You're not saving me, you're saving your own chicken-shit heart—"

The man in the lab coat presses a damp cloth against my nose and mouth, and a sweet, chemical smell wafts from it. I buck against my captors and try to shake the hand. It grips my face harder.

I know whatever they've doused the material with is a sedative. As soon as I lose consciousness, I don't know when—or if—I'll wake up.

I try to hold my breath, but it's a lost cause. I last for maybe a minute and a half before I'm forced to breathe in a deep lungful. I breathe in another. And another.

The soldiers are lowering me to the ground, and someone's brushing my hair back. I follow that arm to its owner. My husband truly appears upset.

Is there no room for my own suffering in that heart of his?

The drug's beginning to affect me. My focus drifts, and when I move, the colors of my surroundings blur for a second too long. But I haven't passed out yet.

A surge of anger has me redoubling my efforts against the hands that hold me down, but I'm too weak and too outnumbered to make much headway.

Still, I don't stop fighting.

"Serenity," Montes says, continuing to pet my hair. "I would never hurt you. It's going to be okay."

Those five lying words. I've said them to soldiers as their lifeblood drained from their veins and their souls slipped from their eyes. It's a statement you say to someone who's lost hope, a lie you voice to make yourself feel better. But the person who is forced to hear it? They alone know the truth.

Sometimes, there is no hope to be had.

An angry tear trickles out. I can't tell if my rage comes from this strange betrayal or from what will happen to me once I'm unaware.

Montes's eyes focus on the tear, and the bastard strokes it away with his thumb. "Don't cry, *nire bihotza*," he says, his voice hoarse—as though this is tough for him. It makes me want to scream.

He has absolutely no idea what pain and loss feel like. The narcissist in me hopes that the king cares for me enough to regret this mistake for a very long time.

But I'm not counting on it.

"This isn't forever," the king says.

My eyes try to focus on him, but the sharpness of my reality is slipping away. I don't know how much time has passed—minutes maybe—but I can tell the drug is working. Darkness is licking the edges of my vision.

The last thing I see is the king's face, and the last thing I hear is his voice. He leans over me, and I feel a hand stroke my face. "We'll only be apart for a short while. Once we cure your sickness, you'll be mine again."

EPILOGUE

THE KING

1 week later

I TELL THE world she's dead.

My enemies don't believe me, but it doesn't matter. She's locked away in the Sleeper far below the surface of the earth, the machine healing her advanced sickness one malignant tumor at a time.

My fierce, violent queen.

I ache for her. This is different from the other times she'd been hospitalized. Now I know she's not coming out until we cure her cancer. That could be years, decades even. That entire time I have to endure it with one side of my bed cold. I have to carry this nation solely on my shoulders after catching a glimpse of what it would be like to have a true partnership with the woman I love.

I gaze into the window of the Sleeper and press my hand against the glass. She looks too serene. I'm used to my queen's frowns, her glares, her narrowed eyes. The way she studies things with cool detachment, the way those old soul eyes of hers assess the world.

This woman does not look like my wife.

I don't think I can bear staring at her face much longer. It's cruel to want something and know you can't have it.

Serenity believed that I never felt the wounds of my war. That I was above it. If only she knew how goddamn bad my heart hurts. Sometimes I can't catch my breath under the weight of all this grief. I lost my closest advisors, my oldest friend, my child, and the love of my very long life all within months of one another.

The world doesn't realize just how fragile their immortal king is at the moment.

But my enemies do. Of course they do.

6 months later

THEY STILL MOURN her, my people. They hated her while she was alive, but her supposed death has made her a martyr. It helps that the rebellions in the West are responsible for some of the most heinous atrocities to date. The devil the people know is better than the one they're learning about, the one the Resistance is regretting aligning with.

It also helps that I've encouraged Serenity's martyrdom. I've leaked a series of clips, much the same way the Resistance once did. But rather than degrading her character, these video segments show the world the Serenity I knew—a woman who wore violence alongside benevolence. I have clips from her interrogation, security feeds from the palace, even rare footage from her time as a soldier and an emissary of the WUN.

They're scrubbed down and shortened so that they cast her in a positive light, and they do the trick. Too late my people want to know about this woman that fought for them, who not only claimed to be one of them, but *was* one of them. And they love me for loving her.

I watch the clips over and over, until I've memorized every word, every expression, every movement of hers.

I'd hoped it would bring me peace.

It only brings more heartache.

2 years later

"CHRIS KLINE, YOU are a hard man to track down."

The man in question currently wears shackles and sits sullenly on one of my couches. He's much rougher around the edges than when I first met him. Hiding does that to a man. Makes him lean and shifty-eyed. But the former general's sanity is still intact, and I can see he's just as hardened as ever.

My guards flank him on either side. If he so much as moves a finger wrong, they'll load his body with bullets.

I settle myself on the couch opposite him and prop one of my ankles over my knee. A butler comes in with two glasses of aged Scotch. He dips down, and I take one from the tray. My butler then turns to Kline, who's watching this all unfold with wary eyes.

I gesture to the drink. "Go on. I'm not trying to poison you. I have far more efficient ways of getting rid of people than that."

Reluctantly he takes the tumbler off the tray, his cuffs clinking together as he does so. It's an awkward maneuver, drinking while shackled, but the former general manages it with ease. He takes a swallow and exhales, his eyes closing for the briefest of seconds.

"That's good stuff," he says.

"It's near the best," I say.

"Why are you sharing your best Scotch with one of your prisoners?" he asks.

Blunt and to the point, just like my wife. I wonder if this is where Serenity picked up some of her personality traits, or if this is just a feature of all North American citizens.

"I'm hoping by the end of this conversation you won't be my prisoner."

The man squints his eyes and leans back. "I reckon that's not going to happen," he says. "I don't like you very much. See, you killed my son, destroyed my country, and married the closest thing I had to a daughter, and now she's dead too."

I swirl my Scotch. "I'm not here to apologize or discuss the past. It's your resume that interests me. How long had you been the general of the WUN?"

"Six years."

"And before that?"

"I was the Secretary of Defense for two years."

I nod. "And you remain loyal to your homeland even now?"

Kline leans forward, resting his forearms on his thighs, his drink still clutched in one of his hands. "From where I sit, you've got me by the balls. Do you really think I'm going to answer that honestly? Add treason to the growing list of charges against me?"

I set my glass of Scotch down carefully on a side table, then I, too, lean forward. "This isn't your old world. I can kill you now just because I feel like it—if I were so inclined. I'm not. I know you're now heading up the Resistance, I know you love my wife, and I know you still want to help your people."

South America has fallen into my enemies' hands, and North America is set to follow. Serenity's beloved homeland is far worse off now than it was two years ago when they surrendered to me.

For the first time ever, someone's taken land from me. I intend to get it back.

"'Love'?" Kline's still stuck on my comment about Serenity.

"Come," I say, standing. "I want to show you something."

He doesn't get a choice. His drink's taken from him; my guards yank him up to his feet and force him to follow me.

I head down to some of the lowest levels of the palace. Here, the drone of many different machines fills the air. It doesn't take long to find Serenity's. I open the outer shell. Inside it is another glass case—a sort of incubator. And inside of that, the woman that holds my heart.

I haven't laid eyes on her in nearly a year, and I have to lock my knees to keep myself upright. But for my purposes, Serenity's old general needs to see this.

"Holy fuck!" Kline reels back soon as he catches a glimpse of her. "She's alive?" There's a strange note in his voice.

"She never died to begin with. But she will if I take her out of this machine."

Kline regains his composure and creeps closer. I can still read the horror on his features, however.

"Why keep her like this?" he asks. "Why not just let her die?"

My eyes are transfixed on that scarred, beautiful face. "Because I love her."

He's shaking his head like he thinks I'm crazy, that what I feel for my wife is something less pure than love. But what does he know? He gave away this very woman to a man he considered his worst enemy.

I'd level the earth before I'd let that same fate befall Serenity.

"I'm working on curing cancer—and repairing radiation-damaged tissue," I say instead. "I'm going to save her life. Once I do, I will have the ability to heal the sick. And I *will* heal them.

"You are a good man, Kline. I believe you have an honest heart. I need men like that. Will you help me repair what I've broken?"

It's been a long time since I've done something that's felt right. Like power, this feeling is addicting. Maybe I'll rewrite my own history along with Serenity's. Maybe one day people won't see me as a man who ruined the world, but the one who saved it.

That won't happen anytime soon, but time is something I have plenty of.

"I worked for you once," Kline says. "I never will again."

Before the sight of Serenity can break me, I close the lid. I turn to Kline, a man who was once my enemy, then my ally, then my enemy again, in hopes that he will be my ally once more.

Serenity trusted this man. I will too.

"I'm not asking you to work for me. I'm asking you, and the Resistance, to work with me."

7 years later

MY TRAITOROUS FORMER advisors have stolen my technology. For the first time ever I feel the anger that comes with trying to kill something that just won't die. That's how I find out they're utilizing the Sleeper.

I've never received direct evidence that they're taking my pills, but while under my rule, I watched their hair thin and their skin wrinkle. Now their thick heads of hair and their youthful faces are all the evidence I need that they're taking the pills.

I am now fighting monsters of my own making.

10 years later

NANOTECHNOLOGY.

That's how we save her.

24 years later

ANOTHER FAILURE. AND just when things were looking up. We'd begun human trials on the latest drug, too.

When I find out, I cradle my head in my hands and I sob.

It wasn't all a loss, I suppose. The drug is able to cure certain types of cancer— just not Serenity's. And, selfish bastard that I am, hers is all I really care about.

I have to accept the fact that even after all this time, I'll have to wait longer.

That doesn't sit well with me, and I take out my aggression on the WUN. I imagine that Serenity would hate me for it. But then, I wouldn't be giving her enough credit. She always had a way of parsing down issues fairly. Maybe she'd understand that the WUN I fight today is not the same one she left.

29 years later

I SIT IN front of the Sleeper, my hands in my pockets.

"My queen, I think we've found the key to curing your cancer."

It's not the only news I have, but it's the one that consumes my thoughts. My hands practically shake from excitement.

Three decades, three long, excruciatingly lonely decades. Three more decades of war. My depravity has gotten worse. And now, finally, I'll be able to hold her in my arms again.

Will we be the same once she wakes? All this work I've done for her, and sometimes I fear that I've changed too much. She will still be the Serenity I left thirty years ago, but will she see me as the same man she gave her life and heart to?

319

"You're getting moved. I'm rebuilding my Mediterranean palace," I say to her. It's the place where we were first married. Far below the palace there's to be a secret room—more of a temple really. And right at the heart of it my queen will rest until the last of her illness is obliterated.

53 years later

THE PLAGUE HITS again, and the death toll this time around is just as merciless as it was the last time it swept through the Eastern Empire.

The WUN and my old advisors who rule it are responsible. We traced the origins back to a series of contaminated food supplies smuggled in.

I've now lived through two epidemics. The first one fashioned me into a wealthy ruler when I sold the cure for profit. I thought I was evil then, but compared to current events, I've actually had to reassess my own suppositions.

Unfortunately for the WUN, a mutated strain of the virus made its way back West. The numbers of our dead are nothing compared to that of the WUN.

It's times like these that I'm glad my queen still sleeps.

Her cancer's been cured, but there are other mutations to her genome caused by radiation that the Sleeper is fixing. It's a slow process, providing gene therapy, and just when it appears all is well, some new issue pops up that the Sleeper must deal with.

I rub my face. Most of the time my thirst for life vanquishes all those things that haunt me. But late at night when I'm alone, like I am now, they come pouring in and I feel the weight of all my regrets and sorrow.

It's moments like these when my skin feels most alien. I'm far too weary for the young body I live in.

I leave my study and head down flight after flight of stairs. The mausoleum is finally complete.

Once my architects finished the project, I delivered a refined version of the memory loss serum to them. No one can know about this place. And for the unfortunates that I hired, that was the price I exacted.

My footsteps echo against the marble stairs as I enter the cavernous, subterranean chamber. The room is covered completely in marble and embellished with gold, lapis lazuli, and indigo tiles. I head down the walkway that leads to Serenity's burnished sarcophagus. At least, that's what it looks like by all outer appearances. But beneath the golden designs that cover it is state-of-the-art machinery. This Sleeper is not only the most beautiful one in existence, it is also the most advanced.

It sits on an island of marble, surrounded by a pool of water. Columns ring the edges of the circular room, and the ceiling arcs high above us.

My shoes click as I head down the marble walkway that bisects the pool. The water is still and smooth. It reflects the dim lighting and, beyond that, the artificial night sky set into the ceiling. So she'd always have the stars to gaze up at.

I sit at the bench that overlooks her sarcophagus.

I still miss her, but already I've forgotten the sharp ache of our love. Now, like the rest of the world, she's more myth than woman. I wouldn't even know what to do with the real Serenity if I were to meet her again.

64 years later

I'VE DONE SOMETHING unforgiveable—two things, actually. Two twisted deeds I already regret. It's times like this when I need Serenity's ferocity. I need her to aim her father's gun at me and demand I change my ways on pain of death.

As fucked up as we were, she tempered the conscienceless part of me.

No one else bothers to stand in my way.

My loneliness is to blame. It eats away at me. Some days I'm not sure I'll survive it. But I'm too afraid to die and too afraid to resurrect my queen.

"I'm sorry, Serenity."

I miss her.

73 years later

SERENITY IS HEALED. Completely.

Every single strand of DNA mutated by radiation has been repaired. Externally she retains her scars, but on a cellular level, she's flawless. It took the better part of the century, but I did indeed cure her.

So why does it feel so wrong?

I rub my mouth with my hand as my stomach contracts, sickened by where we've ended up. I'm still no closer to reclaiming my lost lands and she's still enshrouded by glass and metal. My vicious Sleeping Beauty. This is our violent fairytale.

To the world, she's a martyr and a mascot of all that is good and free.

The irony isn't lost on me.

Dear God, it isn't lost on me.

I stare at her golden sarcophagus.

Not dead, but not alive.

I pinch the bridge of my nose. I need to wake her. I need to let her see sunlight for the first time in nearly seventy-five years.

But.

I can't go back there. Back to a time when I had a weakness. When I lost control, and lost loved ones and territories in the process. The WUN still remains out of my hands. If I woke her now, what would I lose next?

I don't want her to see the man I've become. I don't want to fall for her all over again. It took decades for the pain of her absence to dull.

Here my wife's safe. And so is my heart.

So is my heart.

104 years later

I SLIP DOWN the passageway and head straight for Serenity's subterranean temple. This visit should be like the thousands of others I've made over the last century.

But it isn't.

The sarcophagus lid is askew, and the chamber inside—it's empty.

Serenity's gone.

The QUEEN of All that LIVES

Now, I am become Death, the destroyer of worlds.
—Robert Oppenheimer, quoting the Bhagavad Gita

PROLOGUE

WE FOUND HER.

Finally.

There had always been rumors that the undying king's queen lived. That she slept deep in the earth. That the king, mad with grief, put her there.

I step up to the golden sarcophagus, my men fanning out around it.

They weren't rumors.

The subterranean temple is just as the blueprint said it would be—same size, same location. Only, my information never told me it would look like this. I'm a hardened man, and even I have goosebumps being in this place. The gold, the marble, the shrine set in the middle of the room surrounded by a moat of water. All to encase a supposedly living woman. And not just any woman; we're retrieving a being this king and the rest of the world have all but worshiped for a hundred years.

"You're recording all this?" I say to one of my men, my voice echoing. They're the first words any one of us has breathed since entering the chamber.

He nods, the compact camera he holds focused on the coffin.

Styx would kill a hundred men to be here. Instead he's forced to watch from behind a screen.

I holster my gun and reach out, my hand trailing over the golden ivy that covers the sarcophagus. I find the lip of the lid, and my fingers curl over the edge. I'm almost afraid of what we'll find once we lift this sucker. I know what Serenity Lazuli looks like—everyone does—but the mythical woman has been gone for a century. For all I know, we're about to come face-to-face with her mummified remains.

"On the count of three," I say.

"One." *If the king finds us, we're all dead men.*

"Two." *If what lies inside this casket is everything we hoped for, the war might finally end.*

"Three."

My lips curl back as we push off the lid. Beneath it ...

"Holy shit," I breathe.

Inside rests a woman, her arms crossed over her chest, her eyes closed. I take in her long golden hair, the smooth, pale skin, the deep scar that mars an otherwise beautiful face.

They definitely weren't rumors, and these are definitely not Serenity Lazuli's mummified remains. As we watch, her eyes move beneath closed lids.

The queen lives.

CHAPTER 1

SERENITY

I DRAW IN a breath of air.

Exhale.

I draw in another. And another.

The air tastes good. Is that even possible? To taste air? Because in this moment I swear I can. I take deeper and deeper lungfuls. Light filters in through my closed lids, beckoning like an eager lover.

"She's waking up!"

"I can see that, you wanker."

"Harvey, you capturing all this?"

"Styx is getting the livestream as we speak."

"Would you fuckers shut up? You're going to scare her."

My eyes flutter open. At first, I see nothing. The light is too bright. But then my eyes adjust, slowly. Color bleeds in and my surroundings began to take shape.

I stare up at a metal roof. My brows furrow. The king's ceilings are either gilded molding or exposed wood. Not dented, rust-stained metal. And never so low.

That's when I notice the rocking. My body shakes from side to side. I'm inside a vehicle, I realize.

What the hell is going on?

I brace my hands against the edge of the bed I lay in, my pulse climbing.

Nothing about this is right. People don't wake up like this.

Where am I, and why can't I remember how I got here?

"I can't believe we did it."

I startle at the voice. I have an audience—of course I do. Situations like this don't just happen; people orchestrate them.

I begin to sit up.

"Whoa, whoa, my queen," a man to my right says, placing a hand on my chest, "easy."

I glance down at the hand touching my chest. I follow it back to its owner. A soldier in his late twenties stares back. He's not the king, and these are not the king's men. Which can only mean …

I got fucking abducted.

Again.

"Who are you?" I ask, my voice hard.

I'm going to have to hurt more people, kill more people. That's the only way anyone's going to learn that I make a terrible captive.

The man dips his head. "Jace Bridges, Your Majesty. Former infantryman in the king's army. Current regional commander of the special ops unit, European division, of the First Free Men."

All I got from that was that this man is dangerous. That's helpful to know.

Five other men circle my bed. All soldiers by the looks of them, all equipped with weaponry, all standing between me and freedom. They stare a little too intensely, making me distinctly aware that for all my training, I am still just a woman lying in a bed in the back of some vehicle, surrounded by a bunch of men. There are too many of them and only one of me. I could easily be overpowered.

As my gaze sweeps over the soldiers, they dip their heads and murmur, "Your Majesty."

And all of them show me reverence. This is a first. I'm used to being hated. I don't know what to do with their respect.

One of them holds a camera, its lens trained on me. I frown, unsettled at the sight. If they're here to liberate me, why do I feel like an animal on exhibit?

The First Free Men. I've never heard of the organization, but I hope to God the king has, otherwise I'm going this one alone.

The king.

"Where is Montes?" I demand.

The six of them share a look.

"He's far away, Your Majesty," Jace says. The way he says the words, it's as though they're meant to reassure me.

Where *is* he? And why can't I remember?

"Is he dead?" I ask. And now I really have to control my voice. The thought of my brutal husband ceasing to exist is … unfathomable.

Another look passes between them.

"No, Your Majesty."

I release a shaky breath.

Alive.

I can work with alive.

"Why did you take me?" My eyes pass over the soldiers again.

They look at me wondrously, like I hold the answers to all their problems.

I'm in a car full of eager men. Not good.

Jace leans forward, resting his forearms on his thighs. "How much do you remember?"

Remember? My blood chills. If this is another one of the king's memory serums …

But that cannot be. I wouldn't remember him, I wouldn't remember myself—I wouldn't remember anything before this moment.

And I do. Don't I?

I eye the soldier warily. "Remember what?"

Jace sighs and rubs his face. "Does someone else want to take this on?"

"Shit no," one of the other soldiers says.

My heart is still pounding like mad, but now it has more to do with confusion than adrenaline.

"Your Majesty—"

"Stop calling me that," I interject. I hate the title, hate that the king made me what I am.

Jace inclines his head. "Mrs. Lazuli—"

Naturally, he chooses a name that's even worse.

"Serenity," I say.

"Serenity," he repeats. "My men and I were given the task of finding the lost queen."

I frown.

"We've been searching for you for decades."

I stop breathing.

What in God's name … ?

I look over them again just to memorize their faces.

These men have lost their minds. People don't disappear for decades. *I* don't disappear for decades.

I went to bed last night, right after … right after …

"We found you buried beneath one of the king's palaces. He's kept you there for close to half a century, as far as we can tell."

Now we've gone from decades to fifty years? This is like one of those stories that gets bigger every time it's retold.

"What do you want?" I ask, sitting up a little straighter and eyeing the back doors of the vehicle.

"Jace, she needs proof," one of the other men says.

Jace squeezes the back of his neck. "I don't *have* proof."

"Wait," another soldier says. He reaches into the back pocket of his fatigues and pulls out a folded piece of paper. He tosses it onto my lap.

I raise an eyebrow as I stare down at it.

Nothing about the situation is going as it should. My kidnappers are not demanding things of me; they're beseeching me to understand what they're telling me. To be fair, what they are telling me is insane.

"A piece of paper is supposed to convince me I've been gone for fifty years?" I say.

"Not gone," Jace corrects. "*Asleep*. We found you in one of the king's fabled Sleepers."

My attention snaps to Jace. The Sleeper. I'd almost forgotten about the machine. The last time I had gotten in one of those was right after the king and I lost our child.

The memory has me tightening my lips and squeezing the sheets beneath my fingers. At least I can rule out memory suppressant. I remember that moment in vivid detail, and oh how I would like to forget.

"Open the paper, Serenity," Jace says.

I grab it, mostly because I'm curious. That, and I'm still unarmed and surrounded by six soldiers who have taken a keen interest in me.

I open the crumpled sheet.

Staring back at me … is me.

It's more of a sketch, really. My face is outlined in black and shaded in yellow and navy. The king's colors. I stare directly at the viewer, my face resolute.

I touch my scar as I notice the one on paper. It starts at the corner of my eye and drags down my cheek, making me look dangerous, wicked even. Beneath my image is the phrase, *Freedom or Death*.

I don't know what to make of this. Their proof hasn't convinced me of anything, except that maybe a few of my subjects don't hate me as much as I assumed they did.

"That poster has been in circulation for almost a century."

I fold the paper. "And now it's a century. By the time we arrive to whatever destination you have in mind, you'll tell me I've been gone for a millennia."

"Jace, you're doing great man," one of the other soldiers says. It's a jibe, and it only confuses me more.

"If you want to fucking jump in, be my guest," Jace says.

He returns his attention to me. He rubs his cheek, studying my face. "How am I going to get you to believe me?"

"You're not," I say. I'm not a big fan of trusting strangers, especially ones that kidnap me.

And there it is again. These men *took* me. Perhaps if it had been the first time, or even the second that this had happened to me, I'd be more interested in escape than revenge. But it isn't. When I get the chance, and I will get the chance, I will mow these men down.

My eyes flick to Jace's gun.

His gaze follows mine to his weapon. He covers it with his hand. "My queen, I understand you are confused, but if you get violent, we will have to as well. And I really don't want that."

I meet his eyes, and the corner of my mouth curls slowly. I'm made of violence and pain. He might as well have welcomed me home.

The atmosphere in the vehicle changes subtly. The men are on guard.

"What do you want?" I say.

Jace looks at me square in the eye, and I notice that, just like his comrades, he stares at me like I'm the answer to his problems. "We want you to end the war."

CHAPTER 2

SERENITY

THE LAST I remembered, the war was over.

No—war *had* broken out again. The king's council had turned on him. I had been working with the king to suppress the insurgents in South America.

"You do realize I have been doing exactly that since war broke out."

The soldiers exchange another look.

"Goddamnit," I say, "stop acting like I'm crazy."

The vehicle falls silent for several seconds, the only sound the jiggle of the bed's rickety frame and the men's weapons.

"No one believes you're crazy," Jace finally says.

He sounds so reasonable. That in and of itself is infuriating.

He leans forward. "Look at what you're wearing."

I narrow my eyes at him.

"This isn't a trick. Look at your outfit."

Hesitantly, I do.

I wear a fitted bodice of pale gold silk. A layer of delicate lace flowers overlays it.

I pull the blanket covering my legs aside. The material drips down my body, all the way to my feet. I hadn't noticed it earlier, but now that Jace has forced my eyes to take in my clothing, I realize how unusual my outfit is.

"Do you remember when you put that dress on?" he asks.

I run my fingers over the material. The honest truth is I've never seen this dress in my life.

"Do you?" Jace pushes.

I look up. All six of them are watching me with baited breath. They're waiting for … something.

"No." Without meaning to, I've fisted the soft material.

Jace rubs his hands together. "What is the last thing you remember?"

It's a good question, one I hadn't seriously pondered since I woke up here.

My eyes lose focus as I retrace my final memories. The king and I had been working together to stop his traitorous advisors.

I remember him saying he loved me.

The revelation hits me all over again. It never should've happened, but in my world, a world filled with bloodly, broken bodies, love had grown in the most desolate of places.

I force myself to move past this memory, to the next one. Waking up, the blood-speckled sheets. I worried that the king had seen the evidence of my sickness. I reassured myself that he hadn't.

I searched for him, but I couldn't find him. I was sent to a room on the east wing and told he'd be there. But he wasn't.

It was a trap.

It was a *trap*.

I go cold all over.

The king had me cornered. I jumped three stories into the waiting arms of his guards.

And then ...

"This isn't forever," the king says.

The last thing I see is the king's face, and the last thing I hear is his voice. He leans over me, and I feel a hand stroke my face. "We'll only be apart for a short while. Once we cure your sickness, you'll be mine again."

I choke on a wrathful cry. He betrayed me. Drugged me, forced me to endure the Sleeper until he could cure me of my cancer.

I'd imagined months, years maybe, but decades?

I feel my nostrils flare as a tear drips down my cheek.

Not just decades.

A century, if what these men say is true. Locked away so that he wouldn't have to lose me.

It feels like someone has stacked stones on my chest. I can't seem to catch my breath.

Monsters will be monsters. Why I thought mine was any different, I cannot say.

Perhaps because I am a foolish girl.

I can feel it, my anger, like a storm brewing on the horizon. Right now, my shock and pain are all I can focus on. But my fury is coming, and when it hits, no one is going to be adequately prepared for it.

My eyes return to the soldiers. They all wear looks of pity. They can keep their pity; I don't want it.

I'm no longer skeptical.

"Exactly how long have I been gone?" I ask Jace.

His eyes are sad when he says, "From our best estimates, one hundred and four years."

I AM 124 years old.

I stare at Jace, my nostrils flaring as I breathe through my nose.

One hundred and twenty-four years old.

My brain won't process that. It can't. No one lives that long.

The soldiers are quiet, and I hate that I have an audience. I'm so close to falling apart; I don't want these strangers to see me when that happens.

I turn my hands over in my lap. My skin has retained the smoothness of youth. I run my fingers over my flesh.

Over a century old. I wonder where the years are hidden. They must've left some mark. All things leave marks.

All things, save for the king's inventions. Those remove things—wounds, memories, ... *age.*

An entire century went by, and I saw none of it. The king had kept me in a coffin, not dead but not alive.

I recognize the moment the truth settles on my shoulders.

Loss so big my body can't hold it is expanding, expanding. It tries to crawl up my throat.

Had I thought before I was the loneliest girl in the world? If what these men are telling me is true, and I'm beginning to believe it is, I have nothing left.

Nothing.

The world has passed me by, and the people and time I belong to are now long gone. I haven't seen anything beyond the metal walls of this car, but would I recognize the world outside? The people? A hundred years before I was put in the Sleeper, the world was a far different place from the one I lived in. I have every reason to believe that same logic applies to the future—*present*.

I rub my forehead agitatedly. Everything and everyone I've ever known is gone. Everyone except for the man I love, the man who did this to me.

My surroundings blur as my eyes water. But I will not shed another tear for that abomination. Not now, in front of these men, and not when I'm alone.

He deserves nothing but my wrath.

And what has he been doing this whole time while I rotted away?

I already know the answer.

He's been killing, screwing, ruling.

Betrayal is giving way to rage. Everything I have ever cherished the king has taken from me, either directly or indirectly. My family, my land, my freedom, my life. And I gave him everything. My body, my heart, my soul.

I'm taking them back. I hope he's enjoyed my stone cold heart for the century he's owned it. Next time I see him, I'm going to carve it right out of his chest.

I level my gaze on Jace. "You said you wanted me to end your war?"

He must see the mayhem in my eyes, because he hesitates. Then, slowly, he nods.

There is nowhere Montes can hide where I won't find him. And when I do find him—

"I'll end it."

THE KING

I SIT DOWN heavily on the edge of my bed and loosen my tie. The flight was long, the day even longer, but I can't go to bed. Not yet.

I shrug off my jacket and roll up my sleeves.

Someone knocks on my door.

"Tomorrow," I call. The world is going to have just as many problems then as it does now.

When the footsteps retreat, I move to the back of the room, right to the garish painting of Cupid and Psyche. I grab the edge of the frame and pull it away from the wall. It swings back with ease, and behind it is a door, barred to all, save for me.

I press my thumb into the scanner embedded next to it.

The light blinks green, and then the sealed off entrance hisses open.

I step into the narrow hallway sandwiched between the rooms of the palace, the cold air already settling into my bones. Above me the overhead lights flick on.

I used to believe that secret passageways were the things of spy novels, but during the course of my long reign, these hidden features have saved my life and land a time or two.

My shoes click against the stone floor, and I slide my hands into my pockets as I pass room after room on either side of the hall. One-way mirrors expertly camouflaged as decorations allow me to catch glimpses of my guests.

All those years ago, Serenity taught me a valuable lesson: trust will earn you a knife in the back and a shallow grave. This is my insurance policy against that.

Tonight, the rooms are all empty. I've been gone for a while.

Too long.

I'm drawn down the passageway like a moth to a flame. Even in sleep, Serenity calls to me.

The lights flicker on, one after another, as I gradually descend into the lowest levels of the palace.

It's when I get to the entrance of her mausoleum that I feel the first stirrings of unease. One of the doors hangs slightly open.

I stop, my eyes studying the inconsistency.

This has happened before. There have been times in the past when I've forgotten to close the door tightly. A bad habit borne from the fact that no one but me accesses this place.

I push it open, all senses on alert.

More than a hundred marble steps lie between me and my wife. I take each one slowly, letting the peace of this place soothe my nerves.

The lights here are already on; they're always on. I can't bear the thought of Serenity laying here, alone in the darkness.

As I head down the stairs, the rest of the room unfolds before me. Grotesquely large marble columns hold up the cavernous ceiling, a domed roof at its pinnacle. Gold and indigo tiles are embedded into the walls of this place. And finally, the pool of water, the walkway, and Serenity's golden—

All my breath slips out of me when I catch sight of her sarcophagus.

The lid sits askew.

I can't move for a second; all I can do is stare. I've come here a thousand times, laid my eyes on that Sleeper a thousand more. Never once has the image changed.

I begin to move again. First I walk, then I run.

I reach her sarcophagus, her empty sarcophagus, and my worst fears are confirmed.

Serenity's gone.

CHAPTER 3

SERENITY

"SO WHAT ARE you planning to do with me?" I say, assessing the six soldiers from my bed.

As far as I can tell, these men didn't wake me to let me go. The camera is proof of that, the weapons are proof of that. Hell, the way this situation is unfolding is proof of that. No one's treating me like I'm a victim. They're treating me like I'm an acquisition.

I give them hard looks. These men might be my rescuers, but they're also my captors, no matter how agreeable they've been.

Jace leans back against the metal wall of the vehicle. "Right now," he says, "We're trying to lose the king."

I lean back against the partition that separates the back of the vehicle from the front, getting nice and cozy myself. "And once you lose the king?" I ask.

"We'll take you to our compound."

Just as the Resistance did when they captured me. Yes. This is all very familiar.

"And then?" I ask.

The car rumbles and shakes in the silence.

"And then, once you're ready, we'll hand you over to the West, where you belong."

"Where I belong," I muse.

It rubs me raw to hear these men talk like they have my best intentions in mind. They have no idea where I belong. *I* have no idea where I belong.

The only reason these men are even mentioning the West is because they've either been hired by them or they're going to get money from them when they hand me over.

I don't bother asking if I have any say in these plans. I already know I don't. Of course they didn't factor in the possibility that their slumbering queen might not agree with their schemes. That I might, in fact, violently oppose them. I'm sure they didn't consider that I might have an opinion at all.

But I do.

From the moment my father and I arrived in Geneva all that time ago, I've been passed around between men. The king, the Resistance, and now these men. How cruel must I become before people will begin to see me as a formidable opponent?

"One problem with your plans," I say.

Jace and his men wait for me to speak.

"Every time I've slipped from the king's clutches, he's retrieved me." I meet each soldier's eyes. "Every. Time."

Perhaps it's my imagination, but I swear the men shift a little uneasily in their seats.

"With all due respect, Serenity," Jace says, "we are good at what we do."

"I don't doubt that." The fact that they were able to retrieve me from the king's Sleeper is proof enough. I'm sure Montes hid me somewhere secure. "But the king I knew never did like it when people took away his toys." And I am his toy. I always have been.

"Maybe King Lazuli is not the same man you knew," Jace says.

That, I am certain of. A single year can change a person. A hundred is enough to evolve a man into whatever thing he wants to become. I can't even fathom the weight of all that time.

"Maybe," I agree.

It doesn't matter how much the king has changed; if he didn't care about losing me, these soldiers wouldn't be fleeing from him. They know that, I know that, and, unfortunately for them, the king knows that as well.

I fold my hands over my stomach and settle in. Hunting season has begun, and the only creatures that are sure to die are the six surrounding me.

THE CAR FALLS into silence after that. I have plenty of questions, but I want to sort them out before I voice them.

A hundred and four years went by, and during that time the world still warred, the king still ruled, and while I slept, some portion of the people turned me into a mascot, if the crumpled sheet of paper I saw was anything to go by.

Even now, after all these decades—decades I can't fully wrap my mind around—people know of me, which means the king has likely spoken about me.

No—more than just spoken. He's commodified me, turned me into someone larger than life. Someone people can rally behind.

This is pure conjecture, but I know enough about politics and the king to assume my theory is true.

God, when I see that man, I'm going to gut him, navel to collarbone.

"So the world's still at war?" I ask.

"Off and on for the last century," one of the other men says. "The West and the East make flimsy treaties every once in a while, but they usually disintegrate after several years. A bad bout of plague swept through both hemispheres at the turn-of-the-century—that also led to a temporary cease-fire."

War, plague, vigilante organizations—these are things I'm familiar with. Perhaps this world isn't as different as I assumed it would be. I find that possibility unsettling. I don't want to fit into this world if it means that everyone that lives here is suffering.

I run a hand through my hair. It might be slightly longer than I remembered, but it's by no means as long as it should be. Nor are my nails, now that I look at them.

I squeeze my hand into a fist. I've been groomed, my body meticulously taking care of. And now I have to wonder: is my cancer gone? After all this time, has the king not found a cure? Or has he abandoned the quest altogether? Have my muscles atrophied?

I don't feel weak; I feel strong and ruthless.

I won't get the answers, regardless. These men don't have them, and the man who does … I don't want words with him.

Just revenge.

I'M GETTING RESTLESS.

Propped up in the hospital bed as I am, these men don't see me as a threat. Dangerous, yes, but not a threat.

That's good for me. It means that when I'm ready to act, I'll have an extra several seconds to catch them off guard.

Now I just have to wait, and I hate laying here like an invalid. My legs are getting jittery. I haven't walked in a hundred years. I need to feel the ground beneath my feet.

That's not even my biggest concern, though. My anger has come calling. It causes me to focus on the soldiers' guns and the knives a couple of them carry. It'll be easy enough to divest them of their weapons. They haven't locked me up, which was probably their biggest mistake. Once I make my move, I won't give them the same concessions they've given me.

I squeeze my hands together and rein my rage in. Long ago the king taught me something important about strategy: often not acting when you want to is more effective than the alternative. I'll wait for my opening, and then I'll strike.

There are still things I want to know, questions I won't dare ask these men.

What is the king like?

Does he have a new wife?

Children?

Is he still made of nightmares and lost dreams?

"How, exactly, did you want me to end this war?" I ask.

These men aren't going to let me go. That much is obvious.

"The people love you. All you have to do is convince them to get behind us."

These men think they can use me for their own selfish motives. They need me to win over people for them.

My earlier rage simmers.

"And I'm supposed to go along with this," I say.

They're not even asking for my permission.

You don't ask a prisoner for permission.

"It's what the people want," Jace says.

Spoken like a true conqueror. People who want power convince themselves of the most implausible things. I don't doubt the world wants an end to war, but I do doubt they see the First Free Men as the godsend Jace seems to think they are.

"And what happens when you and the West take over the world?" I ask.

"We intend to work together to rebuild it," Jace answers.

Surprise, surprise, the First Free Men don't want to abdicate the old rulers nearly so much as they want to become ones.

"And how do you intend to do that?" I ask. I work to control my voice.

"Serenity, I'm a soldier, not a politician," Jace says.

And therein lies the problem.

"So you want to use me to help the First Free Men and the WUN achieve world domination, even though you and I don't know what policies either will push once they take over?"

"They won't abuse it the way—"

"*Everyone* abuses power," I say.

I feel it again. That crushing weight on my chest. Greed and power, power and greed—they're the most constant of companions. Once you get a taste of one, you must have the other.

"I'll never do it." I stare him in the eye as I speak. I have been used by everyone—the WUN, the king, the Resistance. And I'm so damn tired of it.

I won't be anyone else's puppet.

I've been so deeply immersed in the conversation that only now do I notice the muffled sounds of chopper blades and engines.

"*Hold on boys, the king's found us,*" the driver shouts from the other side of the partition, the vehicle accelerating even as he speaks.

"You *will* do it," Jace says. "Our leaders will make sure of that."

I smile at him then. People keep making the mistake of thinking that I'm someone they can control.

Before I can respond, a series of bullets spray against the side of the car. The vehicle swerves violently, its rear end fishtailing.

I'm thrown from my bed into the lap of several soldiers. All around me I hear grunts and curses from the other men, none so loud as the driver's. Even though the metal partition muffles his voice, we can still hear his words clearly.

"*They're coming in hot!*" he shouts.

As if that's not obvious.

I use the distraction to steal a gun from the soldier whose lap I've fallen into. He doesn't have time to react as I unholster and aim it. Just as the car corrects itself, I press the barrel into his chest and fire.

The sound of the shot is deafening.

Now the men are scrambling, some trying to stop me, some still confused.

I lift my torso, swivel, and shoot three more men, all while bullets continue to graze the outside of the vehicle.

In seconds the van is filled with blood. Spraying, misting, dripping down limbs, pooling around dying men.

"*What the fuck is happening back there!*" the driver shouts at the same time Jace bellows, "Serenity!" I can hear the fury in the latter's voice.

The car lurches again, and I'm thrown off the now wounded soldiers' laps. My body rolls under the bed.

Two men left, plus the driver.

A moment later, the mobile hospital bed is thrown aside.

I bring my gun up. I don't bother looking at Jace's face. I fire off a shot that buries itself in his stomach. He stumbles back, his hand going to his wound.

"*By order of the king, stop the car and come out with your hands raised.*" The intercommed voice drifts in from somewhere outside.

The king found me, just as I assumed he would. Adrenaline floods my system. I didn't enjoy killing these men, but I will enjoy killing *him*.

Rather than slowing, our vehicle accelerates.

I hear a familiar click. The sound of a gun being cocked. I look up at the final soldier standing. He has a gun trained on me.

"Don't fucking move. I swear I'll shoot," he says. His body is trembling.

Freedom or death—the poster got that much correct about me. I'm not letting these men take me hostage, even if it costs me my life.

Lord knows I hadn't expected to live this long.

The soldier doesn't shoot. I can tell he wants to look at his fallen comrades, the ones that are moaning and those that have gone still, but he's smart enough to know that the moment he takes his eyes off of me, he'll join their ranks.

"We freed you," he says.

"Swapping one prison for another is no freedom," I tell him.

He opens his mouth, but I don't give him time to respond. I turn my gun on him, and I shoot.

The bullet takes him between the eyes. He remains upright for a moment longer, then his legs fold and his body lands with a thump.

I take a moment to catch my breath. Blood is seeping onto my dress. I can feel the warmth of it against my thighs. It sticks to my back, staining the material crimson. The vehicle is a mess of dead men.

I can still hear two clinging to life, their breathing labored. When I catch sight of them, my stolen gun comes up and I pull the trigger twice. It's not just a mercy killing. Dying men have nothing to lose. Even though I'm some long dead queen, and even though they needed me alive, none of that matters much when you're bleeding out.

The vehicle is still canting from side to side, and I can hear the driver yelling, but I can't tell if his words are meant for me or for the men bearing down on us.

I lean my back against the wall. Until the driver is either killed or decides to stop the car, there's not much for me to do except muse over my dark thoughts.

I reach out and exchange my gun for another, wiping the bloodied metal off on my skirts, taking in my surroundings again as I do so. I expected the future to be clean and shiny like a new penny. But I'm not seeing clean and shiny. The interior of this vehicle is rusted and stained. The men's uniforms are faded. And the soldiers themselves had a sinewy, desperate look about them.

I don't believe I like this future very much at all.

Suddenly the car slams to stop. I hear the driver side door being thrown open, followed by the sound of pounding footsteps moving farther and farther away from the vehicle. More gunfire goes off outside.

Time for me to move.

I push my body off the ground, blood seeping between my toes. For the first time in over a century I stand on my own two feet. The gown I wear drapes off my shoulders, and my drenched skirts stick to my legs.

I am a thing made of lace and blood. Swathed in silk and dripping with the dark deeds of men. I suppose I'm finally clothed accordingly.

The adrenaline I felt earlier resurges through my veins, and I grip my gun tighter.

I'd like to say that I can feel all those years I lost, that they left some imprint on my body or my mind. But I can't. Other than my memories feeling a bit foggy, there's no indication that I'd been asleep for decades rather than hours.

That makes this all worse. Because it seems like only hours ago the king told me he loved me. The moment that love became inconvenient for him, that fucker let me waste away. My breathing is coming faster and faster.

My monster, my husband, my captor. Soon he will be my victim.

I always considered Montes the thing of my nightmares. Now I'll be his.

Yes, I think as I step up to the vehicle's rear doors, *I will enjoy killing him*.

CHAPTER 4

SERENITY

"COME OUT WITH your hands up!"

Even the orders of the future remain the same. Has nothing changed at all?

Pressing my back against one of the vehicle's doors, I use my hand to throw open the other. Instead of the gunfire I expect, a dozen different soldiers yell orders to exit the car. Those orders die away when they catch sight of the bodies.

Finally, fearfully, one calls out, "Serenity?"

I close my eyes. "I'm here," I say.

"Is there anyone with you?"

"No one living."

There's a pause as the king's men process that. Whatever they were told about me, I'm guessing that it hasn't prepared them for who I really am.

"You can come out, Your Majesty. We won't shoot."

I open my eyes and push away from the wall and into the open doorway. Sunlight touches my skin for the first time in a very long time. I soak it in. The day is full of firsts.

I step down from the car and onto the dirt road.

A hush falls over my audience as they catch sight of me. Then slowly, one by one, they kneel.

I stop and take them in. I had prepared for their horror, dressed in blood as I am, not their veneration.

There are dozens of soldiers circled around the car I exited. Behind their ranks, several armored vehicles are parked, lights flashing. Above us, a chopper circles.

It's all the same. The machinery might look slightly different, but it doesn't appear to have advanced in all this time. Prosperity breeds progress, and this, this isn't progress.

I fear for the world I have woken to.

Beyond the cars, scraggly rolling hills stretch out as far as the eye can see. I can feel the solitude of this place. The whistle of the wind seems to exacerbate it.

I haven't dropped my gun, but the soldiers don't seem to mind. As soon as they rise, I catch sight of their expressions.

I'm a ghost. A myth. That's the only explanation for the spooked ardor in their eyes.

All the while, rivulets of blood snake down my calves. They're right to be spooked of me.

I scour their ranks, looking for Montes. My eyes pass over dozens of men and a few women. I look them over once, twice. I didn't realize I held onto some sick hope until I feel it vanish.

The king isn't among these soldiers.

Even in the middle of my bloodlust, my heart aches. Last time I was captured, he was there to retrieve me.

A hundred years to change into whatever he wanted to become. A hundred years to fall out of love. A hundred years to forget about the broken, deadly girl he forced into marriage.

The king that rules these people isn't the same king I knew. All my anger and pain are wasted on a man who, in all probability, no longer cares for me. The world's still at war, after all. If I can really end it, the king should have taken me out of the Sleeper long ago.

Reflexively, my hand tightens on my gun.

Behind me is open road, in front of me is vengeance. My twisted heart is breaking, but I'm tempted to leave my heartbreak and revenge to the past and walk away from it all.

I take a step back. The soldiers tense.

"Your Majesty," one of them says, "we're the king's royal guard. You can trust us."

Normally, when people tell you that you can trust them, it means exactly the opposite.

I look around; the soldiers encircle me completely. If I ran, how far would I get before they caught me? How many more men would I have to kill? I don't want to spill more blood. And even if I did, I couldn't possibly take them all out before the king's guard immobilized me. I'd lose whatever precious power I had to wield.

I'm still not free.

"I need your word," I say to the man who spoke.

He pauses. "Anything, Your Majesty."

"Don't let the king put me back in the Sleeper." My voice breaks as I speak. "Kill me first."

"I'll vow to you anything but that."

"Then I can't go with you," I say.

"Your Majesty," he says, all but pleading with me, "what you're asking of me is treason. The king would—"

I press the barrel of the gun to my temple. The soldiers tense once more.

"I need your word," I say. "I need *everyone's* word, or I will pull the trigger," I say.

I hear murmuring from all around me. It takes a minute to make out what they're saying, but eventually I do.

"*Freedom or death.*"

Even out here in the midday heat, my skin prickles.

What have you made of me, Montes?

As my gaze sweeps over all of them, I begin to see them nod. Then, one by one, they take a knee and put their fists over their hearts.

"You have my word," the first soldier says.

"And mine," someone says from behind me.

"And mine."

"And mine."

This lonely space fills with the sound of dozens of oaths.

Slowly, I lower my gun. They don't know me, but now they show me allegiance.

I slip my weapon into the bodice of my dress and approach the king's guards, leaving bloody footprints in my wake.

Time to meet the man of my nightmares.

THE FUTURE IS no place for civilization.

I stare out the window of the chopper that circled high above me only hours ago. Even this far away from the surface of the earth I can see the destruction.

What does a century and a half of war look like? It looks like ghost towns, like rust and wreckage.

Here and there I see evidence of small towns where people must live. Nothing about these settlements follow any sort of city planning. There are no straight lines, and they have none of the symmetry I recall from the time before the war.

The king appears to have left more than just me to rot.

Over the course of the flight, I notice the settlements change. They get bigger, nicer, and they seem to have some of the symmetry that the other ones lacked. Perhaps not everyone is suffering in this new world.

Once we begin to descend, I have an idea of where we're headed. A swath of deep blue ocean stretches below me, broken up by islands every so often.

The king rebuilt his Mediterranean palace.

An unnatural dread settles into my bones. It's going to feel like nothing's changed. I just know it.

As soon as we land, I stand, and the king's guards step into formation.

Dried blood flakes off me. I suppress a grimace. I'm a mess.

The back of the chopper opens, and I follow the soldiers out, the metal floor cool against my bare feet. My hair kicks up around me as I exit the aircraft.

No cameramen wait for me, nor any eager civilians. Instead, an armored car idles off to the side of the runway, and other than the few soldiers that stand in front of it, we are alone.

Still no king.

And now my mind skips back to the first time the king retrieved me, back when I thought he ordered my father to be killed. Even knowing that he was last person I wanted to see, he'd come for me.

Perhaps that's why he didn't show up today.

Because it if there is one person I do want to see, it's Montes.

I WAS RIGHT.

The king's world is all so eerily familiar.

The palace is just as abominably beautiful as his palaces have always been. Just as big, just as grand, just as oppressive. I stare up at it as the armored car I ride in comes to a stop. Exotic, flowering vines grow up the sides of its walls. Beyond the walls, the ocean stretches on and on.

Just as before, no one waits for us.

I slide out of the vehicle before anyone can try to help me out.

My entourage of guards fans out around me.

I can't look away from those tall walls.

"The king's inside?" I ask.

"He is," one of the men says. "He's ordered us to take you to your chambers, where you're to shower and dress."

I feel my upper lip curl. Of course he would want me to wash away all my sins like they never happened.

I follow the soldiers up the marble steps. Before I can cross the threshold, one of the men guarding the door clears his throat. "Your Majesty, your gun."

The cold metal rests between my breasts. "What about it?" I ask.

"You can't bring it inside."

"Says who?" I ask.

"It's the king's policy."

Reluctantly, I reach down my bodice and hand the gun over. I stole that one; I can always steal another.

Walking into the king's palaces always felt like entering someone else's dream. But now, more than ever, it feels surreal as I pass the colossal columns that line the great entryway. I'm in a time and a place that I don't belong. There is a bone deep wrongness to the situation, and I can do nothing about it.

So I settle for getting perverse pleasure dragging my bloodied skirts and dirty feet across the king's pristine floors.

As we wind our way through the halls of this place, I keep my muscles tense. The guards may have promised to keep me safe from the Sleeper, but their allegiance ultimately belongs to the king.

Our footsteps echo through the lonely, abandoned halls. When I was newly married to the king, his corridors bustled with politicians and aides, servants and guards. Now they're eerily empty, the artwork that lines them covered with drop cloths.

Has my terrible king grown eccentric in his old age?

The few posted guards I pass stand stoically. If they're shocked by my presence, they show no sign of it.

Eventually my retinue stops in front of a set of double doors.

"Your chambers, Your Majesty," one of the soldiers says. "Make yourself comfortable. We'll be right outside."

I nod to them and enter the room.

I could still be an emissary and this my suite for all the similarities I see.

My eyes move over a large, gilded mirror, a canopy bed, and elaborately carved table and chairs to match.

I run a hand over and intricately carved piece of furniture. This is too similar to the time I left. It's destabilizing. Confusing.

On the far side of the room, two French doors lead out to a balcony. They have already been thrown open, and a sea breeze rushes over me. I'm sure that if I walked out there right now, I'd see the ocean in all its glory.

Instead I pace.

I'm right back to where I started, here where the tragedies of the world can never touch me. Everything about this place mocks my existence.

He should've just left me to die.

I press my palms to my eyes.

I don't want any of this.

And then there's what I do want. Answers, revenge, repentance.

I have a sick feeling I won't get any of them.

CHAPTER 5

THE KING

SHE'S HERE, IN the palace. Awake.

Even if I didn't hear the cars pull up or receive updates from my soldiers, I would know it.

Every square inch my skin is buzzing in a way it hasn't done for decades. Not since those beautiful eyes of hers closed a hundred years ago. I'm mortified to admit that I've long since forgotten their exact color.

I can't escape her face. It's everywhere—printed onto posters, mounted on billboards, tagged across the sides of walls—but I can escape all those details about Serenity that used to haunt me. I've avoided the footage of her I'd once so liberally dispersed.

Up until now, my feelings for her had moved from a fresh wound, to an old one, to a dull ache, to a fond memory. A perfect memory.

That all ends today.

From the reports coming in, my men say they found her covered in blood. That the vehicle she was pulled from was full of dead men.

I put a fist to my mouth.

My wife's awake.

Awake and on a warpath.

And I'm her target.

SERENITY

ONCE I'M IN the shower, I begin to assess myself.

Other than a few absent freckles, my skin looks the same. And from the brief glimpse I caught of myself in the mirror, I still retain the scar on my face, as well as the thin white ones that crisscross my knuckles.

I might be heartsick, but physically, I feel great. If I'm still riddled with cancer, then my health will change soon enough. For now, I count my blessings. I have few enough of them.

It's only once I leave the shower that I encounter disappointment.

I frown at the lone gown and heels that sit inside the closet. It's the furthest thing to combat gear I can imagine. The lacy lingerie that accompanies them is little better.

It takes me almost five minutes to dress, due largely to the number of holes and straps the deep crimson gown has. I ignore the heels altogether.

A thud at my back has me spinning around. My eyes lock on the gilded mirror that takes up a good portion of one of the walls. The surface of it trembles ever so slightly.

I walk up to the mirror and press my palm against its surface. The tremors die down, and eventually vanish altogether.

This eerie place.

Someone raps on the door. "*Your Majesty*," they say, "*The king will see you now.*"

MORE CAVERNOUS HALLS, more empty corridors. Everything is pristine, but there are no signs of life.

For the first time since I woke, I feel the stirrings of trepidation. I've been angry at the man who put me in the Sleeper, not the one who refused to let me out.

I don't know *this* man.

The guards that surround me carry no weapons. I was so confident that I could steal one off of them, but there are none to steal.

They take me to a room I assume is used for extravagant parties, judging by how large the double doors are.

We stop in front of it, and one of my guards knocks.

No one answers the door and no one responds.

I cast a side glance at the soldiers. They don't appear surprised about this.

What is waiting for me on the other side?

They pause for several more seconds, then reach for the doors.

As soon as they swing open, my breath catches.

If parties were once held in this room, they are no longer. A world map covers the far wall. The same hated strings and blacked out faces are pinned to it. But the two adjacent walls, those are filled from floor to ceiling with photographs and reports.

Conquering has become Montes's obsession, though *obsession* is not nearly a strong enough word for this.

A century to transform a man into whatever thing he wishes to become …

Right in the middle of the room, staring up at his enormous map, his hands clasped behind him, is the one man I hate more than any other.

My tormentor. My lover.

The king.

Tha-thump.

Tha-thump.

Tha-thump.

My pulse pounds in my ears as my eyes land on his back.

There is no word for what I feel. It's too big, the pain too acute. It burns up my throat and pricks my eyes.

In my mind, I held this man yesterday, felt him move inside me yesterday, heard him whisper that he loved me yesterday.

But my yesterday was 104 years ago.

"Your Majesty, the queen."

The king's body is just as still as ever; he gives no signs that he even heard the guard.

The moment stretches on.

Finally, "Leave us."

That same smooth as Scotch voice echoes through the room, and it sounds grander than I've ever heard it.

Now, *now* I feel the weight of all the lost years. It might've seemed as though I went to sleep yesterday, but my ears know they haven't heard that voice in an eternity.

Montes doesn't turn around as the guards retreat. The door closes with a resounding thud behind them, and then it's just me and the undying king.

I don't move. I barely even breathe.

I'm falling apart.

From hate to love to hate once more. My hardened heart was not made to withstand such vast and ever-changing emotions. It's cleaving me to pieces.

Why did he do this?

Why?

WHY?

"You *bastard*," I whisper.

The king's entire body flinches at the sound of my voice.

"Are you even going to face me?" *You fucking coward.*

I hear the scrape of his heel, and then he's turning.

I thought I'd be ready to face him, I thought that this pain-laced fury churning inside me would obliterate any other feelings the sight of him would bring.

God, was I wrong.

Our gazes lock, and it's all right there—the love, the hate, the sorrow and happiness we hold for one another. All that time can go by, yet everything between us is just as raw and intense as it's always been.

My monster. My husband. He's utterly unchanged. He still has the same olive skin, the same dark hair, the same seductive lips and dark, dying eyes. And judging by the way he stares at me, that obsessive love he once harbored might not be completely gone.

He takes a step forward and nearly goes down to one knee, his legs are so unstable. At first I think something's wrong with him. It takes a moment to realize it's the sight of me.

"Serenity," he says, straightening.

Tha-thump.

Tha-thump.

My chest rises and falls faster and faster.

He takes another step towards me. And then another. He doesn't tear his gaze away from me. Not for a second. His face is impassive—all but his eyes. Those depthless eyes that have witnessed so many of his terrible deeds, they devour me. They move over my outfit, and then my face.

Here they linger, touching each one of my features. But it's my scar they finally rest on.

I swore I wouldn't shed another tear for this man, and yet I feel one slip out anyway.

Damn my heart. Even after everything, I love him, and it's ripping me apart.

"You came here to kill me." There's such resignation his voice.

"You motherfucker," I say. "You left me to *rot*." My entire body trembles. Had I once thought I was the colder of the two of us? I've gotten no reaction out of him, and here I am breaking apart in his midst.

The king blinks several times, his eyes a bit too bright. "Your hate—I'd ... forgotten."

He's still coming towards me, and I can tell he wants to touch me. I begin to move, one of my legs crossing behind the other as I circle the king.

"I was your wife," I accuse.

"You still are my wife." That voice of his—so sure, so commanding.

"No, Montes, you forfeited that right a long time ago."

Suddenly, he's no longer casually strolling. He strides forward. "You will *always* be mine, and you will never—"

As soon as he is within range, I cock my arm back and I slam my fist into his face.

He staggers, his hand reaching up to his cheekbone.

I stalk forward, and then I sock him again. And again. Pain radiates out from my knuckles, and I relish it.

Montes falls, and I follow him to the ground. My fists have a mind of their own. They land wherever they can, and the meaty slap of skin meeting skin echoes throughout the room. My tears fall along with them. I didn't realize I could feel like this—angry and desolate—all at once. And with every blow, I wait for that flood of relief to come. I'm meting out my revenge.

But this doesn't feel like revenge. The king keeps taking the hits, and he doesn't raise a hand against them, not even to protect himself.

"Fight back, you bastard," I growl.

He laughs, and those white, white teeth of his are now stained red with his blood.

My husband is insane.

We both are.

Finally, his arms come up, but only so they can encircle me. He pulls my body flush against his. "God, I fucking missed you, Serenity."

And then he kisses me.

CHAPTER 6

SERENITY

I TASTE HIS blood on my lips. This is not how the reunion is supposed to be going.

It was supposed to end swiftly with his death, but in an instant I've gone from killing the man who betrayed me to kissing him. Unwillingly.

One of his hands comes up and palms the back of my head, making it impossible for me to pull away.

I move my own hands to his neck, and I begin to squeeze.

He releases me, but he doesn't try to pull my hands away, just stares up at me with those too bright eyes as I choke the life out of him.

"Death in a dress." He barely gets the words out, but I hear them all the same.

I close my eyes, feeling two more tears slip out, and squeeze tighter. I remember the exact moment he first said those words to me.

"Why do you think I wanted you in the first place? Death in a dress. That's what you were when you descended down those stairs in Geneva. I knew you'd either redeem me or you'd kill me."

With a sob, I let Montes go, casting myself away from him.

I cover my face with my bloody, shaking hands. I can't do it.

I can't do it.

I *love* him. To kill the thing I love … that might just destroy the last bit of my conscience, and there is so little of it left.

I feel another tear drip down my cheek, and I taste it on my lips. Tears and bloodshed, that's all this relationship has given me. All that this life has given me, really.

His hand touches my cheek. "You didn't do it," he says.

I drop my palms away from my face and open my eyes.

He watches me, and there is no indifference in his gaze. Quite the opposite. Whatever he feels for me, the years haven't dulled it, though they might've transformed it into something else.

It's not anger that's riding me now. It's a hurt so vast I can't see any end to it. I could fit entire galaxies into the space it's carved out for itself inside me.

I stand. I look around me. The room had, in all likelihood, once been used for entertaining. But not anymore. This man's vices are devouring him from the inside out. I'm nothing compared to them, just a desperate, angry girl who's been under someone else's thumb for far too long.

I can't be around this. I just … want out.

I back up.

Montes leans back, his arms slung over his knees. If I didn't know him better, I'd say he was completely at ease. But he never did like me walking away from him, and I can see the controlled panic in his eyes.

"The queen I remember never leaves until she's made a threat," he says, watching me back away from him.

He remembers more than I thought he would.

And now, of all things, he wants me to threaten him. Because that's intrinsically something I would do.

I pause, only for a moment, and exhale, suddenly very weary.

"Not for lost causes," I say.

And then I leave him.

THE KING

I DON'T MOVE until the door closes behind her. But once it does, I can't seem to move quickly *enough*.

I pull my phone from my pocket and dial the head of security. "Serenity is not to leave the palace grounds under any circumstances."

My guard is quiet for a beat too long.

"Understood?" I say.

Finally, he says, "Understood, Your Majesty."

I click the phone off and bring it to my lips.

For the first time in a hundred years, my soul flares to life, my heart along with it. And it hurts so fucking bad.

No one's ever been in my situation, so I couldn't have foreseen that love doesn't function as other things do. It took decades for it to fade, and an instant for it to come roaring back.

As far as my heart is concerned, no time has passed.

And yet, Serenity was nothing like my memory. None of my imaginings could've made her so perfectly flawed.

I can now recall the exact color of her irises—somewhere between gunmetal gray and a frigid ice blue. And her anger—part of the reason I didn't stop her from laying into me was that I was mesmerized by that inner fire of hers. My beautiful storm.

I touch the side of my face tenderly. The skin's beginning to swell.

I breathe harshly through my nose to beat back a shout. I did leave her in a machine to rot. She couldn't protest, so I didn't listen. And now she's back with a vengeance.

The fool I was who first laid eyes on her all those years ago did one thing right— he saw redemption within his reach, and he snatched it up for himself.

And then he sabotaged it again, and again.

I'm still brooding when I hear a knock on my door twenty minutes later. I already know who's on the other side. I squeeze my phone tighter as a wave of anger washes over me.

I should've known.

He should've told me.

I pull myself together, breathing in and out through my nose to calm myself down.

I knew this was coming.

"Come in," I call.

This is something else I'll eventually have to explain to Serenity, something else she'll want to kill me for. And maybe this time she'll be successful.

I rub my face. Redemption has always been within my reach. I'm just too damn guilty to accept it.

SERENITY

I THREAD MY hands behind my head and pace once more inside my room.

I've only ever had one job: to take out the king. I failed at that task time and time again.

I can kill easily enough. There are six dead men who can attest to that.

And no one is more deserving of death than the king. The man has done so many unconscionable things.

My stupid, idiotic feelings.

And what now?

A century ago, I had a purpose. Marriage for peace. A voice for my people and all those who were downtrodden. I might not have wanted the life I was forced into, I might've lamented it, but at least then I understood it.

I don't understand this.

The future, the lost, obsessive king and the war he still futilely fights. Why life has made a joke of my existence.

I take a deep breath.

I never had much time for pity. I still don't.

The king and his world have moved on. I'm no longer needed to hold together two hemispheres.

My gaze travels to the window.

I could leave.

I could *leave*. Not as someone else's prisoner, but on my own.

The thought is heady. Freedom has always been just beyond my reach. To finally have it … It would almost make up for my tragic, broken heart.

But if I did leave, I would need boots, fatigues, weapons, food, water and a means to get more. That would take time to acquire, and there's always a possibility that outside these walls, I will be recognized and fought over as a pawn to be played in this war.

It would be a hard life. A life where I couldn't make much of a difference, a life where I was expendable.

A life without the king.

I walk onto the balcony and spread my arms over the marble railing. The ocean stretches out as far as the eye can see.

That life might be what I want, but my existence really was never about what I wanted. I was woken to save the world.

And the best way to do that would be to stay here and work with the very man who destroyed my heart.

I draw in a breath through my nose.

If that is what is needed of me, then that is precisely what I will do.

Even if it breaks me.

349

CHAPTER 7

SERENITY

NOT TOO LONG after I come to my decision, there's a knock on the door. I cross the room, my skirts swishing around my ankles.

When I open the door, my hand tightens on the knob.

Montes stands on the other side, his hands in his pockets. The gesture is so reminiscent of how he's always been that my knees weaken.

It's too soon. It physically hurts staring at his face and feeling like things can never be the same between us.

I may have decided I can't kill Montes, and I may have decided to help fix all those things the king and his war have broken, but I'm not ready to be civil with him. Not yet.

He just stares at me for a long time, not saying anything. His face has already begun to swell, and that leaves me cold.

Fuck love.

I turn on my heel and head back to the desk I was working at. I've been jotting down notes on what I must learn to help the people I now live amongst.

I hear the sound of his footfalls behind me.

"Are you here to torment me?" I say over my shoulder.

"How did you know?" he says. "That's precisely what I had in mind."

"You haven't lost your silver tongue," I note.

"Serenity."

I glance up from my writing, and my gaze meets the king's. Had I noticed how tormented his eyes were? How weary they appeared? But even as I watch, that weariness dissipates. In its place I see a familiar spark in them.

"What you have done is unforgivable," I say.

He moves leisurely towards me, every step deliberate. It feels like the whole world extends outward from him, like the very universe shaped itself around this man. The king's always been larger than life, but now, if anything, he seems grander and more unnatural than he ever was.

He shakes his head. "No, Serenity. When it comes to us, nothing is beyond forgiveness."

I feel my nostrils flare. "You think this is still a game. The world, your power, my life."

He shakes his head again. "No." He keeps those tormented eyes of his trained on me. "I really don't." His voice carries weight. His years, I decide, are sometimes worn in his words.

"Are you planning on putting me back in there?" After the words leave my lips, I swear I don't breathe. It matters very much how he answers this.

Montes steps in close. "No," he says, searching my face.

I shouldn't believe him, he's deceptive to his core, but I feel the truth of his words.

He reaches up, as if to touch my face.

"Don't, Montes, unless you want to lose that hand."

His entire face comes alive at my words. "You haven't changed at all." He says this wondrously.

He always did like the broken things inside me.

His hand is still poised.

"Don't," I repeat, raising my eyebrows to emphasize my point.

"Can't I touch my wife?"

He said those words once before, and this time around they level my heart. Even after all these years, he remembers them.

"What are you doing, Montes?" I ask.

Is it not enough for him to destroy my life?

"Winning you back," he says.

And then, despite all my warnings, he lays his hand against my cheek.

THE KING

SHE SLAPS MY hand away. "I am not some prize to be won."

God, her anger. It makes the blood roar through my veins.

I am *alive*. Alive in a way I haven't been in decades.

To think I lived without this for so long. Unfathomable.

I see hate burning in her eyes. Time has distorted most of my memories of her, but I'm almost positive I've never seen this particular brand of it. This fierce thing I've bound to my side is dying from the inside out.

That I can't take.

I don't give her time to protest before I place both hands on either side of her face.

Now that this fateful day has come, and I have to deal with the fallout of my choices, I find I'm eager for it. Desperate, even.

Serenity tries to pull away, but I won't release her.

I shake my head. "Fight all you want, my queen, you're not going to escape me."

"Fuck you, Montes. Let me go."

She's about to get violent. Even if I hadn't remembered other interactions that spiraled out of control like this, I would be able to sense it.

This terrible angel of mine. I welcome her vengeance.

I squeeze her face, just enough to get her attention. "Serenity, listen—"

She renews her struggles against me. "No," she says. "I know what you're going to say, and I don't want to hear about your suffering."

I nod. "I know," I say quietly. "But you will."

I can tell that this pisses her off, but when I fail to let her go, she stops fighting against me. I think, deep down, she wants to hear me out.

"There is nothing—nothing—I have ever treasured more than you. I let myself forget." I can feel my eyes begin to water, and any other time—*any* other time—I would fight back the reaction. But I won't with Serenity. Let her see her frightening king strip away his barriers for her.

"But you need to know that no one ever made me happy the way you did, and no one ever made me feel the burdens of my war the way losing you did."

Humans should not be able to feel what I have for this woman. Flesh isn't strong enough to house this much sadness. If I wasn't so afraid of death and the reckoning that waits for me on the other side, I'd have exited this world long ago.

She's blinking rapidly. Despite the firm set of her jaw, my bloodthirsty wife is just about as exposed as I've ever seen her.

Breathing quickly through her nose, she wraps her hands around my wrists and removes mine from her face.

"I listened," she says, "but now you need to listen to me: you never gave me a choice in any of this.

"I watched my mom die when I was ten after one of your bombs exploded outside our house. I became a killer when I was twelve because your war destabilized my country. I became a soldier when I was fifteen because my people were dying, and you were winning. I had to take on my father's job when I was sixteen because our government no longer had the ability to hold elections."

Her voice shakes; I can tell she's fighting tears.

"I was forced to seduce you," she continues, "the single man I most hated and feared in the world so that my country could know peace. I saw my father die protecting me from you, I held his murdered body in my arms. Even then, once I escaped you, you made me marry you. And then, when you realized I was dying of cancer, you forced me to sleep in that hellish machine of yours for a hundred years. A *hundred* years.

"So tell me again, Montes, what do you know of suffering?"

The room falls to silence as I take in her pain.

"I know that it makes you come alive, Serenity," I say softly.

She flinches at that.

"I know that loneliness its own kind of loss, and I have been lonely for a long time." I want to reach out and touch her skin again just to assure myself she's real. It's been so long since I've touched anyone. "I know that I want your suffering. I'll cherish it, just as I do everything else about you."

I can see her body trembling as she frowns at me.

The footfalls of several men interrupt us. A moment later, they pound their fists against Serenity's door. Of all times to be interrupted, now might be one of the worst.

I see Serenity's face shut down. All that anger, all that pain, all that vulnerability gets sealed off. Whatever moment the two of us had, it's now gone.

"Come in," I call, not glancing away from her.

Half a dozen soldiers crowd the doorway.

"Your Majesties," one says, bowing, "footage of the queen has been leaked."

SERENITY

MONTES AND I stand in front of a large screen in one of his conference rooms. I try not to think about how little has changed inside these walls. The king's conference rooms are virtually identical to the ones I remember.

And then there's the role I've slipped back into seamlessly. I didn't even realize when I strode down the hall next to Montes that my actions were out of place until I saw him cast me several glances.

He hadn't had a queen to co-rule with him in over a century. Of course the situation must be strange to him. But he didn't say anything, and I wasn't about to relinquish power when that was my reason for staying.

I run my tongue over my teeth now, my arms crossed, as I watch Jace and his team lift the golden lid of what appears to be a coffin.

The camera pans in.

Goosebumps break out along my arms.

There I am.

My body is still, my arms folded over my chest.

If I still had any doubts about what happened to me, I no longer do.

My eyes are closed, my skin startlingly pale against my golden hair. And my face is serene. It's an expression I rarely wear.

I'd been like that for a hundred years. Forced somewhere between death and life.

When Jace and his men lift me out, my head rolls listlessly against one of their shoulders.

I grimace at the sight. I was utterly helpless.

Next to me, the king begins to pace. This shouldn't be as terrible for him as it is for me, and yet I get the impression it is.

Another clip directly follows this one. In it, I'm still asleep. The camera focuses on my eyes. They move rapidly beneath my closed lids. That footage cuts out, replaced by a close up of my hand as my fingers begin to twitch. That, too, cuts away.

This time when the camera settles on me, I'm fully awake.

"Who are you?"

My voice doesn't sound nearly as confused as I know I was. These men were foolish to not have their guns out and pointed the entire time I was under their care.

"Where is Montes?"

I glance over at the king just as he bows his head and closes his eyes.

Remorse is a strange emotion on him, and I find it both angers and placates me. I want him to feel guilt, but then, what I really want, what I can never have, is for him to have made a different choice and us to not be where we are.

The video ends, and the room is left in silence.

"Take it down, along with any new instances that pop up," Montes finally says.

The soldier stationed near us bows and leaves. I watch him go, my eyes narrowed. Somewhere in the time that's lapsed, Montes has gotten rid of his aides and his advisors, along with the men and women of court. Now all that's left are military personnel.

I turn my attention back to the screen. "This situation is bad because ... ?"

"Before this, the world didn't know you still lived. They're have always been rumors, but not proof," Montes says. He nods to the screen. "Now there is."

THE KING

I KNEW THIS was inevitable, I had just hoped to put it off a little longer. All those years ago, when I'd made Serenity a martyr, I never imagined my actions would have such ripple effects. Not until the years melted away and I had to face the reality of waking my wife up.

The world will come for her. Everyone on this godforsaken earth wants to be saved. What that video shows is something just as unnatural as me. From miraculous beginnings come miraculous endings.

"Montes," Serenity says, "I saw one of the posters."

I mask my surprise. So she knows to some extent that she's famous. I barely have time to process that before she continues.

"What, exactly, do people expect of me?" she asks.

Serenity says this like she's actually considering doing something to meet their expectations.

I turn from the screen.

"They see you as a figure who fights for freedom," I say. "I imagine, if presented with the real woman, they'd expect you to do exactly that."

"They want me to end the war," she clarifies.

I hide my surprise once more. How much does Serenity know? And who told her? My men? Those on camera? The situation is already spiraling out of my control.

"I think that's safe to assume," I say carefully.

This is history repeating itself. The instant Serenity's back in the game, people want to play her.

My enemies will either try to capture her or kill her. They've obviously tried to do so already. And there are so many enemies.

The prospect leaves me short of breath. All those reasons I left Serenity deep in the ground come rising up. There she was safe. Awake, she has a target on her back.

"Well then," she says, breaking my reverie, "that makes this simple: you and I are going to end this war."

CHAPTER 8

THE VEIN IN the king's temple begins to throb.

It's pretty blasé of me to just announce this like Montes hasn't been trying to do the very thing for the last century. I also don't mention that ending the war and winning it are two very different things.

The bastard obviously doesn't like my idea. But just when I think he's going to put up some sort of fight, he nods slowly.

Those dark eyes of his gleam, and I worry that whatever he's agreed to is somehow different from what I've proposed. That terrible mouth curls up into a terrible smile the longer we lock eyes, and that terrible face I feared for so long— I'm going to have to deal with it until this is finished.

I'm seriously concerned that I'm getting played at this very moment.

"Tomorrow, we'll begin," he says, picking his words carefully.

I stare at him a beat longer, then it's my turn to nod. "Alright."

The tension between us evaporates when Montes extends an elbow. "Dinner?"

I huff out a laugh and shake my head. I walk away from the king and his elbow. We are so far beyond chivalry.

In a few long strides he's caught up with me.

He places a hand on the small my back as we exit the room.

"You *will* lose that hand if you keep touching me," I say, not looking over at him.

"You've always liked my hands too much to do them any harm," he says, but drops his hold anyway.

"I don't like much of anything about you right now," I say.

As of today, I finally, *truly* begin to understand my father's lessons on diplomacy. Sometimes you have to ally with your enemies for a higher cause. That means not throttling Montes, despite the almost overwhelming urge to do so.

"We'll see how long you say that," he says.

You know what? Fuck diplomacy, and fuck this.

Even as I swivel towards Montes my arm snaps out. My knuckles slam into his jaw, and even though they're already ripped up and even though his face is already bruised and swollen, the hit is incredibly satisfying.

He stumbles back, clutching his jaw.

"You can wait another hundred and four years for me to like you, asshole. It still won't be long enough. Just be happy I didn't kill you when I had a chance."

That dangerous glint enters his eyes as he rubs his jaw. He closes the distance between us until chest brushes mine.

"Yes, about that," he says, his head dipping low. "You didn't kill me when you could've. I wonder why *that* is," he muses, his gaze searching mine.

"One massacre was enough for the day," I say.

He leans in even closer, bending his head so his lips brush my ear. "You can say it or not, but you and I both know the truth." He straightens enough to look me in the eye. "You can't kill me, even now, even though I deserve it—and I *do* deserve it."

I pull back enough to get a good look at him.

The king I knew took, and took, and took because he felt it was his right. And now, what he is essentially saying is that what he did wasn't his right.

I narrow my eyes at him. "Have you grown a conscience?" It's an almost preposterous thing to consider.

"Age gives you wisdom, not a conscience," he says as we wind our way through his halls.

"And where was that wisdom when it came to me?" I ask.

His eyes look anguished when he says, "It was wisdom that kept me from waking you, *nire bihotza*, not the other way around."

MONTES LEADS US outside, where a small table overlooking the sea waits for us. Oil lamps hang from poles around us, already giving the area a warm glow as the sun finishes setting.

I glance over at the king. This Montes ... he isn't exactly the same man I knew. And the change has me confused.

Confused and intrigued.

He pulls my chair out. I ignore the proffered seat and take the one across from it.

He smiles at the sight, though I swear his eyes carry a touch of sadness.

Someone's already set out a bottle of wine.

The setting, the table, the wine—it all harkens back to those instances when the king tried to seduce me and I was unwilling. Or maybe this is just how the king eats, beholding the sea and the sky and everything that he hasn't managed to ruin yet.

"Re-creating our previous dates will not win me back."

He grabs the wine bottle and begins to open it, appraising me as he does so. "So you admit that I can win you back?" The cork pops.

"That's not what I said."

He begins filling my glass with wine, his eyes pinched at the corners like he finds this whole thing very humorous. "It's what you don't say that interests me most."

I pick up my glass. "I'd prefer it if nothing about me interested you." God, it's such a lie.

Montes meets my eyes. "Serenity, the sun would sooner fall from the sky. Even when you slept, I couldn't stay away from you."

The ocean breeze stirs his hair, and I have to look away.

Montes has had a hundred years to perfect not only being the very thing I hate, but also the very thing I love.

I breathe in the briny air and take in the horizon. The sky is the very palest shades of orange and pink. Beneath it, the ocean looks almost metallic blue. It's beautiful. Peaceful. Paradisiacal.

"Is this the same island where we married?" I don't know why I ask. Why I feel nostalgic over a memory I never wanted.

When I face Montes again, I catch him studying me.

"It is," he says.

All those people I met, they're long dead by now. I should be too.

I take a long drink of wine. "Is this where you kept me when I slept?"

"It is."

"Did you ever regret what you did?" I ask, setting my glass down.

He settles into his seat, his frame dwarfing the chair. Even his build hasn't changed. I find myself looking at his deeply tanned forearms. It feels like only days ago I touched that skin like it was mine. I ache to do so again. Even though I can't, the urge won't disappear.

"Every day," he says.

My eyes move from his arms to his face. It's so unlike him to admit this—to feel this. I thought hearing that would make me feel better; it doesn't.

I let out a breath. "And yet you never changed your mind."

"I am over a hundred and fifty years old, Serenity. Much about me has changed, my mind most of all." He says this all slowly, each word weighed down by his long, long existence.

I swallow. My anger still simmers, but it has nothing on the terrible loneliness that crushes me. I am the relic of the forgotten past.

And I'm beginning to understand that I'm not the only one carrying a heavy burden. If the king's demons don't eat him up at night the way mine do, then they at least fall on those great shoulders of his throughout the day.

The waiters come then, bearing plates. I study the men. Their shoulders are wide, their faces hard. Soldiers dressed as servants. Montes no longer employs civilians it seems.

The food they place on the table isn't quite like what I'm used to with the king. It's simple—a cut of meat that rests on the bed of greens with a side of rice. The portion sizes are much smaller than what the king used to dole out.

I stare at it, not making a move for the utensils.

"The food is not going to bite you, Serenity," Montes says.

"How bad off is the world?" I ask.

If the king eats like this, if he's given himself a demotion, what must the common people's lives be like?

"What makes you think it's the world that's different, and not me?"

It's an echo of his previous statement. That he's a changed man.

My gaze flicks up to Montes. He takes a sip of wine, watching me over the rim. He lounges back in his seat, slowly setting his glass down on the table. Everything about him is casual. Everything but his eyes.

I don't want to believe what he's suggesting. Not my narcissistic king, not the bastard who ruined my life and the lives of those I loved. He can't have changed his ways. Because if he truly has, all my righteousness will be for nothing.

I can't do this. My hate is all I have left; I don't want to know that the object of it is no longer worthy of my wrath. And, hypocrite that I am, I'm not ready to hear that leaving me inside the Sleeper was a personal sacrifice he made for the greater good.

The king is the selfish one. Not me.

Dear God, please not me.

"I think I'll eat alone." I grab a bread roll from the basket that rests between us and stand. "Enjoy dinner. I'll see you in the morning."

Montes catches my wrist as I pass him.

I look down my arm, at those long, tapered fingers that completely engulf my wrist. "Let go."

The vein in his temple throbs. "Sit. That's an order."

The king and his orders. He always did like to lord them over everyone. That hasn't changed.

I lean in, getting close to his face. "Fuck you and your orders."

I twist my wrist out of his hold and stride away.

"Serenity!" he calls after me.

But I don't stop walking, and I never look back.

CHAPTER 9

SERENITY

SELF-DOUBT HAS NEVER been one of my character traits, but now as I pad through the empty halls of the king's castle, I can't help but feel it.

When it comes to the king, I have always assumed the worst. Perhaps my assumptions are no longer correct.

Perhaps he's no longer the most abominable person on the planet.

Nodding to the guards posted on either side of my door, I slip inside my bedroom. As soon as the door closes behind me, I lean against it, my head tilted towards the ceiling.

I must be the worst sort of person to be angry at this possibility. If my father were here, he would be shamed by my selfishness.

But my anger always did a great job of masking every other emotion I felt, and right now the main emotion that lurks just beneath it is worry.

How long did I hold out against the king when he was wholly wicked? What will I do now when the king's wicked side is tempered by something just, something good, something I might actually agree with? Believe in?

That is something I fear.

I DON'T WANT to fall asleep.

Despite the guards' promises, I'm still concerned that the king will change his mind and force me back into that Sleeper. I should be thankful for the leaked footage. Now that the world knows I'm alive, Montes can't easily hide his little secret once again.

But it's more than residual concern that keeps me awake. I don't want to go back to sleep after sleeping for a century.

My wants don't seem to matter; my eyes still begin to repeatedly drift close. I fight it until I can't any longer, and then I decide to change for bed. I pad towards the closet, my skirts swishing around my feet.

I stare into the empty closet.

The room I'm staying in still has no clothes.

I mutter an oath beneath my breath and begin unzipping my dress. Just or unjust, the king is still a wily fucker.

The gown slips off of me, sliding to the ground, and I'm left in the lacy lingerie the king provided me with earlier. I step out of the gown pooled at my feet and head for the enormous bed.

Halfway there, I hear a dull thump from the side of the room. I twist around, my body instinctively tensing. My eyes find the source of the noise, my body stiffens.

The surface of the mirror is vibrating once more. As I watch, the vibrations slow, then eventually vanish altogether.

I walk over to the mirror. It's unusually large, taking up a quarter of the wall. I wait for the noise to repeat itself, my eyes fixed on the smooth surface. When the seconds tick by and nothing happens, my exhaustion creeps back up on me.

Ghosts I'm not afraid of. Far too many already haunt my mind.

I pad over to the bed and slide in. It's only once I'm amongst all those sheets made of fine fabrics that I notice how empty the bed feels. It's about to swallow me up it's so large. I've gotten used to the king's body pressed against mine. I never realized that once something like that is gone, you feel its ache like a phantom limb.

I don't want to think about him deep in the night, or pine for his presence the way I'm sure many ladies of the court have.

Monsters like the king don't sleep in beds, they sleep under them. And I don't yearn; I exact vengeance.

THE KING

I ENTER HER room late that evening, long after I know she's fallen asleep.

If I thought it would work, I'd wait for her to invite me herself. But I'm not a complete fool; another hundred years would go by before that would happen. Serenity is vindictive enough to deny both of us this for as long as she seeks to punish me.

I'm not a fool, and I'm not some chivalrous knight here to defend her honor.

I'm her morally depraved husband.

So I'm bending the rules of propriety.

I shrug off my button-down and slacks and round the bed.

Serenity stirs as I slip under the covers. The sheets are warm from her body heat. There were days long gone when I would've ruined entire cities for something as simple as this.

I'd gotten so used to her inhuman coldness as she slept in that sarcophagus. I'd nearly forgotten that Serenity has always been fire and heat and blood and ignited passions. My injuries are a testament to that. The excitement that thrums through my veins is a testament to that.

Those grave robbers resurrected more than an ancient queen when they took Serenity. My heart and my spirit slept with my wife, and those two have now woken. Just as I feared they would.

"Montes," she murmurs in her sleep.

I still at my name.

No time has gone by for her. She hasn't felt that century like I have. I forced myself to exist without her, the fates' punishment for all those years I took from everyone else. Maybe I finally paid my penance.

She rolls against me, her body nestling into my side, her arm wrapping around my torso.

I close my eyes and swallow down what feels like a shard of glass in my throat. Her skin is all over me. I rasp out a pained breath. Nothing has ever felt so good.

My arms come around her hesitantly. I'm never this tentative, but tonight my mythic queen is in my arms, and I haven't been a husband in a very long time.

I move my hand to her hair and stroke those golden locks. I have to breathe through my nose to control my emotions.

I'm not dreaming.

Nothing should feel this good.

I shouldn't be here. I did this to her, to me, to us. And it's not over. Even once she forgives me—and she will, that I'll make sure of—there are my enemies. We're back to square one, where she was my weakness. Only I, in my infinite stupidity, have made her more than my weakness. I have made her a vital player in this war.

My men have been alerted to look for and eliminate threats, and already they've taken care of dozens. But more will come, and I'm no longer smug enough to think I can neutralize all of them.

Even now with her cancer gone, death looms over Serenity. I've brought this upon her—just as I have every one of her other misfortunes.

"*Nire bihotza*, I'm sorry," I whisper, my lips brushing the crown of her head, my shaky fingers running down her arm. "I know you'll never believe it, but I'm so, so sorry."

SERENITY

I STIR, MY body stretching out. The first rays of dawn slide through the windows. It's almost enough to rouse me.

Almost, but not quite.

Montes's arm tightens around my waist, and I settle back into him. For once my king isn't up earlier than me. My lips curl and I drift back asleep against him.

Sometime later, I wake again, my body stretched along Montes's. I blink, taking in the room.

The drapes are the wrong color. The room is the wrong shape and size.

I furrow my brows, confused. I begin to sit up, only to have my king groan and pull me back into him.

Right as I feel the firm press of his skin along mine, everything comes roaring back to me.

The king, that slippery bastard, snuck into my bed during the night. He's been holding me this entire time.

And while I slept, my body has been encouraging him along.

I try to move away, but his embrace only tightens.

I flip over to face him. His eyes open slowly, heavy with sleep, and his hair is ruffled. That ache that's taken up residence in my chest only increases at the sight.

"You have no right," I say, my irritation overriding that horrible burn that imperfect love produces.

He stares at me from across the pillow. I can see my bruises on him, and it shames me all over again that I put my mark on his skin. And then I am ashamed to be ashamed, for if anyone deserves to get roughened up, it's the king.

"You are my wife," he says. "Spouses share a bed."

"Get. Out." I'm beginning to shake as irritation gives way to anger.

Montes's thumb rubs little circles into my back. The man looks downright content. "My roof, my rules," he says. "We go to sleep and wake up together."

"Oh, do we now?" I say. "I wonder what happened to that rule when you put me in a box for a hundred years."

He searches my face. "I never did it to make you suffer."

No, he did it to save me from death.

"*Is* the cancer gone?"

I feel Montes's hand creep up my back and into my hair. He hesitates briefly, then nods. "Everything is gone. The cancer and all other ailments you might have suffered from."

The king made good on his word.

"How long did it take?"

"Three quarters of a century."

Seventy-five years. He waited over seven decades for me to heal.

Seven decades.

Most people I knew never lived to be half that age.

"And was it worth it?" I ask.

His eyes turn heated. Fervent. "*Nothing* has ever been more worth it."

"And yet you never woke me." I slept three extra decades, and I probably would've slept more if I'd never been captured.

Montes pulls me up and onto his chest.

"Yesterday I gave you my repentance," he says, his voice rough. "Today you'll get everything else."

"You going to have to do a little more than repent for a single day, considering you took thirty thousand of them away from me."

An amused smile curls the edges of his lips. I hadn't meant for that to be amusing.

"I'll give you thirty thousand more," he says.

"I don't want thirty thousand more. I want you to let me go." I push against him. That only serves to tighten his grip and rub our bodies together.

His jaw clenches, and his eyelids lower just a smidge. "If you keep doing that, you're going to be coming rather than going."

"I *will* hurt you," I threaten.

"But you won't kill me, and that really is what's important." His thumb skims under a bra strap. "I rather like this on you."

I grab his hand. We stare each other down.

"Montes, you don't get to do this with me," I say. "You gave that up a long time ago."

He leans in close enough that I can feel his breath tickle my skin. "I gave *nothing* up. Be upset at me for making you live when you wanted to die, but don't blame me for this."

He moves the hand I still hold captive to my face, touching my scar. "You fought for me, killed for me. You wore my crown and carried my child. Don't distort what you mean to me, what you've always meant to me.

"And I'm going to keep you in this bed until you understand something: I won't let you go. Everything you are is mine, and everything I am is yours."

"That is something I've always known," I say.

Ever since the day my father died I've understood. So long as the king lives, I will never be free of him.

CHAPTER 10

SERENITY

"DO YOU HAVE anything besides lace that I can wear?" I ask, sitting up and frowning at the empty closet across the room.

Montes gets out of bed. I try and fail to not stare at his backside as he strides away from me.

You know what? Screw it. The man has always taken liberties with me when he shouldn't. I can look at my husband all I want.

He grabs his button-down he's thrown over a side chair and tosses it to me.

I finger the material. "This isn't funny."

"My men have restocked my closet with clothes for you, but wearing them comes with a condition."

A century was not long enough to stamp out the conniving side of this man.

I raise an eyebrow.

"You wear the clothes I provide, you sleep in my bed. Willingly."

My hold tightens on his shirt, wrinkling the material.

Everything with this man comes down to strategy and what he can take. Fortunately for him, I've made a habit of sleeping with the king even when I didn't particularly like him. I have few qualms about repeating the process.

"Fine," I say. "But when you wake up and your balls are missing, just remember that you asked for this."

A slow, smoldering smile breaks out across his face. "And when you wake up with me between your thighs, just remember that you agreed to it."

"You really do have a death wish." The audacity of this man never fails to astound me.

I slide out of bed. Ignoring the shirt he offered me, I put yesterday's dress back on. I can feel his eyes on me as I slide it over my hips.

"What?" I say, pulling the straps up.

His eyes pinch at the corners again, like I amuse him.

Rather than answering me, he grabs his shirt from the bed and pulls it on. I bid goodbye to his abs as he buttons it up.

I find myself watching him just as acutely as he watched me.

He doesn't bother tucking in his shirt or slipping on socks and shoes before coming back to me and taking my hand.

Montes brings it to his lips, kissing the split knuckles that hit his flesh.

I take a deep breath. He's going to keep doing this, whether or not I fight him. So I bear it and try to ignore the brush of his lips.

When he's done, he tugs on my hands and leads me out of my room.

"I don't know anything about you," I say as we walk. "I don't know who you are."

"It doesn't matter," he says.

"It does," I counter. "Do you have a wife?"

He's quiet for a moment, and the only sound is the soft tread of our bare feet and the march of the soldiers that trail us. "She wants to know if I have a wife. I think she's more interested than she lets on."

All that time managed to go by, and yet he still remembers how much I hate it when he refers to me in the third person. "*Montes.*"

"No, my queen," he says, his voice somewhat offended, "there are no others, save for you. There never have been."

I am mortified at the relief I feel. Am I so ready to forgive this man who's betrayed me at every stage of our relationship?

"Kids?" I ask.

He flashes me a skeptical look.

"Oh, don't act like you're a saint."

That vein in his temple begins to pulse. "No wives. No children, Serenity."

I take that all in stride, perversely enjoying the fact that I have upset my king. He has a hard look about him, the expression he wears before he damns someone to death.

My attention diverts from the king when I catch sight of the palace walls. Some of the cloths that covered large frames have now vanished. Now I realize why they were hidden in the first place.

My face stares back at me from half a dozen different places, the grandest of them is the photo from our wedding that once rested in my office. It's an odd picture to be so grand; it's not stiff and formal. But the tenderness captured in that moment—albeit, tenderness I distinctly wasn't feeling at the time—is almost overwhelming on such a grand scale.

The other photos are an odd combination of shots I never saw.

"I couldn't look at them until now," the king admits next to me, noticing my interest.

"Why did you put them up in the first place?" I ask, distracted.

"I had hoped they would bring me happiness. But I was wrong."

My gaze sweeps over the walls again. Not all of the frames have been unveiled. It all seems so very deliberate.

"What about the ones that are still covered?" What else is the king hiding?

Montes peers down at me. "Those are a story for a different day."

A story I'm bound to not like, I think as I stare into his handsome face. The secrets the king keeps are both huge and terrible. At this point, however, I must be impervious to the king's terrors. There's not much more that can frighten me; I've already endured all my fears.

We stop outside a set of double doors. Montes opens one of them for me and we head inside.

His room.

I don't know what I was expecting, but I'm not sure it's this. His room looks essentially the same as the one I stayed in last night. Beautiful, but lacking personality.

This man keeps all those fathomless bits of himself locked tightly up. Not even in his room does he set his personality loose.

I shouldn't be concerning myself with Montes, who I feel at my back even now. I should concern myself with my own fate.

I'm to stay here, in this beautiful, empty palace, full of these opulent, meaningless rooms alongside my terrible, tortured husband.

When I turn, I see Montes standing on the threshold.

He jerks his head to the side of the room. "Your clothes are in the closet. I'll be in the shower. We're in a drought, so if you want to conserve water, I'll allow you to join me."

I narrow my eyes on him. "I'll pass."

His monstrous eyes twinkle as he backs away. My nightmare won't capture me today.

"Then get dressed," he says, unbuttoning his shirt. "We have a war council in an hour."

THE KING

THIS SHOWER MIGHT go on record as one of the fastest I've ever taken. I soap myself up, my skin quickly getting slick with it.

Day two with the awakened queen.

My heart beats fast, and for the first time in decades, I feel young again. Uncertain again. Of my feelings, of hers, of the situation we've now found ourselves in.

She can't escape, I ensured that, but I still don't want her out of my sight. My paranoia is a beast that could swallow me whole if I let it. And I have ample reason to feel this way. I thought Serenity would be safe below my palace. She hadn't been.

And now she's in my room. *Our* room. Ready to gut me alive. Everything that's wicked in me thrills at her savage nature.

I rinse off the suds.

Life with Serenity begins again.

This time around, it will be different. I'm not a good man, and doing the right thing has never come naturally to me, especially when it concerns my wife, but I'm trying. That's why I've decided to keep including her in my official decisions. I want her involved in this war, not only because I have made her a key player in it, but also because my queen thrives best on the front lines.

I turn the spigot off and step out of the shower stall. Grabbing a towel, I wrap it around my waist.

I remember the call I got when they found her. All those dead men. She'd been untouched. That's what happens when you corner my wife. That's what happens when you throw her into the fray.

I'm an idiot for trying to protect her this whole time. She was never the one who needed protecting.

Everyone else was.

CHAPTER 11

SERENITY

MONTES AND I head back to the giant map room together. I cast him my fifth skeptical glance.

"What concerns my vicious little wife?" he asks. He looks down at me fondly. It's so strange, how kind this man can be when he's been so cruel.

"You're wearing fatigues. And combat boots."

Like me.

I found my own standard issue clothes in his room almost immediately. Granted, these are more fitted than the pairs I'm used to, but otherwise they're essentially the same.

That was my first shock—Montes stocking my dresser with fatigues.

The second and bigger shock was that he wore them himself.

"I am," he says.

"I've never seen you in uniform." Not like this. Outfitted like a soldier. He looks good in it.

He runs a hand down his shirt front. "Like I said, many things about me have changed."

I'm finally starting to understand that.

He peers down at me. "You like this." It's not a question.

My eyes drop to his clothes. "It depends."

"Depends?" He raises his eyebrows. "On what?"

"On whether or not it's all for show." Wearing military attire doesn't make you a soldier. Battle does.

"I like what you're wearing," Montes says by way of answer, nodding to my outfit. "It's a reminder that we will be sharing a bed tonight."

My face heats at that. "We shared a bed last night."

"Yes, but this time my willing queen will fall asleep in my arms. I wonder what else she will be willing to do ..."

"Just because I agreed to your terms doesn't mean I'm willing," I say.

Montes gives me a knowing look. "Let's save the lies for the politicians," he says.

I thin my gaze. "You better get some custom armor to wear below your belt, my *king*," I say. "You're going to need it."

That earns me a laugh. "I'll look into it, *nire bihotza*."

Inside the king's enormous map room, a series of long tables have been brought in and arranged in a U-shaped pattern. More startling than the addition of tables is the addition of people. Dozens upon dozens of military officers sit at the thick oak tables, most wearing uniforms and medallions.

Several screens have been pulled down from the ceiling, covering much of the maps. More military officers watch from the other side of those screens.

And amongst them all, I see many women.

My heart beats faster. This is not the same king I remember. Not even close.

When the officers notice me, the noise dies down until room becomes ominously silent. Then, one by one, they stand and salute.

I lean into Montes, looking out at them all. "Did you pay them to do that?"

He places a gentle hand on my back. "No, Serenity. Money can't buy you that kind of loyalty."

Nor can fear, not with these types of men and women. I stare out at their stoic faces. If they've lived through enough battles, things like death and pain don't scare them. That begs the question: how did Montes convince them to join his ranks?

I flash the king a questioning look. Rather than speaking, he urges me forward. I nod to the soldiers I make eye contact with, still confused by the man and situation I find myself in.

This is the first—being inside the king's palace, surrounded by people that look just like me. It's destabilizing.

Montes stops us in the middle of the room, where everyone can see us. "Please sit," he says. The acoustics of the room carry his voice to the far corners.

Dozens of chairs scrape as they do just that.

The king glances down at me. "I would like to introduce you all to my wife, Her Majesty Serenity Lazuli, Queen of the East."

The room is as silent as the dead. Most of the officers school their faces to look impassive. But their eyes say what their expressions don't.

I'm the apparition no one expected.

"She's well over a hundred years old," Montes continues, "but she has slept through most of them."

He lifts his gaze to the room. "I have lied to you all, to the entire world. Serenity never died of her cancer. I had her sedated until I could find a cure for her. By the time that came to pass, I hesitated to wake her for other reasons."

My entire body tightens. I want to devour the words that will fall from his lips, but I have to rein my own emotions in. Whatever he says now is likely some official explanation rather than the actual truth.

My husband is not exactly known for truth telling.

"I was afraid of what would happen to her and the world if she was brought to life. Martyrs don't last long in war."

It takes hearing Montes's explanation to realize I wanted something else, something that burned hot. A reason worthy of a century of sleep.

Not this anesthetized explanation.

"I'm sorry I lied to you all in the process." The king looks back down at me, and now I really don't want his eyes taking in whatever reaction I'm wearing. "She's my wife. I don't want anything to happen to her. I thought that keeping her asleep and safe under my protection would be enough. But the enemy came in here, they stole her from me, and they were going to use her in the way the West uses all their subjects."

Montes's jaw tightens. Now *there* are words to get behind. Now there is the king. Not the king I knew—that one was a man wearing a title.

This is a title wearing a man, power and purpose given flesh.

I can't help but stare in silence. When did the West become the great evil, and this man a fighter for freedom? When did leaving me to sleep become a mercy rather than a death sentence?

And how, exactly, does the West use their subjects?

I find I really don't want to know that answer.

Montes steps away from me. "They came for my wife, trespassed inside my house, and tried to use her against us," he says, pointing a finger to the ground. He pauses for effect. "They will try again. And again. And again. They will try to capture her until they succeed or we stop them."

He orates to the officers like they are clay to mold into whatever shape he desires. And he's good. Really good. His adoration seems genuine, his pain seems genuine, his anger seems genuine.

But is it?

"They give us only one option: we must stop them. And we will." Montes casts his gaze about the room. "This time when we make war with the enemy, we do it for good."

ONE OF THE officers stands, and he seems like the meanest of the bunch from the sharp set of his features. His eyes move from Montes to me. "What does Your Majesty, Serenity Lazuli say to this?"

Suddenly, dozens of eyes are on me.

And I realize I'm not just a woman wearing a title, either. Not to these people. I'm their hope given form.

I walk forward, passing the king, my boots echoing as they click against the floor. I cast a wondrous glance around the room. I throw a look over my shoulder.

The hairs on my arm rise as our gazes lock. Montes, in his infinite darkness, has done the most twisted thing of all: he's fashioned his evil into something good men can get behind.

I face forward once more. "I won't pretend to understand these times or your ways," I say. "But a hundred and fifty years is too long to be at war. I am prepared to do whatever is needed, whatever it is you ask of me, to end it, once and for all."

The officer who spoke stares at me for a long time. Then he brings his fist over his heart, and he thumps it against his chest. The action is savage. He pulls his fist away, then does it again. And then a third time.

A chair scrapes back and the man next to him stands. He too places a fist over his heart and begins to pound it just beneath his decorated breast pocket. Then a woman stands and does the same thing. Then several officers.

One by one, like a wave, they stand and thump their fists over their hearts until the entire room is echoing with the sound.

I feel the devil's breath against my ear. "There is no higher compliment, my queen, than for the officers to give you their honor."

That's what this is?

"What have you done?" I say, staring out at the sea of medaled men and women. I've already agreed to this, to be what the world needs me to be, but I'm still horrified by all that comes with it.

I'm nothing more than a story to these men and women, a face to their beliefs. And they are all but ready to set down their lives for me.

Those terrible eyes of his capture mine, but he doesn't respond.

It's hard to believe everything that led me here wasn't orchestrated by his hand. That my escape and the fallout from it wasn't planned. Montes seems more omnipotent than ever, and the superstitious part of me wants to believe that he can see some endgame the rest of us can't.

But he can't control me, I know that. His reluctance to wake me up has everything to do with that. And I won't bow to him, no matter how drastically he's changed his ways. A long time ago I forgot I slept in bed with the enemy. I paid a hundred years as penance.

I won't make the same mistake twice.

CHAPTER 12

SERENITY

"So LET ME get this straight, the Western United Nations is still called the Western United Nations, and it's run by a group of representatives, just as it always has been."

The officers around me are nodding.

After the meeting in the map room adjourned, Montes and I moved to a smaller conference room with a handful of the officers. All of them are helping me catch up on what I've missed.

It's an impossible task; it took me years to understand the intricacies of my time's politics when I was studying as an emissary. It will take me years more to understand all that's happened between then and now.

"Some of these representatives are Montes's old advisors." This comes from the stern-looking officer that was the first to show affiliation to me in the map room. Heinrich Weber is his name, Montes's grand marshal of arms.

I'm surprised by how quickly he's taken a shining to me, considering how much of a threat I am to the king.

Or maybe he just doesn't yet know my true relationship with Montes.

"I believe you've personally met them," Heinrich adds.

A chill races up my spine.

Wait, *those* old advisors?

Some of them are still alive?

I shoot a glance at Montes, who sits in the chair next to mine. He lounges back in his seat, his thumb running absently over his lower lip, those sinister eyes of his narrowed like he's trying to figure me out. It was never me that was the enigma.

"So there's more than just one of you now?" I ask.

More men that can't be killed, each one more rotten than the last. Of course it's the worst ones that have managed to cheat death.

The corner of Montes's mouth lifts up. "My queen, there has only ever been one of me."

"Thank God for that."

The officers in the room stiffen slightly. It's not like before, when Montes's subjects scuttled about, perpetually in fear of his wrath. However, the king still appears to command their respect, and I'm not very respectful.

Now the other corner of Montes's lips lifts as well. He always did enjoy my insults. And just as always, he seems more captivated by me than the matters at hand.

To be fair, everything I've been learning he's known about for decades. If roles were reversed, I can't say I wouldn't be sickly fascinated with him as well.

I return my attention to some of the papers spread out on the table and the men and women seated around me. "Just what kind of people are these representatives as a whole?"

"The worst kind," Montes says.

I raise my eyebrow and flash him a sardonic look. "Refresh me again on what the worst kind of leaders are."

Tell me how they are different from you, I challenge him with my eyes.

I swear the air thickens as we stare each other down.

"The representatives have a long history of neglecting their people. From our best estimates, there haven't been significant efforts to clean out the radiation from the ground, so radiation-related medical issues are a big problem in the West. It doesn't help that their hospitals are critically understaffed and understocked.

"Food and clean water are also serious issues for them. And I haven't even gotten into the ethics of their leadership."

The more he says, the deeper my frown becomes. I don't know who I'm angrier at—the representatives, who abuse their power more egregiously than even the king, or Montes, who forced me to lay in stasis right when I was on the cusp of helping my people.

"And what about you?" I ask.

"What about me, Serenity?" He lifts an eyebrow.

"How are you any better than the enemy across the sea?"

"Within the last century, over ninety percent of the radiation has been removed from the Eastern Empire," one of the officers says, coming to Montes's rescue.

"Radiation that the king put there," I respond.

"I'm sorry, Your Majesty, but that's just not true," the officer says.

I furrow my brows and tear my gaze away from Montes. "What do you mean?"

"The WUN has dropped several bombs since you last ruled."

Sickly sensation runs through my body. "They dropped ... more bombs?" When I worked with the WUN, that kind of warfare had always been off the table. When you start playing with nukes, you flirt with global extinction.

The officer nods. "They hit a few major city centers in the East."

This is my land all over again, only everything about this story is wrong. My former enemies are the victims, and my homeland is the great evil.

Shock and something like despair fill me. I can't catch my breath. Is there no one decent left? Haven't the innocent suffered enough?

"What did you do to retaliate?" I ask.

"A peace treaty was formed in light of the loss, so that we could redistribute our resources," the officer says.

A peace treaty?

When I meet Montes's eyes this time, I don't like what I see there. It's not haughty, or selfish, or wicked. Finally, finally I see what I'd always hoped to in those eyes of his—repentance, sorrow, loss—and I can't bear it. The years should've made Montes more apathetic, not less.

"Is that true?" I ask.

"I have changed," is all he says.

I wait for him to say more. I find I'm desperate to know the secret to climbing out of the abyss our souls have fallen into. I'm even more desperate to know whether this is what happened to the king. He's already admitted his wisdom grew, not his conscience.

But Montes doesn't speak, and I'm left with one horrible question.

"How many have died?" I ask.

No one in the room answers right away.

Eventually, someone clears their throat. "Since you've been gone, the war has claimed over a billion casualties from the East, and about three hundred million from the West."

It's all hitting me at once. Over a billion lives—parents, children, spouses, siblings. Friends, lovers, comrades. Over a billion of them cut down because bad men decided they wanted to have it all. When that many people are gone, what is the point?

I actually feel a tear roll down my cheek at that. I look over at Montes, and he must see my despair.

I can see wounds in those old eyes of his; my king's finally been touched by his war, and his ghosts are eating him alive.

"The enemy fights more ruthlessly than we do," someone says.

A day ago, I wouldn't have believed it. Now I do.

A billion people gone. You really do reap what you sow. Montes has cultivated fields and fields of violence and watered them with bloodshed. These are his crops.

I draw in a ragged breath. I was never able to fulfill my promise of healing this broken world. Not until now, when so much has already been lost.

Not glancing away from me, Montes says, "Everyone, out. We'll reconvene tomorrow at eight a.m. in the Great Room. Bring with you a comprehensive plan for your respective departments."

The room clears in under a minute, but not before the officers bow and salute us. And even on their stoic faces, I swear I catch a glimpse of hope when their eyes meet mine.

Once they leave, I rotate to the king. "Why did you clear the room?" I ask.

He leans forward in his chair, his forearms going to his thighs. "You don't like having an audience when you feel weak."

My throat constricts at that. This man can be so cruel yet so considerate. And God, does he remember me well.

My gaze slides to the door. "They love you." It's both a statement and a question.

"Not as much as they love you."

It's easy to love a dream. It's much harder to love the reality. Once these people understand who I really am, I doubt they'll remain blindly loyal.

"I thought you believed all the good men were gone," I say. He told me this long ago.

"I was wrong about many things."

I peer at him closely. "Are you a good man?"

A devil-may-care smile flashes across his lips. He wants to touch me; I can feel his desire as though it's a physical thing.

"Does it matter?" he says. "I'm still the King of the East, you're still married to me, and the world's still at war. Good and evil have little to do with it."

Now I lean forward, until there are only inches between our faces. "They have everything to do with it. So which are you?"

He leans forward, closing the last of the distance between us, and just as his lips meet mine, he says, "Both."

THE KING

I AM MARRIED to a lioness. Some dangerous, beautiful creature that cannot be tamed, and she will eat me alive.

As my lips move against hers, and I take my conquered kiss, I expect those claws of hers to come out. She hates me, perhaps now more than ever.

Instead, she kisses me back. And now I'm not just reveling in the taste and the feel of her, but the memory of the time when she wanted this every bit as much as I did.

Eventually, she pushes me away, and the look on her face ... horror and regret. "I'm not doing this with you again, Montes."

I lean forward, refusing to let her put distance between us. "Is this one of your famous facts?" I say.

"Do you really think I'm here sitting next to you because I believe we can resolve our issues?"

Oh, the fire that burns within her. I want to stoke it until I can feel nothing but her heat.

"You're sitting next to me because I didn't give you a choice," I say.

She gives me a hard look. "I'm here to fix what you've destroyed."

What she doesn't realize is that our relationship is one of those things.

I pull my chair as close to her as I can get, until our thighs are pressed against one another. "The terms are the same as they've always been, *nire bihotza*—if you want to fix the world, you'll do it at my side."

I think she understands this. I can see the concession in her eyes. I don't want to be her second priority, and I don't intend to remain one. However, if this gets her to give me another chance, I'll take it.

"What happened once I was gone?" she asks.

I pick up one of her hands. She tries to pull it away, and I flash her a look.

"If you want information from me, you play by my rules." It's as simple as that. "One of those rules is that while I answer your questions, I get to touch you."

She glowers at me, despite the fact that we began our relationship this way. She came to my land prepared to trade secrets for sex.

"Fine," she says. I don't know how she does it, but she manages to make the word sound like a curse.

Satisfaction spreads through me. "Good."

I turn over Serenity's hand, running my fingers across her soft skin. Time has long since wiped away the calluses she wore like jewelry. I find I miss them. I like it best when my savage queen displays her true nature. If I give her long enough in this world, she will wear those calluses once more.

"After you were placed back in the Sleeper, I continued to war with my advisors and some of the surviving regimes of South America," I say, beginning to answer her earlier question.

She listens avidly.

"The West never much liked me, and the Resistance and other militia groups got behind South America's fight. Within a year, what little gains I had made in the WUN were undone, and the political leaders who remained loyal to me were slaughtered."

It should please her that the Resistance pushed me out, but she doesn't look pleased. She looks worried. She must be thinking about the advisors who fled to South America. Those were not men anyone should get behind.

I run my thumb over the soft skin of her inner arm.

"My enemies banded together and retook the West. They called themselves representatives and established their leadership throughout the WUN. Despite the similarities in names, their government is nothing like the one they replaced. Ever since then, we've been at war."

To be honest, I'm more interested in the feel of my hand along her flesh than I am in retelling this bleak history. The world has been the way it is for the last hundred years, and I've had a century to come to terms with it. Meanwhile, I've only had a day to drink up my wife's essence.

"Montes."

I am the ancient one, and yet every time I meet her gaze I can't help but feel I'm looking at someone even older than me.

"How is it that after all this time, you haven't managed to defeat the West?" she asks.

It's the most laughable question. No one tries to lose a war.

"I know you have the resources," she says. "So why, Montes?"

"They fought dirtier than I did."

"No one fights dirtier than you."

I'm still holding one of her hands in my own. I tug on it, pulling her close. "That was true until I met you. They are your people, *nire bihotza*. You care for them, as I care for you. I tried to do right."

Her eyes widen almost imperceptibly. "What are you saying?"

I bring her hand to my mouth and kiss those soft, scarred knuckles of hers, but I don't respond. It should be obvious.

She and I are love and war. Peace and violence. I have taught her how to be a worse person, and she's taught me how to be a better one. I fuel her hate, and she fuels my love.

I've torn the world apart and now I need my queen to help me stitch humanity back together, and my heart along with it.

CHAPTER 13

SERENITY

A SWIMSUIT WAITS for me when we return to our rooms.

"What's this?" I say, picking up the two dainty scraps of material.

The king comes striding in behind me. "I've decided I'm only going to answer your intelligent questions. The inane ones you'll just have to figure out for yourself."

I flash him an annoyed look.

He begins to change next to me, and I realize a swimsuit has been laid out for him as well.

When I don't follow his lead, he says, "You don't have to get in the ocean. You can stay inside the palace, just as you have for the last several decades."

This man knows how to play me even better now than he did a hundred years ago.

"I need to work more, Montes. There's so much I have to catch up on." Of course in his world, the king has time for idle swims when there's work to be done.

"I will allow you to continue to ask me questions while we swim," he says, unzipping his pants. He steps out of his fatigues a moment later. Reflexively, I back up.

He's shirtless and clad only in a pair of boxer briefs, all of that toned, olive skin on display. I feel my body react to the sight of him before my mind can catch up.

The king notices, and his gaze heats. "Provided, of course, that the same rules apply."

"What rules?" I ask, pretending that I don't feel the heat crawling up my cheeks.

"That I get to touch you while I answer them."

I narrow my gaze, still not making a move to put on the suit.

As we stare each other down, he drops his boxer briefs, and I get an eyeful of a very aroused king. He's not embarrassed in the least.

I am. Even after all that we've done together I'm still somewhat modest.

Leisurely he grabs his suit, taking his time to pull it on just so that he can toy with me a little longer. And then he's done changing, and I still haven't moved.

Seeing that I won't be joining him, he heads to the door, but then pauses when he gets there. "Serenity?"

I glance over at him.

"I was lying. You don't get a choice. I'll give you five minutes to change, and then whatever state of dress you're in, my men will bring you to me."

He's so lucky I don't have a gun.

FROM THE MOMENT I leave the back doors of the palace, I can feel Montes's eyes on me.

I scowl first at him, then at the guards that flank me.

I did change into the swimsuit he left for me. I'll give the king that much. Then I went into our closet and put on the most expensive gown I could find. Seed pearls are sewn into intricate designs across the bodice and down the sleeves.

I intend to ruin it in the salty water ahead of me.

Like I told him when we first met, I'm a vindictive bitch.

Not to mention that dresses like this one belong leagues under the sea.

The breeze lifts my gauzy skirts, like the wind wants to rub its phantom fingers over the material. It *is* lovely. That won't stop me from destroying it.

The king is thigh deep in the water, looking like some strange sea god as the waves roll in around him. His hair is swept back from his forehead, and all those fine muscles of his glisten in the sun. Even this far away, I can see him assessing my clothing. Whatever he's thinking, it brings a grin to his face. If I had to guess, I'd say my defiance amuses him.

"You got all dressed up for me," he says when I'm within hearing range. "I'm so honored."

My bare feet sink into the warm sand as I approach him. I don't bother lifting my skirts as the granules tangle in them.

"I'm beginning to believe you are genuinely suicidal," I say.

"You know me better than that," Montes admonishes.

"Do I? The evil king who laid down his arms to heal his people—if that is the man you are, then I don't in fact know you."

But I want to.

The realization comes as a shock, and not a welcome one. The king's seduced me once into forgetting that he was the enemy. If I'm not careful, he'll do it once more. And, unfortunately, I'm even more vulnerable this time around because my feelings for Montes haven't vanished.

A wicked man with a decent heart. That is the worst sort of combo. I have no defense against it.

Seawater begins to climb up my dress as the dry sand gives way to wet.

"Then it's my job to see to it that you do come to know me. Intimately, my queen."

Intimacy. It always is his endgame with me. I won't be able to avoid it.

I walk up to him, the saltwater rising up and up until it's nearly at my waist. My dark king watches me. He's enjoying this—my anger, his control.

"And what do I get out of that situation?" I ask.

If Montes is going to make my ignorance of current events a situation he can take advantage of, then I will use his desire to my benefit.

A wave crashes against us, the surf wrapping my dress around me.

"What does my vicious little wife want?"

"I'm not going to tell you," I say. "Not yet. Give me whatever it is I wish, and I'll give you intimacy."

A tradeoff—one not so different from the one we made when I was just an emissary.

He stares at me for a long time as the waves roll in around him, crashing against his back. I can't read him or the machinations of his twisted mind, but he's entertaining the thought, and that, at least, is something. To even consider what I proposed—

"Agreed."

I can't hide my surprise. The king must want me more desperately than I can imagine.

"We begin now," he says.

My small victory is only just beginning to sink in when his words register.

He closes the last of the distance between us and wraps an arm around my waist. I put my hands on the shoulders reflexively, about to push him away.

"Ah-ah-ah," he says. "You agreed to intimacy. Fight me on this, and you can forget about your pretty little request."

"I didn't mean *now*," I say.

"You never specified that. As far as I'm concerned, intimacy will be on my terms. Or, you can forget about your secretive wish and I will seduce you the old-fashioned way." Which might just be worse because I know myself well enough to understand with perfect clarity that he will pull me under all over again.

He knows he has me when I glare at thin.

"Now," he says, "put your legs around me."

This is absurd.

With a very obvious reluctance, I do so, giving him a not-so-subtle glare the entire time. His other hand cups me from below. He moves us into deeper water.

His eyes drop to my mouth. "Now your lips," he says.

This man is insufferable. Of course he would take complete advantage of his end of the deal.

I will let him have his moment. I'll get mine later.

I lean into him, brushing my lips against his. I can taste the salty ocean on his skin.

I assume that he'll find the kiss wanting—I'm not trying very hard to make it enjoyable—but he's patient, his lips barely moving beneath mine. And then, at some point, he takes over. His grip on me tightens, and the kiss becomes impassioned. Montes's fingers dig into my skin.

I don't know what to do with this fever. A part of me wants to fall just as deeply into it as Montes is, but another part of me wants to fight back, even though I just made a promise otherwise.

The king doesn't give me much of a choice. The arm cradling my back slides up, delving into my hair. I feel his tongue part my lips and then I'm not just tasting water and sea salt; I'm tasting this man's desperation and his toxic, undying love. How terrible that I'm the focus of it.

Finally, he ends the kiss. Both of us are breathing heavy when he pulls away to look at me. His thumb strokes one of my cheekbones. "I intend to do more," he says.

"I know you do." It is just like my husband to take full advantage of the situation.

His eyes drop back to my lips, which already feel swollen. And I see in his gaze the same thing I've been seeing in everyone else's—hope.

But he doesn't say it. He makes no mention of the fact that I can feel his need vibrating through him. He and I both know it's a weakness, and the king hasn't gotten to where he is today by being weak.

"I see you took great pains to destroy this dress," Montes says, moving one of his hands along the collar, his fingers brushing a string of the seed pearls and the tops of my breasts.

"Are you going to put me down?" I ask. He's still holding me to him, and my legs are still idiotically wrapped around his waist.

377

"You should never make deals without stipulations," he says. "For I intend to be intimate with you until you freely give into it."

"That's not going to happen," I say, more to convince myself than to convince him.

"It already has once before," he says, gripping me tightly as the ocean swirls around us. "It will again, my lady of lies."

What I hate most about his words is that he very well could be right. I'm not nearly as underhanded as he is. I can't mask my emotions, not the way some people can.

"I'm not the only one who agreed to a deal without stipulations," I say.

Mirth reenters his eyes. "It is my deepest wish that you will use me as I will use you."

An unbidden shiver runs down my spine at the king's plans for me—for us.

"Be careful what you wish for, Montes."

Because I will use him. Oh, how I will.

CHAPTER 14

SERENITY

"I HAVE SOMETHING to show you," the king says that evening.

I'm not a particularly big fan of Montes's surprises.

He leads me through the palace, and I catch another glimpse of his covered pictures. Our footsteps echo, along with those of our guards. What sort of madness must've overtaken the king for him to sequester himself in this lonely place?

We enter what looks like a small library. Montes presses a button embedded in the wall to our right. At the far end of the room, a screen descends from the ceiling. My eyes flick to him, but he gives me no clue as to what's going on in his twisted mind.

Montes begins to roll up his shirtsleeves with those deft fingers of his. I feel my heart break a little more, watching the careless action. He still does it.

His eyes lift to mine, and whatever he sees makes him pause. His gaze moves to his hands, then up again.

"*Nire bihotza …*"

Whatever he's about to say, I don't let him finish. I stride over to the screen, trying hard to ignore his presence.

It's impossible. It always has been. But it's worse now that the gulf between us is larger than it ever has been.

"You will want to sit for this," he says from behind me.

There's a couch at my back, but I make no move towards it.

"I'm fine."

I hear him cross the room. I badly want to swivel around and watch him, both because I don't trust him and because my eyes can't help but be pulled to every pleasing feature of his. But I keep my gaze steady on the screen.

A moment later, it flickers to life. It looks like a computer's home screen, though it's slightly different than what I'm used to. Montes flips through menu after menu until a photo fills the display.

The image has me sucking in a breath.

General Kline's hardened face stares back at me.

Only, it's *old*.

And now I do turn to face Montes. I can feel my eyes filling, filling. I don't want to cry.

"How?" The word is barely even a whisper.

"You'll see." He looks pointedly at the couch. "You really should sit."

He presses something, and I catch movement in the corner of my eye.

It's not a photo, I realize, dragging my attention away from the king and back to the screen as the image of the general comes to life.

It's a video.

All the air releases from my lungs.

The sight of it, and the realization that the general lived and died all while I slept, is enough to shake my resolve. Without thinking, I sink back into the couch.

I'm not sure I want to see this. Not sure I can bear it.

Behind me I hear the king's footfalls retreating, then the door opens and closes, and I'm alone with a ghost.

"Serenity—" The general rubs his face on the other side of the screen.

He's far away enough from the camera that I can see his leg jiggling. Decades may separate us in time, but I can tell I am not the only one nervous about this video.

He sighs, staring down at his thick, calloused hands. They've seen action. I can tell by how rough they are. Even as old as the general appears to be, he clearly hasn't stopped fighting, hasn't stopped living.

Good for him. I hope he fought death to the bitter end.

"I don't know where to start," he says, frowning. "This situation is all sorts of fucked-up. I don't know when—or if—you'll ever see this. I hope to God the bastard unplugs that damn machine and lets you live or die the way nature intended."

I smile sadly at that. And then his words register.

How did the general know I was in the Sleeper?

Why does Montes have this footage?

They're enemies. Bitter enemies.

"I am going to tell you a story, Serenity, and you're not going to like it." He sighs again, running his thumb over his knuckles. "Two years after you were last seen, I found out that you weren't dead. The official story had always been that you died of cancer."

The general clenches his jaw. "No one believed it, most assumed the king had killed you himself, though there were those who believed that it was a suicide or that you met a violent end at the hands of an enemy.

"There always had been conspiracy theories that you lived, but I never believed them. Not until he showed me ..." General Kline's voice is gravelly with age, but it's lost none of its strength, not even when he's grasping for words.

"I don't know how much you knew before you were ... put under. Right around that time, the Southern WUN rebelled, and the Resistance was a part of that rebellion."

I watch him in wonder. Nothing about this video makes much sense to me. Why he made it, why he's telling me this.

"I didn't make the call to rebel with the South Western territories, but I lived long enough to regret it anyway. The men who've secured control make Montes look like a decent guy, and you know how fucking hard that is to accomplish."

The general runs a hand over his thinning buzz-cut. "The king captured me a couple years after war re-broke out. I was sure I was going to be tortured. Not much love lost between the king and me. Instead he spins me this story about wanting my help, and he shows me something—something every bit as wrong as him."

General Kline grimaces and looks away. "You were so still." His voice lowers. "He had you in this capsule, what I later learned was a Sleeper. And you were alive—unconscious, but alive.

"I'll give the bastard this—he loves you. He's mad with it. Even now. Unfortunately for the rest of the world, I believe he's still willing to destroy anything and everything to get what he wants, and what he wants right now is a cure for that cancer of yours.

"He recruited me and the Resistance to work with him. And we have ever since."

I bring a fist to my mouth. I can't put my finger on what I'm feeling. Relief, definitely. Knowing that the Resistance eventually opposed the advisors that hijacked the WUN makes me feel less disoriented about my own allegiances. But I also feel something else, something that makes me mourn the general more than I already do.

Montes killed his son, and General Kline still found it within himself to work with the king because he knew it would help the greater good. When it came down to it, he was willing to make the same sacrifices he asked of me.

"The king is not a good man," the general continues, "but he's surrounded himself with good men, so there's that. And he's trying to do right. The fucker actually consults me for advice from time to time."

Kline leans forward. "Listen to me carefully, Serenity. The king might win the war, but I don't see him ending it. There is a distinction. That's why the war still rages on. All he knows is violence. It's a good skill for defeating the enemy, but it's useless once the fighting's over. And, Serenity, he knows nothing of peace."

He pauses for a long moment.

"You do. That's all your dad taught you in the bunker. As your general, I'm giving you one final task."

My body tenses, my pulse hiking at Kline's words. I already know whatever he tasks me with, I'll follow the order.

"If the world you wake up to is the one I fear it will be, then you and I both know your duties aren't over."

I already figured this out, and yet coming from the general, the prospect has my stomach clenching.

"You need to help him. Believe me, I know how wrong it is to ask this of you."

I'm sucking in air fast. My veins thrum as they get battle ready.

I understand him. The general and I might be more similar to one another than anyone else. Even my father. Even Montes.

"That man," he continues, "will eventually reconquer the world, and he's primed to ruin it over and over again.

"Serenity—" He levels his gaze on the lens, and I swear even though time and space separate us, he sees me.

"Don't let him."

CHAPTER 15

SERENITY

I SIT THERE long after the video ends.

The general sent me a message from beyond the grave. That's obviously what this is. The final meeting that we never had.

I rub my palms against my eyes, ignoring the wetness that seeps out from under them.

I can't even say what I'm sad about—that the general's gone, that I've been left behind, or that a burden the size of continents has fallen onto my shoulders.

When I exit the room, Montes waits for me.

It's almost implausible, that those two worked together.

The king gives away nothing as he takes me in. I'm sure my eyes are still red.

"Why did you show me that?" I ask, stepping into the hallway and closing the door behind me.

"Why wouldn't I?"

There are so many reasons. The general wasn't kind to the king in his video.

"You've watched it?"

Montes steps in close, that dark hair of his swept back from his face. His features look more regal than ever as he stares down at me.

"I have," the king says.

So he's heard the general's unflattering assessment of him, and he's also heard my final order. I'd be surprised that he showed me the video, except that it benefits Montes. The general essentially tasked me to remain close to the king.

"How long has he been dead?" I ask.

"Sixty, almost seventy years."

I reel from that information, but of course. The general was already old when I knew him. For him to live three extra decades is extraordinary.

"He cared for you," Montes says.

"I know that," I say quietly.

"Does the Resistance still exist?" I ask.

Montes studies me, then slowly shakes his head. "The group splintered into several other organizations about a decade after the general died."

And, given the king's timeline, that happened over half a century ago.

"So they no longer exist?"

"They no longer exist," he affirms.

Time is a spooky thing.

A world without the Resistance … it seems just as implausible as a world without the WUN or the king. They were once a great ally, and then a great enemy, but for them to no longer exist at all?

I've never considered the possibility.

Apparently, even deathless things can be killed.

THE KING LEADS me back down the hall.

"Where are we going?" I ask. My voice echoes in the cavernous space.

"Dinner."

I haven't thought about food in hours and hours, full as I was on this new world and all of its revelations.

I catch more glimpses of abandoned halls and closed doors as we wind our way through the palace. The door we eventually stop at looks like every other, but a faint smell of smoke clings to the area.

He opens it, and I catch a glimpse of the room beyond. A series of antlers decorate the walls. A billiard table sits in front of us, and farther into the room couches surround a grand fireplace. That same smoky smell lingers like a haze in the air.

"What is the name of this room?" I ask, taking it all in.

"The game room."

I smile at the name. "The king and his games," I muse, stepping inside. "I'm surprised the game room and the map room aren't the same." Lord knows the man finds war and strategy vastly entertaining.

Montes whispers in my hair, "Now's a good time to remember that you promised me intimacy. Keep talking as you are, and I will put that mouth to other uses."

Hand it to the king to think of the most creative way to shut me up.

"I see you're still fluent in threats," I say because I can't help myself.

"My queen," he says, stepping away, "it's only a threat if you don't want it to happen."

A part of me *does* in fact want it to happen. My heart's deepest wishes contradict all logic.

I move farther into the room. The space is an ode to highbrow masculinity.

"This place looks nothing like you," I say, taking in the antler chandelier high above us.

Montes heads towards a round table that looks like it was made for card games. He pulls out a chair and leans his hands heavily over the back of it. "I'm glad you think so," he says, his voice genuine. "It was made more for the men I host than for myself."

I run my hand over the green felt of the billiards table I pass as I drift towards him. "Why bring me here?"

"Why not?" he counters.

"I thought we were having dinner."

"We are." He indicates the seat he's pulled out. "Please."

Chivalry—it's just another one of the king's games.

I take a seat across from him because that's just what we do. Montes tries to seduce me with his usual bag of tricks, and I turn him down over and over again. The king's masochistic enough to enjoy the rejection, and I'm petty enough to enjoy dealing it out.

I look around me. This place might not be the worst room in the palace, but it leaves me feeling cold. I wonder what kind of man enjoys a room like this. I imagine he has thick fingers and a large gut. And he'd probably despise a woman like me.

The king takes the seat opposite me and leans back in it, taking in our surroundings just as I'm doing.

"My advisors used to love meeting in rooms like this," he says. "I believe all men want the best of both worlds—to be ruthless savages as well as cultivated thinkers. And that's what this room is, a place where those opposing desires meet."

My eyes move to the king. "Is that what you want?"

"*Nire bihotza*, that's what I *am*."

I suppress a shiver as I take in his dark beauty.

"And what do all women want?" I ask.

Montes appraises me from his seat. Abruptly, he stands and heads over to what looks like a wet bar. He extracts two tumblers and a bottle of amber liquid from beneath it, and sets them on the counter. Uncorking the lid, he begins to pour us drinks.

"It doesn't matter what all women want," he says, "because you are not all women."

"Then what am I?"

His eyes flick up to me. *Mine*, they seem to say.

He returns his attention to his work. "You're right," he says, moving the bottle of liquor from one glass to the other, "I do play games.

He corks the bottle. "That's all life really is—an elaborate game of luck and strategy."

This—*life*—doesn't feel like a game. This feels real and terrible.

He grabs the tumblers and bottle of spirits and heads back to our table. Coming to my side, he hands me one of the glasses.

I wrap my hand around it, feeling the warm brush of his fingers. He doesn't let go.

My gaze rises to meet his. I don't want to look at him, this man that takes up way too much space—in this room, in my head, in my heart.

Montes stares down at me like the universe begins and ends in my eyes.

Nothing can be simple with this man. Not even a drink. I feel that thick, cloying chemistry rise up out of the ether and wrap around us. It doesn't matter that the cancer is gone. With Montes it will always feel like my life has come right up to the edge of death.

He still hasn't given me the drink, and I look pointedly at it.

"You really have no idea what I'm capable of," he says.

The hairs on the nape of my neck stand. I would've said that if anyone knew what the king was capable of, it would be me. But I'm not going to contradict a bad man saying he's worse than I remember.

"And that has you worried," he continues. "It shouldn't. You know of my depravity, but I'm not talking about my evil side."

"Are you going to give me the drink?" I ask, exasperated.

"My lap," he says. He backs up, forcing me to release my hold on the tumbler. He settles back into his seat, his legs splayed out.

You've got to be kidding me.

I see the challenge twinkling in his eyes.

I get up and move over to him, positioning my legs on either side of his chair. Slowly I lower myself and straddle his lap. I take the tumbler out of his hand, and staring at him the entire time, I down its contents.

I hiss out a breath at the burn of it.

"You're wrong, you know," I say, taking the other glass from him and handing him my now empty one. I'm going to need the alcohol. This close to the king, I end up either wanting to fight him or fuck him.

He raises an eyebrow, setting the glass and the bottle of alcohol he holds on the table behind me.

"Your depravity is not what worries me." I've lived through that. That part of the king is predictable. "It's all the other parts of you that do."

That was, after all, what led me to sleep for a hundred years. That wicked soul of his still has a bit of goodness inside it, but when he applies it ... sometimes terrible things happen.

Montes brings his knuckles up and rubs them softly against my cheekbone. "That might be one of the nicest compliments you've given me."

I shake my head and take a sip of my stolen drink.

His fingers wrap around the tumbler and he pulls it from my lips. My hold on the glass is trapped beneath his as he brings it to his own lips, and together we tilt the alcohol into his mouth.

Heat burns low in my belly. I want to say it's from the alcohol, but I can't lie to myself. It's anticipation I feel.

A knock on the door interrupts the moment.

"Come in!" the king calls, not looking away from me.

The door to the room opens, and the king's soldiers come in with dinner.

I begin to get up.

The king's free hand clamps down on my hip. "Stay here."

"Every time you exert a little more intimacy, the interest on my end of the bargain goes up," I say.

"I don't care."

And here we are, locking horns once more.

Behind me I can hear the soldiers. They make quick work of setting out our dinner. I wait until their footsteps retreat. Until the door opens and then clicks shut behind them.

Until I'm alone with my monster once more.

I yank my captive hand out of his, along with the tumbler. I down the second glass's worth of alcohol, then set the empty cup on the table.

Readjusting my hips on the king's lap, I place my hands on his seatback, caging him in.

A very honest smile spreads across Montes's lips as I lean in, my hair dangling between us. "Is this what you want from me?" I ask. I'm tired of fighting every inch he takes, and I'm tired of him toying with me.

Now both of his hands grip my outer thighs, holding me in place. "No," he says.

He closes the last of the distance between our mouths and brushes his against mine. "I want everything you have to give," he murmurs. "And everything you don't."

He's taken my memories, my mortality, my freedom, even my death. I don't know how much more there even is to give.

CHAPTER 16

SERENITY

"YOU'RE DIFFERENT," I say.

I'm sprawled out on my stomach in front of the fireplace in the king's game room, a now half-empty bottle of what I learned is bourbon and two tumblers sitting in front of me.

We've long since finished eating dinner. I don't mention how odd it is to no longer feel nausea or pain when I eat and drink. I'd gotten so used to both that it's strange to not have to deal with them.

The king healed me.

Between the initial betrayal that landed me in the Sleeper and his more recent reluctance to wake me, I let myself forget that Montes spent the better part of a century curing me, far longer than most people even live.

I can't fathom that kind of perseverance. That kind of loyalty.

I watch him as he lights the fire. And I'm not liking where my eyes are landing. It starts with his hands. He has nice hands. Not too thick, not to boney, just ... deft. Capable.

My gaze moves up his forearms. Underneath his bronze skin, his muscles ripple.

It doesn't take long for my attention to move to other parts of him. His dark hair, which is just long enough to have fun with. His corded back, hidden beneath his shirt.

To my utter mortification, he turns then, catching me eyeing him like he was my dinner.

"I know," he says. "I've been telling you this."

I almost forget what I said in the first place.

That he's different.

That's why my emotions can't seem to land on anger. Every time they're about to, I learn something that shakes up my entire worldview.

"I don't trust your word, Montes," I say. "I trust your actions."

I watch as he finishes lighting the fire. Who would've known a man like the king could do anything so practical?

He straightens, dusting off the last of the bark from his hands and thighs. "And what do you think of my actions?"

My mouth tightens, and that's answer enough. I haven't seen him pull any of his usual, horrible stunts where people die and he gets everything he wants.

He heads back over to me and stretches himself at my side. "You're at a loss for words. How unusual."

I peer over at him. "I notice you're still good with them," I say, ignoring how that intense gaze of his is focused entirely on me. I lounge back on my forearms. "If I didn't think you were the devil, I'd say you'd be able to seduce even him."

"You give the oddest compliments," he says, his eyes pinching happily.

He's happy. I'm making him happy. And, for that matter, I'm happy.

Oh God.

Of all ironies to exist, we are the worst one.

I grab the bourbon bottle then, fumbling with the cap.

Montes takes it from me and pours a minuscule amount of alcohol into my cup. Really just a sip.

"I see you're still a control freak," I say. And now I'm just recovering from the fact that this is happening all over again. I'm getting sucked under, lost in his dark eyes and black heart. It takes so little.

Montes laughs, oblivious to the fact that while he maintains control, I'm losing it. "It just so happens that I actually care about how you're going to feel tomorrow. Shocking, I know."

Out of all the thing's he's said, I don't know why that one slips through my defenses.

But it does.

I cover the king's hand with my own, my fingers skimming across his skin. I've wanted to do that little action for a while now. It feels just as good as I knew it would.

Montes stares at the hand touching his.

Slowly, his eyes rise to mine. I see lifetimes and lifetimes of desires in those eyes. They all begin and end with me.

He never stopped loving me. That much is obvious from his expression.

And yet, the same man who stares at me in apparent adoration also shut me away in some desolate corner of this palace for decades and decades.

"When did you forget your feelings for me?" I ask.

His brows pinch, and his eyes grow distant. "When you live without someone for as long I have, love becomes this abstract concept, something you attach to a memory. And when memories are that old, they feel like dreams, and you wonder if any of it was real, or if your mind created it all."

It hurts to hear what he has to say, and yet, I understand, and that's the worst of all.

"Why didn't you just let me die?" He hadn't woken me, after all.

"I am over a hundred and fifty years old, and in all that time only a single woman has been able to move me." He looks over at me then. "You are mine. I would *never* let you die."

I should be horrified by the statement. Instead I feel the tempest of this man's love for me. It survived a century apart, it survived Montes himself, a man who shouldn't even be capable of something like love.

The king lifts himself up from where he lays and he leans over me, forcing me to swivel to face him until I've rolled onto my back.

And then he's there, his presence enveloping me.

I can see his intent in every line of his body, the firelight dancing along his skin.

It's happening all over again. This. Us.

It feels old and new all at once. Montes's intensity will always make me feel like intimacy is something I'm experiencing for the first time, and yet my body now knows his, as does my heart.

He dips his head, his hair trickling my cheeks. The moment those lips touch mine will be the moment of no return.

If I do this, I have to accept that my heart's going to get broken all over again. Because I can't become the king's lover once more without handing him my heart. And this time when Montes shatters my trust, I will be the fool who let it happen.

I'm making peace with that. The world is bigger than me and my heart, it's bigger than my life and the king's. It always has been.

"I'm going to trust you," I say softly, his mouth a hairsbreadth away from mine. "Even though you don't deserve it."

His intense face stares down at me. He presses a hand to my cheek. And then he kisses me.

Ash and fire, blood and death—it's all wrapped up into a single stroke of his lips. Both of us are burning, burning. This is heaven and hell.

His body lowers until it's pressed flush against my own. All the while, his mouth moves against mine. He savors everything about me, every scar, every wicked deed, everything remotely good. And I do the same.

He's not wholly evil. I've always known this about him, and yet it's a sweet lullaby to believe that he is.

My breathing picks up as he begins to run his hands up and down my sides.

Montes begins to move against me. My fingers find the edges of his shirt, and I'm yanking it up even as we continue to kiss.

He helps me out of it, and then it's his turn. His hand moves between us, unbuttoning the top of my fatigues.

Our movements become rushed at that point, our old, tormented souls desperate for each other.

Once we are both free of clothing, Montes settles himself between my legs. He bends his head down and kisses the skin between my breasts.

All those years ago, had I ever imagined people could be this way? That men were good for more than just friendship and fighting?

Montes's fingers slide into my hair, and he tilts my head to gaze down at me.

My broken, broken monster. I run my fingers down his cheek. He's just as beautiful as ever, but beneath his skin are the horrors of a century and a half of life. And not just any life, a tyrant king's life.

He turns his head to kiss my palm.

I know all about broken things. I came from a broken house, and a broken land full of broken people. I have a broken soul and a broken heart. This man doesn't know it, but all his cracks align with mine.

Montes shifts his hips, and I angle mine to meet his, and then he's entering me.

Bliss. I begin to close my eyes at the sensation of it.

"Look at me," he says.

My eyelids open, and I gaze up at the king as the two of us come together for the first time in over a century. It feels like it's just been days to me. I'm sure, to Montes, it feels like lifetimes.

We stay joined, unmoving, for several long seconds. I can feel his heartbeat pounding against my skin, he's so close to me.

"I imagined this moment countless times," he admits. "Feeling you around me again." He slides out slowly, then thrusts back in. "It never did you justice."

His lips brush my cheekbone. "You are better than any dream I had of us."

And we are worse than any of our nightmares. This conundrum we have.

It should never have been this way. The two of us have done so many unforgivable things. But at the end of the day, we are two wrongs that, together, make something right.

CHAPTER 17

SERENITY

I BLINK MY eyes open. Early morning sunlight streams in to the king's rooms.

I can't immediately figure out how I got here. Last night was a blur once we started drinking. I remember what I did with the king well enough for heat to spread to my cheeks. It's what happened after that's hard to remember.

At some point last night, after we'd dozed off, our bodies twined around each other, Montes had woken me up. After feeding me water and some nondescript pill, he led us back to our room.

I shift slightly, and the moment I do so, I feel coarse fabric rub against my skin. I finger the edge of the shirt I wear. It falls to my thighs.

Not mine.

I wear the king's shirt. I must've walked through the palace last night in it. I scrub a hand over my face and muffle a groan. That's not one of my prouder moments.

Whatever he gave me, it must've countered the alcohol because I feel decent. Not great, but decent.

I lay in bed staring out at the room, trying fruitlessly to fall back asleep.

Time and memory are a strange thing. The room I spent my wedding night in, as well as every piece of furniture inside it, are long gone. And yet, I swear it's as though no time has passed.

My head tilts to the side. It's not just the room that's the same. Déjà vu sweeps over me as I stare at the king's muscular back, not for the first time reveling in his masculine beauty.

A duplicate memory assaults my mind. That first morning I had looked over at the king, the light streaming in just like it is now.

It's all the same, and yet it's not.

I reach out and run my hand over his olive skin. That freckle of his is gone, the one I noticed the first time I woke up next to him. I wonder what injury got that one, that tiny freckle that brought me to this man at the beginning of it all. All signs of his mortality have been wiped away by the Sleeper.

He stirs beneath my hand.

I hadn't meant to wake him. I don't want him to wake. Not yet.

But what I want has little to do with the situation. He rolls over.

His eyes meet mine, and a lazy smile spreads across his face as he draws me to him.

He nuzzles my nose. "I dreamed of you and then I woke, and I realized it wasn't a dream after all." His words are sleep-roughened.

His voice, his touch, his expression … I'm remembering last night vividly.

The king must be too, because I see a flare of heat enter his features, and then he rolls us so that I'm on my back and he's covering me.

Almost immediately, my breathing picks up. The girl in me is embarrassed by it. I try to sit up, but Montes's hand presses against my sternum, pushing me back down as he begins to kiss between my breasts.

It doesn't end there.

The kisses continue, and he's dipping down, down …

He spreads my thighs apart. I'm about to push him away, when his lips press against my core.

My breath escapes me all at once.

He groans. "*Nire bihotza*, you taste the same as I remember."

Suddenly, I'm not so keen on pushing him away. And my embarrassment … It's still there, but it's taken a backseat to the more immediate sensations.

Montes wraps his arms under the backs of my thighs, pulling me even closer. His mouth is everywhere, and he's still just as good at this as I remember.

A small cry slips from me. I feel the breath of his husky laughter.

I'm climbing, climbing—and then it halts.

Montes releases my thighs, his body moving up mine. I don't have time to be disappointed; I feel the press of him against me as he slides in.

We stare at each other, twin points in the universe. I think I mean more to him than even I realize. He won't speak his thoughts, not a man like this, one who rarely lets himself get vulnerable. But I see them nonetheless, gleaming in the back of his eyes.

He captures my mouth, and I taste myself on his lips. It's wrong and it's right, it's dirty, it's pure—the king makes all my carefully crafted dichotomies disappear.

He pulls my hips close, deepening each stroke—

Oh God.

I break off the kiss. "Birth control," I rasp.

Birth control.

We forgot last night.

The king freezes, though he's practically trembling in an effort to hold back. We both are.

Montes leans his head against mine. "I have none."

None.

I think about what that means, how that changes my own plans. It doesn't—not really.

But shit, to do this knowingly …

"You are my wife," Montes says. "This is how it's meant to be—how it was always meant to be."

Neither of us has moved.

"I can't," I whisper quietly, divulging this weakness of mine. It might've been a century since he lost his child, but it's still fresh in my mind.

Montes searches my eyes, and something like realization, or wonder, subtly changes his expression. I can only imagine the strangeness of the situation from his perspective—his long lost wife's mind still lives in a past he's nearly forgotten.

"You don't want to carry our child, or you don't want to lose another one?" he asks.

My throat works. I look away.

I am no longer fearful of having the king's child.

I'm fearful for it.

Montes must see it in my expression, my mannerisms.

He lets go of one of my hips, relaxing his hold so that he can tilt my jaw until I meet his gaze.

"*Nire bihotza.*"

Those two words carry a world of meaning. It's a strange mixture of love, and hope, and all other sorts of beautifully heart-wrenching emotions. "This time would not be like the last," he says, and I can tell he means it.

"It can't be." My voice breaks as I speak.

It really can't be. I am becoming Montes, paranoid of losing everything that I love. Because I've lost so much.

His hand brushes my hair back. "It won't be."

I draw in a shuddering breath and shake off somberness that comes with remembering.

And then I'm the one that pulls him to me, pushing this forward.

I've always wanted my pound of flesh, and now I'm taking it.

CHAPTER 18

SERENITY

WE'RE BACK IN the Great Room, the king's mad walls hidden once more by large screens. And once more the space is filled with military officers. I intend to get to know each one, eventually. For now I have to hope that Montes's subjects respect him a whole lot more than the ones that filled his conference room a century ago.

In addition to the U-shaped table that takes over much of the space, there's now a smaller one that faces it, where the king and I sit.

I spend the first several hours of the day listening to officers discuss updates on the war and strategies they're implementing.

This world is strange. The moment I believe it's identical to the one I left, some tidbit filters in that has me second-guessing everything.

Eventually, however, a picture begins to stitch itself together. The world's population has been decimated by war and sickness. Efforts to clean radiation from the water and soil are ongoing. Not as many people are suffering from famine, but that's only because there are so few people left. Even the small annual outputs in the farming industry can sustain them. Aside from outright killing, cancer is the leading cause of death, though every once in a while the plague sweeps through and takes its place.

From what I understand, there are cures for many of the world's health issues, but there isn't enough money to make these cures widespread. The end result is a huge economic gap between the haves and have-nots. People are discontent. They know nothing but war and living on the edge.

I drum my fingers on the table as we hear yet another report from some lieutenant of some battalion on the state of his troops and the intel they've gathered on the enemy. I don't pretend to be the authority on anything, but if I had to guess, I'd say that these officers have been running in circles for as long as anyone can remember, discussing the same strategies, the same concerns, and applying the same answers they always have. And this entire time no one's realized that they need to derail themselves.

I stand, my chair scraping back as I do so. The sound echoes throughout the room, interrupting the speaker. The officer's voice dies away as dozens upon dozens of gazes move to me.

"Is war all we plan on talking about?"

These people don't understand. I can see it in their confused gazes. In a war council you talk about war.

I make eye contact with many of them. "War doesn't end war," I say. "Peace does."

I'm sure they think me an idiot. I'm saying nothing they don't already understand. But knowing something and framing the world through that lens are two very different things.

"You won't win this war by plotting ways to destroy the enemy—necessary though that might be," I say. "You'll win it by forging peace."

Again, I'm saying nothing new.

"Your Majesty, how do you suggest we forge peace?" One of the female officers asks this.

I glance down at the king. "You promised to give me whatever I asked for," I breathe.

His face wipes clean of all expression. He knows he's been had before I speak.

"I will campaign for it and break bread with whomever I must," I say to the room, though my eyes stay trained on the king. "And I will end this, once and for all."

THIS IS WHAT intimacy cost the king.

Power. Control.

He might have allowed me onto his war council, but I know with certainty Montes was never going to place me in a position of true power. Not when I'm so iconic. Not when a position like this often means capture or death.

So I'm carving the position out for myself.

That vein begins to pound in the king's temple as I hijack the meeting. It's not just anger I see rising to the surface. It's panic. The man who controls nearly everything is realizing he just bargained away something he shouldn't have.

I tear my gaze away from Montes to look out at the room. I can feel that wildness stirring beneath my veins, the same excitement that comes before battle. Only this time, it's so much sweeter because I'm solving a problem, not exacerbating it.

"The king will still lead all the current war efforts, but we will be incorporating my strategy into it," I say to the room.

I am no fool. I need Montes's expertise and knowledge. I just want to build my tactics on the foundation he's laid.

"I don't know how much you all know about my past," I say, moving around the table. I can feel the king's eyes like a brand on my back. "But before I slept, before I even married the king, I was a soldier, just like many of you. I was a soldier—and an emissary."

The people sitting in on this meeting look alive and attentive, when only minutes ago many wore bored, listless expressions.

"I was taught to fight, but I was groomed to negotiate."

I throw a glance back at Montes. His eyes burn with his fury and with something brighter, something much more honorable.

"Long ago, I forged a peace treaty with a hostile nation. I will do so again, and I won't give the representatives of the West a choice."

"You still haven't answered how you propose to go about attaining this." Heinrich says this. The grand marshal looks skeptical, as do many of the other men and women gathered here.

The true brilliance of this plan, and the ultimate irony, is that Montes had handed me the answer on a silver platter.

"I appear to already be a symbol of freedom to the people." I pace as I speak. "We are going to encourage that belief, and we're going to win the common people over. I am going to fight for them and speak for them until I become synonymous with victory, regardless of what nation they belong to."

I watch the officers faces as they mull this possibility over. Many appear unsure, but more appear intrigued.

"Ideology will win us this war," I say.

The room is quiet. I don't dare look back at Montes. All I can think is that he is indeed a changed man to have not intervened thus far.

"Whoever is in charge of coordinating the king's political maneuvers," I say, "I want you to schedule a series of meetings." My footfalls echo as I move to the center of the room. "I want to meet with every regional leader—especially those who have a history of disliking the king. Even those that belong to the Western United Nations. And I want to meet with the leaders of every grassroots organization and vigilante group."

Some people are writing furiously. Others are staring at me with bright eyes, and still others look grim. But no one, no one appears unengaged. That, if nothing else, is one accomplishment of this meeting. This struggle needs to mean something to people. And I bet it hasn't in quite some time.

"I plan on creating alliances with each and every one of these leaders."

Someone interrupts. "But what you're saying—some of these men and women are terrorists, most no better than the leaders of West."

I seek out the voice. I smile a little when my eyes find the officer. "I don't plan on catering to their demands. I'm going to convince them to get behind mine."

This lesson I learned from the king. When to compromise, and when not to. For all of Montes's terrible decisions, he's great at getting people to do his bidding without conceding anything himself.

I pause, my gaze sweeping over the men and women in the room. "And finally," I say, "I want to meet with the WUN's representatives—either directly or over video."

CHAPTER 19

SERENITY

"ARE YOU INSANE?"

I turn to face the king.

The last of the room's inhabitants have left, leaving me alone with Montes.

He leans against the double doors that lead out. Only a minute ago he'd been swapping some final comments with his officers. Now that everyone's gone, he's dropped any pretense that this was a joint decision. Though, technically, it was.

I walk over to him slowly. When I get close I say quite slowly, "Fuck. You." All my civility is gone.

He rears back just slightly, enough to let me know I surprised him.

Good. Finally I can let the full spectrum of my feelings show.

I'm one raw, savage girl, and he has *wronged* me.

"You selfish bastard," I continue. "You really thought I would just jump into bed with you without a damn good reason?"

His jaw tightens.

I've learned how to play the king's games, and now the player is getting played.

"You had something I wanted, and I had something you wanted." I am treading in very, very dangerous territory.

Montes hasn't spoken, but that vein in his temple throbs.

I move away from him. The screens have been rolled back up, and I can see all those conquered territories once more. The sight of them still disgusts me.

"You can have your intimacy and I can campaign for peace," I say, rotating to face him, "or it can all go away—the intimacy, the camaraderie—all of it. I will become the bane of your existence."

He doesn't react—not immediately. I feel something like energy gathering behind him.

When he finally begins to stalk towards me, I have to force myself to stay rooted where I am. There's a reason he's been the king for this long. His power moves with him, and right now it's intimidating the hell out of me.

He cocks his head, assessing me like a hunter does prey. "So my little wife decided to try her hand at strategy?" he says, his footsteps echoing through the room. "I am impressed."

I run my tongue over my teeth. Now it's my turn to stay quiet.

He squints at me. "What other schemes have you been up to?"

I look over at the bits and pieces of the maps that I can see. "You're not the one who should be worried about their spouse scheming."

He captures my jaw with his hand and peers into my eyes. I try to jerk away, but he won't release his hold.

His gaze searches mine. "You do have something else up your sleeve," he says.

I do.

I don't look away from him. I don't give him any sign at all on whether or not he's correct.

The air shifts, and I can't tell whether it's anger or passion that fills the room, only that I'm choking on it. Knowing us, it's probably both.

"If you're hiding something from me, I will find out." His voice is steady and quiet. Lethal. People die after hearing that tone.

"And if you're hiding something from me," I say, "then so will I."

His calculating eyes brighten, and a whisper of a smile crosses his face. He inclines his head.

He still grips my jaw. "So my vicious little wife plans on ending the war. And she wants power and autonomy along the way," he says, still studying me.

Yes. That's precisely what I want.

The king taps my jaw with his index finger. His vein is still pounding, and his features are just as uncompromising as I've ever seen them.

He pulls my head in close. "I will keep my end of the bargain."

He kisses me then, a punishing, severe kiss that lets me know just how displeased he is. I revel in it.

As his mouth moves against mine, his fingers drop to the waistband of my pants. He flicks the top button open.

I pull away from the kiss with a gasp, grabbing his wrist.

In response, he presses me closer. "This is what I get for your little stunt. You promised me intimacy," he breathes against my cheek. "I want it."

Surprise and a deviant sort of satisfaction unfurl within me. I enjoy sex, and I enjoy an angry king.

I release his wrist and let his hand dip down into my pants. I gasp again as he begins to work me.

"My vicious little wife, you do me proud," he says. "I should've known." He dips his mouth close to my ear. "You've gotten a taste for playing games after all."

And so I have.

"I WANT TO see it," I say that evening.

The ocean breeze blows my hair. We're back outside, finishing dinner as the sun sets.

The scenery of this place always gets to me. Oranges and reds shimmer off the sea's surface. It's breathtaking, and looking at it, you would never know that across those waters people are suffering.

"See what?" Montes says, lounging back in his seat.

"The place where I slept," I say.

It might be my imagination, but out here in the fading light, the king looks distinctly uncomfortable. He appraises me from across the table.

I wish I could appear just as relaxed as the king, but nothing will loosen my limbs. The thought of seeing my resting place has me wound up.

"Alright, my queen," he finally says.

Just like that. No fighting, no wrangling, no demanding on his part. The fact that he doesn't try to get something from me in return makes me more nervous, not less.

His chair scrapes back and he stands.

Now. He's planning on showing me right now.

I hide my surprise. I hadn't imagined the gratification would be this immediate.

I rise to my feet, dropping my napkin on the table.

Montes comes to my side, and, placing a hand on the small of my back, he steers me forward. We cross the gardens and head back into the towering building.

So it's inside the very palace itself. Part of me had imagined that I would be sleeping in some sort of crypt on the palace grounds, far away from the living.

He leads me down several hallways, and with each turn the setting becomes increasingly familiar.

We end up right back in front of our bedroom.

I raise an eyebrow.

I can't tell whether this is a trick or not.

Montes smiles at my expression, his eyes gleaming. "You thought I'd keep you anywhere else?" he asks as he opens the door.

"You kept me in your room?"

For a second, I imagine myself laid out on the bed, stiff like the dead, before I remember that I was encased in the Sleeper.

"Not exactly." He leaves me at the threshold, and I watch him, puzzled, as he heads to a large framed painting.

A familiar unease washes through me, one that's reserved for unnatural things. There is something frightening about watching this beautiful man share his dark secret. Something *wrong*.

Montes turns back to look at me as he swings the frame back.

My lips part with realization. There's another room. A hidden one. Now that the painting is moved aside, I make out a door camouflaged with the rest of the wall. A discreet thumbprint scanner is embedded next to it.

The king presses his thumb against it, and a second later it blinks green. With a pressurized hiss, the door unlocks. He holds it open for me.

What lies beyond is cloaked in shadow. Suddenly I'm not so sure how much I want to see where I rested. What's to stop the king from forcing me back into the machine?

He notices my hesitation. "Serenity, you don't have to see this."

My paranoia dissipates. If he wanted to put me under, he'd need a doctor and a sedative, and I know he has neither.

I still don't trust him. Not with everything.

I brush past him as I step into the corridor. Around us, dim lights flicker to life. I press my palm against one of the walls and turn my head, following the line of the surface until it disappears into darkness. I squint as my eyes make out …

Windows. Windows that look into the palace's rooms.

"What is this place?" I ask.

Montes's voice comes from behind me. "A king always has secrets. Secrets and enemies. This is where I used come to be alone with you."

The hairs on the back of my neck rise.

"Come." He places a hand against my back and leads me once more.

As we walk, more lights flicker on.

"There's another entrance to this passageway through my office. We believe that's the one your abductors used."

I'm not paying much attention to him, too busy staring in horror at room after room that we pass. He spies on people.

"This is wrong," I murmur.

"It's saved my life several times."

I come to a stop as a thought hits me. "These are one-sided mirrors, aren't they?"

"They are."

There was a mirror in the room I stayed in. Twice I had heard a thump on the other side of it. Twice its surface vibrated.

"You watched me." Horror bleeds to anger.

He appears amused. "When I wanted to see you, I visited." The light glints off his dark eyes. "I did not watch you from behind glass."

I search his face, looking for the lie in his words. I see only honesty. I believe him, and yet …

"Who else has access to these passageways?"

"No one. I alone come and go through them."

I try not to think about the fact that Montes was the only company I kept while I slept.

"Well," I say, "we know at least half a dozen other men know of this place."

"*Knew*," he corrects. "I believe you took care of that situation."

It's an unwelcome reminder. I now have their faces to add to the ghosts that haunt me.

"Someone else was back here. I heard them while I was in my room."

Montes glances down at me, his brows knitted. He searches my face. He must see that I'm not lying because a frown forms. "I will look into it."

I appreciate this about the king. He takes my concerns seriously.

We walk for a while, the passageway twisting every so often as it maneuvers around rooms. The corridor widens as we get to a set of thick double doors.

The king leans away from me to scan his thumb once more. I hear the latch click as it unlocks, and then Montes is opening one of the doors.

My earlier skittishness returns as I stare down at the massive marble staircase that descends away from me and the giant pylons that hold up the roof high above. I lived under the earth for years when the bunker was my home. I should have no qualms about entering this room. But my blood and my bones know this place and they recoil from it.

My curiosity overrides superstition. I take the steps one at a time. My gaze moves up to the domed ceiling that arcs high overhead. Embedded into it, seemingly at random are indigo and gold tiles. Our colors.

The pattern of tiles is not random, I realize after a moment. The fresco has been made to reflect the night sky, and each gold tile represents a star, every cluster a constellation.

The sight makes me press my lips together. He gave me the sky.

The columns that rise around me seem even larger the farther down I descend. They look luminescent under the dim glow of lights.

I can feel the king watching me, this man who attended to me while I was down here. Here he could control me, here he could have me to himself. Here I could be whatever he needed me to be, and I didn't have the agency to defy him.

I glance back up at him.

Those eyes of his are wary, like I am the dangerous one.

I return my attention to the room as I reach the bottom of the stairs. I take in more marble and tile features. A small pool captures my attention. It gleams under the light of this place.

And then my eyes fall on the Sleeper.

Only, it doesn't look like a Sleeper. It looks like a sarcophagus, something rich people used to be buried in long before my time or the king's. Sheathed in gold, intricate flowering designs cover it. A marble bench rests before it, presumably where the king sat when he visited.

I'm drawn towards it, both horrified and mesmerized.

The place is an ode to me, to us. Even the pool of water and the way it dances along the walls reminds me of the first time Montes held me in his arms.

Montes did this all for me. My gaze sweeps over our opulent surroundings.

No, not for me. All of this is much too grand. He did this for *himself*.

"It's a temple," I say. A temple made to honor me.

But this place does me no honor, and I deserve none. I'm a soldier, a killer, a captive queen. But not a god.

His shoes begin to click as he walks down the stairs, the noise echoing throughout the chamber.

"Are you frightened?" he asks.

I don't bother answering.

Instead I reach out a hand and run it along the surface of the Sleeper. This is where I stayed in a state of stasis for lifetime upon lifetime, years stacked one on top of the other. People were borne from the earth and drawn back into it, and still I remained.

Montes's footfalls draw closer, and I'm so very aware of him. My muscles tense when he stops only a handful of feet away.

"Tell me something that makes this better," I say.

"I love you."

Now I rotate to face him.

I regret it immediately.

Montes's eyes go soft.

Will I ever get used to that face wearing that expression when he looks at me? Your nightmares aren't supposed to make you feel cherished.

His eyes rise above me to the room beyond. "This is the evidence of my love. I know you find it terrible, possibly even unethical, but I never saw it that way."

What's worse than not understanding the king is understanding him. Every time I do, I forgive him a little more.

His eyes return to me. "We've been here long enough. Come, my vicious little wife, there's much to do."

And together we return to the land of the living.

CHAPTER 20

SERENITY

THE NEXT MORNING I'm set up in an office, three of the king's officers surrounding me.

Montes left me at the room's entrance, giving the door a parting glance. "The people you need to speak to are inside," he said mysteriously. And then, without elaborating, he stalked away.

I stared at his retreating form, wondering if somehow this was a trick.

But now that I sit with the closest thing the king has to advisors on the dainty couches in the room, I get the impression that the only trick being played is on my archaic notions of the king.

Because by all appearances, he's fully equipped me to see my war strategy through.

The three individuals that sit around me must've been soldiers at one point. That's the only thing that can account for the hard twinkle in their eyes and the strong set of their shoulders. And now they wait for me to make demands of them.

I sit forward on the couch, arms braced against my legs, hands clasped between them. "I need to devise a plan to meet with our enemies, our allies, and anyone else in between who you consider important enough to speak with." I say, getting right to business.

Across from me, one of the officers pulls a file from the briefcase she carries and drops it onto the coffee table resting between us. "We've already put together a list of leaders you'll want to speak with," she says, tapping on the folder. "We've also included a tentative schedule of meetings that can be immediately arranged with your approval.

"We can fly in some of these individuals as early as the end of the week, but there will be quite a few that you'll have to visit yourself."

I pick the folder up and begin thumbing through it. It's dizzying, the amount of information inside. Schedules, names, titles. Most of them mean nothing to me. I've had a hundred years to lose all frame of reference.

I set the file down at my side. In most ways, I am utterly inadequate for this position. I have a century's worth of complicated political history I need to catch up on, a century's worth of knowledge that my allies and my enemies already know about. Ignorance is a great tool to be exploited.

My jaw hardens. I've already been exploited quite enough for one lifetime.

So I begin to look for one of the few names I do know. When I've skimmed through the entire file and don't see it, I set the folder aside.

"What about the First Free Men?"

"What about them?" one of the male officers asks.

I meet his eyes. "Why are they not listed among the groups I'm to speak with?"

"With all due respect Your Majesty, this was the group that broke into this very palace and stole you. The king has issued a KOS—kill on sight—order for their leader."

Montes hasn't lost every last bit of his depravity after all.

I lean forward. "The First Free Men were powerful enough to find the resting place of a woman who was believed to be dead. And they were powerful enough to smuggle her out of the king's palace."

The three officers are quiet, and I'm sure they know what my intentions are.

"Set up a video call with their leader. I want to speak with him or her as soon as possible."

"Your Majesty, Styx Garcia is in hiding," the female officer says. "There's no guarantee we will be able to get communication through to him. And even if we do, there's no guarantee that he will agree to the call."

I am the hundred year old queen he almost captured, the woman that slaughtered six of his men.

I look her square in the eye. "He'll take the call."

IT TAKES FIVE hours for Styx to agree to the call.

At 2:00 a.m. this evening—*morning*, technically—I'll be on the phone with the man who failed to abduct me.

I considered telling the king about it as soon as the call was confirmed. Montes is perhaps the most ruthless strategist that I know, and I can't help but want to pick his brain for advice.

The petty part of me also wants him to know I've openly defied his orders by arranging this.

But, in the end, I decided against it.

Someone else will likely tell him, and soon, but it won't be me.

I lay in bed for a long time, my eyes peeled open. Montes's arm is wrapped around my midsection, my backside pressed tightly to his front. He holds me like nothing short of another apocalypse will tear us apart. It's both comforting and confusing. I don't know how to deal with all these conflicted emotions I feel.

I wait until his arm slips from around my waist and he flips over before I slip out of bed.

I dress quietly, and then, ever so softly, I head out of the room. Even doing this is a risk. Montes used to have a habit of waking up in the middle of the night. He might still.

I can only hope his sleeping habits have changed since we've been apart.

I make my way through the empty corridors of the palace, towards the office I was given.

I flick the lights on and sit down behind my desk. I begin to flip through some of the documents I requested on the First Free Men. There isn't much on them. It makes me think they're even more powerful than everyone believes.

Their leader is Styx Garcia, a thirty-six-year-old combat veteran who fought for the West before being honorably discharged. A photo of him is paper-clipped to the documents.

I pull it out and frown. He would be handsome except that his face is a patchwork of scars. They slice down his eyebrows and cheeks, drag across his nose, and claw upwards along the edge of his jaw.

The sight of all that mottled tissue has me touching my own scar.

And in the midst of it all, he's got a pair of dark, soulless eyes. Just like the king's.

I set the picture aside and read his biography in the file. Like me, he was born and raised in the northern territory of the Western United Nations. He spent over ten years on active duty; far, far longer than the amount of time I had.

At some point after that, though the document doesn't say exactly when, he established the First Free Men. He's been building it ever since.

I close the folder. By all indications, this man is just as power-hungry as all the other corrupt men I've met throughout this war. What I don't understand is why the West would work with him at all.

Somewhere inside the palace, a grandfather clock tolls twice, my cue to leave my office.

My footfalls echo throughout the cavernous halls. This place rubs me the wrong way. There is a hollowness to the corridors that only exaggerates just how empty the place is, and yet I swear I can feel the weight of unseen eyes on me as I head to the king's study.

His room is one of the few in the palace that has absolute privacy—or so I was told. We'll see soon enough.

The king was right yesterday. I am keeping something else from him, something he would rebel against if he knew.

When I reach the door to his office, I press my thumb to the fingerprint scanner. It blinks green like I knew it would, then I'm inside.

I slide behind the king's desk and pull out the set of instructions on setting up a video call from one of the royal computers. It takes five minutes to execute, and then I dial the number Styx's men gave to me.

Almost immediately the call goes through.

The large monitor in front of me flickers, and then I'm staring at Styx Garcia in the flesh.

I appraise this man with narrowed eyes. He has even more scars than his photo let on, none quite so gruesome as the one that's split open one of his nostrils.

This is a very dangerous man. It makes my decision to escape his men that much wiser.

"Your Majesty," he says, dipping his head. "It's an honor."

I nod back to him. "Styx."

He peers up at me as he straightens. His fascination is plain. And on his face, it's an unsettling look.

"Your men woke me," I say. It's as good enough conversation starter as any.

He inclines his head.

My gaze moves behind him, to a stark, dimly-lit cement room. "How did you find me?" I ask.

His eyes are too bright. "With difficulty."

My lips thin. "It's two a.m. here. I want to go to bed. Please give me the straight answer."

He flashes me a distinctly unsettling smile. It has my trigger finger twitching.

"Perhaps if you visit me," he says, "I will tell you in person."

"Oh, for fuck's sake," I say.

This conversation won't get anywhere if he keeps answering like this.

"Are you aware that there's a bounty on my head?" he asks, straightening in his seat.

"I am."

"And still you called," he says.

"And you answered," I reply.

"Why wouldn't I?" He smiles pleasantly, the action contorting all his facial scars. "You're the supposedly dead queen that's come back to life. And you somehow managed to kill half a dozen of my best men when you escaped." His gaze shifts subtly. I can tell he's taking in the hair that spills over my shoulder. "I was very eager to speak with you.

"But," he continues, "that doesn't explain why *you're* calling *me*." He tilts his head, the gesture almost mocking. "Tell me, does the dear King of the East know you're talking to me?"

I tighten my jaw. Styx is just another man that likes to toy with people.

"Tell me about your connection to the West," I say instead.

Styx throws his hands out. "There it is," he says. "Oh, you *are* transparent. You want my connection to the West."

"I do." I don't bother denying it.

"Why?"

"I need to speak with the representatives," I say. "Privately."

Styx folds his hands over his chest. "You don't want your king to know." He says it with such satisfaction. "What makes you think I have the clearance to speak with the representatives?"

"You were going to hand me over to them. Your men said so themselves."

"Hmmm ..." He appraises me.

He sits forward suddenly. "You know, I always believed." He stares at my scar with fascination. When his eyes meet mine again, an unnatural amount of fervor has entered them. "A woman like you can't be killed so easily."

"You have no idea who I am," I say.

Even though a screen and countless miles separate us, my hand is itching for my gun. I don't like the way he looks at me.

To be fair, I don't like the way most people look at me, but the way Styx does it ... In another situation it would've earned him a bullet. It might still, depending on the way the future unfolds.

"I expected you to be violent, Serenity Freeman."

"*Lazuli*," I correct.

"But to watch you gun my men down in seconds ..." He continues on as though I hadn't spoken. "That, that surprised me."

When I don't react, he raises his eyebrows. "You did realize there was someone watching on the other end of that camera, didn't you?"

He's asking the wrong questions and giving the wrong kind of answers to mine. I don't know what I was expecting from him, or what the correct response to my call would be, but this isn't it.

He wants to understand me, I can tell. Capturing me would've allowed him all the time in the world for that, but he's trying to make up for it now.

"I never planned on handing you over to them—the West." The look in his face as he says that ... this man better tread carefully, he's setting all sorts of violent tendencies in me.

He leans back in his seat, watching me, his eyes unblinking. "So, how are you faring?" he asks.

I have a sick, sick admirer in Garcia. I assumed he'd be angry that I killed off his men.

"I'm fine." That was my last attempt at being civil. Entertaining this man's version of small talk is almost more than I can bear.

"What does your husband think of your being awake?" A flash of something enters his eyes. I would say it was jealousy, but I've seen that emotion so rarely that I doubt my own intuition. Not to mention that I don't know this man. To be jealous of a stranger receiving attention from her husband ...

He makes Montes seem normal, and that is an impressive feat.

"We are not friends, Garcia," I say, my voice hard. "You are the leader of the terrorist group that attempted to capture me. Save the personal questions for men who must answer to you."

His jaw tightens, and his gaze flicks off screen. He's the only person I can see in the room, but I bet there are other people behind the camera, people that just overheard their leader get slighted by me.

"Do you know how much money and resources went into finding and retrieving you?" he hisses. This is the first glimpse I've gotten of the real Styx Garcia. "You wouldn't be awake to sit here and insult me if it weren't for me."

The last of my patience evaporates.

I lean forward. "You are a fool if you think you're going to get either my pity or my gratitude." I'm just about done with this man. "You kidnapped me, I killed your men. I don't regret it, and I imagine if our roles were reversed, a man like you would feel the same way." Someone who collects scars the way Styx does has a taste for violence.

"Now," I say, "we can continue with the slights, or we can discuss how we're going to end this war."

That has him straightening. I see the fist that he rests on his desk tighten and then release.

I take a deep breath. "I want to work with you, Garcia, but what I really need is someone who has an in with the West. Do you have that in?"

He folds his hands and taps his two pointer fingers against his chin as he studies me.

"Yes," he finally says.

"I need to speak with them. Can you help me arrange that?"

Another pause. Then, "Yes—for a price."

405

CHAPTER 21

SERENITY

WE TALK FOR an hour. Unfortunately even by the time I end the call, that sickening shine in Garcia's eyes still hasn't waned.

Working with him might be a mistake.

I shut everything down and return it where I found it.

I sit back in the king's chair and bring my folded hands to my lips, musing on the situation I'm creating for myself.

I run my hands through my hair. If the king finds out everything I intend … he might very well change his mind and shove me back in that Sleeper. I don't fear that nearly as much as I fear my plan will fail and the world will bear the fallout from it.

I stand and push the chair in.

I'm halfway to the door when a thought catches me off guard. I pause mid-step.

Slowly, I turn. My eyes land on the large gilded frame that hangs on the back wall of the king's study. I remember something Montes told me, something about a second entrance to my crypt.

I might very well be staring at that second entrance right now.

Hesitantly, I head towards the back of the room and touch the expansive painting. My fingertips run over the brushstrokes before wrapping around the edges of the frame.

I give it a swift tug, but the added force isn't necessary. It swings open with ease.

Just like the other painting, a door and a thumbprint scanner rest behind this one.

This is the second entrance to my crypt, the one the First Free Men came through.

Out of curiosity, I press my thumb to the fingerprint scanner. It's worked once before. I wait an agonizing several seconds, and then …

A green light blinks, and the door hisses as it unlocks, swinging inwards.

The king authorized me to enter his secret passages. It makes sense; if the palace is ever under fire, this might be our best chance at escape. The king and I have already lived through one instance where I was locked out from such a passage.

Still, to give me access to areas where I cannot be watched … my obsessive husband has surprised me.

I step through, shutting the door behind me.

I look down the corridor. The hall stretches out on either side, descending into the darkness beyond the motion activated lights. I begin heading back towards our room.

My footsteps falter as I pass by the first one-way mirror. It's unnerving to think that the king could just stand here and watch someone go about their business without them knowing. I understand his motives, but it's eerie and invasive nonetheless.

I begin to move again, passing several more rooms, each one dark. Eventually, I pass a room whose lights are still on. Without meaning to, I pause and survey it. What I see has me stepping up to the window.

A gun rests on the bed. That alone is eye-catching enough for me to give this room a second look. If only there were a way in. I could use a gun. Any weapon, really. I don't trust Montes, or this place, or these people. It's nothing personal— well, excepting Montes, of course. I was raised to mistrust my surroundings.

I force myself to step away from the window and resume walking. I can't shake my unease. It's this place. The king's madness and depravity is all concentrated here. It's messing with my mind.

My eyes drift down the hall, towards the lights that continue on into the distance.

Lights in the distance … that's not right. The only time they come on is when they're motion activated. And then it hits me.

Shit.

I'm not alone.

I HEAD TOWARDS the illumination. Even if I were the type to hide, it would be pointless. The lights are convenient breadcrumbs for either Montes or myself to follow.

Ahead of me, the hallway is abandoned. But it veers sharply to the right, where the light appears to continue on. That's where the king will be—if, of course, he's still in the passageway.

I pass the double doors that lead to the crypt I was kept in, and I have to steel myself against the warm burn of anger it evokes. My shoes click loudly against the stone. Montes must hear me.

Once I round the corner, I see a figure peering into one of the rooms, his back to me.

I halt in my tracks.

His hair's too short to be Montes.

The king was wrong. He's not the only one who can access these passageways. And now I'm facing a stranger unarmed.

Beyond the man, the overhead lights trail off into darkness.

"*Serenity.*"

A chill runs down my spine.

I know that voice. I'd know it from anywhere.

But … it's impossible. The man last drew breath a hundred years ago.

The figure swivels around.

My eyes take in the slight build, the brown eyes, the skin that's every bit as tan as Montes's. The dark hair that's shorter than I remember it. And finally, that face I hated so much.

My ears didn't deceive me.

Marco, the king's oldest friend and advisor, is alive.

CHAPTER 22

SERENITY

THE KING BROUGHT him back to life while he let me waste away.

The anger churning through me sharpens.

My hands fist, and I begin stalking towards him.

Sensing my violent intentions, Marco puts a hand up. "Whoa, whoa, whoa."

I don't let that stop me. As soon as I'm within swinging range, I lunge for him.

He catches me around the midsection before I can land a blow, pinning my arms to my sides.

I thrash against him. "You fucking murderer! Why did he let you live?"

Gone is the composed leader I've been for the last hour. I'm back to being an angry, lost girl.

"Stop. Serenity," Marco says. "Please. Stop."

To hear that asshole's voice ... I'm seeing red.

What I really need is a gun. Any gun—

Something about Marco's tone has me redirecting my thoughts. Something ... not right.

I seek out his eyes. He's not looking at me the way he used to, like I was just a thorn in his side.

And the way he said my name a few seconds ago ... it's too familiar.

"Let me go," I say.

"Not if you're going to hit me again."

I struggle futilely against him. He's still staring at me, and it's setting off all sorts of unwelcome reactions.

The worst thing the king could do was immortalize me. I'm quickly finding I don't react well to the attention and the adoration.

And that's what I see in Marco's eyes. Adoration.

It shouldn't be there. We hate each other, and unlike the king, there is nothing else to our relationship beyond that.

Marco adjusts his hold on me. He pulls me in close, until our chests are flush against each other.

I bring my knee up, and he only just manages to pivot out of the way. "Jesus. Stop." He shakes me a little. "Serenity, I am not going to hurt you."

It's almost laughable that he thinks I'm the one worried about getting hurt.

"You killed my father, you bastard." I'm shaking I'm so angry.

It had been justice enough to know that Marco had taken his own life with the same hand and the same gun that killed my father.

But now that he's so obviously cheated death and lived while I slept ... the anger resurges.

"I am not the same man," Marco says.

This again.

"Screw you and Montes and all of your fucking excuses!" I spit out, jerking against the hands hold me captive.

I'm tired of evil, immortal people telling me this. Like they're recovering psychopaths. Time can change a person, but it cannot erase their past.

"You will *always* be the person that took the first man I ever loved."

I swear in Marco's eyes I see some mixture of surprise and devastation. "Montes never told me Marco did that."

I rear back, some sick combination of confusion and disgust filling my veins.

He continues on before I can get a word in edgewise. "I'm sorry for you and your father, Serenity, but I am not that man.

"You see," he says carefully, "I am his clone."

THE REVELATION IS enough to make me pause.

"You're a ... ?"

I can't even say it.

Back in the time I left, clones were the things of science fiction, along with flying cars and humanoid robots.

"I am a copy of him," Marco says. "Same DNA. It's no different than twins, except that we never shared a womb and we weren't born at the same time—obviously."

He says this all as if his existence is somehow normal.

"You're not Marco?" I say.

It's still not registering

"I *am* Marco," he says, "just not the one you knew. I was named after him."

Suddenly all the pieces come crashing together. No technology could revive the king's brain-dead friend. So instead Montes made a copy of Marco to keep him company through the years.

That is the saddest thing I might've heard yet.

Marco must sense that I'm no longer a threat. His hold loosens on me.

I stagger away from him.

A *clone*. I'm still wrapping my mind around it.

I look everywhere but Marco, and that's when I remember where exactly we are.

"You were the one watching me," I say as the realization dawns on me. The noises I heard. I'd been in lingerie one of those instances.

My hands clench. "You *saw* me," I accuse, my face flushing. I'm ready to throttle him, the pervert.

He doesn't bother denying it. "I wasn't *trying* to watch you undress."

I narrow my eyes at him.

That *voice*. I can't help but hate it. I recognize that this is not the same man who crossed me years ago. That doesn't change the fact that everything about him reminds me of the pain his twin put me through.

"I just wanted to see you, and the king forbid me from meeting you until he'd broken the news. So I came here," he continues. "He doesn't know that I can access these passageways."

"Why did he hide you from me?" I ask. I'm still angry and more than a little spooked, but I also feel an unbidden wave of pity. Pity for this creature who will always live in his predecessor's shadow, and pity for a king who must create his

409

own friends because no decent human would truly and willingly become that man's companion.

Marco glances at my hands, which are still balled into fists. "I imagine he was trying to prevent this from happening."

The strangeness of the situation is beginning to wear off. I glance beyond Marco's shoulder.

"The king's room is at the end of this hall," Marco says.

I return my attention to him.

"That's what you're looking for, right?" he adds. "You came from the king's study."

It's not good that he knows that. The whole point of being in Montes's office was to draw as few eyes as possible. And now Marco's dangling that piece of information in my face. And I don't know whether he intends to blackmail me with it, but I've had enough of men trying to play me.

I lean forward, momentarily setting aside my disgust for the face this man wears. "I don't know who you are, but I will tell you this: if you threaten me in any way, you will regret it."

I've scared a lot of people in my time. Marco does not appear to be one such person.

He inclines his head. "I won't tell the king you were in here if you don't tell him I was."

I stare at Marco for a long moment, then I turn on my heel and leave.

"I'll be seeing you around, Serenity," he calls to my back.

"For your sake," I say, not bothering to face him, "you better hope not."

CHAPTER 23

SERENITY

I PUSH THE framed painting softly open. Beyond it, the king's bedroom is dark. As quietly as I can, I slip through the doorway and close the door and painting behind me. They shut silently.

I tiptoe across the room, removing my clothing as I go.

It's still odd, sleeping skin on skin with the king. I enjoy it, much to my shame. Too many years spent without touching of any kind has left me famished for it. And Montes is all too ready to provide the contact I desire.

I pull back the sheets and slide into bed.

Several seconds later, the king's arm drapes around my waist and he pulls my back to his front.

"I am king for a reason," he whispers into my hair.

Immediately, I stiffen in his arms. He doesn't sound sleepy. Not even a little bit.

He brushes my hair away from my ear, his touch proprietary. "I will let you have your secrets," he says, "so long as they serve me." His hand skims down my arm, then lays flat against my stomach. Idly, his thumb begins rubbing circles into my skin. "The moment they no longer do, my queen, bargain or no, I'll strip you of your power." His hand continues down my outer thigh. "And I will enjoy it."

"And how will you know when my secrets no longer serve you?" I ask.

He presses me even tighter into him, until his body feels like a cage and I am his prisoner.

He's quiet for several seconds, but not because he's at a loss for words. He's toying with me again. I can tell by the way he's still calmly stroking my skin, building up the tension between us.

"You are not the only one with secrets, my queen."

"Secrets like Marco?"

The king falls silent again, and now I do get the impression he's at a loss for words.

"You met Marco?" His tone changes from threatening to shocked.

"Unfortunately," I say.

He rolls me onto my back so that he can study me. The moon's bright enough to cast him in shades of blue.

"I was going to tell you," he says.

"Just as you were going to wake me from the Sleeper?" I say, the comment biting.

He moves a wisp of my hair from my face. "I felt it better to wait until you had adjusted. You hate me enough as it is. Marco was supposed to make himself scarce."

"Well, Marco has his own ideas."

Now that neither of us is pretending to be asleep, Montes strokes his finger down my nose and across my lips. "What, I wonder, did my vicious queen do to him?"

His hand finds my own and he rubs his thumb over my knuckles. Even in the dim light of the room I can see the smile he cracks when he feels the scabbed skin. "I'm disappointed, Serenity. Here I was hoping someone else might get a taste of your wrath for once."

"I thought you had brought him back to life," I whisper.

He stares at me for a long time. "You thought I had woken him and left you asleep," he clarifies.

It's times like this that I seriously question whether Montes was ever human. It's not just his lifespan that's unnatural. It's the way he sees right through people.

"And you thought I'd be mad when I found out," I say.

"You're not," he says it like a realization.

"I was. And then Marco explained it all to me." Now I'm just disturbed.

The king brushes a kiss along my knuckles. "Your reactions always were so refreshing. How I've forgotten." He presses my hand to his face. "How I wish to remember."

Now I look away. Even though fighting this magnetism we have is futile, I won't go quietly into it.

"Give me your eyes, Serenity." The pitch of his voice gets lower, more intimate.

Reluctantly, I do so.

His gaze holds a million things. He was never one to unburden himself with his feelings, but his eyes rarely lie.

Endless want. Hope. Grief. Love. Regret. Disbelief. I see it all.

I could resist him when he had no weaknesses, when I thought he was pure evil.

But this strange, time-wearied Montes who has lived a lonely existence for lifetimes and lifetimes, I can't fight him. I can't fight this. Us.

"I love you," he says.

"*Montes*," I say. It sounds more like a plea.

He lowers himself to his forearms, his bare skin meeting mine. "I love you," he repeats. "I know that makes you uncomfortable. It's made me uncomfortable for longer than I care to admit. But now I've gone a hundred years without saying those three words, and I've nearly lost the only person I want to say them to. So you're just going to have to listen to them."

He's now petting my hair, combing it back with his fingers. Now all I can see of his face are the sharp slashes of his jaw and the shadows that caress his high cheekbones.

He's terrible and magnificent. My monster. We are the two loneliest people in the universe, but we have each other.

"Tell me you love me," he whispers.

I shake my head. "Never."

"Liar," he says softly, a small smile playing on his lips.

"I told you a long time ago you'd never get all of me," I say.

He reaches over to the side of the bed and clicks on a side lamp. "And I have always told you that you're mine," he says, returning his attention to me. "Every bit of you. Even your love."

He bends down, and I think he's going to kiss me. Instead, he murmurs, "We're going to play a little game."

His lips skim my jaw. "I'll ask you a question, and you'll either answer it honestly, or you'll touch me where I tell you to."

It's an iteration of the drinking game we used to play. Only this one has managed to incorporate our deal into the mix.

"I don't want to play any of your games."

He shifts against me, and I feel it all the way down to my core. The bastard knows what he's doing.

"Too bad," he says.

I exhale. "I really pissed you off today, didn't I?" I can't help the satisfaction unfurls at that thought.

"You caught me off guard," he corrects. "And I'm glad for it. My wife should be my equal. But now, you'll pay for it."

"The king and his games," I murmur.

"Do you love me?"

He wastes no time diving right in.

I lift my chin. "Pass."

He grins, his white, white teeth striking in the dim light. "Kiss me."

I stare at him for a beat, and then, gently, I pull his head down and brush my lips against his. It's over before it's even begun. Not that I'm trying to get out of anything. I know how this ends.

"When was the first time you felt something other than hate for me?" he asks.

It's my turn to play with his hair. I rub a stray lock between my fingers. Montes unconsciously leans into the touch.

"That evening you brought me to the pool house," I say.

"I remember that," he says, gazing down at me fondly.

His memory has aged a hundred years. Will that ever stop shocking me?

"You skipped my turn," I say.

"Tonight you don't get to ask questions," he says.

I frown, digging my hand deeper into his hair. "Is it wrong for me to want to know who you've become?" I ask.

I'm getting better at manipulating words to my will. It's what my father was so good at. What Montes is so good at. And it was almost inevitable that I would pick up this habit.

He's quiet. But then, "Forever is a long time to spend by yourself."

He's terrible and terrifying and monstrous and so ill deserving of any goodness, and yet—

And yet my broken heart bleeds for him. I have the strangest urge to run my hand down his back and comfort him as neither of us has been comforted in a long, long time.

"That's the last question you get to ask," he says quietly.

I don't fight him. His past sounds like a dark place, one he doesn't want to dwell on. I know all about terrible memories; I won't force him to divulge his.

"Do you love me?" he asks, drawing me back to the present.

My brows knit. "I already answered this question."

"And I am asking it again."

I really shouldn't feel bad for him. He's up to his usual tricks.

"Pass," I say.

Another triumphant smile. "Touch me."

I place my hand at the juncture between his jaw and his neck. My thumbs stroke the rough skin of his cheek.

"Lower," he says gruffly.

413

My touch moves down the column of his throat until it rests over his heart. *My* heart. The one he stole all those years ago and now holds captive. I can hear it beating. Long after I die, it will continue to beat in his chest.

His nostrils flare as some emotion overtakes him. "Lower."

I feel my cheeks heat. I know what he wants. I run my hand down his chest, over the ridges of his abs, and I wrap my hand around him.

This is so lewd.

"Happy?" I ask, raising my eyebrows.

"I will be," he says.

I release him. "Next question."

I can tell I'm amusing him. It's no one feature of his, but all of them—the wry twist of his lips, the shine of his eyes, the way his hands dig themselves deeper into my flesh.

"What is your favorite thing about me?"

I search his face. "It's always about you, isn't it?" I don't bother to add any sting to my words. I'm not trying to wound him. But I've taken it upon myself to dole out all the hard truths that Montes needs to hear.

"You follow through on most of your threats," I throw out.

He shakes his head, his eyes glimmering. "I know for a fact you like certain parts of my anatomy better than my follow through. But I'll let that one slide."

How magnanimous of him.

"Do you love me?" he asks.

I give him a hard look. "You're not going to wear me down on this one, Montes. Pass."

His hair tickles mine as his lips brush against the skin of my cheek. "Touch yourself."

"*Montes.*" It's one thing to be intimate with the king. Quite another to do this in front of him.

"We can stop," he says. "Tomorrow morning when we sit in on the meeting with my officers, you can inform them that you are no longer willing to follow through with your role in our war efforts. I will not stop you. I want my queen safe above all else."

He's goading me, but at this point I can't tell if he wants me to dissolve all my plans or to continue doing things for him that make me distinctly uncomfortable.

Knowing how twisted he is, I'd say he be happy with either outcome.

I glare at him and reach between us, placing my hand between my thighs.

He tears his gaze from me and his eyes dip down. I hear his breath hitch.

A moment later he extricates one of his hands from my hair and uses it to cover mine. Wrapping his fingers around mine, he begins to move my hand up and down, up and down.

Now it's my breath that's picking up; I'm inhaling and exhaling in stuttering gasps.

Montes watches the way he works me. The whole thing is embarrassing and exhilarating all at once. If only I could have one uncomplicated emotion towards this man. Everything he does, everything we do, is mired in complexities.

His gaze returns to mine. "Are you not having fun?"

"*Fun,*" I say, my voice breathy, "is not a word I would use to describe your games."

He leans in close, dipping both his fingers and mine into my core. "Then you're not doing it right."

Montes adjusts himself, so that he's right at my entrance. "The game's over—for now."

He takes my lips then. The kiss is rough, almost abrasive. As he does so, he thrusts into me. I'm gasping into his mouth, arching into him.

Gone is the girl who hated the king. Gone is the man who took everything from her. When we are like this, we're just two lost souls coming together.

He moves against me and I stare up at him. I bring a hand up and caress his cheek, swallowing as I do so.

"We lost a child."

I don't know why I say it. Maybe I'm feeling oddly vulnerable with him. Despite everything he's done to me, this man has buried himself in the deepest recesses of my heart. And we've been through things together, things that pulled us close when they should've torn us apart.

Whatever mood rode us a minute ago, it's been replaced with something far heavier.

"We will make another," he says.

It's such an enchanting thought. To create rather than destroy. That even we are capable of it.

I pull him closer. He moves gently against me, his strokes slow and tender.

There is no question how he feels about me. I'm the one holding back, refusing to give in fully. And I don't want to. God, I don't.

After we finish, the king tucks me against him, our skin is damp with sweat. He places a soft kiss behind my ear. "Tonight, you win my queen."

I haven't won anything. I can see that even if I hold out, there is no way this ends well for me.

Montes shifts, clasping me in close. "Now," he says, "sleep."

And I do.

CHAPTER 24

SERENITY

"YOUR ITINERARY IS complete." The officers I met with yesterday are now discussing the peace talks I will be having with the heads of several of the king's territories.

None of them have broached the subject of last night's call with Styx. I doubt they will either.

Montes sits next to me in the conference room, his presence dominating the space.

His leg and arm brush against mine as he settles in, and I can't help but think it's deliberate. That everything about him is deliberate. And these two casual touches serve to remind me that this monstrous man can make my heart flutter even when his attention is focused elsewhere.

The king doesn't need to be here, but of course he wants to be. If he can micromanage every step of this process, he will.

I grab the document set out in front of me in an effort to refocus my energy and attention.

"The queen's tour of the East will begin next week," one of the officers says.

I lean back in my chair, flipping through the itinerary. We're starting my campaign for peace in the East. I have to win my own people over before I can consider swaying the people of the West.

Next to me, Montes reads through his copy, pinching his lower lip. One of his legs begins to jiggle. I take the subtle hints of his aggravation as a good sign.

"How did you pick these places?" I ask.

"Your Majesty, we followed your requests—these are the biggest cities or the ones that have the least loyalty to the East."

Most of the city names I recognize, but some are new. When I get the chance, I will discreetly find a map and plot these places out.

The king closes his copy and tosses it onto the table. "No."

We all look to him.

"Half of your scheduled visits are in wild country. We've long since established that we can't secure many of these locations."

"Yes," the female officers says slowly, "the lack of royal presence in those regions is partially responsible for their fractured loyalty."

"These are exactly the places I want to be," I say.

The king stands and shrugs off his jacket. "No," he repeats.

"Yes," I say just as forcefully.

The vein in his temple pounds. "Goddamnit, Serenity, don't test me."

I stand, my chair screeching as it slides back. "Or what?"

"Or I will lock you in a fucking room where no one can hurt you."

I take a step towards him. "Are you threatening to put me back in the Sleeper?" I ask, my voice low.

He flinches. So the bastard has some remorse after all.

"I'm not going back in there, Montes. Not ever."

"You've said that before, and then you went back into the Sleeper." He says it like I chose to return to the coffin. Like I wasn't forced into it by his own hand.

I step in close. "How *dare* you. Consider yourself lucky I'm unarmed."

Before the discussion can devolve any further, the door to the conference room opens, and Marco strides in.

Marco the clone. My skin still prickles at the thought.

It takes him only a handful of seconds to register that he came in at a bad time.

He puts his hands up. "By all means, don't stop on my account."

I turn back to the king. "So now that I know about Marco, he's allowed to join us?"

"He's my right-hand." To Marco, the king says, "Have you seen the itinerary?"

"I have," Marco says, taking a seat near us and kicking his heels up on the table.

That little gesture makes me like him just a smidgen more.

Montes folds his arms across his chest, widening his stance. "And?"

Marco drums his fingers against the armrests. "And I think it's a good idea."

I try not to smile. I fail.

The king throws me a lethal glare.

"It's not safe," he says, returning his attention to Marco.

"You act like you're not married to the most dangerous one of us," Marco says. He juts his chin towards me. "She woke up in a car full of armed men. When she was retrieved, they were all dead."

I appreciate Marco sticking up for me. He has no reason to. I haven't been kind to him.

The king frowns at his friend.

"Montes," I say, "let me do this."

He fully turns his body towards me, and his nostrils flare as he tries to tamp down his emotions. When I look into his eyes, all I see is agony. I'm someone he loves, someone he respects, someone he cannot bear to lose under any circumstances.

I take it all in, and then I do something uncharacteristic.

I place a hand against the side of his face, in full view of Marco and the officers.

"We need to end this war," I say. "I have a good chance of doing just that, but only if you let me try. I'm not going to hold our deal over your head, and I'm not going to force your hand."—*Yet.*—"I'm asking as your wife and your queen to allow this to happen."

He looks moved, but I'm not sure.

"It can be how it was before," I say quietly. "We rule well together. Let me do this. Nothing bad will happen."

Montes grimaces then closes his eyes. He places his hand over mine, trapping it against his cheek.

"I always knew you'd make a good queen," he murmurs.

He opens his eyes. "Fine. I'll agree to it, provided there's extra security."

I nod, my expression passive. But there's nothing passive about how I feel. The king doesn't readily make concessions, and I don't usually get my way without threatening someone.

The two of us are making progress.

"Serenity?" he says quietly. "You still need to work on your lies. You and I both know that with diplomacy, something bad always happens."

CHAPTER 25

SERENITY

AFTER THE MEETING, the king takes me to the palace gardens.

Montes and his gardens.

The plants that grow here are far different than the ones in Geneva and his other palace in the United Kingdom. They're greener, brighter, more exotic.

"Do you still have your palace in England?" I ask.

Montes glances over me. "I do. Would you like to go back at some point?"

What an absurd question. That place was just another example of the king's decadence, another example that I was just a brightly colored bird in a gilded cage.

My retort is on the tip of my tongue. Only … I find I can't say the words. That terrible home of the king's might be one of the few things about this world that I remember. People need familiarity. I need to feel like I'm not swept out at sea.

"Maybe," I say.

I look over at Montes as he squints off at the sea.

His handsome face is made all the more so by how well I know it. His palaces are not the only thing I am familiar with.

I could reach out and touch his face. I want to. I want to run my finger down the delicate folds of skin that pinch when he squints. For the longest time I've held back my affection. I thought it important to punish the king for being the king and me for wanting him.

I reach out and ever so softly run two fingers along the skin near one of his eyes, smoothing out the crinkled skin.

He turns into my touch. I can tell without speaking that he's surprised and pleased. Both of us stop walking.

My fingers move to his mouth. I trace the edges of his lips. "What happened to all your wickedness?" Even that has changed. Oddly enough, I miss it.

He gives me a what-can-you-do-about-it look. "I got old."

"You don't look old," I say.

We haven't discussed it, but the king must still be taking his pills. He looks identical to how I've always remembered him.

And he hasn't tried to make me take any; it's just further proof that he's not nearly so wicked as he used to be.

Montes touches my temple. "I got old here." His fingers move to the skin over my heart. "And here."

I understand that. Age isn't just a number; it's also how you feel.

Montes takes my hand and tucks it into the crook of his arm. When I try to tug it away, he holds fast to it.

The age-old battle of chivalry versus my stubbornness.

He wins this round.

We resume walking.

"Marco likes you," he says, absently running his thumb over my knuckles.

I don't bother hiding a very real shiver. "That's regrettable."

"It is."

There's something about the way Montes says this that has me glancing over. I can't put my finger on it—

"What do you think of the future?" he asks, changing the course of my thoughts.

"It's disorienting," I say, "though not as different as I imagined it would be. The world does not appear to have made any progress."

"War does that," Montes says. "The only thing that ever gets more impressive are the new ways we find to kill each other."

That's more than a little disheartening to hear.

"In what ways has the weaponry gotten worse?" I ask.

"Mmm," he muses, staring out at the horizon, "I'll let you figure that one out on your own. It's probably in my best interest not to have you knowing about all the new and ingenious ways you can kill me."

I smile at that.

I'm so fucked-up. *We* are so fucked-up.

"So you still think I might kill you?" I ask.

The king stops again.

This moment is too much. The warm, bright sun, the sweet smelling flowers, the sound of the surf crashing. The way the king's staring at me. I am getting gluttonous off of it.

"That's the beauty of being with you," he says. "I never quite know."

A WEEK GOES by in a blur as I prepare for my tour of the East. A tour that begins tomorrow, when we leave for Giza, the first of nearly two dozen cities I'll be visiting.

Most of my time has been spent locked up in meetings. And when I'm not listening to other people discuss world affairs, I'm locking myself away to study them.

The king, being who he is, has decided to hole himself up along with me. He's fashioned himself into my personal mentor.

I pity the world; under his instructions, it will undoubtedly burn.

"So there are thirteen representatives," I say, leaning back in my office chair. Spread out in front of me are photos of a dozen men, each with their name neatly typed beneath.

"Correct," Montes says, "thirteen representatives, but we only know the identities of twelve."

Montes sits on the desk itself, his legs splayed wide, his shirt sleeves rolled up. After being here for over a week, I've noticed he alternates between fatigues and suits. Today is a suit day.

I pull my attention back to the matter at hand. Thirteen representatives, but only twelve identities. That's more than a little odd. "Why don't we know the identity of the thirteenth representative?"

Montes reaches forward and hooks his hand underneath my seat. With surprisingly little effort, he drags my chair forward until I'm sitting between those splayed legs of his.

My eyes are level with his crotch.

"Forcing me to look at your dick is not going to help me learn who the representatives are," I say.

"You could always sit on my lap," he offers.

"Pass," I say absently, my gaze drifting back to the photos. I stand to get a closer look at them.

As I do so, Montes's arms go around my waist. I'm now trapped in his embrace.

"Had I realized how fun diplomacy was," he says, his lips brushing against my hair, "I would've taken it up much sooner."

"No you wouldn't have," I murmur, my attention still locked on the photos. I move them around, reading the various names, and trying to memorize the faces that go with each. "You're an asshole, and assholes don't give a shit about peace."

One of his hands falls heavily over mine, trapping it to the desk.

"You think that what I've done is bad?" he says, his voice deadly quiet.

I don't have to look at him to know I've offended him.

"I will tell you a story about what I've seen in the West," he says. "Girls sold as slaves—some younger than ten. Those went for the highest price. Women taken from their families, raped and sold then raped some more."

Now he has my attention.

"Don't blame me for being hesitant to forge peace between my land and theirs," he finishes.

I feel a muscle jump in my cheek.

I search his eyes. "Is that true? What you just said?"

He frowns, his eyes dropping to my mouth. "It is."

Women and children enslaved? Raped? This is not the West I knew. This is every one of my nightmares made flesh.

"Why?" I know Montes can see the horror on my face.

"You've asked me the same thing," he says. "Power can twist people."

He wraps his hand around mine and begins moving my fingers over the photos. "Gregory Mercer, Ara Istanbulian, Alan Lee, Jeremy Mansfield, Tito Petros, ..." He lists off all twelve of them.

"Each has his own brand of evil. Alan—" Montes moves our hands over the photo of a man with dark hair and beady eyes, "coordinates disappearances. People of importance he doesn't want alive—sometimes he has them killed outright, sometimes he detains them for torture, and sometimes he sends them to state-funded concentration camps."

A lock of hair falls into his eyes as the king speaks.

"Jeremy—" Our hands travel to a photo of a man with pale, blotchy skin and a weak chin, "was the mind behind the development of these concentration camps. All that radiation has led to widespread disease and genetic mutations. He decided some WUN citizens were too sick or unsightly to be left amongst the regular population, so they were moved. It's a great place to send anyone who doesn't fall into line as they should. It also incentivizes violent individuals to join the West's military. If they're stationed at one of these camps, well, anything really goes."

I'm about to ask him why he hasn't taken action sooner. Why evil like this hasn't been stamped out. But before I can, he moves on.

"Tito." Our hands trail to a man I recognize, the Eastern politician who always reminded me of a walrus. He was one of the king's former advisors. "This man knew exactly where all my research laboratories were, as well as my military outposts and warehouses. The WUN had them bombed almost immediately after I placed you in the Sleeper. Then they hit the East's hospitals."

I can understand bombing military outposts and warehouses. I can even understand wiping out laboratories.

But hospitals?

The West has thrown any sort of code of ethics out the window if they're hitting hospitals.

"Ronaldo," the king continues, moving our hands again. "You remember him, don't you?"

God help me, I do.

Once upon a time I'd saved him from death only to find out he was the advisor who'd sanctioned the atomic bombs dropped on the WUN.

I nod.

"As soon as he traded alliances, he was back to his old tricks. He dropped a handful of bombs on the biggest, most successful cities in the East. The damage was so disastrous that many of the cities have not been rebuilt."

His hand moves on. "Gregory sanctioned human trafficking, and he personally has close to a hundred slaves—"

"*Enough*," I say, pulling my hand from the king's.

I'm going to be sick. How does evil get concentrated like this?

Bombed hospitals, slavery, concentration camps—this is ghastly even by my standards.

Beyond my horror is that roaring monster inside me. The one that loves the taste of blood and vengeance.

Already I can feel my hands aching for necks to squeeze and my knuckles for skin to split. I will get my day, I vow it to myself.

Montes turns me in his arms so that we're staring at each other. "You asked me why the thirteenth representative doesn't show himself. The truth is, I don't know. But if I had to guess, I'd say it's because he's either hiding from his enemies—or lying amongst them."

I take that in.

"How haven't you managed to kill them yet?" I ask. That's what the king was good at, after all. Slaughter. And he had so many decades to eliminate these men.

Montes absently plays with a strand of my hair. "You kill one, they elect another." He smooths my hair back in place. "This wouldn't be a problem if all thirteen representatives gathered together—I could wipe them out all at once. But they don't. And if you can't kill them simultaneously, it's not worth the effort."

I return my attention to the photos.

"What *would* cause them all to gather?" I muse aloud, my fingers tilting one of the images to better see the representative.

My hand stills as the answer comes to me.

Slowly my eyes return to the king.

He already knows, I can tell. I say it anyway.

"Victory."

CHAPTER 26

SERENITY

THAT EVENING, THE officers gather in the large dining room for a goodbye dinner. The atmosphere feels celebratory, like they already know I'll accomplish what I set out to do.

I'm not so certain.

I lean back in my chair and finger the velvet tablecloth. It's worn. I don't know how long it takes to age material, but I would guess years, maybe decades if it's well cared for. It makes me wonder about that dress I wore when I so carelessly ran into the sea. It makes me wonder about every grand detail of the king's lifestyle.

I've made a lot of assumptions, about Montes and everyone else. In the past, they've been founded, but I no longer know whether they are or not.

My eyes move across the table I sit at. It's round, which means I get a good view of everyone. And they are all watching me, though some are more discrete than others. There's an energy to the room, and excitement, and I know I'm responsible for it. The dead queen's come back to end war once and for all.

They believe in me far more than I do.

There's no magic to this. In fact, chances are, someone will bury a knife in my back before I'm even halfway through visiting countries. That's what happens to powerful, dangerous people. They lead very short lives.

A heavy arm brushes my back. I glance first at the hand draped over my seatback, then its owner.

Montes is casually talking to Marco, who's seated on his other side.

The soft lighting gentles the king's features. I find my breath catches as I look at him.

He breaks conversation to turn to me. "My queen is quiet," he says softly so that only I hear. "Never a good thing."

"I have nothing to say."

Montes contemplates me. Beyond him I feel Marco's eyes on me as well.

The king stands, his chair scraping behind him. He reaches a hand to me.

I inhale sharply as I stare at Montes's hand.

I am a stranger to this world, this future I must live in. I don't know what to talk about, because I know nothing of this world. And I want to save it, I do, but I don't know how to be a part of it.

Montes figured that out all with a single look, and he's giving me an out.

The entire room's attention focuses on us.

I take the king's hand and I stand.

I can leave. Montes is willing to cut this dinner short. I can see as much in his expression. But I'm not going to run from these people just because I find these types of gatherings uncomfortable and I feel a little lost.

So instead I squeeze the king's hand and then turn to the officers seated around the table. "Tomorrow we begin what will hopefully be the end of this war." That earns a few claps and a couple of whoops from the dinner guests.

I can feel the king's assessing eyes on me; I sense his curiosity. He likes my spontaneity.

"Many of you are used to fighting," I say. "I know that I am."

The king squeezes the hand he still holds.

"But I don't want to spend the rest of my days watching young men die."

The evening's lightness dries up in the room.

"I want to see them grow old, and fat—I want to see men fat because there is so much food to go around."

Several officers nod at that. As I gaze out at their somber faces, I realize that these are my people. A hundred years ago I couldn't relate to the men and women the king surrounded himself with. These men and women I can.

Change is possible.

I pick up my wine glass. "A toast to peace."

I meet the king's mesmerized gaze. A small smile creeps along his face.

People raise their glasses. "To peace!"

AFTER DINNER, WHILE people are moving into the adjoining room to drink and chat, I slip away. I'm sure my exit gains some attention. Once I made my toast and sat back down, I had more interested guests eager to talk to me than I knew what to do with.

It's for that very reason that I take my leave early.

At the end of the day, I am a solitary thing. I'm not sure if this is the result of circumstance, or if I would've been this way had war never altered my life.

As soon as the dining room doors close behind me, the tinkling glasses and jovial conversations cut off.

I head through the cavernous palace, my steps echoing. I pass the massive entry hall, with its long entryway and towering columns, and keep going.

Down the corridors, all those sheets still cover most of the royal paintings. It's vaguely irritating. Why put a picture up at all if it's just going to get covered?

I don't know where I'm headed; I have no place in mind. I just want to keep moving. And the more I walk, the more I notice how much of the walls are covered up.

Whether it's curiosity or irritation that halts my steps, I can't be sure, but I stop in front of a section of wall partially covered by velvet drop cloths.

I reach out, towards the material.

It only seems like a bad idea at the very last second, when I've already bunched the velvet up into my fist. By then, gravity has taken over. The fabric slides off the frame.

A young Marco stares back at me from inside the frame. It's a formal photo, one where he's posed rigidly in a uniform. He can't be more than fourteen or fifteen years old. He has a wispy mustache boys at that age get.

I take a step back. It's hard to look at Marco as a boy. I don't associate his cruelty with this version of him.

I glance down the corridor, noticing over half a dozen similarly covered frames.

Surely they are not all photos of Marco? Not that I would put it past the king. He's obsessive with his affection.

I move to another covered frame and tug the cloth off of it. It's another of Marco, this one when he's older. In it, he and the king are clasping shoulders, laughing at something together.

I move on. My heels click against the floor as I stride down the hall.

This time when I pull down the velvet covering, I'm not prepared.

What lies beneath it has me recoiling.

The person I'm staring at is me.

Only, it's *not*.

It can't be. For one thing, I'm posing in a huge fucker of a dress. I'd knock someone out sooner than I would put that thing on. And I would've remembered it if I'd worn it. I mean, the thing's practically as big as a tank.

For another thing, my scar is gone.

I walk several paces down the hall and pull off another sheet of material.

There I am again, this time as a young teenager. I can't be older than thirteen or fourteen.

And I'm not alone in the photo either.

My arm is slung around the neck of an equally young boy.

But not just any boy. A cloned one.

Marco.

CHAPTER 27

SERENITY

I TAKE A shaky step back.

Oh God, what is this?

"Her name was Trinity."

I startle at the voice. When I swing around, Marco is watching me. His eyes drift to the wall.

My pulse is in my ears. I can hear my own blood whooshing through my veins.

I place a hand to my temple. "Are you saying—?"

"He couldn't bear waking you, so he cloned you," Marco finishes for me.

It takes several seconds to process his words.

"Montes cloned … *me*?" The proof is hanging on the wall, but I don't want to believe it.

Marco steps up to the photo.

My chest is rising and falling faster and faster. "Why would he do that?" I ask.

"Marco. Serenity." That powerful, ageless voice. It's wiped out cities, ordered countless deaths, whispered sweet platitudes in my ear. It's fooled me into loving it.

I stiffen when I hear it.

He cloned me.

It doesn't take long for shock to slide to anger.

I spin to face the king. "You did this?"

The king strides towards us, his eyes taking in the framed photos.

The bastard wouldn't wake me up, but he'd make a copy of me.

I back up when I realize he wants to eliminate the distance between us. "Stay away from me," I warn.

"Marco, leave us," he says as he continues to stride forward.

Marco hesitates, earning an arched brow from Montes. With one last, long look at me, the king's right-hand turns on his heel and leaves.

Montes steps into my personal space, and even when I cock my arm, he doesn't stand down. Instead he lets me throw my punch, but only so that he can catch my fist.

I growl my frustration, trying to tug my hand out of his grasp. "Let me go, you bastard."

"Not until I explain."

I keep yanking on my arm. "I'm tired of your explanations," I say between gritted teeth.

What I don't say is that something in me is broken and bleeding. Something that no Sleeper can heal. I force back a sob.

When he still doesn't let go, I bring my knee up to his crotch. He swivels out of the way.

Now he's mad, his features taut with his anger. He thrusts my body back up against the wall, the force of it making the frames shiver. His hand is at my throat. "Listen to me," he growls.

"Fuck. You." I don't want to listen. I want to bathe in the horror of this moment because this is the Montes that I remember.

"That was forty years ago," he says as though he can read my mind.

"And let me guess," I say. "You're a changed man."

His vein throbs.

Hit the nail right on the head with that one.

"Where is she now?" I ask.

The king's face closes down.

Dead.

I can read that much off of him. For however long she lived, she no longer does.

Goosebumps break out along my skin. It's equally disturbing to think that my clone both lived and died while I slept. And for all the king's unnatural technology, he wasn't able to save her.

"What did you do to her?" I say.

This psycho.

He grimaces. "I didn't *do* anything to her, Serenity. Or can you not tell that from the photos?"

I close my eyes because I can't bear to gaze into his dark, anguished ones. I don't want to know if he loved her. Not on top of all the deception and pain he's given me.

"Why not just wake me up?" I ask. My heart is primed for breaking. I really know nothing but destructive love. So he can tell me whatever pretty words he thinks are going to soothe me, but I doubt there will be any to make this better.

He gives my neck a light squeeze. "*Nire bihotza*, look at me."

I open my eyes, not because I'm interested in following his demands, but because I've never hid from unpleasant truths, and I don't plan on starting now.

"Haven't we already established that I was a fool to not wake you up?"

"We can always establish that more," I say.

Montes cracks a smile, but it quickly disappears. "There was a while where I felt like I'd gone insane from loneliness. The Sleeper was still repairing your body at the time, though I will admit that by then I was afraid of seeing you again. But I was even more afraid of the possibility that you would never get out of the Sleeper, never be healed. So I cloned the two people I missed most."

"You depraved son of a bitch."

Montes played God, deciding who got to live and who didn't.

He frowns, his features hardening at my words, but he doesn't try to defend himself further.

"What happened to her?" I ask.

It's taking a lot not to lash out like a wild animal. My basest nature wants to. But at this point, throwing a fit like a child won't change the past.

I take a deep breath.

"She was killed," Montes says releasing me reluctantly.

"How?"

"She was captured much the same way you were. The West was planning on using her as their puppet.

"She was not like you—not at all." He says this last part quietly.

"We recaptured her." He looks away and rubs his eyes. "But the plane was shot down."

There's real emotion there. Real anguish.

He takes a deep breath. "They thought I'd cloned her to end the war." Montes shakes his head. "It's a good theory, but I had the real thing the entire time."

I search his face. "You cared for her." Just saying those words is a bullet to the gut.

His expression doesn't alter, but it does intensify. "I couldn't *stand* looking at her."

He reaches out and tries to touch my cheek. I step away before he can. His fingers curl into a fist.

"There was only ever one of you," he says. "I didn't want anything else—not in any sense. Once I realized that, I stayed as far away from her as I could. She suffered because of it. But I tried to care for her."

Some bitter combo of disgust and relief flow through me. I find I don't want to be replaceable, and it's a dagger through the heart to know that he must've created her with that in mind. And then there's the unbidden pain that comes when I think of this woman he created after me, created and then abandoned. All she got for it was death.

He must see me withdrawing because he seems desperate to close the space between us.

I back up, shaking my head. "You ruin everything, Montes. *Everything.*"

I turn my back to him and walk away.

I can't be sure, but I swear I hear him whisper, "That's all I know how to do."

CHAPTER 28

SERENITY

LONDON'S GONE, AS is Paris, Cairo, Delhi, Beijing. On and on the list goes.

Today, in the hours before we leave, they show me the footage of it. What little there is left.

I stand in the middle of the Great Room, dozens of men and women as my witness. They didn't need to be here; it's all old news to them. But I think they want to remember, or to try to see it all with new eyes.

I watch the bomb that rips apart the Eiffel Tower. The steel beams that had held for over two centuries now buckle and collapse.

The footage cuts away, only to be replaced by the Burj Khalifa, the tallest building in the world. Or at least, it was.

I don't want to see this. I don't want to see man's greatest achievements blown away in an instant because someone somewhere thought it would be a good idea to destroy the world.

I force my feet to stay rooted to the floor. I owe it to both the people of the East and the West to watch.

"Do you see that glint?" One of the officers has a laser pointer that he aims around a section of the frame taken up by sky.

The bright concentrated section of light flashes in the middle of it. The camera catches similar flare-ups of light glimmering along the windows of the Burj Khalifa. But this one … This one has no business being in the middle of open sky.

"This was one of the first instances where the West used retroreflective material to camouflage their weaponry," the officer says.

I don't get a chance to ask what retroreflective material is before the side of the skyscraper explodes into flame, rows of windows and debris scattered to the four winds. Plumes of dark smoke bloom almost immediately.

The footage is time lapsed, and the next frame shows the building still smoldering, a dark halo of ash and dust enveloping it. We watch this for about thirty seconds.

And then, somewhere in the middle of it, the building begins to fall.

I don't breathe as I watch the world's tallest building collapse onto itself. It happens in a matter of seconds, one story after the next swallowed up by gravity and rubble-filled smoke. Somewhere in the middle of it all, I feel a tear slip out of my eye. It's the atomic bomb all over again. Destruction so vast and so terrible that my very bones ache for humanity.

And then it's over, and I know that within those few seconds, thousands upon thousands of people died. I can hear the observers' screams through the speakers. And though their language is different, and though I've never set foot onto their land and never walked the earth during their lifetimes, I ache for them.

At some point, we are all the same.

"That's enough," Montes says.

The screen shuts off.

I feel my dark king at my back.

"Are you ready?" he asks me.

I turn and take him in. His eyes aren't giving away his mood. But he must feel it, this smoldering anger that burns at the sight of so much carnage.

Behind him the officers wear grim expressions.

I nod to all of them. "Let's end this."

THE PLANE WE board has all the accoutrements I remember. Plush central seating, a bedroom, and a conference table, each sectioned off into separate segments of the cabin.

A dozen men board along with us, one of them Marco. He catches my eye and gives me a tiny, playful wave.

I thin my eyes in response. Divine intervention better strike this plane. That's the only way Marco will leave it unscathed.

"Play nice," Montes whispers in my ear.

"I'm not nice, *my king*," I say disparagingly.

"Well, you're going to have to learn how to be. Marco is my right-hand."

"He can just get used to me." I am, after all, the queen. The title has got to be good for something.

Montes flashes the man in question a penetrating look. "I think he's all too ready to do that," he says, his lips thinning.

Before I'm able to respond, he begins to herd me to the back room. I catch sight of Marco once again, and he watches us, his eyes filled with some emotion I cannot place.

"What are you doing?" I say, reluctantly moving towards the small bedroom.

As soon as we both cross the threshold, Montes slams the door shut. "Getting you alone."

I bump into the bed, and now I think I have an idea of where the king's mind is at. I can still hear the muffled conversations of Montes's men as they get settled.

"If you think—"

He cuts me off with a kiss, holding my face hostage as he does so. It's long and drawn out, and I know he's making a point, especially when he backs us up until we both collapse onto the mattress, my body pinned beneath his.

Only then does he release my mouth. "That is not why I brought you in here, though I would enjoy fucking you senseless ..."

"*Montes*." I'm still so pissed off at him after last night. Kissing me only serves to make my anger burn hotter.

"Do you trust me?" he asks. He has me trapped beneath him.

How does he expect me to answer?

"No, not with most things."

"And should I trust you?" he asks, his face just inches from my own.

"Not with most things," I repeat softly.

"Can you trust that I want to keep you alive?" he asks.

If there is ever one thing I can be sure of, it's Montes's obsession with my life.

"Yes."

"Good," he says. "We're going to dangerous places, and there will be people who want you dead. So you understand my concern." He doesn't release me. Instead he threads his fingers through my own. "You are not going in there unarmed."

I raise my eyebrows. "You're giving me a gun?"

"Can I trust you not to shoot me with it?"

"No." I need some target practice anyway.

He sighs, but there's a twinkle in his eyes. "If you shoot me, there will be very severe repercussions."

"I'm quaking," I say, but I'm excited. I feel naked walking around without my weapons. Being raised on violence has taught me to always be prepared.

Montes releases me and pushes off the bed. He heads to an overhead compartment. Opening it, he pulls out a box. I hear something heavy slide inside it.

A gun.

I stand, my hands itching to touch the heavy metal.

He turns, cradling the box. "Don't make me regret this, Serenity."

I meet his eyes. "You won't." *You will.*

When he hands me the flimsy packaging, I sit down on the edge of the mattress, opening the lid carefully.

Nestled inside is not one gun, but two, each tucked into a belted holster. I recognize one of them immediately.

"It's over a hundred years old, Serenity. The thing jams fairly often."

I run my fingers over my father's gun. So it's not reliable. But Montes would only know that if …

When I look up at him questioningly, he watches me, arms folded.

"I fired it on many occasions," he explains.

When I wanted to be close to you.

The king omits much of what his heart wants to say, but I glean it off of him anyway. And it's twisted that this weapon, which has ended many lives, is a bridge between the king and me. But everything about our relationship is twisted, so it fits.

"The bullets are also long out of production."

I unholster the gun and run my hands over it. From the looks of the thing, it's aged about as well as I have. Which is to say, not at all.

But it's a relic, nonetheless.

Just like me.

"So you gave me another gun," I say, re-holstering my beloved weapon and reaching for the other.

"Everything about its design is essentially the same as the guns you're familiar with," the king says, crossing his legs at the ankles as he leans back against the wall. "And those bullets are the most common ones on the market."

So I can get my hands on more if we find ourselves in a tight situation.

I loop the belt and holsters around my pants. Once everything's secured, I glance up at Montes.

"Thank you," I say. I mean it, too.

I'm still upset and unnerved about my twin, but for once, I'm going to bury the past. I have bigger worries on the horizon.

The king levels a serious look at me. "Don't die on me."

"So many demands," I murmur. "You're setting yourself up for disappointment, Montes."

"I didn't marry you because you were a pretty thing. I married you because you were a wicked one."

Was that a compliment?

"You married me because you're a bastard."

"Yes," he grins, though it lacks any mirth, "that too."

IT TAKES ONLY a couple hours to fly from the king's seaside palace to Giza. Only a couple of hours' time, but there appears to be lifetimes of differences between the land we left and the one we arrive in.

Giza is only a handful of miles from Cairo, one of the cities that the West apparently destroyed. But as we descend and the buildings come into view, I realize just how war-torn and desolate Giza itself is. Half the buildings are in various states of disrepair.

When I step out of the plane, hot, dry desert air greets me, and the very feel of it is nothing like what I'm used to. I squint as a hot gust of air blows my hair around.

The king steps up to me and presses a hand to my back. Several men wait to greet us on the ground. From what I've picked up, these men are the territory's dignitaries, and they will be our guides while we're here.

They take one look at me and begin to bow, their hands clasped together as they do so, like I'm some desperate, answered prayer of theirs.

Montes puts pressure on my lower back, urging me forward. I dig my heels in instead.

"They're acting like I'm a god," I say to him. I can't quite take my eyes off the people in front of us.

"You are a queen and a rebel fighter, and you've been dead a hundred years only to turn up alive. To them you might as well be.

"Now," he continues, putting more pressure on my back, "you need to meet them and act like it."

When I approach them, one by one they clasp my hands and kiss my knuckles.

"It is an honor to meet you." The man who speaks has a heavy accent, yet his English is crisp and sharp. The result is a lilting speech.

"I am honored to be here," I say honestly.

"Where is Akash?" Montes asks, glancing about the group.

From what I read, all of the king's lands have regional leaders. Giza and its surrounding land is managed by Akash Salem.

"Your Majesties," the man who first spoke now sobers, his easy smile disappearing. "On our way here, we received worrisome news concerning Akash and his family."

"What about them?" I ask.

No one seems to want to be the one to break the news. Eventually, however, one does.

He takes a deep breath. "They're missing."

CHAPTER 29

THE KING

"How could this have happened?" I pace up and down one of the rooms in the royal house we're staying at. We've been here mere hours and already I'm itching to drag my wife back onto our plane and return to my palace.

If my regional leaders can be taken, then so can Serenity.

"Akash's servants were found slaughtered and there were signs of forced entry," one of my men says.

My eyes cut to my queen.

She sits in an armchair, her expression stormy. She's been sitting there brooding since we entered the room.

"Serenity," I say, my voice softening.

Her gaze flicks to me, returning from wherever she wandered in her mind.

"Are they dead?" she asks.

One of the men behind me shakes his head. "We don't know, Your Majesty."

She looks to me because she knows I won't euphemize the situation.

"If it's the West,"—and it surely is—"they'll be tortured. All of them. Even the kids."

She flinches at that. Buried beneath all my queen's violence is something soft and righteous.

"How old?" she asks.

"Eight and five," one of the dignitaries says.

She gets up from the couch, and everything about her looks heavy. Evil does that; it weighs you down, makes you weary. I know all about it.

Serenity removes her father's gun from its holster, and everyone tenses just a fraction. She flips it over in her hand.

"How easy we kill," she murmurs. She sets the gun on the table in the center of the room. "It never solves our problems."

Something about her words and her voice has my hackles rising. Only recently Serenity discovered the art of scheming. It's a talent of mine, one I fear she's taken a liking to as well.

"We will get them back," she swears to the room.

"Serenity," I cut in.

There are some promises we cannot make, and that is one of them.

"We will get them back, Montes," she reiterates, her eyes glinting.

I stare her down. We might get them back, yes. But they might not be alive by then.

"Leave us," I tell the men.

Once the room clears, I approach her. "You can't save everyone," I say.

She leans her knuckles against the tabletop and bows her head. "I know," she says softly. She lifts her head and I see resolve in her eyes. "But I owe your subjects, *our* subjects, safety for their allegiance."

It's almost too much, seeing her like this. She might be the best decision I've ever made.

"How did our plans get leaked?" she asks.

"You already know," I say.

Even surrounded by honest men, I have traitors in my midst.

She presses her lips together and swipes her gun off the table, holstering it at her side. She might've hesitated killing me, but she won't when it comes to our enemies.

"If this continues," I say. "I'm pulling the plug on this campaign."

Her eyes flash. "Montes—"

I stride towards her slowly, well aware that when I'm like this, I'm intimidating. Even to her.

And that's the point. She will not question me on this.

"This is your chance at peace," she says.

I shake my head slowly. I've had a hundred years to devise ways to end the war. I know she feels there's some rush to save the world, but we've gotten by without that elusive peace for a century now.

"It's not worth your life," I say.

Just the thought has my knees weakening. At times like this, I feel regret that she's not still in the Sleeper where I can keep her safe. Losing her, *really* losing her, could very well be the end of me.

And then she says something that has my blood curdling.

"But it *is* worth my life, Montes." She looks out the far window. "It is."

SERENITY

I'M ESSENTIALLY ON house arrest.

One little comment was all it took for Montes to double up the original number of guards, bar the doors of the mansion and secure the perimeter of the property.

All so that I never have the chance to put my life on the line. Already our itinerary is being changed to accommodate his paranoia. Less time in each location, extra security around each building we'll be meeting in. He's even pulled extra troops to guard the large stadiums I'll be speaking at.

I can barely piss without someone watching over my shoulder.

Anyone who thinks that with power comes freedom is wrong. I'm a prisoner to it, and it doesn't matter that I never wanted this for myself.

Morning sunlight streams into our bedroom, and I swear it looks different here. A part of me yearns to linger in this place just see all the ways the sun shines differently.

But there are things to do—loyalties to sway.

I sit on an ornate couch in our room, my weaponry and ammunition spread out along the coffee table. Gun oil, cleaning rods, and rags are littered between them.

I'm sure I'm quite a sight, clad in the dress and heels I've been forced to wear, my face painted and my hair coiffed for today's speech.

Cleaning my weapons is my little act of rebellion.

The door to the room opens, and even though I don't look up from my work, I know it's the king that steps through. Perhaps it's the heavy sound of his footfalls, and perhaps it's the power of his presence alone.

I hear him pause. "Should I regret giving you those guns?" he asks.

I lift an eyebrow but otherwise ignore him.

The narcissistic king doesn't like that very much. He strides over and places a hand over mine and the gun that I hold.

"Look at me," he commands.

I lower the weapon and raise my eyes. "What?"

He narrows his. Before I can object he sweeps his hand across the coffee table, brushing aside all the items I have laid out.

I curse as they clatter to the ground, beginning to reach for them.

He catches my wrist. "No."

"In a hundred years you haven't managed to be less of a control freak," I bite out.

"Hazards of being king," he replies, his voice hard.

Only then do I notice he's wearing his crown. Just like the last time I saw him in it, he looks devastatingly deadly.

It's then that I notice he's holding another. And it's not just any crown. By the looks of it, it's *the* crown I wore when I was coronated.

"No," I say.

"Yes," Montes counters.

I stare at the crown in his hands.

"*No*," I repeat more vehemently.

I've already compromised enough with the day's attire. The deep blue gown I wear is far too tight along the bodice and the heels I'm forced to wear will break my ankles if I need to run. I allowed it all without complaint.

But a crown?

"You might find this hard to believe," he says, and now his voice gentles, "but people don't carry the same stigmas they did a hundred years ago. They're not going to see the crown as you see it."

I don't want to concede, I don't want to give this man anything. But the truth is, he might be right. I really don't know this world and the people in it. Perhaps a queen is what they want to see. Their lives and their pasts are so very different from mine. I can't presume to know their hearts.

While I hesitate, Montes places the crown on my head, his hands lingering.

"Does getting your way all the time really make you feel good?" I ask.

The corner of his mouth lifts. "Not nearly as much as your charming personality does."

His hands drift down, towards the low neckline of my dress. Maybe I hear his breath catch, or maybe the action itself is enough.

Does this man's passion ever wane?

"I look forward to your speech," he says. "And I look forward to after."

CHAPTER 30

SERENITY

I AM A fool.

That's all I can think as I climb the steps of the dilapidated stadium, the king at my side, his men fanned around us.

I am a soldier, not a public speaker. At times like these, I'd rather lay my life on the line than stand in front of an audience. And that's just what I will have to do.

Over two dozen times. A speech for every city I visit.

Like I said, I am a fool.

I can hear all those lines I memorized, each one jumbling with the next. The words lodge themselves in my throat.

As we near the top of the stairs, my gaze moves to the horizon.

My heart pounds as I get my first glimpse of the pyramids of Giza.

Or what's left of them.

They're mostly rubble. The ancient blocks that were painstakingly placed one on top of the other thousands of years ago now look like anthills someone's kicked over.

I run my tongue over my teeth, remembering the footage I watched yesterday. And now a renewed sense of purpose drives away my anxiety.

As we summit the steps, the event's coordinators descend on us from all sides, boxing us and our guards in. Most wear headsets and carry fancy equipment.

"My king," one of the women says, "you will go up first, and my queen, he will introduce you shortly thereafter."

Our entire group is shuffled to a small waiting room, where couches and platters of food wait for us.

Montes takes a seat at one of the couches, lounging back against it, his legs splayed wide. He looks completely at ease.

Oh, how I envy him.

Relaxing is the last thing I'll be able to do. I'm already amped up; my body doesn't know the difference between this and going into battle.

We don't wait long. Not five minutes later a woman raps on the door, then opens it a crack. "Your Majesties," she says, "it's time."

WE HEAD OUT of the waiting room, towards the stage. More technicians and event planners crowd our group. The farther we walk, the more king's men break away from our cluster.

I do a double take of the hallway wall when we pass a poster with my face on it. Without realizing it, I've stopped.

It's almost identical to the one the First Free Men showed me. The sight of it is a shock to my system.

I approach the faded image and touch the worn paper. I keep forgetting what I am to these people, perhaps to the entire world.

"Serenity." I feel the king's eyes on me.

"It's old." I state the obvious.

The colors are muted, the paper has yellowed; the poster has obviously been here for months at the very least.

"People have believed in you for a very long time," he says.

I drop my hand, and reluctantly I resume walking, keenly aware of the crown on my head. I can't even fathom how strange this must be for the rest of the world. To find out the woman who symbolized freedom was not just alive after all this time, but also unchanged.

We stop in the wings of the stage. All that's left of our group is now Montes, me, Marco, and two guards that stand some distance away from us.

There we wait, the noise of the crowd drifting in. It sounds big.

I crack my knuckles, then my neck, shaking them out.

Montes leans in, about to make a comment, when a man with an earpiece approaches us.

"Your Majesties," he says, bowing to each of us in turn. "They're ready for you."

The king bends down and brushes a lingering kiss across my lips. It's soft and gentle—sweet. These moments always come as a shock to me.

His crown catches the light as he straightens, and he gives Marco a penetrating look. "Keep her safe."

It's all I can do not throw up my hands. I'm not some simpering damsel needing saving.

As though he knows what I'm thinking, Montes winks at me, and then he's gone.

AFTER THE KING leaves, I'm left alone with Marco. The king's right-hand stands to my side, far too close for my comfort. Despite choosing to ignore him, I know he won't ignore me. He's taken a keen interest in me since we met in the palace's secret passageways.

I wait for him to break the silence, counting off the seconds.

"Nervous?" he asks, as soon as it stretches on for a smidgen too long.

I clench my jaw, but don't respond.

Beyond the stage, I hear the audience roar; it sounds like something infernal and ferocious.

"Why do you despise me?" This time, Marco doesn't pretend to be jovial. His voice sounds sad, dejected.

I close my eyes. I should be thinking about my speech, about an entire hemisphere whose needs I now must represent. Instead my own emotions bubble up.

I'm being unfair to him. And I'm being petty.

"I don't despise you," I sigh out. "I despise the man that came before you." I have to force my next words out. "It's not your fault, but every time I see you, I relive those final moments with my father." And out of all the memories I have of him, that's the one I want to dwell on the least.

One of those people wearing the fancy headsets cuts into our little heart-to-heart. "Serenity, you're on in thirty," he says, waving me forward and saving me from continuing the conversation.

I'm led to a door at the end of the hallway, where he explains down to every minute detail how my entrance and exit should be executed. Then he leaves and I wait once more.

A countdown begins, and my pulse speeds up. These final seconds seem the longest as my adrenaline mounts.

And then the door I stand in front of is thrown open. As I move away from the wings, towards the stage, Giza unfolds before my eyes. I almost stagger back from the number of people gathered. A sea of them stand in the field in front of me, and many more fill the rows upon rows of stadium seats that wrap around it.

And as soon as they see me, they go crazy.

The soldier in me tenses. I almost reach for my gun before logic overrides the reaction.

The king still stands at the podium, and now he turns away from the audience, his deep eyes trained on me.

I walk up to him, and his hand falls to the small of my back. He resumes talking to the crowd, but I'm not listening. The audience has me mesmerized.

This can't be my life.

I've somehow gone from a dying soldier living out her limited days in a bunker to a mythic queen.

It feels like such a farce. Like *I'm* a farce.

I feel the king's eyes on me. He laces his fingers through mine and brushes a kiss against my fingers. When he straightens, he gives me a slight nod then leaves the stage.

Now it's my turn.

I take a deep breath as my gaze travels over the countless faces.

"The last time my eyes took in the world, it was at war," I began. "That was over a century ago."

If the crowd was silent before, now it goes dead.

"I slept for a hundred years and woke only to find the world is still at war. That should not be the way of things."

I take a deep breath, feeling the cameras on me. I'm going to have to be vulnerable, something I'm bad at in the best of situations. And this is far from the best of situations.

"One hundred and twenty-four years ago, I was born in the Western United Nations ..."

I don't know how many minutes pass by the time I bring people up to the present. I'm not even sure what I've told them matters. I wanted them to understand me, to know that for all our differences we are very much the same, but my life story isn't terribly relatable. It's mostly just sad. These people don't want a sad story. They want something to drive away the nightmares, something to hold onto when life gets tough.

"The world can be at peace," I say. "It was, long ago, and it will be again. I will make sure of it."

My gaze travels over them. "I was awoken for a reason. My sleep has ended because it is time to end the war. I can't do it alone. I need each and every one of you. War ends when *we* decide it does. So I ask you this: believe in me and believe in humanity. Fight alongside me when the East needs it, and lay down your arms when our land no longer requires it. If you can do this, then the world will know peace once more."

437

The crowd goes quiet.

I've been too vague. Too optimistic. Too fumbling with my words. I feel it all in the silence.

I'm about to bow my head and walk off stage when one person somewhere out in the crowd begins to pound their fist over their heart.

Another person joins in. And then another.

Soon people are joining in handfuls at a time, then dozens, until eventually, the entire audience is thundering with the sound.

They begin to shout, and I can't make out the words at first. Eventually, the voices align and I hear it.

"Freedom or death! Freedom or death!"

I stare out at them.

A hundred years of life to become whatever it is you want.

And a hundred years of death to become whatever it is they want.

CHAPTER 31

SERENITY

I DRAW IN a shaky breath as soon as I leave the podium and retreat back to the wings of the stage. I see Marco first, watching me with too-bright eyes. He steps towards me, but I brush past him.

I don't want to be around him or anyone else for that matter. I'm not sure what I'm feeling, and I want to sort my emotions out alone. I see the king standing off to the side, engrossed in a conversation with several of his officers. His eyes catch mine as he speaks, following me as I walk down the hall.

Several guards fall into formation, two behind me, two in front.

I'm never alone. Never, never alone. And I really would like to be.

I head back to that little room where I waited earlier with the king. Five minutes is all I need to decompress and deal with the fact that I am no longer some abstract concept on a poster, but now a living, breathing ideology that people can consume.

The corridor outside the room is abandoned. I should be relaxing at the sight; solitude is what I wanted. Instead I find myself tensing up.

Behind me I hear several slick sounds. Something warm and wet sprays across my arms and back.

A trap.

In the next instant I hear the wet gurgle of dying men gasping for breath.

I swivel just as my guards fall to their knees, one clutching her neck.

Beyond them, three men wait for me, two holding bloody knives, and one with his gun leveled on my chest.

He adjusts his aim, then he pulls the trigger.

I HEAR A grunt at my side as the guard next to me takes a bullet to the chest. He staggers in front of me, covering my body even as he chokes for breath. The shooter's gun goes off several more times, and the other soldier flanking me goes down.

In the distance I hear shouts, but they're too far away.

I reach for my gun as they come at me.

I unholster my weapon just as the three reach me. One of my attackers jerks my arm up. I use the motion to align the barrel with the bottom of his chin.

I fire.

The back of his head blows away. Whatever pretty beliefs he had, whatever life he'd made from himself, it's gone within an instant.

As quick as I am, I'm still outnumbered two to one. One of the men forces my hands behind my back while the other covers my mouth with a damp cloth.

Now I'm having flashbacks to when the king pulled the same stunt.

That will *never* happen again.

They are still grappling for my weapon, and now I begin firing, hoping that I can hit some piece of enemy flesh. Blood splatters on my hands and wrists. One of my abductors shouts, releasing me reflexively.

I don't hesitate. I raise my gun and shoot the man point-blank in the face.

The final man, who's still pressing the damp cloth against my face now slams me into the wall in an effort to dislodge my weapon, cursing under his breath as he does so. I can hear the panic began to enter his voice.

I'm likely putting up more of a struggle than they expected.

The drug I'm being forced to inhale starts to take effect. Colors are blurring and my movement is slowing.

I lift my gun wielding arm.

Suddenly, I'm yanked back from the wall. The hallway spins with the movement.

My body begins to sag, each muscle feeling increasingly heavy. I still hold my weapon, but it takes an increasing amount of focus to get my body to move.

"Don't shoot!" the man behind me says.

It takes a second for my eyes to focus.

When they do, I see what my attacker sees: over a dozen different guards and officers, most with their weapons drawn. And right in the middle of them, Montes.

Our eyes find each other. He doesn't show his fear or his anger, not like most men do. But they're both there, simmering just beneath the surface.

I know his men aren't going to shoot, not when my captor is using me as a human shield.

The edges of my vision are starting to darken when I feel the man at my back trying to pry my gun from my grip.

I'm not going out like this.

It takes the rest of my strength just to pull that tiny little trigger. The shot echoes down the hall and the man cries out. I'm not even sure whether or not the bullet hit him or he was just taken by surprise. Either way, it's enough.

I fall out of his hold, and a dozen other guns discharge. And then the last of my attackers meets his grisly end.

I SET MY bloody crown down on the airplane's conference table, the gleam of it somewhat dulled by the blood splatter.

It's been over an hour since the attack, though you wouldn't know it by looking at us all. I'm still coated in blood. Despite the fact that I have worn blood more often than makeup, it never gets less horrifying.

Heinrich Weber, the king's grand marshal, is the last to enter the cabin, the door to the aircraft closing behind him.

"Your Majesties," he bows to me and Montes, the latter who is stalking up the aisle from the back of the plane, a damp hand towel gripped tightly in his hand, "we found several dead employees in the stadium's storage closets," he reports. "From what the investigators have been able to piece together, it's believed that Serenity's attackers disposed of them then took their ID badges and gear."

"That was all it took?" the king says. He kneels in front of me. Placing a hand against my cheek, he begins to wipe down my face with the cloth. I'm so taken by the gesture that I let him tend to me.

"The queen of the entire eastern hemisphere goes to her first—*her first*—speech," he continues, "and all it takes for the enemy to infiltrate is a couple stolen badges?" His ministrations roughen with his anger.

As soon as the towel gets close to my lips, I take it from Montes. I don't want anyone else pressing a damp cloth near my mouth. Not even the king.

He stares into my eyes, one of his hands dropping to my thigh and squeezing it. When he removes his palm, I notice it's stained red from just touching the fabric I wear.

I'm a bloody, bloody mess.

He stares at his hand for a beat, then his fingers curl into a fist.

Someone's going to die. I can feel it. The king's anger has always needed an outlet.

He stands. "Did you discover who the men are affiliated with?"

I begin wiping my arms down. It's a hopeless task. The blood's everywhere.

The officer hesitates. "They're still not sure, but it appears that they were associated with the First Free Men."

I go still.

Styx Garcia.

The man tried to capture me again *after* the deal we made. The thought makes me seethe. Surely there's an explanation for it.

I remember the way Styx looked at me when we last spoke. He wants me for more than just power and political leverage. There is some personal aspect to this.

The king glances back at me, and for a split second I'm almost sure he knows of my talk with Styx. My heart pounds in my ears, but I stare at him unflinchingly.

"These sorts of things will continue to happen so long as the queen visits these places," Marco says, interrupting the moment. He sits on the far side of the room, his eyes on me.

"Then we will call this off," the king says.

A bit of the old tyrant ruler peeks out. I knew that bastard wasn't gone.

I stand, setting aside the now blood-drenched towel. "*Montes.*"

The king isn't the only one who can call the room to heel with his presence. It takes just a single word for all eyes to focus on me.

A century of sleep has given me a strange sort of power, one that I never had when I was just a young foreign queen.

"You think this is just going to go away if you lock me up in one of your palaces?" I say.

His head tilts just the slightest. "No, but it will keep you alive longer than this." He holds up his bloody palm. "I didn't hide you all this time just to watch you die."

Sometimes I get so swept up in his dominance plays that I forget he's just a broken man trying to save his broken woman.

My voice softens. "You've tried hiding me away. The world found me. Why don't we try a different tactic now?"

He holds my gaze.

Finally, he blows out a breath.

He gives a brief nod to the men that await his orders. They seem to relax at the gesture, many of them returning to whatever it was they were previously doing.

The king comes back to my side then. "I'm going to trust you. Don't make me regret it," he says softly, echoing the same words I said to him a week ago.

I had wondered once whether it was possible for people like us to redeem ourselves. Now as I stare at Montes, my conscience whispers, *perhaps*.

Perhaps.

CHAPTER 32

SERENITY

OUR NEXT STOP is in Kabul, a city smack dab in the middle of the East's territories. It's a barren place bordered by huge, austere mountains.

We arrive early that evening, just as the sun is beginning to set.

Endless war has made this city even more desolate than Giza. Most of the dwellings are mudbrick, and the older ones seem to be crumbling where they stand. Then there are the buildings that came *before*. Steel and cement skeletons are all that remain of those.

Here it appears that the city is returning to the earth. We rose, we peaked, and now we fall.

I can't say it isn't beautiful, however. The rosy hue of sunset makes the ruins look deliberate, like some city planner crafted the desolation into the architecture of this place.

As our car winds through the city, I catch glimpses of street art. On this street it's a spray-painted grenade. The artist went to the trouble of adding eyes to the explosive. Eyes and a single curving scar that looks like a teardrop. Beneath it a caption reads, *Freedom or Death*.

I see several more tagged iterations of this propaganda on our drive. Some with just a grenade, others with renditions of my face. In some, I can only tell it's me by the scar they include.

I touch my face. Perhaps I'm the wrong person to encourage peace. From everything I've seen, I'm a war cry. A liberator, but a violent one.

Marco was right—more attempts will be made to capture me or kill me.

I am, after all, a walking revolution.

I SIT OUT on the back patio of Montes's royal residency in Kabul. The mansion rests on the mountainside overlooking the city.

An evening breeze stirs my hair, and I pull the blanket around me closer.

"You know, there are other ways to stay warm." The voice at my back is like the richest honey.

My king has decided to join me.

"If I was trying to stay warm, I wouldn't be out here," I say over my shoulder before returning my gaze to the brutal landscape.

Montes comes to my side, placing two tumblers and a bottle of amber liquid on the table in front of me before pulling out the chair next to mine.

"I don't like it when you're alone," he admits.

I glance over at him, some of the hair that was tucked behind my ear now falling loose. "Why?"

He pours us each a glass and hands one to me. "Another way to keep warm," he explains. From the way he's gazing at me, his eyes will do more to heat me up than the drink will.

"I don't want you to ever feel like you're lost," he says, returning to the previous subject.

That's so oddly sweet of him.

"I've been alone enough for the both of us," he adds. He stares at his glass, as though he can divine his next words in the liquid.

After a moment, he brings it to his mouth and takes a sip. He hisses out a satisfied breath after he takes a swallow.

I follow his lead and take a healthy swig of the alcohol. I almost spit it back out. It scorches the inside of my mouth.

"*Mother*—" I curse. "That's *strong*."

Montes look like he's trying not to laugh. "I hope you never change, Serenity."

I glance over at him again. Between the light streaming out from inside and the lanterns scattered throughout the garden, Montes seems to glow.

Beautiful, haunted man. How is it that I'm only seeing how tragic he is now?

"I hope I do," I say softly.

I squint out at the small, flickering lights of Kabul. "Tell me how you've changed."

He sighs, like it's all too much. And what do I know? If I lived for a century and a half, life might overwhelm me as well.

He bows his head. "I've always felt such … *discontent*. Even as a boy. It didn't matter what I achieved or what I was given. I wanted more. Always more," he murmurs, staring at his glass. "To hunger for success—that's a good trait to possess as a businessman and a conqueror, but it needs to be balanced with temperance, morality, and wisdom. I'm not sure how much I have of any of those. Even now."

His gaze moves up to the stars. "I can't tell you how many nights I wished upon your Pleiades. For you to heal. For you to live. Once you were gone, for the first time in my life, success was overridden by something else."

I feel a lump in my throat. I couldn't speak even if he asked me to.

Montes looks at me. "How have I changed? I fell in love. I needed you, and you were locked away in a Sleeper. And the only way you were getting out of that machine was if I found a cure for cancer. It changed my entire focus. I began to understand loss in a way I hadn't before—I began to feel the weight of your life and your suffering. Of everyone's suffering. I couldn't ignore it. God, did I try, too. But after a time … well, even an old dog like me can form new habits. Better habits."

I'm gripping my glass so tightly I can feel the blood leaving my fingers.

He shakes his head. "You go so long without someone and fear can eat you up. The idea of you sustained me for decades but—and it's inexplicable—I felt that once you were healed I couldn't wake you. And I had all sorts of reasons for it—and so many of them are legitimate—but at the end of the day I don't know, I just couldn't make that one leap."

Montes is finally explaining his decision to me. *Really* explaining it.

I take another swallow of my drink, and this time I don't feel the burn, grappling with my thoughts as I am.

"You and I are the only people who know the world as it once was," he says.

I shiver. Right now I feel like Montes and I are the only two beings in the entire universe, tied together by love and hate, time and memory.

"Us—and your former advisors," I say.

"They aren't people," Montes says.

I take a deep breath. "Neither are we."

We are all just self-fashioned monsters posing as gods.

"You're wrong, Serenity. You and I cling to our humanity more fiercely than anyone else."

He has a point. We cling to it because we know just how close we are to losing it.

"*Your Majesties!*" Heinrich dashes out to the patio. The alarm in his voice has us both standing.

Almost reflexively, Montes steps in front of me.

I frown at his back. I never wanted the old Montes, but he became mine anyway. I want this newer version even less. This is a man whose evil deeds I can truly forget. And I don't want to forget. I want to remember to my last dying breath that even though the king might now be the solution, in the beginning he was the problem.

Just as soon as that thought comes, another follows in its wake.

No one is beyond forgiveness.

Both my parents used to say that, and *that* was something I had almost forgotten.

"We just got word from our men who were supposed to change guard for the regional leader of Kabul," Heinrich says. "They said the place is a bloodbath—our soldiers are dead and the family is gone."

CHAPTER 33

SERENITY

"YOU'RE NOT GOING," the king says.

He and his men are equipping themselves in the living room.

A mercenary king. I hadn't expected that from Montes. I don't know whether I'm more surprised that he's joining the unit assigned to the task, or that his men seem unfazed by this.

After all these years, the king has finally come down from his ivory tower.

"I am if you are," I say, checking the magazine of my gun to make sure my weapons are fully loaded. My new gun isn't. I haven't had a chance to replace the spent bullets I fired off in Giza. I cross the room where box of communal ammunition rests. I pull out my own bullets and compare.

A match.

I begin to slide them into the magazine. The soldiers around me tense, their eyes darting between me and the king.

"Anyone have a spare magazine?" I say.

Just in case we run into any difficulties.

One of the soldiers lifts one sitting next to him and begins to hand it over.

Montes catches his wrist. "*Don't*," he says. "Serenity won't be joining us."

I finish loading my magazine and force it up into the chamber of the gun. "Who's going to stop me?" I ask.

Many of these men saw me kill today, which means they saw my lack of hesitation, and now they're seeing my lack of remorse.

Some of the soldiers look uncomfortable, but I also catch some suppressing grins.

Montes steps forward, crowding me. "Don't force my hand, Serenity." His voice has gone quiet.

"Then don't force mine."

We stare each other down. Us and our impasses. Montes knows just how easy it would be for me to lift my arm and point this gun at him, and I know how easy it would be for him to have his men detain me.

He knows I can hold my own if something bad should happen. I've proven that to him over and over.

"Let me into your world," I say softly. My plea cuts through the tension in a way that none of my previous words could.

Montes's nostrils flare and his lips press together. It used to be that the king couldn't resist me when I got physical. Now it's something else. Every time I tear down an emotional wall of ours, I make headway with him.

"If anything goes wrong—*anything*—I won't be repeating this, and nothing you say or do will stop me."

BY THE TIME we arrive at the home of the woman who ran Kabul's government, all that's left are bodies and blood.

I step over one of the king's fallen soldiers just inside the entrance of the home. His throat has been sliced open. I can still hear the slow drip of his blood as it leaves his body.

The king's men who were on the scene first have secured the perimeter of the house and the surrounding neighborhood, but aside from them, we'll be the first ones inside the home of Nadia and Malik Khan, the regional leader and her husband.

I have my gun out. Even though there are plenty of guards, some who were here before us and some who came with our brigade, it never hurts to be ready.

We move through the residence, our footsteps nearly silent. I take in the sparse furnishings. Even regional leaders live fairly humble lives, if this home is anything to go by. The furniture and decorations are faded, and the wooden tables have lost their polish.

Montes walks slightly ahead of me, his broad shoulders largely obscuring the hall ahead of us.

We head to the back of the house, where the bedrooms are.

More fallen soldiers lay outside the doors, their eyes glassy. These ones have gunshot wounds.

My eyes drift back to the door. Hesitantly, I step inside.

The reports never mentioned that Malik and Nadia had kids, but they very obviously do. Two beds rest against the far wall of the children's room, both empty. The sight of those ruffled sheets is harder to look at than the dead soldiers. I grip my gun tighter.

Someone will die for this.

Once we scan the room, our group moves back out into the hall. We make quick work of the other rooms, until there is just the master bedroom left.

I don't particularly want to go in there. For one thing, the closer I get the stronger the smell of raw meat and death is. The reason for that is obvious—four dead guards line the hall leading up to it.

But there's also the less obvious reason for my reluctance. My intuition is now kicking in. Maybe it's just the partially open door and the darkness beyond it, but my heart rate's picking up.

We enter, and my eyes land on the empty master bed. There are several drops of blood on the sheets, but I have no idea what sort of injury caused them.

My gaze doesn't linger on the bed for long, though.

Not when I catch sight of a crib.

My knees go weak.

Not a baby. Please, not that.

My chest tightens. I really don't want to get any closer.

But, in spite of myself, I creep towards the crib with the rest of the soldiers. There's a bitter, metallic taste in my mouth. The room is too silent.

In front of me, Montes stiffens. "*Nire bihotza—*"

He tries to block my view, but it's too late.

I catch sight of a tiny, unmoving body.

I barely have time to push away from my guards before I vomit.

I'm not the only one either. Grown men and women join me, people who I know have seen horrible things.

My stomach spasms over and over. I try to catch my breath, but I can't.

Montes was right. We might be monsters, but we're not evil.

Not like this.

MY CROWN SITS heavy on my head as I stare out at the crowds the next day.

The first day I wore a crown, my child died. And that's what it will always represent to me. Innocents dying for causes evil people uphold.

As heavy as my crown is, my heart is heavier.

"How badly do you want peace?" I open.

The people of Kabul roar in response.

This city has no official stadium, so I'm giving my speech on an open expanse of land, one where several old buildings once stood. Now all that remains are ruins.

There are cameramen both offstage and on, and I see them move closer as I began to speak. At my back I know there's a large screen magnifying me. I wonder just how much they can see of my expression.

"Good," I say, "because there are people out there that will make you fight for it. They will make you *die* for it."

My eyes flick only briefly to the side of the stage, where Montes watches me.

"What I'm about to tell you—I was advised not to say. But you have a right to know."

I see at least one officer begin to rub his temples.

"The leaders of each of the cities I've been visiting are being taken, one by one."

Already we've begun to notify the other cities and put their leaders on high alert that the West is targeting them. Many have pulled out of the tour altogether. Others have gone into hiding.

Murmurs run through the audience. Up until now, the king has kept quiet on this. His greatest fear was that the news would spark aimless violence among the citizens of the East.

And it might. They still have a right to know. And if I'm to be some great savior of theirs, then I should be the one to deliver the news.

"Someone doesn't want peace. Someone is afraid of what I am doing."

I turn my attention to the cameras because what I'm about to say is for the representatives. "To our enemies, listen carefully: Pray I don't find you. If I do, I will make you pay."

My gaze moves back to my audience; the crowd is roaring with outrage and excitement. "If you are angry, you have a right to be. No one should live in a world where they must fear for their life. But I will also tell you this: death cannot avenge death, and bloodshed cannot avenge bloodshed. Justice must be served, but it shouldn't turn good men into wicked ones."

I take off the crown. I flip it over in my hands. My audience has gone quiet.

"I've also been told that I should wear this. That this is what you want to see." I look up from the crown, towards the people watching me. "This," I hold up the headpiece, "means nothing. I am not above you. I am one of you.

"The world is interested in telling you all the ways we're different. You have the East and the West. Ruler and ruled. Rich and poor.

"But they lie."

I was never a very good orator. But this is different. The words are coming to me, born from a fire in my soul. I'm angry and excited and so very, very full of life.

"I killed many men during my time as a soldier," I say. In the past, admitting something like this would be a disaster. But these people already know I'm no idle ruler. "And I saw many men die. They all bled the same. *We* are all the same. And this," I hold up the crown. "This can go fuck itself." I fling the crown offstage, towards some of the king's soldiers. Much as I'd like to give it back to the people, I fear something as precious as gold would be enough to draw blood between civilians.

The audience bellows at the sight. This is fervor. This *is* revolution.

"We are all the same," I say. "Let's end this war together. As equals."

The crowd begins thumping their chests, the rhythm picking up pace until it's one continuous sound.

My eyes cut to the king, who stands just offstage. He rubs his chin, his eyes glinting as he watches me. When he notices me looking, he inclines his head, and the beginnings of a smile form along his lips.

Our enemies should be afraid.

I am a bomb, and they've just lit the fuse.

CHAPTER 34

SERENITY

WE LEAVE KABUL shortly after the speech, our next stop, Shanghai. The pacing of our itinerary was brutal to begin with, but now that figureheads have been disappearing, we're moving through the tour at a breakneck speed.

I fall asleep fully clothed on the airplane's bed, my face smooshed against the sheets. I rouse only once, when a familiar someone covers me with a blanket.

Montes's fingers trail down my cheek. My eyes open just enough to see him staring intently at me.

"I—" I almost say it then. Those three dreaded words that I've kept from the king for so long. It's equally shocking how natural they come, and how badly they want to be let out.

The king's touch stills.

"I'm happy you're here," I murmur.

"Always," he says, his fingers moving once more.

I'm already falling back asleep, like I didn't almost just surrender the last bit of my heart.

I'm jerked awake when the plane dips sharply to the left. I grip the edges of the mattress to keep from rolling.

The door to the back cabin is closed but on the other side I hear raised voices, their tones laced with controlled panic.

Quickly, I get up, shaking off the last of my grogginess, and stumble to the door.

When I open it I see Montes on the other side, heading straight for my room, presumably to wake me.

"What's going on?" I ask.

"Three enemy aircraft share our airspace," he says, his expression grim.

I glance out the window but see nothing.

"Are they armed?" I ask. It's a ridiculous question. Of course they are.

"Undoubtedly," Montes echoes my thoughts, "but they haven't shot us down yet."

No sooner are the words out of his mouth than I hear a distant hiss.

I've missed out on a hundred years of civilization, and yet in all that time weaponry hasn't changed much. Not if the sound I'm hearing is a—

"Missile incoming," the pilot informs us over an intercom. "Engaging the ABM system."

It's a fancy way of saying we're going to blow that fucker out of the sky. That is, if it doesn't hit us first.

The noise gets louder, and louder, and then—

BOOM!

The sky lights up as a fireball unfurls some distance away from us. A split second later the shock wave hits us, sending the plane canting, and throwing us idiots not belted in across the cabin.

450

I slam into the wall, my body dropping into the row of seats beneath it. When I look up, I see Montes on the floor nearby, crawling towards me.

"Are you okay?" he asks.

I nod. "You?"

"Yeah." He exhales the word out. He jerks his head towards the seats. "Strap in. It's going to get rough."

I right myself and begin to do just that. The plane starts losing altitude rapidly. I grab my stomach as we plummet. An alarm goes off and the overhead lights start to flash.

Montes makes it to the seat next to me and straps himself in.

"Has this happened to you before?" I ask.

He grabs my hand, his face stony. "Yes."

The king's men follow our lead, scrambling into seats and hastily buckling themselves in.

"And how did that end?" I ask. He obviously survived it.

"I was in the Sleeper for a month." He doesn't elaborate, which means it was likely worse than what I might imagine.

I hear another distant hiss start up as our plane continues to drop from the sky.

"ABM system reengaged," the pilot announces.

Another explosion follows the first, rocking the plane further. The people that still aren't buckled go tumbling across the cabin once more. One of them is Marco, and he falls close to my feet.

Fighting my baser impulses, I reach out a hand and drag him up to the seat next to me.

He nods his thanks, buckling his seatbelt right away. I feel the king's eyes on me, but I refuse to look over at him. I don't want to see his gratitude.

Shrapnel pings against the outside of the plane. But it's not until I hear the screeching sound of metal smashing into metal and the aircraft shudders that my eyes move to the window. Outside I see one of the engines catch fire.

How long does good fortune last for people like us? This is Russian roulette, and this might be the shot the kills us.

I squeeze the king's hand and take a calming breath. I don't fear the end. I haven't for a very long time. This isn't the way I'd choose to go, but there are worse ways to die than reclining in a plush chair, the world spread out beneath you.

The alarms are still blaring, the officers all have wide eyes. But no one screams. Montes brings my hand to his mouth and holds our entwined hands there.

I see his lips move. I can't hear his words, but I know what he's saying.

I love you.

I pinch my lips together. Only hours ago I almost said those very words right back to him.

His gaze meets mine. My mouth parts. I feel those words coming back, moving up my throat. They want out.

The plane hits some turbulence, breaking the spell. My gaze cuts away from him as my body's jerked about. The moment's gone, and if we die right now, we'll die with him never hearing those three words fall from my lips.

I can't tell if I feel relief or disappointment.

Both, I think.

Our seats begin to shake as our velocity increases. Above the shrill alarm I swear I hear the rumble of engines. Through the aircraft's tiny windows, I catch a glimpse of fighter jets. If they've come to end us, they got here too late.

But as I watch, they accelerate past us, presumably towards the enemy, who I still haven't seen.

The officers begin to clap and whoop at the sight, like we've been saved. All those jets managed to do was head off one enemy. But now gravity is our more obvious opponent.

Our aircraft continues to plunge straight towards the earth. I hate that I have enough time to feel my mortality slipping through my fingers.

I swear I feel the plane pull up, but I have no way of knowing whether that's just wishful thinking.

The ground is getting closer and closer. Our angle is still bad.

I look at Montes one more time. If I'm going to die, it will be staring into his eyes. We were bound to go down together.

When I meet his gaze, I can see relief, but I don't know what put the expression there.

It turns out that, whatever the reason, he'll live to tell me about it.

The plane levels out at the very last minute.

My gaze is ripped away from him as we slam into the earth. I'm jerked violently against my seatbelt. Part of the ceiling pulls away from the metal frame on impact, cutting off my view of the front half of the cabin.

The world is consumed by an awful screeching noise as the plane slides across the ground. I hear plastic and metal ripping away from the underside of the plane. A few screams join the noise, some panicked, and some high-pitched cries that cut off sharply.

And then, miraculously, we grind to a stop.

For several seconds I do nothing but catch my breath.

I didn't die.

"*Nire bihotza*, my hand."

I hear Montes's voice, and my chest tightens almost painfully.

The king didn't die either.

A choked sound comes out of my mouth as I face him and see that he is, in fact, alive.

I release his hand, a hand I've been squeezing the life out of, and cup the side of his face. I can't put into words what I feel. But now the relief that was so blatant in his eyes earlier seems to be making a home for itself beneath my sternum.

I pull him to me and kiss him roughly. How horrifying that my heart has come to rely on this creature.

I feel his surprise—he still isn't used to my affection, especially when I do it in public. But once his shock wears off, he kisses me back with a possessive intensity I've become familiar with.

Death will come for us both, sooner rather than later, but it won't happen today.

CHAPTER 35

SERENITY

I WATCH THE unfamiliar scenery pass me by. Montes and I sit in the back of the armored vehicle that arrived on scene shortly after we crashed.

Two of the king's men didn't survive the crash landing. One's neck snapped and the other was crushed under the section of ceiling that ripped away from the airplane's frame.

I'm so numb. At some point, you see too many people die. It becomes just one more ache in your heart. Another person taken too soon.

It takes several hours to reach Shanghai. When we do, I can only stare. Many of the buildings are in ruins, but what remains is in use. And the structures are from *before*. They've been kept up for over a century.

We eventually pull up to a high-rise that faces the East China Sea.

I should be taken with the sparkling ocean. I never imagined I'd see an ocean this far east. And it's beautiful. But I can't seem to tear my gaze away from the goliath we've stopped in front of.

We step out of the car, some combo of sewage and ocean air carried along the breeze.

"Have you ever been to the top of a skyscraper?" Montes asks, steering me towards it.

I shake my head. Montes had cornered me inside an abandoned skyscraper once, when I lost my memory, but I never made it close to the top.

"We're going to the top?"

Montes gives me just the barest hint of a smile. Some uncomfortable combination of excitement and trepidation fills me at the possibility, especially so soon after we were shot out of the sky.

The rest of our brigade exits their cars, and we all enter the lobby. The people inside stare and stare. It's probably a shock in itself to see the king of half the world. But their eyes linger the longest on me. And then out of the blue, one of them begins to thump their chest slowly.

Several more join in. Within seconds the whole room is doing it, the tempo increasing to a frantic pace.

This is becoming a habit, I notice.

I nod to them, and I'm sure I look more demure than I am. Montes waves, his other hand pressed against the small of my back.

"You were right," he says, his voice low. "This campaign will help end the war. Look at them. They will die for you."

"I don't want anyone to die for me," I whisper furiously back to him.

"That, my queen, is no longer for you to decide."

THE SOUR TASTE at the back of my throat hasn't disappeared since my enemies tried to shoot us from the sky. It's been decades since the West has pulled such a risky maneuver.

They will pay for it.

Already I've ordered attacks on several Western outposts they thought I didn't know about. I feel the familiar blood hunger. I want the sort of intimate revenge I swore off a long time ago.

It was easy enough to swear it off back then. For a long time I was deadened to most things. And then Serenity woke, and my heart awoke with her. Now it doesn't know how to remove itself from cold strategy.

My eyes fall on my queen as she moves about our quarters, taking in each furnishing and every detail.

No, my heart is no longer cold.

Christ, I want to hide this woman.

If I thought she'd forgive me for it, I would lock her away someplace where my enemies could never find her. But I think that would just about push the last of my luck with Serenity, and I don't want to give her another reason to despise me. She has too many of those already.

She stops in front of one of the windows, placing her fingertips against it.

"I'm used to seeing these without the glass still intact," she says.

"War hasn't destroyed everything," I say.

"No," she agrees, dropping her hand. She casts me an enigmatic look. "Not everything."

She begins removing her weapons and setting them on the small nightstand next to our bed.

Savage woman.

I watch her as she peels off one soiled clothing item after the next, dropping them where she stands. It's obvious her mind is in other places; she's oblivious to my eyes on her.

There's a smudge of dirt just behind her ear—a place she'd never notice or think to clean. I have the oddest desire to wipe it away.

Instead my eyes travel from it to the delicate line of her neck, then down her back. Her body is so small for such a force of nature. Sometimes I forget that. She takes up such a big part of my world.

Bruises speckle her skin. I frown at the sight. She's received each one in the short time since she's woken.

She turns her head in my direction, doing a double take when she realizes I've been watching her. Belatedly she covers herself.

I begin to walk towards her, unbuttoning my shirt as I do so. I decide then and there that whatever she's planning on doing naked, I'll be joining her.

"Don't you think it's a little too late to be shy?" I say.

"Not with you, no."

I can tell she wants to back up as I close the space between us. But she won't. Her pride and her nerves will prevent her from showing weakness. I love this about her, and I take advantage of it, stepping up to her until my chest brushes against her arms.

I pull them away from her body, exposing her. "I'm your husband."

She lifts her chin, staring up at me defiantly. "You haven't been for the last hundred years."

I grab her jaw and tilt her head to the side, so that I see the back of her ear. With my other hand I rub away the smudge I saw earlier.

I turn her head back to face me. "Save your anger for our enemies."

Our gazes hold, and I think I've gotten through to her.

She pulls away, slipping through my fingers once more. She wanders to the bathroom, closing the door behind her—but not all the way. It hangs open several inches.

An invitation.

Several seconds after the faucet turns on, the shower door bangs closed and I hear her suck in a breath, presumably at the temperature.

"You know, you could wait a minute for it to warm," I say, removing the last of my clothes.

"That's a minute's worth of water wasted," she calls back to me.

I close my eyes and savor the moment. Everything's changed—everything except for her. It's almost unbearable. Like a memory come back to life.

With a shuddering exhale, I open my eyes and head into the bathroom.

Her back is to me. She doesn't turn, even when I open the shower door and step inside. I know she knows I'm there, but she doesn't object.

I don't think she hates me nearly as much she wants to.

I push her mane of hair over one of her shoulders and kiss the back of her neck. This is how it was always meant to be between us.

I run my hands over her bruises.

She leans her head back into me, and I wrap an arm around her torso, pulling her even closer. This is the woman I never deserved, and this is the life I always craved.

Letting my eyes drift shut, I brush my mouth against one of her shoulder blades, leaning my forehead against her neck.

I would inhale her in if I could.

"Montes—"

I squeeze her even tighter. Just my name on her lips undoes me.

"Why do you love me?" she asks.

My lungs still and my eyes open. Serenity has turned her head halfway towards me.

Back on the plane I sensed she came close to uttering those very words. And now she wants to explore my feelings for her.

Because she's trying to figure out her own.

My heart will burst, I'm sure of it.

But I let on none of this.

Instead I press a kiss to Serenity's cheek.

"Why does anything happen the way it does?" I ask, resting my chin just above her head. "I don't know. I don't know why that first night in Geneva, when you entered my ballroom with your father, I couldn't take my eyes off of you. Or why, in a hundred years I haven't been able to banish you from my mind." Now I turn her to face me. "Or why, even after all the ways I've changed, I can love you the same way I always have.

"But I do."

God, I do.

CHAPTER 36

THE KING

BECAUSE OF THE attacks, and our quick exits from each territory, we have an extra day built into our schedule and nothing planned to fill it.

If we weren't at war, and if my enemies weren't actively trying to attack us, I would show her all around Shanghai. One day, once this is all over, I will take her to every distant corner of our world and show her sights she's never seen.

But that won't be today.

I let her sleep until noon comes and goes. When she still doesn't wake, the old worries begin to fester. That the cancer has come back. That the Sleeper never fixed her. That her exhaustion comes from within.

So, only hours after I've dressed for the day, I undress and slip back under the covers. I settle between her thighs, my hands snaking around her legs. And then I wake her up with a kiss.

There is no slow rise to consciousness with my wife. One moment she's asleep, the next she's trying to jerk away. I hold her hips in place, enjoying her surprise.

"*Montes.*" She squirms under me.

My lips return to her. Almost unwillingly, she moves against me, like she can't help it.

I groan against her core. I'm not going to last much longer like this.

Before she has a chance to protest, I flip her onto her stomach and move up her torso, my chest pressed to her back.

"Mon—"

With one swift thrust, I'm inside her.

Whatever she was about to say turns into a breathy sigh.

"Morning, my queen," I say against her ear.

My earlier fears concerning her health vanish now that I'm near her.

She relaxes against me, her body pliant beneath mine.

I thread my fingers between hers.

"Say it," I whisper.

It's been a demon riding me, the need to hear those words. I sense she loves me, but I want to hear the words from her.

I *must* hear them from her.

She stiffens beneath me. "No."

I swear I hear true worry in her voice.

She's close to cracking.

I nip the shell of her ear.

I will get her to say it.

And soon.

CREATURE COMFORTS STILL make me feel guilty. I'm not sure that part of me will ever go away. I spent all my formative years as one of the have-nots. I don't know what to do when everything I ever wished for is in the palm of my hand.

So I only reluctantly spend the day in bed with Montes, who appears to have no problem enjoying his creature comforts.

And oh, how he enjoys them. He hasn't even let me out to eat, instead bringing our meals to bed. And when we're not eating ...

Like I said, Montes enjoys his creature comforts.

It's only as the sun begins to set that he lets me slip from his arms.

He watches me as I dress. I feel those eyes, those thirsty, thirsty eyes drink me in.

When I go to grab a shirt, Montes says, "Ah, ah."

I give him a look over my shoulder. "Unless you'd chain me naked that bed, I'm going to have to dress at some point."

Give this man an inch, and he will take miles and miles.

He throws the covers off himself and leaves the bed to stride towards me. "Much as that would please me," he takes the shirt out of my hands and tosses it aside, "I'll have to save the chains for later."

Montes heads to our closet and pulls out a dress with black and gold feathers along the shoulders and what looks like armored scales along the bodice. "We have dinner tonight."

Between the relentless traveling and the attacks, I'd almost forgotten about the hateful dinners sprinkled liberally throughout the tour. We canceled all of the previous ones because they'd been contingent upon the officials of each territory.

"Shanghai's leaders?" Now I feel doubly guilty for spending a day in bed.

"They're fine," Montes says.

My attention returns to the dress.

"What *is* that?" I say, eyeing the gown with equal bits curiosity and revulsion.

"Armor for a queen."

OUR DINNER IS being held in an extravagant building with architecture even older than the skyscrapers, the roofs slanted, the colors deep and vivid.

I walk into the enormous main hall on the king's arm. My dress shivers as I move, the result of all those metal scales rubbing against one another.

The walls around us are gilded in gold, and the columns bracing the ceiling are a vibrant red. It's beautiful and foreign, and it makes me feel like an interloper.

As soon as the two of us catch the attention of the guests already inside, they begin pounding their chests, just like the men and women earlier. I press my lips together.

I never meant to become some sort of celebrity, and I'm unused to the positive attention I've been receiving. In the past, a good portion of the king's subjects didn't like me. I find it's much easier to deal with hate than love.

I dip my head. Even that doesn't stop the strange salutes they're all giving me. Not for several minutes. And once they do stop, it's not over. Not really, because everyone there wants to talk to me.

A waiter passes by, carrying several glasses of wine. I snatch one up, earning me a raised eyebrow from Montes. But for perhaps the first time since we've been together, he doesn't actively try to prevent me from drinking.

An hour goes by like this. Drinking and talking. The king is by my side the entire time, smoothly managing the conversations without letting on that he's doing so.

At some point, we come across Shanghai's regional leader, Zhi Wei, his wife, and several dignitaries he works with. All of them look a little spooked.

They're smart to be afraid. We've marked them for death by coming to their land. I still can't think of that house in Kabul without feeling nauseous.

Zhi bows, his entourage following his lead.

"It's an honor to have you here," he says when he straightens.

It's a curse.

I swallow down the bad taste I have at the back of my throat. I'm cursing these people by coming here.

"Thank you for hosting us," I reply.

He gives a solemn nod.

"We are eager to end the war." Zhi glances briefly at his wife. "We've lost two sons to it."

This part hurts. It always hurts. I think most soldiers don't fear death nearly so much as they fear this—their family's grief. Soldiers know better than most the mind games the dead can play with you.

"I will do everything in my power to make that happen," I say.

We chat with Zhi and his wife a little longer, then we move on to greet more people. I drink and greet, drink and greet. On and on it goes until the alcohol makes my smiles a little more genuine and my body a little less stiff.

I don't notice I've drawn closer to Montes until he brushes a kiss on my temple, a kiss I lean into. I realize then how much of my side is pressed against his, and that my arm is wrapped just as tightly around his waist as his is mine.

A glass clinks at the far end of the room, and for one brief instant, I fear it's another one of those embarrassing kiss requests meant for me and the king.

Instead, the waiter holding the glass clears his throat. "I'd ask all the guests to move into the dining room." He gestures to a room to my left. "Dinner will commence shortly."

Guests begin to meander towards the room, many throwing eager glances in my direction. Each one makes my heart stutter a little. Surely there are types of people that would like this attention, I'm just not one of them.

The king sticks closely to my side. If I had to guess, I'd say that he doesn't like the attention on me any more than I do.

We enter a small, overly ornate room dominated by a large rectangular table and dozens of place settings. Just like the main room, the walls here are gold. It feels like something out of a dream, something I will wake up from.

I scan the room for our seats. It's then that the back of my neck prickles.

I stiffen.

Even with the alcohol dulling my senses, there are some things I can't shake. I've been a soldier too long. Self-preservation and paranoia are two sides of the same coin.

So I covertly place my foot in front of the king, and then I push him. I exert just enough force to have him stumble forward and trip over my leg. He begins to fall, and I go down with him.

The sound of the bullet is explosive. I hear a ping as it hits a silver serving bowl just to the left of Montes.

That's all the time it takes for me to realize—

"They're trying to kill the king!" I shout, grabbing Montes's shoulder and shoving him the rest of the way to the ground. He forces me down along with him.

Distantly, I'm aware of others diving to the ground, but at the moment my attention is limited to the king.

When I try to cover his body with my own, he simply gives me a look and flips us.

He's looking at me with wild eyes as more shots fill the air. It's apparent from the agonized screams that the king was not the only target.

Wood and plaster dance in the air as the bullets tear through walls and furniture. I hear glass shatter as one of the shots rips apart a window. From my vantage point beneath the table I see people tumble to the ground.

My hands slide between me and the king and I grab my gun from the inner thigh holster I wear. All the while the sound of bullets and screams is a dark cadence in my ears.

I try to get up, but Montes isn't budging. I can see the warning in his eyes. *Don't you dare.*

"We need to take out the shooters," I say. I can't hear my own voice above the noise, but Montes must because he gives a slow shake of his head.

"*Stay down.*" I read his lips.

The air is filled with a hazy red mist. I taste it on my lips, and I feel it brush against my face. This isn't a simple execution, this is a butchering.

Montes won't let me up, but I can still see legs beneath the table. I look for pairs that are stationary. Panicked people run or hide. Attackers don't.

I see three separate sets of legs. I'm pulling the trigger before I can think twice about it. They go down, one after the next. When I see their heads and chests come into my line of sight, I shoot those too.

For a moment, I'm not positive I hit the perpetrators. There's the terrible possibility that these were innocents I took out. But the shots cut off abruptly.

An eerie silence follows.

Dust, plaster, and misted blood hang heavy in the air. Around us, scattered bodies lay. The woman closest to me is missing an eye, and across from me the wife of Shanghai's regional leader slumps against the wall, clutching her heart, her blood seeping between her fingers. Her eyes meet mine, and I see her surprise as she gasps in a breath.

Zhi crawls towards her, his body trembling with the effort as he drags his limp lower body across the floor.

The king's face is awash with horror as he takes in the pair as well.

That could've been us. I can tell that thought is running on repeat in his head.

"Montes," I say, gently pushing at him. He still pins me down.

His nostrils flare when his attention returns to me. I push against him again, signaling that I want to get up. I think he's going to refuse, but then, reluctantly, he rolls off of me.

I rise to my feet, Montes joining me a moment later.

Most of our guards have sustained some sort of injury. Those that haven't now move over to our attackers. I begin to follow.

Montes catches my forearm.

459

"*Not yet*," he says. At least, that's what I think he says. My ears are still ringing.

I don't bother arguing with him, I simply yank my arm from his grasp and head towards the rest of the men.

I can feel the king at my back, bearing down on me, and I sense his frustration. He's having trouble controlling an uncontrollable thing.

I reach the king's soldiers just as they're checking the shooters' vitals. I kick away our attacker's weapons, though I'm almost positive all three are dead.

I study our attackers. Two men, one woman. All dressed as waiters. One of them was the very man that ushered us into the dining room.

He'd timed the attack.

As I stare down the three gunmen, I notice several strange lumps around the woman's midsection. Now I crouch down, my hand going to the edge of the woman's shirt. I untuck the fabric and peel it back.

Beneath ...

It's been a hundred years since I last saw an explosive, but unless this is an elaborate hoax, they haven't changed much.

"Bomb," I whisper.

"What was that?" Montes says from behind me.

I stand and began to back away, one of my hands aimlessly groping for the king's.

"Bomb," I say much louder. "The woman is rigged."

The king's guards peer beneath the shirts of the other two shooters. I don't have the same view that they do, but I still see enough. And when their grim gazes meet my own, I have all the confirmation I need.

My eyes move across the room where half a dozen of the survivors stare at me with frightened eyes. Several more moan from the ground. "Everyone needs to evacuate," I say. "*Now.*"

CHAPTER 37

THE KING

I'M TIRED OF this, tired of death always following my queen. We barely escaped with our lives. *Again.*

Immediately after Serenity discovered the bombs, we were evacuated, along with the rest of the surviving guests, leaving only the dead behind.

I lean back in my seat, ignoring the view of Shanghai as it begins to blur past us. If I look back now, I'd still be able to see the tiled roof of the shikumen-style building we were in not five minutes ago.

But I don't glance back; I look at Serenity, really look at her.

Her jaw's tight as she stares out the window. She looks tired, angry—desolate. I can hardly bear it.

I reach out, my thumb rubbing against her cheekbone. She leans into the touch, closing her eyes briefly. There are smears of blood and dust all over her.

I'm so tired of seeing her wear this war paint.

I have only myself to blame. She's a monster I created long before I had her in my clutches. This is the karmic reckoning I've put off for so long.

I want her eyes on me, her eyes and her bloodied, bruised skin.

Without a second's more thought, I drag her onto my lap, refusing to fight the impulse.

"Montes, stop." She pushes halfheartedly against my chest as I reel her in. I'm surprised she's still going through the motions of keeping me away. We both know she no longer wants to. "Let me go."

"*No,*" I whisper harshly.

And then, all at once, Serenity gives in. Her body sags into mine, and she leans her forehead into my chest. I feel her body quake, and automatically I begin to stroke her back, like I'm some caring, good guy and not a heartless son of a bitch. And Serenity clutches me tighter, like she's a fragile, docile thing and not the killing machine *she* is.

She breathes in a ragged gasp, pulling herself together. Slowly she draws her head away from my chest. The look she gives me ... men have lived and died and never seen that look.

BOOM—BOOM-BOOM!

The explosions go off at our backs, one right after another. Serenity's eyes widen.

A second later the car skids from the force of the shockwave.

Shit.

The two of us are thrown forward, and I hear our driver curse.

Out the back windows a fireball lights up the night.

The undying king and his mythical queen were nearly killed as they ate dinner from dainty china. The West would've loved that story.

Next to me, Serenity is transfixed by the explosions, and her expression makes my blood run cold.

Whatever soft emotions overtook her a moment ago, they're gone.

I wish she feared more and lived through less because right now, I don't see desolation—or even anger—on her pretty face.

Just ruthless resolve.

SERENITY

TONIGHT WE SLEEP inside one of the king's garrisons, located just outside Shanghai proper.

Montes is taking no risks.

The two of us lie together in a windowless cement block that's buried dozens of feet below the earth.

Once again, I'm back in the fucking ground.

The subterranean structure is the closest I've ever felt to my bunker. And I hate it. I hate the very thing that's made me *me*. I can't decide whether the king's lavish lifestyle has rubbed off on me, or whether it's simply the knowledge that I've spent lifetimes belowground—it doesn't honestly matter. I'm devastated anyway.

First to find the king is no longer evil, then to find I can no longer passively endure what I once readily accepted.

Who am I?

"A queen."

I startle at the king's voice. Only then do I realize I spoke out loud.

"My wife," he continues. "The woman that's going to change the world—the woman that already has."

I roll over in bed and gaze at Montes.

He brushes my hair off my face, his fingers lingering. When did he get so achingly sweet?

He must sense my inner turmoil because he says, "This is right. What you're doing is right."

Color me shocked. I assumed the king was only going along with my peace campaign because of our deal. But to hear him admit that he essentially believes in me and my cause … it's doing strange things to my heart.

His eyes move above us, around the room. "Was this what it was like, living in that bunker?"

I nod, not bothering to look away from him.

His gaze returns to mine. "I should hate this," he says, "but I would take a lifetime of living underground if it meant you'd be by my side."

I swallow.

I don't want to hear this. I don't want to *feel* this. But only because I do—I really, really do, and I can't fathom this vision breaking my heart. Montes, in his infinite cruelty, did this very thing to me a hundred years ago. He convinced me of all the ways he couldn't live without me. And I fell for him, even if I never admitted it, and I paid for that terrible love with my life.

Now, this wise, *decent* Montes is demanding more than just my body all over again.

I knew this would happen, but oh, how I'm—

"You're *afraid*." The mind reader says this like it's some great revelation.

I open my mouth, fully prepared to lie. "I'm not—"

"Oh," he interrupts, tilting my chin up, "but you are."

My nostril flare as our gazes hold. And hold. And hold.

And then he sees something he shouldn't.

"*My God*," he utters. His chest expands as he takes in air. And then his mouth descends on mine.

And now I have to deal with the very real possibility that I lost my last bit of power, because the king, I think he *knows*.

He knows that I love him.

I WAKE IN the middle of the night to an empty bed. I lay there for several seconds staring up at the cement ceiling before I realize what woke me.

Light.

Just like the bunker I spent many years in, there is no natural light in this subterranean fortress. When the lights are out, you can literally see nothing. But I can see the cement ceiling dimly.

I sit up and search for the source of the light. It comes from the edges of the door, which isn't fully closed. I can hear voices in the distance.

What's happened now? And why wasn't I woken?

Getting out of bed, I hastily pull on a pair of fatigues, wincing when my feet touch the chilly cement floor. I shove on my boots, then leave our room.

Out in the hall, a single sentry stands guard. I nod to him, then head down the corridor toward the sound of voices.

Ahead of me, the hallway bends sharply to the right. I'm almost around the corner when I make out who's speaking.

"How could you not tell me?" I hear the king hiss.

"They never told *me*," Marco replies.

I hadn't seen or heard from the king's right-hand since before we left for the dinner.

"Do you realize how badly that could've gone?"

"How could I not? You forget that I care for her too," Marco says, his voice heated.

"No," Montes's voice is low and lethal, "let's be clear about this: she is not Trinity. She is not yours. Serenity is mine."

I lean my head back against the wall and close my eyes. I've already heard too much. Before either man knows I'm there, I return to our room and slip back in bed.

If I had heard that all correctly, then Marco had loved my clone.

Can this world get any more fucked-up?

Turns out, it can.

CHAPTER 38

SERENITY

SEOUL. OUR NEXT stop.

This is no longer the same tour we started the trip believing it was. The meetings with regional leaders have been cut out completely, our stay in each local has been drastically shortened to just the speeches, and our immediate surroundings are now safe rather than luxurious.

The military aircraft we sit in is a far cry from the king's royal plane. I can see the structure's exposed metal framework as well as the insulated wires that run along the walls and ceiling, and we sway in our seats with every subtle movement the aircraft makes.

This new king. I assess him while he's not watching me. His head dips towards the sheet of papers he reads, one of his legs jiggling like he can't possibly sit still.

He's still a workaholic. Still vain. Still controlling. Still scarily powerful.

Montes glances up, and his eyes heat instantly.

Still in love with me.

"What is my vicious little queen thinking about?" he asks over the drone of the engines.

A hundred years for a man to become whatever it is he wants.

I cock my head. "I think you're afraid of getting everything you ever wanted," I say. "I think you know that once you do, you'll be forced to realize how empty it all was in the end."

He lowers the papers in his hands. I have his full attention now. His eyes are alight with an emotion I can't quite put my finger on. I don't know if it's just his usual intensity or something else.

"My queen came back to me a psychoanalyst."

"You wanted to know my thoughts," I counter.

He watches me for a beat longer, then unbuckles his harness.

"Your Majesty," one of his guards is quick to intervene, "you need to—"

The king raises a hand and quiets his officer. Now we do have some attention drawn our way. And among those eyes are Marco's. I meet his gaze briefly, just long enough for him to look away. And then my attention returns to the king.

Montes crosses over to my seat and kneels before me, his hands resting on my thighs. The gesture is casual, but like anything that has to do with Montes, my mind moves to more intimate things. Stripping off clothes, hot breath against my skin, and more caresses from those hands.

"I don't know," he says softly.

I furrow my brows. "You don't know what?"

His thumb absently strokes my leg. "Whether you are right or not. I've wondered the same thing myself. Whether I could've stopped the war from being drawn out this long."

I search his face.

"But I'm not sure I could have," he adds, "not without staying the same man I was."

It's still there; I see a flash in the back of his eyes even now. The urge to be cruel.

Montes leans forward, and I get to see that face of his up close and personal. If I thought he was intense far away, it's nothing to this—having this man's complete and utter attention.

And then he kisses me, his captive queen.

The entire production draws out. Montes won't release my lips, not even when I try to move away. We have an audience, after all, an audience that only moments ago I was all too willing to entertain. The king has manipulated me yet again.

It's only once he feels me give into the kiss that it sweetens. Eventually I manage to rip my face away from his.

I'm breathing heavily. This man that lays waste to all sorts of things, his head is still close to mine. At some point during our kiss, his hold on my legs tightened. It's almost bruising, but I only now notice it.

My voice is low when I speak. "It doesn't matter what you say, or what you do now, Montes. You're still always going to be the man that ruined the world in the first place."

He draws away, his eyes lingering on my mouth. "I am. And if it meant getting more time with you, I would've ruined it sooner."

As soon as we arrive in Seoul, I sense it. The day feels ominous, like a storm about to break.

My new gun is holstered at my hip. No one's asked me to remove it, but I wouldn't anyway. The West's violence has only increased throughout this trip.

We're taken straight from the airfield to the stadium where I'll be giving my speech. By the end of the day I will be back on that aircraft, heading towards the next location. Trying to stay one move ahead of the West.

Like the other cities I visited, Seoul show signs of the toils of war. Half the buildings are nothing more than rubble. And on many of them I see more posters and wall art depicting my image with the words *Freedom or Death* scrawled beneath. In one instance, I even see two assault rifles crossed beneath my image, like a skull and cross bones.

I've become a freedom fighter.

As our vehicle pulls up to our destination, I catch sight of the stage I'll be speaking from. It's nothing more than a temporary construction set up at the end of one of Seoul's city streets. Some stadium seating appears to have been brought in, but other than that, the people use the topography itself to get a view of the stage.

And the people! I expected a low turnout. We had to change the time of the speech to fit into our rushed itinerary. But, if anything, the place looks overcrowded.

The street in front of the stage is packed with hundreds, if not thousands of bodies. Large skyscrapers border the road on either side, and judging from the people camped out just inside the broken windows of many of them, I can tell that this is the city's improvised seating plan.

The armored vehicle comes to a stop at the fenced-off back of the stage.

"Are you sure you want to do this?" Montes asks, casting a speculative look at our surroundings. He doesn't let on, but I know he's worried. Maybe even downright panicked.

He still hasn't insisted I leave. And now he wants my input.

I reach out and take his hand, drawing his attention to me. Very deliberately, I brush a kiss along his knuckles. "Yes," I say softly.

He stares at our hands for several seconds, then his eyes flick up to me.

I don't thank him for being reasonable, but I know he can see my gratitude.

He nods, but his expression turns grim. "Very well."

He exits the car, holding the door open for me to follow. Almost immediately, a crew of men and women close in on us.

"Your Majesties," one of them says, crowding me and Montes, "we're so very happy to have you here. Please follow me. We have your wardrobes waiting for you in the dressing room."

Wardrobes?

I raise an eyebrow at the king, but he's too busy scowling at anyone that gets too close to me.

We're lead to a makeshift room, which is really not much more than four temporary walls.

Inside it, a stylized black uniform and a tuxedo wait for us.

I remove my outfit from the wall. The uniform looks half paramilitary and half high-fashion. I can't help but grimace when I notice the shoulder and upper arms of the fitted top glitter.

Whatever. At least it's not a dress.

I change, making sure to strap my new gun to my outfit. My father's gun is packed with my things, which are Lord knows where.

That unsettling feeling still lingers in the air. It stays with me even after the king and I are ushered from the room.

We stand together behind a red velvet curtain, the two of us waiting to be introduced to the world.

I glance over at him.

The devil never looked so good. He wears a suit, his hair swept back from his face. And his eyes—a person could lose their soul in their dark depths. He appears just as he did when he waited for me at the base of those steps in Geneva. The monster who'd come in and ruined my life. And now, a hundred years later, I stand at his side, determined to fix everything he's broken.

"Thirty seconds," someone calls out to us.

Montes turns to me. "Are you ready?" Today we're walking out together and facing the crowd as a unified front.

I nod.

He doesn't say anything, just takes me in, looking at me like I'm his own personal apparition before he bows his head and faces forward again.

The people around us begin counting down with their fingers, like this whole production must be executed down to the very second.

Their fingers run out, and then the king and I are walking onto the stage.

Large screens have been set up in between the buildings. I see our faces projected onto them as we step forward. For the first time, I realize that it's not just the king who appears inhuman.

I do too.

The ferocity of the scar that runs down my cheek, the tightness of my jaw, the look in my eye—I'm no natural thing. Murder and violence have made me this way. Loss and war have made me this way.

I look like a savage.

A savage queen. One who doesn't need a crown or even a weapon to appear powerful.

I see it now—this world's faith in me. It's not just that I am an anachronism; the harshness of my face speaks to these people who have only ever known war.

No wonder the West wants me gone.

A century has gone by, and yet even after all that time I am still something to fear.

CHAPTER 39

SERENITY

OUR ENEMIES WAIT until the king and I are separated.

Until I'm vulnerable.

"I did not choose this fate willingly," I say, right in the heat of my speech.

My eyes briefly flick to the wings of the stage, where Montes watches me. He said his piece and then left me win the crowd over.

"Just as many of you did not choose yours," I continue. "But these lives are still ours, and they matter."

The people need to know that whatever dream they held tightly onto, it can happen. Dead queens can be resurrected. Peace can follow war. Good can vanquish evil.

The back of my neck prickles, and my voice wavers.

Something … is amiss.

I swear I hear the quiet drone of an aircraft, but when I look up to the cloudless blue sky, it's utterly empty.

"I don't bleed for the West," I resume speaking. "And I don't bleed for the East. I have and always will bleed for freedom, and I will always fight those who seek to oppress you."

The crowd roars.

High above us, something glints, catching the light of the noonday sun. It jogs my memory. Hadn't I watched something like this back at the king's palace?

My breath catches.

Oh God.

Now I remember.

Optical camouflage, the material that made the enemy all but invisible.

I turn to the officers. Their fingers are at their earpieces. My own hand goes to my gun reflexively.

Then I hear it. The horrible whistling sound of a bomb being dropped.

It's already too late.

BOOM!

The first one explodes to my left, in the middle of our audience. Concrete and metal and flesh blast into the air in a hundred different directions as a rotted-out building is ripped apart. A hundred people die before my eyes, all in an instant. Just like my mother had years ago.

A second explosion follows the first, this to my right. The bomb unfurls like a strange and terrible flower, and the sound that accompanies it is so loud it seems to move through my bones. I can feel the hot breath of it already, though I'm far, far away.

As I watch, several armed soldiers begin rappelling from an aircraft that's still all but invisible.

My eyes find Montes's. He's fighting his guards trying to get to me.

468

A third explosion hits, just off to the side of the stage.

BOOM!

My gaze rips from the king as I'm thrown back, my hair whipping around my face as I tumble through the air. Fire and heat unfurl, and this time, for a split second, it feels as though I'm being boiled alive. And then my body slams into the ground and the intensity of the explosion retreats.

For several seconds I stay down, dizzy and disoriented. I can't seem to suck in enough air.

I push myself up. I can taste blood in my mouth where my teeth cut the inside of my cheek. I spit it out, then run my tongue over my lower lip.

The air is thick with smoke and debris. But even through the haze, I manage to see the king's guards now vehemently trying to force Montes off the stage. He's thrashing wildly against them, and I can't hear what he says, but he only has eyes for me.

I turn my attention to the crowd beyond the stage. Bombs are still being dropped, and I notice a sick symmetry to it. They're roughly outlining the perimeter of the amphitheater and arena, corralling us in. The enemy is now amongst the civilians. I see small flashes of light scattered throughout the crowd where the soldiers are now firing their weapons.

This isn't a battle. It's a massacre.

I spot the microphone I used not a minute ago; it lays on its side some distance away from me.

No one is dying today without working for it.

I stand just as the king's soldiers turn their attention to me.

Unholstering the firearm stashed at my side, I flick off the safety and run to the fallen microphone, swiping it from the floor.

The cameras have shifted their focus to the audience. If the sight wasn't already horrific enough, it's being projected around us. Their screams are a chorus in my ears, and thanks to the video footage, their agony is intimately on display.

"Citizens of the East!" I shout into the mike. The skeptic in me figured the sound systems would be down, but they're not—not yet, anyway. My voice echoes through the speakers, harmonizing with the roar of the fire.

At my words, I see the cameras pan to me. The whole thing is macabre, especially since several of the large screens projecting my face have caught fire. "If you're going to die today, let it be on your terms, not theirs." I raise the hand holding my gun. "And let it be at my side."

I drop the mike and run to the edge of the stage.

"*Serenity!*" the king shouts from far behind me.

I don't bother looking back, and I don't hesitate. I leap into the crowd of bodies.

Down here it's bedlam. Madness. People are screaming as bombs continue to drop. The ground quakes, each explosion like a drumbeat.

There are people on fire. People missing arms and legs. People getting crushed underfoot. People bleeding and dying.

I cut my way through the crowd, my eyes pinioned to the enemy soldiers rappelling down from seemingly nowhere, their aircraft invisible to the naked eye. They slide down their ropes and drop into the crowd.

I aim my weapon at one of them and fire.

Even at this distance, I can tell I clipped them on the shoulder by the way their body jerks. Their hold loosens on the cable, and then they're falling. As soon as they reach the ground, the crowd swallows them up.

My eye catches the large screens. It's a close up of me. My hair is wild, my lip bloody, and cold determination glints from my eyes.

Savage justice.

The footage pans out and I see the king's soldiers cutting their way through the crowd, trying to get to me.

I rip my gaze away to aim my weapon at another enemy soldier descending down the ropes. I pull the trigger again, and again I hit my target.

Say what you will about the future, their guns have improved.

I begin picking the enemy off one by one.

The crowd parts for me, and I get to see exactly what hope looks like on their faces.

Amongst the chaos, something shifts.

I sense him before I see him. And then he's up there on the screen, his dark, ageless face blown up for us all to see.

The king strides through the crowd, straight towards me. I turn away from the screen, and look behind me just as his soldiers reach me.

As they surround me, I see Montes, in the flesh, a gun brandished in his hand.

I've never seen him like this, walking amongst chaos and danger like he's striding down the halls of the palace.

This is not the king I knew. This is not the ruler cloistered away in his ivory tower, nor is it the killer who fought at my side in South America.

He's something else. Something *more*.

The sounds of battle rush back in. I'm no longer feeling so irreverent about jumping into fray. Not now that the king is on the battlefield with me, prime for the plucking. There are no Sleepers nearby, nothing to save him if he gets mortally wounded.

He reaches me then. This close, I see the vein in his temple throbbing and the hard set of his features. "There is no winning this, Serenity."

I know. I knew it before I leaped off that stage. It's just not my nature to run from danger.

The king's eyes leave mine to focus on something over my shoulder. His whole demeanor changes.

I turn in time to see enemy soldiers rushing towards us. They shoot my guards. I hear a grunt of pain as a soldier to my left falls to his knees, clutching his chest.

Next to me Montes growls, and then he lifts his gun and begins shooting at the enemy. I follow his lead, shooting more soldiers converging on us.

"Men, cover the queen!" Montes yells. "Let's get our asses out of here!"

I don't have time to marvel over the king before his men surround us, clearing a path towards the stage.

It takes less than a minute for the enemy to gun down those soldiers covering mine and Montes's front. I don't have time to check their vitals now that the king is exposed.

He won't die.

Not here. Not now.

Turns out, however, that the king is pretty effective at defending himself.

Montes and I back up as we fire. Every target Montes shoots at goes down. His accuracy is even better than mine.

"You've gotten good!" I yell over the noise.

His lips draw back from his teeth as he fires off three more rounds, his arm barely jerking at the gun's kickback.

"I've had a hundred years to practice!" he shouts.

"Not taking a compliment?" I say, pulling the trigger twice more. "How unheard of."

"If we live through this," he says, "I'm spanking you for that."

I smile gruesomely. He's still good at battle-talk.

"If we live through this, I might just let you."

He grins.

Slowly, we make our way through the melee, our guards covering our flanks. When we get to the stage, we have to turn our backs to the fighting.

Gunfire lights up the ground around us. One of the soldiers ahead of me jerks as a bullet tears through his arm, but he doesn't slow. Whoever these soldiers are, they're made of *tough* stuff.

We cross behind the curtains, and the shots cease now that our enemies no longer have a visual on us.

Up ahead, our motorcade waits for us, and the soldiers guarding me and the king now hustle us to one of the vehicles. Montes and I are barely inside when the door slams behind us and the car skids out. Now we're moving targets. Any enemy in the sky could get a bead on us.

I wait for the next explosion to come. The one that will kill me and Montes.

It never happens. One second bleeds into the next, and the sounds of fighting gradually fade away.

"*Nire bihotza.*"

I swivel just as Montes gathers me to him. He holds me tightly in his arms, like I might evaporate.

"We made it," he murmurs into my hair, "We made it."

I let out a breath. Things are not processing, not the way they will once the high wears off. My brain moves sluggishly.

For several seconds we sit there in silence, our car careening down the streets.

"Are you all in one piece?" he asks.

"Yes," I whisper against him. "You?"

"Yeah." A beat of silence passes, and then, "Don't fucking do that again."

There is my cold, cruel husband.

I don't respond.

"Marco and your officers?" I ask instead.

He sighs, knowing I'm evading the topic. "They're already on their way to the aircraft."

I nod.

Montes leans his head back against the seat rest. "No more, Serenity. No more."

Speeches, he means. Speeches and visits.

I nod again.

I might be determined, but I'm not suicidal. We'll figure out another way to sway the people, one a little less deadly.

The drive to the airfield is more than a little eerie. No one shoots at us, no one even seems to notice us.

And that damn tingle skitters up and down my back again.

Not right. Not right. Not right.

This isn't unfolding as it should.

The airfield comes into view, as does the hangar where our aircraft waits. A minute later, our vehicle pulls up to it, the rest of the motorcade filing in around us.

Soldiers hop out, several jogging over to our car. They usher us out, and Montes and I, along with his officers and his men, head towards the taxying aircraft.

We never make it.

I see the pool of blood first, near one of the rear wheels of the aircraft. It doesn't draw attention to itself, but it's shiny, fresh.

My steps falter.

Ambush.

It barely has time to register before the men and women loitering about the hangar withdraw their weapons. The enemy has camouflaged itself to look just like us.

The king's enemies knew that we would fly out of here.

They begin to open fire, and Montes's men go down one after another.

I unholster my weapon for the second time and begin to fire. Two shots in, the chamber clicks empty.

And now I am a sitting duck, no better than a civilian.

Ahead of me, Montes is busy shooting the enemy, his movements fluid. Practiced. My mercenary king is a strange and glorious sight.

The guards that surround us—those that still live—are also firing. I can see some of them calling in for backup, but by the time anyone else arrives, the fight will be over.

None of us are leaving here until the enemy is gone.

Or we're dead.

The bullet takes me by surprise.

My body jerks back from the impact. I don't feel the pain. Not immediately. The itch and burn of the bullet's entrance and the sickening tug of its exit are merely uncomfortable.

I hear the king's shout amongst the barrage of bullets. How loud he must be yelling to cut through all that noise.

I swear seconds slow to a crawl as I stare out blindly at my surroundings. My hand falls to my stomach. I actually *feel* my insides as I press my palm against the wound.

I stagger, then drop to my knees.

Now I feel the pain. Oh God, now I feel it.

That agony is so acute I'm nauseous. The only thing that stops me from vomiting is that the pain closes up my throat. I can barely swallow in air.

I need to move.

I'm hurt and soldiers are still attacking.

I suck in a breath and then another. Sheer force of will has me crawling across the cement. Scattered around me are several bodies, both friend and foe. I hiss in a breath as I grab a gun lying a foot from one of them.

Gritting my teeth, I force myself back to my feet. An agonized cry slips out as the movement tugs at the injury.

My eyes search for Montes.

When I find him, he's mowing the enemy down with his gun, making his way towards me. He holds his bloody left arm close to his side, and I realize I'm not the only one injured.

That is enough to invigorate me.

Someone hurt my monster.

I begin to shoot the men attacking the king, baring my teeth as I do so. I welcome my bloodlust like an old friend.

Enemies go down, one right after the next.

Aim. Fire. Aim. Fire. I'm screaming as I shoot, from rage and from pain.

The gun clicks empty.

I'm breathing heavy. I'll have to bend down to grab another, and I really don't know if I'll make it back up.

I'll shoot from the ground.

I collapse more than kneel onto the cement, and I cry out as my entire body radiates pain.

At the sound of my shout, Montes's head snaps to me. He falters, his eyes burning, burning as he takes me in.

Lately I've seen the king wear many new faces. This is another I've never seen. His nostrils are flared, his mouth parted and his chest heaving.

His mouth moves. *Nire bihotza.*

Seeming to forget about the fight still raging around us, he staggers towards me.

I'm shaking my head.

I'm just grabbing another gun, I want to tell him.

He doesn't stop. One tear falls down his cheek, then another.

A dozen different gun blasts are going off every second, but Montes doesn't hear any of them. He's forgotten about the fight.

I lick my lips. "Mont—"

A bullet rips its way through the king's neck.

Tha-thump.

Tha-thump.

Tha-thump.

My heart palpitates in my ears. And I'm choking, choking.

I try to scream, but nothing comes out.

Montes reaches a hand to his throat. Instantly, his blood envelops it. The king sways on his feet, his gaze locked on mine, then his legs fold out from under him.

A hundred years of war, a hundred years of fighting and waiting, and it all comes to this—a messy death in a hangar.

Montes. I mouth his name.

He's still staring at me, even as his body jerks. Death throes. I've seen them often enough.

This is my last fear, and just like all the others, I have to live through it.

Pain and anguish and rage all gather below my sternum.

I'm falling, falling back into that abyss that I've tried for so long to crawl out of.

I welcome the darkness.

Now a brutal cry tears from my throat. I grab a gun from the nearest dead man, my lips curling back, and then I begin to fire. I kill the closest people in a matter seconds, smiling terribly as blood and bone explode out the back of their bodies.

Freedom or death. It's an apt slogan. I will either live by my own terms or die by them. And I'll take as many of these fuckers with me as I can.

473

Someone clips me in the arm. My torso jerks back, but it only takes a moment to recover. And then I'm pulling the trigger once more.

I can feel the pain screaming across my body; it harmonizes with the screams inside my head. And still I shoot.

The enemy falls, one after another.

My gun clicks empty, but now the ground is full of scattered bodies. I crawl to one of them, pausing to vomit from the pain.

Just as my hand reaches for another weapon, a booted foot kicks the gun away.

Lightheaded and cold from blood loss. I reach a hand down to brace myself against the ground.

I sense more than see the soldiers swarm around me.

Something heavy slams into my head, and the world goes dark.

CHAPTER 40

SERENITY

THE SOUND OF beeping wakes me.

I come to in a narrow hospital bed.

For a girl that hates doctors, I end up in quite a few hospitals. Of course, that's assuming I'm in one at the moment.

It smells like a hospital—that antiseptic smell hasn't apparently changed in the last hundred years.

The moment I try to move, I hear the jangle of metal, and the sharp edge of handcuffs digs into my wrists.

I tug on them again and find each hand has been locked to the metal frame of the bed I lay on.

Imprisoned to a bed. This is going to make going to the bathroom interesting.

I sit up the best I can, ignoring how the metal rubs away skin.

My last memories come rushing back. The explosions, the shootout at the hangar. My stomach was torn open, and then ...

Montes.

I can't catch my breath.

Dead.

The grief is instant, unfurling within me. My heart is shattering, just the way I feared it would.

A tear slides out, and my throat works. I lock my jaw to fight back the anguished cry I want to let loose.

It's unfathomable. My monster can't die. My nightmare can't be over. Not when I was just beginning to enjoy it.

My body shakes as I fight to keep myself together. I know better than to fall apart now. Not now when I'm clearly my enemy's prisoner.

I *will* kill them all. Every single person.

The girl who hates games needs a game plan.

By the time they come for me, I have one.

A SINGLE MAN enters the room. He's some sort of ex-military, even though he wears civilian clothes.

I glare at him. I can't help it. I want to gut him and savor his screams. The killer in me begins to hunger.

Because Montes—

I cut the thought off.

The game plan, I remind myself.

"Your Majesty," the man murmurs, dipping his head.

I'm surprised by the show of reverence.

He closes the door behind him and approaches me.

"You treat all your prisoners this nicely?" I ask, jingling my cuffs as I speak.

"No." He pulls a chair up to the bed. "Just queens, I'm afraid. I'm Chief Officer Collins, head of the Western United Nation's Security Department."

"And you're here to interrogate me?"

Collins gives me a wan smile. "I'm here to talk with you."

"Pretty words," I say.

He leans forward, bracing his elbows on his thighs. "You've done this before," he states, settling himself in.

My eyes wander to the suit he wears. The pleats of it are crisp, but the material has a faded look. "How many items of clothing do you own?" I ask.

He follows my gaze and self-consciously smooths down the material before he returns to looking at me. "We're not here to talk about my wardrobe."

"I bet not many," I continue. "And I bet you're still better off than most of the WUN's citizens."

He gives me a bored look, like he's only listening because he must.

"It was not always like that," I say. I draw in a deep breath and look around at my surroundings. There's not even a window in this closet of a room. "Where am I?" I ask.

"You're in the West," he says carefully.

I figured that much.

"And when am I?" It's an odd question, but judging by the lack of pain, I'm guessing I've recently been removed from a Sleeper.

He threads his fingers together. "You were injured a week ago."

I only lost a week this time.

"Injured by your people," I clarify.

Collins nods. "But you weren't killed."

"How benevolent of them. And where was their compassion when they bombed thousands of innocents that day?"

"Some sacrifices needed to be made—"

"Then *you* die." I snap. "If you think sacrificing any life is necessary, then I want to see you give yours up first."

Collins mouth tightens. "I didn't give the orders for the West to bomb a city block."

"But you're defending them."

I'm not sure why I'm even engaging in this conversation. This man doesn't care.

He leans back in his seat. "The representatives want to work with you."

"Of course they do," I say.

Wars are often based off of ideological differences, and I have become an ideology that can win the war. And I am one that both sides can look to. After all, I was an emissary of the West before I was Queen of the East. Never has such an easy solution just fallen into the laps of so many powerful people.

"Give me one good reason why I should work with them."

"The king is dead."

My nostrils flare and my muscles tense, but other than that, I don't react.

Collins cocks his head. "No words?"

He doesn't want words. He wants me to weep or cheer or give him something that he can take to his bosses to manipulate me with.

Instead, I say, "Montes has cheated death longer than anyone else. I'll need to see a body before I believe it."

476

"You think highly of him." It's not a question, and Collins doesn't state it as though it is, but I'm expected to answer nonetheless.

"Is there a point to this?" I say.

"From what I hear, he's the one that hid you from the world for all this time."

"And?" I say it like I don't give a damn about the betrayal.

"It seems like something unforgivable," Collins elaborates.

I've been in enough of these rooms and talked to enough of these men to know they are always trying to dig under your skin. I'm sure the tactic works when someone can be caught off-guard. But what could I possibly be surprised by at this point? I have lost everything I ever loved.

"And you're assuming I forgave him," I say.

He raises his eyebrows but inclines his head.

"That is not the worst thing the king has done to me." I tilt my head. "What are you trying to do, create dissension between me and the king? He's dead."

But then, as I stare at him, my heart begins to beat faster and faster. Because creating dissension appears to be exactly what he's doing. That would only be useful if …

I feel my shock wash over me. "The king *is* alive."

CHAPTER 41

SERENITY

COLLINS SHAKES HIS head. "I already told you, he's dead."

Now that I'm looking for it, I can see the WUN officer's uncertainty.

He doesn't *know*, which is good enough for me. If Montes could be alive, he likely is—one doesn't survive a century and a half by sheer luck alone.

A surge of hope moves through me.

"Serenity, I urge you to weigh my next words carefully," Collins says, settling into himself. "The representatives are willing to work with you. They want to end the war."

I reign in my excitement. My plan—I'll need to change it now that the king is likely alive.

"If you agree to it, I will take you to them straightaway," he continues.

I narrow my eyes. "And if I refuse?"

He hesitates. "If you refuse, you will be transferred from this military hospital to a work camp." His face softens and his voice lowers, "You don't want that. It's not a good way to go."

I never did well with ultimatums, and I don't want to go along with this one. I'm tired of bad men getting their way.

I'm tired of being used.

"From what I've seen," Collins says, "all you want is peace."

I lean forward, my arms pulled taut against the handcuffs. "Men like the representatives will never give you peace. They will only ever give you tyranny."

I lean back against the metal headboard. "But, you're right. What I most want is the war to end." I draw in a deep breath and try to recall all the tricks my father used as an emissary. I'm going to need them. "So long as what they ask of me is reasonable, I will work with them."

WHAT CAN ONLY be a handful of hours later, I'm being escorted out of the hospital room, my hands bound behind my back.

Collins is by my side, along with several guards that look like they'd have no problem killing me if I so much as moved wrong.

I'm escorted out of the building. The sky above us is a hazy white, like the air has been sapped of its vibrancy.

A swarm of people, most wearing dirty rags, press against the chain-link fence that runs around the perimeter of the property. The moment they see me, they begin to shout and reach for me. I can't tell if their excitement is borne from love or hate.

The guards posted on my side of the fence train their firearms on the civilians. One person out of the crowd, a young man, begins to climb the fence.

The soldiers shout at the civilian, but he's not listening. He's staring at me, yelling something. I never get the chance to find out what he's saying.

A gunshot goes off, and the man is blasted back.

My body jerks at the sight. Now people are screaming for an entirely different reason, and they look angry.

"Come, Serenity," Collins says, pressing me forward. I hadn't realized I stopped to begin with.

I let him lead me forward, tasting bile at the back of my throat.

An armored car waits for us. Collins shoves my head down and into the vehicle before following me inside.

I adjust myself, letting him strap me in, my eyes drifting back to the crowd. They are all so skinny, so malnourished.

God, how they are suffering.

I lean my head back against the seat rests. "The West has a problem on its hands," I say.

For all the king's terrible qualities—and there are many, even now—his people never looked that close to death.

I want to weep. Those are *my* people. They might be several generations removed, but they opened their eyes and drew their first breaths in the same land I did.

They deserve more than what they've been given.

"We do," Collins says, his eyes lingering on the people swarming the vehicle. "But you can help us fix it."

I fully intend to.

IT DOESN'T TAKE long to get away from the crowds. Once we do, the land opens up, stretching out for miles in every direction. Every so often, we pass relics of old cities. Judging by the size of the buildings, they were nothing grand to begin with. The West's biggest metropolises were leveled by the king long ago.

These are just remnants of the land this used to be.

Eventually, those too fall away, and then there's nothing left but long stretches of dead, wild grass.

"Where in the WUN are we?" I ask.

"Northern hemisphere. West Coast."

I can't decide if I'm relieved that we are far away from my hometown or disappointed. I want to see it again, desperately so, but I fear it would look nothing like what I remember. And then I'd have to face the reality that there really is no place for me in this new world.

We drive for a long time. Much longer than I expected. Long enough to leave the grasslands behind and enter a mountain range. As our elevation increases, scraggly brush gives way to trees.

As the car ride passes, I toy with the grand plan I settled on back in the military hospital, a plan I'd been forming even before then. I use the hours to alter it, now that the king likely lives. It puts me in a darker and darker mood.

What I must do might break me.

I forget about my macabre plan the moment the mountains part. The deep blue Pacific stretches across the horizon, and my eyelids flutter as I take it in. Nothing that men can do to one another will ever make this sight less beautiful.

Breathtaking as it is, the ocean captures my attention for only a moment.

Directly ahead of us is a gigantic wall made out of cement and stone. I can see nothing beyond it.

Our vehicle drives up to a heavily guarded gate—a checkpoint of sorts. We're waved through, and then I'm inside.

On the other side of the gates is a city like nothing I've ever seen.

Built into the mountainside overlooking the water, this place doesn't look like a city of the future. It looks like the city of the past. Each structure is made of stone and adobe and plaster—every one beautifully crafted, but all with a handmade look to them.

In spite of the wealth of information I learned since I woke, I never read about this place. I don't even know the name of it.

At the center of the walled city a giant glass dome rises above most other buildings, reminding me of the greenhouse Montes took me to a long time ago.

Even that small reminder of the king causes so many emotions to flood through me—grief, hope, *vengeance*.

Our vehicle makes its way towards the domed building. I'm not surprised when we pull up in front of the behemoth.

"This is where I'll be meeting the representatives?" I ask, looking up at it.

"We call it the Iudicium in the West," Collins says. He steps out of the car then offers a hand to help me out as well, cuffed as I am. "And yes, it is."

I ignore his hand, though as soon as I exit the car, he grips my upper arm anyway. A series of other guards surround us, keeping the crowd at bay.

I've done this before—been paraded through enemy territory. The Queen of the East. What an acquisition.

I spare another glance at the sprawling building before me.

So this is where the representatives work. Corrupt leaders love their palaces.

I only have a moment to take it in before I'm shuffled forward, away from the eyes of the crowd and inside the building.

The doors close behind us, the sound echoing through the chambers I now stand in. Despite the rich furnishings and ample marble that adorns the interior, the place is cold and dark.

I'm led to a set of double doors on the other end of the expansive entry hall. Two guards open them, and then I'm staring into a cavernous, circular room filled with twelve men.

The representatives.

Twelve of them. *Twelve.* I bet this is more than the king has ever heard of gathered in a single room. The only representative missing is the mysterious thirteenth one.

The rest of them sit at the far end, behind a wooden bench, and each wears a different expression when they catch sight of my face. Most appear bored or impassive. A couple seem curious. The rest of them look at me like I killed their sons.

I might've.

"Come in," one says.

Collins forces me forward, and I walk down the aisle, past rows and rows of empty seats. I've only stopped once I stand in front of the representatives.

I recognize each from their photo. Jeremy, the one who established the work camps; Alan, who's likely responsible for kidnapping the regional leaders; Gregory, who legalized human trafficking. On and on I name them, along with the atrocities they've sanctioned.

Some of these men are Montes's former advisors, men who plotted my death. Men that were involved in the death of my unborn child.

A quiet calmness settles over me. This is the place I go to when I kill.

They should never have met with me. They're now all marked. I won't let them live, not so long as I have life in me.

"Serenity Freeman Lazuli, Queen of the East," begins Alan. "Welcome to the West. I hear it was your home once."

"Once," I agree.

A drawn out silence follows that, until someone clears their throat.

"In the hundred years you've been gone, you have become quite a legend," Alan says.

My eyes flick to Montes's old advisors. Their frowns deepen.

The feeling's mutual.

"So I've heard," I say.

"Oh no," Alan says from where he's perched above me, "you've more than just heard. You've incited revolution. You are the world's rallying cry.

"And you've *acted*. Giving speeches, fighting the enemy," he says this with a wry twist of his lips. "It's all quite impressive.

"We talked to a certain paramilitary leader—Styx Garcia. He says you wanted to speak with us. So here you are."

I hide my surprise. He helped set this up?

The others watch me carefully.

"That was before you bombed a peaceful gathering."

This earns me a grim smile from Alan. "I would imagine a true rebel queen would be more eager, not less, to speak with the men that threaten *her people*." He says the last two words with disdain, like I'm a charlatan for supporting the citizens of the East rather than the West.

"And maybe this rebel queen feels she is beyond the point of civilly discussing *her people*," I shoot back.

"You don't have to be our prisoner," Jeremy interrupts. "The war has gone on for too long."

Begrudgingly, I incline my head. "It has," I agree. On this subject we have common ground. Ground I wish to exploit.

My eyes cut to one of the long, narrow windows that line the walls high above us. Through it I can see a sliver of the wall that encircles the city.

I feel the responsibility of this world, of my title, settle onto my shoulders. Today, I will be joining in the machinations of men.

It's time to finally set my terrible plan into motion.

The representatives watch me shrewdly.

"I know why I'm here," I say.

Diplomacy is a treacherous thing when neither party trusts the other but both want to work together. They need me, I need them, and we're all known for our ruthlessness.

"You want the war to end," I continue. "You want Montes dead, and you want me to be the one that kills him."

CHAPTER 42

SERENITY

"WHAT MAKES YOU think Montes is dead?" Alan says.

"Don't take me for a fool," I say. "We would be having a different conversation if that were the case." One where they made demands rather than requests of me.

No one speaks, but in that silence I get affirmation that I am correct.

He lives. My husband *lives*.

Which means he will live long enough to see my deception.

"We want peace," Tito says, training his bulging eyes on me. "You and I know that will never happen while the king lives."

My jaw tightens. I know what these men want. I've been preparing for it. *Planning* for it.

I take a deep breath. "I will kill Montes Lazuli for you," I say, carefully looking each of them in the eye.

My stomach churns sickeningly. I have become the traitor queen I was once accused of being.

The room goes dead silent. Around me, the representatives look surprised, suspicious even. I bet they didn't imagine the woman who's spoken out against them would state their terms then agree to them.

"How do we know your word is good?" Gregory lazily asks.

I can't stop the ironic twist of my lips. It's real rich of them to ask me that like they weren't trying to convince me to work for them only seconds ago.

"Your options are limited here," Gregory continues, "but as soon as you board a plane and see your pretty life again, what will stop you from going back on your word?"

What would my father do?

Convince.

I look around. "Do any of you know about my history?" The king's former advisors do. Way back when, they had to watch the king parade around the sullen girl from the West.

I take a step forward. "Let me tell you all a story." I let my eyes rove over them. "Once there was a girl who lived in a city that no longer exists. She had a mother and a father and friends. And then a strange king came and took each one away from her, one by one. But it wasn't enough. He forced her to marry him. And then, when she was planning on betraying him to his councilmembers, he found out."

The lie slips in easily enough.

I see Montes's old advisors sit up a little straighter. They betrayed the king a century ago. They still might remember the bloodbath that occurred in the conference room when the king learned of his councilmembers' disloyalty. I'm hoping they do.

"Yes," I say. "Why do you think you and your brethren were spared? There are things the Beast of the East and I plotted, things he never got the chance to tell you all. We gave Montes the wrong names that day the councilors were shot dead."

My father, bless his soul, would be proud of me in this moment. Lying is a terrible thing, but it is better than violence, and when it has the power to end a war, it can even be admirable.

"So the king found out his wife had betrayed him. But he couldn't kill her." My gaze moves over the representatives. "No, the evil king had fallen for his wife. So he kept her locked away in a machine, asleep indefinitely. And he never intended to wake her."

I go quiet, letting this alternate history sink in.

"Why would I help him?" I finally ask. "With every fiber of my being, I hate him." I glance down at my boots. "I always have," I say quietly.

The silence that follows this is pensive.

Finally, "We will deliberate," Ronaldo says. "Collins, take the queen to the prison quarters."

Collins hesitates, and it's plain to see that this decision shocks him. He'd been so sure the representatives would treat me well if only I agreed to their demands.

I don't bother telling Collins it's better this way. The king's silk sheets and his sweet words made me forget several times what he was.

There will be no forgetting this.

THE KING

MY EYES BLINK open.

I stare at the ceiling and breathe in deeply. I've been in the Sleeper enough times to know that when I wake up in this manner, it's because I've come from one.

Several officers surround my bed.

Something's wrong.

I push myself up, my brows furrowing. I look for Serenity. She's not here.

I almost choke when I remember.

She took a bullet to the gut. She fell, and she never rose.

I saw her death upon her.

"Tell me," I order my men.

If she's dead, I will not rest until every last Western leader is obliterated.

"The queen is alive," Heinrich says, his face grim. "The representatives have her."

Some things are worse than death—being a prisoner of the West is one of them.

I rise then, heedless of the fact that I'm essentially wearing thin cotton pants and nothing else. Worlds should end for all the anguish I feel.

My men hurriedly stand, trailing after me as I storm through the palace.

"Montes, you should rest," Marco says.

I overturn a nearby table and spin on him. *"Fuck* resting." He of all people should know. "Get the goddamn West on the phone. We're getting her back."

APPARENTLY THE REPRESENTATIVES like to eat where they shit. That's the only explanation for why their prison sits directly below their domed building.

I can tell from the stairwell I'm dragged down that there are floors upon floors of cells down here. Between the West's decimated population and their work camps, I have no idea why they'd ever need so many.

Then again ... bad men have endless enemies.

We move so far below the surface of the earth, that I feel all memory of the sun has been erased from this place. I don't want to be underground so soon after I was released from the Sleeper. It's damp down here. And cold. The chill of the place worms its way into my bones in a matter of minutes.

"Are the East's regional leaders imprisoned here?" I ask Collins.

I don't expect him to answer, but several seconds after I ask, he grunts something like an affirmation.

"Are they okay?"

Again, the silence draws out. Then, "You should worry about yourself," he says gruffly. His answer leaves me more concerned for them, not less.

The cell I'm led to is nothing short of medieval. What isn't covered by bars is inset with stone. There's fetid puddles in several locations, and the entire area reeks of shit and piss and death. There's no bed, and a filthy bucket is the closest thing to a toilet I'm going to get.

You can tell a lot about a territory by the way they treat their prisoners. This doesn't speak well for the men who depend on my loyalty. And it's not endearing me to them.

"I'm sorry," Collins apologizes. He sounds genuine.

I turn to face him. "You shouldn't be." I don't elaborate.

His head dips, like he can't bear looking at me. "I'll be back later." He leaves quickly after that, taking most of the guards along with him.

I pace for a while.

Kill the king.

I've never been able to accomplish this one task. And that's exactly what the representatives want. What they've always wanted. All so that they can continue to torment the world without resistance.

Slavery, concentration camps, crippling poverty. What fearful lives Westerners must live.

All thirteen of those bastards need to die, even the one who wasn't present.

I will end the war, and I *will* kill them.

CHAPTER 43

SERENITY

AFTER A WHILE, I force myself to sit. I lean my back against the wall and rest my forearms on my knees, bowing my head over them. A shiver runs through me. My eyes land on that bucket.

Fuck prisons.

I haven't heard a soul down here.

"*Hello?*" I shout, just to see if any other prisoners are down here.

Silence.

Not even the guards respond, if only to tell me to shut up.

I don't know how long I sit there before I can no longer beat back thoughts of the king. Now that I'm almost sure he's okay, I should feel relieved. That's the last thing I feel. I promised the West his *head*.

If only I could return my heart to the way it was before I met him. Duty and love are often opposing forces. Now is no different. And it doesn't matter what paths the king and I travel together. There is only one way this can end.

The only way it must.

I dread that ending more than I've dreaded anything in my entire life.

I'm dragged from my thoughts when I hear the whispers. Down the hall, up the corridor. Guards gossiping like the women of court.

I lift my head. That's when I notice it.

A storm's brewing.

There's a heaviness to the air, like my captors are bracing themselves for the worst.

A grim smile stretches across my face.

He's coming.

The devil is coming for me.

WHEN COLLINS RETURNS to my cell, I'm waiting, my back against the wall, my legs crossed at the ankles, and my arms folded across my chest.

"The representatives have come to a decision."

And here I was almost positive they'd leave me to molder for at least a day.

He watches me as the iron bars slide back and the cell door opens. The guards come in and spin me around roughly, pushing my chest against the wall. They jerk my hands behind my back then cuff my wrists together.

I'm dragged out of the cell and marched back to the circular room where the representatives wait. I'm cold, I smell like a latrine, and I'm not feeling very diplomatic at the moment.

Just angry. Really, really angry.

Twelve representatives wait for me.

"We would like to work with you," Tito says, his jowls shaking as he speaks. He says this as though they have the upper hand.

485

I might be in shackles, but the representatives are the ones with their hands tied. I die, the king wins. It's as simple as that.

Nothing brings people together like a martyr.

I pretend like I don't grasp this very obvious fact.

"You have thirty days to bring down the king," Tito continues. "We will be monitoring you regularly. In case you have any misgivings, you should be warned: we have moles everywhere. If you decide to go back on your word, we will find out. You won't like what becomes of you; traitors don't receive clean deaths in this land."

The irony of the king's old advisor telling me this isn't lost on me.

"Understood?" he adds.

I give a sharp nod.

"One of our men will seek you out. You will work directly with him.

I look down at my shackled hands.

"If I do this," I say, lifting my head, "it will be filmed and distributed. I want this on record."

For the first time since I met them, I see some of the representatives smile.

"It will be theatrical," I continue, "and it will require your assistance."

"You will have it," Alan says. He pauses before saying, "We will need proof of the kill."

A body. It's the currency of conquerors.

The men look hungry for the king's death.

"You'll get a body," I say, "but I want a peace agreement in return, one with equitable terms for my people."

"That goes without question," Rodrigo says.

Without question my ass. These men would rob an old lady blind if they could get away with it.

"If you agree," Tito continues, "we will release you immediately to the king."

This is happening.

Oh, God, it's really happening.

I nod. The weight of my task settles on my shoulders.

"I agree to your terms."

I STAND IN the middle of the Western city's large central square, my hands still bound behind my back.

Still a queen held for ransom.

On all four corners, soldiers stand at the ready, loosely holding semi-automatic rifles in their arms. I can tell by the deadness in their eyes that these men have killed many people. I can also tell many people have died right where I stand by the brown bloodstains that stain the concrete at my feet.

The rendezvous area doubles as an executioner's square.

Around us, the citizens of this place watch impassively. I bet most of them had to cultivate that bored look, lest their trigger-happy leaders find fault in whatever real expression they wish to wear.

A single camera focuses on me and the representatives who sit at my back. Ahead of me, a large screen has been erected, much like the ones that were mounted at the speech I gave. Right now the screen is blank, save for an emblem of some sort that's projected onto it. I'm guessing it's the flag of the West. It looks nothing like the American flag I grew up with.

We all wait. The wind stirs my hair, the square eerily silent.

I don't understand any of this, the presentation of my handoff, the strategy of it all, and what role I play. For all I know, this is actually an elaborate execution. The stains on the ground seem to suggest that.

The screen flickers to life. A moment later, I see the king's face stretched across it.

I have to lock my knees to stay upright.

Alive. I hadn't fully believed it until now.

His jaw tightens, his dark eyes unreadable.

Now I really have no idea what's going on.

Behind me, one of the representatives begins to speak.

"The thirteen representatives of the West do hereby release Her Majesty, Serenity Freeman Lazuli, to the Eastern Empire. We guarantee the queen safe passage home."

It's the king's turn to speak.

Montes's vein begins to throb. "I, Montes Lazuli, King of the East, do hereby declare before gods and men that in exchange for Her Majesty Serenity Lazuli's safe return to the East, the territory known as Australia will be ceded to the representatives of the West."

Those words are strange, foreign things that should not be strung together in the same sentence.

An entire landmass in return for me.

I can't catch my breath.

An entire *landmass.* And it's now under the care of the creatures at my back.

I look over my shoulder, just to catch a glimpse of the representatives. Most of them wear grim smiles.

Just as I've played the representatives to keep up appearances, they've played me and the king.

Love is a weakness the king has discovered in himself. A weakness the representatives have exploited.

I face forward again and find Montes staring at me. I can feel unbidden tears welling in my eyes.

Now I've had two men in my life choose me over the welfare of a nation. First my father, and now my husband.

Never again will I underestimate this man's devotion. He will ruin countries for me.

Above us, a jet of sorts enters the airspace.

My hair whips about my face as it lowers itself to the ground ahead of me.

"As a sign of good faith, we have allowed one of your aircraft into our city," one of the representatives says.

Montes and I still stare at each other when Collins approaches me and begins to unlock my cuffs. "Stay safe, Serenity," he says quietly. "And be careful."

I don't acknowledge his words. It would probably be bad for him if I did.

I'm marched onto the aircraft. At the last minute I turn around and face the representatives. I catch Ronaldo's eye, and he nods to me.

The West is ruled by thirteen devils, the East, two.

And I am the worst one of them all.

CHAPTER 44

THE KING

IT TAKES NEARLY fifteen hours for the aircraft carrying Serenity to return to the East. This time, I wait for my queen just off to the side of the airstrip.

I have this unreasonable fear that something will be wrong. That my pilot is a traitor. That as soon as the video call ended, the representatives shot her in the back. That the West will ambush the aircraft before it lands.

My worries breed more worries, extrapolating into elaborate scenarios that I know cannot occur, but my heart won't be reasoned with.

Not until I watch her plane touch down.

My pulse gallops.

The aircraft rolls to a stop a short distance away from me and the engines die down. Each minute I wait is an eternity. I managed to stay away from Serenity for over a century, yet I now find I can barely stand the time we're apart.

Finally the engine quiets. The staircase lowers.

A moment later, Serenity stands on the threshold. Her eyes find mine almost immediately. I know what she's thinking, what they're all thinking.

How could he?

How could I indeed? Australia is a territory I've ruled for a 113 years. A good territory.

A territory I'll get back. But I will do it with my queen at my side.

A landmass is not nearly so fragile as a human life. It'll be there tomorrow and the next day and the day after that.

I step away from the soldiers gathered around me, and they all give me plenty of space. This greeting is personal.

I begin to move towards Serenity, my strides quickening the closer I get. She storms down the steps, her eyes trained on mine.

The distance evaporates between us, and then I'm dragging her to me and forcing a kiss on her. I can't say it's all that gentle. I want her to fight back, I want to feel that brutal life force of hers come to life beneath my mouth and my hands.

It does.

She grabs the lapels of my suit, fisting the material in her hands. I feel her shake me roughly, like she can't decide whether she wants to pull me closer or push me away. I'm not going to give her the option.

"You are such an idiot," she whispers when our lips briefly part.

I smile into the kiss. "That is no way to talk to the man who just saved your life."

I allow her to pull away. "You gave them an entire continent."

"I did."

"You're going to lose the respect of your people."

I capture her hand.

Still alive. It's going to take several minutes to believe it.

"And you'll win it back for me."

THE KING MIGHT very well be losing his mind, I think as we pull up to the palace. I'm still going over the last twenty-four hours in my head.

Never has he given up a kingdom for a single person. I doubt he's ever even given up a car for someone.

Not true, I correct. He gave up quite a few things in the past when my life was slipping through his fingers.

But this is unprecedented.

I exit the car with him, staring up at his enormous Mediterranean home. After spending time holed up in a plane, a dungeon, and a Sleeper, I can't bear the thought of a roof pressing down on me.

"Serenity."

My eyes move to the king.

He must be able to read all of my emotions because I see panic in his own. I don't blame him for it. I'm here, but I'm also a million miles away.

I agreed to kill him.

My throat works. "I don't want to go inside. Not yet—please."

I'm so rarely polite, and I see Montes physically react to this.

The king might not be the only one losing their mind.

He gives me a subtle nod, then looks to one of his men. "Have someone get the boat ready, and make sure it's stocked with everything the queen and I might need."

As soon as the order leaves Montes's mouth, one of the guards begins to radio commands to his men.

I'm still stuck on the word *boat*.

I jog my memory, trying to remember if I've ever been aboard a boat. Nothing comes to mind.

A nervous thrill runs through me, chasing away my dark thoughts.

Pressing a hand to the small of my back, Montes steers me around the edge of the palace, towards the back gardens. I can tell he wants to touch me. More than touch. He wants to devour me alive. I can feel his hand trembling with the need.

He's not alone. But it's more than just his body I wish to explore. I want to see inside that twisted mind of his and understand what drove him to give up so much for me.

He gave away a territory for me. I intend to take his head.

A sick sensation courses through me, and I sway a little.

Montes notices. "Once we dock at the end of the day, you will get checked out by the royal physician."

I've passed through quite a few hospitals and seen quite a few doctors since I married the king. My prior phobia of them has only increased.

The king must see the fresh mutiny in my eyes. "That is not a suggestion, Serenity."

I know it's not. Even if I refused the king's order, he'd find a way to force me into a medical examination.

It doesn't mean I like it.

His eyes flick to my stomach, and oh God, I know where his mind drifted. What his motives are.

My hand drifts over my midsection. "I'm not pregnant," I say quietly.

"You don't know that." He looks concerned, but he sounds … hopeful. Of course the greediest, loneliest man in the world would get a taste for companionship and want more.

And he's right. I don't know that I'm not pregnant, but it's doubtful. I took a bullet to the stomach, after all.

Regardless, I'm not having this conversation right now.

I squint off to the horizon, seeing the blue ocean stretch on and on.

"I've never been on a boat," I say.

I'm sure Montes doesn't miss the subject change.

I feel his gaze on me. "Then I hope you enjoy it."

CHAPTER 45

SERENITY

I CLING TO the railing, another wave of nausea rolling over me. I've been on this blasted thing for not even ten minutes and already I feel like this was a grave mistake.

I'm pretty sure I fucking hate boats.

"When we get back, you're seeing the physician *straightaway*."

"I'm *not* pregnant," I growl.

He's trying to goad me. I can hear the smile in his voice.

"The waves are bad here," he says. "Once we get farther out, your—" *pregnant* pause, "*stomach* should settle."

He heads over to me, pulling my form away from the railing and forcing me to sit on one of the plush couches arranged on the deck.

"Keep your eyes on the horizon and rest. I'll be right back."

I sit a little straighter as he moves to the interior of the boat. I don't dare try to follow him out of fear that the close quarters will make the sickness worse.

Montes returns several minutes later with two items—a glass of something fizzy, and a bottle with a cream of some sort.

"For your stomach," he says, handing me the drink, "and to protect your skin," he says, holding up the bottle of salve.

I take it from his hand and read the label.

Sunscreen.

I have vague memories of using this when I was younger, before the world had gone crazy.

"You'll want to put that on your face. Otherwise your skin will burn."

Sunburns, now *that* was something I was familiar with.

I have time to neither try the drink or use the sunscreen before Montes takes my jaw and kisses me roughly. "I have to go man the helm. Remember—eyes on the horizon."

He leaves me there so that he can start up the engine.

He's doing all this because I asked him to. The sunscreen, the drink, the day out at sea. He just wants to see me happy.

Was this what love was like? Not just something to fight and die for, but something that didn't draw attention to itself unless you looked for it?

I think back to my conversation with the representatives. The agreement we made, the one I intend to see through to the bitter end.

My nausea only deepens, and I take a sip of the drink the king gave me.

I find the fluid does help settle my stomach, as does watching the horizon. And once the boat gets moving, the last of my seasickness dissipates completely, and I begin to enjoy myself.

My gaze drifts to Montes. He's shrugged off his suit jacket and rolled up his sleeves. He's also unbuttoned his shirt, so it blows behind him.

Those abs he sported when I met him are still there.

Glorious, wretched man.

Normally I'm taken by how otherworldly he appears, but that's not the case now. Now he seems startlingly human.

I force my attention back to the horizon, where sea meets sky. It's such a far cry from the dank dungeon I was in only a day ago.

The boat slows to a halt.

I glance over at the king just as he removes his shoes. Then his socks.

"What are you doing?" I ask, my eyebrows rising.

"Going for a swim. And my pregnant queen will be joining me."

My annoyance flares. A command given in the third person, and that insinuation again that I'm pregnant.

"I don't have a swimsuit."

Montes actually looks charmed by my words. "That didn't stop you the last time you swam in the ocean with me."

His hands move to his zipper of his slacks.

"*What are you doing?*"

The king sighs, dropping his pants and stepping out of them as he does so. "Remember what I said about inane questions? I'm not answering that."

I glance over my shoulder. The palace is fairly far away, but I don't doubt that there are eyes trained on our location.

Montes's hands go his boxer briefs. With one swift tug, he removes the last of his clothes.

The king has never had many qualms about being naked. That doesn't change as he approaches me.

He takes the drink out of my hand and sets it aside.

I lean back as he enters my personal space. He drops to his knees, his fingers going to the hem of my top.

I grab his wrists. "What are you doing?"

"Undressing you, in case that wasn't apparent," he says, his mouth curving up just a little.

He wants us to swim … naked? My shock is tempered by a good dose of curiosity.

He must sense my interest, because he takes the opportunity to lift my shirt. I raise my arms passively.

"People do this?"

He tosses my shirt aside and squints at me, his head tilting. "My queen, have you never skinny-dipped?"

I don't even know what the term means, though by its context I figure it out real quick.

I'm sure my expression says enough.

"Another new experience," the king says. I can hear the wonder in his voice.

I let him undress me until we both stand together, naked from head to foot.

He spends a moment drinking me in. Then he grabs the sunscreen from its resting spot and squeezes it onto his hands.

I think he's going to put it on his own body, but then he begins to rub my shoulder, dragging his hand down my arm, massaging the sunscreen in to my skin.

I watch him for several seconds, utterly transfixed by him. Montes appears to be enjoying the excuse to touch me.

"What's the point?" I ask. He has pills and machines that can do far more than sunscreen can.

He doesn't look up as he responds, "You don't like doing things my way, so I'm trying to do them your way."

I stare at him in awe. He's a different being entirely from the one I married. One that compromises and works to be good even though it goes against his very nature.

Montes smooths more sunscreen onto me, his hands brushing across my ribs, over my bellybutton, beneath my breasts. I don't bother telling him this last spot probably won't capture the sun. I'm enjoying his hands on me far too much.

He touches me with familiarity, and I'm charmed despite myself. He's taking care of me. Aside from my parents, I've never had anyone take care of me. That's what happens when you're strong. No one thinks to.

"Done." He caps the bottle and, setting it aside, stands. "Now for the fun part."

Without warning, he scoops me up.

I think I know what's coming.

"Montes, put me down," I command. Even as I speak, I wrap my arms around his neck. I know better than to assume he'll listen to me. He just finished making one consolation. Two within such a short timespan would be pushing it.

He just smiles at me, those white, white teeth looking even brighter against his olive complexion. Out here, in the open sun, my skin pressed to his, I notice just how much his body dwarfs mine.

Once, that realization would've made me uneasy. Now it makes me feel safe in a very innate way.

That terrible sensation takes root in my stomach again, partly guilt, but partly something else. It tastes a lot like desperation. Like this man, who has outlived everyone else, will leave me soon.

My heart begins to race, and I wonder if, for the first time in my life, I could be a coward and back out of the promise I made to this world. He gave up a continent, I would give up the world. All for him.

But I can't. I *can't*. It's not in my nature, and unlike the king, I'm not sure I'm capable of really changing.

Montes carries me to the edge of the boat, completely unaware I'm having an existential crisis right now.

He pauses to stare down at me, his gaze latching onto my lips. Right when I think he's going to lean in, he steps off the edge.

For the merest moment, we're falling, and then together we hit the water.

It's cold enough that I almost gasp the ocean into my lungs. And the sensation of liquid running all over my naked skin. It feels … strange and exquisite. I kick away from Montes and come up for air.

The king surfaces a moment later, slicking his hair back. He flashes me a grin. "Welcome to the Aegean. You are now officially swimming in Homer's wine dark sea."

I give him a strange look. I know of Homer, but I don't get the reference.

His eyes soften just a smidge. "When the war is over, I will show you other things that you have missed."

When the war is over. Not *if*.

"You believe we can end it," I say, treading water. He's never admitted this before. I assumed he thought it was a lost cause, especially now that he traded away Australia.

"Let's not talk about war for one afternoon," he says.

I can respect that. He's given me the outdoors, I can give him this.

I move my hand through the water, watching light dance along it.

There's a fullness in my heart, like it might burst. With happiness, I realize. It's all so unbearably wonderful. The sea, the sun, the man staring intensely at me.

"I wish this could last forever," I say, tasting sea salt on my lips as I speak. It's far too wonderful, which means it won't.

I know it won't.

It can. Montes doesn't say it, but it's all there in his eyes.

He swims over and pulls me against him, cradling my body in his arms. And it isn't lewd, or sexy, or erotic.

It's romantic. Intimate.

I see the sunset in the king's eyes, those old eyes that look so young when they gaze at me.

My gaze drops to his neck. I touch the pulse point that throbs to the beat of his heart, trailing a finger over the dark skin there.

"Never have I been so afraid," I admit softly. I can still see the moment; it plays on repeat in my mind. The moment I nearly lost him.

I'm still so, so afraid.

Montes swallows, his face growing serious. "I know the feeling."

He did. Had the Sleeper not existed, the king and I wouldn't be in each other's arms; we'd be six feet under.

As the water laps at us, I shake off the morbid mood. "Sorry—I didn't mean to lead the conversation right back to war."

He presses his thumb against my mouth. "*Nire bihotza,* to hear you feared for my life ... I *want* to know that."

Slowly, I nod.

Montes's thumb begins stroking my lower lip, his brows still puckered.

The sun loves the king. It makes his dark eyes glow amber and his skin brighten. A lock of his wet hair slides over his eye.

This man is mine.

I brush the lock of hair away from his face, allowing my fingers to trail over his features. There's nothing out here but us, the sun, the sea, and the sky.

"This might be the happiest moment of my life," I admit. It isn't grand, and it shouldn't be particularly memorable—nudity aside—but ... but perhaps that's why I enjoy it so much.

It is beautifully normal.

Montes brushes the backs of his fingers against my cheekbone. "I'm certain it's mine."

I raise my eyebrows. "Out of all of them?"

"Out of all of them."

I play with another wet strand of his hair, and he closes his eyes for a second, like he just wants to revel in the feel of it.

"Why?" I ask.

He opens his eyes. "Because for once it's not a memory, and it has you in it."

CHAPTER 46

SERENITY

DOCTORS HAVE BEEN and will be one of the things I hate most passionately. Especially royal ones.

I'm not very good at hiding my distaste. I know the royal physician can sense it as she inspects me for injury.

Back in the WUN, doctors often meant death. And when it comes to the king's medics, they've been known to turn traitor.

But it isn't all bad. The appointment is the perfect excuse to look into an issue that I've been meaning to for some time.

The king holds my hand from the chair he sits in, but make no mistake, this isn't some shining example of his devotion. The bastard is making sure I don't bolt for the door at the soonest possible moment.

The doctor straightens. "Your Majesty, everything looks good."

I'm not surprised.

"The only thing that's left," the doctor continues, "is the blood work."

The blood work Montes insisted on.

When it finally comes back in, she flips through it. "Not pregnant," the physician says.

I give Montes a bored look. *See?*

"Hmmm," he says in response, and I really don't like the look in his eyes. Like he wants to rectify the situation immediately.

When the exam ends, the king leads me out.

Once we return to the main section of the palace, I halt. "Shit," I say.

"What is it?"

I glance behind us. "I left my jacket behind."

"Someone will return it to our rooms." The king begins to steer me forward once more.

I dig my heels in. "I'm just going to grab it," I say.

Montes gives me a peculiar look. He knows me far too well. To willingly suffer through more time in the medical wing is out of character.

"Alright," he says carefully. "I'll be in my office." Giving me a final, poignant glance, we part ways.

I turn around and stride back towards the medical facilities.

Being sneaky is not a forte of mine. I tend to storm into situations guns a-blazing. Unfortunately for me, the king knows this. I just have to hope that other tasks keep him busy enough to ignore my inconsistent behavior.

When I run into the royal physician, she glances up from the paperwork she holds.

"Did you forget something?" she asks.

"My jacket," I say.

"Let's go get it for you," she says, dropping the file on the desk near her. I head back to the room with her.

Something has niggled at my mind for some time, something that I might be able to make use of.

"How many Sleepers does the king have?" I ask as we walk.

"Here?" she says, tucking a wispy strand of white hair behind her ear. "Seven I believe—of course, that's not including the one you were in. Globally, there are twenty-four, again, not including yours."

"And how many of them are occupied?" I ask.

The doctor glances over at me sharply. She doesn't appear all that enthusiastic to answer it.

"Three here, not including yours, and eight others worldwide. Many of the remaining Sleepers are periodically in use depending on the needs of the people."

"How many of those contain long-term occupants? Like me." I began the conversation casually enough, but now there's no masking the fact that I'm probing with a purpose.

She licks her lips. "Two."

"I want to see who's in them."

"Your Majesty, I don't see how this is—"

"You don't need to understand my motives," I interrupt her to say. "All you need to do is follow through with my request."

"You didn't come back for your jacket, did you?" she asks.

"I didn't," I confirm.

The doctor doesn't slow when we pass the room I had my checkup in.

"I'm only authorized to show you one," she cautions.

That makes me all the more eager to find out who's in the remaining Sleeper.

"Fine," I say. "Show me the one."

I STARE DOWN at the occupant of the king's Sleeper.

I was right.

"How long has he been here?" I ask, glancing up at the physician. I'm sure she has a busy schedule, and this is the last place she wants to be, but she is patient, acting as though she has all the time in the world to spend answering my questions.

Then again, if I served the queen, I might make time for her as well.

"For as long as I can remember. And for as long as the doctor before me can remember."

I have no doubt this man has been resting here for just as long as I had. Over a century.

The room he's housed in is not nearly as grand as the temple made for me, but time and lots of money have clearly gone into the richly painted frescos that adorn the walls around us. This is as beautiful a crypt as I've ever seen.

I frown as I return my attention to the man, visible through the Sleeper's porthole.

I'm not the only beloved person Montes kept alive. Marco rests inside the machine—the original one—his face expressionless.

I'd wondered for a while now how the king managed to clone Marco. Where he got the DNA. Now I know.

It just goes to show you how twisted my life has become that I pity the man trapped in this box, I pity him and his fate. Doomed to remain alive even though there is nothing sentient left in his body, not after the bullet he took to the brain all those years ago.

Death must come to all men. It is our due.

Marco hasn't been able to claim it, though his soul has long since left this place.

I still hate the man with a vengeance, and I haven't been kind to his doppelganger, but there are some dignities even my enemies deserve.

When the time is right, I will give this man the death he deserves.

CHAPTER 47

SERENITY

THE NEXT DAY, when I walk into my office, an unassuming envelop sits on my keyboard along with a small packet of matches.

I pick up the envelope. *Serenity* is scrawled along the front of it.

I open it and pull out a sheaf of paper made from thick cardstock.

Rendezvous in your office at 02:00. Burn this message after reading.

Lowering the note, I look around. Someone slipped into my office to drop this off. My hackles rise at the violation of space.

My attention returns to the note.

The first communication from the representatives.

Grabbing one of the matches, I strike it against the desk and bring the flame to the note, watching it burn.

How absurd to think that we could meet in my office. There are cameras in here. I stare up at one of them pensively.

Unless …

It takes me fifteen minutes to find the head of security, who's outside with some type of technician, discussing models and makes of camera equipment.

"Your Majesty," he and the technician bow when they see me, "it's an honor to finally meet you."

"Likewise," I say, trying not to sound too impatient.

"What can I do for you?"

"I would like to go over the last several hours' worth of footage taken from my office."

He appears baffled by the request. "Of course. Right this way."

He leads me to a small auxillary building a short distance away. Inside is a bank of monitors, all showing different images of the palace and the surrounding grounds. He pats the shoulders of the two men manning the desk. "Would you two mind handling Steve? He's on the northwest end of the palace."

They get up, startling when they see me behind their boss. Placing a fist to their chests, they bow and murmur, "Your Majesty." Quickly, they exit the room.

Once they leave, the head of security pulls one of the vacated chairs up and taps on a screen. "This is one of them, and—" he taps on several others, "these are the other three."

Pulling out a keyboard, he begins typing. "You said you wanted to see footage from the last hour?"

"The last several hours would be even better."

He pats the chair next to him. "Take a seat. We'll be here awhile."

IT'S DUMMY FOOTAGE. All three hours of it.

I never see who placed the envelope and matches on my desk, and I never see myself enter and retrieve the letter. Someone went in and tampered with the video feeds.

Even after all this time there are holes in the king's security.

Someone's betraying the king.

We come to the end of the footage.

"That's it," the man says, rubbing the gray scruff of his beard.

He gets up, prepared to leave.

I stand with him, my eyes still locked on the bank of screens. "I want to know the weaknesses in the palace's security, should there ever be an attack."

"Your Majesty," he seems startled, "I assure you, no such thing will—"

I cut him off. "I haven't survived based on luck alone. I want a thorough understanding of this place—how many officers are stationed around the grounds, their hours, tasks, the weaponry they carry, what sorts of emergency exit strategies the king and I have at our disposal. And today, I want to start with the rest of the security footage and audio for the entire palace."

"But your Majesty, the security footage alone will take hours, possibly even days, to go over."

"Then we better get started now."

THE KING

I RUB MY lower lip as I watch Serenity through the very cameras she's inspecting.

My vicious little wife has taken a keen interest in the palace's inner workings.

She's a strange creature; this could just be one more way she feels she has some control over her situation. But it could also be something else.

Something that could come back to bite me in the ass if I don't watch her.

Does she believe an attack is imminent?

Or does she have other reasons?

I already know she visited Marco's Sleeper yesterday when she'd claimed she needed to retrieve her jacket.

I squint at her image.

I steeple my fingers and press them to my mouth. I have to acknowledge what I've always known: I have made Serenity larger than myself. She's only rising to the role I've given her. Not just as queen, but as some sort of savior.

I call in Heinrich.

When he enters my office, I nod to my computer screen, where the footage of Serenity still plays. "Keep an eye on her, and give me updates on everything she does."

My grand marshal inclines his head.

"Is that all?" he asks.

"Yes."

I watch his back as he exits.

"Oh, and Heinrich?"

"If she begins to do suspicious things or breaks palace code, let her."

"Even if it involves your men?"

I nod. "Even if it involves *you*."

499

Serenity might be sneaky, and right now she might be secretive, but I have my men's loyalty.

I want to see what she's up to.

SERENITY

I RUB MY eyes then pinch the bridge of my nose.

By the time 2:00 a.m. rolls around, my brain feels like it's about to explode with all the information I've gleaned today.

Blueprints of the palace and the surrounding grounds are spread out in front of me. Already I've begun circling areas where I know cameras are installed. Some of them will need to be rigged.

I roll up the blueprint and set it aside.

A few minutes later I hear a gentle knock on the door. My pulse speeds up in anticipation.

Time to meet one of the West's moles.

Withdrawing my gun from its holster, I approach the door. Whoever has been planted amongst us, I don't trust them any more than I would an enemy aiming a weapon at my head. Traitors are the worst sort of people.

I would know. I have become one myself.

I open the door. I can't hide my shock when I see who's on the other side.

"*You?*"

Marco.

He brushes past me, and I quickly shut the door behind him.

"I could ask you the same thing," he says.

The king's wife and his closest friend are conspiring against him. It makes me sad, and it makes me feel sorry for Montes, who is so desperate for companionship.

I force my feelings back so I can say, "The king's taken everything I've ever loved from me." It's the truth, and yet it feels like a lie when I say it now.

Marco takes in my office, then rotates to face me.

"What has he done to you?" I ask. The original Marco was many things, but he wasn't a traitor.

"Trinity," the man in front of me says, like her name is explanation enough. "He never loved her, not in any sense of the word."

There hasn't been enough time for me to understand intricate inner workings of the king's house. And when it comes to vendettas the devil is *always* in the details.

"When she died, Montes didn't mourn her. If anything, he was *relieved*," Marco says. "She looked *just* like you, but it never mattered to him. She was just a copy, a poor man's Serenity. I loved her, and he let her die. I can't forgive him for that."

Love and hate, they are so very interconnected.

"The disappearances," I say. "You're the insider that's been telling the WUN of our plans."

All those leaders that had disappeared. We couldn't figure out how the West had known we were going to meet with them.

I swear I see a flash of remorse in Marco's eyes, and then it's gone.

"I am," he admits.

I fight the urge to grab my gun. If it weren't for this man, countless people would still be alive and several regional leaders wouldn't be undergoing God knows what at the hands of the West.

This man is *worse* than the Marco I despised.

It takes me several seconds to get my emotions under control. "So you're going to help me kill the king?" I finally ask. Saying the words aloud makes it all the more real.

He nods.

I move father into the room. I'm getting that prickly sensation at the back of my neck, telling me that something about this situation isn't right.

"Why haven't you done so before now?" I probe.

"I've considered it, as have the representatives. But the king has many ways to sidestep death, and I don't have the clearance or the connections to make sure the king dies and stays dead."

But I do.

I run my tongue over my teeth.

"How do you intend to kill him?" he asks.

Now for the tricky part, the part I've been toying with since I awoke. A plan I'd finalized on the flight back here.

The king is going to die with just as much panache as he lived.

"We're going to burn the palace to the ground."

CHAPTER 48

SERENITY

"WE NEED TO call Styx," Marco says as our meeting winds down.

I pull my head back. "Why?"

All I want to do is to crawl into bed.

"He has access to many of the East's military warehouses."

Shit, does the king know this?

Of course he doesn't.

And now I hate deception because it ties my hands.

"We're going to use the East's weapons against them?" I ask skeptically.

"Would you rather use the West's?" Marco challenges.

It's a loaded question.

"The West has already promised me their firepower," I say, leaning against my desk.

"They are an ocean away. It will be easy for the king to defend the palace against them."

I begrudgingly agree with Marco's assessment.

He gestures to my computer. "May I?"

I work my jaw, then jerk my head *yes*.

Sitting down at my desk, he sets up the screen for a video call.

Within minutes Styx Garcia's face fills the screen.

I frown, my nostrils flaring at the sight of him and all his scars. This is the last thing I want to be doing, surrounding myself with these two men.

"My beautiful queen," Styx says by way of introduction, ignoring Marco altogether, "what an honor to speak with you again."

I feel my upper lip curl. I'd forgotten just how much I disliked this man.

"You answered quickly."

Styx's gaze finally moves to Marco. "I was expecting the call."

My neck prickles again. This shouldn't be how it plays out; I should be the one coordinating. Instead I feel like a lamb being led—led to slaughter.

"Did you enjoy your visit out West?" he asks. "The representatives were very eager to see you once I told them that you wanted to arrange a meeting."

"A videoconference would've sufficed," I say sharply.

"I am just the messenger," he reminds me.

He does have a point.

"Pretty woman, I hear you're going to be a widow soon," Styx says, smiling slyly.

I narrow my eyes at him. That only makes his smile grow.

"Marcus seems to think we need your help," I say.

"You *do* need my help. The moment you kill the king, your men are going to turn on you."

"And you have men willing to defend me?" I ask skeptically.

"Aye, every one of them would die for you," he says. He hasn't blinked since he picked up the call, and it's beginning to unnerve me.

"She also wants to burn the palace down," Marco adds.

The news brightens Styx's eyes. "Ah, my queen, I have explosives for days."

"Explosives that belong to my husband."

Styx cocks his head at my accusatory tone.

"Yes," he says carefully. "And my own." He leans forward. "Speaking of your husband, he's still trying to kill me."

"It's a good thing he doesn't know the extent of your depravity," I play with the strap of my holster, "otherwise he might put more effort into it."

"It's a good thing he doesn't know the extent of *yours*," Styx replies.

Another good point.

"My queen, I will lend assistance to you. And when that day comes, I'll be there to congratulate you in person."

I NEED TO scrub off the evil that shrouds me. I've never done something like this before. I wonder what my father would think. I bet he would be proud. I bet, if he were still alive, this would be the moment he'd think, *she has finally understood my lessons.*

I head back to my room, quietly tiptoeing back in. I shouldn't have bothered. The lights are on, the bed still made.

The king isn't here.

I'm alarmed and relieved and disappointed all at once. I want to see him, but I don't want him to see me. I can't hide nearly enough of myself from his penetrating eyes.

Rather than get into bed, I head out onto the balcony. It's become the place I go to when my heart is all twisted up and my mind is addled.

Immediately I hear the sound of the surf.

My father might be proud of me—if he were here—but I'm filled with self-loathing. I no longer hate the king nearly so much as I hate what I have become and what I must do.

I lean against the railing for who knows how long, letting the night air wash over me. Eventually my gaze drops from the sky to the gardens.

A figure sits on one of the stone benches, his broad back facing me.

Montes.

Has he been there the whole time? What could he possibly be musing about deep into the night?

I push away from the balcony and leave our room. My shoes click down the hallway.

I want to see him, my king. Even though I'm plotting against him, and even though he's bent and broken all wrong, I want to see him.

You see, I love him.

So much.

I can finally admit it to myself now, at the end of things. It's been there for a while. Quite a while. I was just always afraid of it.

I stride out the palace's back doors and head down one of the paths that winds through the garden. My steps slow when I catch sight of the king's form. He sits next to a bubbling fountain, his forearms on his thighs, his head bent.

I am not the only weary one here.

He tilts his head in my direction when he hears my boots click against the stone, but he doesn't turn around.

When I reach him, I touch his shoulder. "What are you doing out here?" I ask quietly.

His hand goes to my arm, like he wants to make sure I'm tethered to him. "My wife wasn't in my bed." He smiles wanly, his focus on the fountain ahead of us. "I'm discovering I can't sleep when you're not in my bed."

I move to sit down next to him, surprised when he doesn't try to pull me onto his lap.

"So you came out here?" I fill in.

"You're not the only one that gets tired of those walls pressing in."

There something frightening about the way he's talking. The way he's acting. I might finally understand why Montes panics when I pull away. I can feel the anxiety there, right beneath my sternum. He's the one whose life will soon end, and he's acting distant, and I'm pursuing him. He's the decent one, and I'm the great evil who will destroy every last thing he holds dear.

When did our roles reverse?

He finally looks at me, and God, the look—I could live and die in it.

"Stop it," I say quietly.

He cups my cheek. "Every time you say that, I know I'm doing something right."

I frown, even as my eyes well with some soft emotion.

"*Nire bihotza*, why are you sad?"

I should be asking him the same thing.

"There's a lot to be sad about."

He shakes his head. "I've had a hundred years to be sad. I don't want to be sad any longer. And I don't want my queen to be, either."

But that's impossible at this point. The two of us have spent too long drowning in horrors of our own making.

That's all we know—pain and bloodshed.

Montes threads his fingers through mine.

I glance down at our joined hands, and amend my earlier statement.

All we know is pain, bloodshed—and *this*.

And it's this last one that will kill us.

CHAPTER 49

SERENITY

THERE'S ONE LAST person I need to speak with, and he will be the one to play the most pivotal role.

I find Heinrich in his office. The grand marshal is on the phone when I enter, his voice gruff. The moment he catches sight of me, he straightens in his chair, rushing the caller off the phone.

I take a seat in one of the guest chairs across from him.

"Your Majesty," he bows his head.

I'm struck all over again by how hardened this man is. He's seen his fair share of carnage. I can tell he respects me, but I bet he also thinks I'm a bit naïve and disillusioned. Me with my grand speeches and rosy ideals.

He doesn't speak, doesn't ask me why I'm here, or what I need.

"How loyal are you to the king?" I finally ask.

He rubs his chin and speculates me from where he sets. "I would die for him. And for you, Your Majesty."

You can't trust people. Even the most decent ones can turn on you for the right price; I know that better than most. But I decide to trust this man because I'm out of options.

"What if I told you that I needed your help to end the war?"

He stares at me for several seconds before saying, "I would ask you what you need from me."

"I was hoping you'd say that."

And then I tell him exactly what I intend to do.

I'm not even finished speaking when he starts shaking his head.

"*No*," he barks out, "I know what I said before, but I won't do this."

"Then I will die, and the world will continue to be at war."

"It's too risky." He's arguing with me, which I take as a good sign. It means he's considering it on some level. "For you *and* for the king. I will be executed for treason," he says.

"How many people has this war already killed?" I say. "How many more people will it kill if we don't end it? You and I both know I can manage it."

"Listen, let's forget for one second that we're not equals. Let me put this plainly: I like you, Serenity. You have a good heart. But this is madness."

"I won't tell the king you came to me. Just forget about this whole plan."

I run my hands through my hair. I need this man backing me.

I try one last time. "When I was nineteen, the general of the Western United Nations, our leader at the time, asked me to marry the king, the man who had killed my family and countless numbers of my countrymen. That was the king's price—if the WUN handed me over, the war would end.

"I couldn't imagine a worse fate, but I agreed to it because I knew the world would be better off.

"I'm asking the same thing of you now," I beseech the grand marshal, "to rise above the ethics of it all to serve the greater good. I know that's not fair of me to ask, but I can't do this alone."

He runs a palm over his buzzed hair. He shifts his weight. Deliberating, deliberating. The entire time, those flinty eyes watch me.

Finally, his jaw tightens, and he blows out a breath. "You have my loyalty, Your Majesty. I will do what you ask."

I feel my muscles loosen. I didn't know how tense I was until he accepted.

"Then this is what I need you to do ..."

THE KING

SOMEONE RAPS AGAINST my closed door.

I drop the report I'm reading, and lean back in my seat. "Come in," I say.

My grand marshal enters the room.

"Your Majesty," Heinrich says, bowing, "I have something alarming to tell you. Something that concerns the queen."

I feel my muscles go tight. "What is it?"

And then he tells me.

The news is a hit to the gut—so much so that it takes me several seconds to get my emotions under control.

Once I do, I lean forward. "You're going to go along with her plan," I say.

"But, Your Majesty—"

"You're going to go along with her plan *and* mine."

THAT NIGHT, WHEN I see Serenity, Heinrich's words echo in my head. I had to go to the gym and beat the shit out of an inanimate object to work off everything I felt. And I felt so goddamn *much*. Neither Serenity nor I can escape what fate has always had in mind for us.

She sits across from me at the small, intimate table. Seeing that loose golden hair of hers framing her bittersweet face, it's a shock to the chest.

I can tell by the way her leg jiggles that she wants to kick her heels up to the edge of the table and slouch in her seat.

Instead she runs a hand over one of the flames. "Why are you looking at me like that?" she asks.

I almost hunted you down and confronted you. I almost threw your damn body in a Sleeper. I almost went on a warpath in this palace. Only a hundred years of wisdom and temperance stopped me.

She's oblivious.

There's a deep ache in my bones that I can't drive away.

Her hand stops over the flame. "Is everything alright?"

I move her hand out of the way. "It's been a long day." I lean forward to kiss her scarred knuckles.

This beloved, wild creature. She doesn't belong here, inside these gilded walls, sitting in front of an intricately carved wooden table set with delicate china.

It was foolish of me to think that she could ever be caged.

I've been running from everything she represents for so very long. And I'm tired of running.

It's time to stop being so afraid.

It's time to accept everything she is.

It's time to set her free.

CHAPTER 50

SERENITY

THE DAYS TURN into weeks. Time bleeds away, stealing hours from me. And as the time slips by, so does the strange happiness that had grown in my heart.

I might never believe Montes is truly a good man, but I'm not sure I ever wanted good. He's complex, and terrible, and at the end of the day he's my monster.

And I have to slay him.

This is what remorse feels like. It's premature, which is almost worse. Because I have time to change the course of my actions, but I won't. I made a promise to the world, one I intend to keep.

Things appear to go back to normal. The king watches me, and I swear he sees everything. But if he does, he doesn't stop me.

I can't even ponder that possibility.

Each day is worse than the last because it brings me closer to the moment I've arranged to kill my husband. I talk with Marco most days, Marco and Heinrich. I plot and plan until every last detail is accounted far.

Tomorrow, at precisely 9:30 a.m., this place will burn, the king along with it.

It's the king's day of reckoning. And mine.

"Everything's in place?" the representatives ask on the other side of the screen. I'm acutely aware that their thirty day timeframe is nearly up.

I nod, and Marco, who sits at my side, says, "It is."

The two of us are holed up in my office, hopefully for the last time.

All those years ago I sat next to my father, and spoke to a different set of representatives.

This is the world gone wrong.

"Good. Our men will begin to move in at nine-twenty. A vessel will be waiting offshore. Marco, you'll radio our men the moment Serenity takes out the king."

I have to breathe through my nose to curb the nausea that rises at the prospect. I have killed countless people; this should be no different. But it's a world apart. The man I love, the monster who's found his conscience, the king who gave up a piece of his empire to hold me in his arms again. Who defied death to have me by his side.

I dread this more than anything I ever have.

"We'll pick you both up from there," the representatives continue. "We won't consider the deed done unless you bring the body."

They're looking at me, even though Marco is just as much a part of this as I am.

I pull myself together. "I'll get you your body."

"Good. Then we'll see you tomorrow. We have a peace agreement to negotiate in the coming days."

Pretty words for ugly intentions. Knowing these men, it won't be a peace agreement so much as terms of surrender. It doesn't matter. I won't be agreeing to anything.

"Get some sleep," one of the representatives says, rousing me from my thoughts. "You'll need it."

BATTLE FATIGUE. IT'S a very real thing. You've seen too much, done too much, and at the end of it all you are so, so weary.

I stare at myself in the bathroom mirror.

I thought I had lost everything.

And I had. I lost everything I loved, even things I didn't realize I could lose—my memory, the past, my hate.

I've become something I loathe, and I don't know how to get back to the girl I was, the one that easily divided the world into right and wrong.

And to be honest, I don't know if I even want to be her anymore. I'd rather be the girl who was never touched by war. Who knew nothing of sleeping with the enemy, who'd never seen what flesh looks like when it was blown open. I want to be a girl who woke with a clear conscience each morning, whose demons didn't plague her late at night.

But I can't have that. Not short of injecting myself with that memory loss serum, and that was no solution. Forgetting doesn't mean it never happened; it means not dealing with the consequences.

And oh, have the consequences stacked up.

I gaze into my reflection, my hands tightening around the edge of the counter.

I may have suffered, I may have changed, but I *know* who I am.

I am the girl from the WUN—the girl born a citizen of the United States of America. I am vengeance and I am salvation.

And tomorrow, the world will know it, once and for all.

NOT LONG AFTER my revelation, I hear Montes enter the bedroom, back from whatever business he was attending to. We've both been keeping late hours.

I hear his footsteps head directly for the bathroom. A moment later, Montes enters.

Our eyes meet in the mirror, and I see such bottomless sadness in his own.

He knows. He must.

He steps up behind me and wraps an arm around my middle. His other hand clasps my neck so that he has me shackled to his body.

My hands tighten along the rim of the counter, but I don't fight his grip.

"I've never known my vicious little queen to be vain," he says.

I pass him an annoyed glance through the mirror. We're both aware that's not what I was doing.

His lips brush the shell of my ear. "Come to bed," he says, his voice husky.

My throat works. "I don't want to fall asleep," I admit.

The idea of what's to come tomorrow has my stomach twisted in knots.

"Who said anything about sleep?" he breathes.

I turn my head to face him, and that's all the opening he needs. He kisses me fervently, his hands moving so that I'm no longer his hostage. They cup either side of my jaw.

I'm gasping into the kiss, and I play it off like it's passion, when all I'm really doing is choking back sobs.

I push against him, forcing him to back up. All the while I rip away at his clothing. I've never been like this, violent with the need to be close to him.

Montes welcomes it with a wolfish smile. He always was just as fucked-up as me.

He helps me shrug off the remnants of his shirt, and then his slacks. And then his large, sculpted body is completely on display. The sight of all that coiled power nearly brings me to my knees.

When my hands reach for the edge of my shirt, he captures them in his own.

"Ah-ah," he says. He hooks his fingers around my shirt collar, and, pausing just long enough to make it dramatic, he rips the garment down the middle.

This is *wrong*. To pursue sex with the man I intend to kill. I know it is, and I wonder if Montes ever had thoughts like this before he took me—in the beginning. Because my plans aren't changing, yet I still want this desperately, and I *will* take it.

He jerks my pants to my ankles then tosses me onto the bed. Now, as I see him prowling towards me, I remember why I'm usually the more subdued of the two of us.

I'm not sure I can handle him in all his intensity. Not here, where all the pretty layers that usually make me hardened have been stripped away with my clothes.

Hell lives inside me, and it's been consuming me for the last several hours.

Montes will see all my ugly intentions the moment we're locked together.

He unlaces one of my boots and tugs it off, throwing it over his shoulder. He does the same to the other. The entire time he watches me, those eyes.

Carelessly, he removes my pants and lets them drop to the floor. My panties follow soon after. Then he's between my legs, looming over me, his chest brushing against my own.

Montes searches my face. "What's bothering you?" he asks.

I need to pull myself together.

Instead of answering, I draw him to me and kiss his lips. My hands find his hair and I take great pains to muss it up.

I hear his rumble of approval deep in his chest. I know he hasn't forgotten his question, and I know he's probably more suspicious now than he was before.

I need to make him forget, to make us both forget.

No sooner does the thought cross my mind than he wraps an arm around my waist and rolls us so that I'm staring down at him.

He unsnaps my bra and throws it to the side of the bed.

"You're no longer shy," he says.

Belatedly I realize that I used to make a habit of covering myself. I don't do that now.

"Does that make you sad?" I ask. In the past, Montes took great pleasure in shocking me when it comes to things between a man and a woman.

He sits up slowly, his abs tightening as he does so, until our chests are pressed together.

"No," he says, touching my scar. "I liked your modesty, but I love this more."

"Why?" I ask.

"Because it means you've accepted me."

My expression is on the verge of collapsing.

Montes saves me from myself; he recaptures my mouth, and we're desperate for each other once more. It's not until he lifts me onto him and he slides into me inch by agonizing inch that our frantic movements slow.

I exhale out my breath once we're fully joined, my arms twined around his neck. I stare into his eyes as I begin to move, my fingers playing absently with his hair.

"Say it," he whispers.

Swallowing back my emotion, I shake my head.

We're wrapped up in each other, our limbs tangled, and now his arms tighten around me. "I know you want to. I see it in your eyes."

I know he can.

"You don't get to have all of me, Montes." I don't know why I say it. Maybe to harken back to the very beginning, because I'm feeling sentimental. Maybe to protect my heart, even though it's too late. I don't know.

I expect his normal retort. He doesn't give me it.

He brushes my hair back from my face. "Alright, Serenity. Alright," he says. His eyes are sad again. "This is enough."

I lean my forehead against his shoulder to hide my expression.

His hand tips my chin back up. He frowns at what he glimpses on my face. "Don't hide from me."

He flips us so that I'm staring up at him.

My terrible, undying king.

Who knew at the beginning of things that it would all come to this?

He makes love to me slowly, drawing out each thrust. He stares at me the entire time.

"*Nire bihotza, nire emaztea, nire bizitza. Maite izango dut nire heriotzaren egun arte*," he says.[1]

"What are you saying?" I ask.

He cups my face. "Just a promise." His thumbs rub my cheeks as he moves in and out of me.

"Now," he thrusts harder, ratching up the sweet burn, "come for me, my queen. I want your cries in my ear."

As if on command, sensation builds. I fight it, wanting to stretch this out for as long as I can.

Montes has other thoughts.

He puts more power behind each stroke and he takes the tip of one of my breasts into his mouth. I squirm against him, panting as I try to stave my climax off.

"Come—for—me." He punctuates each word with a thrust.

All at once, against my will, my orgasm rips through me. I clutch Montes, my back arching as each wave of it washes over me. I feel him swell as his release follows my own.

The two of lock eyes as our sweat-slicked bodies crash against each other. I want this moment to last. But then it ends.

Montes eventually slides out of me, dragging my body onto his.

He holds me to him, stroking my back.

I wrap my arms tightly around him. Our ragged breathing eventually evens.

I don't want this night to end. I never want it to end.

---

[1] Translation: My heart, my wife, my life. I will love you until the day I die.

Running a hand over his chest, I ask, "Montes, do you think we could have ever been good people?"

"My queen is full of deep thoughts tonight."

I don't bother responding.

He tilts my head back to face his. "I think we still can be. I don't think it's too late to try."

I maintain eye contact with him, but it takes so much effort. I want to curl up into him and just let go. I think death, when it comes for me, will be a great release. Oblivion from this cruel world.

"Montes," I say, "I need you to promise me something."

"Why don't you tell me what it is first?" he says softly.

"Promise me you will always try to do good."

He flashes me a quizzical look. "Where is this all coming from?"

"Promise me."

He frowns. "I promise you, I will always try."

That's the most reassurance I'm going to get.

I settle back in his arms. And for the rest of the night, I hold my monster to me.

IT'S EARLY IN the morning, when I finally pull myself out of our bed. The king's breaths have long since evened. I, meanwhile, haven't slept a wink this entire night. Instead I spent the long hours savoring the feel of him.

One last time.

I drag on my fatigues and boots, careful to muffle my movements. I clip on my two guns and then I head out onto our balcony.

I stare up at the stars and let the past wash over me. I carry a terrible history inside myself, one full of loss, but it's the only one I know, so I cherish it.

Over a hundred years ago I stood in almost this exact place, a woman married to her enemy.

How the tides have turned.

I continue to stare up at the dark sky, where everyone I love now lives. Or perhaps they don't. Perhaps death really is the end.

I push away from the railing and leave the room, not allowing myself to give Montes a parting glance.

Today I'm going to have to be strong.

I make my way to my office. I need a place to hide out until all hell breaks loose. Anyone who catches sight of me before then will see that I'm acting cagey as fuck.

Once I'm inside, I pace a little, sit behind my desk for a bit, flip through reports that I'll never get around to addressing.

Slowly the hours creep by.

I'm checking the magazine of my new gun for the thirteenth time when I hear a rumble. I slide it into place with a satisfying click and stand, my head turned towards the door.

I hear a hollow, hissing noise, then—

BOOM!

I stumble back as the earth rocks. The walls shake violently. Books rain down from the shelves that line the room and my monitor topples over, along with a lamp.

I grab the edge of the desk and straighten. Out my window I see bits of the palace arcing through the sky. A large slab of marble slams into the fountain the king and I sat at mere weeks ago.

The screams start up almost immediately.

So it's begun.

CHAPTER 51

SERENITY

I STORM OUT of my office, gun clutched in my hand, my heart beating a mile a minute.

I head down the halls to the main entrance as the sound of gunfire joins the screams.

People run past me, and none seem to notice the queen is amongst them, so focused they are on their own self interests.

The second explosion hits the southwest wall of the palace, the shockwave making me stagger. The screams ratchet up.

I throw open the front doors. I get a clear view of the chaos outside the palace.

Trails of dust and debris arc outwards from the blast sites. Both wings of the palace are enveloped in flame. I can already smell the smoke on the wind.

The West's aircraft are all invisible, as are their missiles. But I can hear them all.

I stand at the palace's threshold, my clothes and hair whipping about.

BOOM!

The explosion hits directly in front of the palace. I'm thrown through the air, across the entrance hall. My body slams into one of the great columns that line the space, the force of it knocking the wind out of my lungs and the gun out of my hand. I fall to the ground, landing hard on my hip.

Those haunting pictures that line the great entrance drop from their perches, smashing against the ground, becoming just one more piece of the growing rubble.

I glance towards my gun, the palms of my hands pressed against the ground.

"Serenity!"

I close my eyes and swallow. I knew he'd come for me.

I am a spider, and I've lured my husband into my web. I don't bother looking above me, where several of the king's cameras are recording this footage.

I push myself to my knees, my hand reaching for my father's gun, the one still strapped to my side.

This is it. The moment I've feared since I left the West.

This will not be some detached act. It has always been personal between Montes and me.

When I look up again, I finally catch sight of my husband through the haze.

The king covers his head, and even amongst the chaos in the room he's trying to make his way to me.

On either side of us, bombs detonate, one after the next after the next, down the entire length of the great hall. Just as planned.

The entire thing happens in slow motion.

The walls blast out, blowing plaster and stone across the room. There is a strange beauty to the synchrony of it all.

The columns that hold up the second story sway, but they don't give out.

I don't wait for the explosions to stop before I stand, drawing my gun. At some point, the blasts threw Montes to the ground. He's halfway to his feet when he catches sight of me, gun in hand.

I'm not running towards him like I should be. I'm not panicking either. My true intentions are finally on display.

This must look like a savage reckoning—the king's brutal queen covered in dust and ash, walking towards him amongst the flames.

Montes doesn't appear betrayed or confused like I thought he would. It's desolation that I see in his eyes.

He's worked so hard for so long to keep me alive. All because that wretched heart of his loved me.

I have to draw on all the worst parts of me to keep my feet moving forward and my arm steady.

Perhaps Montes isn't guilty of all the depravity I initially attributed to him. It doesn't matter. Somewhere along the way, he lost his humanity. Whether or not he flicked that first domino and set events in motion no longer matters. We both have done too many unforgivable things. The blood on his hands, the blood on mine ... It's time for us to pay.

He rises to his feet, his eyes moving from my father's gun to my face. He drinks in my expression, his eyes pained.

"I knew you hated me when we met, Serenity," he says. "I knew you even hated me when I married you. But I never knew it ran this deep."

The blackened lump of coal that is my heart breaks.

Another thunderous boom tears through the hall. The ground shakes and the fire flickers.

For a second, Montes turns his head to the side, listening to the sound of his palace going up in flames. Everything he spent lifetimes building is being torn down before his eyes.

The soldier in me who fought for the WUN, the one who lost her family and nation to this man, she revels in the retribution. The rest of me simply weeps.

Montes's attention returns to me.

Had I thought before that he was majestic? Otherworldly? Now, even when he knows his empire is collapsing right in front of him and his wife has turned traitor, he looks untouchable. His shoulders are straight, his eyes still deep with secrets. That timeless face dares me to finish what I've begun.

"Do it." Montes walks forward, lifting his chin in defiance. "I'm tired of fighting. If you think this is right, then do it."

I taste smoke on my tongue. All around us, the king's mansion burns.

There is no happy ending for people like us.

Cold resolve takes over.

I cock the gun and point it at the king.

All those years ago my father told me a story about my name, my birthright. I was named Serenity for the peace I brought my mother. Peace has been the very thing my life has lacked. And my father told me long ago that in order to find peace, I had to forgive.

In front of me is the one man who has always stood between me and that.

A tear slides down my cheek, and then another.

After all this time and all the awful things we've done to each other, I finally, *truly* understand my father's words.

Montes. The Undying King of the East. My nightmare, my beautiful monster, my enemy and my soul mate.

I forgive him.

My throat tightens up.

This is what happens when you love and hate something.

I know what I have to do. I've always known.

"I love you, Montes," I say.

His eyes widen at my admission.

And then I make good on my age old vendetta—

I pull the trigger and kill the undying king.

CHAPTER 52

SERENITY

THERE ARE MANY types of death.

There's the literal one, the one I am most familiar with. You stab a man in the chest and watch him bleed out. If you do it right, you will see his life and his soul slip out with all that blood.

But then there are other types of death. No one ever talks about those. The death of your identity. The death of your dreams. The death of your innocence.

I know all of death's pseudonyms, because he and I are very good friends. He's been my shadow since I was a child.

And he's here in this room with me and the king.

In an instant, the bullet cuts through skin, bone, and finally muscle. Not just any muscle either. The most important one.

The heart.

To kill the king, I had to kill a part of myself. A hundred years ago he took my heart and never gave it back. Montes might be the only person who would want that rotted organ of mine.

He clutches his chest, his eyes wide with shock. The king staggers, and my lips begin to tremble as I hold back all the emotion that's welling inside me.

I holster my weapon, and grab the gun that I dropped earlier, clipping it back into place as well. And then I approach the king.

I walk amidst the flames to get to him. The most terrible thing in the world might be fire. That's why hell is always imagined as an inferno.

But fire doesn't just burn, it *transforms*. And here in this blazing building, as Montes's palace and his life fall to ashes, it's not the end. Of him. Of us. Of our efforts.

If you can survive the flames, what becomes of you?

The two of us are about to find out.

I hook my arms under the king's shoulders. His eyes have slid shut. I begin to drag him, forcing my muscles to move faster than they ever have.

The clock is ticking, and time is not my friend.

From the wings of the entryway, Marco steps out.

He must've seen the entire thing. His eyes are red, though I can't say whether it's from remorse or the burning smoke that hangs thick throughout this place.

"Let me help you," he says.

I shake my head, not slowing down in the least.

Tick-tock, tick-tock.

"Call the men we're rendezvousing with, then clear a path for me outside. I'll be heading out the back main entrance."

He hesitates.

"Now!" I bark.

That's all the encouragement he needs. He leaves my side, racing back down the long hallway, his form disappearing in the haze.

I begin to move in earnest, straining all my muscles to drag the king as quickly as possible.

I head to the nearest room, a room I requested Heinrich disable the cameras in. Up until now, the representatives have been watching a live feed of the king and me vis-à-vis the palace's security cameras.

That's about to change.

To the representatives, it will appear that the explosions took the system out. But it was deliberate.

Inside the room, five soldiers wait, a gurney at their feet. As soon as the door closes, they rush to help me, loading Montes onto the stretcher.

Beyond them, the mirror at the back of the room has already been shot out. Beyond it, I see the shadowy hall of the king's no-longer-secret passageways. I grab an edge of the gurney alongside the other soldiers, and together we step into the passageway.

And then we run.

Everything down to the last detail of this day has been carefully crafted to look spontaneous. Believable.

But it's all a lie.

The entryway, this guest room—all of it was picked for a specific reason. These were the closest rooms to my crypt. Marco doesn't know that, but I do, and so does Heinrich.

Still, there's a good twenty-five yards between us and my Sleeper and only so long that the human body can return from death unharmed.

Tick-tock. Tick-tock.

"Hurry!" I shout.

We pass through the double doors that lead to the subterranean room, and then we trip down the marble steps in a mad rush to get the king into the Sleeper. As we descend, the moat, the walkway, and then, finally, the golden Sleeper all come into view.

This should work.

I'm betting that it does.

I've learned quite a few things from the king, and one of them is gambling. I doubt the king ever imagined I'd take this to heart, or that he'd pay for it with his life.

The six of us make it down the stairs, and then our footsteps are pounding against the marble floor. The roof above us shivers with each muffled explosion. From what I've learned, this room was designed to survive an earthquake. Or an attack.

Heinrich waits for us next to the Sleeper, a scowl on his face. As soon as we get to him, the soldier and I hoist the king's body into the very Sleeper I lay inside for a hundred years.

And then the victim becomes the villain, and the villain the victim. The king and I have utterly swapped roles.

I only have a moment to stare down at him.

I hope I'll be able to gaze at his face again. I hope, but I doubt it.

The king's men hoist the Sleeper's lid back into place, and the machine flares to life. The readout of this one is on the back of the machine, hidden from view by a removable golden panel.

I go to read it, but Heinrich catches my arm and gives me a warning look. "You don't have time for this."

"I need to know that he's okay."

The grand marshal gives me a look that's scarily similar to the ones General Kline used to give me. "Your Majesty, you have a job to finish. Be strong, so that the men that have died today will not have done so in vain."

If I could, I would stay rooted here until I was positive the king was completely healed, but Heinrich's right.

I draw in a deep breath and nod.

"The body?" I ask.

"It's waiting for you in the passageways, just as we discussed."

I place a hand on the Sleeper. The machine will save my husband. I have to believe that. "Montes stays inside this until I return, or until ... the alternative." I can't have him foiling me this far in.

"I will see you tomorrow, my queen."

I stare at the officer in the eyes. I don't think either of us actually believes that, but I incline my head anyway.

"Be safe my queen," he says.

The last thing I'll be is safe.

CHAPTER 53

SERENITY

THE BODY I drag out of the palace is burned past the point of recognition. The mutilation is intentional since the body is not that of the king.

It's Marco. The original one.

I gave him the death he deserved. As much as I hated the man, I know in my heart of hearts this is how he would want his final death to go. His life for his friend's.

I glance back down at the body. Heinrich's men were really liberal with the lighter fluid.

This isn't going to work.

It can't possibly.

Soon after I exit the palace, I catch sight of Marco—the living one. He jogs up to me, unwittingly grabbing his double's legs and helping me carry him down the back steps.

Around us the palace still burns, and I can hear the sound of gunfire as the king's men fight the ground troops the WUN brought in as a distraction.

So many men will die today. I hope this will be the last bits of death that this war will claim.

"What took you so long?" Marco asks as we cross the gardens, winding our way around the elaborate hedges, some of which are on fire.

I give him a look that plainly says, *Are you fucking kidding me?*

"I'm dragging a grown man," I say.

He grunts, like I have a point.

We make our way to the beach, where a small group waits. Heinrich's men have been ordered to avoid attacking us unless it would appear suspicious not to. But they are legitimately preoccupied at the moment, so the need doesn't arise. Now we just have to avoid getting hit by stray bullets.

When Marco and I arrive on the sand, the WUN men close in on us. Amongst them is Styx Garcia, his scars even more prominent in person.

He stares at me with wonder. "The mythical queen in the flesh." He bows his head, but he can't quite tear his eyes from me. "An honor."

Yeah, whatever.

Some of the soldiers take the body from Marco and me and began to load it into the boat.

"What are you doing here?" I ask Styx. He hasn't stopped staring at me.

"Meeting you in person, as promised. I am escorting you and the king's former right-hand," he gestures to Marco without looking at him, "to the West."

My gaze cuts to Marco, who's openly scowling at Styx.

"Alright," I say with a shrug, brushing past him to board the boat. This is where my control in the situation begins to unravel. If the West thought this was a decent idea, then I'll go along with it. And if I happen to kill the leader of the First Free Men en route, that's on them.

One of the WUN soldiers steps in front of me. "I'm sorry, Your Majesty," one of them says, "but we can't let you bring your weapons onboard."

I glance back at Marco, who shrugs. "It's their policy," he says as he divests himself of his weapons. They hit the shallow water we stand in with a splash.

I've been here before. I'm not leaving my father's gun.

"You're not taking my weapons, and I don't give a shit if you think this flies in the face of diplomacy."

"Your Majesty," one of the soldiers says, "the representatives—"

Fuck the representatives.

"I can walk right back into the palace, douse the flames, and continue to war with the West as the Queen of the East," I say. "You and I both know I have the backing of the people. So I suggest you let me take my damn guns and we get on with it."

They don't look like they're going to get on with anything.

"Let the queen have her weapons," Styx says, crowding in close and covering my hand, which is resting on my holster, with his own.

I tighten my jaw. Those mad eyes of his bore into me, and they contain no little amount of heat.

I can feel Marco stiffening at my side, and I swear I'd say he was acting protective. *He was in love with a woman who looked just like me.* Of course he's being protective.

I shoulder past both of them, stepping onto the boat, and no one else tries to stop me.

Once we're all boarded, the motorboat cuts through the water, moving out into open water. This time, I don't get seasick, though I'm not surprised. At the moment I'm too hopped up on adrenaline and desensitized from the earlier attack to notice something like nausea.

"It is a strange thing," Styx says, looking over at the body. "The king is very badly burned, and yet you appear unharmed."

I expected this.

I raise an eyebrow. "It wouldn't be so strange if you'd been there."

Styx cocks his head. "Perhaps. Or perhaps our sleeping queen is now a scheming queen."

I lean back in my seat and squint up at the sun, ignoring the stares. "I guess we'll just have to find out, won't we?"

The tension on the boat ratchets up at my words.

"We will."

AT SOME POINT we exchange boat for helicopter, then helicopter for aircraft.

I'm pensive as I stare out the window. These might be the last hours of my life. I should savor them. Instead, I spend that time letting my mind drift, unwilling to let my thoughts settle on any one thing.

Marco sits at my side. Every several minutes, he glances over like he wants to talk. Each time he does, I tense. What could we possibly have to say to one another? He betrayed his friend, and I know he thinks I did as well.

"Garcia has been staring at you since we boarded," he finally says.

"I know," I say, not bothering to look away from the window.

Marco's voice lowers. "He's not a good man."

"I know," I repeat. These aren't epiphanies or anything.

Marco grabs my chin and forces me to look at him. "He's been married twice," he says, his voice low. "Both women bore strong resemblances to you. Both died mysteriously."

"What do you want me to do about it, Marco?" I hiss. "Now take your goddamned hand off of me."

Reluctantly, he releases my chin. "I can't protect you once we're in WUN territory."

"I didn't ask you to." I'm insulted he thinks I need protecting, and I'm even more annoyed that he thinks I'm ignorant about Styx's perversions. If there ever was a man who I should be immediately wary of, Styx would be it.

"Just be careful. He's going to come for you at some point. I want you to be ready."

I stare at him for several seconds. My eyes flick up to Styx, who is indeed still watching me, and I nod.

I can already tell Styx is not someone to underestimate.

NOT AN HOUR after our conversation, the aircraft begins its descent.

The walled city comes into view. It looks even more magnificent as we circle it, the bright blue water of the Pacific nicely framing the city nestled in the coastal cliffs.

We touch down shortly after that, bouncing in our seats as the aircraft's tires skid down the runway.

We're here.

As soon as the engines die down, I stand. Resolve steals over me.

I will be the king's Trojan horse.

That's the promise I made all those years ago. To make it past the gates and wreak destruction from the inside out. But unlike Troy, there are no heroes here. Just killers and corpses.

I head down the aisle, and as I pass Styx, his head swivels to follow my movements. I can sense his excitement. Just like the representatives, I'm sure he thinks of me as nothing more than a war prize.

I am exactly that, and I will lead to the downfall of this nation.

CHAPTER 54

SERENITY

ONCE WE EXIT the plane, Marco and I are taken in one direction, the body in another.

Dozens of guards escort us from the airfield. No one from the West mentions what's going on or where they're taking us. Half of me is sure we're being led straight to an execution. But then Marco and I are loaded into armored cars and driven up to the Iudicium, the domed building I'd so recently been in.

On either side of the street people crowd the sidewalks, cheering. Ever since my father and I entered Geneva, I've been on the losing side of those cheers.

Our car pulls up to the Iudicium, and Marco and I are unloaded from the vehicle and led inside. Rather than entering the circular courtroom, our guards steer us to an elevator.

We arrive on the third floor and then we're shuffled down a wing of the building. In the short time I've been here, no one's tried to take my weapons. I wonder how long that will last.

Eventually, the group of us halt in front of a solid wood door. I still have no idea what's going on.

Marco stops alongside me.

"Not you," one of the soldier's barks. "That's the former queen's room."

Former queen. The WUN is already taking efforts to strip me of my titles.

"I'm still Queen of the East, soldier." I say to the guard that spoke. "Do yourself and your leaders a favor and don't piss me off until after we have a signed peace agreement."

The guard dips his head and manages to bite out, "Apologies, Your Majesty."

Marco leans in. "Be careful," he whispers. I don't have time to get a good look at his face before he's led farther down the hall.

Five guards remain at my side, and while one of them is busy unlocking the door, another says, "The representatives would like to give you a chance to sleep before you meet with them. They give you their regards and look forward to speaking with you in person tomorrow."

The door to my room opens, and a luxurious guest suite waits for me on the other side. I assess it like one would a trap.

"Please," one of the guards says, gesturing for me to enter.

I eye him, just to let him know I am no fool. I'm aware that as soon as the door closes behind me, I'll be locked in.

Knowing this doesn't change the fact that I'm supposed to at least attempt to go along with the West's schemes. So I step inside.

"We'll be posted outside your doorway and along the halls for your protection." *So don't try anything.*

"Tomorrow at eight a.m.," the soldier continues, "we will escort you to the representatives."

The soldier doesn't wait for my response. The door closes behind me. Just for the hell of it, I try the doorknob.

It doesn't budge.

Short of shooting my way out of this room, I'm trapped.

I BATHE, WASHING off the smoke and dust that seems as though it's embedded itself into my skin.

After I finish, I shake out my old clothes and put them back on. Briefly I eye the platter of cheeses and cold cuts someone's left out for me, along with a pitcher of water and an uncorked bottle of wine.

If only I trusted the representatives not to poison me. Instead I drink water from the tap. Even if the WUN's water supply doesn't filter out radiation, I'd rather take my chances with it than with these men.

I unholster my guns, and once I make sure the safety's off on both of them, I place the weapons under the pillows of the large bed that dominates the room. Most people that enter this walled city don't come out alive. If they come for me, I'm not dying without a fight.

Pulling back the covers, I slide into bed, combat boots and all. Just to be ready.

Now that I'm in bed, my body at rest, my mind only wants to return to one thing.

The king.

My throat closes up at the thought of him. I should've forced Heinrich to let me see the Sleeper's readout, I should've stayed longer to make sure Montes lived through his wound. I can't bear the thought of that powerful body of his devoid of life. Life that I snuffed out.

My chest tightens. He survived the gunshot. I *have* to believe that.

I cover my eyes with my hand. I shouldn't be worrying about the king when I'm currently sleeping in the lion's den. The odds of me escaping this place aren't good.

I fall asleep without realizing it, and when I wake, it's dark out. I'm disoriented before I remember. The bombs, the king whom I fatally shot, the flight over.

And now this.

The king's reckoning came yesterday. Mine will come today.

Grabbing my guns, I get up and sit at the window that faces out onto the street below. The city is dark beyond. Every so often I see a light glimmer from somewhere far off in the distance.

Even here in the WUN's capital, the world is bleak. I'd hoped that a century would be long enough for my homeland to get back on its feet, but obviously it wasn't.

I lean my head against the window. I should get back to bed; I need the sleep. But I can already tell it won't happen anytime soon. I'm too wired, and even if I wasn't, the West has a habit of snatching people up in the night.

So I watch and I wait.

I'm comfortable with this. There's a lot about war that is simply waiting. Waiting to kill. Waiting to die. Waiting, waiting, waiting.

Hours pass before I hear footsteps moving down the hall, straight towards my room.

I pull out one of my guns but don't bother aiming it. Not yet.

Is it Marco? A representative? My executioner?

My money is on this last one.

The door that's been locked since I entered now creaks open.

I wait as a shadow enters the room. It's big enough for me to know it's a man, probably a soldier on active duty.

I wait, studying the individual while they cross the floor and head towards my bed. Their eyes clearly haven't adjusted, or else they'd know I was no longer in it.

Now I point the gun.

"Were you planning on killing me in my sleep?" I rise to my feet slowly as I speak, gun still trained on my target.

"My queen."

Styx.

He's going to come for you at some point.

I step away from the window, my aim trained on Styx's chest. "Or were you simply going to rape me?"

Styx isn't like Montes. He might want me just as the king did all those years ago, but at least then the king had struggled with the morality of the situation. This man hasn't. I sense that if he gets the chance, he'll assault me and he'll enjoy it.

Just knowing that has me putting pressure on the trigger.

"I came to talk," he says. I see his silhouette lean against the wall next to my bed.

"And that's why you knocked." If I shot this man now, how would that affect my meeting with the representatives? It's very, very tempting.

"I still can't believe you're real," he says in a hushed tone. "That you have a personality behind that face. I've wondered what you would be like. I didn't imagine this."

He takes a step forward, out of the shadows. The moonlight catches the contours of his face. It brings out his scars. He looks more monster than man.

"That's the last step you get," I say. "Move towards me again, and you're going to bleed."

He lifts his hands in the air, like that'll appease me. "I wanted to speak privately with you."

"There's no such thing as privacy here, Garcia."

"I don't want to talk about politics," he says.

That leaves personal affairs. "We have nothing else to talk about."

"Come now, my queen, we will be working closely together in the coming days, and you need friends in this world." He's the worst type of predator. I'm amazed that after everything he's seen of me, and after that sneaky entrance of his, he still thinks he can convince me to let down my guard.

"You think I've never come across men like you? You think I haven't *killed* men like you?" I say. "There are cemeteries of them beneath this earth."

"Are you trying to scare me?" He hasn't dropped his jovial act.

"My first victims were exactly like you. Big men who thought that they could take advantage of a little girl. They picked the wrong girl."

Attached to Garcia's side I can see the handle of a wicked knife. It's the kind of weapon that you used to subdue someone. Place it right next to their jugular and you'll get a person to cooperate real well.

I have no doubt he was going to use that on me.

"I don't know who you think I am," Styx says, starting to sound aggravated, "but I came here to get to know you. Nothing more."

"I don't want to know anything about you," I say, "and I sure as hell don't want you know anything about me."

525

In the moonlight, I see his expression tighten. Any minute now he's going to get violent. Fortunately for me, a bullet moves faster than a full grown man.

"Now," I say, "get the fuck out of my room, or I will shoot your dick off." I'm tempted to anyway. I have an unhealthy amount of violence for predators.

The seconds tick by, and he doesn't move. Just when I'm about to pull the trigger, the corner of his mouth lifts. "You will be fun to tame." His voice—hell, his entire demeanor—changes.

Shoot him, shoot him, shoot him, my heart chants.

I can't. Not yet, anyway.

My upper lip curls. "Get. Out."

He inclines his head. Still keeping his hands in the air, he backs up, towards the door. The barrel of my gun follows him. I know enough about men to know that this one is obscenely dangerous. Not the same way Montes is. Styx is not terribly strategic or calculating.

He's just evil.

"I'll see you in a few hours," he says when he reaches for the knob. "Sleep well."

As soon as he leaves the room, I sag against the window.

That was far too close a call.

IT'S ONLY ONCE the sun peaks out from between the mountains that someone else comes for me.

These footfalls are not quiet, which is a relief. If Styx Garcia came for me again, I wouldn't give him the benefit of the doubt.

The door to my room opens, and I see a familiar face. Chief Officer Collins stands with a group of soldiers out in the hallway.

"It's good to see you again, Your Majesty," Collins says by way of greeting.

The feeling isn't mutual.

He and the soldiers march me to the Iudicium's main room, the same place where, only weeks ago, I agreed to kill the king.

Twelve representatives wait for me. I bite back my disappointment when I see that thirteenth seat once again unoccupied.

My plan hinged on having all thirteen representatives gathered in a single room.

When I'd plotted with Heinrich, I'd been so sure the cocky SOBs would finally unveil their elusive thirteenth representative.

I stare up at them, no longer in shackles like I was last time, but it doesn't take handcuffs to be someone's prisoner. How stupid they must think I am to get myself in this situation.

"You decided to come into the West armed." Tito is the first to speak, his bulging eyes staring at my firearms.

"And you decided to lock the Queen of the East in a guestroom," I say. I glance at the several guards that still surround me. "I was brought here under the assumption that we were going to discuss a peace treaty between our two hemispheres as allies would."

"Yes, we will discuss the treaty momentarily," Alan says. "Please," he gestures to the benches that face them, "be seated."

"I prefer to stand." My eyes move over the representatives. "What, exactly, is the hold up?"

"We're waiting for the bloodwork and dental records to come back," Alan says.

I stare stoically at him.

He leans forward. "You didn't think we were just going to assume the body you gave us was the king's, did you?"

I don't respond.

"Once it all checks out," Alan continues, "we will begin negotiations."

Not five minutes later, someone knocks on the double doors at my back.

"Ah," Alan says, "that should be the medical examiner. Let him in, let him in."

I can feel Ronaldo's eyes on me. "Troy," the traitor-turned-representative says to one of his soldiers, "keep a bead on the queen. If the results don't match the king, please shoot her where she stands."

A soldier to my right removes his gun from its holster, the barrel of it pointed at my temple.

My situation settles over my shoulders.

I'm not leaving here alive. And now all I can think about is my monstrous king.

He's going to wake up and I'm going to be dead, and I can't guarantee that the world will survive it.

A man in a lab coat strides down the aisle, stopping just a few feet away from me.

"The results?" one of representatives inquires.

The man's eyes slide to me, then back to the line of men sitting above us.

"It checks out. The body is that of Montes Lazuli."

CHAPTER 55

SERENITY

IT TAKES A moment to register.

The DNA matches?

Impossible.

Is the man lying? That's the most obvious possibility.

The soldier to my right lowers his weapon.

"Do you swear before God and men that this is the truth?" Ronaldo asks the medical examiner. I can tell he's hoping it isn't.

"I do," the medical examiner says. "My technicians can verify it. The remains belong to the former king."

The representatives look almost disappointed.

The remains are the king's.

"It seems our suspicions were misplaced," one of them says to me. "Our apologies. Surely you understand ..."

The king is ... dead?

I give no sign of it, but my fallen heart is falling apart. It fell for a fallen king amongst the ruins of this fallen world. And all of that has now fallen into the hands of these men.

No, I refuse to believe that. There was a mix up of some sort. The king can't be dead. Otherwise, these men win, and they don't get to win. That is not how this world ends.

The double doors swing open again.

I swivel to see who's entered this time.

Styx Garcia strides down the aisle behind us, his eyes devouring me.

I fight the urge to touch my gun.

What's he doing here?

This is not going according to plan.

"You're late," one of the representatives says.

"I couldn't fall asleep." He stares at me proprietarily. "Jet lag."

I watch him with narrowed eyes as he passes me and heads back behind the representatives, taking the final, empty seat.

I don't breathe.

Styx Garcia is the thirteenth representative.

"YOU'RE SURPRISED," STYX notes, scooting his chair in.

I don't bother denying it.

He leans forward. "How do you think I managed to find you in the first place?"

"The First Free Men?" Did the group even exist, or was it just an elaborate ruse meant to throw off the East?

"A real organization that I also run. Convenient when the West needs mercenaries to get a job done without any of the messy political ties."

Removing me from the Sleeper had been one of those jobs.

"My queen, I will admit, I didn't think you had it in you to kill the king," Styx says, changing the subject. "You're a more dangerous woman than even I gave you credit for."

I'm going to die. I can sense it.

"We are in a quandary, Serenity," Ronaldo interjects. "We could just kill you— that would be the easiest.

"But that still leaves the problem of swaying public opinion. It seems they like you.

"Fortunately, Styx here has a solution."

The representative in question leans back in his chair, his sick eyes on me.

You will be fun to tame.

He doesn't even have to say what the solution is.

We will be working closely together in the coming days.

My anger feasts on the indignity of their proposal. I've already been given once to a man. That will never happen again.

I'm done with the deception.

I let them see my empty, empty eyes. Killer's eyes.

In the distance, I hear a muffled sound. The ground shivers then resettles.

I am chaos. I am the undoing of man. And all the world will fall to my feet.

That's what this feels like. That's what everything since my awakening feels like. And today it ends.

CHAPTER 56

SERENITY

I SEE THE first stirrings of unease. The representatives didn't really think it was going to be that easy did they?

How do you take down the West? You gather all thirteen representatives together. How do you gather thirteen representatives together?

You make them believe they've won.

More vibrations follow the first.

"I've been a thorn in a lot of men's sides for quite a while," I say. "You know the problem with my existence? I've always been just useful enough to keep alive."

Ronaldo stands. "Guards—"

"Your time is over." I speak over him. "Those pretty walls of yours are coming down."

"Seize her!"

I smile viciously as the adrenaline begins to move through me.

High above us, the glass dome explodes. That's my cue that the clock's begun. Heinrich is going to blow this place up, and if I don't escape in the next fifteen minutes, I'll get blown up along with it.

The representatives and guards shield their heads as shards of glass rain down on us. From beyond the opening, the king's soldiers begin to rappel down.

I use the distraction to unholster the gun.

And then I fire.

I go for the armed guards nearest me first. The gunshots echo throughout the room as my aim moves from one temple to the next. Troy doesn't even have time to react before my bullet lodges itself in his temple, his blood splattering against the bench directly in front of Ronaldo.

The traitorous former advisor now stares at the blood in shock. His eyes move from it to me. The barrel of my gun is trained on his forehead.

He was a marked man the moment he turned on the king.

I pull the trigger.

Ronaldo's head whips back as my bullet catches him between the eyes. His body collapses half-on, half-off his chair.

Outside, distant gunshots echo my own.

The Western soldiers around me are now recovering, but even as they reach for their weapons, the king's men are dropping to the ground and firing at the enemy soldiers and representatives.

Collins takes a bullet to the gut, as does the medical examiner. Alan's body seems to dance as he's pumped full of bullets.

Many of the other WUN commanders duck behind their desks. What big men they are now that they can't control their enemies.

I round the bench, gun aimed. It's like fish in a barrel; the representatives are all lined up, some of them reaching for weapons they've stashed near their seats.

I shoot Gregory and Jeremy in the head, the two men responsible for human trafficking and concentration camps, and they die where they stand.

At the end of the row, Styx stands, gun in hand, a dark look on his face as he stares out at the room.

I train my gun on his forehead. This is a kill I'm going to enjoy.

As if sensing my attention, he turns.

And smiles.

A split second later a large body rams into my backside, tackling me to the ground. I grunt as the soldier pins me down.

"Drop your weapon," the man on top of me says.

When I don't immediately comply, he grabs my hand and slams it repeatedly into the ground until I release the gun.

Styx heads down the bench, shooting soldiers as he moves. I see the king's men go down.

"Get up!" Styx shouts to some of the representatives he passes, kicking one as he goes.

A couple of the men do shakily stand. A few others remain crouched.

Amongst the madness, Styx levels his gaze on me.

He lifts his gun, the barrel focused somewhere between my chest and that of the guard pinning me down.

Styx and I stare at each other, and I can tell he's having an internal debate about what to do with me.

Before he comes to a decision, I hear the familiar clank of heavy metal right outside the doors.

I close my eyes and breathe out. Saved by a freaking grena—

BOOM!

The blast unbalances my captor and he releases my wrists to stabilize himself.

This might be the only opening I'll get.

I reach for my discarded gun. My fingers lock on the cold metal, and I point it at the guard's face. He only has time to widen his eyes before I pull the trigger.

His blood splatters down on me, his body collapsing on mine.

I grunt as I force his dead weight off of me. Styx slips between fighting men, heading for a side exit.

He's getting away!

I can't let that happen. All thirteen men must be either captured or killed, otherwise, today will have been for nothing.

I've barely gotten my feet under me when I stare down another gun.

Tito, Montes's traitorous former advisor, trains his weapon on my chest. Sweat dips down his ruddy face. His hand trembles just the slightest.

"You better aim for the head," I say, rising slowly. "You don't want me coming back."

But it's not my head that gets blown away.

One moment Tito's bulgy eyes are glaring at me. The next, they're gone, along with a good portion of his face.

I follow the bullet's trajectory back to its owner.

My knees almost give out.

Impossible.

Standing just inside the threshold of the room is the very man I shot through the heart.

The love of my fucked-up life.

Montes Lazuli, the truly undying king.

THE KING

SHE'S WAR AND peace and love and hate. She's my death and my salvation, and right now, standing amongst all these massacred bodies, she's staring at me like I'm the mythic one.

"Montes?" Her voice shakes. Uncertainty is an endearing emotion on my wife.

"You're shit at keeping secrets, my queen," I say.

Finally I can speak on this subject.

And finally I can breathe easy, knowing Serenity's alright.

Bloody, but alright.

Her mouth is slightly parted, and her brows are furrowed. I know my queen well enough to know she's trying to piece together what she feels is an impossible series of events.

One of the representatives nearest her moves, and she shoots him without question.

Deadly, savage woman.

I make my way towards her, shooting anyone I don't recognize. Already my men have taken out most of the enemy soldiers and representatives in here.

Now I just need to get to my wife. My scheming, violent wife who concocted this elaborate, *foolhardy* plan so that war could end and I could live.

Even after everything I put her through, she did this for me. It is without a doubt the single greatest show of love I've ever received.

Which makes me all the more frantic to keep her safe.

I feel Marco at my back, covering for me.

The three leaders left standing now balk at the two of us.

Marco never was the West's mole, he was a double agent working for me.

Serenity sees Marco as well, and she appears equally confused. But quickly her gaze returns to me, her eyes dropping to my heart.

In my peripherals, I see the last of the West's representatives and their royal guard go down. I breathe a little easier as I step up to Serenity.

"How?" she asks.

I whisper in her ear, "I surround myself with loyal men."

Loyal men, and loyal women.

SERENITY

ALL OF MY elaborate plans, all of my late nights, all of the details I worked hours on ironing out. Montes had known, and he'd kept it from me.

I want to be angry, but my heart's not letting me have my moment of indignation. It's far too happy that the king is alive. Alive and … not all that upset himself, considering that I shot him.

"How long have you known?" I ask. There had been nights where he gazed at me with such sad eyes, and I could've sworn he'd seen right through me.

He stays quiet.

"How long?" I repeat.

"Serenity, you are not that good at being subtle."

Goddamnit, had he known the whole time?

Around us, the gunfire has ceased, and the only ones left standing are the king's men.

"And you just let me go along with my plan?"

Montes's eyes are stormy. "It was ... *difficult*. All the details were so very reckless. And I wasn't looking forward to getting shot. But yes."

My eyes dip to his heart. Tentatively, I place a hand on his chest. I feel the organ thump beneath my palm. "Your gunshot wound?" An injury like that should've left him in the Sleeper for a week.

He covers my hand with his own. "I wore a bullet proof vest."

I tilt my head up to him. "But there was blood."

"It isn't hard to rig a blood bag to my outfit. You yourself managed to get ahold of an entire body."

The wrong body.

His body. The second impossible detail about this situation. "The bloodwork, the dental records—they said it was you."

"It *was* me."

I furrow my brows.

"I didn't just clone you and Marco."

The full force of what he's saying hits me. That single Sleeper I wasn't authorized to view. It had housed his double.

"You killed your clone?"

Smoke curls around Montes. He looks for all the world like some terrible deity come to feast on the violence. Only, he's here to save me, to avenge me.

He gives me an indulgent look. "You've killed dozens and dozens of men and you're worried that I killed my twin? My queen, you are a strange creature. But to answer your question, the body was braindead to begin with. I didn't want to chance another version of me ever getting loose."

That was something we could agree upon.

He continues. "I'd planned on faking my death for some time—"

BOOM!

I'm nearly thrown off my feet as the explosion rocks the ground, the sound of it deafening. Montes grabs my arm, bracing me.

The roof above us groans sickeningly, and more glass shards rain down on us.

I glance at the king.

"Is Heinrich still planning on bombing—?"

Montes nods sharply. "We need to go."

CHAPTER 57

SERENITY

THE TWO OF us dash out to the front of the building, the hot breath of air from the blasts whipping my hair about. From here we have a panoramic view of the walled city.

There are fires everywhere, and people are running, panicking.

More bombs go off, one right after another. I see chunks of the seaside buildings blown out from the side of the mountain. A few of them are blasted so far out I see them hit the water.

As I watch, one of the walls circling the city goes down with a thunderous boom. A plume of dirt and debris billow up into the air.

Troy indeed.

I'm breathing heavily, all but ready to cease fighting, when I remember.

The regional leaders and their children. They might be in the dungeons below the building.

My pulse accelerates. Oh God, they're trapped.

I begin to back up.

Montes looks over at me, a warning in his eyes when he sees what I'm doing. "Serenity—"

"The prisoners—they're below the building." I can't even fathom how close I came to forgetting, swept up in the action as I had been.

"Call Heinrich, tell him to hold fire."

I don't wait for Montes to respond. I swivel on my heel, dashing back the way I came, drawn back to the dungeons below the building.

The king curses, and I hear *martyr* amongst the oaths.

I don't care what he thinks. There are children down there.

I head back through the main entryway, hopping over dead bodies. The king isn't at my back, so I take it he's getting ahold of Heinrich rather than chasing after me.

Ignoring the elevator, which could be out of commission, I storm down the stairs, descending deeper and deeper into the earth.

I ignore the prickly sensation that breaks out along my skin as I feel the walls press in on me. My boots echo as they slap against the ground.

When I see royal detention center stamped over one of the levels I descend to, I exit out the nearest doorway.

The light from the stairwell pours out onto the dungeon's floor. Beyond it, lightbulbs are spaced thirty feet apart.

I slow, my boots echoing. I try not to shiver as I head farther into the wet, subterranean chamber. This chill never gets any easier to bear.

I move down the first row of cells. There are at least three more rows, and several more floors. I'd better hope the king gets ahold of Heinrich soon, or else I'm a dead woman.

A pebble skitters in the distance.

I readjust my grip on my gun. "Hello?"

My voice echoes. I hear whispers in the distance, then silence.

"My name is Serenity Lazuli. I'm here to help."

"Serenity?" someone calls out weakly.

I jog towards the voice, which is one row over.

The family is in a cell at the far end of the row, where the shadows seem deepest. A man, a woman, and two children huddle in the corner of it.

The regional leader of Kabul and her family.

"Nadia, Malik?" I ask them.

Nadia nods her head jerkily.

"I'm going to get you all out of here." My eyes drop to the lock. It and the rest of the cage is made out of iron.

"Back up," I say, lifting my gun. This is no safe extraction, but I'm out of options.

I fire off two shots before the lock splits open.

For once, this feels like the right thing, saving instead of killing.

I swing open the cell door, and the family files out.

Malik clasps my hand in his. "Thank you, thank you." His whisper is hoarse. I don't want to imagine what these four have been through since they got here.

I nod to them. "Go to the end of this hall and up the stairs as quickly as you can. I have to get the rest of the prisoners out." I pause. "There are other missing regional leaders. Do you know anything about their whereabouts?"

"They're not on this floor," Nadia says. "We were it."

That's good to know.

We separate at the stairwell, Nadia and her family going up while I continue downwards.

I only just exit the stairwell when I hear sobs, coming from somewhere deep within.

"Hello?" I call out, striding down the first row.

The crying cuts off, but the prisoner doesn't respond.

I tense when I hear footfalls behind me.

"I knew I would find you here," a familiar voice says.

I turn.

Styx Garcia stands between me and the only exit out of here. He holds a gun, its barrel trained on my forehead.

I don't know why the terrible ones always fixate on me. I suppose they think I'm a challenge. But I'm not.

I'm just death.

I adjust the grip on my own weapon. I have no idea how many bullets—if any—I have left.

"You fool," I say. "You should've never come back for me."

"You know why I like you?" he says, his eyes unnaturally bright in the dim light. "Because even when you're cornered and held at gunpoint, you still have this confidence. I'm sure if I stripped you, I'd find a pair of brass balls between those pretty little legs."

I begin to lift my weapon.

"Ah-ah," he says, cocking his gun. "Lift that thing any higher, and I will blow your face away."

I don't believe he'll shoot me in the head. I've seen too much of this man's fucked-up interest in me to think he'd give me the easy way out. He wants me alive.

At least, for a time.

"... And if you're dead, then who will free these prisoners?"

I lower my weapon back down.

"Good girl," he says, and it's so damn patronizing. "Now drop the weapon."

My jaw tightens, but I don't release the gun.

He takes a step forward, and my hand twitches. If he gets much closer, I will risk death to bury a bullet in that scarred flesh of his.

"Drop it," he repeats.

"You're a dead man, Styx," I say. "You'll never leave this place alive."

The corner of his mouth lifts.

The gunshot echoes down the cellblock.

I grunt and stagger back as the bullet hits my upper arm. I feel it enter, feel it rip through sinew, then exit out the other side. My gun arm.

My other hand goes to it just as the blood begins to pour out of the wound. I hiss out a breath at the pain.

"You should worry about your own life, my queen." He says my title like an endearment. Considering he just shot me, he's doing himself no favors.

Styx heads down the cellblock, towards me. "Ever since I was little, I heard about the great Serenity Freeman, a child of the West, sacrificed for the lusts of the East." His eyes are far too bright as he speaks. There's more than just a touch of madness in them. "I saw the footage of you bathed in blood. I saw your horror and your violence. I saw your sacrifice. It made me want to be a soldier.

"And that *scar*." He lifts his gun and drags the barrel of it down his cheek, tracing the phantom path of my scar as he stares at it.

I'm beginning to sweat from the pain, and the cold subterranean air is only getting colder with the blood loss. It drips between my fingers and down my wrist onto the dank ground.

"It was inspiring," he continues. "The strong carry scars."

I had imagined Garcia dangerous before, when I first saw his mutilated face. But now there's the extra knowledge that his scars might've been inspired by mine.

I begin to lift my injured arm again, the handle of my gun slick with blood.

"You aim that weapon and I will shoot you again."

"Fuck you," I say.

He closes the last of the space between us. "I won't kill you," he says softly, confirming my earlier thoughts. He studies me for a moment, and then his gaze drops to my injury.

He presses his gun into my wound. "But you might wish I had by the end of it all."

I stagger back, but now he grabs me with his other hand, keeping me rooted in place.

I try to jerk away from him as the barrel of his gun digs into the ragged flesh. My jaw clenches through the pain, and my nostrils flare.

"The representatives are gone, aren't they? All but me. That makes me the sole ruler of the West."

He presses harder, watching me the entire time. He's so busy keeping eye contact that he doesn't notice me lifting my gun. This evil, crazed man. He's so lost in my pain that he's not paying attention to things he should.

"How would you like to be my queen?"

The edges of my vision darken.

Aiming for his groin, I pull the trigger.

Click.

Fuck. Whatever ammunition I had, it's now gone.

The sound breaks Styx from his trance. He glances down at my gun, aimed at him. His grip tightens as he realizes I meant to kill him.

I pull my head back, then jerk it forward, head-butting him.

He releases his hold on me and staggers back, placing a hand to his forehead.

I follow him, reaching for my father's gun. This ends now.

My fingers barely skim the handle when Styx lifts his gun and shoots at my holster.

I jerk back in surprise as the bullet whizzes past my hand, only just missing it.

Styx storms forward, gun now trained on my chest, his expression murderous. "And I thought we were finally coming to an understanding, my queen."

He yanks my father's gun from its holster and tosses it aside.

I know he's about to hit me. I can see how badly he wants to pull his hand back and pistol whip me. My muscles tense.

But he doesn't hit me, and I get a glimpse of how he's managed to gain this much power. For a psycho, he has a good measure of control.

Instead, he presses the barrel against my temple. "Where were we?"

I stare unflinchingly back at him. I think he wants me to be scared, but he's picked the wrong girl to try to frighten. I don't fear men like him.

I hunt men like him.

"Ah, yes, I remember," he says. "You could be my queen, but only—if—you—behave." He punctuates the last words by tapping the barrel his gun against my temple.

I glare at him as the blood that still coats the end of his weapon now smears against my skin.

He drags the barrel down, further smearing my blood across my face. He draws it over my cheekbone and across my mouth.

Then he pauses.

He taps my teeth with his weapon. "Are you going to behave?"

"Fuck. You."

He smiles. "Dear, sweet Serenity, let me rephrase: you will behave, or I'll start giving you more scars." He leans in close. "And I will make them very, very distincti—"

The gunshot takes us both by surprise.

Styx and I stare at each other, and I have no idea how I look, but the thirteenth representative appears shocked. He glances down between the two of us.

There's nothing. No bullet holes. No blood. No pain.

But then Styx staggers forward, his body slumping against mine. And I realize, there is blood, it's just not mine.

I disarm Styx easily enough, and then I'm holding both his upper body and his gun with my good arm. Behind him I see a man, who's nothing more than a shadow against the light spilling down into the prison from the stairwell.

But I know who it is. I would recognize that silhouette anywhere.

Montes prowls forward slowly.

"*No one* threatens my queen."

The king's voice is poison-laced wine. It's the same voice that asked me to dance in a gilded ballroom over a hundred years ago. It's the same voice that broke the world.

The voice that shattered my heart before he claimed it.

His shoes click against the cobblestone floor, his gun still smoking as he approaches us.

I release Styx, whose body slides out of my arms. The thirteenth representative groans as he hits the ground.

"For months I had to listen to you disrespect my queen."

Shit. It *had* been months.

He stops at Styx's feet. Using a booted foot, he forces the injured man onto his back. A line of blood trickles out of Styx's mouth, and his breathing is labored.

Punctured lung. I've heard the sound enough times.

"And you thought you could just take her?" Montes continues. "From me?"

This is out of my hands. The king has few demons left, but the ones that survived his transformation—those, he's about to feed.

Montes steps up to me. His face goes grim when he sees my wound. "Are you okay?"

I run my tongue over my teeth, then nod.

He pulls me to him and kisses my forehead. He doesn't chastise me for running down here. I think Montes knows exactly how to fan the flames of my love.

When he lets me go, the atmosphere in the dungeon changes to something dark and violent.

The devil has come to feast.

Montes towers over Styx. "I was ready to torture you before, but now ..." He crouches down. "I could hurt you, then heal you, then hurt you some more. On and on until I die." He pauses. "I've lived for a century and a half. I could make you immortal, only so that you'd live lifetimes of torture."

What Montes is suggesting is beyond horrific.

Styx's gaze moves to me, and for once I actually see fear on his face. He never believed he was going to lose his power. And now he's facing a man and a fate that might be worse than death.

The king aims his weapon. "We could start now."

"Please—"

The gunshot cuts Styx's plea short.

The representative's body goes still, and I realize that sometimes Montes's empty threats are not just lobbed at me. The fresh bullet hole carved between the Styx's eyes is proof of that.

And that's how the thirteenth and final representative falls.

WE FREE THE rest of the prisoners, and then there's the gruesome task of carting Styx's body topside, where twelve others are already laid out.

Only then do the West's soldiers believe leadership has fallen. And only then does the military cease fire.

As soon as Montes and I are well out of range, Heinrich lights up the Iudicium.

Now, an hour later, the building the representatives reigned in is nothing more than a pile of stone and ash.

It probably wasn't necessary, but I'd insisted on it. I didn't want that monument, where so many evil men gathered, to remain standing.

I lean against one of the West's military vehicles that's long since been abandoned. Montes has fished out a first aid kit from inside it, and now he bends over my upper arm, bracing it with one hand and cleaning my wound with the other.

I keep jerking away from him every time he wipes the antiseptic over it.

"This would all be over with much sooner if you let a proper medic tend to you," the king says conversationally.

I refused any other type of medical care. The bullet had just skimmed my skin; it was nothing more than a flesh wound.

"I don't want a proper medic. I want you." I won't lie, I'm enjoying my husband taking care of me.

Montes dips his head back towards his work, but not before I catch the edge of a smile. I think he's enjoying taking care of me too.

"You know," he says, grabbing a roll of gauze, "it was all intentional."

I furrow my brows, not understanding.

"How and when you woke up," he clarifies.

Now he has my full attention.

"After Trinity died, Marco did want revenge."

My eyes move to the king's right-hand. He's busy discussing something with the cameramen who are setting up a stage and a screen.

"He spent decades gaining the West's trust, then decades more solidifying that trust. He leaked information approved by me. It benefitted me to have Marco feed them certain select pieces of classified information because in return, I learned of their plans.

"I created my double around that time," Montes says, "thinking that ultimately I'd need to fake my death. That was also when I began making plans to wake you.

"I didn't want to expose you to this world," he says.

My mouth tightens.

"I was afraid that after all that waiting, you'd still just be killed like Trinity," he continues. "I couldn't bear that possibility. But you needed to wake up and the war needed to end and those two things were appearing more and more mutually inclusive."

Montes finishes wrapping my wound, tying off the gauze.

"So eventually," he continues, "I let Marco pass along information on your resting place. And thus set in motion all that has happened."

He had woken me. It took him years to wait for the right moment, but that's exactly what he did.

You know the thing about strategy? he said all those years ago. *It takes knowing when to act and when to be patient.*

What he's saying reframes everything.

He'd been planning an end to war for a very long time. "How could you have possibly known what was to come?" I ask.

"I discovered what you did—that the key to winning the West was taking out the representatives. And only victory would do that.

"I never imagined sending you in—it was always going to be Marco—but then you made a deal with the representatives and I couldn't undo the situation—short of calling the whole thing off. Much as I wanted to do that, I had faith in you."

My throat works. There aren't any words that can convey everything I feel, so I wrap my hand around my monster's neck and kiss him instead.

He believed in me enough to put both our lives on the line. Enough to ignore his controlling nature and his obsessive need to shelter me. I can think of no greater show of love from this man.

ONCE I'M PATCHED up, the king and I gather at the city's central square, the same place I stood at only weeks ago. Like then, cameras hone in on me. A microphone rests in front of us.

I know I am a sight—bloodied, dirty, tired. The king, for all his unearthliness, looks little better.

My eyes move over the city.

Much of it lays in ruins, the buildings smoldering, the wall encircling it little more than rubble.

I wish I could say that everyone who stared back at me was happy, that this felt like some great milestone for them, but the truth is that this city was home to many people, and now there's nothing but destruction here.

There are many people beyond this city who won't be pleased, and there will be many more who won't know how to react.

But then there are the multitudes that will be freed from work camps and multitudes more living on the edge of survival who will now begin to receive aid. The neglected cities of the West might finally, finally know peace.

But beyond that, there is one thing that can bridge everyone that lives in this time.

I lean into the microphone. "Citizens of the world: the war is over."

CHAPTER 58

SERENITY

MY GUNSHOT WOUND takes an agonizing month to heal. It's the first serious injury since I met the king that's healed without the aid of the Sleeper.

I insisted on it. He acquiesced.

I think we're finally getting somewhere.

He kisses it now, his lips running over the scar, his hands sliding up my sides.

The scar that cuts down my face I'd always thought of as a permanent tear for the lives this war took. I wear this latest one with pride, because it marks the day it ended. For good.

Even as the king and I sit out here in the sand yards away from one of his island homes, the surf crashing close to our toes, my mind is pulled to the future.

We only get one more day before we head off to the Western hemisphere and begin the toiling task of rebuilding this broken world.

I'm starting with medical relief and efforts to clean any remaining radiation from the earth and groundwater, the very things that a long time ago the king tried to deny my people. Then will come subsistence, much of it government-subsidized.

Montes is not too thrilled about this last one, but I still sleep with my gun, and he's a smart enough man.

True infrastructure will eventually be put back in place. Continents, regions, cities—they all need local leadership. The end of the war marks the beginning of the arduous task of rebuilding the governments the world lost long ago.

The king smooths my brow, tiny granules of sand sprinkling down my forehead and nose as he does so.

"I can tell you're going to be a bigger workaholic than I am," he says.

His face is cast in shades of blue from the moon above. I cup it, letting my thumb stroke the rough skin of his cheek.

Montes's gaze turns heated. "Say it."

The heart is such a vulnerable thing. Encased beneath skin and muscle and bone, you think it wouldn't be. But it is. Even ours.

I still have to grapple with the words; I drag them out kicking and screaming.

"I love you," I say.

Montes closes his eyes.

"Again," he says.

I'm not sure how many times he's heard these words in his lifetime. I imagine whatever the number, it's far smaller than the amount he needed to hear them.

We have plenty of time to rectify that.

"I love you," I say.

Plenty of time, but not forever.

I won't take the king's pills, and I've asked him stop taking them as well. I don't know if he has, but I haven't seen the pill bottles around.

People aren't meant to live as long as us. And people aren't meant to experience the horrors we have.

Bloodshed, death, hate—I used to wake every morning to this. It's actually quite odd not to. Perhaps that's why I've thrown myself into my work, so that I don't forget.

High overhead I catch a glimpse of the stars.

I'd always imagined the dead resided in the heavens, and here and now I feel both closer and farther from them than ever before.

My eyes search the night sky, looking for one constellation in particular. I smile when I find it.

The Pleiades, the wishing stars. I hear an echo of my mother's voice even now, pointing them out to me.

The king rolls onto his side, placing a hand on my abdomen. He follows my gaze up to the star cluster.

"Have you ever heard the story of the lost Pleiad?" Montes's fingers are gathering the material of my shirt, lifting it as he talks.

I narrow my gaze on him. "If you're about to lie to me ..."

Montes has developed a bad habit of teasing me. Apparently I'm gullible. Considering, however, I'm also violent, he never takes it too far.

He laughs. "*Nire bihotza*, I'm not. This is *true*. Apparently there are seven stars—Seven Sisters—but you can only see six of them in the night sky. The seventh is 'lost'."

We're both quiet for a moment while I ponder his words. The night air stirs my hair. Mine and the king's.

He leans in close to my ear. "It's because I caught her," he whispers.

My eyes return to the constellation.

"Make a wish," I whisper.

He stares at me for several seconds, then softly says, "I don't need to anymore."

Montes is no good man, and I am no good woman. We grapple day in and day out with our demons. Long ago, I married a monster, and the king's war made one out of me. And all our terrible edges fit together, and together we've become something else, something better.

The world is at peace, and for once, so am I.

After all this time, I finally found serenity.

EPILOGUE

5 years later

THE KING

I FLIP OVER and stare down at my queen. Often I wake early—a habit I've developed over the decades. I used to spend those early hours working, squeezing another hour in if I could. It used to fuel me when I needed a distraction from my lonely life.

Now I tend to use the time to marvel over the fact that this *is* my life. After all the turmoil, all the violence and poor decisions, somehow the wrongs were made right.

Serenity made them right.

I run a hand over the swollen slope of her stomach. This is something else to marvel over.

Only a few more weeks. It's just simply not possible to be this excited.

Or this petrified. Or this protective.

I'll be a father for the first time at the ripe age of 174. I can barely fathom it.

"Mmmm." Serenity stretches beneath my touch.

"*Nire bihotza*, today's a big day for you," I whisper.

Her eyes snap open. "Shit."

She sits up, her gaze moving to the windows. The sun is just rising. "What time is it? Did the alarm not go off?"

"Ssssh. It's still early. Go back to sleep." She hasn't gotten enough of it. I don't believe being eight months pregnant is particularly comfortable.

Instead of going back to sleep, her hand lazily combs through my hair. Then it freezes. She leans forward and peers at my hair more closely.

"You have a gray hair." She says this wondrously.

My grip on her tightens just a fraction as I nod. I'd noticed it a week ago. This is also something that petrifies me.

I know Serenity's wanted me to stop taking my pills for a while now. At first I couldn't—old habits die hard and all that. And then one day I woke up and realized that I wanted to get old with this woman. I wanted our skin to sag together and our faces to wear wrinkles together the same way Serenity currently wears her scars.

So I stopped.

"I'm surprised I haven't gotten any sooner," I say, "considering who I'm married to."

She swats me. "You should just be thankful I've stopped sleeping with my gun."

I roll over her. "Oh, I am."

And then I decide she doesn't need sleep nearly as much as she needs me.

TODAY I WEAR my hated crown.

One final time.

Five hundred men and women gather in the room before me and the king, regional leaders from all over the world.

It took Montes nearly a hundred and fifty years to conquer the world. It took me only five to give it back.

"Today marks a turning point," I say to the group spread out before me in the auditorium.

From this day forward, our world won't be ruled by monarchs. The road ends here. With us.

I remove the crown from my head. Next to me, Montes mirrors my movements. I would've thought he'd fight this more, but the man is weary of ruling. At last.

I don't spare the headpiece more than a passing glance.

"Today we hand the world over to you."

There will be a single government made up of regional leaders appointed from each territory. All will work and vote together on issues that afflict the world.

Like every government that came before it, this one won't be perfect—it could even be a disaster. Only time will tell.

I look over at Montes. My beautiful monster.

I wasn't looking for redemption in this man—or from him, for that matter. But that's what I got.

I return my attention to the hundreds gathered in this room.

There's a place for me here, in this future I never expected to be a part of. I no longer straddle two hemispheres and two time periods. Instead, I am the woman that loves both the West and the East, the woman that will always fight for the blighted and broken, the impoverished and the oppressed. I'm the woman that came from the past to help the future.

I'm no longer the loneliest girl the world, the woman who fits in nowhere.

Now I'm the woman who fits in everywhere, and I'm the woman that believes in freedom and justice, and above all—

Hope.

TO MY READERS

TO SAY I am sad to leave this world and these characters is an epic understatement. I'm not sure I've enjoyed writing a series quite as much as this one. And the things it made me feel! I hope I'm not alone in that.

Everything about these characters and this world got under my skin, essentially from the start. When Montes first came to me, he was wholly wicked, and Serenity wholly good. They were never supposed to fall in love. It wasn't just Serenity who fought it, it was me. But, as you know by now, these characters did fall in love, and the story became something else entirely from what I'd planned.

I hope you enjoyed reading *The Fallen World* series. I'm sorry to say that I don't plan on revisiting this world again. However, I do have plans in the future to write a four book post-apocalyptic series, though only time will tell when I'll release those! Until then, I hope you'll consider joining my newsletter at laurathalassa.com so that we can share more stories together in the future.

Until then—

Hugs and happy reading,

Laura

Never want to miss a release?
Click here to sign up for Laura Thalassa's mailing list for the latest news on her upcoming novels.

Be sure to check out Laura Thalassa's post-apocalyptic romance series

Pestilence

Out now!
Click here to buy it on Amazon

Be sure to check out Laura Thalassa's new adult paranormal romance series

Rhapsodic

Out now!
Click here to buy it on Amazon

Be sure to check out Laura Thalassa's young adult paranormal romance series

The Unearthly

Out now!
Click here to buy it on Amazon

Other books by Laura Thalassa

THE FOUR HORSEMEN SERIES:
Pestilence

THE BARGAINER SERIES:
Rhapsodic
A Strange Hymn
The Emperor of Evening Stars
Dark Harmony

THE FALLEN WORLD SERIES:
The Queen of All that Dies
The Queen of Traitors
The Queen of All that Lives

THE UNEARTHLY SERIES:
The Unearthly
The Coveted
The Cursed
The Forsaken
The Damned

THE VANISHING GIRL SERIES:
The Vanishing Girl
The Decaying Empire

THE INFERNARI SERIES:
Blood and Sin

NOVELLAS:
Reaping Angels

Found in the forest when she was young, Laura Thalassa was raised by fairies, kidnapped by werewolves, and given over to vampires as repayment for a hundred year debt. She's been brought back to life twice, and, with a single kiss, she woke her true love from eternal sleep. She now lives happily ever after with her undead prince in a castle in the woods.

… or something like that anyway.

When not writing, Laura can be found scarfing down guacamole, hoarding chocolate for the apocalypse, or curled up on the couch with a good book.

Printed in the USA
CPSIA information can be obtained
at www.ICGtesting.com
LVHW090845220224
772532LV00003B/178